Sagan's Warning

Dion's smile vanished, lips compressing to a thin line. He looked down at the hand, at the five marks on the inside of the palm that were swollen and red. Swiftly, he snatched his hand from Sagan's grasp. The fingers curled in, hiding the scars.

"You've seen him," Sagan repeated harshly.

"Who is he?" Dion asked in a low voice.

"Your cousin, my liege," said Sagan. "Your first cousin. The only son of your late uncle, the king."

"Son?" Dion stared, incredulous. "Are you saying that . . . Is my cousin the rightful heir to the throne?"

"No, Your Majesty," answered the Warlord grimly. "He has no legitimate claim to it. But, I fear, sire, that this will not stop him. . . ."

Bantam Spectra Books by Margaret Weis and Tracy Hickman
Ask your bookseller for the ones you have missed

From Margaret Weis

STAR OF THE GUARDIANS
The Lost King
King's Test
King's Sacrifice
Ghost Legion

and by Margaret Weis and Tracy Hickman

THE DARKSWORD TRILOGY
Forging the Darksword
Doom of the Darksword
Triumph of the Darksword

Darksword Adventures

ROSE OF THE PROPHET
The Will of the Wanderer
The Paladin of the Night
The Prophet of Akhran

THE DEATH GATE CYCLE
Dragon Wing
Elven Star
Fire Sea
Serpent Mage
The Hand of Chaos

STAR OF THE GUARDIANS

Volume Four

GHOST LEGION

BY

MARGARET WEIS

BANTAM BOOKS
NEW YORK • TORONTO • LONDON • SYDNEY • AUCKLAND

GHOST LEGION
A Bantam Book / July 1993

SPECTRA and the portrayal of a boxed "s" are trademarks of Bantam Books,
a division of Bantam Doubleday Dell Publishing Group, Inc.

Grateful acknowledgment is made for permission to reprint excerpts from "The Second Coming" by William Butler Yeats. Reprinted with permission of Macmillan Publishing Company from THE POEMS OF W. B. YEATS: A NEW EDITION, edited
by Richard J. Finneran. Copyright 1924 by Macmillan Publishing Company, renewed
1952 by Bertha Georgie Yeats.

ISBN 0-553-56331-9

Published simultaneously in the United States and Canada

Bantam Books are published by Bantam Books, a division of Bantam
Doubleday Dell Publishing Group, Inc. Its trademark, consisting of the
words "Bantam Books" and the portrayal of a rooster, is Registered in
U.S. Patent and Trademark Office and in other countries. Marca Reg-
istrada. Bantam Books, 1540 Broadway, New York, New York 10036.

PRINTED IN THE UNITED STATES OF AMERICA
RAD 0 9 8 7 6 5 4 3 2 1

To all who love.
And have been loved.

The king and his people are like the head and the body. Where the head is infirm, the body is infirm. Where a virtuous king does not rule, the people are unsound and lack good morals.

John Gower,
The Major Latin Works of John Gower

Upon the king! let us our lives, our souls,
Our debts, our careful wives,
Our children and our sins lay on the king!
We must bear all, O hard condition,
Twin-born with greatness, subject to the breath
Of every fool, whose sense no more can feel
But his own wringing! What infinite heart's-ease
Must kings neglect, that private men enjoy!

William Shakespeare,
King Henry V, Act IV, Scene i

Book One

But say I could repent, and could obtain,
By act of grace, my former state; how soon
Would height recall high thoughts, how soon unsay
What feigned submission swore; ease would recant
Vows made in pain, as violent and void—
For never can true reconcilement grow
Where wounds of deadly hate have pierced so deep—
Which would but lead me to a worse relapse
And heavier fall . . .

John Milton, Paradise Lost

Chapter ·=⊃◯⊂=· One

> ... is there no place
> Left for repentance, none for pardon left?
>> John Milton, *Paradise Lost*

The monk's cell was dark and chill, small and narrow. Walls, ceiling, and floor were made of stone. It held a crude bed, a desk, a chair, and a small altar for personal use when the bells roused the brethren from their slumbers, called them to matins—midnight prayers.

The service had long ago been said. It was only an hour before dawning, during that restless part of sleep when dreams come most vividly, most terribly.

The sleeper in the crude bed was obviously entering into the shadowed world of one of these dreams. He stirred on his pillow, moving his head from side to side like a blind man, groping through his endless darkness. He stretched forth one hand suddenly, the right hand, and grasped an object that was not there, except for him, in the dream. His fingers closed over it, as they would close over the hilt on a sword. An expression of pain contorted his face. He groaned and caught his breath.

The one who watched over his sleep sighed and shifted restlessly in the chair on which she sat. She reached out a hand to waken him, checked herself. She would have wept for him— wept in pity and frustration—but for two things: the knowledge that her tears would irritate him and the fact that the dead are not permitted the comfort of tears, just as they are not permitted the comfort of a touch.

She could only sigh again and settle back in the chair that she occupied by instinct rather than by need, for she no longer possessed a body whose needs and aches and pains had to be considered. Her spirit could have floated upon the air, with less substance than the smoke of the flickering flame dancing upon the oil of the altar's small incense burner. She preferred to sit in the chair. It was an action of the living and it seemed to make her one again with the world of the living.

Night after night, she had occupied that chair. Night after night, she'd watched over his sleep, guarded it—except that she made a poor guard, for she could not drive away the dreams that tormented him by night, just as she could not comfort him for the regret that tormented him by day. But her anger intensified as she watched his suffering this night. She bit her lip and frowned and appeared to make up her mind to some action, for she rose to her feet and was taking a step toward the door of the cell when suddenly the sleeper sat upright, his eyes open, wide, and staring, a hoarse cry in his throat.

Startled, afraid at first that he'd seen her, Maigrey stumbled backward through the chair, the desk, into the corner of the cell. Then she realized he wasn't awake; nor was he staring at her, but at something beyond her. Something in the dream.

He sat on the edge of his bed. He wore the habit of his calling even when asleep; the cell was cold and the cassock and a loosely woven shabby blanket were all he had to protect himself against the dank chill. He dragged off the blanket, threw it to the floor, and stood up.

He raised the unseen weapon in either defense or salute— Maigrey could not be certain—and he spoke words that held some meaning to him, apparently, but which she couldn't make out.

She crept forward, out of her dark corner, instinct drawing her to his side, as she had gone to his side during countless battles faced together in their lifetime. Pity burned in her, pity and anger and frustration. She was tempted to thwart the prohibition that had been placed upon her, tempted to break the covenant she had made and speak to him.

She was close, so close to him, yet she knew the bitter pain of never being able to get close enough. His mortal flesh stood like a prison door, barring her entry. But their spirits had been closer than most; the mind-link that bound them together in life had not, apparently, been shattered, even by death.

Maigrey felt a jolt surge through her, a spark that arced from him to her, and she was sharing the vision, the dream ... the reality. But she understood instantly what she saw and heard. He did not, and there was no way she could warn him.

He spoke again and stretched out his left hand.

The action woke him up. He was confused at first; confused and alarmed, and he fell back in an instinctive defensive posture, sword hand raised. It was then, by the feeble flame burning on the dish of oil, that he saw where he was, saw that the right hand holding the weapon was, in reality, empty.

Sagan straightened and frowned and looked around. His frown grew deeper, darker. He raised his right hand to wipe the cold sweat from his face, caught a glimpse of the palm in the shadowy light. His eyes widened; he stared in disbelief. Falling to his knees before the altar, he held his hand to the light of the flame.

Maigrey, looking to see, shook her head, whispered in soft anger, "No! How could You? This is not fair!"

On Sagan's right hand—five scars. Five scars of five puncture wounds made by the needles of the bloodsword—the weapon of the Blood Royal.

Three years had passed since Derek Sagan had been constrained by Abdiel to throw the bloodsword into a lake of water and of flame. Three years had passed since he had put his hand to that weapon. The palm was callused, roughened by the hard physical labor he'd endured since, smoothed by being pressed together in hour upon hour of passionate, desperate prayer. The scars had all but disappeared—from his hand, if not his soul.

But by the fire's light, this night, the scars were fresh, as if he'd just now released the bloodsword. A clear liquid, streaked with red, oozed from the wounds.

Sagan stared, disbelieving, pondering. Then he clenched his fist over the scars. He returned to his bed, lay facing the wall, his face grim and hard as the stone.

And, though he did not know it, he was now alone. The silent guardian of his sleep had left him.

······

The radiant personage strode through the vast and echoing hallways of white marble and gold. Intent, earnest, all thoughts bent on the errand, the personage was only gradually aware of a shadow across the path. The radiant being turned eyes outward, instead of inward, and the shadow took on form and substance, took on the semblance of the living being it had once been, became a thin human male clad in faded blue denim jeans and a blue denim work shirt. The man was tall and stooped, his face pleasant and careworn and sad.

"Child of God," said the radiant personage.

"Platus," the man gave his name, with a quiet but dignified inclination of the head.

"What may I do for you, Platus?" asked the radiant being.

"If . . . if I could talk to her," Platus suggested softly.

"Do you think it would do any good?" the personage asked after a moment's serious consideration.

"I understand her," said Platus. "I believe I can reason with her."

"I don't know, my son," said the radiant being doubtfully. "Much is at stake."

"Yes . . . yes, I know. If I could just try . . ."

The radiant personage gave the matter thought, then indicated approval. "Perhaps it would be best. Go, then, and may His blessing go with you."

Platus accepted the task and the blessing and continued on the way which the radiant personage would have taken, the radiant being turning aside to tend to other duties.

The martial tread of booted feet and the faint metallic jingle of armor echoed disturbingly through the peaceful vaults. Platus made his way toward the sound, walking slowly, taking his time. He could have reached his destination with the swiftness of a thought, for he was not bound by constraints of time or place or distance. But as his thoughts themselves were lumbering and slow-paced, so he matched his speed to them. Platus was far from being as assured as he'd assured the radiant being.

When he had, at least, some vague outline of his arguments readied, Platus drew near the echoing footfalls. He came upon Maigrey, pacing the empty halls, which were empty to her only because she refused to populate them. Every line of her body was expressive of anger, defiance.

She wore in death the silver armor she'd worn in life. Her right hand rested on the hilt of the bloodsword strapped at her waist. The long, pale hair flowed over her shoulders, drifted around her in the air she still breathed, air she created.

Aware of another presence, she turned on her heel, advanced on him, her face stern with resolve. But she had obviously expected someone else.

Seeing only her brother, Maigrey paused; a momentary confusion checked her swift steps. The hesitation passed swiftly, however. She continued on, the warlike sound of her clicking heels jarring Platus, seeming to jar the very stars.

"So, they sent you," she said.

"I offered to come," he returned mildly.

This answer was nonplussing, to judge by the fact that she was silent a moment, inwardly struggling.

"I want to know why they are tormenting him like this," she demanded at last.

"Maigrey, it is not our place to question—"

"It is!" she flared. "He doesn't need to be involved! He was at peace. . . ."

"Was he, Maigrey?" Platus asked quietly.

She raged on. "I see their intent. Not satisfied that they have brought him low, humbled and crushed him, they want to destroy him."

"Maigrey, that's not true—"

"You probably approve of it!" she accused him bitterly

"It isn't my place to approve or disapprove," Platus said, uncomfortable. "And it isn't their intent to hurt him. He hurts himself. . . ." He paused, began again. "Maigrey, what is done is done because of the failings of mortal men."

"Do you approve?"

"I am afraid," Platus said after a moment. "Afraid for Dion. If Sagan . . ." He fell silent.

"If Sagan falls, you were going to say. You don't trust him!"

Platus smiled sadly. "It is difficult to trust one's killer, sister."

Maigrey glared at him, as at an opponent who takes advantage of a misstep and thrusts the sword point home. Turning away in disgust, she began to pace again. "I want to talk to someone else."

Platus checked a sigh. "They are displeased. . . ."

"They don't trust me either, I suppose."

"You came very close to breaking your covenant with God this time, Maigrey," he told her gently.

She halted, stood a moment, her head bowed. Then, lifting her gaze, she looked earnestly at her brother. "If you could see Sagan, Platus! If you could see how he suffers! Why don't they hear his prayers? Why don't they grant him the peace he's earned and longs for—"

"They *have* heard his prayers, Maigrey. Words of repentance come from his lips, but not his heart. Sagan is filled with rage and resentment, doubts and questioning. He did not enter the church humbly, baring his bleeding soul to the healing light. He skulked into the church like a hurt animal, using it as a place to hide and lick his cuts. And consequently, the wounds have not healed, but fester and pain him still."

"And whose fault is that?" Maigrey cried. "When he asked for forgiveness was there an answer? No, only silence." She resumed her distraught pacing. "As for the covenant I made, I *will* break it. I must. That's what I came to tell them." She paused. "Though I don't consider it truly broken, for I don't consider it truly made. It was a trick, a trick meant to keep me from helping Sagan. They only want their revenge, they want to see him suffer—"

"You're not being just, Maigrey," Platus interrupted sternly. "You know that isn't true. Man brings his suffering on himself. They grieve to see it, as they grieve to see your suffering, my sister. I grieve to see you bound to him. I sometimes think it would be best if you would let go—"

"I can't!" Maigrey turned on him, her hand on the hilt of her sword. "I won't."

"No, I know you can't. Nor should you." Platus sighed. "Derek Sagan stands upon a precipice. Your hand is all that holds him back, keeps him from falling past redemption. You are the one bright star in his darkness. But now you must consider this, Maigrey—if you fall, what will happen to him?"

She was angry. Her lips parted to make a sharp retort.

Platus held his ground before her anger, did not return it. Once he, too, had been unable to let go.

Maigrey wavered, broke, lowered her defense.

Platus slid in past it. "The covenant was not a trick, sister. You knew when you made it that sincere repentance was his only hope. Together you walked the paths of darkness, as the prophecy said. Now he must walk the path alone. You can light the way for him, but you can't lead him by the hand. He has to find the path to redemption himself."

"Or lose it utterly," Maigrey said, trembling. "And it's not fair!" Her fists clenched. "They slant the path upward, make it easy to fall, far more difficult to climb. They place temptation in his way. They did not show me *this* when they urged me to make the covenant.

"And what *of* Dion?" she demanded before Platus could answer. "What about the danger *he's* in? Aren't you worried about him?"

"I have faith in Dion, Maigrey, to do what's right—"

"Implying that I don't have faith in Sagan!" she retorted bitterly.

"Do you?" Platus asked.

"Yes," Maigrey answered, eyes gray as a storm-ridden sea. "I have faith in him. In *them*, I don't!" She pointed her gloved and armored hand at her brother. "And you can tell them that. And you can tell them something else. That if he falls, I go with him."

"Maigrey—" he began, but she cut him off.

"Don't worry. I will keep the covenant, for the time being. I will not speak to Sagan or reveal my presence to him. But remind them of this, Brother—I made no such promise concerning Dion. And if I can help him . . ."

With a sharp, cold nod, she turned, the pale hair whipping about her like a fierce wind. Hand on the hilt of the bloodsword, she stalked away, the stamp of her booted feet striking like steel against an anvil through the vast vault of heaven.

"You may help Dion," Platus said softly. "But who will help you?"

Chapter ⋅⋅❖⋅⋅ Two

Home—none. Wife—none. Kids—none. . . .
The Magnificent Seven

Xris adjusted his eyesight to night vision; the "meat" locker was impenetrably dark. Corasians, with their sophisticated sensing devices, have no need or use for light to see by. In some areas—the munitions factory Xris had just been in, for example—the Corasians install lights for use by their human slaves. Lights were unnecessary in the locker. The "meat" had no need to see, were probably thankful they couldn't.

Xris's augmented hearing detected no sounds except those of intense human misery and terror, and those he was coldly and purposefully ignoring. He knew that he'd tripped the security alarm, if it could be called that. He couldn't hear it, no matter how sensitive his augmented hearing. Each individual Corasian is a single part of a collective whole, as individual cells make up an entire body. The deaths of the two Corasian guards, gunned down by Xris at the back entrance to the tunnels, had set off an alert that vibrated or jangled or twitched—however these fiends reacted—throughout every other Corasian in the place.

He was counting on the fact that the Corasians would be forced to search innumerable levels to find him, and once they did find his tracks, his body readings would throw them off—hopefully for the few precious moments he needed. Expecting a human—the two dead Corasians would have reported that they were being attacked by a human—the enemy would be looking for human readings. They wouldn't be looking for a human who was mostly machine.

Keeping watch for the telltale red glow that presaged the coming of the fiery, amoebic Corasians, Xris stopped in front of a computer terminal located at a junction of intersecting tunnels and activated the system. He knew how it operated, the uncreative Corasians having been forced to steal their technology from the human life-forms in the neighboring galaxy. Xris had encountered a Corasian computer system one other time before on a mission with the late Lady Maigrey and he knew what to expect—a system that was out of date and primitive. He called up inventory.

The Corasians kept strict records. The "meat" was a valuable commodity, to be shipped out to those planets in dire need of either food or slave labor—or slave labor that would ultimately become food. Each "carcass" was numbered when it arrived and carried that number through to final consumption.

Xris located the number—her number. Activating his own internal computer, the cyborg brought up the diagram of the locker tunnels, studied the screen embedded in his wrist, and located her cell. One level up and three compartments down, to the right. He moved, just as the red glow began to light the far tunnel behind him.

He found her—that was the easy part. Now for the hard. She wasn't alone. She was inside a cell with five others—a man and two women and two children.

Xris shorted out the force field, walked into the cell.

Dull-eyed, stupefied with terror, the six stared at him. They didn't believe in him . . . at first. Then she recognized him. Her eyes widened, color flooded her pale cheeks. Her lips parted. She rose to her feet.

The others didn't know him, but they understood. Hope lit their eyes. The kindest thing he could do for them was to end it, swiftly.

"Sorry," he said. "I can only manage one."

He reached out, took hold of her, pulled her to his side.

"If my team was with me, I could—"

He stopped. Explanation was time-consuming, unnecessary.

"My children," pleaded the man, shoving a pair of ragged, sleepy, and frightened kids toward Xris. "It doesn't matter about me, but take them with you. Please, for the love of God—"

She was pleading with him, too. Urging him to take the others, no matter that it would endanger them all. And there was no arguing with her.

A needle flicked out of the palm of his mechanical hand, punctured her skin. She was startled at the sudden sharp pain, but before she could cry out, he shot her full of the drug. She sagged against him. Her eyes closed; her body went limp.

He picked her up with his mechanical arm, thinking, The last time I touched her with this hand, she flinched.

"Shoot us, then," said one of the women, gathering the children close, holding them tight. "That's the least you can do."

Yeah. It was. It would take time, time he didn't have. But it was the least he could do. Xris took aim and shot them, shot them all.

Then, carrying her in his arms, he headed for the exit.

A red glow flooded the tunnel, blocked the way. The Corasians opened fire. Laser light flared around him.

"Hit," came a synthesized voice. "Two kills."

"Damn," Xris muttered.

He holstered his lasgun, checked the clock, shook his head. He had to get out faster. He needed to cut at least forty seconds off his time.

Deactivating the dummy in his arm, he dropped it to the floor and crossed over to the control panel located on a far wall of the target range. He hit a switch. The red glow died. The holograph people and the children disappeared. Forty seconds. Where the hell was he going to pick up forty seconds?

A blue light began to blink above the door.

"Visitors," the synthesized voice informed him.

Xris looked out the observation window, saw two people—at least he guessed one was a person—standing in the hallway. Raoul and the Little One.

The cyborg muttered a curse beneath his breath. He hadn't expected them back this soon. He had planned to be long gone before they came.

He considered sending them up to report to Harry; then it occurred to the cyborg that Harry was probably the one who'd sent them down here to report to him. If Xris refused to see them, they would grow suspicious, and the last thing Xris wanted was to rouse suspicions in these two—particularly the Little One. Best to see them, hear them out, act as if nothing was up, give them their orders, send them away.

He hit the switch, opened the door.

The two entered. Xris shut the door behind them.

"We'll talk in here," he said. "I can seal it off."

Raoul nodded complacently. Raoul would have nodded complacently if Xris had told him he was intending to blow off his head. Raoul was an Adonian—a human race noted for their beauty. He was also a Loti, so called because he lived, thrived, and survived on mind-altering drugs. He drifted through life in a state of euphoria, never frightened, never upset, never disturbed by anything. At least, that was how Raoul claimed he lived.

Xris was beginning to wonder.

During the past three years, Raoul had worked with Xris, been one of the team. They'd handled several dangerous assignments and Xris had seen Raoul in action, seen the Loti react to the unexpected swiftly, alertly—too swiftly and too alertly for a doped-up Loti. And yet he never lost the glassy-eyed gaze, the vacuous expression, the isn't-the-world-a-beautiful-place smile. Not even when it seemed likely that they were all about to die.

Raoul glanced around in bored fashion as he minced inside the target room, shuddered delicately. "A Corasian meat locker. How truly ghastly."

Purple-drenched eyelids fluttered. He smoothed his long black hair, which had been ruffled by the slight breeze created by the opening of the door. "You do find the most remarkably ugly places in which to play your games, Xris Cyborg."

Xris shrugged. Pulling out a particularly noxious form of cigarette known as a twist, he stuck it in his mouth, lit it, breathed in the foul-smelling smoke. "A little target practice, that's all."

He was aware of a sudden change in Raoul's partner, known only as the Little One. Two bright and intense eyes shifted their curious gaze from the target range to Xris's face.

If Raoul was a mystery, his partner was an enigma.

No one had ever seen the Little One; no one had ever heard him speak. No one knew his race, creed, color. All anyone had ever seen of him was the raincoat, a pair of small humanoid hands, and those penetrating eyes—the only portion of the small creature's face visible from between the pointed collar of the overlarge raincoat in which the empath habitually enveloped himself. All topped by a battered fedora.

Xris couldn't even say for sure that the Little One was a he, except that Raoul termed him a he. But, given the Loti's own androgynous state, Xris wasn't at all certain Raoul knew the difference.

The Little One was getting too damned interested in Xris's insides.

The cyborg did what he could to adjust his thought processes, but this wasn't as easy as adjusting a cybernetic leg or hand. Too bad. His brain should be a machine, like the rest of him.

Erase. Shut down. Switch off.

No more pain. No more hurt. Disk drive empty.

"Too bad your late boss didn't set up a target range for poisoners," he commented, taking a drag on the twist.

"What an extraordinarily interesting idea," said Raoul, struck. "Still, I don't quite see how it could have been possible—considering the quiet nature of my profession—to create that atmosphere of violence and excitement that you all seem to find so attractive—"

Raoul paused at this point, glanced down at the Little One. The Loti looked back at Xris, and the shimmering, drug-vacant eyes didn't appear to be quite as vacant as the cyborg would have liked.

"The Little One says you are not seeking thrills this day, Xris Cyborg," said Raoul, flipping his black hair over his shoulders with a graceful motion of his delicate hands.

He looked around at the target range, at the elaborate sets designed to replicate perfectly the inside of a Corasian "meat" locker, at the scoreboard that registered two kills for the Corasians, at the dummy—dressed to resemble a human female—lying huddled on the floor of the cell.

"You are practicing here with serious intent," Raoul observed.

"Special job," Xris commented briefly, hoping this would end it. He took the butt end of the twist out of his mouth, ground it on the concrete floor with his good foot.

Raoul gave him an exasperated glance. Reaching down gingerly, he picked up the twist between thumb and index finger, and—making a face—threw it in the trash compactor.

"What about your assignment?" Xris asked, changing the subject. "Since you're back early, I take it you completed it satisfactorily."

"Most satisfactorily." Raoul gave him a charming smile. "The Little One says you are going alone."

Xris fixed the Little One with a look that caused the empath to literally shrivel up. The raincoat actually seemed to deflate; the eyes disappeared beneath the brim of the fedora.

"I thought he was an empath—soaked up feelings. Since when did he get to be a goddam mind reader?"

"It comes with age, among his people."

"What?" Xris grunted, eyed the fedora. "You serious?"

"As serious as possible in an absurd world. But I think you are attempting to change the subject, Xris Cyborg. You are going alone on a mission that is fraught with deadly peril. This is not good," chided Raoul, gently sighing. "This is not worthy of you. Or wise of you. And so the others will feel, once I tell them—"

"You're not going to tell them!" Xris snapped, taking another twist out of his pocket. He thrust it into his mouth, didn't bother to light it. "Better get used to this place 'cause I'm locking you in here. Don't worry. I'll send Harry for you in the morning. He'll let you out in time to wash your hair and put on your makeup. By which time I'll be long gone."

"On your way to Corasia, by yourself. A suicide mission. And to rescue one person—"

Raoul glanced down at the Little One, who—undeterred by Xris's fierce warning stare—apparently said something to his partner in whatever mysterious way they managed to communicate.

"Your wife," said Raoul softly.

"Tell him he's lucky I don't stuff him in there," Xris snarled, pointing to the trash.

"How have we deserved this of you, Xris Cyborg?" Raoul asked. The Loti's eyes filled with tears. "What faith have we broken with you that you do not keep faith with us? How have we failed you?"

"Shit!" Xris took the twist out of his mouth, threw it on the floor. "Don't start crying. In the first place this is personal, none of your goddam business. In the second place, I don't need you. Any of you, but especially I don't need a whacked-out poisoner and a snoop! I'll take care of this little matter and I'll be back before you know I'm gone. You can tell that to the others. Tell them I'm taking some time off, a well-deserved vacation."

Raoul opened his peach-colored lips.

"Not another word!" Xris warned. "Or by God I will stuff him in the trash. And you with him." He leaned back on the console. "Now, make your report."

Raoul exchanged glances with the top of the fedora, which was about all that could now be seen of the Little One. Apparently deciding that Xris meant what he said, the Loti removed a lace hankie from his blue beaded evening bag, dabbed his eyes—careful not to disturb his mascara—and then spread the hankie carefully over the control panel to dry.

"We met, as arranged, at the Exile Café. They had arrived ahead of me, by two days. An expensive room, near the top. I had the impression that they had never been there before, but naturally I did not ask."

"Who are they?"

"John Does. Nobodies." Raoul raised a disdainful plucked eyebrow. "Experienced starpilots. The Little One says they have military backgrounds, some mercenary work, nothing of interest. They gave me their names, of course, but the Little One says that the names were false."

"And who are they working for?"

"They claimed to be members of a prodemocracy organization unhappy with the return to a monarchy. The Little One says that, too, is false. They have no strong political beliefs as would be manifest if they were dedicated members of such an organization. Instead, they were acting a part, repeating what they had been told to say."

Xris took out another twist, examined it absently, shifted his gaze to the Little One. "He pick up on any real names? Places?"

"A group calling itself the Ghost Legion. The thought crossed the mind of each person at various times. Does that nomenclature mean anything to you, Xris Cyborg?"

Xris shrugged. "Could be anything from a paramilitary organization to a dance troupe. I'll pass it along. These characters you met were obviously just flunkies. Did you get any kind of a line on the people higher up?"

"Something rather strange. I led the discussion to commanders, leaders." Raoul flushed a delicate pink. "I am afraid I was forced to denigrate you and your leadership capabilities, Xris Cyborg. If anything of what I said should happen to come back—"

Xris waved his good hand. "Think nothing of it. What'd you find out?"

"The Little One descried a name."

"Yeah? And?"

Raoul lifted himself on his patent leather dancing pumps, swayed forward, and whispered "Starfire!" in breathless, dramatic tones.

Xris lit his twist, took a puff.

Raoul waited, regarded the cyborg expectantly.

Xris took the twist out of his mouth. "Yeah? So?"

Raoul's purple-lined eyes opened wide. "Do you not find that odd, Xris Cyborg?"

He snorted. "That you're talking about commanders and these former military pilots think of their king? The commander-in-chief?"

"But they are plotting to overthrow him, Xris Cyborg. Why would they think of him?"

"Ever heard of a guilty conscience?"

Raoul stared blankly.

The cyborg shook his head. "Skip it. Was what you offered them satisfactory?"

"I assume so. They examined the layouts to make certain all was there. But the Little One says that they lacked the technical expertise to truly understand what it was they were looking at."

"That's what we counted on. These guys are just the middlemen. Their job is to transport the goods to the experts. I hope you sold your soul dearly?"

"They were quite munificent," remarked Raoul, with a smile and a fluttering motion of his hands toward the beaded bag. "I will, of course, deposit this in the corporate account. After we deduct our expenses, of course."

"Of course," Xris said dryly. "I suppose that new outfit of yours is on the list. Kind of subdued for you, isn't it?"

Raoul looked down solemnly at his crushed purple velvet toreador pants, mauve hosiery, and matching purple sequined jacket.

"I thought I should present a serious image. I should look earnest in my desire—"

"—to betray king and country." Xris grinned, stuck the twist in his mouth. "So this is what the well-dressed traitor is wearing this year. Any indication of when they plan to strike?"

"The Little One says they intended to transmit the information we provided to another location, have it checked over."

"That should keep 'em busy awhile. Where do they plan to send it?"

"The Little One was unable to ascertain. A coded sequence. I doubt if these people know where they're sending it."

"Probably not. Well, we got a fish on the line. I hope this makes Dixter happy." He paused. Raoul was shaking his head, regardless of the harm the movement did to his hairstyle. "What's the matter?"

"I find it difficult to believe that any group would attempt to attack this facility. My former employer, the late Snaga Ohme, used to say that not even the renowned forces under the command of the dead Warlord Derek Sagan could lay siege to this place with any hope of achieving success."

"Your former employer was right." Xris cast an approving glance around. "It might be harder to break into His Majesty's palace, but I doubt it. Shields and the force field protect us from air attack. Life expectancy on the outer grounds is thirty seconds—if you watch where you step. Inside, we can pick up fleas crawling across the floor. Yeah, your former employer knew how to build a damn fine house for himself. Still, not even all this fancy technology kept *him* alive. He let his guard down once, maybe, but once was all it took."

"Yes, that is true." Raoul sighed and flashed a blissful smile. "And so we appear to let our guard down and wait to see who lunges at us."

"That's what we were hired for. Damn dull, if you ask me, but I couldn't very well say no to the Lord of the Admiralty."

Xris began packing up his gear—specially designed missiles that fired from either a gun or his cybernetic weapons hand. He'd developed them three years ago, when he'd been hired by the Starlady to fight Corasians. The missiles had worked then, saved their lives. He'd modified them, refined them, sold his design for them to the Royal Military. He was a wealthy man now. Which was good, since it was going to take a large portion of that wealth to get him into and out of Corasia alive.

"When are you leaving?" Raoul asked, watching the cyborg's preparations.

"Tonight."

"The others will notice you are gone."

"By the time they do, it won't matter. Might as well make yourself comfortable. You may be here for a while."

"This is not in the contract, Xris Cyborg," said Raoul, seating himself on the edge of the control panel. Taking a small mirror from the beaded bag, the Loti studied himself in it, frowned slightly. He removed a silver tube from the bag, opened it, and began to trace a peach-colored line around his lips. "You are always very insistent on the contract."

"There's a clause about an act of God in the contract," Xris told him. "Look it up. Besides, you don't need me for this job. Hell, you got half the Royal Military out there, the other half on call. Tell Lee he's in charge. Nothing's going to happen. Whoever they are, they won't be ready to make their move for a long, long time. Shit, it'll take them a military month to figure out those phony layouts we provided. By then I'll be back—"

"You won't be back," said Raoul complacently. He regarded the cyborg from beneath languidly drooping, half-closed, purple eyelids. "Not if you go alone. You don't have a chance. You will die. And so will she."

Xris said nothing.

Raoul sat on the control panel, swinging his shapely legs back and forth. The empath was huddled underneath a fake fiberglass boulder. He looked remarkably dejected, hopeless, despairing.

"If he's picking up on my mental state, no wonder," Xris muttered, suddenly angry.

He stalked over to the sliding door, moving with his awkward gait, trying to force the natural human part of his body to work faster, be better than the stronger, indestructible mechanical part. He had almost reached the door when Raoul slid off the control panel, flitted over toward Xris. The Loti sidled near.

"A kiss for luck, my friend."

"No, you don't." Xris stiff-armed Raoul, shoved the Loti's head against a wall, being careful to use his mechanical hand near the Loti's mouth. "I know about the lip gloss, remember? What's in it today?"

"A sleeping potion." Raoul gasped a little in pain, though the smile never left his face. If anything, the smile was rather more blissful. "You would not have slept long. We could have discussed the matter. Please, do not crush the velvet. I—"

"Xris!" Harry's voice boomed out into the target range. "You better get the hell up here! Our security monitors just went berserk! And is that empath down there with you? Bring him along."

Xris glared at Raoul.

The Loti gave him a charming, pouting smile. "Don't blame me. I have no idea what is transpiring. And I am not responsible. Perhaps it is, as you said, an act of God."

The cyborg cursed beneath his breath, released the Loti. "Nothing I can do or say will keep you from telling them, will it?"

"Nothing short of murder, Xris Cyborg."

"Try that lip gloss trick on me again and—"

"Xris!" Harry sounded tense.

"Yeah, I'm coming. I'm coming. And I've got the empath."

The cyborg was on the move. Raoul, rubbing his bruised jaw and making certain his velvet had not been damaged, flitted after him. The Little One trotted alongside, moving as fast as his short legs and the long hem of the raincoat, which was continually tripping him up, permitted.

"Why do you want the empath?" Xris spoke into his commlink. He was heading for the elevator and the upper levels of the late Snaga Ohme's mansion. "What's going on? What have you got?"

"If you ask me," Harry said grimly, "I think it's ghosts."

Chapter ❦ Three

. . . toward his design, moves like a ghost.
William Shakespeare, *Macbeth*, Act II, Scene i

Sir John Dixter, Lord of the Admiralty, sat in his resplendent suite of offices, located on the top floor of the newly constructed Royal Military Headquarters building, and gazed out one of the floor-to-ceiling windows. The view was breathtaking, magnificent, and all other laudatory adjectives. The Glitter Palace, His Majesty's royal residence, stood directly opposite. Its multifaceted crystal walls—strong and stalwart—sparkled radiantly, with jewellike beauty, in the sunlight. And directly beneath the palace, its shining mirror image, reflected in the rippling surface of a cobalt-blue lake, shimmered and danced.

From his vantage point, Dixter could see the entire city of Minas Tares. It was lunch hour, and many of the government workers were in the streets, taking their noon meals in the restaurants and wine bars, spending their brief noon hour shopping, conducting business, or dropping by the day-care centers to play with their children.

The winding, artfully designed streets were crowded, but the crowds were orderly, went about their business or pleasure quietly. Directly below his window, a well-shepherded group of tourists stood gawking at the palace. Tourists were permitted on King's Island, but they were closely monitored, herded about in small groups and permitted entry only to certain areas.

A monorail system provided transportation to and from City Royal, a bustling metropolis located about ten kilometers from King's Island. The two were separated by a bay, connected by monorail. Most of those who worked on King's Island lived in City Royal, which was also the jumping-off point for tourists.

Dixter eyed the tourists closely—as closely as possible from twenty stories up. He scanned the crowd for the one who might attempt to edge away from it, to sidle off down a back street . . .

His nose practically pressed against the windowpane, the admiral realized what he was doing, flushed and glanced around swiftly, hoping Bennett had not seen him.

John Dixter was being paranoid and he knew it.

"But then, I have reason to be," he murmured, easing up on himself, remembering the Revolution—a time he hadn't paid attention to small details and his world had exploded in flames around him. That had been twenty-some years ago. But John Dixter would never forget.

When His Majesty Dion Starfire first came to power three years ago, it had been recommended that King's Island be transformed into a security zone, barring entry to everyone except those who had business there. Twenty years ago, John Dixter had seen the Glitter Palace in flames, its walls covered with blood, and he had been inclined to favor such precautions. Dion had adamantly refused. He would not separate himself from his people; he would not become some godlike figure perched high on a mountain peak, speaking to them through the vidscreen.

His Majesty liked to travel and was constantly on the move. And wherever he went, he drew enormous crowds and was always as accessible as it was possible for a man surrounded by armed guards and burdened with a tight, down-to-the-second traveling schedule to be accessible. He often held public audiences on the worlds he visited, inviting those with grievances or petitions to present them in person.

This hour with the public was an hour from hell for the Royal Guard, responsible for the king's life, despite the fact that people admitted into the Royal Presence were carefully screened—generally by their own governments in advance of His Majesty's visit—and searched practically inside out for weapons.

"I put my trust in God," Dion told an unhappy Dixter when the admiral had made his formal protest.

The king had smiled when he spoke, and so Dixter wasn't certain whether His Majesty was being reassuring or ironic.

The admiral was serious. "Begging your pardon, sir," he said in a low tone, "but I knew another king who used to say that."

Dion had reached out, placed his hand on the hand of his old friend. "God watches over me, sir."

"That may be true," Dixter later remarked to Cato, captain of the Royal Guard, when they were discussing the matter. "But who is watching over God?"

"Derek Sagan," said Cato with a shrug.

The story made its way around the barracks and was greatly appreciated by the Royal Guard, most of whom had served under the deceased Warlord. Dixter himself had smiled at the captain's witticism, though he rather thought that Cato had been more serious than otherwise.

"I will not be seen living in fear," His Majesty had stated on his first ascending to the throne. "My intent is to project an image of calmness, tranquillity. If the people see that I and my family feel secure, unafraid, then the people will feel secure, unafraid. I must be seen to be in control of my present and of my future."

And it had worked. It was working. Dion had seized control of the reins of state and was hanging on to them grimly. He had established a constitutional monarchy, formed a parliament. Each day was a struggle, however. Each day brought some new crisis for the young king. Each day it seemed he might lose his grip, be jounced from the saddle to fall in the mud. And there were many riding behind him, waiting to trample him when he fell.

"And he loves it," said Dixter now to himself.

As the days progressed he watched the young king in awe, amazed that someone in his early twenties could act and think with the wisdom of far older years. Dion knew when to bring quarreling factions together, knew when to keep them apart. He knew when to talk, when to keep silent. Knew when to threaten, to bully; knew when to plead, cajole. Politics never wore him out. It acted on him like a stimulating drug. He would emerge from a grueling session looking refreshed, invigorated, while others in attendance would come out weary, drained, exhausted.

The tour guide below was pointing out the location of the king's private rooms, describing the myriad luxuries in a rapid-fire monotone, machine-gunning the tourists with accounts of the royal china, the royal silverware, the royal tablecloths and bed linens, the royal jewels, the royal shoes, royal this and royal that and royal so forth. The tourists, ducking beneath the hail of statistics, looked up at the faraway windows in awe.

Dixter looked at the windows in musing sorrow.

It was behind those windows, when Dion was away from the cams and the vids and the media, away from the "balm, the scepter and the ball, the sword, the mace, the crown imperial. . .", as Shakespeare termed it in *Henry V*, that the drug wore off, the reaction set in. It was there, in his home, where he faced his most difficult challenge. The young man who, at twenty-one, could bring warring star systems together in peace could not manage to spend fifteen minutes together peacefully with his wife.

The door opened noiselessly. Dixter's aide-de-camp, Bennett, glided into the room, unobtrusively began to set to rights everything the Lord of the Admiralty had knocked askew.

"Magnificent view, my lord," remarked Bennett, noting Dixter's fixed stare.

"Is it?" Dixter blinked, looked at what he had been looking at. "Oh, yes. I suppose it is." He smiled ruefully. "You'll never guess what I was seeing, Bennett."

"No, my lord," said Bennett in tones which indicated that though he might not be able to guess, nothing would surprise him.

"I was in that trailer on the planet Vangelis. Sitting in that little cubicle of an office, looking out over the tarmac. Do you remember?"

"I remember the heat, my lord."

"Was it hot? Yes, I suppose it was. I didn't notice the heat. We'd been in hotter places."

"True, my lord." Bennett continued his tidying up, rearranging chairs that had been moved during a conference, emptying coffee cups, whisking away paper napkins.

"I was thinking about that day Tusk brought him in to see me. 'Dion' he said his name was. He didn't know his last name. I remember that red-gold hair, those blue, blue eyes. Do you know, Bennett—when I think back on that moment, it seems to me that everything in my life was gray up until then. I don't remember seeing colors before then. Not for years." He sighed, rubbed his eyes, which ached from staring fixedly into the sun's glare.

Bennett cast a surreptitious glance at his commander. Others addressed him as "Sir John" or "Lord Dixter," but to Bennett he was always the "general," just as he had been for the fifteen or so years the sergeant-major had been in Dixter's service.

Bennett had memories of his own. He looked at John Dixter, resplendent in his uniform that had at least started out immaculate. A uniform decorated with medals—medals of honor awarded him by innumerable star systems, primary among them being the lion's-head sun that had been pinned onto his chest by the young king's own hand. Dion's first official act.

Bennett looked around the enormous office, took in the desk that was practically as large as the trailer on Vangelis to which the general had been referring. The sergeant-major thought back to the first time he'd met John Dixter, in a bar on Laskar. It had been shortly after the Revolution. As a suspected royalist, Dixter was on the run. There was a price on his head. He made his living as a mercenary, operating out of Laskar. This bar was the only bar on Laskar Dixter ever entered. The only bar where he ever got truly drunk. That night, Dixter told Bennett—a complete stranger—why.

In this bar, years before the Revolution, John Dixter had met the one woman he would ever love—the Lady Maigrey. The one woman he could never have, for she was Blood Royal and John Dixter was . . . ordinary. He told Bennett how he had loved her, how he'd lost her the night of the Revolution. What he hadn't told Bennett, what the general had not foreseen, was that years later he would find her again.

Only to lose her again.

Perhaps it was just as well he hadn't foreseen. Dixter was drunk enough that night as it was.

And so the sergeant-major had carried the general home that night and had not left his side since. Remembering Dixter then—dressed in a faded, tattered uniform, slumped over the bar—and seeing him now, Lord of the Admiralty, Bennett was forced to blink back a most unmilitary moisture in his eyes. The sergeant-major marched across the room, cleared his throat with a loud harrumph, and stared hard at the general.

"What is that stain on your uniform, my lord?"

Dixter glanced vaguely in the direction of his aide's disapproving gaze. "Where? Oh, that. Coffee, I would imagine."

"You appear to have set your elbow in it, my lord."

"It's those confounded small cups. Like drinking out of an eggshell. I can't get a grip on that fancy gold-plated handle and I end up sloshing coffee into the saucer. Then I hit it with my arm. . . . What the devil are you doing?"

"You will have to change jackets, my lord."

"For a little coffee stain?"

"And the cheese pastry on your lapel, my lord."

"Confound it, Bennett, I'm not scheduled to see anyone—"

A trilling whine interrupted. Bennett was forced to leave off struggling with his general in order to answer the phone. While he did so, Dixter left the window, returned to his desk. He took the opportunity to dip a napkin in a glass of water, rub ineffectually at the stain.

Bennett's eyebrows telegraphed his disapproval, but he was prevented from saying anything until he ended the conversation.

"Urgent communiqué coming in for you, my lord. Your personal access code."

Dixter frowned, stuffed the napkin in the water glass, and headed for the commlink room. Very few people in the galaxy had access to the admiral's personal access code, which provided the highest level of security available. An urgent message from one of them boded nothing good.

Entering the commlink room—located adjacent to his office—Dixter dismissed the personnel working there, shut and sealed the door. Bennett, with a long-suffering sigh, remained behind in the general's office to mop up the spilled water.

Dixter gave his identification, provided voice and hand print and DNA scan to gain access to the message. The descrambling took several seconds, during which the general waited with grim patience. He had a good idea who was calling and wished he'd thought to take an antacid tablet after breakfast.

A man's face appeared on the vidscreen—a bald head, acid-splashed skin, overhanging forehead, and deep, shadowed eyes—one real, one cybernetic. The burning sensation in Dixter's stomach increased.

Xris nodded curtly as Dixter's image registered on the cyborg's own screen. No preliminary, time-wasting formalities for the cyborg. He was direct and to the point.

"Something took the bait, boss."

"They made an attempt? Did you catch them?"

Xris grimaced. "You might say they ended up catching us, boss. Swallowed us hook, line, pole, and boat. The good news is you were right on two counts—you've got a leak and someone is after the bomb. The bad news is—they found it. Something entered the vault. Took the bomb."

Dixter stared, shocked. "Good God, man! That's not possible! And you let them get away—"

Xris grunted. "Hold on, boss. You've got to hear me out.

You'll get my full report in writing, but I thought I better deliver it first in person. Let you know I'm sober."

Dixter attempted to contain his impatience. "What happened?"

Reaching into his pocket, the cyborg drew out a twist, stuck it in his mouth, lit it.

"We made the transfer, moved the space-rotation bomb from the palace to Snaga Ohme's. You know how it went from your end. Top secret. Same from ours. As you and I arranged, Raoul let it be known among certain circles here on Laskar that he was for sale. A couple of people wanted to buy, but they turned out to be just after information on new product lines.

"Then we hit dirt. These guys weren't interested in the latest in plasma grenade launchers. They wanted blueprints of the house, details about the security systems. Raoul gave them the stuff, enough of it real to look good to an expert. Not real enough to use. I don't know why they needed it. Any of it." Xris drew in smoke. "Waste of their money, our time."

"Obviously not," said Dixter dryly. "It worked for them. You must have made a mistake, Xris, given them too much real information."

The cyborg snorted, blew smoke through his nose. "I don't get paid to make mistakes, boss. Hell, I could have given them a layout of the inside of Raoul's head and it would have been one and the same. Take a look at the monitor readings. They should be coming through by now."

Dixter walked over to another machine, studied the information that was being transmitted halfway across the galaxy.

He stared at it, frowned. "Print it," he ordered the computer, unwilling to believe what he saw on the screen.

The printout was no different, however. He studied it wordlessly, then looked back at the cyborg. "If it were any other man, I'd say you were seeing ghosts. . . ."

"Ghosts." Xris stubbed the end of the twist out on the console. "Funny you should mention ghosts. Look, if it makes you feel any better, boss, we didn't believe it either. We figured, like you are, probably, that the equipment must have malfunctioned. We checked it, more than once. It's working fine."

The cyborg stopped, took another twist from his pocket, but he didn't light it. He stared at it, switched the stare to Dixter. "And then we found proof. You want it from the beginning?"

Dixter sighed, rubbed his forehead, nodded.

Xris continued. "Front gate security saw, registered nothing. Same with the entrance—all the entrances. Nothing. Nada. Zip. The first we know we're being invaded, the motion detectors inside the house start registering movement. Like you see there."

"But how can you be sure? There's no corroboration from the other monitors, is there?"

"Nothing on visual, nothing on audio."

"What confirms it?"

"A drop in barometric pressure—in certain areas only—and a corresponding movement of the air in places where no air should be moving."

"The drop in pressure accompanies the disturbance," Dixter observed, studying the report. "So do the air currents."

"That's what convinced us we weren't crazy. We fed all this stuff into the computer, had it chart the results. Take a look at that. Look at the path it makes."

Dixter examined another document, transmitted by the cyborg—a diagram of Snaga Ohme's vast estate. A line had been drawn in red, a line that followed the movement detected by the various sensors. Dixter stared at it; his jaw went slack.

"Ghosts, you said, boss," Xris commented.

The path started at an outside wall, went through a nullgrav-steel-lined marble wall into the house, and traveled through room after room, moving straight through walls, ceilings, floors. It never deviated from its chosen course; no obstruction stopped it. It headed straight in one direction: the vault.

"As you see, to even reach the house itself, this thing had to pass through the force field that surrounds the estate, had to go through the garden, where life expectancy is thirty seconds if you're lucky. Motion detectors sensed movement in the garden, but they didn't get any corroborating evidence from other detectors, and so they didn't react, other than to register it.

"That's why it didn't trip any of the thousand or so booby traps, not that they would have done any damage. Couldn't. The thing moved too damn fast. It made it safely to the house, slid right through a fortified exterior wall that could withstand a direct hit from a lascannon and not buckle. Nothing stopped it. Nothing even fazed it, apparently."

"Was the vault on the layout Raoul passed on?"

"Sure. No reason not to. A lot of people already know about it. Snaga Ohme was proud of the contraption. He used to take special clients to see it. According to the Loti, Ohme once claimed he could detonate an atomic bomb next to it and the blast wouldn't so much as put a dent in the walls. He was exaggerating, of course, but probably not by much. What we *didn't* put on there was the security surrounding it, not to mention the vault's own internal security systems."

"And you say this ... whatever it was ... got past all that and inside the vault. What did it do once it was inside? Did *it* take the bomb?"

"Maybe it took it. Maybe it vaporized it. Maybe it ate it. We got the thing on vid. All I know is that one minute the damn bomb's there and the next it isn't."

"And this ... thing ... was responsible. Damn it, how do we know for sure?"

"Maybe we don't. We got two firm indications, boss: First, we registered an increase in the radiation level around the vault. Not much. But enough to make us suspicious, especially tracing the path the thing took. We examined the vault's superstructure. There'd been an alteration in the metal itself, a chemical change, enough to generate radioactivity. And only in that one place, directly in line with the path."

"That's the first. What was the second?"

Xris looked grim. "The bomb was moved."

"Moved?"

"Jostled, handled. Not far—a fraction of a fraction of a centimeter before it vanished. But enough to set off the alarm. That was the only alarm this thing did set off, by the way. And that was only because we've had the bomb surrounded by every conceivable type of sensing device, all sensitive enough to register a hair falling on it. The guards reacted instantly, entered the vault. They found nothing. Nothing except that the bomb was gone."

"The guards didn't see anything? Hear anything?"

"Now, that's another strange thing, boss. The guards didn't see or hear anything, but one of them reported *feeling* something. About a split second before the alarm went off. She said she felt as if she'd been shoved into a compression chamber. The feeling passed immediately. She shows no physical damage, no chemical alteration. No increase in radiation level, no aftereffects. But notice where she was standing, boss."

Dixter looked, gave a low whistle. The guard's position had

been indicated on the diagram. She had been standing directly in the red-lined path.

"You mean whatever this was went right *through* her?" Dixter was aghast.

"Through her, through nullgrav steel vault walls, into the vault, and out again. Look, motion detectors pick it up here, on the opposite side. It passed on through the rest of the house, exited here, through another fortified wall. Back out into the garden, through the force field, and presumably back to wherever it came from."

Dixter passed his hand over his face, scratched his chin. "Do you realize what you're saying, Xris? This thing goes through solid steel walls with leaving so much as a trace, then actually manages to touch and move an object? Damn it, it's not possible!"

The cyborg chewed on the twist. "What can I say, boss? I agree completely. It's not possible. But it happened."

"It took the bomb. Through solid matter."

"Yeah, and . . . I wonder if you've considered something else."

Xris lit the twist, puffed on it absently, flicked the ash to the floor. He stared at Dixter speculatively.

"What?" the admiral asked grimly.

"Whoever has that bomb now," Xris said, letting the smoke trickle slowly from his lips, "knows it's a fake."

The pain in Dixter's stomach jabbed him. He winced, pressed his hand to his side.

"Damnation," Dixter swore. He bent over the computer readouts, studied them, willing them to change, to make sense. They didn't.

"What was that you said about ghosts?" Dixter asked suddenly, thinking back to something Xris had said earlier. "You said it was funny I should mention it."

"Oh, yeah. When Raoul was meeting with these jokers who bought the information, the Little One—you remember the Little One?"

"The empath in the raincoat."

"Yeah. Well, the Little One picks up on the name of an organization these guys are all carrying around in their heads. Ghost Legion. Ever heard of it?"

"No, but that doesn't mean much. You think there's a connection?"

"It's one hell of a coincidence if there's not. These guys buy a layout of the house and grounds and three days later something goes right through us. Yeah, I'd say there was a connection."

"But, like you said earlier"—Dixter waved a hand—"if they have this type of capability, what did they need with layouts? Why bother?"

"Maybe they're trying to tell us something, boss. Send us a message. Maybe we got caught in our own trap."

Dixter shook his head. "That doesn't make sense."

Xris took the twist out of his mouth, tossed it onto the floor. "Let me know when any of this makes sense, will you, boss?"

Dixter was thinking. "I suppose the next step is to investigate this Ghost Legion. Will you—"

"Sorry, boss. Count me out. I've got . . . other business."

"Xris, this is important," Dixter said quietly.

"So's my business. I'm leaving tonight, as a matter of fact."

"I could order you to stay for complete debriefing. I could have you arrested."

"Wouldn't be pleasant for either of us, boss. Besides"—Xris smiled ruefully—"I'm about as debriefed as I can get. The others, too. I've sent you my complete report, plus Raoul's and the Little One's, plus the reports of everyone else in this place. Damn machines saw more than any of us. Spend your time debriefing them. Like I said, I'm leaving."

"I don't suppose you'd care to elaborate. . . ."

A series of beeps came over the commlink—the cyborg's mechanical arm, running through a routine systems check. Xris made a few minor adjustments, looked back at Dixter.

"Yeah, all right, boss. I could use your help, in fact. I plan to make a quick trip out of the galaxy. If your perimeter patrols spot me, I'd appreciate it if they didn't shoot me, either on the way out or on the way back."

"You're going into Corasia?"

Xris took a twist out of his pocket, studied it with interest.

Dixter tried again. "This wouldn't have anything to do with those humans taken prisoner during the raid on the Nargosi outpost, would it?"

Xris lit the twist, drew the smoke into his lungs, blew it back out.

"I can't give you permission to go behind enemy lines, Xris," Dixter said gravely.

"Fine, then. Skip it. Forget I said anything."

"Are you going alone? You can at least tell me that much."

Xris considered; apparently decided he could. "I was. But that's all changed—thanks to Raoul and his big lip-glossed mouth. The whole team's going. Though what the hell I'm going to do with a poisoner and an empath is beyond me."

Dixter thought the matter over. "If someone could rescue those people . . ." He nodded. "I'll pass the word along. Nothing official, of course. I can't do that."

Xris looked intently at Dixter, actually almost smiled. "Thanks, boss."

Dixter shook his head. "You know the odds. If you get into trouble, I'll have to deny I ever heard of you. The treaty and all that."

Xris grinned. "If we get into trouble, you won't need to bother. Nobody'll ever hear of us again. Though I wish I could stick around and help you on this other job. Damnedest thing I ever saw—or didn't see. I could give you the names of some good people . . ."

"Thanks, but I have someone in mind. You know him, in fact. Tusca. Former Scimitar pilot. You rescued him from the Corasians—"

"During that job we did for the Starlady. Yeah, I remember. You know, boss, it's mostly because of Lady Maigrey I'm doing this other. Something she said to me. She had a way of sticking to your mind."

"She did indeed," said John Dixter. "Godspeed, Xris."

"Same to you, boss."

The image of the cyborg vanished. The vidscreen went blank. Dixter stood staring at it a long time without moving. Then he wiped his hand across his face again, grimaced at the pain in his stomach. He stuffed the printouts under his arm, to be studied again at his leisure, coded the information contained in the computer under the highest possible security, then summoned back the operator.

"Have that new material in there gone over by experts," he ordered.

"Yes, sir. What type of experts, sir?"

Dixter pondered, frowning. "Damn it, I don't know!" He exploded, frustrated. "Expert experts. We seem to be inundated with them around here. Maybe they can do something useful for a change."

The officer stared at him, startled. The admiral was noted for being easygoing, unflappable.

Dixter drew a deep breath, raised his hand in a mollifying gesture. "I . . . I'm sorry, Captain. I didn't mean to bark at you. My guess is we're dealing with some type of newfangled probe. Start there. Oh, and bring in a parapsychologist."

The captain raised her eyebrows. "Parapsychologist, sir?"

"Yes." Dixter smiled. "Parapsychologist. A person who studies the supernatural."

"I know what one is, sir," said the officer stiffly.

"Then no doubt you'll be able to find me one, Captain."

"Very good, sir," said the officer, mystified.

Dixter left the commroom and bumped into Bennett, who had been hovering near the door.

"Are you feeling quite well, my lord?"

"Not particularly," Dixter growled. He sat down at this desk, began rummaging around among the papers.

"The antacid tablets are in the top drawer to the right, my lord."

Dixter grunted, found the tablets, ate two, munched on them disconsolately. "Get hold of Tusk."

"I beg your pardon. Who, my lord?"

Relaxing, the pain in his stomach subsiding momentarily, Dixter managed a grin. "You know who, Bennett. Don't give me that look. I'm not planning to run off and start the old mercenary trade again. Not that I don't think of it sometimes," he added wistfully.

Bennett sniffed. His regulation mustache quivered in disapproval.

Dixter shook his head, shook off memories. "I need Tusk to do a job for me, that's all."

Bennett appeared resigned. "Do you have any idea where Mendaharin Tusca can be located, my lord?"

"Last I heard from him, he was living on Vangelis, running a shuttle service with that blowhard . . . what was his name . . . Link."

"Vangelis, my lord." Bennett lifted an eyebrow. "Odd, that you happened to be discussing that very planet in rather nostalgic terms this morning, isn't it, my lord?"

"Just get hold of Tusk."

"Very good, my lord. And you will remember to change your jacket, won't you, my lord?"

Dixter glowered. Bennett left, stiff-backed, expressing silent disapproval. The Lord of the Admiralty remained seated at his desk, not changing his jacket, risking his aide's ire. The insides of Dixter's mouth were chalky with the taste of antacid. He picked up a cup of cold coffee, swished the liquid around, swallowed it. Too bad he couldn't coat the inside of his head with soothing relief.

Bennett was back. "Sorry, my lord, but phone service to the residence of Mendaharin Tusca has been disconnected."

"Tell the phone company this is the Lord of the Admiralty calling, extremely urgent, and that they jolly well better connect it back up again," Dixter snapped.

"I informed them of that, my lord. They said that the service was disconnected for nonpayment of a considerable sum owed to them. The equipment was repossessed, removed from the premises."

Dixter grimaced. The antacid was apparently under counterattack from the cold coffee and, by all indications, was fighting a losing battle. "Try XJ, then."

"My lord?"

"XJ-27. Tusk's shipboard computer. Find the call number under Interplanetary Vehicle licensing and registration. Tusk's a legit businessman now. He'd have to be licensed."

Having known Tusk nearly as long as he'd known the general, Bennett appeared to have his doubts, but he left on his assignment. Dixter wasn't feeling any too confident himself. He was already starting to contemplate, with a certain amount of enjoyment (if he didn't count the space travel, which he detested), flying to Vangelis to talk to Tusk in person, when Bennett returned.

"I managed to reach the computer, my lord. Tusca is not available at the moment. It appears that he is . . . um . . . babysitting. The computer promised to have him contact you when he puts in an appearance. I gather he is expected at any moment, my lord."

"Good. Thank you, Bennett. Let me know when that call comes through."

"Yes, my lord. Is there anything else, my lord?"

Dixter sighed. There was something else, but he didn't know whether to do it now or wait until he had more information. He decided he'd better do it now.

"Set up an appointment for me with His Majesty."

"Very good, my lord. Knowing His Majesty's busy schedule, I probably cannot arrange a meeting sooner than tomorrow. Will that be suitable, or should I say it is an emergency?"

"No, that'll be suitable." Dixter was relieved.

It wasn't an emergency, not really. Some sort of weird probe had penetrated their security, had walked off with the space-rotation bomb hidden in the late Snaga Ohme's vault, and by now probably knew that the bomb they had stolen was nothing more than an interesting paperweight. His elaborate entrapment scheme had partly failed, partly succeeded. He knew now, for certain, that someone was after the bomb. He also knew that there was a breach in the navy's own security.

Keeping the operation under as much secrecy as it would have been for real, he'd used Xris's commandos to transport a fake space-rotation bomb to a new, supposedly more secure location. As he'd figured, the information that the bomb had been moved had been leaked. Someone had known where it was and how to go after it. But his plans for catching the informant and his or her cohorts had failed.

Or had it?

"Ghost Legion," he muttered.

Bennett had returned and was hovering again. "The meeting with His Majesty is scheduled for tomorrow, 0800. And now, my lord, about that jacket—"

"Screw the damn jacket!" snarled Dixter. He reached for the printouts, knocked over the coffee cup, spilled coffee on his pants.

Chapter ·✦◑✦· Four

> What beckoning ghost ... invites my step ...
> Alexander Pope, *Elegy to an Unfortunate Lady*

Tusk climbed, hand over hand, up the ladder that led to the Scimitar's hatch. He stopped once about halfway up to adjust the child carrier he wore strapped to his back and to admonish the small child inside.

"Remember, be quiet and don't touch anything. Grandpa XJ doesn't like it."

The child nodded solemnly, wide-eyed at the prospect of treading on sacred and forbidden ground. It was not often he was allowed inside the Scimitar. The bright lights and myriad buttons and dials—some of them actually on his level—were too great a temptation for two and a half. Then there was the disembodied voice, the awful and mysterious Grandpa XJ, who was the god of the Scimitar, who had power over light and air and a certain sealed compartment beneath the plastileather sofa.

Tusk reached the hatch located on the top of the spaceplane, and pounded on it. "Open up, XJ. It's me."

The hatch whirred open with a suddenness that surprised Tusk, who had been expecting an argument or at least a barrage of sarcastic remarks from the computer. Flashing one last warning glance at the toddler, Tusk crawled through the hatch and descended into the spaceplane.

Those who had flown in this plane three years earlier—His Majesty among them, as proclaimed by an engraved plaque bolted to the bulkheads (Link's idea)—would not have recognized it now. Once a fighting warbird, the Scimitar had undergone a remarkable and expensive transformation, was now (as Nola put it) a cockatoo.

The bubble on top, which had once been the gun turret, was the "observation dome." Only one passenger could sit up there and "observe" at a time, and that was a rather tight fit, due to the fact that the gun was still in place, though Tusk had built

36

a cabinet around it and it now masqueraded as a drink holder. But the observation dome was popular with travelers and was one of the spaceplane's selling points.

The sleeping area—once a repository for tools and mags and vids, coils of wire, empty bottles of jump-juice, and a couple of hammocks suspended from the overhead—was now "homey and inviting" as Link termed it, though Tusk thought privately it looked like the waiting room in a dentist's office.

The weapons storage compartments were plastileather settees. The deck had been carpeted (used). A large-screen vid provided entertainment for the space-weary traveler. Link would have added an artificial fireplace, for "ambiance," but Tusk had threatened to throw him out the airlock if he did. The only improvement of which Tusk thoroughly approved was the new wet bar. He took care to keep it well stocked, much to XJ's ire. The computer ceased to grumble, however, after discovering how much profit they made off liquor sales.

Unfortunately, that was the only area in which they were showing a profit. Business was good. The swift-flying shuttle was popular with those who either needed to be somewhere in a hurry or wanted to get there without customs and immigration taking notice of them on arrival. Such people were willing to spend extra to obtain one or the other convenience, or both. With careful money management and sound investments, "Tusk's Link to the Stars" (as Nola had cleverly dubbed it) could have made its two owner-operators comfortable, if not wealthy.

But Link's idea of a sound investment was a hot tip on a horse in the seventh. Tusk's notion of money management was to spend what he had when he had it and to save it when he didn't. Nola could have handled the accounting, but she was working full time, trying to raise a toddler, and pregnant again. XJ-27 yammered and raved and ranted about their bleak financial state, but unless the customer paid with credit, the computer could rarely get its microchips on the money. And most of their customers paid in cash, to leave no record of the transaction.

Some children are frightened by the bogeyman or ghosts or the monster that lives in the closet. Young John was terrified of the dark and ghoulish nemesis known in the Tusca household as the Collection Agent.

Reaching the dentist-office level of the Scimitar, Tusk slid his arms out of the straps of the backpack child carrier, lowered his son silently and stealthily to the deck, and put his finger to his lips.

"XJ," called Tusk, trying to sound nonchalant. "There been any calls for me?"

"One. It was— What's that?"

"What's what?" Tusk asked innocently. Winking at his son, the pilot walked over to the bar, began to clang bottles together loudly. "We're low on scotch. . . ."

"Someone else is breathing," stated XJ irascibly. "And I detect the distinct smell of wet diaper. You've brought that brat of yours in here!"

Young John sat on the deck, thumb in his mouth, waiting patiently to make his move. The son of a starpilot and a former TRUC driver turned guerrilla fighter, John Tusca knew the value of a diversion and was waiting until the shooting started.

Tusk was about to deny the charge, then changed his mind. "It's only for an hour or so. Nola's got a doctor's appointment and we couldn't get a sitter. And he's not wet. He's potty trained now. At least most of the time. Who called?"

"I'm not saying," the computer snapped. "This is not Dingdong School. Remove the little twerp and we'll discuss business."

"Damn it, XJ! My kid's not a 'twerp' or a 'brat.' He's my son—a person, just like me—"

"Now *there's* a recommendation!" XJ gave a mechanical snort.

"—and he needs to be treated with respect!" Tusk finished loudly. "You're gonna give him an inferiority complex or something, talking about him like that. Babies can understand a lot more than we think they can. Now, who the devil called? Was it important?"

"Extremely. Urgent, in fact. And I admit the brat makes more sense than you do, most of the time, but he doesn't belong on my plane. He touches my buttons," XJ complained peevishly.

"I'll touch your buttons!" Tusk stalked over to the railing that separated the bridge from the plastileather-and-used-carpet lounge area and peered down into the cockpit. "What do you mean, *your* plane? We're partners—you and me and Link. And damn it, XJ, if a client called and we miss a run because you're—"

"A run?" XJ sputtered. "How're you going to make a run with junior there? 'Sorry, folks, we can't make the jump to lightspeed. It gives the baby hiccups.' I was never so humiliated! It's a wonder I didn't short out."

"Would you forget that? He was real little then. Nola'll be back any minute. Now, who called? Was it Lovason? He said he might have an important drop to make later on in the week—"

"No, it was not Lovason. And why'd you have to go and get pregnant again anyway? Jeez, don't you two ever do anything except—"

This diversion was better than expected. Young John made his move. Keeping low, so as not to draw fire, crawling on belly, elbows, and knees, he made it all the way across the deck to one of the settees. Then there came a lull in the firing. John pulled himself upright, sat with his back against the settee, had his thumb in his mouth by the time his father glanced around.

"John, where— Oh, there you are. Don't mess with that."

John regarded his father with the expression of blank and baffled innocence that is a small child's first line of defense.

"Okay, there's a good boy. He's not bothering anything, XJ, so don't get your circuits in a knot. As for why we got pregnant again, if it's any of your goddam business, which it isn't, Nola's not getting any younger, and the doctor said if we wanted—"

A panel in the bottom of the settee slid open. Young John reached in his hand. His pudgy fingers found the cookie, wrapped around it, conveyed it to his mouth. He munched on it silently, under the cover of friendly fire.

"Don't give me that," XJ was saying. "I think you two just screwed up, no pun intended. And how you expect to feed another mouth, when you've got creditors lined up from here to Hell's Outpost, not to mention the fact that they've canceled your medical insurance—"

"Canceled the insurance?" Tusk gaped. "When? How?"

"Stop jabbering. The insurance company likes to be paid. They're funny that way."

Tusk groaned. "Was that due this month? I thought—"

"No, you didn't. That's your problem. Besides, it was due two months ago. And if you think I'm—" XJ stopped in mid-sentence. The computer's tone altered. "Yes, my lord. Yes, good talking to you again, my lord. He's here now, my lord. Just this moment stepped in. Please hold for a second, my lord, and I'll put him right on."

"Who is it?" Tusk asked, sliding down the ladder into the cockpit. "My lord who?"

He cast one worried glance over his shoulder at the baby, but young John was leaning with his back against a settee, staring at nothing with the grave intensity of two years. His mother would have noticed that he was far too quiet and well-behaved to be up to anything good. His father congratulated himself on how adept he was at child-rearing. He couldn't understand why Nola always complained about John getting into things he wasn't supposed to. Tusk never had that problem.

He sat down in the pilot's seat to take the incoming call.

Young John reached back into the secret compartment, took two cookies.

"General Dixter," said XJ, sounding subdued. "Pardon me, Sir John Dixter. On the viewscreen."

"General Dix—" Tusk made a strangled sound. "Was he the one—? You didn't tell—? Sir!"

The Lord of the Admiralty appeared on the screen, gorgeous and almost unrecognizable in white uniform, decorated with stars, rows of gleaming medals, gold braid on the shoulder, all of which made him look imposing, severe, and unfamiliar. This was not the general Tusk had served under during his years as a mercenary, not the man who'd sat in that hot trailer in the middle of the desert, drinking Laskarian brandy and talking about a king's child, born on a night of fire and blood.

"General! Sir!" Tusk jumped to his feet, saluted. He was acutely aware of his own sweat-soaked fatigues.

"He's addressed as 'my lord,' fool!" XJ intoned in a low audio that, nevertheless, carried quite well.

"I—I mean m-my lord," Tusk stammered.

Dixter smiled, the same warm and generous smile Tusk remembered, the smile that always had something a little sad about it. "Belay that, Tusk. We've known each other too long for that."

Now Tusk saw the cheese pastry stain on the Lord of the Admiralty's lapel, the coffee stain on the right elbow. Tusk relaxed, grinned, and sat down.

"Good to see you, sir," he said.

"It's good to see you, Tusk. Damn good." Dixter himself appeared to relax; the brown eyes in their maze of wrinkles warmed. "How's Nola?"

"Fine, sir. She'll be along any minute. You can say hello.

Well, no, you can't. I forgot. She can't squeeze through the hatch. We're . . . er . . . expecting again."

"Are you? Congratulations! And how's my godson?"

"Growing like a weed, sir. I can get him, if you'd like—"

"No, you don't!" snapped XJ. "Don't bring that rug rat down into my cockpit!"

"Oh, stow it!" Tusk started to stand up again, always proud to show off his son.

"Perhaps in a moment," Dixter said, raising his hand. He continued to smile, but the tense expression was back. "I didn't call just to visit, though God knows it's been long enough since we have. Too long. I get busy. . . ."

He ran his hand through his graying hair, then came back abruptly to business. "I need information, Tusk. I want you to do a little investigating for me. I'm interested in knowing more about a group that calls itself the Ghost Legion. It may be a terrorist group, it may be a paramilitary— What is it? You know something?"

"Sure, sir. I'm surprised you haven't heard about them. They've been advertising. I got some electronic mail from them. Link, too. They're looking for starpilots."

"Indeed," Dixter murmured, his forehead creasing in a slight frown.

"I guess you haven't been paying much attention to the Help Wanteds lately, sir," Tusk said.

Dixter was lost in thought, didn't appear to have heard. When he caught on, he looked rueful, smiled again. "No. No, I haven't. You think that's where they found your name?"

Tusk looked startled. "I suppose. I never gave it much thought. I get lots of mail."

"Mostly threatening to cut off our water," XJ commented.

Tusk shot the computer a vicious glance.

"What's their line?" Dixter asked. "Who are they? Where are they from? I don't suppose you'd have a recording of their message?"

"Yeah, as a matter of fact I do, sir. You see, it sounded like a pretty good deal and, well, things haven't been going real great around here, what with Nola being pregnant again and all, and, well,"—Tusk appeared embarrassed—"I thought I might look into it."

He began to sort through his vid files, kept talking as he searched.

"According to their pitch, sir, these people live on a technologically underdeveloped planet that's suddenly come into a lot of wealth—some valuable type of resource—and they're afraid that bigger, stronger neighbors will try to muscle in. This Ghost Legion—that's what they call themselves—is looking to hire pilots to help them defend their planet."

"But the Royal Navy would provide them protection, if they had a legitimate grievance."

Tusk shook his head. "Begging your pardon, sir, but you know how that works. The Royal Navy can't intervene until a planet's been attacked. By that time, it's generally too late. Plus, you can't stay there forever. You've got a whole damn galaxy to watch. Who's going to mind the store when you're gone? Every planet's got the right to maintain its own defense, sir."

"Of course," said John Dixter, preoccupied. "What's the name of this planet?"

"I forget, sir. Something strange. I can send you the recording. . . ."

"Yes, I'd like to see it." He frowned. "You *and* Link. . . ."

"What's wrong with that, sir?"

"I don't know. It seems odd, that's all. You each received the mail separately? Not under the name of the shuttle service you run?"

"Yeah, that's right. Mine came through XJ, here. My system at home is . . . uh . . . out of commission."

The computer made a rude noise.

"And Link's came through his own spaceplane. . . ." Tusk gave a low whistle. "You know, there *is* something odd about that, sir. I never thought about it before. They sent it to Link's plane. He hasn't flown that plane in two years. Can't. Some loan shark's got a lien on it. But he's rigged up a betting system on his computer—you put in the horse, it figures the odds. It works about twenty percent of the time, like you might expect for Link. He keeps changin' the program. Anyway, he was fooling with it when he found this Ghost Legion ad."

"Damn right, it's odd," Dixter said grimly. "How did they get your names and numbers? *I* never gave them out. You must have known that, Tusk. Too many of you were wanted men."

"Yeah. The late and unlamented Derek Sagan would have given a starship to get his hands on those files. Speakin' of which, maybe—"

"No," said Dixter. "All his old files on you mercenaries were purged after his death. No one—"

"Excuse me, sir," XJ interrupted, "but there could be a completely logical and innocent explanation. Both Tusk and Link hold pilot's licenses on this planet. It is quite conceivable that this Ghost Legion simply sent out this flier to that mailing list."

Tusk shook his head. "We're both registered under the business. It would have come addressed to 'Tusk's Link to the Stars.' It didn't. It came directly to me and directly to Link. You've got me curious now, sir. I'll do some checking."

Dixter nodded. "Good. That's what I was hoping for. Be discreet. You're interested in finding out about the job, nothing more. Do you keep up with any of the others from the old outfit?"

"Gorbag the Jarun, Reefer. I think I could get hold of them. You want to know if they got the same mail, huh, sir?"

"Yes. And, Tusk, I'd think twice about signing up with them."

"I don't suppose you'd like to tell me why, sir."

"I wish to God I knew," Dixter said.

Tusk waited a moment, to see if anything more was forthcoming. It wasn't.

"Yeah. Well, sir, maybe I can help. I'll be in touch, soon as I find out anything."

"Thank you. I'll transmit my private access number. It's on a scrambler, so don't worry about eavesdroppers. The government will pay you for your time and reimburse you for any expenses. Give Nola and young John my love."

"Yes, sir. Thank you, sir."

"And Tusk, be careful."

"Sure, sir," said Tusk, startled.

Dixter's image faded. Tusk sat, staring at the screen in wonder.

"What the hell's up, you suppose?"

"Beats me. Doesn't sound like it's going to make us much money, though," added XJ gloomily. "And when I think of what it's going to cost us, getting hold of those reprobate friends of yours. They're all probably in prison somewhere—"

"Quit complaining. Dixter said he'd reimburse us."

"That's true. He did say that, didn't he?" The computer's lights gleamed. "If we handle this right, we can soak the Royal Treasury for a bundle."

"Yeah, then *I'll* be the one in prison."

"At least that would stop this endless cycle of baby production. Speaking of which," XJ cut in before Tusk could yell, "Nola's outside the spaceplane. She's been shouting at you for the last five minutes."

"Damn!"

Now that Tusk was paying attention, he could hear her. Getting up from the pilot's chair, he climbed the ladder into the living quarters and headed for the second ladder that led up and out of the spaceplane.

"And take your brat with you!" XJ yelled.

Tusk grunted something it was probably just as well the computer didn't hear. Catching hold of young John, Tusk tucked his son under his arm and nimbly climbed the ladder.

"Bye, Grandpa." The toddler waved at the plane's interior.

"Grandpa!" XJ repeated in disgust. "Still, the kid *is* going to need a role model."

The computer slid the hatch shut. Left alone, XJ took a quick inventory, made a note.

"Buy more cookies."

Chapter ·◆◄○►◆· Five

Best image of myself and dearer half
          —John Milton, *Paradise Lost*

Tusk emerged into the bright sunshine of Vangelis, blinked and paused a moment to adjust his eyes after the spaceplane's cool and shadowy interior. Then he slid down the ladder, young John tucked under one arm, the toddler jouncing and grinning at the fun of the descent and the sight of his mother, waiting for them on the tarmac below.

"He's not a sack of potatoes, you know," said Nola, rescuing her son from his precarious position. "What if you slipped?" She hugged the child, presented her cheek to her husband to be kissed.

"I never slip. I'm surefooted, like a panther." Tusk grinned, kissed her, patted her rotund stomach. "What'd the doctor say?"

Nola looked at him quizzically. Her nose wrinkled, which sent her freckles dancing across her face. "I think you better sit down. Maybe we should wait until we get home."

"Can't. Got some work to do. Dixter called. What'd the doctor say?"

"Dixter? General Dixter?" Nola was amazed. "What did he want?"

"Tell you later. Now, what—"

"All right. But let's get the kid out of the sun. Besides, I have to go to the bathroom."

"We can go back in the plane . . . Oops, no. Sorry, I forgot." Tusk patted his wife's stomach again. "You're as big as a cruise liner. I don't remember you being this big with John. Here, we can go to the clubhouse. Get a beer."

"*You* can have a beer." Nola sighed. "Water for me."

They walked across the baking hot tarmac, heading for the small prefab hut that was known semi-sarcastically as the clubhouse. Tusk and Link kept the plane in a private spaceport, located on the distant outskirts of Mareksville, one of the planet's larger and more prosperous cities. The spaceport was run-down, its tarmac cracked and broken. It had no hangars—not that Tusk and Link could have afforded the luxury of a hangar anyway— and no lights. Since most of those who utilized this runway didn't care to be seen, this last was not an inconvenience.

No government claimed the land on which the spaceport stood, so it was outside any government regulations. Occasionally it would occur to some newly elected official that it might be a good idea if the spaceport were shut down, but the people of Vangelis—having only recently overthrown a tyrannical oligarchy—were strong in the belief that a good government— like good children—should be seen and not heard.

This time of day, the clubhouse—which consisted of a soft-drink machine, a beer machine, one human WC, one alien WC, numerous wooden tables and wobbly-legged chairs, and several ancient pinball machines—was empty. The beer was cold, the place was moderately clean and moderately air-conditioned. At least it was cooler inside than out. But then, as Tusk said, an oven would be cooler inside than out.

Nola went to the bathroom. Tusk got himself a beer, his wife a bottle of water, and the kid fruit juice that would mostly end up on his shirt. John toddled happily among the chairs that were like a jungle to him, pushing them under the tables and pulling them out, returning to his parents whenever in need of a drink.

"So what did the doctor say?" Tusk was beginning to get worried.

Nola sat down, placed her sunburned freckled brown hand over her husband's smooth-skinned black hand, and looked him in the eye.

"Twins."

Tusk's jaw dropped.

"'Fraid so, darling," Nola said briskly. "They run in your family. Your mother told me so, last time she came to visit. So it's all your fault."

"Twins," repeated Tusk dazedly.

Nola's expression softened. She stroked his hand. "I'm sorry, dear."

Tusk forced a smile. "Hell, like you said, it's my fault—"

"No, I don't mean about that. I'm sorry for having this baby. These babies. Now, of all times."

"We both agreed, remember? And I was there during the proceedings. A major participant." Tusk kissed his wife, took hold of her hand, squeezed it tightly. "I'm thrilled, honey. I really am."

"Things were looking so good, back then—"

"Don't worry, sweetheart. We'll make it. We'll be fine." He thought about the medical insurance—or lack of it. "We'll be fine," he said again. "We've been in worse situations than this."

"Yes, but usually people were shooting at us," Nola said, teasing.

Tusk didn't laugh, however. He was staring at the half-full beer bottle, moving it back and forth restlessly on the tabletop. Nola knew the signs.

"Tusk—" she began, but at that moment son John came over, demanding orange juice.

Nola gave the child a drink, then caught hold of him as he was about to toddle off, examined him closely.

"Tusk, you've been feeding him cookies! And you know what sweets can do to his teeth!"

"No, I haven't!" Tusk protested.

"Well, someone has," said Nola severely. She turned the boy around for exhibition. "Look at this. Cookie crumbs all down the front of his shirt. And here's half of a cookie stuffed into his pants."

"It wasn't me," said Tusk, surveying the incriminating evidence. "Maybe it was Nan at the Laundromat."

"Who gave you the cookies, Johnny?" Nola asked, lifting the child into her lap.

Caught by the enemy, young John made a valiant effort to protect his source.

"Pinball," he said—a new word and one of which he was inordinately proud. He looked hopefully at his father, attempting at the same time to squirm out of the interrogator's grasp. "Daddy play."

"Not now." Tusk reached out and ruffled the child's thick black hair. "Maybe later."

"John, who gave you the cookies? No, no more orange juice. Tell mama."

So it was to be torture. John eyed the orange juice that had been scooted across the table, just out of reach. He left his comrade to his fate.

"Dranpa," said the child, reaching out his hands for the bottle.

"Grandpa?" Nola stared at Tusk. "Who's he talking about?" She gave John a drink of juice.

"Beats me," said Tusk, puzzled. Then, "I know. XJ!"

"You're kidding!"

"Why, that hypocritical old fart. Going on and on about how much he hates the kid and slipping him cookies on the sly." Tusk rubbed his hands. "This is too good. I'll hang on to this. Maybe catch XJ in the act. He'll owe me big on this one!"

"When you do, let me know. I'm going to have a little talk with 'Dranpa.' There you go, Johnny. Go play." Nola set the child down on the floor, absentmindedly ate the rest of his cookie. "What's wrong, Tusk?"

He glanced up. "Tell mama?" He smiled at her.

"Or no more beer." She took hold of the can, smiled back.

"I was thinking about starting work again," Tusk said, not looking at her.

Nola paled a little beneath the freckles. "You mean mercenary work?"

Tusk nodded. Lifting his beer, he drank it, made a face. "Damn stuff's warm."

"Is that what Dixter called you about?"

"Yes. No. Well, sort of. He wants me to check out this organization he heard about. The Ghost Legion. I told you about them, showed you the vid they sent."

"Yes, but you're not seriously considering going?" She looked at him anxiously.

Tusk took her hand again. "We're up against it, sweetheart. I found out today that we don't have any medical coverage—"

"Oh, Tusk . . ." Nola sighed.

"Just one job. Until we can get back on our feet."

"But what about Link? The plane? He's half-owner. . . ."

"They're mainly interested in pilots. I'll leave Link the plane. He can continue the business. He doesn't need me to run it. The customers like him. You and XJ can keep an eye on him, make sure he doesn't gamble away all the profits."

"But if Dixter wants you to check this Ghost Whatzit out, he must think there's something wrong with it."

"Naw. Just routine."

Not for the first time, Tusk blessed his ebony complexion. If he'd been a white-skinned human, he'd have been red to the eyeballs and Nola would have spotted his lie in an instant.

As it was, she was staring at him, hard. "Routine, huh? Dixter has a staff of a couple of thousand people, not to mention spies of every shape, race, and nationality, and he comes to you to run a *routine* check?" Her eyes narrowed. "There's something you're not telling me."

"I swear. Just routine. Maybe he heard we were hard up and wanted to throw some bucks our way. This Ghost Legion's offering big money, Nola. Big, big money. More'n I could earn in a year. And it'd be all ours. No splitting it with Link. We'll invest it, live off it until we get the business going again."

"*If* you come back alive," Nola said somberly.

If I don't, there's the death benefits they've promised to pay to the surviving family members, was what Tusk almost said, but he snapped his mouth shut. More than half-afraid she might see in his eyes what he was thinking (she'd done that to him, more than once), Tusk took this opportunity to excuse himself.

"I'm going to the head."

He stayed in there long enough to change back into the old jaunty, devil-may-care Mendaharin Tusca, former mercenary who'd defeated a powerful Warlord, defeated evil aliens from a distant galaxy, helped put a king on his throne. Yep. Those had been the days. Just him and XJ-27. As long as he'd had money enough to buy jump-juice and spare parts for his spaceplane, Tusk hadn't given a damn about anything. Now he had a wife, a child, two more kids on the way. . . . It'd be good to go back, just for a little while.

Coming out, he found Nola sitting in the chair, holding her son in her overlarge lap, singing to him quietly. Tusk stopped a moment to look at them. John was yawning, rubbing his eyes fretfully. It was nap time. Nola laid his head against her breast, began to rock him back and forth. He struggled against sleep a moment, then gave in. His eyelids drooped. Nola lay her cheek against the curly head, held her child close.

Tears stung Tusk's eyes. He couldn't believe how much he loved her, how precious she was to him, how precious his son was. Yeah, he'd beaten a Warlord, been a king-maker. But who'd fought at his side? She had. The thought of leaving her, leaving his son, leaving them both for a long time, maybe forever . . .

He turned abruptly, put a coin in the machine, got another

beer. He held on to it tightly, drew a couple of deep breaths, drank a swallow to clear the choking sensation in his throat.

Back to the old life. The old, lonely, empty life.

Going over to Nola, he put his hand on her shoulder, pulled her close to him. She pressed her head against his thigh.

"What are you thinking?" he asked, stroking her hair.

She wore her hair clipped short because of the heat. He thought back to the first time he'd seen her, sitting in Dixter's sweltering office. Short, pudgy, freckle-faced, snippy . . . Tusk had taken an immediate dislike to her. She hadn't thought much of him.

Nola was smiling.

"I was thinking about the time when we were on Sagan's ship, getting ready to fight the Corasians. I was thinking about what you said to me." She raised her head, looked up at him. "Do you remember? You said, 'All I know is that when I'm with you, I can do things I never thought I could do. If there's a way to beat this thing, it'll take us together to do it.'"

She couldn't go on. Lowering her head over the baby's, she began to cry.

"Don't," he whispered. "Don't, sweetheart."

"Damn hormones!" she sobbed.

"I won't go," Tusk said, bending down to put his arms around her and around his slumbering son. "Not without you. I don't know what made me think I ever could."

Chapter ❊❊❊ Six

... married past redemption.
John Dryden, *Marriage à la Mode*

Dion Starfire stood in front of the full-length mirror, studying his reflection. He observed himself critically, carefully adjusting the sleeves of the black uniform jacket to permit only a proper fraction of white shirt cuff to show beneath them. The knife-edged crease of his black trousers fell in a correct line to the tops of the high-gloss black shoes. The jacket was darted in at the waist, emphasizing the king's fine physique.

He shook out his red-gold hair, thick and luxuriant. He wore it long, rampant, like a lion's mane. The red hair had become his symbol; that and the lion-faced sun. The two were often combined by political cartoonists. Red hair was quite the fashion these days. The galaxy over, young men were wearing their hair long and having it dyed.

He could see, in the mirror, the reflection of the servbot approaching, carrying a purple sash.

"No," Dion told the 'bot, not taking his eyes from his image. "I'm not wearing either that or the medals today."

"Very good, sir. May I inquire if His Majesty plans to wear the full regalia for the formal dinner?"

The servbot had been programmed at the finest training facility for gentleman's gentlemen in the galaxy. It was familiar with all forms of etiquette practiced galaxy-wide, could recommend the proper neckwear for any occasion, knew what wine went with what dish, kept His Majesty's social calendar for the next five years in its computer brain, and would kill on command.

"Yes. The media will be there."

The blue eyes, the Starfire eyes, with their intense and startling gaze, the reflected eyes regarded him—the real him—with a cold and unblinking stare. It occurred to Dion that they didn't know him; the eyes might have been staring at a stranger. They didn't know him any better than he knew them.

His own reflection. Everywhere he went, that's all he saw. In mirrors, in people's eyes, in camera lenses. On screens, on monitors. In mags, in the vids. Flat, without depth, dimension. Distant, cold, unreachable, untouchable. Unreal. A shadow . . . colorized.

The door to his dressing room opened behind him. Dion saw it open in the mirror, saw the reflection of the person entering. His wife. She, too, was perfectly dressed, perfectly coifed. They rarely saw each other when each was not perfect.

He did not turn around, kept his eyes on the eyes in the mirror.

"Good morning, madam," he said, with a politic smile.

"Good morning, sir," Astarte replied coolly, with a very slight lowering of her eyelids, a slight bow of the elegant head.

Formalities must be observed, with others present, even if it was only a servbot. Reporters had attempted to conceal cams in such 'bots before now. Though the odds on one succeeding were extremely slim, their Majesties knew better than to take chances.

Astarte entered the room, stood gazing at Dion in silence, a cosmetic smile on her lips, a look in her eyes that her husband knew well.

"That will be all, Simmons. I'll be leaving within the hour."

"Very good, sir. Your Majesties." The 'bot flickered its lights in deference to the king and queen and trundled out of the dressing room, gently and unobtrusively closing the door behind it.

"You're leaving this morning?" Astarte demanded once they were alone. "Where are you going?"

"I beg your pardon, madam." Dion, adjusting his cuffs, spoke to her reflection. "I requested D'argent to provide you with a copy of my travel itinerary. If he hasn't done so, I will—"

"Oh, he's done so." Astarte said with a sigh, folding her slender arms across her chest.

Dion shrugged, as if he couldn't understand the fuss. "Then you know I am traveling to the Academy, for the formal dedication ceremony. I am the founder. It is my duty."

"I know *where* you're going. . . ."

"Then why did you ask, madam?"

"We could have gone together," Astarte said quietly.

A slight flush stained Dion's pale cheeks. He glanced down, away from his reflection, made a pretense of buttoning one of the golden buttons on his cuff.

"Yes, my dear, I thought of that. I sent my secretary to discuss the schedule with your secretary. D'argent reported back to me that there were conflicts—"

"My secretary! Your secretary!" Astarte came to stand beside him, looked at him, not at the mirror. "Why don't we ever talk to each other? I could have rearranged things, put some things off, rescheduled. Nothing was that important. We could have traveled together." She put her hand on her husband's arm.

Dion flinched away from her touch, moved a step away from her. He realized what he'd done only when he saw her hand hanging immobile in the empty space between them. He saw her face . . . in the mirror.

Astarte was beautiful. He looked at her reflection and knew she was beautiful. Her long, shining black hair was worn in the twists and coils that had some sort of religious significance—he didn't know what, he'd never asked—and perfectly framed her small, delicate oval face. Her eyes were wide and the color of port wine, made dark by the long, black lashes. Her mouth was perfectly formed, the lips sensually curved. She was full-breasted, slender-waisted, with slim hips. She was short in stature, but extremely well-proportioned, and, by careful attention to her clothes, appeared taller than she was.

The daughter of a warrior mother—DiLuna, ruler of the wealthy and powerful star system of Ceres—Astarte had not been at all what Dion had expected when he had married her, sight unseen, almost three years previous. Her mother was a tall, long-limbed warrior woman, strong as most males, fierce, proud, a hard bargainer. Most of her numerous daughters (DiLuna scorned to give birth to a male child) were like their mother.

Astarte was different. Perhaps this difference was because she was High Priestess for her people. Or perhaps she'd become High Priestess because of the difference. Dion didn't know. Again, he hadn't asked. She was the embodiment of womanhood, the nurturing mother.

With nothing to nurture.

Dion knew immediately where this quarrel was leading—the same place their quarrels always led. The bedroom.

"I'm sorry things didn't work out, madam. I was only going by what D'argent told me. What your secretary told him. Perhaps next time. And now, if you will excuse me, I have several calls to make before I leave."

He started toward the door. He took two steps, but she was there in front of him, her hand on his arm. This time he forced himself to hold still.

"Yes, madam," he said, trying to keep irritation from showing its edge in his voice, "what is it you want? I fear you must be quick—"

"Why haven't you been in our bed for a month, Dion?" she demanded. Her eyes were wide, trying to draw him inside. "Why?" She tightened her grip.

Dion, mindful of the reflection, gave a practiced smile. "You know how busy I've been, madam. I'm up until all hours. I know you're busy, too. I don't want to disturb you—"

"Disturb me! I talk of making love to you and you talk of 'disturbing' me! We will never have a child if you are not a husband to me."

"I've been a husband to you, madam," Dion said, breaking free of his wife's grip. Turning from her, he reached for a pair of white gloves that he'd almost forgotten. He began to pull one on. "For one and a half, two years, I performed my duty faithfully."

"Duty!" Astarte repeated, following him, forcing herself into his line of sight. "That's what it is to you—duty!"

"And what is it to you?" he asked quietly, lifting his gaze from the gloves.

"I—" Astarte began, but she stopped. Tilting back her head, chin high, she stared at him, said nothing.

Dion nodded, picked up the other glove. "We discussed this on our wedding night. You don't love me, madam. I don't love you. We've never made a secret of that to each other. This was a political marriage, made for the sake of uniting the galaxy. Your mother got what she wanted. I got what I wanted—"

"But what about me?" Astarte asked softly.

Dion raised his head again, glanced at her briefly. His mouth twisted in a bitter smile. "You are queen of the galaxy, my dear." He turned from her again, ready to leave. "And now, if you will excuse me—"

Astarte again caught hold of his arm, pulled him around to face her. "We are the talk of the media. 'When will a royal heir be born?' 'Almost three years, and the queen is not pregnant.' 'Is it him?' 'Is it her?' 'The king undergoes medical tests.' 'The queen undergoes medical tests.' 'Nothing is wrong with either of them.' Nothing except that we sleep in separate bedrooms!"

"There are ways, madam." Dion was carefully maintaining patience, control. "We've discussed this before. Artificial insemination—"

"That is against my religion!" Astarte shouted at him. "You know that!"

"It's not against mine," Dion returned. "And keep your voice down."

"Let them hear!" Astarte waved her hand toward the door. "Let the whole palace hear! A child must be born of the union between husband and wife. Not between wife and test tube! And that is another thing. You promised you would advocate the worship of the Goddess. You promised you would help encourage her worship throughout the galaxy. Another promise broken! Like your promise to be faithful to your wife."

Dion's face paled in anger; his eyes shone bright and hard and they had gone ice blue, like a frozen lake beneath winter clouds. He drew in a deep breath, let it out slowly.

"I have been faithful to you, madam," he said, his voice shaking with tension, the need to remain in control. "You know I have."

"With your body, maybe, sir." Astarte released her hold on him suddenly, pushed him away, as if she were flinging him away. "Not with your soul."

Dion stared at her. His lips compressed tightly, holding back words he might have been tempted to speak. She gazed at him, head tilted upward, her chin thrust slightly forward. Slowly she straightened, stiffened. Her arms crossed over her chest. Her gaze did not falter. It was Dion who lowered his eyes. Giving a stiff, cool nod, he turned and opened the door, stepped out into the hallway.

Two sets of the Royal Guard came to attention—the King's Guard, who stood outside His Majesty's door and accompanied him wherever he went, and the Queen's Guard, who did the same for Her Majesty.

Returning their salute, Dion placed himself in the center of their ranks. The guards closed in around him and proceeded down the corridor, heading for His Majesty's private suite of offices.

Astarte remained in the dressing room, staring after him. The women who formed the Queen's Guard (warriors from Astarte's own planet) kept their faces immobile, impassive, as had the men who formed the King's Guard. All pretending they had not heard.

When the rhythmic tread of booted feet had faded, when the king had entered his own private lift, to be whisked away to the public part of the Glitter Palace, Astarte finally left the room. The Queen's Guard closed around Her Majesty, the tall forms of the female warriors towering over their diminutive ruler.

Disciplined gazes facing forward, keeping close and careful watch, none of them noticed the single tear that slid down Astarte's cheek, a tear that dried on her skin, for she did not deign to lift her hand to brush it away.

··◆═〉◯〈═◆··

Dion entered his office through a door accessible only from the king's quarters. The king's quarters were cordoned off under tight security, not so much for protection as for privacy. Only friends of the royal family—such as John Dixter, and relatives such as the queen's mother, were permitted to enter the king's quarters.

Their Majesties' private offices were located in what was known as the public part of the Glitter Palace. Actually, the general public stood about as much chance of getting into this part of the palace as they would have of breaking into the vault where the crown jewels were kept. It was here that Their Majesties conducted their daily business, here where they did their entertaining. People could even be housed in this wing of the palace, in spacious and luxurious apartments. Dixter had an apartment here. So did DiLuna, which she used whenever she came to visit her daughter. The closest the public came was a look at the exterior of the palace and a vid that they could view at the end of the excursion.

Entering his office, leaving the King's Guard to take up their posts outside the door, Dion was finally able to relax. He pulled off the sweat-damp gloves, tossed them on the desk, ran a hand through his hair. He was startled to notice he was shaking, his hand trembling. He would have liked to have flung himself into his chair, rested his aching head in his hands, devoted time to being alone, to being unhappy, to being frustrated and angry.

But such simple luxuries were denied him. He thought of what he'd said to his wife. Queen of the Galaxy. She could have anything she wanted. And so could he. Anything—except what he wanted most.

He pressed a button. A vidscreen flickered to life.

"Good morning, Your Majesty," came the cool tones of his private secretary.

"Good morning, D'argent." Dion smiled slightly.

D'argent's calm voice and expression spread like a soothing balm over the king's fresh wounds. Nothing ever disturbed D'argent, nothing rattled him, panicked him. No matter what the crisis, the secretary remained calm, detached, removed.

The palace still talked of the time, shortly after the coronation—when the strict security measures that surrounded the king had yet to be established—that a fusion bomb had been discovered, planted under D'argent's desk. If it had exploded, it would have taken out half the palace. His Majesty and the Royal Family were whisked to safety. The entire staff was evacuated, with the exception of D'argent. The secretary refused to leave. His Majesty had important files that had to be saved if this computer system was destroyed.

The bomb squad dismantled the bomb while D'argent remained seated nearby, transferring material into a computer system far removed from the palace. He had been forced to do the work manually: The material was classified, and he could not use voice entry, due to the presence of the bomb squad. He had not made a single error.

The outer door to Dion's office opened: D'argent glided inside. He was of medium height, blond, slender, always dressed in a white linen suit, white shirt, and white shoes. Only his necktie changed color daily, on some sort of scheme known only to himself. Dion often wondered if the variation in color had some sort of relevant meaning to the man's life, for the king occasionally detected a pattern in the shifting colors. Dion could have asked, but D'argent had a way of surrounding himself with an impenetrable shield, generated by his own calm demeanor and vast efficiency.

D'argent's personal life was open to complete inspection, as were all those who served the king. D'argent resided, with a male companion, in a private suite in the palace. He was rarely seen out of either his office or his rooms, except for daily exercise that he took in the gym. He was known to be in exceptional physical condition, was a keen and deadly shot with a lasgun, and a reputed expert in the martial arts.

Today, D'argent's necktie was green. He had worn green for

three days now. Prior to that, the necktie had been alternately
yellow one day and red the next, for a full week.

D'argent performed the morning ritual. He brought Dion a
cup of hot oolong tea. He placed a sprig of fresh flowers in a
vase on His Majesty's desk. This day, it was a tropical violet.
Yesterday had been lavender. (The flowers, too, went by a pattern, but it was even more complex than the ties.) Ordinarily he
would have switched on the computer at Dion's desk, brought
in the day's important mail which required the king's personal
attention. Today, knowing Dion was preparing to leave,
D'argent left the computer off. They would deal with the mail
on board ship.

"Sir John Dixter is waiting, sir. Shall I send him in?"

"Do I have an appointment with him?"

"No, sire. He requested a meeting yesterday, after you'd
gone. I took the liberty of saying you would see him first thing
this morning."

No apologies. D'argent would not have taken up the king's
time unless the matter was vital. Although how the secretary
determined what was vital and what wasn't was, once again, a
mystery. He had never failed, however.

He poured the fragrant tea.

"Bring him in. I don't suppose he gave you any indication of
what this was about?"

"No, sir."

D'argent glided away, soft-footed, and returned steering John
Dixter around the formal furniture groupings, across the wide
expanse of carpet, to a massive, ornately carved desk.

"Sir John Dixter," announced the secretary formally.

Dion rose to his feet. Dixter bowed awkwardly.

The king extended his hand, shook the older man's hand
warmly. Dion was conscious of Dixter's scrutiny, the affection-
ate gaze of a father. The king was comforted, felt less alone.
And it was not often he felt less alone.

Once Dixter was seated, D'argent remained an instant, to
make certain that the Lord of the Admiralty was comfortable,
then departed. The secretary was back again with coffee—in a
sturdy, substantial mug—for the admiral. D'argent poured,
stirred in cream and sugar; then, having ascertained by a glance
at His Majesty that his services were not required, D'argent
glided from the room, shut the door behind him.

Dixter sipped at the coffee cautiously, smiled.

"This is exactly how I take it. How does he remember?"

Dion shook his head. The tension was starting to drain from him. "I have no idea. But he does it with everyone. How have you been, my lord?"

"Fine, Your Majesty. Fine. Thank you for asking." Dixter cleared his throat, flushed, shifted uncomfortably.

Gone was the unrestraint of earlier times, though Dion was far less formal with his long-time friend than he was with others, using the singular pronoun "I" during their private talks, not the all-inclusive royal "we." But barriers existed between them now; both knew it and acknowledged the change as necessary. One was obvious—a barrier of light shining from a golden crown. The other was less tangible, but perhaps thicker, more impenetrable—the boy that Dixter had once called son was now a man. Now his king.

"How are you, Your Majesty?" Dixter wasn't asking the question out of politeness. He sipped at his coffee, regarded the king over the mug's rim, his expression grave, concerned.

"In excellent health, I'm happy to say," Dion answered coolly, faintly irritated with himself that he hadn't masked his inner turmoil. "I'm traveling to the Academy today. Tonight's the dedication ceremony. The renovation is complete. We've expanded the library. The new wing is being called the Platus Morianna Wing. And I'm dedicating a memorial to Lord Sagan and Lady Maigrey. I think they'd be pleased."

"Yes, sire," said Dixter guardedly, setting his coffee mug down on the stand at his elbow. "I'm sure they would be very pleased."

"I wish they could see the Academy, those who attended it so long ago. I'd like them to see how it's come back to life. But they're all dead—all the Blood Royal. Either dead or they've hidden themselves so well that they've managed to avoid all our searching."

"They're dead, Your Majesty," said John Dixter. He stared at the coffee. "Those who managed to survive the purge—and there weren't many—died later at Sagan's hands. He had his revenge on them for betraying him. May God have mercy on his soul."

Dion looked at his old friend sharply, thinking he detected an odd note in the man's voice. But the admiral's face was expressionless. He picked up his coffee again, swallowed it, smiled faintly, savoring the flavor.

Dion reprimanded himself. *I'm starting to suspect everyone of playing devious games, of having ulterior motives. Dixter obviously meant nothing more by that remark than what he said.*

"Is Her Majesty going with you, sire?" Dixter asked.

Dion wasn't paying attention. The admiral was forced to repeat the question.

"No," Dion said shortly.

He rose to his feet, walked over to the window. The curtains were drawn; the king preferred to work in an environment that was shaded, cool, restful. He parted the curtains slightly. A shaft of sunlight, bright and glaring, illuminated him, made his red hair burn like vibrant flame.

"What did you need to see me about, my lord?" Dion asked, glancing around. "Please be seated."

No one sat when the king stood. Dion returned to his desk, sat down. Dixter settled back in his chair.

"You recall the intelligence reports we received—reports stating that a group was seriously interested in attempting to acquire the space-rotation bomb?"

"Yes, I remember." Dion frowned, clasped his hands on top of his desk. His right thumb began to massage the knuckle of his left forefinger, a trick he'd acquired to conceal any nervousness. "You followed through on our plan to draw them out?"

"Yes, Your Majesty. I hired Xris and his squad of commandos to make the phony transfer to Snaga Ohme's. They made it look good, kept it strictly classified, top security. The word leaked out. We now know the person involved, know where the breach occurred. Unfortunately, we were a little late. He disappeared before we could get our hands on him.

"The group made contact with Xris's man—the Loti, Raoul, the supposed weak link. Three ex-starpilots paid a large sum of money for plans of Snaga Ohme's house, the garden, security layout—all what you might expect. Raoul provided it—again, enough to make it look good. His partner, the empath, went along, raided these pilot's minds. Apparently, Your Majesty, the group behind this is known as the—"

"Ghost Legion," said Dion.

Dixter's jaw went slack. "You knew about this?"

Dion shook his head. "No, I didn't know about it. I've never heard of it. And yet, I have heard of it. Or maybe it would be more correct to say I've *heard* it." Unclasping his hands, he stared down at the scars—five of them—that marred his right palm.

Dixter noticed the gesture, guessed at the implication. "When you use the bloodsword."

"Yes. Thoughts, strange thoughts, come into my mind. Odd images, weird occurrences. Not a voice, not like Abdiel's." Dion frowned at the memory that was still painful and would likely always be. "It's as if some other consciousness were brushing against mine. I see shadows of whatever it's thinking. That name came into my mind the instant before you said it. Yet, I swear, I'd never heard it before. I don't know what it means or what it is."

He was silent, pondering. Then—shrugging—he shook off the cold spectral touch that seemed to be brushing the back of his neck. "I'm sorry, my lord. This is all irrelevant."

"Maybe not," said Dixter dryly. "You see, Your Majesty, they were successful."

Dion stared. "They successfully raided Snaga Ohme's! That's not possible. Why, that would take an army, and even then—"

"It wasn't an army, Your Majesty. We don't know what it was, to be honest. No one saw it. No one heard it. Nothing except the bomb was removed. No one was hurt. The reports have been analyzed, but all I've been getting back from the so-called experts are theories, some more far-fetched than others. Everything from a new type of probe to microscopic spacecraft to ghosts. I've transferred the files to you. You can read for yourself."

"They stole the bomb?"

"I'm afraid so, Your Majesty."

Dion sat in silence a moment, absorbing. "They know now they were tricked, that it was a trap. They know now the bomb wasn't real. And since the real bomb wasn't there, they'll keep searching for it."

"And they've shown us, sire, that there's not anywhere they can't go."

"But, my lord, as XJ used to say, it's a hell of a big galaxy. They could look for centuries and not find it. What have they accomplished? Besides letting us know they're after it?"

"That may be all they wanted to do, sire."

"But what for? What do they gain?"

Dixter rubbed his brow. "Let's say that you're a killer who's committed the perfect crime. No one can trace you. But when the detective starts getting close, you begin to feel pressured. You begin to imagine flaws and you go back and try to cover them up. And *that's* what gives you away."

"Thanks for the analogy," Dion said dryly.

Dixter flushed. "I'm sorry, Your Majesty. I was reading Nero Wolfe last night and this idea came into my mind."

"So you think they're hoping to pressure us into making another move? Pressure us into making a mistake?"

Dixter sighed. "To be honest, Your Majesty, I haven't a clue what they're hoping to do. But that seems the most logical."

"What have you done, then?"

"We're still investigating. But I've gone outside of official channels. I've asked Tusk to look into it."

"Tusk?" Dion smiled, memory flooding over him. "How is he? And Nola? And the baby? Your godson, if I remember right."

"Yes, Your Majesty." Dixter was pleased to be reminded. "Healthwise, they're all fine. Financially, it's a different story."

"I was afraid that would happen, once he got involved with Link. So Tusk is trying to track down this Ghost Legion."

"Doesn't need to. They tracked him down. They're advertising openly, apparently. Looking for pilots. That's all in the report."

"Hitting a little close, aren't they, sir? Though I haven't seen Tusk in years; but if they know he was once connected with me—"

"Maybe, sire. Maybe not. It might be coincidence. Tusk wasn't the only one. They contacted Link, too." Dixter's mouth twisted wryly.

"But how did they get those names? You kept those files secret, as I remember."

"Yes, that's another strange thing. Those files *were* secret."

"The security leak again."

"Had to be."

"And then they use them blatantly, openly." Dion shook his head. "That doesn't make sense. What's Tusk doing?"

"He's going to act as if he's interested, see who they are, what they're offering."

The commlink buzzed.

"Yes, D'argent?" Dion answered.

"Begging your pardon for the interruption, sir, but it is time we were going."

"Yes, D'argent. Thank you."

John Dixter was already getting to his feet. "I'm sorry to have to drop this on you before your trip, Your Majesty. But I thought you should know."

"I'll study those reports while I'm en route. You'll inform me immediately about what Tusk finds out."

"Yes, Your Majesty."

The king escorted the admiral to the door. Once there, Dixter paused, started to speak, hesitated.

"What is it, sir?" Dion asked. "You've got something else on your mind. You have, ever since you came in here."

"Just a suggestion, Your Majesty." Dixter looked at the king intently. "I think you should discuss this with the archbishop."

Dion stared incredulously. Then he laughed. "The archbishop? Are you buying in on this ghost theory, my lord? Do you think we should call in an exorcist?"

"No, Your Majesty," said John Dixter gravely, "but I think Archbishop Fideles knows someone who should be called in."

Dion's laughter died. He kept his expression carefully blank. "I can't think to whom you're referring, but I'll keep your suggestion in mind. Thank you for coming, sir."

Dixter was about to say something else, but the cool glitter of blue eyes warned that further discussion would not be welcome.

The door slid open. D'argent was there. King and Lord of the Admiralty exchanged farewells. D'argent escorted Dixter to the outer door.

Dion returned to his office. The door slid shut. He leaned back against it, began to rub the five scars on the palm of his hand.

They had begun to pain him, of late.

Chapter ◆━◇◇━◆ Seven

. . . dead,
Breathless and bleeding on the ground.
William Shakespeare, *Henry IV*, Part One, Act V,
Scene iv

Tusk drove his wife and slumbering child back to the small house. A monetary gift from His Majesty—in recognition of the heroic services of both Nola Rian and Mendaharin Tusca—had enabled them to buy it. The house now had a second mortgage, in order to make a down payment on a new anti-grav drive on the Scimitar.

At least, thought Tusk, steering the battered hoverjeep over the cracked tarmac of the spaceport, the money he made from this job of Dixter's should take care of next month's house payment. After that . . . well, something would turn up.

Parking the jeep was always an adventure. Its air cushion system occasionally malfunctioned, causing it to shut off abruptly. When this happened—as it did now—the craft dropped to the ground with a bone-jarring thud. Certain his spine was sticking up through his skull, Tusk climbed painfully out of the jeep, clambered up the Scimitar's hull to the hatch.

"That brat with you?" XJ asked suspiciously when Tusk slid down the interior ladder.

"No, he's taking a nap," Tusk answered. It was on the tip of his tongue to ask for a cookie, but he choked it back. That bit of information was worth a fortune. He'd wait until he needed something badly, then spring his knowledge of the cookie scam on the unsuspecting "grandpa."

He continued his search through his disk library, looking for the disk the Ghost Legion had sent him. It would be toward the back, behind the entertainment disks he kept for the passengers.

"Heard from Link?" he asked the computer.

"He checked in to see if there were any runs to make. I said we had a line of customers from here to Akara, and he said fine, he'd go back to sleep. Late night." XJ sounded ominous.

Tusk grunted. He found the disk, inserted it into the machine. "You didn't say anything to him about Dixter, did you?"

"You want to see a fool? Look in a mirror," the computer snapped. "Don't look this direction." It lapsed into gloomy silence.

Tusk ignored it, watched the vid, studied it carefully this time. It was the standard pitch. A very professional, but mild-mannered officer—Captain Dallen Masters, by name—assured Tusk by name (computer-programmed drop-in) that he (Captain Masters) had heard wonderful things about Tusk's ability as a pilot, which is why Tusk had been sent this invitation, which had gone to only a select few in the galaxy. Captain Masters would be both pleased and proud if Tusk would consider joining their ranks. Captain Masters assured him—Tusk—that he (Masters) lived for nothing more than to fly with him—Tusk.

"That's interesting," Tusk muttered, watching. "He used only my alias, not my full name."

"So?" XJ-27 had entered its remote unit. It hovered near the vidscreen, tiny arms wiggling, lights flickering. "What does that prove?"

"I dunno." Tusk shrugged. "That Dixter was right, that they picked up the names from his old files of pilots for hire. If they'd found me, say, through the Warlord's official files I'd have been listed by my full name: Mendaharin Tusca, Captain—"

"Deserter." XJ cackled. "AWOL. Wanted for questioning in connection with theft of Scimitar. Reward for information leading to apprehension and conviction. They're looking for a few good men, not a few good convicts."

"What the hell does that matter? That's ancient history now. Sagan's dead and the past is dead with him. Besides"—Tusk puffed out his chest—"those of us who risked our lives to fight the evil dictatorship are heroes now. I've got the Royal Star."

"You're a royal pain. You stumbled into that mess ass backward, which was the only way you managed to survive. That and the fact that I was around to pull your ass out—"

"Shut up. They're gonna give an info number here in a minute. Make sure you get it down."

A number began to flash repeatedly on the screen. Captain Dallen Masters implied that he wouldn't truly consider life worth living if he didn't hear from Tusk in the immediate future, if not sooner. He signed off with a dignified salute.

"You get that number?"

"Yeah, I got it. This better be a toll-free call."

"It is. Besides, Dixter said he'd reimburse us." Tusk headed for the cockpit.

"That's true," remarked XJ.

Tusk turned, glared at the remote. "You're not planning to charge Dixter for a toll-free call, are you? Because if you are—"

"The thought never flashed across my circuit boards," protested XJ-27, lights blinking in indignation. "I see it occurred to you, though."

"It did not. I know how you think." Tusk took a seat in the pilot's chair. "You connected yet?"

"Connecting now. Here it comes. Feel free to talk as long as you want," added XJ, unusually magnanimous. "After all, we're not paying for it."

"Yeah, but I bet Dixter does," Tusk said, but he said it under his breath.

"It wants to know what language you want to communicate in," reported XJ.

"Standard military," said Tusk.

Captain Masters himself appeared on the screen. "Thank you for calling the Ghost Legion," came the clipped voice. "We are now accepting recruits. If you are a licensed starpilot, interested in adventure and the chance to earn more money than you ever dreamed possible, transmit one thousand golden eagles to the account number now being entered into your computer and we will send you the coordinates to which you will report for evaluation. The sum pays for processing your records and is not refundable. Begin transmission now."

The image flashed off, the screen went blank. Tusk whistled.

"One thousand birds. Whew. I guess they want to make sure you're serious. Well, what are you waiting for? Send it."

"Have you been at the jump-juice again?" XJ nearly shorted itself out. "We haven't got one golden eagle, much less one thousand in the account— Well, I'm fried."

"What?" Tusk sat forward, alarmed.

"There's ten thousand eagles in that account. I would swear that—"

"Dixter," said Tusk, leaning back and folding his arms.

"Oh, yeah. What *am* I thinking of?" XJ's lights beamed. "Why, this'll buy me that new software—"

"Send the damn money, will you?" Tusk ordered.

"Thank you . . . **Tusk**." Captain Masters returned to the

screen. "We have received your payment of one thousand golden eagles. You will report to the coordinates now being transmitted to your computer. One of our representatives will meet you on arrival. According to our calculations, based on your current location in the galaxy, we estimate that the trip will take you"—slight pause—"a military-time week.

"If you have not arrived by midnight on the"—another pause, then he gave a date which was exactly a week from the day Tusk was calling—"we must assume that you are not interested and your appointment will be canceled. To arrange for another appointment after this date will require payment of an additional one thousand eagles.

"We look forward to meeting with you, Tusk."

The image faded.

"Did he send coordinates?" Tusk asked.

"Yep. Give me a minute." XJ was silent; then it exploded in a mechanical snort. "Jeez, what a scam. I wish I'd thought of this one."

"Why? What are the coordinates? Where do they take us?"

"Hell's Outpost."

"You're kidding." Tusk frowned, stared at the blank screen thoughtfully. "You sure?"

"Yes, I'm sure. I ran the damn things twice. It's on the edge of the galaxy. Do you realize"—the computer did some quick calculating—"that if we wanted to get there by that date we'd have to leave now. I mean within the next hour, and even *that* would be cutting it fine. It's a scam. A quick way to earn a thousand golden eagles. I wonder what happens to the poor slobs who fall for it."

"Maybe we'll find out," said Tusk. "Get hold of Dixter."

"You're not serious?"

"Just do it," Tusk said, wondering uncomfortably what Nola would say if he called with, *Hey, sweetheart, I'm leaving, blasting off for Hell's Outpost, send you a postcard, love ya, babe. Bye.* The thought made him wince.

"I've got him," XJ reported.

Tusk sat up straight. "That was fast."

"He gave us his direct number. Went straight through."

Dixter's face appeared on the screen. "Yes, Tusk? What have you found out?"

Tusk reported. He described the first message, then the follow-up. "What do you want me to do, sir?" he finished. "I can make the flight, but I'll have to leave within the hour. You know, a pilot'd have to be desperate as hell to consider somethin' like this. There aren't many who could cut ties and lift off in an hour of receiving those coordinates."

"It certainly is suggestive. . . ." said Dixter thoughtfully.

"Of a rip-off," inserted XJ. "They've just made a thousand eagles without turning a hand. We'll probably get a 'Thank you, sucker' card in the mail!"

"I wonder what would happen if I showed up," Tusk pondered out loud.

"They'd pin a sign on your back that says 'Kick me.' "

"It would be interesting to find out," said Dixter. "But it could also be dangerous." He was silent again, considering. "Let's not make the jump until we know a little bit more about what's ahead. We can always contact them again, schedule another appointment. I'd like you to do some more investigating, if you don't mind, Tusk."

Tusk let out his breath. "Sure thing, sir." He shrugged, as if it didn't matter.

"First, have Link contact them. See if he gets the same response, the same coordinates, the same time restriction. Next, get in touch with some of the other members of the old outfit. Find out if any of them have followed up on this, maybe even gone through with it, joined up. I'll do some checking on my end. Let me know what you discover. Keep my name and His Majesty's out of this. You're doing this strictly on your own."

"Yes, sir. Anything else, sir?"

"No, I think that covers everything."

"Uh, excuse me for asking, sir—I know you're busy and all—but how is Dion? His Majesty, I mean."

"Fine, Tusk. I spoke to him this morning, advised him of what you're doing. He sends his regards to you and Nola."

"Does he?" Tusk brightened, felt warmed. "Well, uh, send ours back. Regards. However you're supposed to say that to a king."

Dixter very carefully did not smile. "I will, Tusk. Let me know what you find out. ASAP."

The image faded.

"He looks tired," said Tusk.

"He always looks tired. He's looked tired ever since we've known him."

"I wonder what the hell's going on. What he knows that he's not telling. Dangerous, he says, but he doesn't say why. And the king himself's involved. Not much like the old days. The Dixter in the old days would have told us everything."

"Must have been a Dixter I didn't know," XJ retorted. "Most of the time the general said 'shoot this' and we shot it. Or it shot us. We never asked *why*, just *how much*. You're getting old. Old and soft."

Old and soft. Cookie crumbs. A small, freckled, chocolate-complected face on Nola's breast. Her swollen belly. Twins.

Shoot it. It shoots us. The pain. The bright, blinding explosion. The bright, blinding pain . . .

"I said, should I wake up Link?" XJ repeated loudly.

Tusk stirred. "Yeah. Go ahead. And find out how much money he lost last night. Not that he'll tell you the truth."

XJ busied itself. In the background Tusk could hear the buzz of a commlink, hear Link's muffled, sleep-slurred response. "Yeah? Wha? Wha' time 'sit?" The computer's strident, snappish answer.

Tusk sat with his arms folded across his chest, staring at the blank vidscreen. The ensuing irritable conversation between Link and the computer was nothing more than a drone in his mind, like the drone of the ship's engines on a long flight. At first it was all he heard; then he didn't hear it at all. XJ spoke to him two or three times before he realized the computer had—so to speak—returned.

Tusk shifted his gaze to the monkey-face box that was XJ-27. "You say something?"

"I said, you're glad Dixter let you off the hook."

"Glad?" Tusk repeated, as if he didn't understand.

"You're glad Dixter didn't send you on this job. I heard that sigh you gave. And don't tell me it was a sigh of regret. I know better."

A tingle started at the base of Tusk's spine, down in his buttocks. It crept up his back. His heart started to race; he began to sweat, to breathe too fast. He put his hand to his chest, a hand that shook, felt the scar tissue, tough and roped, beneath his fatigues. He was always surprised to feel it, always surprised to feel solid bone instead of mush. He was always surprised to look down at his hand and not find it covered with blood.

He didn't remember much about that time: the time Abdiel's mind-dead had blown a hole in his chest; the time Xris the cyborg had carried him back aboard the plane; the time Dion had healed him in what the church was now calling a bona fide miracle. Tusk didn't remember much of anything, but something inside Tusk did. It remembered at night, in his sleep; it remembered at times like this; it remembered now.

He stood up abruptly, grabbed hold of his flight jacket, and pulled it on, though it was scorching hot in the mid-afternoon sun. He could have cooked a full-course breakfast on the metal hood of the hoverjeep and he was shivering with chills.

"Where're you going?" XJ demanded. "We have work to do."

"I'm doin' it. I'm going to Link's."

XJ whirred in anger. "You can get juiced just as well here as you can there."

Tusk stopped, gritted his teeth, tried to stop the tremors. He wasn't at all certain he could make it up the ladder. "Look, I want to see for myself what they tell Link. You try to reach Gorbag the Jarun, Reefer, and any of the rest of the old outfit you can think of. Make it casual. Like we're checking this Ghost Legion out, just to see if it's as good as it looks."

"You're getting old," XJ repeated. "Old and soft. You were glad."

Tusk climbed the ladder, stomped up the rungs, felt the metal vibrate beneath his fingers. XJ had the hatch open by the time Tusk reached it.

"Call Nola, will you? Tell her I may not be home for dinner."

"Old," muttered XJ. "Old and soft."

The computer waited until it could no longer register the sound of the whining clunk of the hovercraft's engine. Then it raised Nola on the commlink.

"This is me, Nola. Tusk won't be home for dinner tonight. . . . Yeah, he's got the shakes again. Bad this time. He's gone over to Link's. . . . *Over* a year. It was that job Dixter wanted him to do. . . . Naw, Tusk's not gonna do it, but it looked like for a while he might. . . . What? Oh, sure, it figures, Dixter. Dion. No wonder. Brought it all back. . . . Me? Of course I was sympathetic and tactful! *Tact* is my middle name. I told him he was getting old and soft. . . . No, he didn't say anything. . . . What? *Twins?* Oh, great. Fine. Yeah, that's just dandy. Look, if you two haven't figured out what's causing this yet, I'll be happy to buy you a manual!"

XJ ended the transmission with a vicious click. "Twins!" the computer repeated in a gloomy tone, and immediately called up the computerized grocery service, ordered out two cases of cookies.

Chapter ·◄►◼◄►· Eight

There's fennel for you, and columbines; there's rue for
you; and here's some for me . . .
> William Shakespeare, *Hamlet*, Act IV, Scene v

Three years ago, and almost eighteen years before that, the
Academy had been a ghostly place. Once it had been an institution of learning for the children of the Blood Royal. Brought
here at an early age, the children, whose genetically altered
bloodlines gave them special talent for leadership (or at least
that had been the plan), were raised in an atmosphere dedicated to learning.

The site had been chosen with care. The Academy was built
on a planet whose atmosphere and environs were as close to
old Earth (pre-devastation Earth) as the designers could possibly find and far from all major cities, trade routes, and any
other type of disturbing influence.

Built among rolling, thickly forested hills, the Academy's halls
and libraries and classrooms stood solemn and quiet, each connected with the rest by winding paths which led through groves
of towering oak and poplar and aspen, gardens of flowers and
vegetables (the students and professors were required to grow
much of their own food), rambling brooks and placid lakes.

Following the downfall and purge of the Blood Royal during
the revolution, the Academy was abandoned. Attempts at various times to use the buildings and grounds for other
purposes—from public housing to a retirement center—had all
failed. It was rumored to be haunted, if not by genuine, chain-
rattling ghosts, then by the ghosts of childish voices reciting
Shakespeare or the multiplication tables, ghosts of youthful
voices discussing quantum mechanics or, in the spring, Walt
Whitman and D. H. Lawrence. Perhaps it really was only the
rubbing of tree limbs, one against the other, that created the
odd sounds, but no one could stay on the Academy grounds
long without hearing them. Most left, immediately.

But now all that had changed.

One of Dion's first official acts, following his coronation, had been to reestablish the Academy, open it as an institution of higher learning for any student creatively gifted, academically talented enough to qualify for admission.

Old buildings had been lovingly renovated, new buildings added, their designers careful to coordinate them with the old. Grants were established, many in the names of those who had died in the fight to end the corrupt republic, bring the rightful heir to the throne.

A memorial chapel, located in the new wing of the library, the Platus Morianna wing—had been set aside, by the king's command, to honor the dead. It was this wing, this chapel, that were to be dedicated today.

The ceremony was to take place in the evening. Before that, in the afternoon, Dion was accorded the honor of a private tour of the Academy grounds. The new buildings had been completed and open for use for several months prior to the dedication, the king's busy schedule having precluded him from coming earlier. But the buildings had all been closed the day before His Majesty's arrival for cleaning and decorating, done by the students themselves.

The dean of students was the proud guide. She walked His Majesty relentlessly over every centimeter of the new structures, pointed out every new feature of the new library, and would have undoubtedly exhibited each new volume individually had time allowed. His Majesty was interested and attentive, however, and if Dion's eyes occasionally strayed out the windows, to the crowds to students massed outside to catch a glimpse of their king (and he was *their* king, being the same age as most of them), no one noticed the lapse except D'argent, who noticed everything, and the captain of the Royal Guard, whose duty it was to watch over His Majesty's every move.

And perhaps by the headmaster, a quiet and unassuming man, who reminded Dion of his own mentor, Platus.

"You have done a splendid job, Dean, Headmaster," said Dion when they were nearing the end of the tour. "This is exactly what we had in mind. We couldn't be more pleased."

"Thank you, Your Majesty." The headmaster smiled with quiet pride. Both he and the dean were dressed in their academic gowns—long, flowing-sleeved black robes with silk-lined hoods, which had been a tradition among scholars for centuries.

"Working on this project has been a true labor of love for me and for my staff. We deeply appreciate Your Majesty's support."

They had emerged from the new music conservatory and were standing at the end of a corridor, on ground level. "But where is the memorial chapel?" Dion asked.

"Ah, we have saved the best until last, Your Majesty. This way."

The headmaster, accompanied by the dean, and the king, accompanied by the ever-present, ever-vigilant Royal Guard and the quiet, unobtrusive D'argent, proceeded to the end of the corridor.

There were no other rooms in this part of the building, no windows. The walls were painted in soft, subdued colors; the lights gradually dimmed as the party proceeded down the corridor, giving an effect both soothing to the eye, calming to the soul. At the end of the corridor stood a large double door, carved of oak, bearing the emblem of the lion's-head sun, the king's standard. The doors had no handles, no locks.

"As Your Majesty requested," said the headmaster. "It is open to all, day and night."

Dion gave the doors a gentle push, walked inside.

The chapel was a round room, cloistered, but light and airy. Its walls were of marble, whose stern aspect was softened by a row of slender columns forming a series of arches around the chapel's outer perimeter. Diffused light, from a glass dome in the ceiling, cast the columns' shadows against the marble walls behind them, forming a delicate pattern of light and darkness.

Beneath the skylight was a fountain, carved of limestone, unadorned, plain and simple in design. The name PLATUS MORIANNA was engraved in the stone.

Dion walked up to the fountain, stood a moment in silence, his head bowed, his thoughts with the gentle man who had raised him, who had given his life for him.

The headmaster held back a moment, out of respect. Then he came forward to stand by Dion's side.

"The chapel is quite popular with the students, Your Majesty. Several traditions have already sprung up concerning it. It is said, for example, that the sound of the falling water has a soothing effect upon troubled spirits. Those who are depressed or unhappy, sad or worried, have taken to coming here. They sit there, on the fountain's base, and many swear that they hear a soft voice in the water, offering counsel and sympathy."

Dion stood still, listened to the musical sound of the gently splashing water, imagined the water was washing over him, cooling the fever and soothing the turmoil in his soul. He had the impression that, if he sat here long enough, he, too, would hear Platus's voice, receive his wise council.

"I've experienced the feeling myself," added the headmaster, noting Dion's softened expression.

"Platus would have liked this," said Dion quietly. He could almost hear words in the varying modulations and tones of the plashing drops. If only he were by himself, if only he had time to truly listen, time to truly ask . . .

He supposed he could order everyone to leave. He was king; they would obey. He had the feeling that the headmaster might even understand. Dion was tempted . . . but he abandoned the idea.

He had not yet seen Kamil, nor had any word from her, received any message. Somehow, somewhere, they must meet. He needed to see her. And so he dared not deviate from his well-publicized schedule, lest she should be waiting for him, and he miss the opportunity of finding her.

The water spoke to him no more. He roused himself, was able to attend again to the headmaster's conversation.

Directly opposite the fountain, opposite the door through which they had entered, the circular line of columns ended, forming an alcove, with the marble wall behind. On this wall hung two portraits.

One was of Derek Sagan, Warlord of the fallen republic, a member of the Blood Royal and cousin to the king. The other was a portrait of Maigrey Morianna, outlawed royalist, member of the Blood Royal, cousin of the king. The portraits were uncannily lifelike, so lifelike that Dion's heart constricted painfully when he looked at them, and he heard, behind him, his captain of the guard Cato—an unemotional, stern, and disciplined soldier, who had served many years under Sagan's command—murmur in awe.

"Remarkable, aren't they? Your Majesty hasn't seen them before?" inquired the Dean.

"I saw only the sketches and the preliminary watercolors. The artist, what was his name?"

"Youll, Your Majesty, Stephen Youll."

"Youll offered to show the finished work to me, of course, but he said that he would prefer it if I saw them after they were properly hung. These . . . this is incredible." Dion for the moment forgot the voice of the king, spoke as himself.

"Quite a remarkable man, Youll," said the headmaster, gazing at the paintings with the pride of ownership, as well as appreciation for their beauty. "I had a chance to meet him when he supervised the hanging. A former spacepilot, he told me. He fought with the Warlord in the battle against the Corasians at Vangelis."

"That was one reason I chose him for this commission," said Dion. "He had served under Derek Sagan on board the old *Phoenix*. He knew both Sagan and the Lady Maigrey. To all the other artists, they were just . . . names. This man remembered them. He knew them as I knew them. That was what I wanted."

"It seems Your Majesty has succeeded," said the headmaster.

The Warlord had been painted in his golden Romanesque armor, fiery red cape, with the phoenix emblem—a controversial choice of costume. But then the placing of the Warlord's picture had been extremely controversial, since he was known to have murdered numerous innocent people, including the king's own guardian, Platus Morianna.

True, Sagan had redeemed himself by his heroic actions in the final battle against the Corasians. During this battle, having become separated from the rest of the fleet, he had fought alone and outnumbered. His spaceplane had been destroyed. He was declared missing in action and presumed dead. But there remained those who had little cause to either love or honor his memory.

"Was there any trouble on campus over this, Dean?" asked Dion, thinking of the debate that had raged in the media when he had announced that he was building a memorial to honor Derek Sagan.

"Some of the students protested, Your Majesty. Was he a fallen angel redeemed or a demon damned? That subject was debated at length," answered the dean. "As you might imagine, the argument became more muddled as some of the true details of the late President Peter Robes and his ghastly ties with the mind-seizer, Abdiel, were made public."

"On one point everyone was in agreement," inserted the headmaster. "Such an honor, granted after death to a man who had wronged you, is very much to Your Majesty's credit."

Dion bowed slightly, a lowering of the eyes and an inclination of the head, acknowledging the compliment and letting it pass. He concentrated instead on the portrait. The face was exactly as he remembered: dark, stern, impassive. He recalled Platus's words, spoken before he died, spoken before Sagan had killed him—"... his face, deep scars of thunder had intrenched," from Milton's *Paradise Lost*. Fallen angel redeemed ... demon damned. Or perhaps the question had not yet been resolved.

The dark eyes of the painting stared back at Dion and he was once again that awkward, dazzled, and confused boy of seventeen, standing before the two of them, standing before Sagan and Lady Maigrey. In Saigan's eyes, cool appraisal, doubt, scorn. In her eyes ...

Dion's gaze shifted to the other portrait. The artist had portrayed Maigrey in her silver armor, matching Sagan's. Her robes were blue and adorned with the eight-pointed star which had been the symbol of the Guardians. Around her neck she wore the starjewel, and in the painting it shimmered with an argent flame. The last time he had seen the jewel had been to place it reverently on her body; its fire had burned pale, cold as the fire of distant stars. He looked into her eyes and he saw now what he had seen the first time he'd met her: understanding, cool pity, sorrow.

"It's almost eerie, the way the two seem to be looking at each other, isn't it, Your Majesty?" commented the headmaster.

"Yes, it is," agreed Dion politely. He looked again, thinking that he might have been mistaken. No. He wasn't. They weren't looking at each other. They were both watching him.

"The story of their ill-fated love is well-known and, in fact, Your Majesty, this alcove has started to acquire a certain romantic history of its own."

"Indeed?" Dion glanced surreptitiously at his watch, though he knew well that the silent and observant D'argent would be keeping track of the time and would politely and graciously intervene when necessary to keep His Majesty on schedule.

"The chapel has become a trysting place for lovers," the headmaster was continuing. "Particularly those who have quarreled or separated. They meet here, or leave small bouquets of flowers beneath one painting or the other. ... Why, gracious me, there's one there now. I must apologize, Your Majesty. I wanted this kept neat. ..."

The embarrassed headmaster, robes flapping like sails, was bearing down upon the small flower lying on the floor beneath the portrait of Lady Maigrey.

D'argent, swift, graceful, unobtrusive, cut in front of the

headmaster, retrieved the flower with a gracious, murmured "Allow me, sir."

The headmaster bobbed his thanks, was shaking his head over the incident.

"Please, think nothing of it," said Dion graciously.

D'argent turned to the king, offered the flower. "Perhaps Your Majesty would like to keep this as a souvenir," suggested the secretary.

Accepting the white, waxen blossom, Dion placed it in the buttonhole on the lapel of his uniform. The heady, spicy fragrance took his breath away.

"This is truly a beautiful place," he said, looking around once again. "Truly beautiful."

Dion suddenly wished for, longed for it to be night. It was with great effort that he forced himself to attend to his duties.

The headmaster and dean were extremely pleased to receive His Majesty's warm praise. They would have gone on discussing and exhibiting the chapel for the next hour had not D'argent, whose sharp eyes had noted the king's sudden lapse of interest, quickly intervened.

"His Majesty's schedule prohibits ... His Majesty should rest ... aware that the headmaster has other duties in connection with this evening's ceremonies ..."

Dion heard very little, made the automatic, proper responses that he could have made if he had been drugged, drunk, or somnambulant. Fortunately, he'd had long experience in practicing the control of his emotions, was careful to conceal irritation, boredom. He could maintain a steady pulse rate; could regulate the beating of his heart, prevent the rush of blood to his face.

Passing the fountain, he glanced at himself in the pool of blue water. His reflection, though marred somewhat by the constant motion of the falling water, was the reflection of the mirror in his dressing room: cool, detached, unaffected. He wondered that he heard the fountain's voice no longer, for, in his mind, it should have been singing an aria in celebration of love.

Dion did not fully regain consciousness until he was alone, back in the headmaster's house, which had been turned over to the king and his retinue for his use during his stay. Pleading fatigue and the desire to rest and go over his speech for the dedication ceremony that night, the king retired to his bedroom. The door had barely closed behind him before he removed the camellia from his lapel, pressed it to his lips.

He touched the commlink worn on his wrist, allowing him to speak either to his secretary or to the captain of the Royal Guard.

"D'argent."

The secretary responded immediately, entered, shut the door behind him.

"Yes, sir."

"All is arranged? She'll dine with me this evening?"

"Yes, sir. The dedication ceremony ends at midnight. Princess Kamil Olefsky and her party will arrive at 0100 hours for a late dinner. I gave the Royal Correspondent that information, as you requested."

"How was it received?"

"Since the princess is known to be a longtime friend of Your Majesty's and her father is one of your most valued and trusted allies, nothing untoward was said. They requested the usual: the names of those she would be bringing with her, what they would be wearing, the menu, the wines. The Royal Correspondent gave them all the details."

"And you have arranged for the princess and her friends to spend the night here."

"Yes, sir. This house has numerous guest rooms, which are being made ready."

"Very good, D'argent," said Dion, trying to sound nonchalant, though at the moment not even he could control his swift racing pulse.

"Is there anything further I can do for you, sir?"

"No, thank you, D'argent. I'm going to read over the speech now."

The private secretary bowed again, left.

Dion lifted the copy of his dedicatory speech from the table, sat down in a comfortable chair, and started to read. He made it through one sentence, then the hand holding the speech sank to the chair's arm, all thoughts of the ceremony faded away.

In Dion's mind, it was already night. He was alone, at last, with the woman he had loved in secrecy and in silence for almost three years. And in all that time he had been faithful to his wife, as he had told Astarte. Faithful in body, if not in soul.

But the hunger was strong. Duty and honor had not sated his appetite, filled him as he had hoped they would.

The gleaming crown was losing some of its luster; the scepter was growing heavy for him to bear alone.

Chapter ·—◦═◦○═◦═◦·· Nine

Before God, I might not this believe
Without the sensible and true avouch
Of mine own eyes.
    William Shakespeare, *Hamlet*, Act I, Scene i

Dion sat on the stage in the crowded auditorium, sat with the outward assurance and regal presence of a member of the Blood Royal—the image in the mirror. Inwardly, anticipation teased him with its delightful pain, tempted him into rash and completely stupid, juvenile acts. What if he leapt from the stage and went dashing down the center aisle, singing that lewd song Link had once taught him, a song he'd forgotten until this very moment? He almost giggled at the thought, actually caught himself grinning. Appalled, he corrected himself, corrected the image.

The speakers droned on. Half-blinded by the glare of stage lights, he could not find Kamil in the audience, though he had been searching ever since he'd entered—to a thunderous ovation—almost an hour ago. It was foolish of him to hope to find her, he supposed, since there must be several thousand people in the auditorium. How could he discover out of that number, in the darkness, one head of cropped silver hair, one pair of golden eyes? Still, he searched. It gave him something to do, something to think about besides the coming night. . . .

And now it was time for his presentation. The headmaster was introducing him. The audience was on its feet, cheering. The orchestra played the Royal Anthem—adapted from the Fate motive of Tschaikovsky's Fifth Symphony—as Dion ascended the podium and began to give his speech. He spoke the beginning words by rote, spoke them without really thinking about them until he came to the name of Lady Maigrey.

Her name fell from his lips and, at that moment, he saw Kamil. A spotlight had been playing over the crowd for the benefit of the vidcams recording the historic occasion. The light illuminated her, shone on her silver hair, her white gown.

79

The effect was startling, magical. Dion felt like an inept sorcerer who accidentally stumbles on the correct incantation or the wanderer who falls into the ring of mushrooms, finds himself standing before the fairy queen.

Kamil knew he saw her. She smiled at him, a secret smile for just the two of them, but it sent an arc of blue flame flaring from one to the other. The flame jolted through Dion's body, left him dazed, shaking. Someone behind him coughed. He realized he'd been standing silent, staring dumbly, his speech cut off in the middle of a sentence.

He looked down at his notes. They made no sense. He couldn't read them. He was drying up, literally. Not a drop of saliva was in his mouth; his throat was closing. The spotlight moved on, Kamil vanished, swallowed up by darkness. Dion was suddenly conscious of the audience, conscious of thousands of eyes on him, and they seemed malevolent, vicious, the eyes of the pack waiting for him to fall.

His stomach wrenched; his knees went weak. He clutched at the podium to keep from falling. How long had he been standing here? Hours, days? His face burned with shame. The mirror image was cracking, glass falling . . .

And then he saw her.

Dion blinked, stared.

Lady Maigrey, clad in silver armor, her pale hair shining, stood in the center aisle directly opposite Dion. She smiled at him, and he began to speak.

He spoke to her and to her alone.

He told her how much he valued her advice, her wisdom, what it had meant to him. He told her about her brother, about Platus, his influence, his living example of a true gentle man. He talked to her about Derek Sagan, about lessons learned, about failing, repentance, redemption. He forgot the audience, spoke to Maigrey, as if the two of them were by themselves. And when he concluded, when his heart and soul were empty, he waited for her to answer, was amazed and disappointed when she did not.

She was gone.

The spotlight flowed over the crowd. The aisle where she'd been standing was empty. He stared into darkness, into a hushed silence. He was like one who awakens in a strange place. He had no idea where he was. He looked around, lost and confused.

He turned to step from the podium, staggered. Sweating beneath the heavy uniform, he began to shake with chills in the cool air. He was limp, wrenched, wrung out. The headmaster came to him swiftly, gave him his hand, assisted His Majesty's faltering steps.

"Wonderful, sire!" the headmaster said in broken tones. "I've been sobbing like a child."

"Thank you," Dion murmured, still not certain what was going on.

He heard a strange rustling sound, couldn't imagine what it was. Then he saw. In solemn and reverent silence, a silence more eloquent than the loudest applause, the audience was rising to its feet, rising to pay homage to the fallen ... and to their king.

※

Dion was backstage. He had no idea how he had arrived here. He assumed—hoped—he had made a dignified exit.

Captain Cato was here to meet him. Dion clasped the soldier's arm, thankful to feel warmth, flesh, solid bone, strong muscle.

"Thank you, Your Majesty," Cato said to him softly. Tears shone on the soldier's ordinarily stern and implacable face. "Thank you for what you said about my lord."

Dion wondered what that had been. For the life of him, he couldn't remember a word.

"You were standing in the wings, Cato. Did you see her?" Dion asked in a low voice.

"Who, Your Majesty?"

"Lady Maigrey."

The captain looked puzzled and suddenly concerned. "No, Your Majesty."

Dion was angry. The man must have seen her. Why was he lying?...

D'argent came gliding up. "Your Majesty, are you feeling well?"

Dion put his shaking hand to his forehead. He must sound like an idiot. Her appearance had been a trick of the spotlight or a trick of his mind, reacting to save him from stage fright. But even as he said this, he saw her again in his memory, and he knew he could not banish that vision with logic, disbelief.

Dion roused himself with an effort. From the wings, he'd

been staring once again down the center aisle, searching for the ephemeral figure in silver armor.

"Your Majesty," D'Argent persisted tactfully.

"No. I'm not well." Dion smiled wanly, shook his head. "I hadn't realized this would be so difficult for me. Talking about them ... the memories ..."

He turned to D'argent, who was holding the king's overcoat, top hat, and white silk scarf. "I won't be attending the reception, D'argent. Make my excuses."

He attempted to put on the coat; his arm missed the sleeve. He was shivering uncontrollably.

"I'm certain they will understand, sir."

They had no choice but to understand. He was king.

D'argent assisted him with the coat, holding it patiently while Dion fumbled his way into it. Made of finest cashmere, the coat was thick and warm, but it did nothing to alleviate the chilling sensation that numbed his fingers and limbs. He pulled on a pair of gloves, winced in pain as he tugged one over his right hand.

"Will you be keeping your dinner engagement tonight, sir?" D'argent asked.

"Yes!" Dion grasped at Kamil as at a lifeline. He realized then how desperate he sounded, softened his tone. "I just need to rest a little while. Get away from the crowds."

"Certainly, sir."

The Royal Guard escorted him outside, to the waiting limo-jet. Cato and his men effectively kept the crowds, the reporters, the vidcams, the robocams at a distance. Fortunately, due to Academy policy that restricted visitors from outside, the number of the press in attendance had been cut considerably from what His Majesty would have faced on other worlds. Those who were here were going about their jobs halfheartedly, mainly in the hope of something to spice up what they considered leftover news.

The death of Derek Sagan had caused a brief stir three years ago, when it happened. The death of Maigrey Morianna had received minor mention. A week later, they were forgotten. This was due primarily to the efforts of Dion, who understood that these two would not have wanted their story sensationalized, their sacrifices made trivial, their faults and their virtues mouthed over by those who could never hope to understand.

The true memorial was in the hearts of those who had known them, who remembered them.

Who remembered them. . . .

Dion settled back into the comfortable leather seat of the limo-jet, tried to relax, but he continued to shiver, despite the fact that the limo had been warmed, awaiting his arrival. He was alone, D'argent having remained behind to soothe any ruffled feelings occasioned by His Majesty's absence from the reception line. Cato and four members of the Royal Guard rode in a separate compartment up front, behind the driver. Other guards followed in their own specially designed armed hovercraft.

Dion stared out the window, watched the snow—illuminated by the lights on the side panels—fly at him out of the darkness. The sight of the white flakes spiraling through the air was mesmerizing, almost dizzying. He lay back wearily in the seat.

And he saw Maigrey again, her silver image burned into his mind, like the afterimage seen when looking directly into the sun.

She had come at first to reassure him, to steady him. She'd remained with him throughout that entire ordeal. She'd left him when he no longer needed her. But before she had gone, her expression had altered. No longer reassuring, she was solemn, urgent, dire. She had raised her right hand in token of . . . what? Warning?

Dion tore his fascinated gaze from the whipping snow. He yanked off his glove, looked at his own right hand.

The five scars were swollen, red, burned with pain, as they had the first time he'd grasped the bloodsword under Sagan's instruction, plunged the needles of the bloodsword into his hand.

Dion rubbed the wounds. He hadn't used the bloodsword in a month. Ever since that disturbing interruption, that strange intrusion into his thoughts. Ever since the words *Ghost Legion* had come unbidden into his mind.

He closed his fist tight over the wounds, and thought only of tonight and golden eyes.

Chapter ❖❖❖ Ten

Let us roll our strength and all
Our sweetness up into one ball,
And tear our pleasures with rough strife
Through the iron gates of life . . .
 Andrew Marvell, "To His Coy Mistress"

The chosen few fortunate enough to enjoy a private dinner with His Majesty, Dion Starfire, told the press the day afterward that the king had seemed quiet, preoccupied. He was charming—His Majesty couldn't be anything *but* charming, according to the young women in attendance. He made them feel at ease, after the first terrible few moments of shyness and abashment. He talked easily and readily on subjects that interested them, knew as much or more about their various home planets as they did, and generally won the hearts of the five young women present.

But they each noticed that he would occasionally lapse into silence which he would break only when the lack of conversation was beginning to intimidate his guests. Had any of these young women been extremely astute observers, they would have seen that Princess Kamil Olefsky often introduced the topic herself and her voice seemed to jolt the king out of his solemn reverie. But the friends of the princess's, and not particularly close friends at that, were too absorbed with their own inner flutterings and confusion about which of the myriad spoons to use to notice much beyond how handsome His Majesty was up close and what remarkable eyes he had.

The evening ended with champagne and chocolates, and then His Majesty's private secretary appeared, with an invitation to show them all to their guest suites. The girls shared two large rooms, with the exception of the princess, who was given a suite of her own in another wing. None of them missed her. They spent the time doing their hair, removing their makeup, and discussing the highlights of the evening.

D'argent, bringing in an additional supply of fresh towels,

was arranging them in the bathroom when he heard one girl say to another, "You know, even though they're supposed to be such old friends, the king didn't pay much attention to Kamil tonight, did he? He hardly ever spoke to her and I don't believe he looked at her once."

"It's all political," stated her friend, speaking as an expert. "The king needs to keep on good terms with her father, who's backing him on this alliance they're trying to forge with the vapor-breathers. His Majesty probably felt like he had to do this."

"I never heard that they were close friends," said another. "The king met her once when he was staying on her planet. It's not like they were brought up together or anything."

"His wife is so beautiful! Why would he even look at another woman?" This said with a sigh.

D'argent smiled to himself. Having informed the young women that, due to security reasons, it would be inadvisable for them to wander the halls during the night, he moved on to the princess's bedroom.

He was not surprised to find she was not in it. Smiling again to himself, but this time shaking his head, the secretary retired to his own bed. He did not, as was customary with him when traveling with the king, stop in His Majesty's rooms to see if Dion needed anything before retiring.

··◄══❍══►··

They met in the rose garden.

The meeting had not been prearranged. No covert glances or whispered words, no nods of the head, no folded notes passed between them during dinner. After dessert, she left with the others. She was alone in her room. The king was alone in his. Both rooms had long French doors opening out into the rose garden. Both people in those rooms seemed suddenly in need of fresh air, in need of escaping the confines of walls. Never mind that it had been snowing.

He did not admit to himself that he went out in search of her; that he knew, hoped, guessed that she, who came from a snowy climate, would seek solace in a midnight walk in a quiet, snow-filled garden. When he rounded the trunk of the giant oak tree and saw her sitting on a marble bench, he wasn't surprised to find her. And she, when she heard his softly indrawn breath, was not surprised to look up and see him.

They said nothing at first. Whatever had drawn them to meet here drew them together here. He held out his arms and she came to him. For long moments they stood in silence, clasped in close embrace, her body warm beneath the enveloping fur cloak, her silver hair, wet with snow, shining in the moonlight.

"I knew you'd be here," he said.

"I knew you'd come," she said.

They kissed and the aching desire that each had known and felt and dreamed about for so many days and nights burned through them, strengthened their hold on each other . . . frightened them.

Kamil did not pull away from him; his hold was too longed-for, too wonderful to break. But she averted her face, lowered her head to his shoulder.

"This is wrong," she whispered.

"No!" Dion ran his hand over her cropped silver hair, pressed her closer still. "No. We love. And love can't be wrong. Love makes all things right."

She could have argued, but she didn't want to. She believed him. How could there be harm in this? In two people finding comfort, renewal, joy in each other? She lifted her head and raised her hands, took hold of him and kissed him fiercely, passionately.

His unspoken question was answered in that moment. It was all too perfect. The Creator himself seemed to bless their union. It was meant to be.

And now that they knew the longed-for moment of their love was close at hand, theirs for the taking, they paused to savor the anticipation, to enjoy the delicious ache of wanting, knowing that it would soon be satisfied.

She laid her head against his breast, listened to the rapid beating of his heart, his quick breathing. Her gaze went to the snow-shrouded paths of the slumbering garden, to the marble statues, frozen forever in one moment of their lives, unable to take the next breath, unable to blink or stir and move beyond. Beneath the statues, around them, stood the roses, pruned, bound, their summer's growth and glory ruthlessly cut back, only to flourish stronger in the spring. Towering above the statues and the roses were the trees, masquerading for dead, their branches black lace against the moonlit sky, whose black clouds were gilded in silver.

"I love this garden," she told him. "I work here, you know.

We all have to give so many hours of volunteer work to the Academy. I've loved this garden ever since the first time I walked in it. The headmaster opens it to the students, but not many come here. It's too far away from the rest of campus. And now," she added with a sigh, crowding closer, "it will be even more blessed to me."

He held her fast, the pain in his heart both wonderful and terrible. Wonderful in that they had time yet to come, terrible in that the time must be short and then they would be forced to part. And she would be here, walking in the garden, alone. And he would be here, walking in the garden, only in his tortured memory.

"Do you know," Kamil continued softly, "I often think of Maigrey and Sagan meeting here. They must have, when they were students in the Academy. I don't know why, but I sense them together, in the rose garden, when I don't sense their presence anywhere else. Perhaps that's because I saw her here, only a few months ago."

She spoke in such a calm and matter-of-fact tone that it took Dion a moment to assimilate her meaning. Even then he thought perhaps she'd mixed up her pronouns, was talking about someone else. He drew back, looked at her, looked into the golden eyes that were like sunlight, even in the snowy darkness.

"Who?" he asked.

"Lady Maigrey," said Kamil. "Oh, now, don't look like that!" She laughed, though a little self-consciously. "I haven't been taking any mind-altering drugs. It was last summer. I was working here in the afternoon. It was hot; no one else was around. I don't know what made me look up, because there was no sound. I saw a woman dressed in a blue gown standing in the path. She was looking at the roses. She had her hand out, as if she might touch one, but she didn't. I stared at her, trying to think who would be walking in the garden at this time of day. I put down my spade and stood up and started to go to speak to her. But when I looked again, she was gone."

"A visitor," said Dion.

"You're shivering," said Kamil. "We should go inside . . ."

". . . where it's warm," he murmured, kissing her again.

But they made no move, not yet. It was too wonderful to build the flame, then bank it, let it burn as long as possible.

"I thought it was just a visitor," said Kamil softly, her heart beating against his. "But when I saw her portrait, I knew that it was her. I'd never seen her before that, you know."

"You must have," Dion remonstrated, with a halfhearted laugh to cover his own disquiet. "On the vids, at your father's house."

"You know how my father feels about technological monstrosities." Kamil laughed, shook the snow from her hair. "No, I'd never seen a picture of her before. Truly."

Dion smiled.

Kamil grasped hold of the lapels of his coat, half teasing, half earnest. "Don't look smug. Tell me you've never seen her spirit. Tell me she doesn't come to you. The king she gave her life to protect."

Kamil's manner changed; she was serious, thoughtful. She looked, once again, into the garden. "The only thing I wonder is, why wasn't he with her? They loved each other so much. They were parted in life. I can't imagine that they would remain apart after death. . . ."

Dion shut his eyes against the sting of sudden tears.

"Don't!" he said.

Kamil shifted her gaze to him, saw him pale and shaken. "I'm sorry," she whispered remorsefully. "I'm so sorry . . . I didn't mean . . . Oh, my darling! I love you so much. I want only to make you happy."

"You do! You will!" he said fiercely, harshly, his passion overpowering him.

It was growing darker in the garden. Storm clouds covered the moon; snow began to fall again, hard and thick, sticking in their eyelashes, melting on their skin. Laughing, they turned and, arms around each other, clinging together, they slid and stumbled on the slick stones of the path, returning to Dion's bedroom, to warmth and darkness and exquisite happiness.

Outside, in the night, the snow fell, soft and cold.

--◆>)◯(<◆--

Afterward, they lay in the dark, her head resting on his chest, talking.

"Astarte wants a child," said Dion. "That's all she wants from me. If I gave her that, she'd be happy. Her mother would be happy. The whole damn galaxy would be happy. As if it's any of their business."

"You can't blame them, Dion," said Kamil. "Think of the upheaval and confusion and near disaster they've gone through. The people are grateful for this respite. They want it to go on. Your child is a future for them, a future they can look forward to with hope. It would give them a sense of continuity."

"I know," said Dion. "I understand. I truly do. Believe me, I'd like nothing better than to give them what they want. We've tried, God knows. But I don't want to think about that. Neither do you. Not here, not now."

But he did think about it and he continued to talk about it. It was so comforting to talk about it! She listened, though it was uncomfortable for her, because she knew he needed her to listen.

"We've been to every doctor imaginable. We're both healthy. Absolutely no reason we can't have a hundred royal heirs. They say it's stress. Or maybe space travel. Or maybe space travel's good for us. She won't be artificially inseminated; it's against her religion. Something about the Goddess blessing only true unions of mind and body."

Dion sat up, his back to Kamil. He ran his hand through his sweat-damp hair, dark and blood-colored in the moonlight. "There can be no thought of divorce. It would mean war. And I won't let the deaths of millions pay the price of my happiness."

"I know, Dion. I understand. I don't expect it." Kamil sat up with him, leaned against him, her arms around him, her cheek resting on his bare back. "We talked about this before. Remember?"

He smiled ruefully. "Yes—the night I told you I couldn't keep my promise to marry you. I thought you'd despise me. Maybe I hoped you would. It would have been easier. . . ."

"Despise you?" Kamil smiled. "For doing your duty? I am the daughter of a ruler. I know that duty to the people comes first. That was the earliest lesson my parents taught me. What was our love, what was our commitment, compared to the commitment you had made the people?"

"I could have wriggled out, Kamil. There were ways."

"*Then* I would have despised you."

He put his arm around her, kissed the silver hair.

"This is all I want," she told him. "This will be enough."

Dion sighed and lay back down, drawing her down with him. His expression grave, troubled, he stared into the darkness, into the moonlight reflected off the snow, shining on the ceiling. The silver light came and went as the clouds raced past. Shadows slid over Dion, hiding him from her sight. Kamil lay listening to his quiet breathing, the beating of his heart.

The shadows slipped past. His face, pale and strong, like carven marble, emerged from the darkness. Kamil was reminded suddenly and chillingly of a dream, the first night she'd met him.

They strode into battle together, as had been the custom in her land in ancient times. He the warrior, she his shieldmaid, guarding his unarmed side. Together they fought and fought well, vanquished foe after foe. He was the leader of his army, his flowing red-golden hair a bright banner that was always in the vanguard.

And then they met an enemy beyond belief, a dreadful wave of evil and darkness that crashed into them, beat on the shield. Dion fought, held his enemies at bay, sword and body covered with blood, his own and that of his foes. But wounds and exhaustion overcame him. He slipped and fell. His enemies towered over him, moved in for the kill. Kamil stood before him, held the shield as best she could, offered him a chance, a brief respite. The enemies struck blow after blow, shattered her shield arm, drove her to her knees.

Behind them, the army wavered, the bright banner they had followed dimmed by darkness. Kamil fell, but the shield lay over Dion, over them both. They looked at each other and in that moment knew that they could lie together in the darkness, safe, hidden, and their enemies would ride over them. Ride to victory, destroying those who came behind. Already they could hear them, crying out in despair, shouting for their king.

He looked at her and saw she understood. Rising, he threw aside the shield and cried a challenge to his foe. His army surged around him and he led them forward, and the last she saw of him was the flowing bright hair, shining on them like a new-made sun. And he vanished. And she lay in the darkness, alone.

Kamil began to cry, softly, against her will. She gulped, held her grief inside, though the tears burned her throat. Hoping he wouldn't notice—for how could she explain?—she tried to ease herself out of his grasp, to wipe the tears away, but he felt the wetness on his skin and turned immediately to her.

"Hush, don't. I'm sorry. I didn't mean to hurt you," he said, misunderstanding. He was serious, remorseful. "I was the first lover you've had, wasn't I?"

She pressed her face against his arm, unable to stop the tears now, unable to speak to correct his mistake, then thinking that perhaps he wasn't far from wrong.

He was silent, stroking her hair, then said, his face flushing, "Somehow, I hadn't expected . . . I mean, I thought . . . here, on this campus . . ."

"Oh, Dion." Kamil raised her head, looked at him, managed a tremulous smile. "How could you imagine there would be anyone else? I love you . . . only you."

He held her close, crushing her to him. She clasped him tightly, fiercely, their bodies crowding together, as if they could overcome the flesh that was a physical barrier to their souls' joining. But flesh compensated by giving them pleasure.

Passion stirred. They teased it a moment, then relaxed and lay back, content to enjoy the simmer before the burning.

"We've talked about me too much," he said. "Tell me what you do every day, what courses you're taking; tell me about the people you talk to, who see you every day; tell me where you go, what you think . . ."

"I don't *go* anywhere, except to class," Kamil said, laughing slightly, warm with pleasure at his interest. She snuggled near. "It was hard for me at first. I was far behind all the others. Our people don't believe in formal schooling, you know. And so I've had to work hard to catch up. But I love it . . . now."

"Now?" He looked at her.

"I was homesick in the beginning. That . . . that was a hard time. You were just married . . . and I couldn't help but be jealous. Not of her, exactly. I wasn't afraid that you would love her more than you love me." She put her hand on his lips, stopping him when he would have spoken. "I never doubted you. I was jealous of her time with you, of knowing you two were loving, touching. . . ."

"Touching, maybe," said Dion grimly. "Not loving."

They were both silent. The moonlight disappeared. The wind rose, the storm returned. Bits of ice pelted the windowpanes.

"Don't stop talking," he said abruptly. "Keep on. I want to know. I want to be able to picture you in my mind. What do you eat for breakfast? Do you fix it yourself or go to the cafeteria?"

"Oh, Dion!" She laughed.

"I'm serious." He made it evident with a kiss. "Tell me."

She told him. She told him every part of her daily routine, told him about her classes, what she was studying, told him about the professors, about the people she knew, about the books she was reading, her dislike of philosophy, her love of mathematics. She told him what she ate for breakfast.

He lay very quiet, very still, his breathing soft and regular. She might have thought he'd fallen asleep, except she could see his eyes, wide open, staring into the darkness and seeing not darkness but seeing her, walking through her day.

She thought of his day in comparison—the crushing responsibilities, the life-and-death decisions, the person he had to become, the king she'd seen tonight, so different from the man holding her. She was remorseful. She didn't often give in to self-pity, but sometimes, in the evening, when the air was soft and fragrant with the scent of the roses and she saw young couples walking together, she felt sorry for herself.

After this, no more. There was no self-pity in his expression, no regret. Only an inexpressible sadness that brought the dream-image of the warrior back to her. She banished it hurriedly, afraid she'd start to cry again.

"And what," Dion asked, the first words he'd spoken in a long time, "is the point of all these studies in astrophysics and quantum mechanics? What do you plan to do?"

"Can't you guess?" she asked, flushing.

He propped himself up on one elbow, intrigued by the sudden air of mystery. "You don't plan to give your life to the church, do you? Become a nun?"

"Of course. That's it!" Kamil said, pulling playfully on his hair. That started a scuffle which ended with her breathless and laughing, pinned up against the headboard.

"Tell me the truth," he mock-threatened, pretending to be stern. "Tell all, lady. I command you."

"You'll laugh at me," she protested.

"You didn't laugh at me when I said I wanted to be king."

"No," Kamil returned softly. "I didn't laugh."

He kissed her and this time the passion was too strong. It was some time before they returned to what they had been discussing. Kamil was achingly, sweetly, drowsy in his arms.

"No more trying to change the subject," he said, his voice warm and husky with the pleasant tiredness. He yawned, kissed her gently. "Tell me about your plans. And don't fall asleep. I won't waste this night in sleep."

"It's almost dawn. I should go soon, before anyone sees me."

But she made no move to go. The thought of leaving this rumpled warmth, of hurrying, cold and shivering, through the halls to her own empty room, darkened her heart. "I made the decision last holiday. I'd gone home and there was a visitor. Tomi Corbett. You remember her?"

"The captain of that cruise liner Lady Maigrey pirated and flew into Corasia. Yes, I remember Corbett. What was she doing on your planet?"

"My father met her during the battle, when the fleet was forced to fight its way out of the Corasian galaxy."

"That's right. I'd forgotten. He took some of his troops over to her ship, in case it was boarded. Funny, I hadn't thought of her in ages."

"They became good friends. He invites her to visit every year, when she can get leave. She's a colonel in the Royal Space Corps now. She says you and General Dixter helped her."

"She deserved it," Dion commented quietly. "So you met her . . ."

"Yes." Kamil plaited the sheet beneath her fingers. "She was telling me about the Space Corps Academy. And, well, that's what I want to do. I want to train to be a spacepilot. Like Tomi. And Lady Maigrey."

Dion said nothing.

"I know what you're thinking," Kamil went on, truly believing she did. "You're thinking I don't have a chance. And I know how hard it is . . . what an honor to be chosen. I know that millions apply and only a handful make it. But my professors say my grades are high enough—I've got a straight 4.0. And I took the practice entrance exam already and my score was one of the highest. A candidate has to have influence to get a commission, but," she added with a breathless little laugh, "I'm friends with His Majesty the king and I thought he might—"

"Well, he won't," said Dion.

He pulled his arm out from beneath her, sat up in bed. Throwing back the sheets, he stood up, his back to her, and reached for his robe. "I might as well sign your death warrant."

Kamil stared at him, startled, unable to speak. She felt as if he had thrown the snow in her face.

He tied the robe around his waist, turned back to face her.
"I can imagine how exciting Colonel Corbett made it all sound.
Glamorous, heroic. I've seen how glamorous and exciting it
is. I've seen men die out there. I've heard their screams.... I
still hear them sometimes. I won't lose you, Kamil! I won't!"

You don't have me, Dion. The words came to her mind, but
they never passed beyond. It was the duty of the shieldmaid to
guard her warrior from hurt, not inflict it. But her plans and
hopes were hard to give up. They filled the emptiness of her
nights.

She climbed out of bed and went to him, holding out her
arms. She was shivering. He took hold of her, enveloped her in
the robe, wrapped it around them both.

"Stay here at the Academy," he said. "Stay here where it's
safe. Where I can come and be with you."

"Can you?" She looked up at him, eager, yearning. "Can you
truly come?"

"Yes, I promise. I've been thinking. I've endowed this Academy. I hold an honorary degree. I could be a guest lecturer, offer to present a series of lectures on—"

"Love," she suggested, teasing.

"No." He smiled. "That lecture is for one alone."

"I do love you!" she cried suddenly, clinging.

"And I you!"

They held each other fast in the darkness that was rapidly
brightening to a sullen, stormy dawn.

"I have to go," said Kamil. Gathering up her clothes, she
hurried into the bathroom.

Dion walked over to the windows, pressed his right hand
against the chill glass. The scars ached dully; the coolness
against them was welcome. He stood staring out into the snow-
laden garden. He wouldn't have been surprised to see Maigrey
walking the paths. He found himself hoping to see her again.

"Do you understand?" he said to her. "Perhaps not. You and
Sagan loved, but love wasn't enough for either of you. Your ambition, your pride were too important. You couldn't reach for
the crown without dropping the rose. I have the crown. I have
what you sought. I want the rose now, too. I don't ask for it all.
I know my duty and I will do it." His fist clenched. "But surely
I've earned this much happiness!"

A hand touched his arm, a cheek leaned against his shoulder.

"Is she out there?" Kamil asked quietly.

Dion shook his head, flushed, somewhat abashed. "No. No one is out there."

"But they soon will be." Kamil was dressed. She lifted the hood of her fur cloak, raised it up over her head.

"You can't go out in the snow," Dion said, suddenly understanding her purpose.

"Why ever not?" She looked amazed, waved a deprecating hand at the drifts. "This is nothing compared to what we have back home."

"I know. I was there," said Dion dryly. "But for one thing you'd leave tracks in the garden. Someone would see them. We should behave with dignity, at least."

Kamil blushed, lowered her head.

"Princess Olefsky." Dion took hold of her hand, led her formally to the bedroom door, through it, and out into the headmaster's main living area, with its massive bookcases and strange curios. Reaching an outer door, Dion started to open it.

"My guard will escort you to your room."

Kamil hung back. "Oh, Dion, are you certain?"

"I trust these men with my life, Kamil," he said quietly. "On a daily basis. I can trust them with my honor."

She looked at him, looked at the closed door, and shook her head.

"We'll be careful, discreet," he said to her. "But I will *not* sneak around. I am, after all, the king."

He kissed her lips, her forehead. Lifting her gloved hand, he kissed the palm, closed her fingers over it. Then he opened the door. The King's Guard snapped to attention, bodies and faces rigid.

"Centurion," Dion said to one of the men on duty, "escort the princess back to her room."

"Yes, my liege."

Kamil's complexion was the color of the roses as they bloomed in the summer. She kept her head lowered, the hood falling forward to hide her face. She cast one swift and loving glance back at Dion, then hurried down the hallway toward her room, the guard following a pace behind.

Dion watched her leave. She was flustered, embarrassed. She moved awkwardly, stumbling over her long dress, and would have taken a turn down the wrong hallway had not the guard respectfully corrected her.

Dion thought of her walking through the grass of her homeland with her long, manlike strides, her arms swinging free, her head held high. Not like this. Not ashamed, not embarrassed.

He gave in to a moment's rebellious anger. Why couldn't she be his? Why couldn't he say to the universe: *She's mine. I love her!*

He shut the door, shut it carefully, to keep from slamming it. Gritting his teeth, he leaned against the door until the fire-tinged dimness cleared from his eyes, his mind.

Duty, responsibility. He was, after all, the king. Today he would return home to the palace.

Return home to his wife.

"This will be enough," he said to himself with a long, indrawn sigh. "This will be enough. . . ."

Chapter ❈❖❈ Eleven

I would that you were all to me,
You that are just so much, no more.
Robert Browning, "Two in the Campagna"

Astarte Starfire, wife of the king, queen of the galaxy, High Priestess of both her own people and of a growing following throughout the galaxy, lay in her bed alone and stared into the darkness. The sheets were rumpled in the place beside her, still warm from his presence. She could put out her hand and feel the warmth, feel it rapidly cooling.

Dion's fragrance was there, too. She wondered about that; she had often wondered, from the first time she'd met him—on their wedding day. He used no perfume, yet there was a sweetness about him, a . . . softening of the air around him, for lack of a better way to describe it. Like a spring morning. She came to think she was the only one who smelled it. When she had questioned her women about the mysterious fragrance, her retinue looked blank.

He was gone.

It was the middle of the night and she was alone.

His excuse was that he was troubled with bad dreams, he didn't want to disturb her. That was true. Often, after they were first married, she'd heard him muttering to himself in his sleep, moving restlessly, waking with a gasp and a start. She had tried to comfort him, but he would rebuff her, sometimes coldly, sometimes gently, but always letting her know her interference was unwelcome. She was an intruder. She'd been relieved when he had moved into a separate room, though his absence from her bed had meant scene after scene with her mother.

Astarte stared into the darkness. Her hand left the rumpled sheet that no longer held his warmth, pressed over her belly. He had made love to her.

Made love to her? She laughed, but it turned to a sob.

She lay there, her hand flat over her flat belly, fingers knead-

ing the smooth, bare flesh. "No, you didn't make love to *me*.
You made love to her! My body. But she is in your mind!"

Dion had made love to his wife, dutifully, every night for a
week after his return from the Academy. The first night, Astarte
had been thrilled with joy. There had been a feverishness about
him, desire. His lovemaking had been fierce, passionate. It was
only after he'd left, with a chill kiss, to return to his own bedroom, that she'd realized he'd been loving someone else.

His ardor had quickly cooled. Their lovemaking now was
brief, perfunctory. She had no pleasure from it, guessed that
what pleasure he received was from the fantasy he conjured up
to enable him to perform. He kept his eyes closed the entire
time. Astarte imagined herself ripping out his eyes, to see what
other woman's image was on the inside of the lids. Her imaginings grew quite violent, and they scared her.

She thought of confronting him, but she kept silent because
she knew what he was trying to do. He was trying to give her
the baby she longed for.

Perhaps this time . . .

She closed her eyes, dozed.

He was with her again, as he had been just a few moments
ago. He was "performing his duty" and she was lying beneath
him, enduring it, hating it, wishing it would soon end. And it
did and she felt the rushing warmth inside her. She opened her
eyes and looked into his face . . .

And it wasn't his face.

Astarte caught her breath in a horrified gasp. She struggled
under the weight of a heavy body, trying frantically to push him
away. He was laughing at her.

"My child! Mine!" he said . . . and she found herself sitting
up in her bed, flailing with her arms at the air.

She shuddered, curled up in a ball, her hand clutching her
tight, flat belly. She guessed, then, that she was pregnant. "But
what does this vision mean? Whose face did I see? It was his.
And it wasn't his. Blessed Goddess, what are you trying to tell
me?"

Astarte rolled over on her back. Her tears dried on her
cheeks unheeded. She was devout. The vision came from the
Goddess. It was not the first she'd experienced. The visions did
not come often, nor did they come when sought, but when they
did come to her, what they revealed to her always came to pass.
But what did it mean?

Hastily, with trembling fingers, she lit her lamp and sat up, fumbling for her robe. Catching hold of it, she wrapped it around her body. Hurrying from her sumptuously furnished room, oblivious to the luxuries that surrounded her, she entered a door hidden behind a rich tapestry, a small door that led to a small room off the main one.

Her chapel, private and secret, all things in it placed here by her own hands. If she had been forced to name a favorite room in a palace of many magnificent rooms, this small, windowless alcove would have been it.

She lit a candle, a white beeswax that stood in a plain wooden candle holder. The Goddess liked simple things, things "of the land, of the hand," as the saying went. The candle's light fell upon the altar's centerpiece—a statue of the Goddess herself. It was old, far older than Astarte, having been given to her by her mother's mother, a High Priestess like herself.

The statue portrayed two women. One woman was clad in long white robes. In her right hand she held a sheaf of grain; her left hand rested upon a child who stood before her. Back to back with this woman was a woman clad in armor and helm, who held a sword in her right hand, a shield in the other. The dual image of the Goddess—on one side the nurturing mother; on the other, the warrior who would defend her children.

The statue of the Goddess stood on every altar in every home of Astarte's people. The Goddess had been worshiped there for centuries, ever since the sickness had taken most of the men, left those who survived weak and precious, nurtured like hothouse plants for their seed. In most homes, the Goddess's statue had only one face—the face the woman chose as her own. For Astarte's mother, the Goddess wore the face of the Warrior. For Astarte herself, the Goddess was the gentle, loving Nurturer. But now Astarte reached out, turned the Goddess slowly around.

There was a time when a woman had to fight to save what was valuable not only to her, but to those who trusted in her.

The alabaster statue regarded Astarte with clear, empty eyes. Astarte had hardly ever looked at this side of it; she knew every line and carved fold in the garment on the other side. She had often thought this side cold and hard; it reminded her too much of her own mother. Now she saw that if the Goddess was cold, it was because She had to freeze her heart against sympathy for those who would do Her people harm. If She was hard, it was armor against the wounds that She must both give and take.

Astarte stared at the Warrior a long time, then, sighing, turned the statue back around. She felt warmed, comforted by the familiar sight of the Mother. Lifting a sprig of dried sage, she crushed the leaves in her palm, scattered them in a small brass dish, and set them on fire. She breathed in the sweet incense, wafted some of the smoke over to the Goddess with her hand.

"Blessed Mother," Astarte prayed, "thank you for the vision. I do not understand, but I will heed its warning. Praise to your unspoken name."

She lifted a small brass lid, placed it over the smoking sage, quenched the smoke. Slowly, reaching out her hand, she turned the statue back around. The Warrior stared back at her with the empty eyes of one who must kill.

Astarte sat back on her heels. She had never made an offering to the Warrior and, though she knew what was required—blood—she could not bring herself to make it.

"I know what you want me to do," she said to the Warrior. "You want me to spy on him. You want me to have him followed. You want me to turn men loyal to him into his betrayers. Or if that isn't possible—and I pray to the Goddess it would not be—then you would have me hire a snake to slither after him. And then what? You demand photos of the two of them. Pictures of their lovemaking, laid upon this altar. You would have me confront him. You want the anger, the shame, the hatred. Hating me, hating himself.

"This is not me," she said to the Warrior, pleading with those empty eyes to understand.

They did not. *You don't love him,* they said.

"No, but I honor him," she explained. "Respect him."

She would have loved him; she had started to love him. But that was over now.

When had she first begun to love him? Perhaps in those early months of marriage, which were like a dream to her now. Two strangers, forced together by circumstance, forced to play a never-ending role upon a stage before the devouring eyes of billions. Finding themselves maintaining the roles, even when the curtain was down, the stage empty, except for themselves upon it.

During that time, she caught glimpses of the man behind the

mask, the man beneath the crown, the man inside the purple robe. Strong, decisive; and at the same time weak, vulnerable, tormented by inner doubt. Making decisions, making right decisions, and a part of him amazed when he was right. Punishing himself severely on those rare occasions when he was wrong. Learning from his mistakes and going on, fearful of making more, yet always finding the courage to continue.

She was beginning to love him. She wanted him for her own, and it was then that she realized he was unattainable. She could not win his love, because it belonged to someone else. And now his love for this other woman, which had so long been platonic, had been consummated. Astarte knew it as well as if she had seen them together.

The danger was great. He was one more step removed from her and, if this went on, he would be lost to her—and to his people—forever. The child he had just fathered this night would not be born. Or if it was, it would belong to another. Perhaps the man in the vision. . . .

"What, then, am I to do? I must save him." Astarte's hand went to her belly again, slid inside her robe to press against her bare flesh. He was not the only one she had to save.

The empty eyes of the Warrior held no answers, or else held answers she rejected. Their cold stare was unnerving. Impulsively, Astarte reached out to turn the statue back around. Halfway, she stopped. She had never seen it like this before. The Warrior and the Mother, standing back to back. To nurture *and* defend, to fight *and* care. Was it possible? Was this what the Goddess was telling her?

Lessons of DiLuna returned to her daughter. Astarte recalled nights spent listening to the warrior women talk. A warrior did not always rush forth to meet the enemy, weapons raised, screaming defiance. Sometimes it was best to retreat, to seem to surrender, to fall back and let the enemy come to you.

Astarte pondered. Her plan was hazy, not yet clear in her mind, but it could work. And then she understood suddenly why it would work.

"I know Dion. Deep inside, he despises the deception. He's fought against this illicit love; that was why he remained faithful to me for so long. But he is human. In the end, his love for her proved too strong. During one of those times when he was weak, vulnerable, one of those times when he sought shelter, she was there. He turned to her."

Astarte would have been less than human herself if she did not feel the twinge of jealousy's cruel bite. She thought of him in bed with his lover, of the kisses and caresses given to her that his wife had never known, of pleasure taken with his eyes open. Astarte was the Warrior then, could have watched her enemy's body sliding off her sword and known the emptiness of the statue's alabaster eyes.

An emptiness that would always be with her.

"No," she said, "I can't think about that. Not now. Not ever. If I let that poison work on me, it will kill me." She pressed her hand against her stomach. "Kill us all."

She offered thanks once again. Dousing the candle, she rose to her feet. She felt comforted, her decision made. It would be painful, painful for both of them. But she would be merciful as she could, keep her strokes swift and clean, end it quickly.

Chapter ⇢◦◦◦⇠ Twelve

Turning and turning in the widening gyre . . .
        William Butler Yeats, "The Second Coming"

Tusk crept slowly out of the hoverjeep, moving carefully so as not to jar his aching head. Squinting—the dark sun-goggles were still permitting far too much sunlight to burn into his eyeballs—Tusk fumbled around the outside of the Scimitar until his hands closed over the ladder rungs, then he crawled slowly up the ladder to the Scimitar's hatch.

"XJ, lemme in!"

The roar reverberated around inside his skull like lasgun fire, ricocheting off four walls. He groaned and lay sprawled on the hatch. It was still early morning, but Vangelis' broiling sun was already heating up the spaceplane's shining metal surface. Sweat rolled down Tusk's body. It occurred to him that if he lay here any longer, he'd fry like a piece of raw meat on a griddle.

"XJ, damn it, you know I'm out here!" Tusk pleaded. "I'm not feelin' too good. I feel kinda like I might throw up. . . ."

"Not on my paint!" snapped the computer.

The hatch whirred open. Tusk lowered himself gratefully into the cool darkness, descended cautiously down the ladder, placed his foot gently on the deck. Even then the vibration sent waves of pain crashing over his head.

"Juiced," said XJ in disgust.

"Shud'up," Tusk mumbled.

Holding one hand over the goggles in case they should slip and permit even the dim lights shining inside the plane to pierce his brain, he stretched his other hand out in front of him and groped his way to one of the couches. Bumping into it, he fell onto it with a groan.

"You didn't go home last night," stated XJ.

Tusk made a brief circuit of his memory. "Shit," he said, sitting up and regretting it instantly. "I didn't, did I?"

"Don't worry. I called Nola, told her where you were."

"You did?" Tusk sank back down, pleasantly surprised.

That didn't last long. The more he thought about XJ being nice to him, the less he liked it. He dragged himself to a sitting position again.

"What do you want from me?" he croaked, hanging on to the couch for dear life.

"Jeez, you're so suspicious. Can I . . . can I get you a cold compress?"

"Stop it!" Tusk snarled, bounding to his feet. He put his hand on his head to keep it from blasting off. "So I had the shakes yesterday! Big deal. It happens. See if you can reach Dixter."

"I try to be nice. And this is the thanks I get." XJ sulked. "Next time, I won't call. I'll let you go home to Nola. I hope she skins you alive—"

"Anything'd be better than this. How can something that makes you feel so good turn around and make you feel so awful? It's like God's standin' there with His hand out saying, 'Glad you enjoyed yourself. Now pay up.' "

"Philosophy. From a juicer. It's what I live for."

"Shut up. And while you're shutting up, get hold of Dixter."

"Dixter! Hah! You expect me to believe that you and Link actually discovered some useful bit of information last night? What'd you do, peel the label off the jump-juice bottle and find a prize underneath?"

"Just call Dixter, damn it." Tusk moaned. "And turn the lights off while you're at it."

Clinging to the railing, he lowered himself into the cockpit, fumbled his way to his chair. He lurched into it, rested his elbows on the console, lowered his head to his hands.

Dixter's face appeared on the screen. "Yes, Tusk?"

Tusk lifted his head with an effort. "Oh, hullo, sir."

"Hello, son." Dixter was slightly taken aback by the sight of Tusk sitting in the spaceplane in the dark wearing sun-goggles. "Hard night?" he asked sympathetically.

"Yeah, you'd think I'd learn." Tusk remembered the goggles, took them off. He rubbed his eyes, cleared his throat. "Hang in there with me a minute, sir. Now, let's see. Where did I leave off? Did I tell you that Link got this same message?"

Dixter nodded.

"Yeah, right. I went over to his place last night. He answered the message, same as I did. And he got exactly the same instructions, the only difference being that his name was inserted in all the right places. If he wants to join this Ghost Legion, he's got to go to Hell's Outpost."

"I see."

"Link's like me. He figures this stinks like last week's mackerel. So we try to get hold of Gorbag. Last we knew, he was living on Jarun, where he was born. Well, he was out, but we talked to his mate. She says that yeah, he got one of these vids, too, and it was exactly the same message, except that they used a Jarun pilot instead of that Captain Masters to make the pitch.

"Well, you know Gorbag, sir. Nothing scares him. So he flies off to Hell's Outpost to take a look."

"When was this?" Dixter asked.

"About three months ago, Standard Military Time. He came home madder'n hell. Said it was a scam." Tusk shook his head. "Like he couldn't see this coming? But then old Gorbag never was too bright. Says he met these pilots and they wined him and dined him or whatever you do with a Jarun and then they gave him some more coordinates and told him to be there ASAP.

"So he waddles on back to his plane and runs the coordinates and finds out—surprise, surprise—that it's a planet in some godforsaken part of the galaxy that's nowhere near a Lane. And, according to the star charts, the world is nothing but a hunk of dead rock floating in space with no living thing on it, not so much as a bowl full of organic soup."

Tusk's stomach lurched. He was sorry he'd brought that up. He paused a moment for his insides to settle down, wiped sweat from his forehead. Dixter waited patiently.

"Where was I?" Tusk mumbled.

"Soup," said XJ helpfully. "Get it while it's hot."

Tusk glared at the computer. "Anyway, that's what the Jarun found. He went back to the Exile Café, to tell these pilots he didn't think this joke was so funny and maybe bounce them around on their heads some to relieve his hurt feelings and, of course, they were long gone. So he's out of fuel and a thousand golden eagles and feels like a damn fool."

"But that's all," said Dixter.

"Yes, sir."

"Then, Tusk, what's the point? They took him for a thousand eagles, but that's an elaborate scam to only pull in that much. They didn't set him up to be hijacked way out there by himself in space; they must have surely known he'd run the coordinates before he flew them."

"Beats me, sir." Tusk massaged his aching temples.

"I'd like to talk to Gorbag. You have his number?"

"Sure, sir, but he's not there."

"Not there?"

"No, sir. Shortly after this, he got a call from a planet on the Corasian perimeter. They're all nervous as a stepped-on cat after that Corasian attack on the outpost. Hiring mercenaries right and left to back up their own defenses. He flew off to join up."

"I see. Has his mate heard from him?"

"Naw. But he's been sending home his paycheck and so she figures he's okay."

"But he hasn't talked to her, hasn't told her where his is?"

"No, sir, but why would he? She knew where he was going. She's got no reason to think he's not there. And if the Corasians are sniffing around, you guys in the navy are bound to want to keep a lid on transmissions."

"Yes, I suppose you're right. Still . . ." Dixter's voice trailed off.

Tusk looked at the admiral in concern. "You want us to do anything else, sir? Link's offered to go check it out. We can't leave right now, of course, 'cause we got a job lined up, but—"

"No," said Dixter, shaking his head. "No, I doubt if you'd find out any more than we already have and it might prove—" He stopped, frowned again. "Don't do anything. And don't mention any of this, will you?"

"Sure, sir." Tusk shrugged.

"You didn't happen to get hold of those coordinates they gave Gorbag, did you?"

"Yeah, as a matter of fact we did, sir." Tusk was pleased with himself. "The Jarun had 'em filed in his log. His mate looked it up, gave them to us. I'll have XJ transmit them."

"Thanks, son. Thanks for everything. You and Link both."

"Happy to be of assistance. You know, sir," Tusk added, just as Dixter was about to sign off, "something did strike me as kinda funny about this."

"Yes, what?" Dixter was back and interested.

"It's probably not important—"

"Doesn't matter. Tell me."

"That planet. When we looked it up in the files, we found

out it had a name. Not a number, like you'd suppose with a hunk of worthless rock. But a name. Someone'd gone to the trouble to name the damn thing."

"What did they call it?"

"Val . . . Valum . . . What the devil was that?" Tusk reached into one pocket of his work shirt, fished around, came up empty. He dove into the other pocket. "I wrote it down, 'cause I knew I'd never remember. Yeah, here it is. I'll spell it. V-a-l-l-o-m-b-r-o-s-a. You got that?"

"Yes." Dixter copied it, spelled it back.

"That's it." Tusk nodded. "Mean anything to you?"

"No, but then who knows what language it's in? I'll run it, let you know what I find out. And Tusk . . ." Dixter's tone was serious, his face grave. "Let me know if they contact you again."

"You think they will, sir?" Tusk was astonished. "Why should they? It's obvious I didn't fall for their little scam."

"I know. But it wouldn't surprise me. Take it easy, son. My love to Nola and the baby." Dixter's image vanished from the screen.

"Wonder what he thinks we've tied into?" Tusk muttered, staring at the blank screen. "Sounds more like a case for the Better Business Bureau than a Lord of the Admiralty."

"Who knows?" said XJ. "Maybe he doesn't have enough wars to keep him busy these days. What was that crap about having a job lined up?"

Tusk was feeling better. He could almost see. "No crap. Looks like we have work. Steady."

"No! Steady work! You better back up all my systems. I may black out from the shock."

"Some women contacted Link yesterday, wants us to transport her and a partner a couple times a week to Akara."

"Rough place. What're they carrying?"

"Briefcases." Tusk glowered. "That's all you need to know. And that's what you'll put in the log."

"Sure thing. You know me. Tact and discretion are the tag end of my serial number."

Tusk snorted. "Tact and discretion, my ass. The only place you'll find those two words is in your spell checker. Say," he added in wheedling tones, "I could sure use a cuppa coffee. How about makin' it for me . . ."

"Go soak your head," snapped XJ.

"Sir John Dixter would like to see you, Your Majesty," said D'argent, entering the king's office with morning tea. "He says that it is urgent."

"Can we fit him in?" Dion glanced up from reading a condensed report on the rapidly deteriorating situation in the star system of Muruva, where six planets had just overthrown the dictatorial rule of a seventh. Unfortunately, each one of the planets had decided that now that they were free, they could freely butcher their other five neighbors, and they were proceeding to do just that.

D'argent consulted the schedule. "You have two meetings scheduled this morning—one with the Muruvan ambassadors and one with the representatives of the League of Underdeveloped Planets."

Dion considered briefly. "I'll see the Muruvan ambassadors. Put off the representatives of the league until this afternoon. Back up all my other afternoon appointments an hour."

"The news conference that we're beaming to Muruva, sir? Shall I reschedule?"

"No, I need to come down hard on the Muruvans and I need to do it fast, before the fools nuke each other." Dion glanced at the time. "Send in my advisers on Muruva, then send in the ambassadors. And if they start fistfights in the antechamber like they did at the spaceport last night, call Cato and have him clap the paralyzers on them. I won't put up with this nonsense."

"Yes, sir," replied D'argent, smiling faintly. He glided silently out of the office.

Later that morning, seven angry and quarreling Muruvan ambassadors were ushered into His Majesty's presence and—after a conference—seven chastened and thoughtful ambassadors were led out.

John Dixter watched them go. They were harried and flustered. The king was cool and even grimly smiling.

"Are we sending in troops, Your Majesty?" asked Dixter, taking a seat, refusing any refreshment.

"They have thirty days," said Dion, "to settle their differences peacefully. If not, then we'll keep the peace for them. And the first thing we'll do is end all 'outside interference' in their affairs."

"Blockade," said Dixter.

"The major trading partners have all agreed to honor it. The Muruvans could find themselves in serious economic trouble if they don't shake hands and make up. My advisers tell me that the Muruvans' hatred for one another doesn't extend as far as their wallets. I think it's deeper than that, but we'll see what transpires. I take it you have further information on that matter we previously discussed?"

"Yes, Your Majesty." Dixter spent a moment leaving Muruva, assimilating this thoughts. "I heard from Tusk."

The admiral repeated his conversation with the mercenary. Dion listened in silence, absently rubbing the scars on the palm of his right hand. If Dixter noticed this, he pretended he didn't.

"So why not have Tusk and Link check this out, my lord?"

"Because they're too close, Your Majesty. Too close to you," answered Dixter.

Dion shook his head. "You honestly believe that someone would go to all this trouble just for the chance of getting hold of Tusk? To do what?"

"I think that may be part of it, sire. What their objective is, I can't tell you. I can't even venture a guess. One thing I do know, Gorbag isn't working for any of the Outer Systems. I checked."

"So you think . . . what?"

"I think this is how the 'scam' works. These Ghost Legion representatives contact pilots and offer to make a deal if they'll fly to Hell's Outpost. They've got to figure that only those seriously interested or desperate enough will fork over a thousand eagles and make that trip. Already, you see, they're culling their list.

"Once the pilots reach Hell's Outpost, the representatives look them over. Probably gather all sorts of information, scan their planes, that sort of thing. Then they feed the pilots these weird coordinates. If the pilot swallows it, they've got him or her. Probably meet them once they get there. If they don't, like Gorbag, they see to it that he's offered another job. And when he takes it, they intercept him, make it worth his while to join up."

"Again I ask you, my lord," Dion persisted, "to do what?"

"I don't know, sire, but they're up to something. Following Tusk's lead on Gorbag, I did some checking on the other people I had under my command. All of them have received this same message. About a hundred of them flew to Hell's Outpost. Since then, they either took the Ghost Legion up on their offer—in which case they left one night and never came back—or they took other jobs and—same scenario—they've now dropped out of sight. But they're sending home money. Lots of money."

"Someone's building his or her own space corps."

"Looks that way. And it's big. And selective. They've only taken the best. Some people went to Hell's Outpost and are now wandering around in plain sight looking for work. Never got a call. And this Ghost Legion didn't use my list alone. They've apparently searched the galaxy."

"And could you hide a force that big?"

"Easily, Your Majesty. Especially on someplace like this planet Tusk found. Off Lanes, on the outer fringes. A hunk of cold rock. Not even the Corasians would be interested in it. And that's how it checks out. I studied the reports. But as Tusk says, there are a few things odd about it."

Dixter referred to notes. "It was discovered thirty years ago by the famous space explorer Garth Pantha. You wouldn't remember him; you were too young. But almost everyone my age would, who watched the vids. Pantha was not only a damn fine spacepilot, but a brilliant physicist and natural scientist, and"— Dixter smiled—"one hell of a charmer.

"He was a celebrity. Had his own vid show. Because of his celebrity status, he moved in high circles. Very high circles. He was a favorite of your uncle's. King Amodius made Pantha a knight of the realm."

"Then he was Blood Royal."

"Yes. But the really interesting thing about Pantha was not the living of his life, as the poet says, but the manner of his leaving it. He died in some sort of mysterious space accident about eight years before the Revolution. The galaxy was stunned by the news. His death made headlines for days after. They even had a final transmission, showing him calmly reporting that he'd had engine failure and requesting assistance. But since he was way out in some remote part of space, he knew no one'd reach him in time. He said good-bye to his wife and family. It was a real heartbreaker.

"The Royal Space Corps sent out rescue planes, but when they reached his last known coordinates there was nothing there. Some time later, they found the wreckage of his spacecraft. Of course, no one ever knew what really happened, but Pantha'd always said that if he was marooned in space facing a slow death, he'd end it with a bang. And that's likely what he did."

"I see," said Dion thoughtfully. "And when he died was he near the Ghost Legion's coordinates?"

"No, Your Majesty," said John Dixter. "Nowhere in the area."

Dion frowned. "Then I fail to see . . ."

"I know, I know." Dixter sighed, rubbed his hand across his face. "It doesn't seem to get us anywhere. And maybe Garth Pantha doesn't have a damn thing to do with any of this. But as Tusk said, there's something odd about all this. Pantha discovered scores of new planets, new systems. And he gave lots of them names. It made good copy for his vid show. And this one he called Vallombrosa, which is one of the old languages—Italian, I think. It means—"

"Vale of Shades," said Dion.

Dixter stared. "I'm impressed, Your Majesty. You came up with that faster than the computer did."

"The computer didn't study with Platus," said Dion, smiling at the memory. "Milton. *Paradise Lost.* Satan 'called his legions, Angel forms, who lay entranced thick as autumnal leaves that strew the brooks in Vallombrosa . . .' Vale of Shades."

"Or, as we would say today, 'Valley of Ghosts,' " said John Dixter quietly.

Dion looked up. "Ghosts again."

"Yes, Your Majesty." Dixter was grim. "Ghosts again."

"And you consider this important?"

"I think it's damn important. Look at what's gone on. The Ghost Legion seeks information about Snaga Ohme's. Ghostly somethings evade the very latest in security devices and break into Snaga Ohme's. The Ghost Legion is recruiting and, for all we know, hiring the very best spacepilots. And they give as coordinates a dead planet called the Valley of Ghosts by a dead explorer."

The admiral leaned forward, illustrated his words with a motion of his index finger on the desk. "And what really scares me is that no matter where we start the circle, Dion, it ends up with you. The space-rotation bomb, Tusk and Link—even the fact that Pantha was once friends with your family. I don't understand it, I admit that. But I don't like it. Somewhere there's a key. We're missing it. I think we need to find that key, and find it fast."

"And you're suggesting . . . ?"

"Talk to Archbishop Fideles, son. Ask him to pass this information on to . . . whoever might be interested." Dixter spoke earnestly, forgetting they weren't both back in that trailer on Vangelis. "I mean"—the admiral flushed red—"I mean Your Majesty."

Dion smiled. "It sounded good to hear you call me son. It's been a long time." He fell silent. The smile faded. The room grew darker. A cloud, passing over the sun.

At length Dion sighed and raised his head, looked at Dixter. "How did you know?"

"Know what?" Dixter asked mildly.

"That *he's* still alive." It was obvious, from the inflection, that they weren't discussing the archbishop.

Dixter rubbed his grizzled jaw. "I didn't, Dion. Nothing certain. Call it a hunch. Or deduction. Derek Sagan considered suicide a mortal sin. And he wasn't the type to subconsciously put himself in the way of death. He was too good a fighter. His instincts would keep him alive, if nothing else. No, I never did believe Sagan died in our escape from Corasia. He meant us to think he died. And if he *is* alive, there'd be only one place he'd go, in the end—to the place where he began."

Dion nodded slowly. "Yes, that's how I figured it. I even asked Fideles about Sagan once, the day of the coronation. I said, point-blank, 'Have you had any word from Lord Sagan?' "

"What was the archbishop's answer?"

" 'He is with God,' Fideles told me. And then I asked, 'Is he dead?' But Fideles refused to tell me any more."

Dixter shrugged. "I'd say that pretty well confirms it."

"But where does this get us?" Dion argued. "If Sagan has forsaken the world, then he might as well be dead."

"Unless he hasn't truly forsaken it, Your Majesty. Unless he's part of this conspiracy."

Dion was silent. His hand rubbed the scars, back and forth, back and forth. He was looking at Dixter but not really seeing him. In his mind he had returned to that ghastly moon of death, to the last time he'd seen Derek Sagan standing at Maigrey's bier.

"No," said Dion after a moment. "I can't believe that. You

were there. You saw what he suffered. When she died, part of him died, too."

"Maybe it grew back," Dixter suggested dryly.

Dion frowned, displeased.

The admiral shook his head, sighed. The memory was a painful one for him as well.

"I saw Sagan then, Dion. But I also saw him twenty-odd years ago, too, when he led the revolution that overthrew the crown. If he wasn't directly responsible for the deaths of the king and your parents, Derek Sagan was the moving force behind it. And there was no question but that he tortured and murdered Tusk's father and any of the rest of the Guardians he could lay his hands on. Including—" Dixter stopped, glanced at the king, fell silent.

"Including Platus," said Dion grimly. "I know. I was there. I watched. . . ." He stared back again, in time. "Odd. Platus quoted Milton that very night. . . ."

"Full circle," Dixter muttered.

Dion shook his head. "No, I won't believe it. But," he added, forestalling Dixter, "I will discuss the matter with the archbishop. Not that I think we'll find out anything. He's a man of the cloth, not a man of the sword."

"You never know," said Dixter, standing up, preparing to take his leave. "Not so long ago, Archbishop Fideles was Brother Daniel, a nurse on *Phoenix*. He served on a ship of war, and while he may not have wielded a sword himself, he knew and understood those who did. He's not as unworldly as some people believe. Tell him that you yourself are in danger, Your Majesty. You . . . and the galaxy. I think he'll help."

"Aren't you exaggerating?" Dion asked, smiling.

"No, son," said Dixter solemnly, this time not bothering to correct himself. "I'm not."

The admiral bowed and left. Dion sat a long time at his desk, then touched a switch. "D'argent, I want to speak to the archbishop, the Abbey of St. Francis."

But D'argent was forced to report to His Majesty that the archbishop was gone from the abbey and no one had any idea where he was or how he could be reached.

Chapter ❖ Thirteen

Which way I fly is Hell; myself am Hell;
And, in the lowest deep, a lower deep
Still threatening to devour me opens wide,
To which the Hell I suffer seems a Heaven.
                              John Milton, *Paradise Lost*

Actually, Archbishop Fideles had not yet left the monastery when the king's summons came through. The archbishop was scheduled to leave and would have been on his private space transport, but his plans had been disrupted by an unexpected visitor.

Fideles had sent the brother who served as his aide off on an errand to pick up a breviary the archbishop had forgotten, and so the outer office was empty and Fideles was alone when the respectful knock came at the closed door.

The archbishop had his hand on the door's handle, having been just about to walk out. Thinking it was the aide misunderstanding instructions to meet the archbishop at his transport (the aide was an extremely devout brother, who tended to have his thoughts on heaven rather than on his more mundane and worldly duties, and was thus often and easily confused), Fideles flung open the door, a mild rebuke on his lips.

He was astounded to find not the wide-eyed and abashed Brother Petra ("Oh, dear. I was to meet Your Excellency at the *transport*, wasn't I?") but one of the lay brothers—those who had come to the abbey to dedicate their lives to the service of God but who, for various reasons, would never be permitted to take the vows or perform the duties of a priest.

The brother stood in respectful silence, his head bowed, his arms folded into the sleeves of the cassock that was frayed and threadbare—cast-off clothing from other brothers. It was not required of the lay brother that he dress in such humble garments; he chose to do so himself. Nor was it required of him that he keep his cowl pulled low over his face or shun the company and conversation of his brethren. That, too, he had taken

114

upon himself, just as he took upon himself the hardest, most grueling, difficult, and demeaning tasks in the abbey.

Fideles was too astonished by the sight of this brother, standing in his doorway, to speak. Despite the fact that he could not see his face, the archbishop knew the man immediately, knew him by his above-average height and the extraordinary girth of chest and shoulders—though somewhat thin from fasting— visible beneath the shabby robes.

He was called Paenitens—the Penitent One. That was his formal name among the brethren. Privately, he was known as the Unforgiven. He had another name, too, his true name. But that name was known to only two people, himself and the archbishop, and to God.

"Brother Penitent!" said Fideles, marveling. "I . . . I am extremely glad to see you!"

Extremely amazed to see you would have been nearer the truth, but Fideles trusted God would forgive him the lie. Never before had Penitent sought his archbishop. Generally, the lay brother went out of his way to avoid a meeting. Fideles could not recall the last time they had spoken, though he had often seen the silent, unsociable man working at his solitary labors about the abbey.

"I am pleased, very pleased, to see you, Brother," the archbishop repeated, somewhat flustered. "I have long wanted to speak with you, but now, I am afraid, is not a good time. As you see, I was just on my way off-planet. The matter is quite urgent or else I— I'm really afraid I cannot take time—"

"I am aware of this, Holiness," said the lay brother. Talking seemed to require an effort of him, as if speech were a power not often used, almost forgotten. "That is why I came. I must speak with you now, before you leave."

The archbishop was already late, but he found he could not refuse this dark and commanding presence any more than he could have refused Death, if he'd discovered that grim figure standing in his doorway.

"Certainly, Brother," Fideles said.

Dropping his small article of luggage on the floor, the archbishop stood aside, allowing the brother to enter the office. Fideles started to shut the door when a hand emerged from the rough robes, prevented him. Penitent glanced around behind him, into the empty outer chambers.

"We will be alone?" he asked.

"Yes, I believe so. I forgot my breviary and Brother Petra has gone to fetch it. He is *supposed* to meet me at the transport. . . ."

Brother Penitent nodded silently, stepped inside the room, and stood waiting in silence, unmoving, hands again clasped beneath the sleeves of his cassock. Fideles shut the door and returned to his desk.

"Please be seated, Brother," said the archbishop. Placing his hands on the desk, he was about to sit down himself.

"There is not time, Holiness," intoned the brother.

Fideles levered himself back to a standing position. He was suddenly worried and alarmed, certain some dire catastrophe had befallen. "What is it, Brother? What has happened?"

The lay brother did not respond to the question directly, did not appear to want the waste of words that would be required.

He said only, "You must take me with you, Holiness."

Abbot Fideles was completely and totally confounded. He was also troubled. "Brother," he said, his refusal reluctant, "were it any other occasion, I would, of course, be glad for your company, but I have agreed to undertake this mission in secret and I—"

"I know the secret, Holiness." Brother Penitent's tone was low, his shoulders bowed, as if he bore some heavy burden. "I know where you are going and why."

"That is not possible," said the archbishop.

Brother Penitent did not appear to hear him, continued speaking relentlessly. "You have been requested to come immediately to a sanitarium run by the Sisters of Magdelen on a planet in the Central Systems. The sister superior herself contacted you directly, convinced you that the matter was of the utmost urgency and should be kept confidential, even to the extent of prohibiting you from telling anyone where you are going or why."

"How do you know this?" Fideles demanded, amazed both at the knowledge and the calm with which Brother Penitent recited it. "The message was sent through private channels."

Again the words came slowly to Brother Penitent's lips. "Let us say . . . God revealed it to me."

"Did He?" asked Fideles, struck by the hesitating manner of a man who had never in his life hesitated to do or face or say anything.

Brother Penitent reached up his hand, slowly and deliberately removed the cowl, lifted his head, fixed his eyes upon the archbishop. The man's face was so deeply lined it appeared to be scarred. His black hair was streaked with gray and fell lank and long and unkempt on his shoulders. His mouth was thin-lipped, mirthless. But it was the eyes that arrested Fideles, caused his heart to wrench with pity. The man's eyes were empty, dark. The archbishop remembered those eyes when they had been vibrant, burning, alive.

Brother Penitent said simply, "Let us say that He did."

Uneasy, bewildered, the archbishop pondered what to do and, trying to find some clue, studied the brother standing before him. Fideles became aware of a tension within Penitent, a tautness that made the man's body quiver.

Fideles was suddenly afraid, but of what or of whom he couldn't say. And that made the fear more awful. Yet he was not the type to give way to fear or crumble beneath it. He had served as a nurse on a ship of war, served with courage and distinction, had been cited for bravery under fire. He had been forced, more than once, to make terrible decisions—decisions that meant life or death.

The archbishop, troubled and upset, prayed for guidance. Brother Penitent had done things during his life that were wrong. He had committed crimes of a most dark and fearful nature. But he had repented of these deeds and had since spent his life since in seeking God's forgiveness. And if Brother Penitent chose to be mysterious about this, then the archbishop must consider that God worked in mysterious ways.

Penitent had never before asked anything of his archbishop . . . or of anyone. The lay brother knew details of the mission that no one could have possibly known unless by divine intervention. There were some—Prior John among them—who would have said that such intervention came from a dark and unholy source. But as soon as this thought crossed Fideles's mind, he knew the decision he must make. His faith in God remained steadfast.

"Of course, then, Brother, you must come with me," Archbishop Fideles said resolutely. "Are you packed? Do you need to bring anything?"

Brother Penitent did not reply. Drawing his cowl up over his head, pulling it low over his face, he indicated silently he was ready to proceed, empty-handed as he was.

Fideles left the abbey, satisfied that he had done what the

Creator wanted. The two boarded the transport. At the last minute, Brother Petra arrived, apologetic, out of breath, and clutching the breviary, which he almost forgot to hand over, so astounded was he at the sight of the archbishop's strange companion.

"Tell Prior John that Brother Penitent goes with me" was all the archbishop had time to say, and he needn't have said that much, he reflected, for the news would be circulated through the small, cloistered community the moment Brother Petra had recovered breath enough to tell it.

Again Fideles reminded himself he was doing God's will.

The transport headed out into deep space. And it was here, among the stars, that the archbishop realized he was human after all, and that to be human was to continually battle against doubt.

He had his breviary, but in his distracted state of mind, he'd gone off and left his luggage sitting beside the office door.

Chapter ❖ Fourteen

Cleanliness is, indeed, next to godliness.
                              Charles Wesley, *Sermons*

Tusk—looking sharp and professional in the neatly pressed combat fatigues he wore when he was transporting clients—stood at the foot of the Scimitar's ladder, greeting his latest customers.

"Name's Tusk," he said, extending his hand.

"Don Perrin," said a man, blond, broad-shouldered, good-looking.

"Cynthia Zorn," said a woman, blond, long-legged, and good-looking.

They shook hands all around.

"Commander Link's already on board," said Tusk, "getting everything ready. We should lift off right on time. Can I give you a hand with your gear?"

The man and woman had arrived in a sleek new limo-jet. The driver had unpacked travel cases from the trunk, placed them on the ground.

"Thank you," said Don. "Oh, uh, here, Charles, let me handle that."

The driver had hold of something large and metallic, heavy and ungainly, and was attempting to wrestle it out of the backseat of the limo. He was making little progress and was obviously relieved to stand aside and let Don take over. Tusk grabbed hold of the two travel cases, which were light and small, hefted them easily, and waited to see what would eventually emerge from the limo.

"You two vacuum cleaner salesmen?" he asked when Don had the thing out and resting on the tarmac.

The woman laughed. "In a manner of speaking."

Don, flushed with his efforts, grinned. "I know she's not very pretty, but she's good at what she does."

"Uh-huh," said Tusk, eyeing a large metal canister that stood about one and a half meters tall and came complete with coiled hose, nozzle, and various appendages. "What does 'she' do?"

"Her name is Mrs. Mopup. Get it? *Mop up?* She's the Housewife's Dream. Or househusband's," Don added, casting an apologetic glance at his partner."

Cynthia smiled. "Haven't you seen our vid ads? Or heard our jingle? 'Let Mrs. Mopup mop up after your poppet?' It's quite catchy."

"No, sorry," said Tusk, trying to keep a straight face. They were customers, after all. "But then," he added, hurriedly, "we don't own a vid at home. The wife doesn't believe in them. Thinks the kid would spend too much time watching it instead of studying."

The vid set was, in fact, now siting in Mike's Friendly Pawnshop.

"I can't believe you haven't seen it." Cynthia seemed genuinely crushed.

Tusk made amends. "But I'll bet my wife would sure go for one of those things."

"I know she would!" Cynthia brightened. "We could make you a really good deal. Twenty-five percent off."

"Uh, sure," said Tusk. If nothing else, Nola would get a laugh out of the contraption.

"Thank you, Charles," Don said to the limo driver, who tipped his hat, shut the trunk, and drove off. Don Perrin and the woman started for the Scimitar.

"Come along, Mrs. Mopup," ordered Cynthia, and the 'bot trundled after them.

Tusk trailed behind, carrying the luggage and thinking what he would do to Link once he got his hands on him. Steady job! A coupla salesmen! Shit, we'll probably be lucky if they don't try to pay us in Mrs. Mopups! Still, he reflected, eyeing the two, who were walking along in front of him, there's something kinda fishy about all this. People pay us for a quiet trip and no interference from the locals. Unless they're going to a planet where vacuum cleaners are illegal, why spend the money on *us*? Why not just take a commercial liner? And I'll wager Cynthia didn't buy that smooth-fitting flight suit she's wearing off her commission selling Mrs. Mopups door-to-door. To say nothing of Charles and the limo.

The couple had reached the Scimitar and were frowning at the ladder that led to the hatch. Mrs. Mopup rolled to a halt beside them. Tusk, thinking he understood their concern, hurried to catch up.

"Don't worry. I can stow the 'bot in a storage compartment down below." He pointed them out.

"By herself?" asked Cynthia, her eyes widening.

"Well," said Tusk, grinning, "there're some spare parts and a busted anti-grav unit in there. Maybe she could strike up a conversation with them."

"Oh, dear, no," said Cynthia, shaking her head. "Mrs. Mopup wouldn't enjoy that at all. She has to come with us, Don," she added, turning to her companion.

"Of course she does," Don said heartily, though he looked a bit daunted at the prospect of hauling Mrs. Mopup up the ladder.

He started to lift the 'bot, but Tusk stopped him.

"Wait. I got a winch. We'll hoist her up." He looked at Cynthia dubiously. "If she wouldn't mind . . ."

"Heavens, no." Cynthia laughed. "She's only a robot."

"Yeah," muttered Tusk. "Well, I'll have to rig it up. It'll take a while. You two want to wait on board? The bar's well stocked. . . ."

"No, thank you," said Cynthia. "We'll stay with Mrs. Mopup. Won't we, Don?"

"Sure," said Don agreeably. "She might get lonely. But you can bring me a scotch on the rocks, Tusk, when you come down."

Tusk, dazed, nodded. "Sure thing. You want something to drink, ma'am?"

"No, thank you," said Cynthia, smiling.

It was on the tip of Tusk's tongue to ask if Mrs. Mopup would prefer a glass of premium or regular, but he passed up the temptation. He had the feeling the joke wouldn't be appreciated. "Wait here. I'll be back in a minute."

He ascended the ladder, carrying the luggage. "Hey, Link. Come give me a hand, will you?" Tusk hollered through the open hatch.

Link appeared below. Tusk tossed down the luggage, dropped down himself.

"Where the hell did you find these two? The nuthouse?" Tusk demanded in a low tone. He followed after Link, who was stowing the travel cases in a compartment beneath a couch. "I gotta rig up a block and tackle, haul a goddam vacuum cleaner up the side of the plane 'cause 'she' wouldn't like being shut up by 'herself' in the storage compartment!"

Link straightened, looked at Tusk. "You been on the juice?"

"No," said Tusk grimly, "but I got a feeling that I will be after spending the day with Cynthia and Mrs. Mopup."

"Mrs. Whos-it?"

"Mopup. Hey, XJ," Tusk bawled, going to open the bar, "have I got a girlfriend for you. Wait till you meet her. She's just your type. Comes with a hose and everything."

Only when Mrs. Mopup was safely hoisted into the Scimitar did Don and Cynthia agree to board themselves. Cynthia climbed nimbly up the ladder and lowered herself through the hatch as if she had been doing this sort of thing all her life. Don was a little more clumsy, but then he'd had four scotch on the rocks while waiting for the ascension of Mrs. Mopup.

Cynthia was charmed at the Scimitar's interior, was equally charmed to see Link again. Handsome and dashing as ever, the spacepilot was a born flirt and lady's man. Tusk, watching out of the corner of his eye as he fixed Don his fifth scotch on the rocks, suddenly had a pretty good idea why Cynthia had chosen to take her vacuum cleaner into space with them.

Tusk glanced at Don, hoping this wasn't going to create problems. But either Don and Cynthia were strictly business partners or else Don wasn't the jealous type, for he was lounging back on the couch, his drink in his hand, taking in everything with a wide smile.

Link showed the passengers how to strap themselves in and gallantly helped Cynthia with the buckles when she couldn't manage them herself. Tusk ascertained their destination, punched the coordinates into a sulking XJ.

"We have sunk low before," said the computer, "but never this low."

"Shut up," Tusk growled. "Tact and discretion, remember?"

"I am thankful," XJ added in sepulchral tones, "that none of my old comrades-in-arms can see me now. I, who was once under the command of Warlord Derek Sagan . . ."

"You, who were a goddam deserter," Tusk muttered.

". . . reduced to dispensing scotch—good scotch—to traveling salesmen."

"Say, XJ," said Link, swinging himself down the ladder into the cockpit and flopping into the co-pilot's seat. "I think Mrs. Mopup likes you. Treat me nice and I'll fix you two kids up."

"A comedian," snapped the computer. "I'm having to put up with two traveling salesman and a comedian. We better make a bundle off this!" Lights flashing ominously, XJ turned its concentration to liftoff.

Tusk took the opportunity, over the roar of the engines, to lean over the console, nudge Link on the elbow.

"Where'd you meet her?"

"The Seldom Inn," Link answered. "Hey, it's not what you think. She's a class dame. This Mrs. Mopup contraption was all her idea. She built the prototype, started the company. She's president now. They're a multimillion-dollar outfit. Did you ever hear the jingle she wrote? It's real cute. It goes—"

Tusk snorted. "Spare me. So why's she using us? Why not her own private spaceplane?"

"This is sort of a test run, you might say. She's thinking of expanding off-world, but she's not sure whether to risk it or not. She's got a meeting with a big corporation on Akara, who may be interested in distributing Mrs. Mopup to millions of lucky housewives galaxy-wide."

"Don't forget the househusbands," Tusk said, grinning.

"Yeah," said Link. He leaned closer, winked. "To tell you the truth, I wouldn't mind being her househusband. She could support me in the style to which I've become accustomed. Plus she'd help me recover from my broken heart. I'll never forgive you for stealing Nola away from me."

"Broken heart, my ass. Nola had too much sense to marry you. Not, I recall, that you ever asked her."

"Just doing you a favor, old pal. How could she have said no to *me*? Say, do you think I could teach Mrs. Mopup to shoot craps?"

Tusk described in detail just what Link could teach Mrs. Mopup. By this time, the Scimitar was in space. The planet of Vangelis was nothing more than a yellow-orange globe hanging suspended against the star-studded blackness. Tusk turned over the piloting to Link, went back up to the living quarters to see if his passengers had survived liftoff. It could be pretty upsetting to those who had never flown in a spaceplane before.

He found Don sucking ice and Cynthia calmly reading a mag. Mrs. Mopup, lashed to a beam so that she wouldn't roll around and bang into something, was blinking contentedly and appeared ready to tackle the first housecleaning chore that came her way.

"Uh, everyone doin' okay?" asked Tusk, somewhat taken aback at the nonplussed attitude of his passengers. "The liftoff can be kind of rugged—"

"Quite smooth, really," said Cynthia, laying down the mag. "Is it all right if I get out of this thing now?" She undid the straps with a deft hand. "And I'll just release Mrs. Mopup. You don't mind if she walks about some, do you? It keeps her battery charged."

"Sure," said Tusk, blinking. "I mean, no. Hell, I don't mind—"

"All right if I fix myself another?" asked Don, already out of his safety harness and heading for the bar. "No offense, friend, but you go a little light on the scotch."

"Help yourself," said Tusk, ignoring an irate mechanical squawk from the vicinity of the computer.

Cynthia, on her knees, released Mrs. Mopup's bindings, freed the robot. She said something to it that Tusk couldn't hear, wasn't interested in anyway. Mrs. Mopup took a spin around the living area.

"Probably looking for dust bunnies," Tusk muttered to himself.

Cynthia rose to her feet. She and Don stood watching the robot with the fond expression of new parents seeing baby take his first steps.

"The trip'll last about six hours," said Tusk. "Relax, make yourselves comfortable. I'll be up front if you need—"

Turning, he almost fell over Mrs. Mopup, who had rolled up behind him. One of her nozzles was pointed directly at him.

Tusk deftly recovered his balance, stopped, stared, then laughed. "Hey, did you two know that this attachment looks exactly like a lasgun?"

"That's because it *is* a lasgun," said Don conversationally. He leaned on the bar, swirling the ice in his glass.

Mrs. Mopup sighted the lasgun directly on Tusk's forehead.

"She's a remarkable shot," said Cynthia, regarding the robot with maternal pride. "Never misses, in fact."

Tusk attempted another laugh, coughed when it got stuck in his throat. "The ideal baby-sitter. All right, I gotta admit that this was good for a few grins, but now—"

He attempted to sidestep Mrs. Mopup. The robot whirred, lights blinked. The lasgun followed him, never lowering its aim, locked onto his forehead.

Tusk looked from the robot to Don.

"No laughing matter, I'm afraid," said Don, taking a healthy swallow of his scotch.

Tusk switched to Cynthia.

"Indeed not," she said coolly. "You see, I've locked Mrs. Mopup on to you. If you do anything Mrs. Mopup doesn't like, she'll shoot you without hesitation. Call your co-pilot up here."

"Link, turn the plane over to XJ and come on up here a moment, will you?" Tusk called, lifting his hands slowly in the air.

He was examining the 'bot closely, trying to decide if he was being played for the galaxy's biggest idiot or if he really was being held hostage by an armed vacuum cleaner. The more he studied it, the deadlier that lasgun looked.

"Yeah, what do you want?" Link climbed up, saw Tusk and the robot, and began to chuckle. Only Tusk noticed that the pilot had slipped his hand into the pocket of his fatigues. "What are you doing with the 'bot, Tusk? Playing cowboys and aliens—"

"Shut up, you ninny!" Tusk hissed. "This gun's real. Look at it! It's locked on to me! And it's gonna shoot me if I do something it doesn't like." He glanced over at Don. "Just what's included on the list of things Mrs. Mopup doesn't like? Leaving wet towels on the deck?"

Don said, smiling, "She takes offense at little things—like going for your lasgun. Or disturbing us while we're flying your plane. Or maybe trying to jump us in our sleep."

"Fly . . . sleep . . ." Link apparently couldn't get his brain working long enough to form a complete sentence. "What—"

"—the devil's going on up there?" XJ demanded. "Are these guys from the collection agency? I suppose you forgot to pay the light bill again, Tusk—"

The spaceplane suddenly went dark. Tusk dove for the deck, rolled. A flash of light blinded him; pain seared up his shoulder. Another flash of light, a yelp from Link and a metallic clatter of a boltgun hitting the deck told Tusk that their scheme hadn't worked. The 'bot had fired in two different directions damn near simultaneously.

"Did I fail to mention that Mrs. Mopup's locked on to both of you? And she can fire her weapons from anywhere in a three-hundred-and-sixty-degree radius." That was Cynthia.

"And she can detect you quite well in the dark. Movement,

body temperature, brain waves, heartbeat, that sort of thing." That was Don, crunching ice.

"Yeah, but she almost missed," said Tusk, sitting up. He was shaking and sweating and his arm hurt like hell.

"No, no." Cynthia was soothing. "I set her on incapacitate. I can switch to kill, but I'd prefer not to."

"Can we have some light?" Don asked. "I can't see to pour."

"Turn the lights on, XJ," Tusk ordered sullenly.

"I will not," snapped the computer. "And if you salesmen are thinking about hijacking this plane, you've got another think coming. I won't cooperate. After all, what can you do—kill me?"

"No, but they could kill us, XJ," called out Link.

"Oh, now, that *would* be a loss." The computer sneered.

"Actually, we wouldn't need to shoot anyone," said Cynthia. "Mrs. Mopup is quite adept at invading other computer systems, erasing their memories, and seizing control. All we'd have to do is plug her in . . ."

The lights came on.

Tusk leaned back against a bulkhead. Gritting his teeth against the burning pain, he examined his charred and bleeding shoulder. The wound wasn't serious; the laser beam had seared through flesh and muscle, missed the bone. He glanced across the deck at Link, who was still standing, but wringing an injured hand. The small boltgun he always carried concealed in his pocket lay on the deck beside him.

"Look, I don't get this," said Tusk, rising slowly to his feet, careful to keep his hands in plain sight. Mrs. Mopup had him covered all the way. "What's going on? Why hijack us? Link and I aren't the curious type. We'd have taken you wherever you wanted to go, no questions asked."

"Probably not," said Don, fiddling with the liquor dispenser. "Hell's Outpost? The Exile Café?"

Tusk stared; his jaw went slack.

"Just think of us as your friendly neighborhood recruiting officers," added Cynthia, heading for the Scimitar's cockpit. "Coming, Commander Perrin?"

"Sure thing, Captain Zorn." Don paused to hand Tusk his empty glass. "I think you're out of scotch."

Chapter ❧❀❧ Fifteen

Draw near with faith, and take this holy Sacrament to your comfort; and make your humble confession to Almighty God . . .

Book of Common Prayer, "The Invitation"

Sister Superior was a brisk, business-suited woman, who greeted the archbishop at the front entrance to the hospital with a firm handshake, as if she were greeting any brother of the Order, not its titular head.

In keeping with the sister's mysterious and urgent request that he make his visit anonymously, Fideles was cloaked and wore plain and simple robes. He had removed all vestments and other symbols that might indicate his high ranking in the Church and kept his hood up over his head so that he would not be recognized. Fortunately, brothers of the Order of Adamant were frequent visitors to the hospital; the staff was too busy to pay them much attention.

Sister Superior could not quite hide her surprise and displeasure at the sight of the roughly garbed, silent brother accompanying the archbishop.

"Perhaps, Father, your companion can rest in the coffee shop while we conduct our business," she suggested, pointedly.

"Thank you, Reverend Mother, but I require Brother Penitent to be witness to this meeting," said the archbishop.

Sister Superior frowned, but made no further argument in the presence of the staff and patients. She gave them a hurried and perfunctory tour of the sanitarium on the way to her office, which was located on an upper floor. It was sunny and airy, like the rest of the large and imposing building.

"Quite impressive," said the archbishop upon entering. "You appear to have an excellent facility here, Reverend Mother."

"Thank you, Holiness. Please be seated." Sister Superior indicated several comfortable chairs, arranged in an informal grouping near one of the windows. "Will you have something to drink? Tea, coffee, a glass of water? Although I would forgo the water, if I were you. It tastes of iodine."

Her voice had a nervous edge. She was obviously upset and preoccupied, as evidenced by the fact that, although she offered them coffee, she had evidently neglected to make any. The machine was turned off, the pot cold and empty.

Noting the archbishop's gaze and slight smile, Sister Superior shook her head. "I'm sorry. I drink tea myself. I meant to brew a pot this morning. . . . It will only take a moment—"

"Thank you, I don't care for anything right now, Reverend Mother," Fideles said.

Sister Superior looked to Brother Penitent, who merely shook his head.

"Then, if you will excuse me a moment . . ." She walked to the office door. "Sister Irene, you may take your luncheon break now. Shut the outer door, will you? We're not to be disturbed."

Closing her own door, she took the trouble to lock it securely, then returned to sit in a chair opposite that of the archbishop. Her hands twisted together; her face was tense, strained.

Fideles cast a glance at Penitent, hoping to gauge what he thought of this extraordinary behavior. The brother's face was, however, averted from the light, further concealed by the shadow of the deep cowl. He kept his eyes lowered, his hands folded in his sleeves, and seemed oblivious to what was going on around him.

Sister Superior looked at him again, frowned again. Sitting forward on the edge of her chair, she turned to address the archbishop. "Forgive me for appearing to question your decision, Holiness, but, as I indicated in my message to you, this matter is of an extremely delicate and highly sensitive nature. I cannot emphasize this enough."

Her fist clenched as she spoke. Her face, in the light, was drawn and haggard. She blinked a little too often, probably from a lack of sleep.

Fideles grew more and more uneasy.

Sister Superior was not, according to reports, a woman who would be easily agitated. Upon receiving such an extraordinary summons from her, the archbishop had examined her record. She had been a hospital administrator before joining the Church, following His Majesty's reestablishment of the Order.

Having received her ordination into the priesthood, she had been assigned to take over the sanitarium, which was suffering from lack of funds and mismanagement.

In the two years since she'd joined the staff, she had turned things around completely. She was reputed to be tough, efficient, pragmatic. And here she sat, on the edge of her chair, obviously shaken to the very core of her being.

Fideles was forced to clear his throat before he could reply. "I appreciate your concern, Reverend Mother, but I have a special reason for wanting Brother Penitent present. I cannot explain, but I answer for his discretion."

"But you have no idea what this involves, Holiness—"

Fideles raised his hand. The gesture was a mild one, but it was enough to remind the sister that she was arguing with her superior.

"Very well," she said abruptly and ungraciously. "Before I tell you why I summoned you, Holiness, I must relate something of the background of the hospital. It may seem irrelevant, but it has a bearing on what you will shortly hear.

"The sanitarium is an old structure, dating back about seventy years. The building and grounds are fine enough now, but back then, I'm told, they were considered magnificent. The hospital was originally built to serve exclusively the needs of the Blood Royal, who—by reason of their special genetic makeup—could not very well go to ordinary medical facilities. The night of the Revolution, almost a hundred members of the Blood Royal were staying here. That night, the sanitarium was surrounded by the Revolutionary Guard. Those members of the staff who were not Blood Royal were told to go home. When they returned to work the next day, the patients and the rest of the staff were gone. They had been 'relocated.'

"After the Revolution," continued the sister, "the sanitarium was taken over by the government and run with the usual bureaucratic inefficiency, from which we're slowly trying to recover."

"You appear to be doing an excellent job," said Fideles politely.

Sister Superior responded with a curt nod, obviously too intent on her story to even appreciate the compliment.

"Last week, a patient came to us. A woman in her late sixties. She is dying. She knows she is dying. She is a doctor and has correctly and accurately diagnosed her own condition. There is no cure. She knows that, too. She has only a few weeks of life remaining and came to us in order to spend them in what peace painkillers can offer.

"A common enough story, you might think. But there are circumstances that make it odd. The woman has traveled a great distance to reach us. She had been living on a world light-years from this one. There are excellent medical facilities on her own world. In fact, the doctors there are far more familiar with the treatment of this malady—which is indigenous to their region—than we are. She came here for a reason, however. She had, you see, once worked at this hospital, prior to the Revolution."

"Is the doctor Blood Royal?" Fideles asked.

"No," answered Sister Superior, startled by the question. "Of course not. All the Blood Royal are dead, with the exception of His Majesty, God save him."

"God save him," echoed Fideles.

Sister Superior appeared to be slightly rattled by the unexpected question, which had scattered her thoughts. She was silent a moment, forced to collect them.

"We wondered, naturally, why the woman had gone to such lengths to return here, having undertaken what for her, in her condition, must have been a painful and uncomfortable trip. She replied that she always remembered her days here fondly, and that she wanted to be buried here. But she was disturbed by something, disturbed to the point that it was rendering our treatment of her ineffectual. She refused to talk to the staff psychiatrist, but when she found out I was a priest, she asked to make her confession to me. I agreed. I heard her confession and"—Sister Superior sighed, her hands twisted together again—"it was after I heard it that I sent for you."

"But, Reverend Mother," said Fideles somewhat sternly, "if this secret was imparted to you during confession, you may not repeat it, even to myself."

"I am aware of that, Holiness," Sister Superior said quietly. "And that is why I have prevailed upon the doctor to tell you her story herself. Her illness and suffering have left her confused; she is not certain whether what she knows is important or not. I have convinced her that, in my opinion, it is of the utmost importance. She has, therefore, agreed to talk to *you*. I will take *you* to her room."

Again the emphasis upon *you*, again another sharp look at

the lay brother. Fideles also looked at Penitent, silently inquiring whether or not he would accompany them.

Aware of the scrutiny, Penitent lifted his head. His face shocked Fideles. The skin was pale, the lips compressed into a straight, grim line. He nodded once and stood up.

The archbishop rose, indicated their readiness to proceed.

"This way, then," said Sister Superior. Pausing at the door, she whispered, more to herself than to them, "I pray God I am doing the right thing."

--◄■►◘◄■►--

Memories of his days serving as nurse aboard the Warlord's battleship *Phoenix* returned to Fideles forcibly when they entered the sickroom, brought back by the clean, sharp smell of antiseptic and alcohol, of crisp, sterile sheets. The patient was in a private room, located in a nearly empty corridor. She was sitting up in a wheelchair that had been rolled over to provide her a view out the window. On the spacious lawns below, a group of convalescent children were enjoying the warm day. Sunlight streamed in. A nurse sat nearby, reading a book.

The patient was calm, at ease. When they entered, she looked around at them and smiled. The archbishop moved forward, offered her a few words of blessing and of comfort, which she received with a gentle nod and murmured thanks.

Sister Superior dismissed the nurse, shut the door. All was quiet in the room, save for the distant laughter of the children outside.

"Would you be more comfortable in bed, Doctor?" asked Sister Superior.

"No, thank you, Reverend Mother. I prefer to stay here until the sun goes down."

The three drew up chairs to sit near her. The doctor did not evince surprise at the presence of the silent lay brother, nor did she appear daunted at the prospect of telling her story to no less a personage than His Holiness the archbishop. She had made her peace with God and had that ethereal, distant look of one who has left the shores of this life, is slipping away slowly to another.

"They take beautiful care of me here," she said, smiling at the sister, who was fussing with the pillows, refilling a water glass. "I am content. I'm glad I came back. Glad to see the place filled with life, doing good work once more. I remembered it ... the night after. Empty. Silent. So very silent."

None of them said a word. Sister Superior ceased her ministrations, took a chair. The dying woman looked around at them.

"I was afraid, when I first came here. But I am not afraid any longer."

"It is quite natural for us to fear death—" began Fideles.

The doctor shook her head. "No, it wasn't death I feared. I've known I am dying a long time, long enough to come to terms with my illness. It was him. I was afraid of him. But he can't reach me now. The gulf that separates us is too wide."

Brother Penitent, not saying a word, reached out his hand, took hold of the woman's right hand in his own, and turned it palm up to the light. Sister Superior was taken aback, looked shocked at this strange proceeding. But the doctor made no complaint, did not try to remove her hand.

"No, Brother," she said. "I am not Blood Royal. But my mother was."

Penitent released her hand, sat back in his chair.

Fideles, understanding, not understanding, felt chilled.

"I was a doctor here, in the years just prior to the Revolution. I specialized in mental disorders among the Blood Royal. Yes, there were mental disorders, though the Blood Royal themselves always refused to admit it. Probably just as well, since they were rulers of most of the inhabited worlds in the galaxy. They dared not show any weakness. Because of the need for secrecy, therefore, we went to great lengths to protect our patients' identities, to avoid scandal on their home planets.

"One day, a patient came to us who demanded even greater security than that we already practiced. She was brought into the sanitarium in the dead of night. Masked and heavily cloaked, she was taken immediately to a private suite of rooms which had been fitted up especially for her. Only four people knew her name: the hospital administrator, myself, and two trained nurses who traveled with her. She rarely left her room. No one else in the hospital ever even saw her.

"The woman was in her twenties when she came to us. She was Blood Royal, extraordinarily beautiful, and quite insane. A chemical imbalance in her brain drove her into violent, frenzied rages. She had, in fact, committed murder. The crime was hushed up. Few knew of it. But the family realized then that they could no longer care for her. And so she was brought here.

Her illness could be treated, but only by the constant adminis-
tration of corrective drugs. And due to the wild fluctuations of
the chemicals in her body, she had to be carefully monitored,
the drugs continually altered and modified to produce the de-
sired effect.

"When she was stable, the woman was brilliant, charming,
captivating. When the drugs ceased to have any effect, she de-
generated into a murderous beast. There was no hope of a
cure. Her family had no choice but to have her locked away.

"The woman was permitted visitors, however. She had only
one—her brother. He was some twenty years older, but completely devoted to her. Their parents had been in their middle
years when she was born. Both parents had died in her youth.
She and her brother had been everything to each other. He visited her once each month, without fail, though he was a busy
man. These visits—which had to be cloaked in secrecy—must
have wreaked havoc on his personal life. But he loved her and
she adored him. She lived each month for the day he spent
with her.

"We thought their relationship touching, beautiful. None of
us knew, until too late, that it was black, corrupt at heart."

The doctor paused, took a sip of water. Outside, the sun was
sinking behind a stand of fir trees. Long shadows stretched
over the green lawn. The children were taken indoors.

"It was our policy, if the patient was stable, to permit her to
go on outings with her brother. These were always short in du-
ration, only a few hours at the most, and the time was spent on
her brother's private yacht. At first, I must admit, we were reluctant to permit these outings, but no harm ever came of
them. In fact, the patient seemed to derive some good from
them.

"One month, about five years before the Revolution, the
brother came as usual, took his sister away, spent the day with
her as usual. She returned in remarkably happy spirits. I
thought nothing of it until, during routine tests, I noticed a
marked change in the woman's blood chemistry. She was pregnant."

Fideles started, appalled. Wherever he thought the tale
might have been heading, he had not expected this. "Surely
not . . ." He fell silent, unable to voice aloud the dreadful suspicion.

"I am afraid so, Holiness," said the doctor quietly. "The

woman admitted to us quite freely that her brother was the baby's father. Their incestuous relationship had been going on for years, ever since she had seduced him when she was eighteen. She had always before taken precautions to avoid getting pregnant. It had occurred to her, however, that her brother had not married for love of her. He needed an heir, and she had decided that she would give him one, assuming—in her unbalanced mental state—he could easily contrive to legitimatize the birth.

"We were horrified. And to his credit, so was the woman's brother. Of course, we sent for him, told him what had happened. Ashamed, wretched, he nearly collapsed—he himself was fifty at the time and suffered from a heart condition. He was obsessed with his sister, you see; an obsession strengthened by the fact that she was locked away from him.

"We recommended abortion—for the mother's sake, since we could no longer give her the chemicals she needed to ease her condition without risking harm to the unborn child. The brother refused to give his consent. He believed that this pregnancy was a punishment, a judgment from God on his sins. The brother promised to care for the infant when it was born. Then he left. He did not visit his sister, though she was wild to see him. He never came to her again."

The doctor stared out the window; her face grew grave.

"That was a terrible time. The worst I would ever know, until the Revolution. All during her pregnancy, the woman had to be kept under constant surveillance, often physically restrained, to prevent her from harming herself or others. At first her thoughts were centered on her brother. Then, fortunately—or so we thought at the time—she focused her attention on her unborn child. The mention of her baby would often calm her when nothing else would.

"The birth was difficult for her. But the child—a boy—was healthy and strong. We informed the brother immediately, as we had promised, and the day following the baby's birth a man—one of the brother's most loyal and trusted friends—arrived to take the baby away.

"Perhaps his removal of the baby was all for the best." The doctor sighed. "I knew the child could not be left in the mother's care, of course, but her mental condition had seemed to improve during the later stages of her pregnancy, and I was hoping that maybe a few months spent with her baby might effect a permanent change for the better. I still think it might have. I was never to know.

"I resumed the woman's chemical treatment immediately, but the difficulty of the delivery, the trauma of losing her baby and her dearly loved brother, were too much. Though we did everything possible, she wasted away before our eyes and eventually died."

The doctor looked around at them all. None had moved or spoken, beyond Fideles's brief exclamation of shock.

"As you might guess," the doctor said softly, "I held myself responsible. The tragedy haunted me. I submitted my resignation, but the administrators persuaded me to stay on. Then came the Revolution. I was not on duty that night, when the soldiers entered the hospital. They rounded up all the patients and staff members, loaded them aboard shuttles, and took them God knows where. To their deaths, we were told later. Certainly I never saw or heard of any of them again.

"I was warned that they were searching for me, since my mother was Blood Royal. I was so despondent, I considered turning myself in. A very dear friend convinced me that I had no right to throw away my life, which could be of service to others. The only way to save myself was to put the past completely out of my mind. I did so. He and I fled off-planet. We were married; I changed my name, acquired a new identity. I refused to let myself think about the past, until I was forced to do so, when the young king came to power."

The doctor's gaze shifted to Penitent, as if she thought he might be the only one to understand.

"A few months ago, when I learned I was dying, I began to have dreams about the wretched woman and her child. I saw the boy in my dreams—not as he was, a babe in arms—but as a man. He came to me, night after night. He said nothing, but he cast a shadow over my soul, blotted out the light. He stood before me, his hand uplifted, and I knew that he was blocking my way to the next life. I could not die in peace until I made my peace with him. The only way I can help him is to tell my story. I am the only one left alive who knows it, you see."

"But surely the hospital's records—" Fideles began.

"We falsified them," said the doctor. "The brother commanded it, and he had the power and the authority to see to it that his command was carried out. And it was not a great crime." The doctor smiled wanly. "We merely wrote 'unknown' in the space under *Name of Natural Father*. We did it for our patient's sake, not for his. If someone had found out the truth, she might have been in terrible danger. As it turned out, it didn't matter. All records were destroyed. All those who knew the truth disappeared the night of the Revolution."

The doctor exhaled softly, turned to the archbishop. "Holiness, I want . . . I must . . . tell *you* the truth. I want to tell you the name. I have not told anyone else except the sister, during my confession. She convinced me that I should reveal this to you."

She glanced at Sister Superior, who indicated her agreement.

Fideles had formed an idea, but he couldn't believe it, hoped against hope that he was wrong. It was too ghastly, too dreadful.

"Of course I will hear it, if this will give you ease. . . ."

"I must tell you first, Holiness, that I have kept silent all these years because to do otherwise would have been to betray the oath I took when I became a doctor to keep my patients' secrets in confidence. I kept the secret while both of them still lived. But they are dead now, and no harm can come to them if I continue to keep their secret . . . and great harm might come to the living."

"I understand, Doctor," said Fideles, an aching of dread in his breast.

He looked at Penitent, wondered what he was thinking, but the robed figure sat unmoving, hands folded in his sleeves, head covered and face concealed in the shadows.

"The woman's name was Jezreel. Her brother's name was Amodius," said the doctor calmly, quietly. "Amodius Starfire. Late king, former ruler of the galaxy."

They all sat still and quiet, souls subdued, troubled by the sad and sordid tale of incestuous love, tragic death, denial, and concealment. They continued to remain motionless, each involved with inner thoughts or—in the archbishop's case—a prayer to God to forgive the sins of those He held now in His care, until the doctor began to cough and exhibit signs of extreme fatigue. The reverend mother was on her feet immediately, administering medicine, assisting her patient back into her bed.

"We will take our leave," said the archbishop, about to stand up.

A burning touch on his wrist caused him to flinch. He looked down, astonished, to see Brother Penitent's fingertips on his forearm.

The lay brother's face was hidden in the shadows. His voice, when he spoke, was low and halting. "A question."

"I am sorry, Brother," began Sister Superior, "but you see that the doctor is quite unable—"

The doctor put aside the sister's ministering hands. "I can answer," she said. "What is it, Brother?"

"The name of the man who took the child. You know that as well, don't you? You would not have given up the baby to a stranger."

"You are right," said the doctor readily, though she seemed perplexed by the question. "We knew the man by name and by sight. And we ran various tests, to double-check his identity— eye scan, DNA analysis. He was who he said he was. Not that we had much doubt. He was quite well-known. His name was Pantha. The famous planetary explorer. Garth Pantha."

Brother Penitent said nothing more. The doctor lay back on her pillows, weary but at peace.

Fideles rose, came to stand beside her, rested his hand on her wasted one. "You have done what was right. 'O send out thy light and thy truth, that they may lead me. . . .' *Dominicus tecum.* God be with you, daughter."

"He is, Holiness. And," the doctor added, looking up at him intently, "you have my permission to tell the king, if you think it wise."

"Rest now," said Sister Superior gently.

Fideles followed the reverend mother out of the room. Brother Penitent came silently behind, his hands once again folded in the sleeves of his robes. Outside, in the corridor, Sister Superior sent the nurse back to sit with the patient.

The hallway was empty; the three were alone.

The Reverend Mother looked from the archbishop to the lay brother. She clasped her hands tightly. "What do you think, Holiness?"

Fideles sighed, shook his head. "I believe her. Watching her, listening to her—it is difficult not to. Still, parts of it seem hardly creditable. The man in the dream—"

"Hallucination," said Sister Superior. "Such things are not uncommon, considering the nature of this disease. Add to that a guilty conscience, a terrible secret that has obviously been preying on her mind."

Brother Penitent stirred. Fideles looked at him hopefully, thinking he might have something to say that would clarify this strange tale. But Penitent remained silent.

"Is there any way to verify her story?" Fideles asked, glancing again at Brother Penitent.

He made no response.

Sister Superior shook her head. "I don't see how. As she said, the records were destroyed, and they had been falsified to begin with. I know this is presumptuous of me to ask, Holiness, but will you tell the king?"

"I do not know, Reverend Mother," said Fideles. "I cannot see that spreading such a tale would serve any useful purpose. I must ask for God's guidance in this matter."

Sister Superior nodded once, abruptly. "I will add my prayers to yours, Holiness. I will show you out now. This way, please."

The reverend mother took leave of them at the front entrance.

"God be with us," she said.

"May He indeed," responded Brother Penitent grimly and unexpectedly.

Chapter ❖❖❖ Sixteen

> Words, sir, never influence the course of the cards, or the course of the dice.... I play my game to the end in spite of words ...
>
> Charles Dickens, *Little Dorrit*

The flight to Hell's Outpost was uneventful, not because Tusk wanted it to be, but because he didn't have any choice in the matter. He spent most of the trip lounging around on either the couches or the beds that the couches converted into, admiring Cynthia's skills as a pilot and Don's ability to drink scotch, all the while trying to forget that a vacuum cleaner would just as soon shoot him as sweep the rugs.

Tusk had endeavored to figure out how Mrs. Mopup worked, hoping in this way to be able to come up with a plan to thwart the lethal little 'bot. But he was forced to give up. If he'd had access to XJ-27, he might have accomplished the task, but he wasn't permitted anywhere near the cockpit: It upset Mrs. Mopup.

Near as Tusk could figure out, the 'bot apparently locked on to him and Link in a manner similar to that of a heat-seeking missile. But how could it tell the difference between the two of them and good old Don and Cynthia? Was it really distinguishing between certain body temperatures, heartbeats, brain waves ... a combination of all three ... none of the above? Tusk hadn't a clue.

He couldn't discuss it with Link; the two of them were only permitted to talk together for a few moments each day. They were forced to sleep in shifts—one awake while the other slept, presumably so as not to task Mrs. Mopup's patience. Although, Tusk noted sourly, the 'bot had given every appearance of being fully capable of dealing with both of them.

"Oh, yes, quite capable," said Don, downing scotch. "But it puts a strain on her."

Don and Cynthia continued to be friendly, outgoing, willing to talk about anything except the only subjects in which Tusk was interested: Who are you really? Why are you doing this? And what exactly is it that you're doing?

The two knew a lot about Tusk—that much became obvious almost immediately after they'd left Vangelis.

Keeping a wary eye on the ever-observant Mrs. Mopup, Tusk was lounging near the cockpit as close as he could get—which was standing on the deck above it, staring down at it wistfully.

Cynthia had just ordered a subdued and chastened XJ to find a Lane that would take them to Hell's Outpost.

Tusk, overhearing, spoke up. "Say, my wife's gonna be worried as hell when I'm not back tonight like I was supposed to be. Why don't you let me call her, tell her I'm going to be late? You two can listen in on the conversation. She's six months pregnant and—"

"Yes, we know," said Cynthia, watching numbers flash past her; XJ meekly provided the required information. "A real shame, too. Oh, not that she's pregnant. Congratulations and all that. But the timing was bad. You see, we have a high regard for your wife. She was on our list of recruits, but the pregnancy forced us to cross her off."

"There'll still be a spot open for her, if she wants to go back to work after the kids come," said Don, relaxing in the co-pilot's chair.

"Uh, thanks, but I think she saw enough 'work' during the counter-revolution to last her the rest of her life. Same with me, if you take my meaning," Tusk added, but either they didn't or they were deliberately ignoring him or it didn't make any difference to them one way or the other.

Cynthia told XJ to prepare for the Jump. Don leaned back in his chair, put his feet up on the console—thereby breaking one of the computer's most inviolable laws, second only to leaving wet towels on deck.

Tusk glanced at XJ, saw its light flare. The computer made a sort of electronic, strangled, choking sound, but at that moment Mrs. Mopup emitted a short, sharp buzz. XJ's lights flickered in a moment of wild indecision, then blinked dismally and went out.

"That call?" Tusk urged. "Before we hit hyperspace? My wife's gonna be real worried. . . ."

"No, she won't," said Cynthia. "We already prepared a message to send to Nola, recorded in your voice, saying that you've had trouble with the Scimitar and that you'll be stranded on Akara until you can raise the money for spare parts."

"Recorded? My voice?" Tusk gaped. "When'd you do that?"

"The same time we got all the rest of the information on you that we fed into Mrs. Mopup," said Don. "Fix me another, will you?" He held out his empty glass to Tusk. "I'll take bourbon, since you ran out of scotch."

Gloomily, Tusk took the glass and stomped sullenly over to the liquor dispenser, his fleeting hope of getting a message to Admiral Dixter gone. The moment she heard his voice—his real voice—Nola would have known immediately something was wrong and Tusk, with a few well-chosen words, could have given his wife a pretty good idea what. She would have put in a call to Dixter and, while Tusk couldn't think of a whole hell of a lot the Lord of the Admiralty could do to help, still, he'd have known where Tusk was and maybe what was going on— even if Tusk didn't.

But now . . . Yeah, they'd done their homework. Tusk was always having to lay over on some planet or another to make repairs. Nola wouldn't think to question it. She probably wouldn't even call; interplanetary communication cost money and she wasn't the insecure type of wife who needed to hear her husband's voice every night before she went to sleep. Nor was she the least bit jealous.

All of which made for a fine marriage, Tusk thought, but is damn inconvenient when you've been hijacked.

He resolved then and there to work out a series of coded communications with Nola when—and if—he made it back. This wouldn't do him a lot of good now, but devising them kept him busy during the Jump, after which he could do nothing but lie on his uncomfortable bed and fume and try to think of some way of tricking Don into dropping a wet towel on the deck.

"You ever been to Hell's Outpost?" Tusk asked Link during one of the few times during the day they were permitted to talk together. (Cynthia referred to it as the "happy hour.")

"Nope," said Link. "Got more sense."

Tusk could have debated that one. Considering the fact that, from what he'd heard, there were no gambling casinos on Hell's Outpost, he decided Link was probably telling the truth.

"You?" Link asked.

Tusk shook his head. "Never any reason to." He cast a meaningful glance at Don. "I've never been *that* desperate. And I don't intend to start."

"You guys got the wrong idea," said Don. He always joined them during happy hour, along with Mrs. Mopup, who planted herself in between the three of them and held their drinks on a tray. "Sure, I know Hell's Outpost has a bad rep, but in reality it's a convenient, quiet, and safe place to do business. There are only two prerequisites: If you go expecting to be hired, you've got to be the best, and if you go expecting to hire the best, you've got to have cash."

"Hire to do what, though?" Tusk grunted.

"Whatever needs to be done," Don said, shrugging. "Nothing all that bad. Cynthia and I—we don't look like shady characters, do we?"

Cynthia, relaxing in the pilot's seat, reading a fashion mag, looked up at Tusk and smiled in a warm and friendly manner.

"Naw." Tusk waved a hand. "Just damn near murdered us. Not to mention kidnapping, hijacking, and God knows what else you have in mind."

"More bourbon?"

Tusk handed over his glass. Don filled it, helped himself. Sitting back down, he rested his glass on top of Mrs. Mopup, grinned.

"I swear. You got us all wrong. What've you lost? A week's time. You've had a nice little paid vacation. You're rested, relaxed—"

"Wait a minute. What was that again? *Paid?*" Link perked up.

"Well, sure. We intend to make this worth your while."

"*If* we play the game. . . ."

"Tusk, my friend"—Don leaned forward, earnest, sincere, honest as any vacuum cleaner salesman—"you don't even have to roll the dice. We just want you to listen to us. We want the chance to make you an offer."

Make you an offer.

Words Tusk was to hear again, almost exactly twenty-four hours later, on Hell's Outpost, in the Exile Café.

◄━❐◯❑━►

Tusk wasn't certain what he'd expected Hell's Outpost to be like, but on arrival he was disappointed. He'd been imagining (no matter what good old Don said to the contrary) a sin city similar to Laskar, where anything or anyone could be had for a price and every morning when you woke up you checked to make certain someone hadn't stuck a knife in your ribs the night before.

Hell's Outpost, located on the fringes of the galaxy, was as Don had said, a quiet, safe, and convenient place to conduct business. People went there on business—serious business. They didn't have the time for nonsense.

The main structure located on the cold, gray, and atmosphereless moon was a building known as the Exile Café. Shaped like half a giant egg upended on the moon's surface, the café was a collection of rooms—also shaped like half-eggs—built around a central large bar area. The rooms were private—extremely private. People paid a lot of money to conduct business in these rooms in private.

In the bar area sat other people, who were there for various private reasons of their own. Some of them were looking for work. Others had work and were looking for the means to complete it. Still others were just resting. People in the rooms could view the people in the bar by means of vidscreens. Different colored lights on the tables indicated whether or not the person being viewed was available for hire or merely passing time between jobs.

Weapons were permitted inside the Exile Café—a person had the right to advertise his/her skills. But the weapons were not to be used. That was the law and it was broken on penalty of immediate death. As far as anyone knew, the law had never been broken.

Aware of this, Tusk toyed with the idea of giving Don and Cynthia the slip once they got into the café. How could they stop him? But he was forced to abandon the idea. First the law was good only *inside* the café and it was a long and lonely walk there and back.

"A lot could happen to a guy," said Cynthia.

Second, Don and Mrs. Mopup were staying on board Tusk's Scimitar.

"We'll keep an eye on it for you. I'd hate like hell for you to come back and find out something'd happened to your spaceplane," said Don, settling into the pilot's seat, his feet on the console, a glass of scotch (he'd restocked in the Exile Café) in his hand. "Mrs. Mopup and I'll take good care of it. Don't worry about a thing. Enjoy yourself."

"Thanks," Tusk muttered, and exchanged glances with Link, who shrugged and shook his head.

So much for that idea.

As they entered the atmosphere dome, shed their pressurized suits, and stored them in lockers, Tusk had to admit he wasn't certain he'd have gone through with ducking out anyway. By now he was damn curious to know what was going on. And he was even beginning to get the feeling he might not only live through it, but maybe even profit by it.

All comers to the Exile Café entered through the lobby—a small room decorated in red velvet with a long, curved blond-wood desk, an android greeter who probably doubled as bouncer, and banks of vidscreens and cams. The vidscreens showed those who were inside the bar to those outside; the cams showed those who were outside to those inside. Those in the private rooms remained private.

Cynthia and the 'droid clerk exchanged greetings and she was informed of the house rules, which she apparently knew already. She had her eyeball scanned, and the 'droid made a call, and then they were all invited to walk inside. Tusk, listening with one ear, heard nothing to make him nervous.

He and Link, escorted by Cynthia, walked into a sensory deprivation chamber that effectively mixed him up so thoroughly once he was inside that he had no notion of how to find his way back out. He wondered what would happen if he tried to exit through the entrance, and decided that the chamber might well deprive him of more than his senses.

An android waiter, built to resemble a human male down to the last detail—which could be determined by the bulge in his G-string—approached Cynthia and greeted her by name.

"Well-programmed," said Link to Tusk.

"Yeah, but for what?" Tusk returned.

"You name it," said Cynthia, smiling. She arched a friendly eyebrow. "This way, gentlemen."

The waiter led them through the bar, with its crowds of humans and aliens and bright, multicolored globes that seemed to illuminate everything until you wanted to see something. Faces were distorted by the weird play of light against shadow. Tusk wouldn't have recognized Nola if she'd been sitting at the table across from him, so there was no point in searching the place for someone he knew. The tables were arranged in a maze. The flickering lights made him almost dizzy, but not quite; the shadows disoriented him completely. He had no idea which way was front, back, up, or down.

"No such thing as a fast getaway in this joint," said Link in Tusk's ear.

Tusk grunted.

The android—whose body was thoughtfully and tastefully painted with luminous paint, or they would have lost him completely—led the way to an anti-gravator. Cynthia stepped inside, was immediately floated upward. Tusk sailed up after her, Link drifting up beside him. The waiter ascended after them either keeping an eye on them or on Cynthia.

She caught hold of a ring on what Tusk counted as the eighth floor, pulled herself over to a door. She motioned. They followed. Emerging from the lift, they entered a long, narrow corridor flanked by innumerable locked doors. She marched them down the corridor. Coming to a door, she stopped, waited.

A cam mounted over the door scanned her eyeball. The door slid open, revealing what looked like a room in an expensive hotel, except that it had no bed, only a desk with several chairs around it, a vidscreen on the desk, a couch, a table. Another closed door led to what was probably a bathroom. A tall and handsome dark-haired man in uniform stood by a large window, staring down at the bar about eight floors beneath. At the sound of the door, he turned, smiled.

"Mendaharin Tusca," said Cynthia. "Captain Richard Dhure. Go right on in," she added. "I'll be back to pick you up when the interview's over."

"This is Captain Link," said Tusk, getting a firm grip on Link's arm. "Captain Link, meet Captain . . . what was that?"

"Dhure," said the captain, smiling in a warm and friendly manner. "Glad to meet you, Captain Link. Just come on in, will you, Tusca? Cynthia will escort Captain Link to his interview—"

"Sorry," said Link, his arm draped over Tusk's shoulder. "But we can't be separated. We're twins. It wouldn't be good for us. Upsets our psyche."

"Twins?" said Captain Dhure, eyeing them.

"Mom was white, dad was black," explained Tusk. "They wanted one each—to match."

"I see." Dhure grinned, playing along. "Well, you gentlemen won't be apart for long. Cynthia, Captain Link is going to be late for his interview." The smile was still there, but the tone indicated the game was over.

Link shrugged, let his arm fall. "See you, bro."

"Yeah," said Tusk, with a grim glance at Dhure. "If I don't, I'll come looking for you."

"Same here. Well, I guess it's you and me, sweetheart," said Link, sauntering on down the corridor after Cynthia. "Couldn't wait to get me alone, eh?"

Tusk stood in the doorway, determined to be as uncooperative as possible, curious to see what the captain would do. Instead of pulling a lasgun and threatening to blast him—which is what Tusk had expected—Dhure left his post by the window, crossed over to Tusk, shook hands.

"Really glad to meet you at last, Tusca," he said. "Come in."

With gentle pressure, he led Tusk into the room, steered him over to the desk, and indicated a chair. The door automatically shut and locked behind them.

"Please, be seated. Can I get you anything? Something to eat, drink? It's on our tab, of course."

"And you know what you can do with it," said Tusk, refusing to sit down. "What the hell is going on?"

"Thirty minutes," said Dhure, spreading his hands. "That's all I ask. Surely, since you came this far—"

"Not voluntarily," Tusk growled, still standing.

"You want an explanation. I'll give it to you. You're in no danger. In thirty minutes, if you want, you'll be free to walk out of here with money in your pocket to make up for the inconvenience. Cynthia will take you and Captain Link back to your plane, pick up Don. The four of you will shake hands, and that will be that. Just hear me out. That's all I ask. It could be well worth your while."

Tusk stood, irresolute. He could continue to act like a jerk and get exactly nowhere—that much was obvious. He'd showed them all what a tough guy he was. Now maybe it was time to give in, learn something that might help Dixter. At least that's what he told himself, not wanting to admit that he didn't have a whole hell of a lot of choice in the matter.

"All right," Tusk said, sitting down and stretching his legs, "I'm listening. Thirty minutes."

Actually it took about ten. The deal they offered was good—but not too good. Big bucks generally meant big risks and didn't amount to anything if the money ended up covering your funeral expenses.

"We're in need of experienced pilots," said Dhure. "Combat trained. We're starting to feel threatened from a few powerful neighbors. We have the spaceplanes and the people to fly them, but every single person in the corps is a rookie. From commanders on down. Never fired a shot. In short, what we need are veterans to come in and teach us how to do things."

"Let me get this straight," said Tusk. "You got planes and you got pilots but your pilots have no combat training?"

"Right." Dhure nodded, tilted his chair back. "I know, it doesn't make much sense. But, face it, there are a lot of plausible explanations. Let's suppose that somewhere back in old Earth's history—say maybe around 1960—that a computer malfunction leads to a big nuclear disaster—millions of people dead, more dying slowly of radiation poisoning, the environment poisoned for decades. People are terrified. They ban all nuclear reactors, prevent the building of atomic power stations. They get so scared that they shut down NASA. No more rocket launches and no more computer science. What would have happened?"

"Some of the planet might be left by now?"

"And about a bizillion of us squatting on our little square patch of it," said Dhure.

Tusk shifted in his chair. "So you're saying that this is what happened to your home planet—uh, pardon me, but I didn't catch the name."

"Vallombrosa. Don't suppose you ever heard of it."

"No, can't say that I have," Tusk answered, unable to figure out a way to say *Yes, I've heard of it and you're lying through your teeth* that wouldn't get him killed. "So you're saying that this is what happened?"

"Something like that," Dhure hedged. "Our history is complicated. I'll lend you a book on it sometime, if you're really interested."

"Thanks." Tusk waved a hand vaguely toward what he assumed might be the center of the galaxy. "You know, of course, that the Royal Navy will come in and offer you protection."

"We prefer to handle our own affairs. Every system has the right to defend itself."

True enough, Tusk remarked to himself, but not to declare

war on your neighbors, Captain Dhure, which is probably what you're planning. But that's not my problem.

"What I don't understand is, why go to all this trouble? To get me and Link, I mean."

"Because you're the best, Tusca," said Dhure. "We've seen your record. We want you."

"Yeah, I know I'm great," Tusk said modestly, "but there are at least a million—well, say maybe fifty thousand—other pilots out there as good as me. And you wouldn't have had to shoot 'em to get 'em to come." He put his hand tenderly over his injured arm.

"I'm really sorry about that," said Dhure sincerely. "That was a test."

"A test!"

"Yes. We heard you'd lost your nerve. We were told that the action you saw a few years ago had taken it out of you. We heard you were on the juice, good for nothing except ferrying salesmen. I'm happy to know our reports weren't true. You handled yourself extremely well under fire."

Tusk sat, eyeing Dhure. "You want to dance?"

Dhure stared. "I beg your pardon?"

"I asked if you wanted to dance."

A slight frown creased the captain's forehead. "Maybe I'm missing something, but—"

Tusk shrugged, sat back in his chair. "You've been bobbing and weaving and dodging so much I figure we might as well have some music to go with it."

Dhure threw back his head and laughed. "Damn, I *do* like you," he said when he could speak. "I guess I asked for that. All right, cards on the table. I admit it. We were disappointed when you didn't respond to our ads. And, yes, we *did* go out of our way to get hold of you. You have one rather special qualification which could make you extremely valuable to us."

"My good looks or my winning personality?" Tusk guessed.

Dhure began tracing a circle on the desk with his right forefinger, all the while looking at Tusk.

"How's your friend—the king?"

So that's it. Dixter was right. "Okay, I guess," Tusk said, shrugging. "If you believe the vids."

"Let's say I don't." Dhure was still friendly, but there was an edge to him now. The smile was on his mouth, not in his eyes.

The circle he was drawing closed in a little tighter. "Of your own personal knowledge. Off the record, of course."

"Oh, of course. Let's see. The last time me and the wife were in the palace, which was . . . mmmm . . . a week ago Thursday. We'd taken the yacht out for a spin and thought we'd drop by the palace and raise a glass of the bubbly with our good buddy His Majesty—"

"Cut the crap, Tusca."

"You cut it." Tusk sat up straight, feet on the floor. "Sure, I knew the king. When he wasn't a king. Now he is and it's different. Maybe you think that because I helped put him on the throne he gives me permission to sit my ass down in the Royal Presence. But that only happens in books. We said good-bye to each other three years ago and we meant it."

"Even after the so-called 'miracle healing'? A lot of your friends have mentioned that in connection with you—"

"Healing!" Tusk snorted. "Good doctors and a better PR agent."

"You're saying it didn't happen?"

"Hell, how should I know? I was mostly dead! When I woke up I was in all kinds of pain, had tubes stuck up every part of me that was readily available and a few that they had to work at, and some machine was doin' my breathin' for me. That sound like a goddam miracle to you?"

"That wasn't quite the way we heard it. . . ."

"No, well, I don't suppose it was. Tubes up your butt don't make the nightly news. Miracle healings do."

"One reason you and the king split, eh." Dhure looked deeply sympathetic. "He tried to get you to play along. But you obviously still keep in contact. He sent you a baby gift—"

"His secretary signed the card and spelled my name wrong." Tusk bounded up, suddenly angry, slammed a hand on the desk. "And where the hell do you get off, spying on me and my family?"

"Easy, Tusca, easy," Dhure said in soothing tones.

Tusk drew in a seething breath. Shutting his mouth over a few more choice remarks, he jammed his hands in his pockets, took a turn around the room. He looked at the solid steel walls, at the bar below with its eerie shadows, and reminded himself that a killer vacuum cleaner had hold of his plane and that, somewhere else, Cynthia had hold of Link. And they knew too damn much about Nola. . . .

By the time he'd made the circuit, returned to the desk, he was breathing almost normally, only shaking slightly. After all, he reminded himself, you've been expecting something like this in regard to Dion. It was only a matter of time. You know what to do.

"Look, I'm sorry I snapped at you," Tusk said to Dhure in a low voice, hands tight fists in his pockets. "But if you're expecting me to cut some deal for you with His Majesty, you can forget it. I'm the last person the king'd listen to. Honest, I'd hurt your cause more than help it."

Dhure said nothing, but it was obvious he wasn't buying.

Tusk drew in a deep breath, let it out. "You ever see any plays by a guy named Shakespeare? Yeah, well, me neither. But one day the wife watches one on the educational channel. Says we should get cultured, because of the kid, you know. Well, there was this one. Henry the Fourth or Fifth or something like that. Anyway, it was about this prince, who was a really cool guy and went out drinkin' and partyin' every night with all his friends—until the day he turned king. And that day all his friends came up to him and were getting ready to clap him on the shoulder and congratulate him and he turned to one of them, to the man who'd been his best friend, and said, 'I know thee not, old man.' That's how they talked, back then."

Dhure said nothing. He'd quit drawing the circle. His hand was still. The room was still.

" 'I know thee not, old man,' " Tusk repeated softly, staring at the shifting shadows in the bar below. "That's what the king said to his friends. He was ashamed of them, you see. They reminded him of what he'd been, and he couldn't stand that."

"Despite the fact that you saved his life?"

"You do know a lot, don't you?" Tusk glowered.

"Evidently not enough."

"Yeah, well, don't you get it yet? The 'healing' made us even, then. His Majesty doesn't owe me a damn thing. And I don't owe him."

"I see." Dhure started drawing the circle again.

Tusk sat back down in the chair. Tense, wary, he kept his eyes on the captain.

"Gosh. That's too bad." Dhure looked up with another sympathetic smile. "The young man's head swelled once they put the crown on it, eh?"

"Something like that," Tusk mumbled.

"You can't blame us for trying. It never hurts to have connections. We could have used a friend in high places. Still, at least we're left with one hell of a pilot. What do you say, Tusk? Do we have a deal?"

"If I say no, what happens?"

"We're sorry, of course. But you go back to the wife and kid and we go back to looking for good pilots."

"That's it?"

"That's it."

"Well, then. No. Thanks and all that. But no."

Dhure looked mildly disappointed. "We'd be willing to wait until after the baby came, of course."

"It's not that. You said I lost my nerve. I don't think so, but . . . well, it's hard to explain. . . . Getting shot at just isn't fun anymore. You know what *is* fun? Givin' my kid a bath. Taking him to the zoo, carrying him home in my arms when he falls asleep."

"I understand." Dhure stood up.

Tusk did, too. Quickly.

The captain held out his hand. "Sorry to lose you, Tusca. You'll find a little something in your spaceplane to compensate you for your time and trouble. If you ever change your mind, you know how to reach us."

"Thanks." Tusk shook hands, somewhat dazed.

"You can just go right on out. Cynthia'll be waiting in the corridor to take you back."

Dhure nodded, sat down at the desk. Turning on a computer, he commanded it to delete the file on one Mendaharin Tusca.

Tusk walked out the door. Cynthia was waiting for him, along with Link.

"No go?" she said.

"Sorry," said Tusk.

"Me, too." She sighed, smiled. "I'll walk you back to the exit. You can find your way from there, can't you?"

Tusk supposed they could. He glanced at Link. The pilot shook his head. Neither said a word—except good-bye to a still smiling, still friendly Cynthia—until they had reached their spaceplane.

Don was gone. So was the scotch. And so was Mrs. Mopup. Tusk and Link sat and stared at one another.

"What the hell was that all about?" Link demanded.

"Ten thousand credits," said XJ smugly. "He was going to

make it five, but I insisted on ten. On account of your injury. And mental stress."

"What mental stress?" Tusk asked irritably.

"*My* mental stress! I'm the only one with a brain. Ten thousand credits. In the account. I checked. They're good for it. Best week's work you two losers ever did, either of you. So what'd they'd want?"

"Two damn good pilots," said Tusk.

"No, really. What'd they'd want?" XJ persisted.

Tusk grinned, then looked back at Link. The grin faded. "A direct line to the king."

"That was it, then." Link was disappointed. "You sure?"

"Hell, yes, I'm sure. Didn't they ask you about him?"

"Naw. That's a shame, too, 'cause he and I are real close friends."

"Come off it, Link." Tusk snorted. "This is me, remember?"

"So!" Link was belligerent. "Just because you two had a falling out doesn't mean he's forgotten his old pal Link."

"Yeah, how many times have *you* been invited to the palace lately?"

"Well, the king's a busy guy. Plus that crowd he hangs around with—dukes and earls and stuff. He knows they're not my type. You ready to shove off?"

"Sure," said Tusk. "Unless you got more business—"

"Nope. They offered me a good deal—even raised the ante to try to get me to join—but I said no, thanks. I figured you'd never agree, what with Nola and all, and I couldn't go off and leave you in the lurch, could I?"

Tusk grunted. "You couldn't go off and leave me stuck with a pile of debts and no money without me coming looking for you is what you mean."

"Well, that, too." Link grinned. Leaning back in the co-pilot's chair, he put his feet on the console.

The lights flickered. A humming sound ran through the metal. Tusk snatched his hands back from the control panel just in time.

Link wasn't so lucky. Letting out a shriek, he jerked his feet off the console, shot out of his chair, and began hopping around the lower deck, slapping frantically at his tingling legs.

"Jeez!" he swore, glaring at the computer. "What'd you do that for? You damn near fried me!"

"No boots on the console!" snapped XJ.

"Damn! I knew there was something I meant to do," Tusk said in a low voice, being careful to keep from touching any metal. "I meant to ask how much Cynthia wanted for Mrs. Mopup."

--◁■つ◯Cఆ▷--

"And that was that, sir," Tusk said a week later. He'd returned safely to Vangelis, was making his report to John Dixter. "They thought I had an in with His Majesty. When they found out different, they lost their enthusiasm over me real quick."

"Do you suppose they believed you?" Dixter asked, dubious.

"They got no reason not to," said Tusk quietly.

Dixter was silent a moment, studied him intently. "I'm sorry, son. I assumed you understood. Dion thought, for your own protection—"

Tusk felt his skin burn. "Forget it, sir. I'm the one who should be apologizing. It's all right. Really. And, anyway, it looks like he was right."

"Yes, it looks that way." Dixter sounded unconvinced, but he couldn't argue with the facts and so he let it go, moved on to other subjects. "This Ghost Legion. Did they say anything about it? Why the name, for example?"

"Cynthia told me. It's 'cause they call their spaceplanes Gray Ghosts. I'd score 'em zero for originality, but nothing worse."

"It sounds plausible," Dixter admitted. "And that man— Captain Dhure. He told you the planet's name was Vallombrosa."

"Yeah, I didn't call him on that one. Couldn't very well let him know I'd been checking up on him, though it would have served him right, all the checking they'd done on me. My guess is you look for a planet on the opposite side of the galaxy from Vallomwhatever and you'll find someone getting ready to go to war against someone else."

"You're probably right," said Dixter thoughtfully. "Still . . ."

"Yes, sir?"

The admiral shook his head. "Nothing. Thanks for the information, Tusk. Report to me immediately if you hear from them again."

"Don't think there's much chance of that, sir. Unless they want to sell me a vacuum cleaner." Tusk grinned.

"I wouldn't be so certain," said Dixter, and ended the transmission.

Chapter ❖ Seventeen

But in that he died, he died unto sin once; but in that he liveth, he liveth unto God.

The Bible, Romans 6:9

It was morning in the Abbey of St. Francis. Bells rang, calling the brothers to prayer. Slowly, devotedly, the robed and hooded figures—priests, monks, novitiates, and lay brothers—left whatever tasks they were performing and entered the cathedral to join together in praise of the Creator, to ask His blessing on this new day. At the close of service, the small news of the religious community was given out by Prior John and daily problems and other matters were voiced and dealt with. The brethren were dismissed to go to breakfast, then continue about their duties.

But on that day, one of their number was missing.

"Where is Brother Penitent?" demanded Prior John.

No one knew. No one had seen him. He had not been to breakfast, to take in silence his cup of milk and an orange and a wedge of fresh-baked bread, to sit apart in a corner that had become his own. His absence from a meal was not unusual, however; he was known to fast on frequent occasions, to mortify his flesh as a gift to God. But he had never, though weak from self-enforced hunger, missed a day of work.

Ordinarily Brother Penitent would have been about his duties—lifting sick and infirm brethren in his strong arms, bathing them, changing bed linens, or digging in the garden, fighting the never-ending battle against weeds that, like evil, were rooted out of one place only to flourish in another.

Or perhaps he might be working in the dark subterranean basement, repairing the giant machines—a mystery to most of the brethren—that maintained the abbey's life-support systems, critical in a world of domed cities, stinging, dust-laden wind, and a sun that did not warm the garish red-rock landscape.

Today Brother Penitent had not gone to his work, had not reported to Prior John to find out what task was to be assigned to him. Not once in the three years since he had been in the monastery had Brother Penitent neglected his duties. Silent, grim, he often drove himself until he was on the verge of exhaustion, indomitable will alone aiding his weary footsteps back to his comfortless cell. He would stop working only when the bells called him to his prayers.

Brother Penitent always stopped to pray, falling to his knees wherever he might be. But he never entered the great cathedral. Not once in three years had he set foot inside its holy walls. He shunned it, rather; went out of his way to avoid it, would refuse to do any work inside it. Not even Archbishop Fideles had been able to prevail upon Penitent to accept God's forgiveness and enter His house.

Which is one reason why Brother Penitent had become known unofficially among the other brethren as the Unforgiven.

Today, however, he had not even been seen at his prayers.

This break in their daily regimen caused a small flurry of excitement among the brethren, similar to the day the dome's seal had cracked and permitted the outside bone-chilling and poisonous air to hiss into the abbey. Brothers scattered in all directions, searching the grounds and buildings, and none reported finding their missing brother. Finally one of the young novitiates thought to look through the small iron grille in the door of Brother Penitent's cell. The novitiate, wide-eyed, returned to Prior John and reported what he had seen.

Brother Penitent was discovered sitting on his bed in the cramped and narrow cell in the *dortoir* of the monastery, staring at the palm of his right hand and talking to nothing but the empty air.

"What do You want of me?" They could hear him shout, his voice tense, frustrated. "What do You want of me? I have nothing left to give!"

··✦✧◯✦✧··

Archbishop Fideles sat in his office, behind his desk, staring not at his hand but at a communiqué he held in his hand. The communiqué had been delivered by special courier, a royal courier who was waiting for the archbishop on his return from his trip to the hospital.

Disturbed and deeply troubled by the strange tale of the

doctor, Fideles viewed the Royal Seal on the courier's missive with misgiving. His Majesty was very much on the archbishop's mind, and now to discover that the king had been trying in vain to reach the archbishop seemed an ominous coincidence.

If it *was* coincidence.

The archbishop read the communiqué—which was marked classified, top-secret—in perplexity. It was a compilation of reports dealing with incidents far removed from and unrelated to the business of the Church: a mysterious invasion of the house of the late Adonian weapons dealer, Snaga Ohme; an attempt to steal the space-rotation bomb by a group calling itself Ghost Legion; a report from a Mendaharin Tusca that he'd been contacted by said Ghost Legion; the abduction and return of said Tusca; a mysterious planet known as Vallombrosa; a famed explorer . . .

"Grand Dieu!" breathed Archbishop Fideles, dropping the communiqué to the desk and staring at it in perplexity.

"Holiness?" A rap on the door, a timid voice breaking in on his thoughts.

The abbey did not hold with such modern conveniences as commlinks or intercom devices or even telephones, except for communication with the outside world, deemed necessary to the head of a far-flung Order. Within the abbey walls, business was carried on much as it had been carried on centuries earlier—by word of mouth.

"I left orders not to be disturbed," called Fideles harshly. He never spoke to anyone harshly.

"I . . . I know, Holiness. Forgive me." Brother Petra sounded rattled. "But this is . . . an emergency . . . Prior John . . ."

"It's about Brother Penitent, Holiness." Prior John's stern tones came through the door. A man of extreme self-importance, the prior ran the affairs of the abbey with implacable efficiency. He considered his own affairs must naturally take precedence over any others. "Our brother is acting very strangely. Stranger than usual," the prior thought fit to add.

"What now?" Fideles sighed and cast a reproachful glance heavenward, for which he immediately asked forgiveness. Catching hold of the missive, not sorry to forget it for the moment, he slid it into the drawer of his desk. "Enter, with God's blessing."

Prior John swept inside.

"Yes, what is it?" asked Fideles, now truly concerned at the sight of the priest's set and rigid face. "Is our brother taken ill?"

"I think he has gone mad, Holiness," stated the prior solemnly. "If you remember, I advised against his admittance. We knew nothing about him, about his past, his background—"

"It was my decision, as I again remind you, Prior. A decision that, as head of this Order, I had every right to make." Fideles spoke impatiently, sharply. "Tell me what has happened!"

Prior John, chastened by the rebuke, drew himself up straight, clasped his hands together over the front of his surplice. "Brother Penitent did not report to his work this morning. I sent the others to look for him, to find out what was amiss. One of the novitiates discovered Brother Penitent still in his cell. He did not answer to the young man's knocks.

"When I arrived, I found our brother sitting on his bed talking to himself, apparently oblivious to my presence outside his door. Thinking he was sick, naturally I took it upon myself to enter." He paused, perhaps waiting for approbation.

"Naturally," said Fideles dryly. "And what did Brother Penitent do?"

"He leapt to his feet, like a man possessed, Holiness." Prior John gave every appearance of never being able to recover from the shock. "And he yelled at me in a thundering voice, with such a black look on his face that I thought he was going to strike me."

"Did he?" asked Fideles, growing more and more alarmed.

"No," said Prior John, sounding disappointed. "But he spoke to me in the devil's tongue. Undoubtedly using profane language. I consider it fortunate that I did not understand him."

God keep me from choking this man, prayed Fideles, eyeing the prior grimly. Aloud he said, "I doubt if Brother Penitent would take our Creator's name in vain. Perhaps, if you could remember what the words were, I could make some sense of them—"

"Fortunately, Holiness, I have a good ear." Prior John repeated the words, with an expression that left no doubt he considered that he was placing his soul in jeopardy by merely pronouncing them.

The words came out garbled, but Fideles understood them easily, having spent a year of his life in the Warlord's service on board a ship of war. The language was Standard Military, a jargon used by soldiers of all races and nationalities—both human and alien.

What is the meaning of this intrusion, Captain? was the phrase Brother Penitent had shouted at the astonished prior. *I did not send for you. Return to your duties.*

What was happening? Was the prior right? *Was* Brother Penitent going mad?

"Where is our brother now?" Fideles asked, concerned, preparing to go to him.

But Prior John was not to be hurried with his tale, of which he was—as usual—the hero. "I managed to calm him. Otherwise, I do not know what violence he might have done to himself or to others. I spoke to him sternly. *I* have never been one to coddle him. I reminded him of his duty to me—his superior. At this, he grew sullen, refused to answer my questions. Therefore, I brought him to you. He is waiting in the chamber outside. But I thought it right to prepare you—"

"For God's sake, man!" cried Fideles, jumping up, slamming his fist on the desk. "Stop driveling and send him in!" He shoved past the shocked and disapproving prior, hastened to the door, and threw it open.

Brother Penitent, hood drawn low over his face, hands folded in his sleeves, stood silent and unmoving in the antechamber. Brother Petra, looking nervous and extremely unhappy, huddled in a corner, as far from the supposed madman as was possible to get.

"I will deal with the matter now, Prior," Fideles said, regaining control. "Thank you for bringing it to my attention. Please forgive me if I spoke sharply to you, but I am certain you can understand my concern for our brother's welfare."

The offended prior bowed stiffly, turned on his heel, and stalked out the door.

Brother Penitent entered the office. Archbishop Fideles spoke a few words to Brother Petra, who left immediately and—to judge by his expression—gratefully. Shutting the outer door to the antechamber, Fideles returned to his own office, shut his own door, and locked it.

He faced the brother, who kept his head bowed, said nothing. The archbishop found himself at a loss for words, had no idea where to begin or how to continue if and when he got started. He could, he decided at last, only trust to God to lead him.

"What is troubling you, Brother Penitent? I hope you know that you can trust me."

The lay brother did not respond.

Fideles moistened his dry mouth. "Please, sit down."

The brother did not move.

"I'm glad you came," the archbishop continued. "I was going to send for you. I have received a communiqué from His Majesty, the king."

Brother Penitent raised his head. The eyes were dark, but no longer empty. The eyes asked, as plainly as if he had spoken aloud, *What has that to do with me?*

"The communiqué was addressed to me," continued Fideles, "but I don't believe it was intended for me." He drew in a deep breath, looked at the brother intently. "His Majesty intended it for Lord Derek Sagan."

"Derek Sagan is dead," said Brother Penitent quietly, impassively.

The archbishop reached out his hand, laid it upon Penitent's forearm. He felt bone and muscle, strong still, from backbreaking, self-imposed labor. Within, he felt the quiver, the tension.

"I do not think so," said the archbishop with a faint smile, "for he spoke, just now, to the captain of his guard."

The man's face was unnaturally pale, gaunt, haggard. The eyes were red-rimmed, from lack of sleep, and sunken in their sockets. Fideles was fearful, at first, that Penitent would attempt to continue the deception, but at last the dark eyes closed in resignation, the head bowed.

Suddenly, frowning, he looked up.

"How did the king know?" His voice was hard with suspicion.

"I did not betray you, my lord," said Fideles.

Sagan's mouth twisted. Fideles realized suddenly that he'd used the old title. *My lord.* It came easily, too easily. Fideles knew then how often he had started to address Sagan by it, been forced to bite it back. The air of authority, of command, welled out from underneath the habit of humility and meek compliance. Sagan wore the robes with sincerity, of that the archbishop had no doubt. But there was no denying who and what he was, what he had once been.

"Dion is Blood Royal, Brother," Fideles added, flushing self-consciously. "You know more about what extraordinary qualities. that gives him than I do, but I believe I have heard it said that the Blood Royal have an affinity for each other. And the two of you were close. . . ."

Sagan remained standing, head bowed again, considering. Then he raised his head, looked at Fideles. The eyes' redness made them appear that much darker by contrast. And they were no longer empty. In their depths, a fire burned.

"Would you bring the Warlord back to life?" he asked, and lifted a warding hand when Fideles would have answered. "Think well, Holiness—for if you resurrect him, you bring him back with all his faults—"

"And all his virtues," said the archbishop earnestly. "It is not my hand that draws you back, Brother, but God's."

Saga gave a bitter laugh. "I wonder."

"You said He spoke to you, told you of—"

"I lied." Sagan smiled grimly, turned his right hand, palm up, to the light.

Five scars that looked like puncture wounds marred the man's hardened and callused palm. The scars were obviously old, yet now they were red and swollen and oozed a clear liquid.

Fideles know what had created the scars. They were made by the bloodsword, by five needles on the sword's hilt that penetrated the skin, flooding the body with micro machines that connected brain and nerves to the sword, creating a weapon that responded as swiftly as thought.

"I don't understand, my lord!" Fideles stared at him. "You destroyed the bloodsword! Years ago. I saw you throw it into the fiery water myself. And when you entered the Order, you took a vow before God never again to lay your hand on tools of violence. . . ."

"Look at it, Holiness," Sagan demanded harshly. "Look at the marks of my past. And I ask you again, will you bring the Warlord back to life?"

Fideles did not understand what was going on, but he was wise enough to know that there were some things he was not meant to understand. He had come a child to the Order. He did not remember hearing his mother's voice, or his father's; he remembered hearing only God's. His faith had been tested in many ways and though he had slipped on the path and fallen more than once, he had always risen to his feet and continued on, bruised and hurting, but stronger for his struggles. Young as he was—and he was now only in his early thirties—these struggles were why he had been chosen by the king to restore the Church, to bring worship of the Creator back to those who had previously been informed, by an "enlightened" government, that He was a myth.

Fideles took the man's hand, the scarred hand, in his own. The flesh was chill, as if, in truth, he touched the hand of a corpse. He looked at the scars, the scars of war, of violence, of ambition. And on top of those scars, fresh scars—calluses, rubbed by the wooden handle of a shovel, raw from scrubbing floors, thin from fasting.

"These wounds are on the surface, Brother. I see those in your soul and they are still open and bleeding. You've sought to heal them with prayer, with overwork, with self-denial and self-abuse. . . ."

Sagan's hand closed to a fist.

Fideles's hand laid gently over it. "It hasn't worked, has it? You are not dead. You've been hiding in the tomb. Until you come out and expose these wounds to the light, they will never close, never heal. God has rolled aside the stone. It is not my choice, nor His—but yours."

The archbishop let loose the hand. Turning away, he walked around behind his desk. He seated himself, opened the drawer, reached in, and drew out the communiqué he had been reading when Prior John burst in.

Fideles lifted the sheaf of papers, held them out to Sagan. "Will you come back to life? To help those who need you?"

Sagan accepted the papers reluctantly, but he did not glance at them. He remained standing. "Don't you want to know why I lied, Holiness?"

"If you want to tell me," said the archbishop. "But first I think you should read this. It may make a difference." He looked at the man intently, noticed the lips were parched, cracked. "Can I get you something, Brother? How long has it been since you ate or drank anything?"

"I don't know," Sagan said impatiently. "I can't remember." He looked at the papers. His lips tightened into a thin, dark line. "You would have me do this, Holiness?"

"Yes, I would," said Fideles steadily.

"God help you, then," Sagan muttered. He sat down in a chair on the opposite side of the desk from the archbishop and silently began to read.

Fideles found he was trembling. He murmured a prayer that

was one of both thanksgiving and misgiving. Rising quietly, fearful of disturbing the Warlord's concentration, the arch-bishop left his desk, glided over to a sideboard where stood an iced pitcher of water. He poured a glass, brought it back, placed it on the desk within Sagan's reach.

He drank of it thirstily, then, absorbed in his reading, appeared to forget the water was there.

At first he had scanned the material swiftly, his thoughts unfocused, seemingly unable to concentrate. Then his attention was caught, held. The lines in the haggard face—which had aged far too much in three years—deepened.

Fideles, sighing again, picked up his breviary to read the daily office, discovered he was too upset to give his mind to the words, and let the book fall. He watched the Warlord, watched him read, tried to guess his place in the text, which the arch-bishop found himself remembering with startling clarity.

We have yet to determine the nature of the invader that penetrated the sophisticated detection systems of Snaga Ohme. But be it probe or microships or "ghosts," it stole the fake space-rotation bomb planted there. It has undoubtedly learned that the bomb is a fake and even now, perhaps, is searching for the real one. And how are we to stop it if we don't know what it is? Can't see it? Hear it? Touch it? . . .

Captain Dhure questioned Tusca about his relationship with the king, but did not press the point. Perhaps Dhure believed Tusca's explanation of a falling out. Neither Tusca nor Link has been contacted by this Ghost Legion since. . . .

Vallombrosa: Vale of Shades. Unmanned probes have confirmed what was already indicated on the charts—it is a lifeless planet existing in a lifeless region of the galaxy. Yet its coordinates were given to Tusca and to other pilots—including those we sent as spies—as a rendezvous site. We can only assume that once the pilots reach that location, they are given a different set of coordinates. We can't be certain, however, since our spies have not returned. We have lost all contact with them. . . .

For your information, Holiness, I have included what we know of the history of the planet Vallombrosa. It was discovered by the galactic explorer—

"Pantha!" Sagan breathed, the first word he'd uttered.

"Garth Pantha," said Fideles quietly, his hands folded on top of his breviary. "I, too, was struck by the name. Of course, we would naturally be sensitive to it, having just heard such a name mentioned in connection with the doctor's strange tale. Probably coincidence. . . ."

"I do not believe in coincidence," said the Warlord. He placed the report on the desk, began to rub the inside of his right palm.

"What does it mean, then?" Fideles asked, perplexed. "What does it all mean?"

Sagan was staring intently at nothing that the archbishop could see; the dark eyes narrowed, as if attempting to bring something far distant into focus. The Warlord continued rubbing his hand, as one rubs a sore and aching tooth.

"It means the bastard son of Amodius is alive," he said. "And he is making ready to lay claim to the throne."

"But . . . how do you know?" Fideles was appalled. "You can't know for certain!"

"Yes, I can." Sagan shifted his gaze—and his thoughts—from the far to the near. He looked at the palm of his hand. "I've seen him. Spoken to him. *He* was the one who sent me to that hospital. His voice . . . not God's."

"The Creator have mercy!" Fideles shuddered. He sat in silence long moments, pondering, fingers caressing the leather-bound breviary, seeking reassurance, guidance. "I didn't want to do this. But it seems we have no choice. His Majesty must be informed . . . of everything."

Derek Sagan said nothing. He had withdrawn back into himself—head and eyes lowered, hands folded into the sleeves of the robe, cowl pulled up over his head. The Warlord was gone, if he had ever truly been present. Brother Penitent had returned.

The archbishop continued, "I will send you, Brother—"

"No!"

The word was softly spoken, yet it vibrated through Fideles's taut nerves like an electrical jolt. His fingers twitched. He shoved the breviary to one side, leaned over the desk.

"I understand your reluctance, my lord, but you *must* be the one to go to him. I don't understand what is happening. I am not Blood Royal. You are, and you are the only one His Majesty would believe, the only one who can answer his questions."

The hooded head lifted, but all the archbishop could see within the shadows were the burning eyes.

"Dion would believe Lord Sagan. But Lord Sagan is dead." The voice was dark as the shadows. "Let him die, Holiness! I'm warning you! Let him die!"

"I cannot do that, my lord," said Fideles. "His Majesty may be in danger—"

"He *is* in danger! And I will only escalate his danger!"

Sagan's right hand closed to a fist, slammed down, shattered the glass. Water flooded the desk, soaked everything on it, including the report, including the breviary.

Neither man moved.

The water crept to the edge of the desk. Still neither did anything to stop it.

A drop fell to the floor, then another, and another, measuring the silence. Slowly Sagan unclenched his hand. Traces of blood mingled with the water.

"I am sorry, Holiness. Forgive me."

"It is not from me you should be seeking forgiveness," said Fideles sternly. "Have these three years meant nothing to you? Have your prayers to Him been movements of your lips only?"

"Prayers!" Sagan gave a bitter laugh. "No, my prayers to Him have been sincere. He has cast them back in my face! What does He want from me?"

"Have you asked Him?"

Sagan lunged across the desk, grasped hold of Fideles's arm. Nails dug deep into flesh, fingers crushed and bruised. His words burst out in fierce anger, terrible passion. "God has taken my very soul and left me empty! What more does He want of me?"

Fideles did not blanch. He closed his hand over the man's wrist, held him fast.

"I do not know, my brother," he said. "Unless it be to find the soul that you have lost."

Sagan released his grip involuntarily, as if the fingers had suddenly lost their strength. Slowly he straightened. His breathing was heavy, labored. The sleeves of his cassock were wet from the spilled water and blood.

Fideles felt no pain now. Later, he would see the bruises—ugly, discolored. The marks on his arm would last for weeks.

"I have taken a vow of obedience, Holiness," said Sagan in a lifeless voice, his face averted. "If you command it, I will go."

"And thus force *me* to take responsibility?" Fideles asked wryly.

Sagan's lip curled, but he did not reply.

"Very well." Fideles rose to his feet. "God's will in this is clear. Brother Penitent, I command you to go to His Majesty and tell him all that we have discovered, plus any additional information you deem essential. Further, you will consider yourself at His Majesty's disposal and undertake any task His Majesty may require of you—so long as it does not conflict with your vows, of course."

The Warlord cast the archbishop a long look. "Think well what you ask. I give you one chance to reconsider."

The shadow of that look crossed the archbishop's heart, chilled his blood. Lifting the wet breviary, he held it tightly in his hands, to keep them from shaking.

"*Vade cum Deo,*" he said. "Go with God."

"Thank you, Holiness," said Sagan, voice cold and empty, "but I travel alone." Bowing, he left the room.

Fideles sank back down into his chair. Oblivious to the water, the broken glass, the blood, he clasped his hands on top of the wet desk.

"Blessed Father, have we lost him? Was he ever ours to lose? Yet what else could I do? *Deus eum adjuvat.* God help him. *Deus nos adjuvat!* God help us all!"

Chapter ·☗·☗·☗· Eighteen

Her court was pure, her life serene;
God gave her peace; her land reposed;
A thousand claims to reverence closed
In her as Mother, Wife, and Queen.
           Alfred, Lord Tennyson, "To the Queen"

"Is the transport ready?" Dion asked his secretary, who had entered the office with his accustomed air of tranquillity.

"Yes, sir," replied D'argent. He crossed the large room, making no sound on the thick carpet, laid a file down in front of the king, lifted another. "For your signature, sir. These few here must be done by hand, not electronic. The Lord of the Admiralty is on the commlink. He would like to talk to you before we depart, and Her Majesty requests to see you, as well."

Dixter. Her Majesty. Dion frowned. He was—or had been—in an excellent humor. The day he'd been anticipating for weeks had finally arrived. He'd watched the sunrise and felt its light flood through his veins. Tonight he would be with Kamil. He wanted nothing to ruin this day, nothing to dim the sunshine—not the Lord of the Admiralty, certainly not Astarte. Dion picked up an old-fashioned ink pen, began signing forms—mostly ceremonial in nature: official proclamations of various planetary holidays and celebrations, presentations of awards, gifts and grants, and so forth.

"I will speak with Dixter first. Inform Her Majesty that I will be at her disposal after that. How much time do we have?"

"An hour, if we are to arrive there on schedule, sir."

Dion handed back the folder. The secretary glided from the room. The king flicked on the commlink.

"Good morning, Admiral. No, I haven't heard from the archbishop. The courier left only a few days ago. Yes, I will let you know as soon as I hear anything. I will be at the Academy if you need to reach me."

Dion flicked on another line. "I am free to see Her Majesty now, D'argent."

Rising to his feet, he buttoned his black jacket, shook back his mane of red-gold hair, and had a smile prepared for his wife when she entered the room.

"Good morning, madam. You look lovely today. The blue of that gown brings out your eyes. You are dressed for traveling. What do you have planned?"

Astarte crossed the room, came over to her husband. Taking his hand, she inclined her face toward him. He leaned down, formally kissed her on the cheek. Her skin was cool, her fingers chill in his grasp. She was dressed in a suit of ice-blue lamb's wool, tailored to complement her short stature and exquisite figure. Her black hair was done in its elaborate coif. She used little makeup. Her complexion was flawless. She added only some color on her eyelids, to bring out their purplish hue, and a touch of coral on her lips.

Dion never failed to marvel at her beauty, as he never failed to marvel at the beauty of the cold, glittering jewels on display for the tourists in the Jewel Room on the lower, public levels of the palace. He let go of her hand, though he continued to smile down at her.

"Is there something I can do for you, madam? Before I leave?"

"You are going back to the Academy?" she asked him abruptly.

Dion stiffened, though he was careful to keep his facial expression impassive, blandly smiling. He knew his words sounded stilted, but he held no conversation with his wife— even on the most innocent of topics—that did not sound stilted.

"Yes, madam. Your husband is lecturing the students on the duties of a king." His smile broadened, though he thought his face might crack. He essayed a small joke. "I trust those who fall asleep will be polite enough to keep their snoring to a minimum."

Astarte had no answering smile; she seemed not to have heard him. Looking up at him, eyes dark with an unusual intensity, she said to him, "Don't go."

Dion was startled, uneasy. In all their years of marriage, she'd never made such a request. Why now? Did she suspect? And during the moment of silence that had passed while he was wondering, he realized that he should have been saying something to allay those suspicions.

"Madam, that is—"

"Wait, no, let me finish." Astarte reached out to him. Almost shyly, she took hold of his hand, clasped it fast. Her voice was shaking; she talked too fast.

"I'll cancel my appointments. You cancel yours. We'll go away, just the two of us. That vid star, what's his name, Rusty Love, has been begging us to accept the use of his villa on Adonis. The surroundings are beautiful. It stands on a cliff overlooking the sea. It is completely isolated, away from the press and the people. We could swim and take long walks. You will teach me to play the harp, as you once promised. We won't mention politics, wars, religion. For two days or three, we will be two ordinary people. Please, my husband. We need to get away from this. We need to . . . to be alone. We need to talk."

Dion stared at her, taken aback. He had never seen her so earnest, so impassioned about anything. Her mention of the harp touched him. In those first early, lonely days of their marriage, when they were strangers to each other, trying to learn to be husband and wife, he had played the harp for her. She loved music and those moments were the first moments of pleasure they had ever truly shared.

As time went by, those moments had become the last.

The transport was waiting. He had only to give D'argent new instructions, have the course changed, have the arrangements made. The Academy would understand. More than that, they'd be well pleased. The royal couple taking time out to be with each other. Romance blooms on Adonis.

He should do this. It was his duty: his duty to his wife, to his people. He felt Astarte's hand grow warmer in his grasp. The color deepened in her cheeks, lightened her eyes. She had seen the mirror image crack. She knew she had touched some vulnerable part of him.

She knows about Kamil, he realized. It is impossible, but she knows. And she is offering me this way out. No accusations. No recriminations. It will never be mentioned between us. But if I go with her now, I will be promising to forsake Kamil. And Kamil will know. She'll know when she sees the vids tonight. None of the three of us will ever have to say a word. It will all be ended, as swiftly and cleanly as a knife-thrust through the heart.

And he saw himself in their loveless bed, making love forever with his eyes closed.

Kamil! Desire flamed through him, ached, burned. He had

dreamed so long of their meeting, tasted the delicious torment of anticipation. He needed the soothing rest that came from their easy comradeship, their conversation, her teasing, her laughter. He had made so many sacrifices, given up so much.

No, this he would keep. This was his. He would see to it that Astarte was placated. Damn it, if she'd only get pregnant! That was all she wanted from him.

"Your offer is very tempting, my dear," he said, withdrawing his hand from hers. "It all sounds wonderful. We will certainly take such a trip. Six month's time, perhaps. When both our schedules are free. I'll have D'argent make the arrange—"

"Don't do this, Dion!" Astarte pleaded. Her face was white, the color drained. "I beg you!"

"It is impossible to alter my plans at this late date. I assure you, madam." Dion turned away, walked over to his desk, placed his hand on one of the folders. "My obligations preclude it . . . as do yours, I believe."

He waited, tense, for the tears, the recriminations.

Astarte said nothing. She stood unmoving, looking at him, her expression one of such unutterable sadness that Dion was struck by it. Without a word, with only that singular look, she left the room.

Dion stared after her. He felt vaguely uncomfortable; muffled voices in his soul spoke of trust and honor, but he swiftly muzzled their mouths. He listened only to love's voice, to its sweet song. Love made all wrongs right.

He attempted to return to his work, but he couldn't concentrate. He kept seeing, not Kamil's face, as he wanted to see, but that sad look of Astarte's.

He shoved his work aside. "D'argent, we're leaving early."

He needed, suddenly, to be out in the sunshine.

-◄■○●■►-

His Majesty's shuttlecraft, one of those formerly attached to the old *Phoenix*, was safely and securely docked at the far end of the Academy's small spaceport. Dion chose to use the shuttle as home base during his stay this time, although the headmaster had kindly offered his own house for His Majesty's use once again. Though regretting walks in the rose garden—it was spring on the Academy's home planet—Dion had politely refused.

He would be on the planet for at least a week while he gave

his series of lectures. And during that time he could not abrogate his responsibilities, but needed to remain in control of events transpiring in his realm. He was planning to meet with emissaries from numerous neighboring star systems during his visit, as well as heads of several major corporations. The Academy needed money and the king had promised to try to persuade these wealthy magnates to invest in a commodity with a guaranteed return: education.

Consequently, Dion was busy from morning to night. The shuttlecraft's beautifully-appointed antechamber was filled with people waiting to be received by His Majesty. His lectures were well attended and well received, for though this might be an excuse to be with Kamil, Dion took the subject of kingship seriously. He had done a great deal of research, and his thoughtful and insightful comments impressed everyone, including those skeptics who has assumed this was a publicity stunt.

But at night, when the last diplomat had been placated, the last news briefing held, the last adoring students shooed from the tarmac, Dion ordered the shuttlecraft doors shut and sealed. By day, he belonged to his subjects. At night, he belonged to himself . . . and to Kamil.

No one noticed her amid the flood of people traipsing up and down the shuttlecraft's steps. Once on board, she stayed on board, keeping quietly to herself in the sealed-off private quarters belonging to the king. Her days were long and lonely, passed in anticipation of the nights.

Their love for each other deepened and strengthened during this time, the first time they'd spent more than a few stolen hours together.

"I was a puzzle with pieces missing, until now," said Kamil, embracing Dion. "I couldn't put any part of myself together. My soul was filled with holes, with jagged edges. You came and rearranged everything and filled up the empty places."

"You are the only person who cares about me—*me*," said Dion, stroking the short-cut silvery hair that was silky and warm beneath his hand. "To all the others I am a something—a king, a commander, a ruler, an idol, a father figure (he did not mention husband). But to you I'm a man. Just a man."

"Perhaps," she teased, "that's because when I first saw you, you were naked as a newborn child. I'll never forget that moment. I was sitting in the shadows of the trees on the shoreline when I heard splashing and saw you pull yourself up out of the water, your body white as marble against the deep blue, your hair flaring like flame when you shook the water out. You laughed out loud for the sheer joy of being alive and my heart laughed with you. You took my breath away. I'd never seen any man like you—young and strong and beautiful.

"I didn't know who you were, where you'd come from. I thought, perhaps, you were a god. But then you began to play in the water like a child, and I knew you were not a god, but a man, someone I could love, not worship. I had to meet you; I couldn't let you go. I saw your clothes lying on the other side of the lake and I hurried over and picked them up and brought them back. And then you saw me. You turned red as fire." Kamil laughed at the memory.

"You didn't seem all that impressed," Dion told her, blushing all over again at the thought. "You accused me of wanting to steal your fish."

"Instead you stole my heart," whispered Kamil.

But in their bliss was pain: the pain of knowing that their time together was short.

"I can't help but be angry," Dion said one night, the two of them sitting down to a late supper. "Why were we brought together if we were not meant to *be* together? I need you, Kamil. I need you by my side. You are the only person I can talk to, the only one who understands. You are the shieldwife in my dream—the one who guards my weak side. I would to God you *were* my wife! Why, why did I let myself get entangled in this travesty of a marriage?"

"You did what you had to do, what you needed to do at the time," Kamil said quietly. Moving around to stand behind his chair, she rubbed his shoulders. "You're too tense. Relax."

He raised his head to kiss her. She kissed the back of his neck, continued their earlier conversation. "And you know that if you had it to do all over again, you would do the same thing. Without DiLuna's fleet, you would have lost the battle to the Corasians. Lady Maigrey's sacrifice would have been for nothing, Sagan's death meaningless. They gave their lives to make you king. What is your sacrifice, compared to theirs?"

He twisted around to face her. "You make me feel like that naked kid stranded on that rock again. You're right." Taking hold of her hand, he brought the palm to his lips, kissed it, pressed it against his cheek. "Do you see *why* I need you? Someday—"

"No, don't say that. Don't even think it," she said quickly, putting her hand over his mouth. "To wish for that wishes harm on someone else. And a wish like that is a cursed wish, so my father says, and, once wished aloud, it could turn on the one who spoke it."

Dion assured her he'd meant no harm to anyone. D'argent served their meal; no servants traveled with the king on this trip. The secretary lingered to make certain all was well, and was on his way out to leave the two in private when he was summoned to the bridge by Captain Cato.

Chapter ❦ Nineteen

Angels and ministers of grace defend us!
Be thou a spirit of health or goblin damn'd,
Bring with thee airs from heaven or blasts from hell,
Be thy intents wicked or charitable,
Thou com'st in such a questionable shape
That I will speak to thee ...
　　　　　William Shakespeare, *Hamlet*, Act 1, Scene iv

The robed and hooded figure approached the shuttlecraft long after darkness had fallen. He came on foot, startling the guards by emerging out of the shadows around the brightly lit spaceport. He had, it appeared, taken care to avoid the flooding lights that illuminated the tarmac and turned night to white, artificial day. He seemed to wish to avoid, too, the ever-watchful eyes of the remote press cams, who kept eager watch on all those visiting His Majesty.

The hooded man kept his voice low, was careful to remain in the shadows as he spoke to His Majesty's guards. He was clad in the long black cassock that marked a brother of the Order of Adamant. He kept his cowl pulled over his head; his face was hidden in darkness. He walked hunched over, stooped, but the guards had the impression that he was a tall man, powerfully built.

He spoke only two words—"Archbishop Fideles"—and handed the guards his credentials.

Taking these, leaving the priest, standing within the perimeter of the circle of steel that surrounded the king, the guard hurried to the shuttlecraft, relayed the disk, which contained the archbishop's personal request that His Majesty receive this messenger immediately.

Cato ascertained that the credentials were bona fide, but he was reluctant to disturb His Majesty. Instead, the captain disturbed D'argent. The two met privately—at Cato's insistence—inside the secretary's small, yet elegantly appointed quarters aboard the shuttlecraft.

"There's something strange about this monk or whatever he is, sir," said Cato. "Everything checks out, but ... I don't know ... I think we should tell him to come back in the morning."

D'argent regarded Cato with interest. "I've never heard you talk like this, Captain. Is the man dangerous, do you think?"

Cato answered without hesitation. "Yes, he's dangerous. But maybe not to His Majesty. Not directly, anyhow." The captain smiled ruefully, shook his head. "I know I'm not making a lot of sense, D'argent. But I'd like to see this monk in broad daylight. I'd like to see his face. We asked him to remove his hood, but he refused. Said he'd taken a vow.... It's odd." Cato paused, frowning.

"What's odd?"

"I swear there's something familiar about this man! My hand itched to yank off that hood. I didn't," Cato added hurriedly, noting D'argent's look of consternation. "But I thought about it."

"I'm glad you restrained yourself, Captain," the secretary said severely. "The archbishop would have considered such an act of violence against one of his own messengers an insult."

"I know." The captain's expression was grave. "But that wasn't the reason I didn't touch him."

"What was the reason, Captain?"

"I didn't dare," said Cato softly. "Look, sir, it's like this. Have you ever stood near a high-voltage electrical wire? You hear the hum of the power surging through it. You can feel the aura of that power. It makes the hair stand up on your arms."

D'argent nodded to show he understood.

"Well, sir," said Cato, "I would as soon think of touching a high-tension wire as touch that strange monk outside."

D'argent studied the captain intently. Cato had served the king ever since he had come to the throne, had been a centurion under Lord Sagan's command fifteen years before that. The captain was levelheaded, pragmatic, certainly not given to flights of fancy, premonitions, or dark forebodings. Cato had dealt with thousands, millions of people—humans and aliens—over the course of his service to the king. Some of them had been violent, some had presented a real and cogent threat. Cato had handled all emergencies with efficiency and dispatch. No talk then of high-tension wires.

D'argent was uneasy. "You scanned him for weapons, I presume?"

"Of course, sir. Nothing. He's clean."

"You can't give me any other reason for your suspicions, Captain?"

"Logical reasons, you mean?" Cato's mouth tightened. "No, sir, I can't. It's just . . . when he spoke to me . . . when I heard his voice . . . something went right through me. A jolt, a kind of shiver. I've never felt the like."

D'argent sighed. "I'm sorry, Captain, but unless you can come up with some valid reason for keeping this monk away from His Majesty, I'll have to admit him, if that is what the king commands. His Majesty has been expecting a messenger from the archbishop. And the archbishop's messenger requests a private audience with His Majesty."

"That, in any case, we should *not* allow," said Cato grimly.

D'argent continued to ponder, then shook his head. "We may not have much choice. It will be up to His Majesty." Crossing over to a console, he flicked on the commlink.

Dion's voice. "Yes, D'argent? What is it?"

"Excuse me for disturbing you, sir, but the messenger from Archbishop Fideles is here and requests a private audience with you this evening."

"He's here now? Who is it?"

"A Brother Penitent, sir. His credentials check out. The archbishop has sent a personal message, requests you talk with his representative immediately upon arrival. The matter is, according to the archbishop, extremely urgent."

There was a moment's silence. Kamil's voice could be heard in the background, low and reassuring. D'argent couldn't make out her words, but he guessed from the tone that she was urging the king to see this visitor. Never mind that she had spent the day alone, looking forward to this time together, these few precious, stolen moments. D'argent smiled sadly, sighed briefly.

When Dion's voice returned, he sounded troubled. "Very well. Escort this Brother Penitent to the meeting room. Bring him food and drink and anything else he requires. I'll be there in a few moments."

"Very good, sir. And excuse me, sir, but Captain Cato recommends that you keep the Royal Guard with you during the interview. There's something about this Brother Penitent Cato doesn't trust."

"The archbishop requested a private audience with his representative?"

"Yes, sire."

"Then the audience will be private, D'argent. So inform the captain."

"Yes, Your Majesty." D'argent glanced over at Cato, shrugged.

The centurion shook his head.

D'argent himself accompanied Cato back outside the shuttlecraft. The secretary was curious not only to see this formidable personage who had given the veteran captain of the guard a "jolt," but to make certain that the roving cams of the media had not fastened onto this midnight visitor.

At first D'argent could see no sign of anything out of the routine. The guards walked their patrol, human eyes double-checking, backing up electronic surveillance. The centurions had hustled their visitor off to the mobile command unit, were keeping him well concealed.

Reasonably satisfied that none of the media had spotted the monk, yet thinking it might be just as well to be prepared with a press release tomorrow in case they had, D'argent entered the mobile command unit to get a look at the messenger.

Brother Penitent stood alone, patient, silent, his face hidden, his head lowered, his hands clasped within the sleeves of his cassock. D'argent noted the shabby material, well worn, almost threadbare in places. This man was not a monk, not a priest. He had not taken orders. He was a lay brother, one who might almost be classified as a servant. A strange emissary from the head of the Church to the king of the galaxy.

Yet, as Cato said, there was something about this man . . .

"If you will accompany me, please, Brother," D'argent said respectfully. "His Majesty will see you now."

The brother inclined his head, made no remark. Flanked by Captain Cato and two of his men, they left the command unit, walked across the tarmac to the shuttlecraft. The night was still, the air clear and soft with the smells of new life coming to the land. A myriad of stars were scattered across the black vault of the sky.

Their footsteps crunched on the gravel that was scattered—like the stars, except in a more lowly setting—on the concrete pavement. D'argent's footfalls were quiet, his tread delicate. The centurions' footfalls were measured, rhythmic, as if they walked a parade ground. And so, too, D'argent noticed, startled, were the footfalls of the lay brother.

The secretary glanced down, saw the brother, in his frayed robes and leather sandals, unconsciously matching his strides in military precision to those of the centurions.

D'argent wondered that Cato did not notice this odd occurrence, could not think of any subtle way of drawing the captain's attention to it. The secretary was not even certain that he should; there could be many plausible explanations for the fact that a monk marched like a soldier.

By this time they had reached the shuttlecraft. Most interior and exterior lights had been dimmed for the night. Hatches opened silently, absorbed D'argent and the strange visitor into the shadows, closed and sealed silently behind them.

"This way, please," said D'argent.

He led Brother Penitent into the shuttlecraft's interior, down a narrow corridor, to His Majesty's audience chamber. The brother followed silently, without hesitation. He did not raise his head, appeared to take no interest in his surroundings, hardly seemed to look where he was going.

D'argent, glancing continually and uneasily over his shoulder, had the sudden, uncanny impression that this was because the brother knew exactly where he was. That he could have walked the decks blindfolded.

"In here," said D'argent. The door slid open. The secretary stood to one side. "His Majesty will be with you shortly. Can I bring you anything, Brother? Something to eat, perhaps? A glass of wine?"

A negative movement of the hooded head was the only response.

D'argent glanced significantly at Cato, who had come up behind him. The captain nodded and left. The door slid shut, sealed, locking the strange brother alone inside. The captain and his men would keep the monk under constant surveillance through the room's hidden cameras.

Dion emerged from his private quarters, walked down the corridor to the audience chamber. Though the hour was late, he was not casually dressed for this meeting. He had taken care to change his clothes, was wearing his black uniform, his purple sash and lion's-head pin. He was troubled. Fideles would not have sent a personal messenger, would not have claimed urgency unless the matter was serious.

He found D'argent waiting for him. The normally unflappable secretary was disturbed, shaken.

"What is it, D'argent?" Dion asked, pausing outside the door before entering. "Did the press get hold of this?"

"No, Your Majesty. I don't believe so. Might I suggest, sir, that you take a look at this Brother Penitent before you—"

"Stop, Your Majesty!" Captain Cato's shout echoed off the metal bulkheads. The captain and his men came running down the corridor, lasguns in hand. "Don't go in there, sire!"

Weapons drawn, the King's Guard surrounded him.

"Why? What's happened?" Dion demanded.

"Either something's gone wrong with the surveillance equipment or that man in there has somehow managed to shut it down."

Dion caught his breath, stared at the closed door. For an instant he couldn't move, couldn't think. A blackness came over him, blotted out all light. A roaring sound in his head deafened him. The captain, the shuttle, the door began drifting out of reach, receding into the distance, falling farther and farther away from him. . . .

"Sire!" D'argent caught hold of the king.

The secretary's firm touch dispelled the faintness, brought Dion back.

Cato had his hand on the door's emergency manual release. "You men escort His Majesty back to his quarters—"

"Belay that, Captain," the king ordered sharply. He felt chilled, numb, as if all the warmth of life had drained from his body. "The surveillance equipment has probably malfunctioned. One of the technicians can check it out in the morning. Stand aside."

"But, Your Majesty—"

Dion stared at the man.

"Yes, Your Majesty." Reluctantly Cato moved away from the door, though he did not lower his weapon. "If Your Majesty will permit me to enter first—"

"That will not be necessary, Captain. I will go alone, as the archbishop requested. Post the guard, as usual, then return to your duties."

"Yes, Your Majesty."

Dion shifted his gaze to his secretary, who had been holding on to the king's arm.

D'argent flushed, removed his hand. "Sire, if you would allow me to accompany you—"

"Thank you, D'argent, but that will be all for this evening. You may return to your room."

The secretary had no choice but to bow and leave, first exchanging a worried glance with Cato, who had no choice but to bow and do as the king commanded.

Dion was alone. His face set rigid, limbs so cold he had lost all power of feeling, he placed his nerveless hand on the manual override, but at that moment the door slid open.

All other electronic systems in the room had gone dead. No lights shone, not even the emergency lights.

The robed and hooded man stood by the window. His back was turned; he did not look around. His tall figure was a black nothingness bounded by the cold white shimmer of the stars.

Dion shut his eyes, gathering his strength, his courage. Drawing in a deep breath, trying to ease the painful throbbing of his heart, he walked into the room.

The door shut and sealed behind him.

A single light flashed on overhead. The white beam, harsh and bright, illuminated the king. He was blinded, could no longer see the man by the window. But he heard the rustle of his robes, guessed that the man had turned, was studying him.

Dion stood unblinking in the harsh light, stood unmoving during the harsher surveillance.

Brother Penitent left the window, walked to the king. He blotted out the light. His shadow passed over Dion, like the wings of a dark angel.

He knelt, sank to one knee. "God keep Your Majesty," he said, his tone cool, impassive.

"Thank you . . . Lord Sagan," Dion answered "Please rise, my lord."

"I am Brother Paenitens," Sagan corrected, humbly standing. He lifted his hands, removed the cowl from his head. "Derek Sagan is dead."

Dion stared, astounded at the change only a few years had wrought. The thick black hair was completely silver gray at the temples; the lines in the face were deeply, severely etched; the eyes bitter, shadowed.

"My appearance shocks you," said Sagan dryly. "I thought I looked rather well . . . for a corpse."

Too late, Dion realized he'd allowed his feelings to show. He adjusted his face, carefully concealing the pity and compassion that would be met with scorn. He changed the subject; a king's prerogative.

"Yet I know Lord Sagan *is* alive and he is here, for only he would be familiar enough with his own shuttlecraft to disable the monitors and manipulate the electronics."

Sagan stood in the darkness, well out of the single shaft of white light, but Dion could still see, on the man's thin lips, the twisted smile.

"Cato is an excellent officer," commented the Warlord. "Intelligent, astute. He recognized me, although he doesn't realize it. His mind rebels against what his heart is trying to tell him. If I had remained longer under his surveillance, he would have figured out the truth."

"He would die before he betrayed your secret."

"I am aware of that, my liege," said Sagan quietly. "But Brother Paenitens entered this shuttlecraft and Brother Paenitens will leave it."

Dion caught himself about to sigh, checked it. The mark of the man's suffering was plain upon his face. Dion could not hope to understand it, could only pray to God that he would be spared such anguish. But wasn't repentance supposed to bring peace to a trouble soul? What terrible battle still raged in this one?

"As you wish, my lord. I may call you that? So long as you are here? It seems . . . more natural."

Sagan shrugged, did not reply. He had turned away and was once more staring out the window.

How many times have I seen him thus? Dion asked himself silently, his heart aching with memories, some of them disturbing and painful. But that was long ago, when he and I traveled among the stars. Here, the stars shine down upon us and we stand in darkness.

"It is good to see you again, my lord." Dion spoke awkwardly, uncertain how to proceed. "What have you been——"

"Pardon, my liege," said Sagan, turning around. "But His Holiness did not send me all this distance to make polite conversation."

"Very well, my lord," Dion replied coolly, "what news have you brought? It must be important for you to come yourself."

"My news is vital. You are in danger, my liege. The crown itself is in peril."

Dion shrugged, smiled. "Danger is part of a ruler's life, my

lord, as you well know. I receive threats against my life daily.
I've survived four assassination attempts. Nevertheless, I thank
the archbishop for his concern. What is the source of this present danger, my lord?"

"You know the source," Sagan answered unexpectedly.
Reaching out his right hand, he took hold of Dion's, held it—
palm up—to the light. "You've seen him."

Dion's smile vanished, lips compressing to a thin line. He
looked down at his hand, at the five marks on the inside of the
palm that were swollen and red. Swiftly he snatched it from
Sagan's grasp. The fingers curled in, hiding the scars.

"Who is he?" Dion asked in a low voice.

"Your cousin, my liege," said Sagan. "Your first cousin. The
only son of your late uncle, the king."

"Son?" Dion stared, incredulous. "My uncle was never married. He died childless."

"He died unmarried. Not childless. He fathered a son."

"Are you saying . . . Is my cousin the rightful heir to the
throne?"

"No, Your Majesty," answered the Warlord grimly. "He has
no legitimate claim to it. But I fear, sire, that this will not stop
him. . . ."

Chapter ❊◦❊◦❊ Twenty

And like a devilish engine recoils
Upon himself; horror and doubt distract
His troubled thoughts, and from the bottom stir
The Hell within him ...

John Milton, *Paradise Lost*

"And that is the story, my liege." Sagan concluded his report.

"My God!" Dion raised his head. He was pale, shaken. "Is this possible? Can this doctor be believed?"

"A deathbed confession, my liege?" Sagan asked wryly. "Made to the archbishop himself? Yes, I believe it. More importantly"—he raised his right hand, palm out—"I believe *this*."

Dion made no reply. Sickened in body and in soul, he tried to wade through the chaotic thoughts that swirled in his mind like oil on the surface of turgid water. He was nauseated; there was a foul taste in his mouth. He glanced up vaguely as Sagan rose to his feet, began to pace the room.

"How could no one have known?" Dion demanded. "You, my lord! Didn't you suspect?"

Sagan stopped pacing, regarded the king with amazement. "My liege, I was not even born yet when Princess Jezreel disappeared from the palace. I believe I heard mention of her, on occasion, but I honestly can't recall in what regard.

"Forgive me for saying this, Your Majesty," he added dryly, "but I despised the entire Starfire family. I cared little what happened in their personal lives."

Dion stirred in resentful anger. "My father—" he began.

"Your father was the best of a bad lot," Sagan interrupted impatiently, "who had sense enough to do one worthwhile thing in his entire life. He married your mother."

Dion considered it politic to revert back to the original subject, unpleasant though it might be.

"But how could such crimes be hidden? If, as the doctor

said, my . . . my"—Dion licked his dry lips—"aunt had committed murder—"

"Covering it up would not have been difficult," said Sagan. "You must understand something, my liege. Nothing could ever be permitted to taint the Blood Royal. How could the genetic scientists admit they'd made a mistake? What scandal, what panic would this have caused among the populace? How could they be told that there was a possibility such powerful beings as ourselves were subject to the weaknesses of ordinary mortals? What faults we had were held to be on the side of the angels, not demons.

"Of course the terrible incident had to be concealed. I am certain it was handled with aplomb, dispatch. The murdered victim's body disposed of quietly, quickly. Your aunt hustled off, with some excuse made for her disappearance—anything from a publicly announced decision to join a nunnery to the staging of her own funeral would have been easy for the king's handlers to manage. After that, they take care that the princess is rarely mentioned, her name not avoided, but never brought up. She fades from sight, fades from memory. From all memories except one."

Dion shuddered. He slumped in his chair. He was suffocating, unbuttoned the collar of the heavy jacket. Sweat trickled down his scalp; his body chilled.

Sagan stared out the window, out into the stars. "The one thing in all of this I don't understand, the one factor that does not compute, is Pantha."

Dion looked up. "Who is this Pantha? I mean, I know who he is or was, but why is he so important? He's been dead for years."

"Because—dead or not—he is the link between two seemingly disparate, unconnected occurrences: the birth of the king's illegitimate son twenty-eight years ago, and the rise of a force calling itself the Ghost Legion twenty-eight years later. What planet does this Legion give as its home base? Vallombrosa—Vale of Shades. And who discovered Vallombrosa? Garth Pantha."

"And he took the baby," said Dion, his interest caught.

"And that's what doesn't make sense. Consider this, Your Majesty." Sagan left the window, came to stand before the king. "Pantha was an intergalactic hero. From what I've read, he deserved his reputation. He was Blood Royal. He had fame, wealth. He was a skilled pilot, a brilliant scientist. He was a man of insatiable curiosity, who lived for exploration, discovery. He had no family, no settled home, but was constantly on the move, constantly seeking adventure."

"I see your point," murmured Dion. "Why would such a man saddle himself with a child?"

"And shortly afterward disappear."

"According to Dixter, Pantha was marooned in deep space. Evidence indicated he blew up his spaceplane rather than die a slow death—"

"Not Pantha." Sagan shook his head. "I remember that I was skeptical at the time. He was the type who would have fought to survive to the last breath. Such a 'death' would have been easy to fake. No body. Only remnants of his plane, drifting in space."

"Was his death investigated?"

"Of course, my liege. It created an enormous sensation, the mystery of the century. The evidence that he'd blown himself up was circumstantial, at best. One simple fact finally made everyone believe he truly was dead."

"And that was?"

Sagan shrugged. "No one ever saw or heard from him again."

Dion considered this, pondering.

"If he'd been a recluse during his life," Sagan continued, "if he had detested notoriety, avoided it, people would have accepted the notion that he staged his own death in order to disappear from view. But Pantha was a celebrity. He adored attention, courted it. He was a vid star. His name was a household word for billions throughout the galaxy. For such a man to vanish from the public eye, there could be only one explanation—he was dead."

"Either that," said Dion slowly, "or he had discovered something so valuable that it would make up for everything he would lose, something he had no intention of sharing with anyone else."

"A king's son," said Sagan quietly.

"An illegitimate king's son," Dion countered. "A product of an incestuous relationship that would never be countenanced by any society in the galaxy!"

"Yet the boy is a child of the Blood Royal. True, your cousin might be a feebleminded genetic mess. But he might also be a genetic wonder."

Dion stared down at his hand, at the swollen scars. He began to rub the palm.

"Burns, doesn't it, my liege?" said Sagan.

"Yes," Dion replied, frustrated. "It burns and aches. Every time I use the bloodsword the pain grows worse. And the dreams are more frequent. But how did you know?"

Sagan held out his arm, pulled back the long sleeve of his robe to reveal his own hand. He turned it palm up.

"You, too, then," Dion said. "But how? How is he doing this?"

"Through the bloodsword. As I once told you, those who use it can—if they are strong—gain ascendancy over the minds of others. Your cousin hasn't managed that. Yet he has touched us."

"The bloodsword? But how would he get hold of one?. . ." Dion paused, answered his own question. "Pantha's."

"Precisely. Perhaps the most valid evidence we have that Garth Pantha did *not* perish in space twenty-eight years ago."

"But you haven't used the bloodsword! Yours was destroyed, unless . . ." Dion hesitated.

"Unless I have reverted back to my old ways? No, my liege." Sagan let the long, loose flowing sleeve fall, smoothed the coarse fabric over his arm, hiding his hand. "I took a vow, when I took my new name, that I would never in this life set my hand to a tool of death. It is a vow I have not broken, nor will I. But I used the bloodsword for many years. Our cousin—he is my relation, too, by the way, though distantly—would have little difficulty establishing an affinity with me, a crude sort of mind-link. After all, *you* knew I was not truly dead."

"But why is he doing this, my lord? What does he want?"

"Think back, Dion," said Sagan slowly. "Think back to a seventeen-year-old boy who stole a spaceplane and flew to meet a Warlord who had been responsible for the deaths of hundreds, including a man this boy loved. Do you remember that boy, Dion? When he came to me, he placed in jeopardy not only his own life, but those of his friends. Why did that boy risk it? Why did he come to me? Why seek me out?"

"I wanted to know the truth," said Dion defensively, feeling vaguely as if he'd been accused of a crime. "Who I was. What I was."

"Your only reason, my liege?"

Dion remained silent, not answering.

Sagan reached out, took hold of the king's hand. He touched the sore palm, probed the scars. The Warlord's touch was gentle, yet Dion flinched.

"You were drawn to me like a comet is drawn to its sun. You didn't know why you came, what you sought ... until you set foot on my ship. Then you felt it. Then you knew. You wanted what I had, Dion. That is why you came. And that is why your cousin has come."

" 'The taint in our blood,' as Lady Maigrey said to me once." Dion smiled faintly, sadly, at the memory. He shook his head, drew back from the past, returned to the present. "But if that is true, my lord, why has this cousin—if that's really who and what he is—waited? It seems to me that he would have chosen— My lord?"

Sagan did not respond. He had abruptly walked away. His back was turned; he was staring out the window. Dion saw, by the lambent light of the stars, that the Warlord's right fist was clenched tight, so tight it trembled with the force. The knuckles of the clenched hand were white, as if the bones were laid bare. His face, reflected in the steelglass, was cold, hard, and bleak.

Bleak as the moon on which Maigrey had died, cold as the bier of stones he had made for her.

Dion's heart ached. He hadn't thought, when he'd spoken her name, of the pain this must bring to the man who had loved her, who had been doomed to watch her die in his arms.

What can I say? Dion wondered. What comfort can I offer? What words exist that can possibly assuage such bitter grief? I should not even be seeing this, he realized. Sagan wouldn't thank me for intruding. He doesn't want my sympathy; certainly not my pity.

Dion crossed to the opposite side of the chamber, poured himself a glass of water. He drank it slowly. The thought came to him of what it would be like to lose Kamil. More terrible than that, to know that he was responsible for her death. The memory of a dream came to him, of his shieldmaid falling at his side, of blows raining down on her, of himself helpless, unable to protect her. . . .

"The question is, my liege, what do you do now?" Sagan's voice was harsh, unexpectedly close.

Dion's hand jerked; he nearly spilled the water. Hastily, he set the glass down, banished the dream, turned to face the Warlord, who had come up behind him silently, unobserved.

"What do you mean, what do I do?" Dion asked, irritated at having been caught off guard. "What *can* I do? If this cousin even exists—and we have no proof that he does, only conjecture—we don't know where he is—"

"He exists, Your Majesty. Have no doubt of that. And he's told us where: Vallombrosa."

"Nonsense. It's a dead planet. There's nothing there—"

"On the contrary, my liege. We have been made to *think* there is nothing there."

"Very well, my lord, what would *you* do?" Dion demanded, losing patience. "What is your advice and counsel?"

Sagan fell silent, studied him, measured him. "Do you truly want it?"

"Yes, my lord." Dion sighed. "I presume that this is the reason you chose to come to me in the first place."

"I did not choose to come. I was commanded to come," Sagan returned bitterly. "But now that I am here, I will give you my advice, though I don't expect you to take it."

The Warlord drew forth a leather thong that he wore around his neck, well hidden by the thick folds of the cowl that lay on his shoulders. He gave the thong a swift, sharp tug. It broke, came off in his hand. He held out the thong—and the unlovely jewel that dangled from it—to Dion.

"This is my counsel, my liege. Take the starjewel and place it in the space-rotation bomb. The jewel is the triggering device; it will activate the bomb. Travel to Vallombrosa and launch the bomb into the planet's heart. Detonate it, destroy everything for a radius of a million miles. And when you have done that, Sovereign, send in your army and your navy and command them to destroy everything for a million miles more."

Dion stared at the Warlord, aghast. "You can't be serious! If Vallombrosa *is* populated, then I would be committing genocide, slaughtering untold members of innocent people! You know I couldn't possibly do such a thing. And neither would you, my lord."

Sagan held the starjewel in his hand. Once, long ago, the beautiful rare jewel, carved in the shape of an eight-pointed star, had shone as brightly as the true stars in the night sky above. Now it was blacker than the very night itself.

"Do not be so quick to judge me, Dion," the Warlord said

gravely, his gaze on the jewel. He suddenly clenched his fist over it. "The danger is real. If it were me, I would be very tempted to end it. . . ."

Dion shook his head. "We know nothing for certain. We don't know if this cousin is even alive, much less that he intends me harm—"

"If he did not, my liege, would he be doing this?" The Warlord held up his scarred palm.

"He wants to get our attention," Dion admitted. "That much is obvious. If only my uncle . . . Damn it, how could he do such a thing? He was deeply religious—"

"Oh, yes, he was religious. He leaned on his religion, used it as a crutch to prop up his own weakness. I've no doubt that every morning after spending the night coupling with his sister, Amodius prayed for God's forgiveness. And he blamed God when he lacked the strength to give up his obsession. Witness what he does when the illicit relationship bears fruit. Instead of taking responsibility, he hands it back to God. 'A judgment for his sins.' A judgment, all right. But it will not fall on his head. It will fall on yours."

Sagan thrust the starjewel into a pocket of his robes. "At least *my* father admitted, accepted, and paid for his sin."

Dion recalled, then, that Derek Sagan himself was the product of an illicit relationship, a brutal crime, a father who could not control his passions. . . .

"Unless, of course, Amodius was more devious than we give him credit for," Sagan added quietly, almost to himself.

"What do you mean, my lord?" Dion came out of a troubled reverie.

"He could have deposited the child anonymously on someone's doorstep. Cast the baby adrift in a boat of rushes, so to speak. What are the odds that anyone who found the child would have discovered his true identity?"

"You found me," Dion pointed out.

"Ah, but you were *meant* to be found," Sagan said dryly. "By giving his son to Garth Pantha, who knew the child's heritage, knew his lineage, Amodius also meant his boy to be 'found.' Think about it. Do you begin to understand what I mean about the danger?"

"Yes," Dion conceded. "And if our cousin is this dangerous, it seems to me that our wisest course would be to keep the space-rotation bomb safely hidden from him. Not send it to him."

"Judging by Dixter's reports, it may not remain hidden for long," Sagan remarked gravely.

"The so-called ghosts? Do you know what they are?"

"I have an idea, but I would prefer not to speculate. It is imperative, however, that we learn the truth."

"You must go to him," said Dion quietly.

"Yes, my liege, I must go to him."

"Are you certain? If you're right, you could be in danger—"

"Not me, my liege," stated Sagan, mouth twisting. "*I* am the one he wants."

Dion let out a held breath, slowly, softly. "Yes. I see. Of course, you're right. All of this: sending you to hear the doctor, the 'Ghost Legion,' the attack on Snaga Ohme's—"

"—done deliberately to draw me out."

"But he must believe you to be dead. . . ."

"I repeat—you knew I was alive. He does, too."

"But why? What does he want?" Dion demanded.

"He seeks me as you sought me. And for the same reason."

"And you think he'll trust you?"

"I can make him trust me, my liege."

And you can make *me* trust you, Dion added silently. But do I? Is your ambition truly dead . . . or is it merely hidden beneath those shabby robes? Who are you? Lord Sagan or Brother Paenitens? Do *you* know for certain? What is it that *you* want? . . .

"What do I want?" Sagan asked, repeating aloud the words the king had spoken only in his thoughts.

The Warlord did not answer, but turned his back, walked over to the window, stared out at the stars. At length he said, "I chose penitence as my name when I left the world. I meant to repent, to seek God's forgiveness, my own redemption." He glanced around. "Do you know what the other brethren in the abbey call me? The Unforgiven. They know the truth, you see. There has been no answer to my prayers. No response. Only silence. Empty, terribly silence. Has the Lady Maigrey come to you, my liege?"

Startled at the strange and unexpected question, Dion grappled for an answer. "I . . . I thought I saw her . . . her spirit, that is . . . the night of the dedication."

He thought back; the memory returned to him and he was

surprised at how vivid it was. "She said nothing to me, but I felt comforted. She stayed with me until the end of my speech and, before she left, she raised her hand—as if in warning. Of course," he added, realizing suddenly how foolish he must sound, "I was under a great deal of stress. And I was thinking about her. Small wonder that I imagined I saw her—"

"She has not come to me," said Sagan in quiet, impassive tones.

Dion made no response, had no idea what to say.

The Warlord turned his gaze back to the night. "I want to hear one word from the Creator, an answer to my prayers." He clenched his fist. "Even if it is only to tell me that there is no hope. That I am damned!"

Dion caught a glimpse of the man's soul, saw it a vast, black scape of desperation and anger, bitter regret and despair. And he was doomed to walk the charred and desolate plains alone now, lacking, apparently, even the guiding hand of his own faith. For these last three years, he had tread the barren ground in abject humility and penitence, sacrificing his pride and ambition at every roadside shrine. And, in return, no balm, no comfort, no spring of sweet water. Nothing—Dion saw suddenly, clearly—but another temptation. A luring voice to draw him off the path and into a night from which the Warlord might never return.

Dion had been raised an atheist, but he had been forced to abandon his complacent atheistic view of the universe. An atheist assumes he has all the answers. At seventeen, Dion had assumed *he* had all the answers. Innumerable perplexing and inexplicable occurrences had taught him otherwise. And now he was left with only questions.

Did I truly heal Tusk? Or was his own will to live responsible for what had looked like a miracle? Did I truly see the spirit of Lady Maigrey? Or was the eerie vision nothing more than an electrical short circuit in my brain? Is this sudden appearance of a mysterious cousin some sort of cosmic test? Or is it a random event, brought about by the inability of a weak man to control a sordid obsession? Is it a judgment? Or just some stupid, shabby—albeit potentially dangerous—happening?

Whatever it is, Sagan is right. I have to have answers. I have to know the truth.

And so does he.

"Very well, my lord," Dion said. "You will go, discover if my cousin truly lives. If so, find out what he means by these seemingly threatening actions. What does he want of us? We may have misjudged him. I hope we have. Contact Sir John Dixter for anything you might need—"

"Is it necessary to inform Dixter, Your Majesty?" Sagan asked, expression darkening.

"Yes, it is," said Dion, firm, resolute.

The Warlord gave the king a measuring glance. "Very well, my liege. I suppose it is for the best. But no one else must know. No one! Not your best friend, not your secretary, not the captain of the guard, not your wife . . . not your mistress."

Dion wondered uneasily if Sagan knew the truth or if he was merely emphasizing a point. Too late, it occurred to the king—feeling his skin flushed and burning—that if Sagan didn't know the truth before, he probably knew now.

"If word of this were to leak out . . ." the Warlord continued ominously.

"I quite understand, my lord." Dion ended the matter.

Sagan did not pursue it. "At any rate, I doubt if Dixter could lay his hand on what I want as readily as I can myself—a spaceplane, unmarked, unarmed. An older model, the type used by interplanetary missionaries prior to the Revolution."

Dion smiled wanly. "I doubt if the navy has those currently in stock. But perhaps some sort of concealed weaponry—"

"Your Majesty forgets the vows that I have taken," the Warlord interrupted. "Or perhaps he imagines that *I* have forgotten?"

Dion made no reply. He stood silent, on his guard, carefully keeping—this time—his thoughts to himself.

Sagan smiled, chill and dark. "Still, there is information I will need that Dixter might be able to acquire for me. Tell him that I will be in contact."

The Warlord gazed at Dion searchingly, intently. "He will demand your sanction, my liege. To give it, you must place implicit trust in me. Do you, my liege? If not, then I cannot be of use to you. Brother Paenitens will leave and never return."

Dion hesitated. He recalled the glimpse of that abandoned soul. He's testing me again, Dion thought, suddenly resentful. And the question came to him, unbidden: He may be, but who is testing him?

"I will give Dixter instructions to provide you with whatever you need, my lord."

Drawing the hood of his cowl up over his head, the Warlord—now once more a humble churchman—inclined his hooded head in silent acquiescence. Dion placed his hand on the manual override that would operate the door, was startled to feel Sagan's own strong, gaunt hand close over his wrist.

"A word of caution, Dion. From now on, do not use the bloodsword."

Dion regarded the Warlord coldly. "You have no need to worry, my lord. I can protect myself from him."

Sagan glanced pointedly at the king's hand. "Your cousin has entered your mind, Your Majesty. Have you entered his?"

"Thank you, my lord, for coming," said Dion. "You have leave to go."

Brother Paenitens pulled his hood lower over his head. "God bless and keep Your Majesty," he intoned, bowing low. His voice was muffled. Dion couldn't tell whether or not the blessing was meant in earnest or made in bitter mocking.

"Wait, my lord." Dion stopped Sagan as he was about to open the door. "What should I tell the archbishop? He'll be expecting your return. What should I say?"

Sagan raised his head; the dark eyes, with their flickering flame, met the king's.

"Ask him to pray for me, Your Majesty."

Bowing again, Brother Paenitens was gone.

Chapter ·─◆◇◆─· Twenty-one

Thou hast not half the power to do me harm
As I have to be hurt.
William Shakespeare, *Othello*, Act V, Scene ii

Dion advanced several paces down the corridor until, rounding a corner, he was out of sight of his guards. Then he came
to a stop. The door to his stateroom stood before him, closed
and sealed. Behind it, Kamil waited patiently for him. His dinner was cold by now, but that didn't matter. He had no appetite
left.

He remained standing where he was, needing to be by himself, to assimilate his thoughts, try to recover from the shock of
this news. It reminded Dion of the time he'd been wounded
during the adrenaline-pumped excitement of battle on board
the *Defiant*. He hadn't even known he'd been hit until someone
pointed it out, until he saw the blood staining his sleeve.

While he'd been talking with Sagan, the tension of the constant mental struggle waged between the two strong, opposing
wills had forced Dion to keep his thoughts focused on the combat. Sagan would have been quick to take advantage of any display of weakness on Dion's part, quick to rout, conquer, and
bend the younger man to doing the elder's will.

Dion was exhausted after the encounter, emotionally and
mentally drained. But at least he'd held his ground, stood firm,
refused to retreat from his convictions.

"I wonder if he respects me for it?" Dion asked himself wearily. "I wonder if he will ever respect me? And why do I care
what he thinks of me anyway? Why am I constantly seeking his
approval? I have the power he had and more. I am what he
wanted to be. And I attained my success through peaceful
means, not the bloody war he urged me to fight. I hope to be
a better ruler, a better man than he was. Yet, once, just once,
I'd like to hear him say to me, 'Well done.' "

Dion sighed. "I wish I could talk to Kamil about it. Perhaps
I will. She wouldn't tell anyone. She'd die before she'd betray

me. But then, I'd have to tell her everything—about my uncle. . . ." Dion grimaced, sickened, repulsed. "She wouldn't think any less of me. It wasn't *my* fault. I wonder if my father knew anything about what was going on? Still, it's a shameful, sordid, repugnant thing to have to reveal about one's own kin. No, Sagan's right . . ."

Do not tell your wife . . . or your mistress.

The Warlord's remonstration came back to Dion; again it made his face burn.

He was guessing, Dion decided. He couldn't possibly know the truth.

Dion stood up straight, critically examined his reflection in a steel bulkhead. He decided his face would pass even Kamil's loving scrutiny, and started to place his hand upon the security plate that would scan his palm, permit him to enter.

What makes your crime different from your uncle's?

Dion drew his hand away abruptly. Who had spoken? Sagan? Or some part deep inside of him; some part the moralists would undoubtedly term his conscience?

"Of course it's different," he reassured himself. "Our love is not incestuous! Not a sick obsession. It's love. I love Kamil and she loves me. We were meant to be together. Only a trick of fate keeps us apart. We're not hurting anyone else. And how can I break vows that held no meaning for me to begin with? Our love is right. Everything else in the universe may be wrong, but our love is right. . . ."

Resolutely, he placed his hand on the scanning pad. His identification verified, the door slid open.

Kamil shut the book she had been reading. She advanced toward him with a smile that soon faded. Apparently he had not arranged his face as carefully as he had hoped.

"What is it, Dion? What's happened? You can't tell me," she said quickly, sparing him the need to respond. "I'm sorry. I shouldn't have asked. Do you want me to leave? I—"

"My dear!" Dion took her in his arms, held her close, absorbing her strength, her comfort. "No, don't go. Not now. Not ever. I can't tell you what's going on. But it doesn't matter. Just let me hold you."

They clung to each other in silence. Dion could imagine her shield, held over him, protecting him from the blows aimed at him, giving him time to recover his strength, pick up his weapons, and return to the battle.

I will take this time, he decided. I should return to the palace, I suppose. I should inform Dixter of what I've learned. I should place the admiral in touch with Sagan.

But that can wait until tomorrow. Until the morning. It's bad enough that I must cut short my time with Kamil. I will have this night with her. I need this night. . . .

"Your Majesty." A voice, over the commlink.

Dion kissed Kamil's hair. Holding her, keeping her near, he answered. "Yes, D'argent?"

"Admiral Dixter needs to speak with you, Your Majesty. He is on the vidcom. It's . . . confidential."

Dion sighed. Kamil slid out from his embrace. "No, don't go!" he whispered. "Can't this wait until morning, D'argent?"

"The Admiral says the matter is one of extreme urgency, Your Majesty."

"I better talk to him. Hopefully I won't be long."

"I'll be here."

"I wish . . ." he said, pausing, "I wish sometimes I was . . . we were . . . ordinary. Like Tusk and Nola. Together all the time. Our biggest worry whether or not the collection agency was going to repossess the vid machine."

She didn't answer, lowered her eyes.

Dion sighed again. "It's humanity's curse, I suppose—never to be happy with what we have. Always wanting something else. When I was nobody, I didn't want to be. Now that I'm king, I wish I was nobody again."

"Go deal with your latest crisis, Your Majesty," Kamil told him softly. Kissing him on the cheek, she picked up her book and disappeared into the bedroom.

Arranging his face again, Dion walked back out into the corridor. D'argent was waiting for him, as was the captain of the guard.

"Yes, Captain?" said Dion, moving toward the communications room.

"The electrical disruption of the systems in the audience chamber has been fixed."

"Very good, Captain."

"We didn't fix it, Your Majesty," said Cato dourly. "It . . . seems to have fixed itself, so to speak."

"As long as it's working, Captain. I wouldn't be overly concerned with it. Instruct the technicians to examine it when we return to base."

"Yes, Your Majesty." Cato paused, stared at his king, as if wanting to add something else.

Dion met the captain's eyes, held them.

Cato's gaze wavered uncertainly.

"Was there something else on your mind, Captain?" Dion asked, pausing outside the door to the communications room.

"No . . . no, Your Majesty."

"Then you have leave to return to your duties, Captain," said the king.

"The admiral has requested that this conversation be kept strictly confidential, sir," D'argent repeated. "You will need to access the transmission yourself, highest level security. I will be in room, if you desire anything."

"Thank you, D'argent," said Dion, keeping his voice even, level.

He entered the room, shut and sealed the door, and began to go through the complicated process of opening the secured channel. It took some time. He waited with enforced patience while all systems checked and double-checked that the channel was secure, waited still longer while the transmission was scrambled, coded at Admiral Dixter's end, then descrambled, decoded at Dion's end. The king hoped the transmission wasn't a long one; he could be here for hours.

As it turned out, it was short. All too short.

"Your Majesty." Dixter's face appeared on the vidscreen. He looked exhausted; his skin was gray, face haggard. "I have bad news, I am afraid."

"Of course," Dion muttered to himself. "Nobody ever comes to me with urgent, top-secret good news. Yes, sir, what is it?" he asked aloud, bracing himself.

"The queen has left, Your Majesty."

Dion stared, perplexed, not understanding. So what if Astarte had left the palace? She left all the time. Her schedule of public appearances was almost as demanding as the king's.

He frowned. "I am afraid, admiral, that I fail to see—"

Dixter shook his head, forgot, in his worry, that he was speaking to his king. "What I'm trying to say, son, is that your wife has left *you*."

Chapter ❖ Twenty-two

> So farewell hope, and with hope, farewell fear,
> Farewell remorse! All Good to me is lost . . .
> > John Milton, *Paradise Lost*

Sagan walked rapidly across the tarmac, keeping to the shadows, leaving as he had come. He walked with his head covered, his arms crossed, hands clasping his wrists beneath the long, flowing sleeves of his habit, as was the custom among the brethren of the Order of Adamant.

He did not, however, walk toward the transport which had brought him to this planet, a transport owned by the Church, operated by a hired crew that ferried the priests of St. Francis to wherever in the galaxy their calling took them. Sagan had need of thought and he did not care to do his thinking under the curious stares of the night watch.

The hour was extremely late. An ancient clock in one of the towers chimed twice; the bell's echoes were almost immediately swallowed up by the darkness. The spaceport, though brightly lit, was quiet. No flights were expected in or out until morning. Sagan skirted the lights, kept out of sight of the night watchman, who was chatting companionably with one of the cleaning crew.

Numerous paths and walkways led from the spaceport to the Academy buildings. Some were old, others new, added during the phase of building and reconstruction that had been started under the auspices of the new king. Sagan chose one of the older paths, one he could walk without thinking about where it would take him, retracing the footsteps of the brash and arrogant youth who had walked that path some thirty years before.

The campus was deserted, halls of learning empty, classrooms dark. The night was clear; the path was easy to see, lit at intervals by glowing lamps that shed circles of light along the walkway and by the lambent light of moon and stars. Sagan did not walk aimlessly. He had his destination in mind and, though it was in one of the new buildings, he had, with characteristic

197

foresight and planning, studied a revised map of the Academy grounds and determined the route to take to reach it. His feet kept stolidly to the path; his thoughts were free to rampage.

He was angry, and he found it convenient to focus his anger on Dion. Why couldn't he see the danger—the extreme danger—he was in? They were all in?

"Certainly I didn't expect you to attack and destroy Vallombrosa without warning," he muttered. "I knew when I proposed such a plan you would reject it . . . as you should," he admitted somewhat grudgingly. "Though it would have been simple. Detonate the bomb in what, by all accounts, is an uninhabited region of the galaxy. Tell the people you are acting to rid the galaxy of a heinous weapon. Outwardly you appear the champion of peace; all the while destroying your enemy completely, utterly, with no one left alive to tell the tale.

"No, Dion, I didn't expect you to take the easy way out. I would have been disappointed in you if you had," he added, with the shadow of a dark smile on his lips.

The smile straightened to a thin, narrow line. "But you should have taken the starjewel. You should have taken it three years ago, when I offered it. You should have taken it now. A foolish move, my king. Not logical, not practical. It is all very well for a king to hold an olive branch in one hand, but he must hold steel in the other."

Three years ago. He had offered Dion the starjewel. Offered it over Maigrey's grave.

He thought back, tried to recall the king's words to him then, but he couldn't. Time had stopped for Derek Sagan the moment he had looked into her eyes and seen only the cold reflection of the stars. What had happened to him after that came to him in brief flashes, illuminated vividly by jagged bursts of pain. The rest was lost in a dark, chaotic storm of agony, grief, and howling silence. He remembered offering the starjewel, remembered that Dion had refused to take it. But what words he had used, what reason he gave were obliterated.

The king had left the Warlord alone with the dead. Sagan's body and mind had acted, dragging his unwilling soul along behind. He had fought hordes of Corasians in his efforts to return to his own galaxy. Fought them brilliantly, or so he presumed, simply because he would not have survived otherwise. He had been wounded—severely, they told him later. He didn't know. He didn't remember.

It was Brother Miguel who had found him, and they had proven to be each other's salvation. The sole survivor of Abdiel's plot to trap Sagan, Brother Miguel had seen his brethren murdered at the hands of the fearsome mind-dead. The brother had escaped by a mere fluke and, terror-stricken, had fled to the tombs far below the abbey, where he had hidden in fear until he had been discovered by Brother Fideles.

Fideles's hand had drawn Miguel back from the edge of madness, reminded him that his faith and trust must rest in God. Strengthened somewhat, Miguel had at last summoned the courage to leave his hiding place. He had discovered the mind-dead gone, the abbey deserted, except for the ghosts of his dear dead companions.

Dazed and bewildered, Miguel had wandered the desolate halls, envying the dead, feeling horribly guilty that he himself had survived. He had nowhere to go, for the abbey was built far from any city; the planet's atmosphere was harsh and lethal for those humans who ventured into it without sophisticated survival apparatus. The apparatus was present in the abbey, but Brother Miguel—having never before used it—had only the vaguest idea how to operate it.

The young brother might well have sunk back into the madness from which he'd only just emerged, had not the spaceplane crash-landed outside the abbey's walls.

The noise and flames brought Miguel rushing to one of the windows. He saw the plane on fire, saw a figure—silhouetted black against the flames—stagger out of it, fall to the ground.

All thoughts of himself had vanished in his concern for the wounded man. Miguel had struggled into the breathing mask, praying to God to show him how to use it. Thanks to either God's intervention or the instructions printed on the side of the oxygen tank, Miguel managed to equip himself to brave the harsh, unbreathable atmosphere. He had even had the presence of mind to remember to take an additional breathing device for the injured pilot.

Miguel half-dragged, half-carried the wounded pilot back to the abbey. Both were safe inside the sheltering walls when the spaceplane blew up in a rolling ball of fire.

Miguel had no idea who the pilot was, would never know the truth. The brother was, at first, overwhelmed at the extent of the man's injuries, thought he must surely die. Miguel was not a doctor, but he had worked in the infirmary, and he treated the pilot with what medicines he had available, supplementing these with devotion and fervent prayer.

He had succeeded and the day his patient's fever broke and he opened his eyes and looked in wonder around him, Brother Miguel knew two people had been saved, not just one. He had gone down on his knees and wept and whispered, "Thank God!"

Brother Miguel had afterward reported to Brother Fideles, on Fideles' return to the abbey (following a mysterious journey, the details of which he was always somewhat vague about relating), that the pilot's first words were an echo of Miguel's.

"Thank God."

It was well, perhaps, that Miguel, caught up in his own joy, had not noticed the tone in which these words were said. He had not realized that they were spoken in sarcasm, more a curse than a blessing; a bitter denunciation, hurled in God's teeth.

It was not until some weeks later that Derek Sagan, kneeling at the tomb of his father, had come to accept the fact that he was alive and that God expected something more of him. He'd assumed, at the time, it was to do penance for his sins, for sins of pride and of arrogance, for daring to think he—puny mortal—knew God's mind, for daring to act in God's stead, judging who should live and who should die.

And so, for three long years, he had done penance. He had lain down in the dust, he had fasted, scourged his flesh, worked selflessly to the point of collapse, and prayed, always prayed.

Never an answer. Never a word. No relief from the torment of the emptiness within him, the absence of her voice. Even during those long years when she was in exile, when the mind-link had been broken, still he heard her voice in his soul, like the strains of a half-remembered, well-loved aria.

That God should have abandoned him did not overly surprise Sagan. That Maigrey should have left him to fight this battle alone was devastating, galling.

Faith seeped away. Anger and doubt crept in to fill the void. And now this . . . this temptation. For Sagan recognized it for what it was. He alone recognized it, apparently. Dion hadn't—though the Warlord had tried to make the king see his danger. Nor had the archbishop. Well, he had warned them. He had given them every chance. They would have no one to blame but themselves.

He stopped, raised his head, which had been bowed in thought. He had reached his destination.

The memorial's white stone glimmered softly against a background of night-shadowed trees, coldly shining stars. Sagan advanced swiftly up the path, placed his hand upon the wooden door, gave it a small shove to ascertain if it was locked.

It was not. Then he noticed the placard, which stated that the building was always open to any who might be seeking a place of solace, whether by day or by night. Noiselessly, Sagan pushed on the double doors and passed inside, careful to shut them quietly behind him.

Music, counterpointed by the gentle comforting murmur of a fountain, spread a soothing balm across his raw wounds, the festering sores that would not heal. He recognized, within the part of him that was functioning on the categorical level, the "Sanctus" from Mozart's Great Mass in C Minor.

As he moved farther inside the chapel, the same part of his mind noted with approval the simplicity and elegance of the design, the dignified tribute to all those who had lost their lives during the escape from the Corasian galaxy. His gaze passed rapidly over the small plaque on the fountain, illuminated in the light of the flickering flames that were never doused, never allowed to go out. He cast one brief and uninterested glance at his own portrait hanging on the wall, though one corner of his mouth twisted at the irony of his memorialization as a dead hero.

A person is said to feel a chill when walking on the site of his own grave, but Sagan felt nothing as he passed by the plaque listing the date of his unhappy, unwanted birth and the year of his presumed, glorious death. In a sense he *had* died that year. So be it.

He came to stand before her portrait.

It was very good, very like her, he decided in that same part of his mind that had led him here, the part that had noted and approved the architecture, the choice of music. The artist had portrayed her essence—loving eye guiding living hand and brush, imbuing his subject with his own feelings toward it. Unlike the cold, uncaring eye of the camera that freeze-dries a single split-second of a person's existence.

The artist—what was his name—Youll (Sagan had some vague recollection of him as a spacepilot)—had even painstakingly painted, in accurate detail, the scar on Maigrey's face, as if he understood that this was an integral part of her being, not a flaw to be glossed over with brush-stroke cosmetics.

Sagan stared at the portrait and tried, Pygmalion-like, to will the gray and solemn eyes of the artist's creation to come to life, to meet his. But they did not see him, stared off at a point beyond him, past him, as if they no longer had any concern for the constricted world of a mortal.

Sagan's fist clenched beneath his sleeve. "You came . . . to him, to Dion!" he said in a voice choked, smothered, gasping for breath. "And never to me. Dear God! Why not to *me*?"

No answer. The eyes gazed with that maddening calm into the past, the future, the present—all one for them now. Sagan's fury and frustration burned. He was reminded suddenly, with vivid clarity, of the night of the Revolution, the night she'd opposed him, thwarted his ambitious designs, prevented him from claiming the newborn king. He'd struck her down in a moment of rage very like the one he was feeling now.

His anger blinded him. For long moments he could not see for the red tinge and smoke of the flames that burned him up inside. Slowly, he mastered himself. Slowly, rational thought regained control. It was a portrait, he told himself. Paint smeared on canvas. Nothing more.

Yet he cast it one more dark and accusatory gaze, then started to turn away. Something white—bright, vivid white— lay on the dark and polished floor at his feet.

It was a rose—a white rose.

Odd, that such a thing should be here. He thought back, tried to recall if the rose had been lying on the floor when he'd first entered, was fairly certain it had not, although he was forced to admit that his own robed shadow might very well have obscured it from view. He bent down and picked it up.

The rose was freshly cut, apparently, for the edges of its petals were only just beginning to go limp. A small piece of paper was twined around its stem, using the thorns as anchor. Hardly knowing what he was doing, acting primarily out of a need for some type of distraction from his pain, Sagan unraveled the paper, glanced over the words written there.

I am forbidden to see or communicate with you. I have no choice but to obey. To do otherwise would imperil both of us and those we love. But know that I am with you always.

Have faith, as I do, that someday we will be together at
last, and we will never again be parted.

Sagan stared at the slip of paper, its message punctured here
and there with tiny holes left by the thorns. He was baffled,
amazed, incredulous, doubting. He was about to read through it
again, though its words were etched indelibly on his mind and
always would be, beyond even death's power to wipe them out.

A voice—real, flesh and blood—startled him.

"I . . . Forgive me, Brother. But I think . . . that note you're
holding . . . it's mine."

The voice was timid, hesitant. Desperation had driven it to
speak. Sagan lifted his head. A young man, probably a student,
stood near. He was tall and thin, overly thin, and his gaze was
fixed with feverish intensity on the white rose in Sagan's hand.

Wordlessly, Sagan held the rose and the note out to the
young man. He leapt for them, snatched them up in shaking
hands. Holding the note eagerly to the light of the flame, he
read it and, with a shuddering sob, pressed note and rose to his
breast and burst into tears.

Sagan stood impassively, watched mutely, his hands once
again folded inside his sleeves.

Glancing up to find this silent presence observing him, the
young man flushed in shame. Hastily he wiped his eyes, seemed
to think his emotional outburst called for some explanation.

"I was rude to you, Father," he said, with a gulp. "I didn't
mean to be. I'm not myself. I don't usually fall apart like this.
But . . . I've been waiting so long. I haven't been able to eat or
sleep . . ."

He was forced to stop, to clear his throat. Sagan remained
standing before the young man, willing him to continue.

"We were betrothed." The young man held the rose tenderly
as if it were the embodiment of his beloved. "But our planets
have declared war on each other. We hope the king can stop it,
but . . . who knows? It's all so complicated. Her father demanded that she return home. He's some sort of high-up official,
and she agreed to go, thinking she could do more good if she
was with him. But that was weeks ago. I haven't heard from her,
not a word. She was to send me a message; her roommate was
to leave it here for me. Night after night . . . and nothing. I
thought . . . I began to be afraid that she didn't . . . But now . . ."

He clasped the precious note and the rose tightly, oblivious to the thorns that must be piercing his flesh.

"Now I know she still loves me. And she's right. I must have faith. We'll work things out. And we'll be together again."

He wiped his eyes and, now that he was calmer, it appeared to occur to him that this was a strange time and a strange place in which to find a priest. He eyed the priest with newly awakened, somewhat suspicious curiosity.

Sagan—conscious of the proximity of his portrait—retreated into the shadows, drew his hood over his head.

"I'm sorry to rant on like this, Father," the young man said. "I didn't mean to disturb you, but I didn't think anyone would be here this time of night. There generally isn't. . . ."

He left the sentence hanging, an open invitation for Sagan to offer his own explanation. Sagan said nothing, stood silent in the shadows.

"Well, I guess . . . that is . . . Good night, then, Father," said the young man, uncomfortable in that stern, forbidding presence. "I'm . . . sorry if I . . . if I was rude. It was just . . . well, you know how it is."

Then, realizing that perhaps a priest who has taken vows of celibacy *wouldn't* know (or at least *shouldn't* know), the young man flushed again. He started to say something else, gave it up as a bad try, and hurriedly departed, still clutching his note and the rose.

Sagan remained standing in the darkness, his thoughts abstracted, wondering. Finally, unable to arrive at a satisfactory conclusion, he glanced back at her portrait.

If he had hoped for some clue, some answer, he was disappointed. The gray eyes that saw nothing saw everything . . . except him.

Lips pressed together in a hard, grim line, Sagan turned away and walked rapidly toward the door, stalking past the fountain, whose babbling he was beginning to find irritating. Hand on the door, he paused.

A single white rose petal lay on the floor.

Bending down, Sagan picked it up. He held it, smoothed it between his fingers. "So . . . you are forbidden to communicate with me. If that is true, it means that God has abandoned me, that I am damned, and there is no hope.

"And, therefore," he added grimly, "nothing that I do from now on matters."

Book Two

'Tis not the balm, the scepter, and the ball,
The sword, the mace, the crown imperial,
The intertissued robe of gold and pearl,
The farced title running fore the king,
The throne he sits on, nor the tide of pomp
That beats upon the high shore of this world—
No, not all these, thrice-gorgeous ceremony,
Not all these laid in bed majestical,
Can sleep so soundly as the wretched slave, . . .
And but for ceremony, such a wretch,
Winding up days with toil and nights with sleep,
Had the forehead and vantage of a king.
        William Shakespeare, Henry V, Act IV, Scene i

Chapter ❦ One

In me is no delay; with thee to go,
Is to stay here; without thee here to stay,
Is to go hence unwilling; thou to me
Art all things under Heaven . . .

John Milton, *Paradise Lost*

The radiant being thundered through heaven's hallways, bright light robed with vast darkness, mercy in one hand, law in the other.

Defiant, resolute, certain of the justness of her cause, Maigrey stood alone to face the Immortal Wrath.

"Because the dead are permitted to know the mind of God, because you are given knowledge of past, present, and future, you, who were known in life as Lady Maigrey Morianna, made a covenant with Our Lord that you would not reveal yourself to those still living who might profit from your knowledge, to their own detriment and that of the universe."

"Yes, yes," Maigrey snapped. "I know what I did and why I did it. Which is something that perhaps you don't. I *may* have been given to know the mind of God—though now I doubt it," she added pointedly. "But I doubt if He knows mine!"

"Doubt," said the radiant being, voice soft and frightening in its intensity. "Yes, you doubt. It is your doubt that blocks your knowledge. Doubt casts a shadow over you, a shadow our light cannot penetrate. Doubt and pride will be your downfall in eternity, as they were in your life. You think, in your pride, that you know better than the Creator how to handle the complexities of the universe?"

Maigrey wavered, her righteous anger faltering a little under the personage's argument.

"No, I don't think that," she admitted, chastened. "It's just . . . well, I don't believe you're being fair. And I didn't break the covenant, not really. Sagan thought that I'd abandoned him—"

"As you did in life?"

Though she had no flesh, no blood, Maigrey felt the blood

burn in her face. She put her hand to the scar that existed only in her mind.

"I couldn't let him believe that of me again," she said in a low voice. "But I kept my word. I didn't appear to him. As for him finding that message, you know it was not written by me. I can't help it if he thought otherwise. . . ."

"A technicality," said the radiant being dryly. "You are clever, Lady Maigrey—I use your name because you are closer to what you were than what you should be. But your cleverness has this time proved your undoing. As you surmised, he knew the message came from you. But he did not take hope or comfort from it. He has misconstrued it, has now lost all hope because of it. Now he is reckless and fey. And you have yourself to blame. It was to avert just this possibility that you were asked to make the covenant."

"I do admit I made a mistake," Maigrey said earnestly. "But if you will only grant me leave to go to him, I can fix it—"

"No. You have done enough," said the personage in severe tones. "Too much. It cannot be permitted."

"You permitted my brother to come to me!" Maigrey flared. "You sent Platus to stop me when I was going to kill myself."

"*We* sent him? Are you certain of that? Have you never wondered why your brother walks these hallways instead of seeking the peace that we offer him?"

Maigrey stared, astonished. Her brother—rebelling against a Divine Edict. She couldn't believe it, and yet, she could. By saving her, Platus had, in reality, saved Dion. And Dion meant more to Platus than his own soul.

"What is it you want me to do?" she asked, quieter, thoughtful.

"You will not return to the physical dimension. You will remain here, in our sight and mind. You will not interfere in the lives of any of those you left behind. One exception only is made and that because of a responsibility you accepted in life."

"My goddaughter, Kamil. There is little I can do for her now. But the others, Dion, Sagan . . . how can you ask me to abandon them? Especially now. . . ."

"You will see them—through the mind of God. Submit yourself to His will, Lady Maigrey. Be ruled by His wisdom, not your own misleading passions."

Maigrey shook her head slowly.

The radiant personage was stern. "Would you tamper with their freedom of choice? With their free will?"

"Why not? You're doing it," she retorted.

"You defy us, then." The radiant being did not make the statement in anger, but in sorrow.

"I will do what I think is best," Maigrey said, hedging, somewhat daunted by the power of the forces aligned against her. "That is *my* free choice."

"This is true. We may not stop you. But know this, Lady Maigrey. If once you leave our presence, the Mind of God will be closed to you. You will see only as a mortal. And if you cross over to the physical dimension, if you attempt to physically alter or change that which was meant to be, you will be damned. You will not be permitted to return to this blessed realm, except by a path that is long and difficult and filled with pain. Many are those who have perished on it, to live in dreadful torment and agony, bereft of all hope of comfort, peace, redemption. That is the fate you face. And you face it alone."

The path opened up at her feet. Maigrey looked down it, and her soul shrank back from the sight. But, as she had been trained, she did not show her fear. Her lips pressed together firmly; her grip on the hilt of the bloodsword tightened.

"It is your choice," admonished the radiant being. "But beware that if you tamper with what you do not understand, you may do irreparable damage. And if you do, you will be punished."

She thought long moments. Then "So be it," she said, and left.

Chapter ·────◦━◦○━◦◦───· Two

I think the King is but a man ...
William Shakespeare, *Henry V,* Act IV, Scene i

"Send for John Dixter," ordered Dion.

"Yes, sir." D'argent started to leave the king's office, paused. "Are you certain, sir? You've only just returned to the palace. Your Majesty should rest—"

"Find him!" Dion said through clenched teeth.

D'argent bowed silently and left.

Dion bowed his head. Elbows on his desk, he massaged his forehead, rubbed burning eyes, throbbing temples. Ordinarily he had no problems with space travel, but he had been ill this trip. He hadn't been able to eat; what food he swallowed made him sick. He couldn't sleep, but lay awake hours, staring into the darkness. Stress, nerves, said his doctor, and had prescribed rest, a vacation. Easy to say, but how did one take a vacation from oneself? Where could he go that despair and heartache would not follow in his baggage train?

The king had left the Academy almost immediately after receiving Dixter's message. Dion had taken time only to explain matters to Kamil.

At first he'd considered not telling her. The news hadn't leaked out; there was a possibility he could contain the explosion, minimize the damage, prevent anyone from finding out. He knew Kamil. He was almost certain that she would blame herself.

But he decided to tell her the truth. One reason—he couldn't lie to her. He couldn't keep anything from her. If he was wounded, his shieldmaid had to know, in order to know how to protect both of them. And, too, he feared that he might not be able to keep this news from the press, that she would find out from the evening news, hear it gossiped among her friends. She would not only blame herself, then, but she would assume that Dion blamed her. . . .

No, far better to tell her everything. He remembered every

word of their last meeting. Repeated it to himself now, as he had repeated it over and over again in the long and empty hours of the night.

Once again, he held her in his arms.

"Astarte has left me. I have to return to the palace."

"Oh, Dion, this is my fault!" Kamil responded, as he had known she would.

"Don't jump to conclusions, dearest," he told her. "Don't make this more difficult."

She said softly, "You must go, of course. I understand. And . . . and if you can't come back . . . I'll understand that, too. You won't need to say anything. . . . "

"Oh, God!" With a smothered groan, he gripped her tightly, clasped her to him, his love for her a fire that warmed him and seared him. *I won't give you up!* was what he longed to say, but his broken words were only, "How can I give you up?"

She made no reply. They clung to each other. This was the end.

Or maybe not.

That had occasioned the restless, sleepless hours. There might still be a way. Now, of all times in his life, he needed Kamil, needed her love, support, understanding. There had to be a way. . . .

"Dion . . ."

He raised his head, looked up. "Hello, sir," he said. "I didn't hear you come in."

Dixter settled himself in the comfortable chair opposite the king's desk, eyed Dion intently. "I heard the reports of your illness. Shouldn't you be in bed?" he asked with characteristic bluntness.

Dion smiled wanly. "Just a touch of space sickness. I'll be all right. And, actually, it proved a convenient excuse for canceling my appointments." He drew in a deep breath, sat up straight, back rigid. His face was the face of the mirror. "Tell me everything. How bad is it?"

"Not as bad as it could have been, Your Majesty," Dixter said gravely. He rubbed his grizzled chin, appeared embarrassed.

"Look, sir," said Dion, "let's drop the formalities. This isn't going to be easy on either of us. I'm sorry you had to be involved—"

"Better me than someone else, Dion," said Dixter. "Astarte came to me because she knew you and I were old friends. She doesn't want scandal, any more than you do, than we all do. She's an intelligent woman. She knows how critical this time is for you. She knows the wolves are out there, waiting for you to stumble, waiting to rip your throat out."

"Then why is she doing this?" Dion demanded irritably.

"I think you better read this, son." Dixter held out a letter. "She left this for you, in my care."

Dion took it, stared at it. It would contain reproaches, accusations. It would be bitter, vindictive. Very well. Then he could reply with justified anger. Anger felt good to him at the moment. Far better than guilt.

He opened the letter. Rising to his feet (motioning Dixter to remain seated), Dion walked over to the window, held the letter to the sunlight to see it better. Actually, his desk lamp was perfectly adequate, provided excellent light, but he needed the excuse to keep his face to himself.

The letter was written in ink, by hand—Astarte's hand, neat, small, precise, beautiful—much like herself.

My husband,

They have wronged us. Politics brought together two who were not meant to be together. We were both very young. We were given no choice. We were given no help. Like those in a fairy tale, when the story ended, they shut the book on our lives and assumed that we would live happily ever after. Yes, they have wronged us.

I have wronged you. I knew, on our wedding night, that you loved another. That was all right. I loved someone else, too. Or at least I thought I did. The Goddess, in her divine wisdom, showed me I was wrong. I should have told you. I think it would have made a difference between us. But I was proud, too proud to admit I had a rival. I thought, woman-like, that I could win you over. Yes, I have wronged you.

You have wronged me. You have broken the vows you took—to honor, respect. You did not respect me enough to make me your friend, if you could not make me your lover. You have not respected me enough to confide in me. You could have told me the truth, that you loved someone else. Yes, it would have hurt me, but how much more have you hurt me, hurt us both, by your cold silence? Worst of all, you have made no effort to give up this love. You have defended it with every weapon you can lay your hand on, you use them to drive me away. What do you fear? That you might, accidentally, love me . . . just a little? That you might be unfaithful to her? Yes, you have wronged me.

I do not intend to create a scene or a scandal. I am leaving to give us both time to think calmly, now that the truth has been spoken. I do this now, because I know our marriage has reached a crisis point. I will tell the media that I am returning home to celebrate the Spring Blooming Festival, which is a holiday of great significance to my people, honoring, as it does, the redemptive power of the Goddess. Our people would be pleased if their king would come to participate in the festival.

Will you, my husband? Will you take this opportunity to say anew vows that now lie dead beneath winter snows? Will you reach out to one who feels affection for you? She is prepared to forgive you your wrongs, if you can find it in your heart to forgive hers.

The letter was signed, *In honor and respect, your wife.*

And below, penned in a more agitated style, was the postscript, *This will be between ourselves!*

Slowly, Dion folded the letter up. Slowly, he slipped it back into its envelope, slowly slid the envelope deep inside the breast pocket of his uniform coat. He waited a moment before turning around, not because he needed time to conceal his emotions—that was impossible; they ran far too deep. He waited because he was looking, for the first time, into that mirror image of himself.

"Your Majesty . . ." Dixter said, concerned.

"I'm all right," Dion replied. Drawing in a deep breath, he turned, walked back to his desk, resumed his seat. "Do you know what she wrote, sir? Did she show you the letter?"

"No, son, of course not. But I have a pretty good idea. She told me everything. She seemed to need someone to talk to. She's very lonely, Dion."

"I know. Damn it, I know! Everything she said was true. And more. A lot more. She had the grace to spare me the worst." He hesitated, then said, "I *have* been having an affair."

"Olefsky's daughter," Dixter said quietly.

Dion started up out of his chair, alarmed, amazed. "How could you know? Did she know, say anything—"

Dixter flushed. "I'm sorry. *I* shouldn't have said anything. It was just a guess on my part, Dion. Nola told me all about your relationship, years ago, when she heard you were going to be married to someone else. She was worried about you, wanted me to keep an eye on you. Your secret's safe with me."

"Safe with you. Safe with D'argent, safe with Cato, safe with his men, safe with Olefsky and his wife . . ."

"Not one of these people would betray you, son."

"No," said Dion, "but what must they think of me? I am their king. I'm supposed to be the example—"

"You're also human, Dion," said Dixter with a gentle smile.

"And how can one be both?" Dion walked away from his desk, returned to the window. "Strange, that this should come right on the heels of the other. An object lesson from God, Sagan would say."

"Sagan." Hearing the name, Dixter leaned forward. "You heard from the archbishop?"

"I heard from Sagan, spoke to him."

"He *is* alive," Dixter murmured.

"Very much," said Dion dryly. "More than he wants to be, I think. He had an interesting tale to tell. As if I don't have problems enough. Apparently I'm not the only reprobate in the family."

Dion related the doctor's confession. John Dixter listened in attentive silence and if he was shocked or repulsed, he kept his feelings concealed. At the conclusion, he only shook his head.

"It's hard to believe. And yet, it isn't. Many of the Blood Royal came to think that they were above the laws which governed ordinary men. Your uncle, the king, for one. Sagan, for another."

"Me—for a third?" Dion said, glancing at Dixter. "And yet, if I were an ordinary man, I would not be in this situation. I would be married to Kamil. . . . "

"You made the choice, Your Majesty."

"Yes. I made the choice. But now we have additional worries," he said briskly. He reported Sagan's speculations and deductions concerning Pantha, the child, Vallombrosa.

Dixter frowned, shook his head again when Dion told him of the Warlord's advice to destroy the planet outright. The admiral nodded, appeared to agree with Dion's refusal to accept the

starjewel, arm the space-rotation bomb. Yet nevertheless, at the
end of the king's report, Dixter again rubbed his chin, sighed.

"And now we can do nothing but wait."

"And trust in Sagan," Dion said.

John Dixter heard the ironic tone, shook his head. "That's
the part I don't like. What did you think of him?"

"Dangerous. Maybe more dangerous now than he ever was.
Then he had a purpose, a mission, a divine calling. Now he has
nothing, consequently nothing to lose. He thinks even God has
abandoned him."

"And yet you *do* trust him." It was a statement, calmly made.

"Yes," said Dion, after a thoughtful pause. "I trust him. I
can't tell you why. Maybe because . . . what other choice do I
have?"

"Several." Dixter shrugged. "Not the least of which is the
one he made you himself. Oh, maybe not explode the bomb on
them, but we could send in warships, a show of force—"

"Against an uninhabited planet? Send the fleet into a dead
part of space? We'd look like fools."

"Call it a training exercise, maneuvers—"

"The media would jump on it like starving hounds. They'd
be bound to uncover something—this Ghost Legion, if nothing
else. We'll let Sagan confront my cousin, find out what he
wants. Find out if he even exists. Then, when we know the
facts, we can deal with the matter."

"And then Sagan can make *his* choice," Dixter said softly.

"What did you say?" Dion looked up. "I'm sorry, sir, I'm
afraid I was thinking about something else."

"Nothing." Dixter waved a deprecating hand. "Just talking to
myself. A bad habit. Comes with getting old. With Your Majesty's permission . . ."

"Certainly, my lord." Dion stood up. The interview was at an
end.

Dixter rose to his feet. "I'll double the guard around the
space-rotation bomb. And I'll post a few ships in the general vicinity of Vallombrosa. The worsening situation on Maluvura
will give us a good excuse. It's near there."

But John Dixter didn't leave. He stood gazing thoughtfully at
the king. He was obviously wanting to add something, say
something further.

If I were an ordinary man, Dion said to himself, if I were
Tusk, for example, Dixter would rest his hand on my shoulder,

offer some bit of wise advice. He wouldn't expect me to take it, not really. He'd just be saying it to let me know he cares. That he understands.

But he can't understand. He knows that; he is coming to realize it now. And so he won't say anything. What man dares offer sympathy to his king?

What king dare accept it?

"Good-bye, sir," said Dion. "Thank you for coming. As I said before, I am sorry you were involved."

After Dixter had gone, Dion stood a moment in silent thought; then, sighing softly, he summoned his secretary.

"Establish communication with the planet Ceres," he told D'argent. "I want to speak to . . . my wife."

Chapter ❖ Three

Giving honor unto the wife, as unto the weaker vessel.
The Bible, 1 Peter 3:7

Dion sat at his desk, studying—or trying to study—the latest proposals for a peaceful settlement on Muruva. He was wondering, in reality, what was taking D'argent so long to reach Astarte, had placed his hand on the commlink twice to find out and, twice, had withdrawn it. His secretary knew quite well what he was doing, how to manage it discreetly. Better than Dion, who—now that he thought about it—had very little idea where Astarte was, how she could be reached.

Almost an hour passed.

Something's wrong, Dion realized, giving up all pretense at working. He was on his way to find out what, when the door opened and D'argent entered.

The secretary's cheeks were flushed, the quiet, calm demeanor disturbed.

"Forgive the delay, sir. I am unable to reach Her Majesty."

"Yes, and . . ."

D'argent's lips tightened. It was the first time Dion could recall having seen his secretary angry. "The Baroness DiLuna wishes to speak to you, sir."

"So much for keeping this between ourselves," Dion muttered, speaking before he thought. "Her Majesty ran home to her mother!"

"Not precisely, sir," D'argent replied, his expression softening somewhat. He had always liked the queen. "According to my contacts on Ceres, Her Majesty has returned to the Temple of the Goddess, which, although it is located in the central city-state of Ceres, is high in the mountains. It is isolated, at some distance from the palace. Her Majesty was raised in the temple, sir. She is High Priestess. It would be natural for her to go there, rather than to the palace of her mother. The two of them have never been particularly close. As you might guess, Her

Majesty is not the type of daughter the baroness would be proud to have 'sired,' so to speak."

Dion knew the relationship between mother and daughter was tense. The baroness visited infrequently, and when she did, Astarte was quiet and reserved, seemed to retreat into herself. Dion—who had always been on friendly terms with the baroness, as long as he didn't have to be around her a great deal of the time—recalled that he had noticed his wife's unhappiness during one of her mother's visits, but had never bothered to discuss it with her, never cared enough to find out the reason.

"I assume you attempted to reach Her Majesty at the temple. If that's possible . . . It's not closed to outside communication, is it?"

"Oh, no, sir. It is quite large, as large as a city itself, and they have an extremely sophisticated communications network. They are the central authority for a religion that has a vast number of followers, not only on their home planet, but throughout their system, as well as several systems nearby. Mostly due to the efforts of Her Majesty, the religion is spreading. Her Majesty is quite popular with the people, sir."

Is that meant as a subtle rebuke? Dion wondered, eyeing his secretary with a momentary flicker of displeasure. Well, what if it is? he asked himself. I have earned it.

"You can't get through to her there, I take it."

"No, sir. All channels to the temple and vicinity are closed. The excuse is some sort of solar disturbance, but I am convinced that they are being jammed."

"The baroness."

"Undoubtedly, sir. Her Majesty may have no idea that this is happening."

"How would DiLuna find out, then?" Dion asked, still suspicious.

"Her Majesty's guards, sir, are far more loyal to the baroness than they are to Her Majesty."

"I see." Dion pondered.

Something else he hadn't known. He had always assumed that his wife and the warrior women who dogged her every step were all part of the same sisterhood. Now he was being forced to take a different view of the matter.

She's lonely, Dixter had said. Dion had wondered at the time how that could be possible. He was beginning to understand.

"I'll talk to the baroness," he said, heading for the room adjoining his office, his own personal and private communications center.

"It won't be pleasant, sir," predicted D'argent ominously, leaving to make the necessary arrangements.

No, thought Dion, but then I've asked for this, too. He was not extremely apprehensive, however. He had earned the warrior woman's respect by piloting a spaceplane during the Battle of the Void, as their flight from Corasia had come to be called. As commander he could have remained in relative safety on the bridge of *Phoenix*, but he had chosen to lead his troops into battle. DiLuna gloried in combat and figured that, because he had chosen to fight, he felt the same.

Dion had never disillusioned her, never told her—or anyone—that he'd been testing himself. The first time he'd flown combat against the Corasians, he'd panicked, been captured, taken prisoner. Maigrey and Sagan had been forced to risk their lives to rescue him. A hot rush of shame suffused his body whenever he recalled that incident. He was determined, the first chance he had, to prove himself to them.

But by then Maigrey was dead, had given her life to save his. Sagan had vanished. Dion had been left to prove himself to himself. He'd done it. He had overcome his fear, fought well—as both Sagan and Tusk had taught him.

If he hadn't, he would not have been king. He'd made up his mind to that. It was the least he owed them.

Ever since that time, DiLuna had thought quite highly of her son-in-law; more highly of him than of her daughter, apparently.

"Baroness DiLuna," he said, and added the formal greeting in her own language, when her image came on the vidscreen. "It is a pleasure to see you again."

She was an imposing woman. Over sixty years old, she had borne daughters who had themselves borne daughters, who were nearly of an age to bear daughters themselves. Her scalplock was pure white, no longer jet-black, but her black eyes were as fierce and proud as they had been in her youth. Tall, strong, well-muscled, she still trained her warriors—men as well as women—in hand-to-hand combat herself, offering a purse of golden eagles to anyone who could best her. Few had been known to win and those few were immediately promoted to either her own personal guard (the women) or her bed (the men).

"My liege lord." She acknowledged Dion with an abrupt jerk of her head that set her gunmetal earrings to jangling discordantly.

No bow, no formal greeting in return. The expression on her leathery, heavily lined, and battle-scarred face was unreadable. Dion could make nothing of it except for, perhaps, a faint hint of elation, triumph.

That boded ill, and he was on his guard.

"It is a pleasure, as always, to speak with you, Baroness," he said, using her formal title in her own language, of which the common Standard Military term of "baroness" was, in reality, only a crude translation, "but I am endeavoring to reach Her Majesty. She is, I believe, residing in the Temple of the Goddess. How long do you anticipate these solar interferences to last?"

"A long time," said DiLuna, black eyes glinting. "Perhaps indefinitely. Who can say? Our sun is unstable. Such manifestations often occur when the Goddess is displeased."

Dion stirred in silent anger. Ceres' sun was as placid as was possible for a burning mass of gases and molten rock to be. But he maintained his calm, refusing to let DiLuna provoke him to anger—one method she often used to defeat an unwary opponent.

"This is most inconvenient. Naturally, I am concerned about my queen's safety and well-being—"

"Since when?" DiLuna's lip curled.

Dion was hit. She'd drawn first blood, while he'd been standing flat-footed. So this was how Astarte kept her promise to keep this quarrel between themselves. Dion could do nothing, however, but pretend he had not been wounded, hope the bloodstain wouldn't show.

"Truly, this interference is most annoying," Dion said coolly. "I was unable to hear your last remarks, Baroness DiLuna. I have enjoyed speaking with you, but I am hoping to speak to Her Majesty. Perhaps she could come to the palace, since it appears that *your* communications channels are not affected—"

"That is not possible, my liege lord. My daughter prays to the Goddess for the salvation of her marriage and the destruction of her rival."

Her words entered Dion like sharp steel, drew life's blood this time. He could not breathe, for the pain and the fear that suddenly engulfed him. *Destruction of her rival!* His one thought, which he clung to as a stable point in the reeling room, was that he could not, he must not let this woman know she had mortally wounded him.

"I want to speak to Astarte," he said coldly, thickly. "My wife."

"That is not possible. You have no wife. You broke the sacred vows of marriage and by that act you insulted not only my daughter, but her people, her nation, her Goddess. We consider this an act of war. We therefore declare ourselves independent of your rule and authority and will establish our own monarchy."

"War!" Dion repeated, unable to believe what he was hearing. "You would send your people to war!"

"In a minute, my liege. But"—DiLuna smiled, in smug triumph—"I doubt if that will be necessary. The scandal alone would topple you, Dion Starfire. But it can all be smoothed over. I believe I could persuade my daughter to forgive and forget, *if* you will accede to our demands. First, you will make my daughter queen, not queen-consort. She will share equally in the rule of the galaxy and, upon your death, will succeed to the throne. Second, you will make the worship of the Goddess the official religion of the galaxy and require all your subjects to follow it. Third, you will pay us a large sum of money—the exact amount to be agreed upon later—as reparation for the harm you have done our world. There are certain other conditions, but we will discuss those when the main terms have been met."

Dion had relaxed somewhat. He was able to smile himself, the smile of the mirror. "These demands are impossible, Baroness. Make them public and the rest of the galaxy will think that you have gone insane. Your own people will not tolerate this. You will do them incalculable harm."

He was calmer now, able to think, react rationally. "Baroness, I will not deny that Her Majesty and I are having problems. What marriage doesn't? But they are *our* problems. It is up to us to work them out. I want to speak to—"

"These wretched flares. Your transmission is breaking apart," called DiLuna loudly. "I could hear nothing of what you just said, my liege lord. We will speak on this matter again."

"I want—" Dion began, but the image of the baroness dissolved. "Damn!" He struck the console with his hand. Turning, he walked away, came back. He depressed a button on the commlink. "Reopen that channel," he commanded D'argent. "Belay that," he said in the next breath.

Straightening, he ran his hand through his hair, glared in anger and frustration at the vidscreen. What a stupid, ugly, sordid little mess. And it was Astarte's fault! Why the devil had she run off? Why hadn't she confronted him directly?

Her letter had touched him, had made him see his error. He had been prepared to admit his guilt and make a very real attempt to start to build a relationship. But now . . . she had lied to him, she had promised to keep this secret, but she had obviously told her mother. Astarte might have known how DiLuna would have reacted. . . .

Of course she knew! This was part of a plot. She was in league with her mother to gain more power for herself, untold wealth for her planet. Dion had never supposed his wife had wanted more power; she had always seemed content with her own duties, which were considerable.

"But then I never really knew her," he said to himself. Thirty minutes previous, he would have made that statement in a remorseful tone. Now he said it in anger.

He tried to decide what to do. He had no doubt DiLuna meant what she said. She would make the scandal public, she would . . .

A spark fell on the withered hopes and dreams in his heart. The flame burst into life, rushed throughout his body, blood crackling with excitement.

Divorce. This was his chance, God-sent. He could divorce Astarte, marry Kamil.

He kept very still and let the fire spread, fanned the flames, warmed himself at the blaze, tried not to be blinded by the smoke.

"Say that I refuse my wife's demands. If she truly expects me to give in, she will have no recourse but to go public. The parliament will react in shock. Astarte has no claim to the throne; she's not Blood Royal. The people don't want a religion—any religion—*imposed* on them. And they certainly won't want to hand over large sums of money to an aggressive and warlike race.

"As for her accusations against me—Astarte has no proof." Dion tamped down the flames, deliberately poured cold water on the fire to permit himself to think clearly. "No," he determined at last. "She has no proof. She couldn't possibly. As Dixter said, no one who knows of the affair would betray me. I will simply deny the allegations.

"Astarte is popular with the people, but their favor will wane when she shows herself willing to risk our marriage in an attempt to grab more power."

Dion reached into his pocket, took out the letter. "And to think I almost fell for this, madam."

He tore the letter in half, tore it in half again, dropped it into the disposer canister, where it was reduced, in a fraction of a second, to ash.

Chapter ·••◦•• Four

With the dead, there is no rivalry.
              Lord Macaulay, "Lord Bacon"

"You have done what, Mother?" Astarte rose from her throne, faced DiLuna in shocked outrage. Footsteps emphasizing each word, the queen walked slowly and deliberately down the stone stairs of the dais, advancing on her mother. "How could you? How *could* you! You have ruined everything!"

DiLuna stood over six feet tall, hard and strong as steel, arm muscles firm and well delineated, chest muscles smooth and pronounced, thigh and leg muscles hard as any youth's. Her daughter was not quite five-foot-four, soft-skinned and soft-muscled, fragile. Yet it was DiLuna who fell back a pace before this white-faced, flaring-eyed fury, whom she barely recognized. Or perhaps she did recognize her. Perhaps, for the first time since the frail child had been born to her, DiLuna saw something of her own steel in her daughter.

"How dare you?" Astarte demanded again, taking advantage of her mother's momentary shocked dumbness. "You knew my wishes! How dare you countermand them?"

DiLuna recovered herself, smiled indulgently. "You silly little chick! I did it for your own good, of course." Her voice hardened. "If you have no pride, *I* do. Did you think I would let this man disgrace you? Disgrace me? Disgrace our family? Our people? No, by the Goddess! He will pay for his betrayal!"

"What betrayal?" Astarte asked. She was suddenly cool, wary. "What are you talking about, Mother?"

Turning away, clasping her hands, Astarte walked across the gray marble floor of the temple to stand by the wide-open doorway. She pretended to be absorbed in the view from the columned portico, pretended to gaze at the beautiful panorama of trees and flowers, sweeping downward into a lovely valley, then upward to majestic mountains. In reality, her eyes, hidden by the long lashes, were darting sideways, keeping anxious watch on her mother.

"I said nothing of any betrayal," Astarte continued. "We have grown apart, that is all. The pressures of his schedule and mine. This separation was meant to give us both time to think. Now, thanks to you, Mother," she added bitterly, "that is ruined. His Majesty is probably furious with me now. And I don't blame him!"

"Bah!" DiLuna snorted. "You know perfectly well he has been sleeping with another woman."

"I know no such thing," Astarte returned.

"Then you are a blind mole! Your women know."

So that's it, Astarte realized. That's how she found out. I should have known. Damn! Damn! Damn!

Her small fist curled, clenched tight against her stomach. She took care to keep her unhappiness and disquiet concealed.

I have to be strong, she reminded herself. I have to be strong or I will lose everything . . . if I have not already lost him. . . ,

"But don't worry, Daughter," DiLuna was continuing. "Your rival is one problem that can be easily managed."

Astarte stiffened; her stomach muscles clenched. A foul taste, as if she'd been chewing on the bitter leaves of rue, coated her tongue, dried it, made it difficult to speak. She moistened her lips, waited until she was certain her voice would sound natural.

"What are you talking about now, Mother?" she asked, with affected irritation.

"Ridding you of your rival, of course."

Astarte swallowed, drew in a breath. "I have no rival. This is all in your mind."

"You have, and I will give you her name. Maigrey Kamil Olefsky. She and the king have been meeting at the Academy. He was with her, in fact, the night you left him."

Astarte was thankful she was standing next to a column. Without its support, she might have fallen.

"You need take no part in this, Daughter," DiLuna advised her. "I will make all the arrangements. It is lawful."

"A law that has not been used in centuries, a law that dates back to a time of barbarism," Astarte said in a low voice.

"Yet it is written," said DiLuna, shrugging. "His Majesty himself decreed that local custom shall take precedence over galactic law."

"Not when it comes to murder." Clasping her hands together hard to keep them from trembling, Astarte turned around.

Head held high, she faced her mother. "In any case, I am the one who has the right to claim the blood price."

"That is true," DiLuna was forced to concede.

She eyed her daughter dubiously; then, suddenly smiling, the baroness patted her daughter's smooth pale cheek in what she probably considered a caress. But DiLuna's touch was rough and calloused; her long, sharp nails were cold as real nails made of iron. Astarte held herself rigid beneath the touch that had never in her life been loving, gentle.

"Little Dove," said DiLuna softly, "what do you know of such things? Let Mother arrange it, take care of it for you."

Astarte reflected. She could use her power as High Priestess to order her mother to keep out of her affairs, take no action whatsoever.

DiLuna would counter that this was a political matter, not a religious one, and she would be right. Their society had always been extremely careful to keep the two separate. Astarte might reply that the Goddess had everything to do with the marriage covenant, the bearing of children, the continuation of the race. But in her case, where the marriage had been made for strictly political reasons, the point was debatable. And DiLuna was not one who would be interested in debating.

"Give me until tomorrow at this time, Mother," Astarte begged, suddenly meek and contrite. "I want to pray for guidance. This . . . this is so unexpected." She allowed the tremor to show in her voice. "You can't ask me to make a decision on this now."

"Poor Little Dove." DiLuna's iron nails pressed into Astarte's flesh. "Pray to the Goddess. She will comfort you and reassure you. What I do is right. The Goddess will agree with me that this man who deceived you, who sows his seed in another and keeps your womb barren, must be humbled, chastised, brought low. Who knows but that he has not already fathered a child with this bitch? No, this threat must be averted."

"Mother, please leave me now." Astarte could scarcely breathe, barely forced the words out. Her mother's touch, her words, the images they conjured twisted inside her; jealousy's poison worked on her.

What if he had? What if this . . . this woman is pregnant? Her mind blurred, her thoughts swirled and eddied among dark places. Perhaps Mother is right. Better this woman should die. . . .

Astarte seemed to hear the voice of the Goddess; the Holy Mother was stern, sad and disappointed.

Don't you remember the vision? The warning?

Realizing what she'd been thinking, Astarte was appalled at the depths to which she had sunk. She struggled upward, until she once again found herself in calm water.

DiLuna was gone. She had seen the fierce jealous anger in her daughter's face, had obviously assumed this was a propitious time to depart.

Astarte, recovering her strength, left the outer temple, and retired to the inner sanctuary, kept sacred to the priests, priestesses, and their acolytes. No one else was permitted to enter this holy chamber—not DiLuna, not Astarte's "bodyguards"—in reality her mother's spies. Here the queen was certain of being alone, here she could meditate undisturbed, for when the High Priestess was in the Holy Sanctuary, no one else was permitted to enter.

The Temple of the Goddess was a vast complex, the center of worship for millions of followers. It was built on the steppes of the sacred mountain. The Goddess had descended these steppes, so it was believed, from heaven, to deliver her children safely into this blessed land.

Astarte knew the truth, as did all her people. It was on these steppes the early space travelers had landed. But her race had always found it easy to blend the harsh, gray colors of fact with the softer, more beautiful shades of mythology.

No one knew quite when the worship of the Goddess began. Various sociologists had written innumerable learned treatises on the subject, but no two ever agreed, and few paid attention to them anyway. The religion's seeds may have been brought from old Earth, and were related to the ancient religions that revered the All-Mother. But it did not take root and flourish in this culture until the strange illness decimated the male population, left the females to struggle in the new world on their own. With their men weakened, debilitated, dying, it was not surprising that the women came to view their deity in a strong female form.

Even now, years after the hormone-based disease had been isolated and conquered, with the male population thriving, the people of Ceres and its surrounding systems retained their matriarchal culture and their worship of the Goddess. Men as well as women served Her; the priests practicing their own rites and ceremonies. Young boys as well as young girls were required to give a year of their lives to the Goddess, learning to respect life and the land that gave it, both of which were the Goddess's special province. Women were held in high esteem in the society; the crime of rape was practically unknown.

But there was darkness in the past, arising from the early bad times when society was in chaos, the women fighting among themselves to propagate their race. The few fertile men who survived became valuable commodities, a source of wealth and power to the women who owned them. A wife would share her husband and his seed with other women—for a price.

But if the husband decided to indulge in a little private pleasure on the side—spent without being paid, as the saying went—his wife was entitled to remuneration. The price was often paid in blood, the injured wife having the legal right to kill her rival.

The custom belonged to the history books now. Most people on Ceres would be shocked to hear of the commission of such a barbarous act. But it was a part of their heritage and, knowing and respecting their past as they did, they would most likely (however reluctantly) approve the deed.

DiLuna knew this, and so did Astarte. The realization of how easy it would be to have her rival put out of the way appalled her. That—and the temptation to do so.

She entered the chapel. Several novices, young girls, were placing fresh garlands of flowers and fruit at the feet of the statue of the Goddess. They bowed in awed reverence to the High Priestess. Urged by the cluckings and whispered scoldings of their priestess overseer, they blushingly hastened to leave the chapel.

When they were gone, Astarte made the customary offerings at the altar, then knelt at the Goddess's feet. This statue was ancient, the oldest in all of Ceres, dating back to the very beginning of the religion. It portrayed the Goddess in her mothering, nurturing form; the warrior image would come later. The perfume of the freshly cut flowers and the fragrance of the fruit mingled with the sweet smell of incense.

Astarte took time to rearrange one of the garlands. Nervous, childish hands had dropped it in the wrong place. Remembering a time when she had been one of those young girls, remembering how she had loved and adored this statue which, to her, had been the only true aspect of the Goddess, Astarte sighed. She had learned a lot since then.

"What am I to do, Blessed Lady?" Astarte prayed aloud. She was not afraid of being overheard here; not even her mother's spies would dare commit such sacrilege. "I could return to my husband. It would mean a bitter argument with my mother. She could not prevent my leaving, but she would certainly make it difficult, keep me here as long as possible.

But going back to Dion now would avail me little. The damage has been done. He would never believe that I was not in on this plot with my mother. He would never trust me, never respect me, and I could not blame him. And if anything were to happen to this woman he loves, he would accuse me. And he would hate me for it—always."

Shivering, Astarte lifted one of the flowers, smoothed its petals. "I see your guiding hand in this, Blessed Lady. I know my mother. She was planning to murder this woman without my knowledge. I would have never discovered her plot if you had not brought me here. I will not fail you, Holy Mother. I will not fail my husband . . . or myself."

Rising to her feet, Astarte made a deep reverence to the statue, whose eyes gleamed warm and approving in the flickering altar light. "My way is clear, Holy Mother. Grant me strength."

She left, heading for her own private quarters in the temple complex. Due to the "solar disturbance," Astarte would not be able to communicate with the Glitter Palace, but she guessed it would be possible to transmit messages to other, ordinary places in the galaxy.

On her way to her own private communications center, the queen did, for her, an unusual thing. She stopped to pay homage—with a prayer and a gift of a golden dagger with a jeweled hilt—to the statue of the Warror Goddess, who reigned over a small, dark chapel of her own.

Chapter ❖ Five

The world is big enough for us. No ghosts need apply.
> Sir Arthur Conan Doyle,
> "The Adventure of the Sussex Vampire"

The lone spaceplane flew upon its strange journey, heading deliberately for a part of space in which no life existed. A part of space that was, according to record, uninhabitable, unsuited for the maintenance of human life, one that had never even nurtured alien life.

The spaceplane itself was unprepossessing in appearance, being one of those simple, cheaply but well-made volksrockets valued by traveling salesman, rock-star groupies, and missionaries. This particular spaceplane had obviously, from its religious markings, been used by a missionary of the Order of Adamant in the early, pre-Revolution days. It was unarmed, of course, and was badly in need of exterior maintenance, having been resurrected from a wayside combination space museum and petting zoo.

It had taken seventy-two hours for Sagan to locate the plane, on Omega 11, make necessary repairs, and refit it with the special and complex instruments delivered by courier from Admiral Dixter. Sagan had not slept those seventy-two hours. He was impelled by an urgency that had no tangible source, but was like a nagging tug at his sleeve, a foot tapping impatiently.

I am waiting for you, a voice seemed to say, *but I will not wait long.*

Sagan had worked in solitude, careful not to attract the attention of Omega's inhabitants. He had put away the clergyman's habit and vestments, which might have excited comment. Dressed in military fatigues purchased from an army surplus store, he looked like any other aging spacer, who had taken it into his head to build a rocket ship in his garage. Omega 11 was a middle-class suburban planet, circling a much larger, more important planet—Omega 12—and its people were not inclined to be overly curious. A group of neighborhood children, lining up in a vacant lot to watch the volksrocket being towed to the spaceport, had been Sagan's only audience.

He traveled hyperspace to as near Vallombrosa as the Lanes would take him, left them at the same point the explorer Garth Pantha had left them on his journey. Sagan had entered Pantha's old log (part of the courier's delivery from Admiral Dixter) into the spaceplane's computer. It was a voice log, deliberately recorded by Pantha for playback on his own vidshow. Sagan listened to the entire log often; the gravelly voice with the honey drawl became a familiar companion on the long trip, as familiar to him as the notes of Bach's Concerto No. 2 in F, one of the several "Brandenburg Concertos" he had brought to fill the silence that was now so terribly silent.

He listened to Pantha's narrative with the ear of one who not only enjoyed music but who subconsciously analyzed musical cadences and intricate patterns. Hearing the log over and over again, Sagan was interested to note that, at one point in the narrative, Pantha's discourse grated on the ear, as if the conductor and entire orchestra had skipped a measure.

"Computer, analyze voice patterns," Sagan commanded. "Specifically, was this section of the voice log data entered at the same time as the rest of the log?"

The computer's response was negative. The original log entry had been erased and this entry substituted. The splicing had been expertly done. Sagan himself had not noticed it at first. Constant repetition, familiarization with the rhythms and patterns of Pantha's speech, and the Warlord's own finely tuned musical ear had caught the slight discrepancy.

The original log entry concerning Vallombrosa had been altered by Pantha, presumably at a later date. He had entered his initial discovery of Vallombrosa and information concerning it in his log; then he had, for some reason, altered the log.

Sagan sat back in the pilot's chair, leaned his elbows on the armrests, placed his fingertips together, and gazed out over them at tiny specks, like glittering dust, that were as Vallombrosa's suns.

"Why did you alter it? What did you discover that you decided to keep hidden? Or perhaps not completely hidden. Perhaps you gave us a clue. The name. Vallombrosa. Vale of Shades. Valley of Ghosts. You told us that much—a clever little joke for your own private amusement."

He pondered on the problem long, considering this, discarding that. One of the first things he threw out was the information gathered from the unmanned space probes. That information was false, he decided, although how it had been altered, who or what had found the means to tamper with the probes without revealing themselves to the probes was a fascinating problem. At length he gave up trying to solve it and went to bed. He would have answers tomorrow, for he would, by his calculations, be near enough to the planet to take his own readings—unless something decided to tamper with him.

The next day, something did.

His first indication of the strange presence came moments before he would reach the point where his instruments could begin long-range scanning of the planet. He was standing in the small galley, brewing a pot of oolong tea (a luxury he had denied himself during his years at the abbey) when he experienced a most remarkable and unusual sensation.

He felt compressed, as if each bone and muscle in his body were being compacted, as if his limbs were now made of lead, as if every gram of body weight was suddenly equivalent to a kilogram. The sensation passed immediately, almost before his brain could register it, and he might have ignored it except that there was an odd déjà vu quality about it, as if it had happened to him before.

At almost precisely the same instant, sensor alarms sounded. He looked swiftly about the interior of the small spaceplane. Movement caught his eye—the breviary lying on his nightstand rose into the air, then fell back down. The book had moved only the barest fraction of a centimeter, but the book had certainly moved.

Forgetting the tea, Sagan advanced to the console, to eagerly examine the instruments, which were not standard equipment on a volksrocket. Whatever had been in his plane was now apparently gone. All instrument readings—from motion detectors to heat sensors—were back to normal. But there *had* been something on board. It had left its trace. He began to compare the data with the readings taken from the security devices guarding the dwelling place of the late Snaga Ohme.

Sagan studied again Xris's vid report (compliments of Dixter), and he understood why the odd feeling of being compressed had seemed familiar to him. It *had* happened before—only not to him. He came to that part of Xris's report, played it back.

"Now, that's another strange thing, boss," the cyborg was saying. "The guards didn't see or hear anything, but one of them reported *feeling* something. About a split second before the alarm went off. She said she felt as if she'd been shoved into a compression chamber. The feeling passed immediately. She shows no physical damage, no chemical alteration. No increase in radiation level, no aftereffects. But notice where she was standing, boss."

According to Dixter's files, the guard had been standing right in the path the "ghosts" had taken to enter the sealed vault. Sagan reran the report, time and again, matched it with his own instrument readings.

Xris: "The first we know we're being invaded, the motion detectors inside the house start registering movement. Like you see there."

Sagan's own motion detectors had picked up movement inside the spaceplane.

Xris: "A drop in barometric pressure—in certain areas only— and a corresponding movement of the air in places where no air should be moving."

Sagan's instruments registered the same.

Xris: "The thing moved too damn fast. It made it safely to the house, slid right through a fortified exterior wall that could withstand a direct hit from a lascannon and not buckle. Nothing stopped it. Nothing even phased it, apparently."

It had passed through the hull of a spaceplane—not a plane intended for combat, admittedly, but one meant to withstand the rigors of space travel.

Xris: ". . . We registered an increase in the radiation level around the vault. Not much. But enough to make us suspicious, especially tracing the path the thing took. We examined the vault's superstructure. There'd been an alteration in the metal itself, a chemical change, enough to generate radioactivity. And only in that one place, directly in line with the path."

Sagan examined the plane's superstructure, the console's, the nightstand on which the breviary rested. An increase in radioactivity.

Xris: "The bomb was moved."

Dixter: "Moved?"

Xris: "Jostled, handled. Not much—a fraction of a fraction of a centimeter before it vanished. But enough to set off the alarm."

And the book had moved. Another man might have doubted his own senses, told himself he was seeing things, but Sagan had no such self-doubts. He had trained himself to be observant, had trained himself to trust those observations once he'd analyzed them. He knew he hadn't been seeing things. Ghostly hands had touched that book. The same ghostly hands that had touched the fake bomb.

The same ghostly hands that had, apparently, touched him. He was beginning to get a faint glimmer of what might have happened to the space probes.

He took his seat in the pilot's chair. The plane was now within instrument range of the planet. Whatever was going to happen should happen now. He was either going to be permitted to find out the truth ... or he was going to be stopped.

Sagan waited, alert, tense. He was not particularly fearful. Whatever it was, whoever it was, wanted him here. He had, in a sense, received an invitation to this party. But there was always the chance (however slight) that he had miscalculated, misjudged this person, the entire situation. It could be that the Warlord was wanted ... wanted out of the way.

And here he was, in an unarmed spaceplane. It didn't even have any shields. Although from what he'd seen (or not seen) of these "ghosts," shields were not likely to offer any protection.

He was well within range. His instruments were picking up and recording data on the planet known as Vallombrosa. Nothing had happened to him. He stood up, roamed about the small plane, returned to the galley. In his preoccupation, he'd let the tea steep too long. It was bitter. He poured it out, started to make another pot. Glancing over at his instruments, studying the preliminary findings, he smiled grimly, nodded.

He was being given the chance to draw aside the curtain, to open the lid on the box. He was being given the chance to see the truth.

Vallombrosa was itself deserted. But there was life, life that was not on the planet. Space stations circled it, huge space stations, each probably capable of housing thousands of people.

A Valley of Ghosts that was really quite lively.

And then Sagan, drinking his tea, noticed the anomaly.

The planet was unusually dense, far denser than it should have been, according to calculations based on its size and composition. The gravitational gradient was also way off. Surface gravity was noticeably higher than that of a planet of comparable size. What was more interesting, the gravity was fluctuating wildly. The gravity around a planet such as this should have been relatively even, smooth, with only occasional variations created by the flow of magma beneath the surface. By contrast, the gravity around this planet was erratic, dipping and surging like a storm-tossed sea.

Sagan ran more computations, double-checking his data. He had no doubt. Information on this anomaly was the material Pantha had originally entered in his log.

It was also the information he had deleted. The explorer had lied, deliberately falsified the records. He had made the planet appear ordinary, less than ordinary. He had made no mention of the anomaly.

And now Sagan was beginning to understand why. He began to transmit the collected data back to Admiral Dixter. Sagan presumed the "ghosts" would allow him to do this, wouldn't jam his signal. The time for—the need for—secrecy must be nearly at an end.

Transmission concluded, he sank back in the pilot's chair, with its cracked plastic and exposed bits of foam rubber, and stared unseeing at the flashing numbers, the instruments that were continuing to gather and spew forth data. The discovery, its terrifying import, the sudden rush of understanding as piece after piece of the puzzle locked into place, overwhelmed him with its enormity.

Warlord Derek Sagan was not a man to be easily over-whelmed. He rubbed his palm, which had begun to itch and burn, moved his fingers to touch the starjewel that he wore, once again, around his neck.

A light began to flash on the console. Communication was being established with the planet. Blips on his screen indicated the presence of several spaceplanes, probably escorts.

"Welcome, my lord Sagan," said the voice, a voice he'd heard often in his dreams and thus had no difficulty recognizing, "welcome to Vallombrosa—Valley of Ghosts."

Ghosts, indeed.

Chapter ❖❖ Six

Places you are tied down to—none. People with a hold on you—none. Men you step aside for—none.

The Magnificent Seven

The hotel on Ceres was high class, one of those four-star joints in the galaxy guidebooks. It catered to off-worlders, too, apparently, Xris noted, standing in line at the reception desk. The enormous lobby—replete with a fountain of dancing water adorned by musical metal spheres that soared and dipped in the air above the fountain—could have been used as a Catalog for Life-forms in the Milky Way.

Some sort of convention was taking place, judging by the name tags plastered on the lapels, scales, skin, and fur of the breasts, heads, feet, and tails of the individuals walking, creeping, or crawling through the lobby and adjacent meeting areas and ballrooms.

No one, except a harried-looking bellman, gave Xris so much as a raised eyebrow—unusual for the cyborg, whose acid-burned face and metal body parts, with their flashing LED lights, generally rated stealthy sideways glances, outright suspicious glares, or pitying, averted eyes. And the bellman, once he had been convinced that Xris had only one piece of luggage and that he would carry it himself, disdainfully turned his attention to the next, presumably tipping, customer.

"Single room. Name of Xris," said the cyborg when he reached the desk.

Another indication of a high-class joint—real live clerks. None of this stick-your-card-in-a-machine-and-get-a-room-for-the-night business.

The clerk handed over a key (an antique, honest-to-God key), along with the information that the room was paid for and all expenses would be covered.

Xris took the key and shouldered his way through the crowd in the lobby. His room was located on the ground floor—as he always specified. He never knew when he might have to make a quick exit and at such times it was damn inconvenient to stand around waiting for the elevator.

He entered his room, gave it the once-over for listening devices, hidden cams, explosives—the usual precautions. Finding it clean, in more ways than one, he opened his luggage case, took out a bottle of jump-juice, poured a jigger full into one of the water glasses, and continued his inspection.

Taking care to keep from being seen, he drew aside the window curtain. French doors opened onto a small, walled-off patio. Beyond that was an ornamental garden, graced with fountains and fancifully pruned shrubbery. In the distance, on the horizon, he could see the tops of mountains, bathed with a soft pink twilight tinge. The view was spectacular, but Xris wasn't noticing such things as mountains or flower beds. He was considering escape routes, possible sites for an ambush, hiding places for eavesdroppers or more sinister types.

The room appeared secure and was in a good, though not great, location. Xris was pleased, not particularly surprised. He'd done enough work for John Dixter to know that the admiral would be careful about such details. It was simply that the location for this meeting was so damn odd. Why rendezvous on Ceres? The message hadn't specified, but then, it wouldn't. Special code. Highest priority. Payment already deposited in his account. Xris wasn't even certain it was Dixter who had called him, yet who else would could it be?

Either Dixter . . . or the king.

Xris grinned at that one, shook his head. Taking out a twist, he stuck the black and noxious cigarette in his mouth and lit it. A swallow of jump-juice, then he yanked off his long-range weapons hand, packed it away in the specially designed compartment in his cybernetic leg. Taking out another weapons hand—this one designed for short-range work, tight, close quarters, all noise kept to a minimum—he attached it to his arm, checked it over to make sure all systems were operational.

He was sitting comfortably in his chair, drinking the jump-juice, when a particularly large and raucous group of conventioneers tramped past his room. He might have paid no attention except that his acute, enhanced hearing caught the faint sound of soft footfalls, perhaps using the others for cover, stop outside his door. There was silence a moment, then a knock—a swift, sharp rap.

"I didn't order room service," Xris called.

Nothing. No response.

Xris shifted slightly in his chair.

The knock was repeated.

"I said, I didn't order room service." He raised the volume. The correct response was, "Maintenance. Here to fix your vid."

The knock was repeated again, more sharply, peremptorily. It was beginning to sound irritated.

Xris adjusted his augmented vision in an attempt to see through the door, but the door and wall were shielded to prevent just such an occurrence. This *was* a high-class joint. He was glad Dixter was paying the bill.

Xris concentrated on his other senses. He didn't hear anything that sounded threatening—the whine of power packs charging up, or the slight *snick* made by the loading of a bolt gun. The silence meant next to nothing, however. The poisoner, Raoul, for example, could very quietly kiss you to death.

"Who is it?" Xris tried, for variety.

Not moving from where he sat—at an angle to the door, on the opposite side of the room from the door—Xris shifted his glass from his right hand to his left—his weapons hand. Propping his feet up on the bed, he leaned back comfortably in his chair.

"I am not room service. Let me in!" demanded a voice, with a hint of anger.

Xris was more curious now than worried. No hired gun worth the price of a bolt would stand outside his victim's room beating on the door. Yet this was obviously some kind of setup. An agent from Dixter or the king would have known the proper code response.

"Come on in, then," Xris called, hitting the manual remote control. "I've unlocked it."

Anyone intent on killing him would have to first locate him in the room, react to the fact that he was seated and not standing, then shoot at an angle—and all the while Xris would have the killer in his sights, in easy range of a deadly little poisoned dart that could be fired from the third knuckle of the cyborg's weapon's hand.

The door slid open. A woman entered.

She was short, for a human female, dressed in a smart black suit, expensive, well tailored, with a long, fingertip-length black jacket and a knee-length skirt revealing remarkable legs. She wore a black, wide-brimmed hat, trimmed in a black lace veil that covered her face. The ends of the veil were wrapped around her neck. Her hands were encased in soft black kid leather gloves.

The door shut behind her. The woman remaining standing just inside it, the veiled face turned expectantly toward Xris. She said no word, and it took Xris a moment to figure out what the hell was going on.

She was waiting expectantly for him to stand up, to rise when she entered the room.

He knew, then, who she was, if not how or why. Even though her face was hidden by the veil, there was no mistaking that dignified, regal stance, with the head slightly thrown back, the chin tilted upward. Things began to make sense, even as they didn't.

Xris thought he deserved a moment to recover from the shock. At length, setting down his drink (and deactivating the dart in his hand), he rose to his feet.

"Your Majesty," he said.

The queen appeared not displeased to be recognized. She unwrapped the veil from her face with graceful, deliberate motions, took off the hat, and carefully placed it upon the foot of the bed. She did not glance in the mirror—as nine out of ten women Xris knew would have, to pat their hair back in place— but seemed to take it for granted that she would look extraordinary, whether her hair was mussed or not.

And she did . . . look extraordinary.

Xris was impressed. He had seen Astarte, queen of the galaxy, on the vids, of course, but he had always figured that the cams were careful to capture her good side or that she'd hired a damn fine makeup artist. This woman was all over good sides and, as far as Xris could tell (and he'd become something of an expert, from hanging around Raoul), the queen wore very little makeup. The rose dusting on the high cheekbones, the coral-brushed lips, the port-wine eyes did not come from over the cosmetic counter.

"You're not surprised I knew who you were," Xris commented, to see what she would say.

"Of course not. You must have deduced that I would be the only person—other than His Majesty—capable of retrieving data on you from the classified files." The queen was pulling off her gloves with the same careful, deliberate motions. "Admittedly, I do not have security clearance; I am a royal consort and therefore have no military command status. However, it was quite simple for me to obtain access to . . . certain computers. And then it was only a matter of time and patience before I found what I was seeking.

"There, sir. Have I supplied you with enough information to satisfy any doubts? I trust the answer is yes," she went on, before Xris could reply, "because I won't tell you any more. I may have need to resort to this stratagem again and I wouldn't want you to spoil it for me."

She laid the gloves on the table, stood regarding Xris with a forthright, direct look that was cool, businesslike, and extremely disconcerting. She barely came to the cyborg's shoulder. His mechanical hand could have crunched her like a bug, yet she obviously had no doubt who was in command of the situation. And, according to her, it wasn't Xris.

He found his voice, which seemed to have seized up on him, and shrugged.

"It's not up to me to say whether Your Majesty does or doesn't have the right to poke around in your husband's classified files, but I would be interested in knowing how you happened to go looking for me. Or did Your Majesty just start at the bottom of the alphabet and pick the first name you came across?"

"A fair question," she said after a moment's thought and cool appraisal. "You may sit down." She made a regal gesture. "Don't smoke."

Xris had taken a twist out of his pocket. Now he looked at it, looked at her, then stuck the twist back in his pocket again. The queen walked over to the window. Parting the curtains, she glanced out.

"There's no one out there, Your Majesty, unless you were followed," Xris offered.

"No, I wasn't followed," said the queen. "I'm my mother's daughter, after all."

This meant nothing to Xris, beyond the fact that she said it with a hard and bitter edge to her voice. She let the curtain fall, turned back to face him.

"I heard His Majesty speak of you. He told me the story of how the Lady Maigrey hired you and your team. How you went with her into that terrible moon in the Corasian galaxy. How you risked your own life to save the life of Tusca, His

Majesty's best friend. You helped the Lady Maigrey. She trusted you. It occurred to me, when I needed help, that I could trust you, as well."

The wine-colored eyes lifted to meet his. She was breathtaking. Xris would have taken off his cloak—had he owned a cloak—thrown it in the mud at her feet. Hell, he would have thrown himself into the mud at her feet, begged her to walk on him. But he reminded himself sternly that business was business and he'd better keep this on a business footing—which meant standing on his own two.

"Look, Your Majesty, the Lady Maigrey and I had a deal, a business deal, a contract—"

"You will be well paid, of course," said Astarte, with a slight smile. "I regret that I cannot give you a written contract, but there must be no record of our involvement. I am going to be asking you to do certain things and you will not know precisely why, nor will I be able to tell you. Is this going to be a problem?"

She was cool, very cool. This was some sort of test and "yes" wasn't the right answer.

"So long as you're not going to ask me to do anything that would make me a traitor," Xris said bluntly. "I live by my own rules, generally; I'm my own boss. I've been known to bend the law when I thought it needed bending, or break it on occasion—"

"Such as this last trip you made across enemy lines?" Astarte asked, interrupting. "To rescue your wife, wasn't it? Did you succeed? I hope you did. That was a strong point in your favor."

Xris stared at her, his brain feeling the way his body felt when his battery pack shut down—helpless, paralyzed. He opened his mouth, but no words came out. The silence was broken instead by a series of small beeps. Lights flashed—his weapons arm, undergoing a routine systems check.

"I'm sorry," Astarte said, not even glancing at it. "I shouldn't have interrupted you. You were saying?"

Xris had no idea. All he could remember was the substance. "I won't do anything to hurt the king," he said harshly. "He's all right. I think he's doing an okay job. If you have anything like that in mind, sister, you better pick up your hat and gloves and start walking."

He was rough on her, purposefully so. Her face flushed, but not in shame.

"I am not your sister. Nor will you address me as such." Astarte's voice lowered; she looked almost sad. "What I hire you to do will not harm His Majesty. You might say, in a way, it will save his life. Or what he values more than life."

She said the last in a soft tone, so soft only the cyborg's augmented hearing could have registered it. She began to droop, wilt like a cut rose. Had Xris's arms been flesh and blood instead of metal, he might have taken her into those arms, patted her on the back, told her to have a good cry. Had she been flesh and blood, instead of queen of the galaxy, she might have done so.

As it was, Xris shifted uncomfortably, began fiddling unnecessarily with the controls on his cybernetic leg.

She asked, in the same low tone, "Did you rescue your wife?"

"Yes," Xris said briefly.

Astarte waited a moment, giving him a chance to add details, something he'd never do as long as his artificial heart kept pumping what passed for blood through his body. But he did wonder what had prompted the question, which must have been tripping on the heels of whatever thoughts had gone before it.

He couldn't begin to guess what she had in mind. If he'd been watching the vids, reading the mags, keeping up with the latest gossip, he might have been able to figure it out. Too bad Raoul and the Little One weren't with him. Raoul would have known what was coming down. The Adonian could have named every garment in the queen's wardrobe, complete with accessories. And the little empath would have been invaluable. Not that it took an empath to sense that beneath the purple velvet mantle of royalty, sophistication, and power, this queen, who had—presumably—the resources of a vast empire at her disposal, was desperate, afraid, alone.

Which meant she'll pay big, he told himself. And he'd probably earn it. From what he remembered from college history class, those who got mixed up in court intrigues did not live long and happy lives. But that was a small consideration; almost no consideration at all. Xris's life wasn't so great that he'd turn down good money to prolong it.

Flesh-and-blood women. They could be grateful to a machine that saved them, but never love one. No matter what they said.

He'd been silent so long that Astarte was looking anxious, apparently thinking he was still having doubts about her. "I swear to you, by the Goddess whom I serve, that I would never ask you or anyone to harm the king." She laid her hand on his arm. Her flesh-and-blood hand. His cybernetic arm. "You must believe me."

Xris smiled, shrugged. "Sure. Okay. I believe you. Feels strange, doesn't it, Your Majesty?" he added. "You expect it to be warm, like normal flesh."

"I didn't," she replied. "Also included in your file were complete diagrams showing how you've been put together. I studied them extensively."

Xris regarded her thoughtfully. Maybe he'd been wrong about her. Her touch was just as cold to his sensors as his own metal. Maybe colder.

She removed her hand, slowly, and turned away. Picking up her gloves, she put them on, smoothed them out. She then lifted her wide-brimmed hat, placed it on her head—this time looking at herself in the mirror—and adjusted the veil.

"All women in mourning on this planet must hide their faces for thirty days. You have your own spaceplane. Where is it parked?"

"Spaceport Central. Gate 16-X. Look, Your Majesty, now that you know that you can trust me and I know that I can trust you, why don't you tell me what's going on?"

She tied the veil around her neck. "We will leave now, taking the monorail to the spaceport. You are a transport pilot in my employ. My lover died off-world. I have hired you to bring her body back home for burial."

"Nice cover story, but I mean, what's really going on?"

"No. Not now. Not here." She glanced around at him. "Maybe not ever. You will follow orders."

Astarte looked back at herself, made a minor adjustment to the hat. "When we reach the spaceport, you will go straight to the plane. I will gain clearance for our departure, as well as our return. The journey will be short: forty-eight hours. I will make all the other arrangements, including having the coffin loaded onto your plane."

"Coffin, huh? What's in it? Are they likely to X-ray it?"

"Nothing is in it. I told you. We are going to pick up my lover's body. Are you ready?" She turned to face him, her head back, chin tilted.

Xris took a last, quick swallow of the jump-juice, stuck the bottle back into his luggage. Since that was the only item he'd unpacked, he was ready. He pulled a twist out of his pocket, stuck it in his mouth.

"You will not smoke," she said.

Xris eyed her, considering.

"Royal command?"

"If you want to think of it that way."

"Huh-uh. And speaking of royal commands, just what or who's going to be in the coffin coming back, Your Majesty?"

He couldn't see her face. The veil concealed her features, hid them behind an intricate pattern of lacy black net. But he could see the coral lips part in a cool smile.

"That depends on you," she said. "And now we should go. Time is critical."

She turned, faced the door, stood waiting expectantly for him to open it for her.

Xris opened it.

She walked out, head high, without a backward look. She assumed he would follow.

"Damn," Xris muttered, half-exasperated, half-admiring.

He looked at the twist in his hand. Shrugging, he took the rest of the pack out of his pocket, tossed it on the floor, and followed. He'd been meaning to quit anyway.

Chapter ·◆●○●◆· Seven

KING: Where is the crown? Who took it from my pillow?
WARWICK: When we withdrew, my liege, we left it here.
KING: The Prince hath taken it hence. Go, seek him out.
Is he so hasty that he doth suppose
My sleep my death?

William Shakespeare, *King Henry IV,* Part Two,
Act IV, Scene v

Twelve hours had passed since the voice had welcomed Sagan to the Valley of Ghosts. Twelve hours and no further communication. He spent the time retrieving more data on the planet, its double suns, and its artificial moons—the orbiting space stations.

The lid was off the box; one mystery was solved—only to find a nest of boxes inside. Thousands of people, concealed from the knowledge of the rest of the galaxy. Easy enough to spirit away one bastard child. But an entire civilization? It was not difficult figuring out what had happened to the probes. The "ghosts" that had moved the breviary had undoubtedly "moved" the probes as well. But how do you keep thousands of people silent? How do you keep them from saying to the rest of the galaxy, "We're here!"?

A strong leader could do it. A leader to whom all were unswervingly loyal, faithful. One of the Blood Royal. . . .

At least Sagan was no longer alone in space. Activity in the area had picked up. Sleek fighter planes, of a new design based on his old Scimitar, flashed past every hour or so, keeping an eye on him. At one point he caught a glimpse of a fleet of warships and support craft. Visual observation showed him very little: the flash of sunlight off a ship's prow, occasional streaks of tracer fire, the winking of running lights. His monitors gave him a detailed description, however. The numbers were impressive, consisting of battle cruisers, tankers, carriers, supply ships. Impressive, but not *that* impressive. It was not a force large enough to conquer a galaxy. Nor did it appear well trained or well organized.

A particularly ragged formation flew past. Sagan caught himself on his feet, his face grim, his hand on the commlink controls, about to give the pilots a brief lesson in flying. Recalling where he was—what he was—he stopped himself. Sitting back in his chair, he smiled over old memories.

But the smile was twisted by pain, a sweet honey drink laced with bitter poison—temptation, longing, sudden ardent desire. Once more he was on the old *Phoenix*, standing before the viewscreen on the bridge, watching the exercises, fuming in impotent rage, shaking his head at some piece of stupidity, holding his breath over near disaster averted at the last minute, finally taking his spaceplane out himself and showing by example what he wanted, feeling that inner satisfaction when some terrified recruit overcame fear and confusion and actually did what he was supposed to do—that was life. That had been his life. And it could be again; Sagan recognized a shining red apple when he saw one. He didn't need to see the grinning serpent coiled around it.

He stared at the wheeling, flashing planes, the huge mothering ships that would receive their children home. In that life there was noise. In that life he would no longer hear the roaring silence.

And in that instant, it all vanished.

Ships, planes, stars, sun, planet. Everything went black around him. He darted a swift look at his instrument panel, but whatever was happening to him was sending the instruments berserk.

It happened too fast for fear. His first and most immediate reaction was: "What the—" A shattering crash cut that brief thought short.

The impact sent him sprawling across the console, knocked the breath from his body. The sharp edges of various knobs and switches jabbed into him, bruising and cutting him. The volksrocket jolted and jounced, then lurched to a stop that was as sudden as the initial impact, slammed Sagan into the steelglass viewscreen.

The plane wobbled, then settled to rest. The Warlord lay where he was for a moment, dazed and shaken. Gradually he recovered his breath. His head began to throb in pain. He shoved himself up off the console. Putting his hand to his scalp, he felt blood, warm and sticky.

He sank into a chair, to give himself time to recover and try to assess what had happened. A glance out the viewscreen showed him it was night and he was on land . . . or a reasonable facsimile thereof. The lights on his plane shone on the leaves and thick boles of several huge trees—probably what he'd crashed into. Instrument readings, now back to normal, indicated that he was definitely on land. Judging by the strange gravitational fluctuations being recorded, he was on Vallombrosa. But how he'd arrived here in such a short time from outer space made for extremely interesting speculation.

Thinking back on the entire startling few moments, he had the distinct impression that his plane had been snagged, flung through time and space like a rock from a slingshot.

Well, demanded a voice in his mind, *are you coming?*

Someone was waiting for him, waiting impatiently.

Sagan stood up. The pain in his head subsided to a dull throbbing that he relegated to the inner core of his being, ignored. He washed the blood from his face, stripped off the battle fatigues, stowed them in the trash compactor. He dressed himself once again in the plain and shabby cassock of the humble Brother Paenitens.

The outside atmosphere was breathable. He opened the hatch, found a splintered tree limb lying across it, blocking his way. Heaving the tree to one side, he kicked his way through a tangle of broken branches, walked down the stairs to the ground.

Dark night. And cold. No wind, but the air temperature was chill. There would be thick, heavy frost by morning. The sky was cloudless, spanned by a rift of stars. His plane had landed (been *dropped* might be a more appropriate term) on the fringes of a forest of deciduous trees. Last year's rotting leaves matted the ground. And there were evergreens, too; he could smell the sharp, clean scent of pine.

Looking around, he saw that the spaceplane rested on the gently sloping side of a steep hill, extending upward. The tree line ended not far beyond. A vast expanse of smooth, cropped grass was clearly visible in the darkness, a lighter grayish color against the tree-covered hills surrounding it. At the top burned a fire.

The fire was the only indication of life, of habitation anywhere around. The blaze was enormous. Flames leapt high into the air. He could hear the crackling roar from where he stood, several hundred meters away. A man stood before the fire, silhouetted black against it. Calmly waiting. Calmly watching. Yet with that hint of impatience that drifted through the air like the smoke.

Sagan drew his cowl up over his head, clasped his hands over his wrists beneath the sleeves of his cassock. He began to climb the hill, moving toward the fire.

Suddenly he had the strange impression that he was not walking alone. He was being followed. The hair on the right side of the back of his neck prickled; the skin on his right shoulder and back twitched, as if any second he expected a touch—a hand . . . a blade. He listened, heard nothing. The soft, thick grass underfoot would muffle all but the most careless sounds. Sagan cursed the hood that blocked his peripheral vision, continued walking at an even, measured pace.

The man standing in front of the fire had not moved.

Sagan left the forest behind and with it any cover for his pursuer, who was still keeping close behind him—or so he sensed. The follower must be counting on his own silent movements not to betray him; that and the fact that Warlord's vision was partially obscured by the cowl.

But why track him at all? Why not watch from the cover of the trees? If the man waiting at the fire felt the need to guard the Warlord, why the stealth?

Sagan moved his hands silently from out of the sleeves, loosened the starjewel he wore on the leather thong around his neck.

The starjewel fell to the ground.

Muttering to himself, the Warlord halted, bent to retrieve it. He jerked his head, flung back the cowl, looked around to see behind him.

Nothing. No one. Yet in the instant of his turning, he'd caught, out of the corner of his eye, a flash of silver armor.

He picked up the starjewel, hung it back around his neck, working slowly, deliberately, giving himself time to think. Had he truly seen that flash? Or was it his imagination? He looked to the fire.

The figure standing by the blaze stirred impatiently, peered into the darkness to see what was causing the delay.

Sagan shook his head. With a wry half-smile, he replaced the

cowl over his head, straightened, walked on, quickening his
pace.

He stepped into the circle of light.

The figure remained standing where he was, aware that he
was under inspection. A man of about twenty-eight years, with
saturnine features, square-jawed, hawk-nosed, arched brows.
His glistening blue-black hair was pulled tight from his face,
gathered in a blunt-cut tail at the back of his head, in the fashion of Earth's ancient Oriental warriors.

He was clad in a richly embroidered tunic, worn over a long,
flowing sleeved blouse. The tunic's stiff, extended shoulders
enhanced muscular shoulders of his own, a wide chest, and
strong arms. His stance was straight, upright, open. His posture
was regal, self-confident.

Not much like his father, was Sagan's first thought.

Of course, when the Warlord had met the king, Amodius was
in middle age, sickly, bowed down by the burdens of an empire
that were rapidly burying him. But if Sagan had previously had
any doubts as to this younger man's heritage, they were resolved when he saw the eyes; the Starfire blue eyes, brilliant,
sharp, and many-faceted. And at his side he wore the
bloodsword.

Derek Sagan halted within the outer edge of the circle of
light. He said nothing, made no move.

The man left the fire, strode rapidly down the gentle slope of
the hill, came to stand in front of the Warlord. Reaching out his
hands—his movements graceful, respectful—he took hold of
the hood covering Sagan's head and laid it back, revealing his
face.

The Starfire eyes regarded Sagan intently, taking in every
line, every shadow.

"It *is* you," the man said at last. "I knew you would come.
Welcome, my lord. Welcome."

He extended his hands. Sagan's hands opened. The young
man grasped them in a firm, strong grip.

"Welcome, my lord," he said again.

"What are you called?" Sagan asked, studying the younger
man's face, attempting to trace some feature he knew, find a
family resemblance.

This young man and Dion were first cousins. Coming from
an incestuous liaison between brother and sister, they were
linked genetically closer than most first cousins. And there *was*

a resemblance. But beyond the eyes, which could have been exchanged two for two, the resemblance was subtle—a way of tilting the head, an echo in the voice, the lift of the hand.

"I am Flaim," said the younger man, with a glance at the blazing fire and a smile that included Sagan in the jest. "The name was my poor mother's choice. She was something of a romantic, Pantha tells me. I have a poem she wrote shortly after my birth, explaining the name. It is a long, rambling piece, filled with images of purifying fires, exploding suns consuming the universe, that sort of thing. Probably all sexual in nature; a psychiatrist would find it most enlightening.

"Yes," he added, in response to Sagan's frowning, questioning look, "I am aware of the truth about my past. Pantha has never made a secret of it. Why should he? I have no need to be ashamed. In this age, are we to allow ourselves to be governed by out-of-date taboos handed down from our forefathers? We might as well be wearing their animal skins and living in their caves.

"But come, my lord." Flaim gestured toward a large pavilion set on a rise beyond the crackling blaze. "Come inside, rest yourself. Take food and drink. We have much to talk about, you and I." He took hold of the Warlord's hand. "I have heard so much about you. It is good to meet you at last."

Sagan made no response, and his silence did not seem to disappoint Flaim. He smiled again, a warm smile, brilliant as the eyes, and, keeping hold of the Warlord's hand, led him with charming grace to a large striped tent that had been erected on a level plot of ground near the fire. The tent flap was raised, attached to two spearlike poles thrust into the ground. A glowing brazier inside kept the pavilion warm. Colorful rugs covered the ground, tasseled bolsters provided arm rests when seated.

As they entered, a man emerged from the shadows at the back of the pavilion. Flaim motioned to him.

"Garth Pantha. Lord Derek Sagan. I don't believe you two ever met," said Flaim, his gaze shifting from one to the other, curious to note the reaction of each.

"No, I never had the pleasure," said Pantha, extending his hand. His voice was the deep, rich baritone that so enthralled his millions of fans, and though he must be nearing ninety, he stood erect, walked firmly, had obviously kept himself in superb physical condition.

Sagan saw the accumulation of years in the wise scrutiny of

the dark eyes, in the white hair that was a marked contrast to the black skin, in the tightening of the flesh across the finely sculpted bones of the face.

"I never had the pleasure of meeting you, my lord," Pantha repeated, "but I do feel that I know you. I have followed your exploits with interest. I remember hearing about you and your Golden Squadron. I said to myself, 'There goes a dangerous young man, one who knows what he wants and will take it.' "

Pantha smiled, shrugged. "Too bad I did not share my concerns about you with Amodius. Not that he would have listened. And I must admit that the Revolution caught even me by surprise. I discounted Abdiel, you see. As did others. . . ."

His keen gaze probed, sought to penetrate.

Sagan met the gaze, blocked it, turned it.

"Needless to say I am quite familiar with your exploits, sir," the Warlord returned. He added, with a significant glance at the world around him, "Though obviously not all of them."

Pantha chuckled. "Well put. I trust you studied your instrument readings on your way here. I would be interested to know what you deduced—"

"Enough, my friend," Flaim interrupted, placing his hand on the Warlord's shoulder. "The two of you can discuss scientific anomalies at a later time." He drew Sagan away from Pantha, who—with a glance of fond indulgence—bowed and faded back into the shadows.

But Sagan saw the old man's eyes gleaming in the firelight.

"Seat yourself, my lord. Forgive the informality of our surroundings." Flaim watched over the Warlord anxiously, eager to promote his comfort. "I intended that our first meeting should take place in absolute privacy—as much for your sake as my own. The alcazar where I reside is a large building. There are those on my staff who would know you by sight. You want people to believe you dead. I respect that, you see. Whether and when you reveal the truth shall be your decision."

Sagan stretched out on the rugs, reclined against the armrest. He refused an offer of food, but accepted water. Flaim himself poured the water into a silver tankard, placed it within the Warlord's reach. Assured that he could do nothing more to add to Sagan's comfort, Flaim sat down cross-legged, with the ease and elasticity of a youth. His face was sideways to the firelight. Sagan's face was turned toward the light. Pantha sat in the shadows, near his prince.

"By the way," Flaim said, placing his hands on his knees, "did you see something move out in the night as you were coming our direction? I saw it, and I thought you did as well, for you stopped and turned. What was it? Do you have any idea? Was someone out there?"

If so, Sagan thought, sipping at his water, you don't appear to be much worried. No guards in sight. And just what did you see? Or think you saw? Her? It's possible, I suppose. You are Blood Royal. . . .

"I heard something rustle in the brush," he said aloud. "I assumed it was some animal."

Flaim appeared dubious, regarded Sagan in thoughtful silence, as if wondering how to say politely that he knew the Warlord was a liar.

"It could have been one of *them*, my prince," said Pantha from out of the shadows.

Flaim's brow cleared. "Yes, you are right. I hadn't considered that. Of course they would be curious. And now, my lord," he continued, leaning forward eagerly, "tell me, why have you come?"

Sagan carefully replaced the tankard upon the multi-colored rug on which he reclined. Lifting his gaze, he looked into the Starfire blue eyes, spoke quietly, calmly.

"I come in search of a king."

Flaim seemed in an instant the embodiment of his name. The heat was palpable.

"You have found him, my lord," he said softly.

Sagan's heart constricted with a strange pain. He saw a resemblance at last, a striking resemblance, but not to Dion. The Warlord saw himself.

He hadn't expected this, wasn't prepared to face it.

"That remains to be seen," he said coolly, looking down at the water, seeing his reflection again in the smooth surface. "I have questions, many questions. And there is the rite of initiation."

"Yes, my lord. So Pantha told me. I am ready."

"He did not tell you too much?" Sagan's eyes narrowed. He looked at the old man.

"Only what is permitted, my lord," Pantha said. "Flaim needs nothing more, as you will see."

Yes, Sagan concluded, I can well believe that. Still, we will see. . . .

"And now it is my turn to ask a question: What is it that *you* want, Flaim Starfire?" Sagan asked.

"What do you think, my lord?" Flaim's answer was illuminated by his blazing smile. "The throne, the crown. I want to be king."

"Gaining that will be difficult."

"Of course." Flaim shrugged, nonchalant. "My cousin Dion knows about me, doesn't he? You told him what you discovered at the hospital. You told him the doctor's story."

"I told him. He was already aware of you, though." Sagan glanced pointedly at the bloodsword.

Flaim caressed the hilt with his hand. "We've seen each other, but not communicated. Not as you and I have, my lord. I decided it would be best if information about me came from you. He would believe you. But that wasn't the only reason I arranged the hospital scenario. I wanted to pique your curiosity, my lord."

"Scenario." Sagan frowned. "Was her story a lie?"

"Oh, no, my lord." Flaim was suddenly serious, earnest. "The doctor told the truth. She *was* with my mother. Pantha knew her. He was the one who later found her. He can tell you."

Sagan glanced back into the shadows, to the old man's gleaming eyes.

"I made certain, my lord," Pantha said, "that I found out the name of every person on the staff. I kept files, complete dossiers on each. I knew, you see, that someday my prince might need these people to come forward as witnesses."

Sagan stirred, but said nothing.

"But, as I told you, I was not expecting the Revolution. It upset our plans considerably—"

"*Our* plans?" Sagan interrupted.

"Mine . . . Amodius's. Oh"—Pantha waved a hand, barely visible in the shadows—"Amodius didn't instruct me in so many words, but I knew him. He was ambitious, more than most would credit him. Why would he give *me* the child, if he was not certain that I would raise him to be a king, and that someday I would bring the boy back to claim his rightful inheritance?"

"Not rightful," Sagan corrected mildly.

"And why not?" Pantha demanded, with a flare of anger. "Taboos of the dark ages!"

"Taboos with a reason."

"Bah!" Pantha waved that away. "Such societal laws made sense to our benighted ancestors, but that was before genetic engineering. Are we saddled with any of the rest of their archaic ideas? They used to believe that man could not travel faster than the speed of light. They used to believe that they were the only creatures with intelligence living in the galaxy. We no longer subscribe to those outdated notions. Why should we be forced to follow their outmoded codes of morality?"

"Pantha, my friend," interposed Flaim, suddenly cool and imperious, with a hint of steel, "please desist. Now is not the time."

The older man said nothing further, subsided back into the shadows. Flaim turned to the Warlord.

"You must forgive my dear friend's ardor. He is right, of course, and, as I said, I am not ashamed of my parentage. But I understand that the taboo against incest is a gut-level feeling for many humans, not something that can be argued away rationally. It comes with the same cave-man instincts that pump adrenaline into our blood, enabling us to run away from the lion.

"Pantha would have me reveal my birth openly, but I can see where it would cause problems. I have therefore concocted documents which prove my father's secret marriage to a woman of whom he was enamored in his youth. What was her name, my friend?" Flaim turned to Pantha. "I can never recall it."

"Magdelena of Artemis 6," answered the old man. "You know the story, naturally, my lord."

"Yes," said Sagan. "I know Amodius loved this woman, openly courted her. I also know that she died of the plague which swept over that planet."

"Of course she did," said Flaim. "But who's to remember that now? We play with the truth, keep the elements of the truth alive. She goes insane. Her family locks her away, gives out to the media that she's died of the plague. But Amodius, faithful to the love of his life, visits her monthly, fathers a child. . . . "

"Why didn't he introduce the baby into court as the legitimate heir, then?"

Flaim shrugged. "Who knows? Many reasons. Perhaps Amodius wanted to make certain I was strong and healthy. Perhaps he hoped my mother might recover her sanity and could herself be introduced as queen. Does it matter? Because then comes the Revolution. Amodius and my uncle are murdered. Pantha, fearing for my life, keeps me hidden away. Much as the Lady Maigrey and her friends kept my cousin Dion hidden. You see, my lord, the seeds of the romantic tale are already planted in the people's minds. They will accept my story without hesitation."

"Ingenious," Sagan admitted. "And quite convenient of the doctor to die and make a deathbed confession at this point in time. How did you manage to find her?"

"Pantha discovered her." Flaim glanced at his mentor.

"The Revolution was a devastating blow to me," Pantha conceded. "When I heard the reports—"

"You had a base established for yourself here on Vallombrosa prior to your 'death,' I take it?" Sagan interrupted.

"Of course. The planet's 'inhabitants' performed the work for me, built a place for me to live. But you will hear more of them later. As I was saying, I was here on Vallombrosa when I heard the reports. I feared the worst—that the hospital, all the records, all witnesses had been destroyed. I hastened to the planet, traveling in disguise, of course, for I was supposed to be dead.

"Investigation led me to believe that this doctor had escaped the pogrom. I traced her—a long and tedious task. Eventually I learned the name of the man with whom she fled. Fortunately, since he was not Blood Royal and therefore in no danger, he saw no need to change his name. She simply altered hers to his.

"A study of passenger ship records enabled me to discover the name of the planet on which they disembarked. I found them and kept them in sight, hoping that the day would come when the doctor would be of use. And it did."

Sagan shook his head. "The doctor could testify that Amodius had fathered a son. But she also knew that Flaim was not only illegitimate—which would in itself prevent him from ascending to the throne—but that Flaim was the product of an incestuous union. I don't see how this helps you."

"I must admit that at first I wasn't certain myself. I had various ideas. Perhaps we could 'persuade' the doctor to go along with our story. A risky procedure, but . . . who knows?" Pantha shrugged. "Everyone has a price. Fortunately, we did not have to resort to that. Three circumstances made our next move ob-

vious: the fall of the corrupt government of Peter Robes;
Flaim's young cousin coming to power; and you, my lord, dis-
associating yourself from him."

"I felt your disappointment, my lord," said Flaim earnestly.
"I understood. Dion was not what you hoped he would be. But
then, he didn't even know his own name until four years ago.
I have always known who I am. I was raised to be a king."

He looked to Pantha and smiled. The younger man reached
out and clasped the old man's hand. Pantha nodded; the firelight in the dark eyes shimmered a moment. Then, clearing his
throat, Pantha continued speaking, in a low and husky voice.

"You see, my lord, at that point, it was no longer a question
of having to prove my prince's claim to the universe. We had
only to prove it to you."

Sagan was silent, thoughtful. He shifted his weight, trying to
get comfortable. There is an art to reclining on rugs and cushions, just as there is an art to kneeling all night in prayer on a
cold stone floor.

"You find the doctor. The doctor has contracted a deadly disease." Sagan pursued the subject with interest. "What did you
do then?"

"I discovered that she was a convert to the religion of the
Order of Adamant. From there on, my course of action was
plain. It *was* fortunate for us that she became infected with this
particular disease. The progression of the illness is slow. It does
not debilitate the mind, but leaves it—in its weakened
condition—open to outside influences. It was a simple matter
to induce the 'dreams,' drive her to make her confession."

"*Fortunate?*" Sagan asked.

Pantha smiled, shrugged. "Many of her patients were infected. The odds were against her, and she knew it. She was
not surprised to find she had accidentally contracted it. Nor did
she ever suspect otherwise"

Sagan nodded. "The doctor's death was necessary," he conceded. "But now two other people beside myself know the
truth. The reverend mother, who heard the confession, and the
archbishop."

"The reverend mother has suffered a most unfortunate accident," Pantha said gently.

Sagan frowned, said pointedly, "The archbishop is a friend of
mine. I trust he will not have an 'accident.'"

"Oh, no! Most assuredly," Flaim answered, looking surprised.

"We would never— That is, we know you will be able to deal with the situation."

Yes, I can deal with it, Sagan thought. I dealt with it in the past.

"Why did you bring me here?" he asked slowly. Holding up his hand, he halted the immediate response. "First, know this. If you're expecting me to use my influence to convince Dion to abdicate the throne, forget it. He will never do so. He is strong, stronger than you think, perhaps. His loyalty to his people is great. He will not be easily coerced or intimidated. And so long as he has the space-rotation bomb in his possession, you are powerless to touch him."

"I understand, my lord," said Flaim. "Do not imagine that I underestimate my young cousin. The same blood burns in our veins. But Dion's very strength is also his weakness. He has the space-rotation bomb, that is true. But he will not use it. Am I right in this, my lord?"

Sagan made no response.

Flaim, smiling to indicate that the secret was safely held between the two of them, went on.

"What do I want from you, my lord? Your support, of course. Your expertise, your knowledge. Your leadership. I will make you Lord Commander of my forces. My armies are immense, powerful. My people are fiercely loyal and committed to one thing—making me king. And then there is *our* secret weapon. You had a brief—but I would guess impressive—demonstration of it upon your arrival."

"You plan to go to war, then."

"No, my lord. I do not want to." Flaim shook his head emphatically. "Cousin Dion once made an extremely interesting point. It is not wise to declare war upon one's own people, he said. You start out with half your subjects hating you. I would avoid that, as he did."

Sagan was beginning to understand.

"My cousin must publicly abdicate," Flaim continued. "He must publicly acknowledge my right to rule. That will make it all so much simpler, don't you agree?"

"Yes, but as I said before, Dion will never do so."

"As circumstances stand now, no, he wouldn't. But circumstances have been known to change."

And he will tell me no more, Sagan said to himself. Not until

I commit to him, and perhaps not even then. He will tell me only what I need to know. As I would do. . . ."

"You understand, of course, that I can make no decision until I give you the rite," Sagan said. "If you are not worthy—"

"I will be, my lord," Flaim said, rising to his feet. "You will see. I will prove myself."

"Very well, then." Sagan stood, somewhat slowly and stiffly. "Tomorrow, at the suns' zenith. We must use this tent, I presume?"

"Yes, my lord. Whatever you need. You have only to instruct Pantha and me—"

"You will come alone." Sagan glanced at Pantha, who bowed in silent acknowledgment.

"Certainly, my lord. And now, allow me to show you to your quarters." With grace and dignity, Flaim led the way outside the pavilion, pointed out several smaller tents placed around it.

"Thank you," said Sagan, grimacing and putting his hand to the small of his back, "but I would prefer sleeping in my own bed. And I must spend time alone, in private meditation."

"As you wish, my lord." Flaim smiled ingratiatingly. "I will escort you back. Who knows what strange beings may lurk about here at night?"

"Ghosts, perhaps," the Warlord suggested.

"Perhaps," responded Flaim with a quick, intense look.

Sagan's face remained impassive.

Flaim turned to Pantha. "I will see to it that our guest is made comfortable and has all he requires. Good night, my friend."

Taking the hint, Pantha bowed, wished Sagan a healthful sleep, and took his leave, heading for the tent closest to the fire. The blaze was beginning to die down, the massive logs starting to crumble in upon themselves. Gray ashes drifted upward, floated on the night wind. It must have been one of these that brushed softly against the Warlord's hand as he walked past the dying blaze.

He and Flaim continued down the hill. When they had reached the spaceplane safely, the prince expressed his wishes for a pleasant evening's repose.

The Warlord returned the compliment. He was about to enter the volksrocket when Flaim stopped him.

"Do not be surprised to find that you are unable to send any more transmissions, my lord. From this point on, I have taken the liberty of having them blocked. I want my cousin to know my strength. I want him to worry. But now he's learned enough from you. Let him wonder. A sensible precaution, I think."

"Yes," Sagan agreed. "One that I would have taken myself."

Flaim expression turned thoughtful. "Did you ever reach the point where you could afford to trust people, my lord?"

Yes, Sagan answered silently, but by that time, it was too late.

"No, Your Highness," he said aloud. "That is the price one pays."

Flaim nodded, the matter—for him—resolved. Smiling his good night, he walked up the hill. Sagan watched him go, his strides long and confident, his head thrown back, his hand resting upon the hilt of the bloodsword at his waist.

Sagan waited until the bastard prince had vanished into the shadows. Then the Warlord entered the volksrocket, shut and sealed the hatch. All was quiet within. So very, very quiet.

But he sensed a difference about the silence now. It quivered, like a plucked string on the piano, whose note has faded away past hearing, yet which continues to resonate, sings softly for those who listen.

"Well, my lady," he said aloud, "what do you think of our 'cousin'?"

He received no reply, unless it was the sudden stillness, as if a gloved hand had muffled the singing string.

Chapter ···❧❦❧··· Eight

Of all the plagues a lover bears,
Sure rivals are the worst.
I can endure my own despair,
But not another's hope.
  William Walsh, "Song, Of All the Torments"

Kamil stopped by her dormitory room, ostensibly to drop off her books and change her clothes after morning classes. But her main reason for returning, though she tried hard to pretend to herself it wasn't, was to check to see if some message had come from Dion. She had not heard from him since the night he'd told her Astarte had left him, when he had to return at once, do what he could to contain the damage.

"I cannot permit the scandal," he had said to Kamil, holding her in his arms as if he would shield her from the blow he himself was forced to strike. "It could bring down the throne.

"Why can't they stay out of my personal life?" he'd demanded impatiently. "People who wouldn't give a damn if I ordered the destruction of a million of their fellow citizens would rise up and howl for my blood on hearing that my wife has left me!"

Kamil had been confused, frightened—for him, he looked so dreadfully pale. Thinking back on it, she couldn't remember what she'd said, or if she'd said anything coherent. And the next moment, he'd kissed her, fiercely, despairingly, murmured something about this being their final good-bye.

Then, "I can't bear it!" he'd whispered, his cheek pressed against hers. "I can't bear to let you go!"

But he had let her go, and she had let him go.

Days had passed, and she hadn't heard a word. She'd monitored the news broadcasts, watched the gossip mags anxiously, but discovered nothing. And at length she had begun to breathe easier, though her heart was heavy enough to cut off her breathing altogether. For if no scandal broke, then Dion had managed to salvage his marriage. Her good-bye to him had been a final one, after all.

Kamil told herself she didn't want to hear from him, that it was better to end it clean, swift, like a laser beam through the heart. But she couldn't stop herself from hastening back to her room, looking first thing at her answering machine. She couldn't stop herself from feeling the aching pain, disappointment, when there was no message there.

This day, she had given herself a stern lecture.

"It's over. You're only hurting yourself by carrying on like this. You haven't eaten in three days. You damn near failed that last calc test. A fine spacepilot *you'll* make!" she scolded herself derisively. "You're being weak and silly, longing for something you can never have, letting it ruin your life.

"I won't. Today I won't look at that stupid machine. I'll sensibly put down my books and sensibly change my clothes and sensibly eat lunch and then, sensibly, I'll go work in the rose garden. And tonight, when I go to the library, I'll sensibly study. I won't hide in the stacks and cry."

Entering the small room, firm with resolve, strong with purpose, she tossed her books on her bed and started to change her clothes, looking everywhere *except* at the answering machine. Unfortunately, the denim jeans and work shirt she wore when working in the garden were hanging over the back of a chair that happened to be standing beside her desk, on which rested the machine.

Kamil was about to shut her eyes and try to snag her clothes without looking at the device when she told herself that this was stupid, irrational behavior for an adult. She walked over to the chair calmly, calmly and sensibly picked up the shirt and jeans, and promptly dropped them on the floor.

The light was flashing over "mail."

Kamil's heart jumped, actually ceased to beat for an instant, leaving her suddenly dizzy and light-headed.

"My mother," she said in a trembling voice. "Of course, that's all it is—a letter from mother. I'll be glad to hear from . . . mother."

Firmly she depressed the button, waited with impatience for the machine to process the electronic impulses, translate them into hard copy. The paper began to slide out. Kamil glanced at it. She had actually managed to convince herself that she would see her mother's gigantic, bold scrawl.

But the letter was typewritten, like a form letter. Her hopes rose, though she did her best to trample them back down. For security reasons, Dion always sent his letters to her this way, to make them look like any other everyday piece of mail. And then Kamil saw, at the end, a handwritten note. It was only a few words, but she immediately recognized the writing. Shivering, she clasped her hands together tightly to keep herself from snatching up the paper before the message was complete. And then, even when it was finished, she waited a moment to pick it up.

"He's writing to tell me it's over. That's kind of him. Good for me. Closure, as my psychology professor would say. I need this for closure. Then I can put this behind me and go forward."

Kamil drew a deep breath, let it out, and read the letter.

Beloved.

This marriage was a travesty from the beginning. I tried to save it. As God is my witness (if He does indeed care about the follies of mortals, which I must admit I doubt), then I have made every attempt, short of abandoning my dignity as a human being, to reconcile with my wife.

I know now that she does not want reconciliation. She wants only power and she is using this means to try to wrest it from me. I have no doubt her mother is behind this, but my wife goes along with it. She may even be the instigator. I will not submit to their threats, their coercion. It will mean war, something I have always tried to prevent, but they have brought it on themselves.

I will divorce her. Then you and I can be married— what was always meant to be.

We must be patient, however.

The letter was unsigned. But, at the bottom, in a postscript added hastily, was this note in his handwriting.

I am sorry, my dear, but a queen cannot be a starpilot.

"Oh, Dion!" Kamil cried, and burst into tears.

"Now, really, this is nonsense!" she said after a few moments. "First you cry when he leaves you, now you cry when he says he wants to marry you."

Drying her eyes, she blew her nose, then read through the precious letter again and again.

" 'Threats' 'coercion.' Poor Dion. It must have been terrible for him. He is truly angry. 'Her mother is behind this.' . . . Well, I don't doubt that, from what Father has told me about the baroness.

"And we're to be married!" Kamil sighed.

She closed her eyes, letting the joy well up within her, wash over her. Opening her eyes, she started to read through the letter again, when her gaze fell upon the postscript.

I am sorry, my dear, but a queen cannot be a starpilot.

"A queen." The word came as a sharp jab. Kamil's joy began to seep out, a trickle of fear seeped in. "Queen," she repeated. Her hands, holding the letter, had suddenly grown cold. "I can't be a queen! I won't be any good at it. Gracious, charming, graceful. Always expected to say the proper thing at the proper moment. Everyone watching me."

Kamil looked down at herself, sitting on the chair in her underwear, which she only wore when she came to the Academy. Such female underpinnings as bra and panties were considered superfluous on her own planet. She looked at herself in the mirror, tried to picture herself in one of the dresses she'd seen Astarte wearing—complete with hat and gloves—and Kamil shut her eyes again. The image was too ludicrous. She could imagine every one of her fourteen brothers, lined up laughing at her.

And behind them, the rest of the galaxy.

"Now you *are* being silly!" She caught hold of herself, gave herself a mental shake. "Dion loves me. I love him. And now we're going to be together, our love out in the open, for everyone to see. No longer hiding. No longer ashamed or afraid. *That's* what matters. Not what clothes I'll wear.

"I'll be a queen. I'll go to concerts and dedicate art galleries and visit hospitals and wave and smile and smile and smile . . . in a hat."

Kamil sighed. She rested one elbow on the desk, her head in her hand, and started to read through the letter one more time.

A knock at her door and the simultaneous opening of that door caused her to sit upright, give her wet eyes a quick swipe. She slid the letter underneath the answering machine.

"Glad you're here," said her next-door neighbor, wandering in and making herself at home on the bed. "My head's splitting. If I have to look at another equation I'll jump out my window. You want some lunch? I hear the food in the cafeteria's almost edible today."

"No, thanks," said Kamil, devoutly wishing her next-door neighbor on the next-door planet. "Rose garden time." Hopping up, she grabbed hold of the denim shirt and put it on, buttoned it hurriedly. "I'm behind on my hours. The calc test, you know."

"You can go gardening after you eat."

"I'm not hungry. I don't know where you heard that rumor about the food, but I walked past the cafeteria today. One smell was enough to kill my appetite forever. Besides, I want to finish the weeding before the afternoon sun gets too hot."

"All right. Go kill aphids. Whatever turns you on. By the way, you've got the shirt buttoned up wrong."

"Damn!" Kamil swore, unbuttoned it, started over again. Her eyes stung with tears, for no reason at all. Her fingers fumbled at the buttons.

"You okay?" her neighbor asked. "You look kind of green."

"Fine. Really, I'm fine." Kamil bent down to pull on her jeans. "Uh, you better get going. The molded gelatin salad'll be all gone."

"Only if the gods are merciful!"

The next-door neighbor wandered out. Kamil shut and locked the door. Turning around, she thought at first she would lie down on her bed and cry until she had all tears out of her system.

"No," she said suddenly. "I won't! I never used to cry. I wonder what's come over me? No, I will go sensibly and calmly to work in the roses, get all dirty and sweaty and tired. And then I'll come back here and take a hot shower and go sensibly and calmly to bed."

Before she left, she started to sensibly destroy the letter. Dion had admonished her to destroy all the mail he sent her. But she discovered she couldn't. This was too precious. She had the strange feeling that if she destroyed it, she might end up destroying her hope. Folding the missive, she kissed it and placed it over her heart, in the pocket of her denim shirt.

The headmaster's rose garden was deserted this time of day—one reason Kamil chose to work in it. In the mornings, classes of art students roamed its picturesque paths, making drawings of the famous statues—Michaelangelo's *Pieta* and Rodin's *The Burghers of Calais*—or painting the first early spring flowers. In the late afternoons, the rose garden was a meeting and wandering place for couples of all ages. In the early evenings, before dinner, the headmaster sometimes invited chosen members of the student body to join him in the garden for sherry.

But hardly anyone ever visited the garden in the afternoon. During this hour, the headmaster took his nap—an institution that had become almost sacred to the Academy residents. No one dared disturb the headmaster's nap.

Vehicles approaching the house cut their engines and coasted down the long and winding drive. Students passing anywhere near nudged one another and lowered their voices. The nap even became a time-telling device. Such and such would be done or people would plan to meet at the "nap time."

The most remarkable thing about this was that the headmaster, the meekest and mildest of men, had no idea that his own private and personal nap had become a campus institution. His housekeeper—one Ms. Magwitch—ruled the house wherein the headmaster slept, and it was she and her umbrella—an instrument long and highly underrated as a lethal weapon—who first imposed the reign of silence.

One delivery person had been foolish enough to ring the doorbell, which noise supposedly roused the headmaster from his slumbers (such that he actually blinked, turned his head, and murmured, "What?"). The poor delivery man was met at the door by the infuriated Magwitch, complete with umbrella. The delivery person still shuddered when he spoke of it.

Kamil had arranged a truce with Ms. Magwitch, to the effect that Kamil would be allowed to work in the garden during nap time provided that she used no shears or rake or any other loud instruments of destruction. Kamil had agreed. Most gardening chores are best done by hand anyway.

The roses were not yet in bloom, but new growth was shooting up and so were the weeds. Dead stalks had to be trimmed, while certain bushes, which appeared about to succomb to last winter's frost, were given tender care and a word of encouragement.

Kamil paused in her labors, stood up to rest her back, which ached from bending over the flower beds. Though the roses were not blooming, other planets were. The garden was celebrating spring. The vivid reds and yellows of the tulips and daffodils, the deep purples of the lilacs, set against the bright greens of newborn leaves, was like an exuberant shout of joy after winter's long silence.

Kamil felt like shouting herself, and only the awful image of Magwitch and the umbrella kept her decorously silent. The garden was a blessed place to her, bringing back wonderful memories of the night she and Dion had first expressed their love for each other. Now it would be doubly blessed, for it was here that they would be married. She would be his, he would be hers, they would be one.

Kamil spread her arms wide.

"I will marry you, Dion," she pledged softly to the spring and the azure sky and flaming sun and the new life all around her. "I will marry you and love you and—"

Strong hands grabbed her arms in a firm grip, twisted them painfully, forced them behind her back. Strong hands tied a thick piece of cloth around her mouth, yanked it between her teeth, gagging her.

"Don't make a sound," whispered a harsh voice, unnecessarily.

Kamil was so exceptionally shocked by the sudden attack that she couldn't scream, couldn't even whimper. Her mind was bewildered. Her body limp, unresisting. All was over in those first few seconds, and by that time her arms were pinned, her captor had a tight hold on her.

A young woman appeared from around one of the bisecting garden paths, came to stand in front of Kamil. She recognized the woman—a fellow student.

Kamil went limp with relief. This must be some sort of prank. Then she stiffened with anger. If so, it wasn't funny! She didn't know the young woman very well; she'd only seen her around campus. She stood out among the other students, not only because of her height and unusually strong physical development for a human female, but because of her haughty pride and standoffish attitude. She kept to herself, viewed everyone else on campus with contempt.

She dressed in leather armor, which looked rather ridiculous for campus wear. Her head was shaved, except for the scalplock that was traditional among females of her planet, Ceres, the same planet that Dion's wife . . .

Astarte . . . Ceres . . . DiLuna . . .

Baroness DiLuna and her women warriors . . .

Kamil understood. She had only to glance down at the long nails, digging into her arms to know that the person holding her captive was also a woman. And this was no joke. Kamil began to choke, tried to catch her breath. But the gag constricted her breathing.

"Loosen it, Phileda," ordered the woman holding Kamil. "We don't want her to die on us. Not yet."

Phileda—who had been eyeing Kamil warily—reached out and jerked the gag loose, enough to permit Kamil to breath.

"You are Maigrey Kamil Olefsky?" asked the woman holding her.

Kamil didn't respond.

Phileda answered, "She is, Portia. I recognize her. Maigrey Kamil Olefsky, we have received an order for your execution on the charge of adultery." The woman drew a long-bladed knife; sharp-edged steel flashed in the sunlight.

"First, however," said Portia, her voice grating in Kamil's ear, "we have been told that you received, this day, a message from the king. We have orders to intercept it. It is not in your room—we searched. Where is it?"

Kamil stared at the woman, unable to believe any of this was happening. She shook her head. "I don't know—"

"Search her," ordered Portia, holding on to Kamil more tightly.

Phileda reached a hand toward Kamil.

Stunned and confused, with only a muddled idea of what was happening to her, Kamil might well have died without making a sound. But the hand reaching for the letter acted like an electric shock, jolted her to action.

They must not have the letter! It doesn't matter what they do to me. Dion's crown, his honor, perhaps his very life are in my keeping. . . .

Kamil Olefsky had been raised with fourteen brothers. Most of them were older than she was, larger, stronger, of a boisterous, fun-loving nature. She'd learned at an early age how to fight against overwhelming odds. Add to this the fact that she herself came from a warrior planet. She'd been trained in hand-to-hand combat since she was first able to pick up her mother's heavy war shield.

Using the woman holding her as a brace, Kamil lifted both feet and kicked out violently at the woman coming toward her. Her feet slammed into the solar plexus. Phileda groaned, bent double.

Kamil's feet hit the ground. She jerked her upper body forward, rolling her captor over her shoulder, throwing Portia into her compatriot, sending them both tumbling to the ground.

Kamil was off running. Fumbling in her pocket, she grabbed hold of the letter, held it clasped tightly in her hand, looking for a likely place to hide it.

The garden paths twisted and wound and turned around on each other. She came upon a diverging path. A few steps and she would be out of sight of the women, who had already regained their feet, were coming after her. This would be her only chance. She'd caught them off guard once. It wouldn't happen again.

A strange whirring sound came from behind her. Kamil hadn't time to wonder what it was. She started to race around the path. This direction would take her close to the garden wall. She could jump it and—

A leather thong whipped around her legs and ankles, tripping her, sent her crashing headlong to the ground. She squirmed to a sitting position, tried frantically to free herself. The thong, weighted by two ornately carved ivory balls, was far too tangled and tight.

The letter. No matter what happens to you. Hide the letter.

Kamil tried to shove it into the roots of a rosebush, ignoring the sharp thorns that tore long scratches in her flesh. And then the two women were on her.

One kicked her in the face, sent her reeling backward. The other stomped a booted foot down on Kamil's wrist.

Bone crunched. Pain shot through her arm. Kamil's fingers, clasping the letter, went limp.

"Finish her," Portia ordered, reaching for the letter.

Phileda loomed over Kamil. The knife flashed.

Involuntarily, Kamil turned her head away. She had time to whisper brokenly, "Dion, I—"

Two bursts of light, coming in rapid succession, exploded above her, blinding her. Heat washed over her body. She smelled burned flesh, heard soft thuds, a crash in one of the rosebushes.

She couldn't see, had no idea what has happening. Fearfully, she waited for the stab of the knife.

It didn't come.

Heavy footsteps crunched through the gravel, moving toward her.

Kamil blinked, trying to clear the red burst of the blazing light from her eyes. She started to push herself up to a sitting position, but pain flashed through her right arm. She collapsed.

Someone picked her up, using steel hands, apparently. She felt the cool touch of metal on her skin.

"Take it easy, sister," said a deep voice that had a faint mechanical sound to it. "Your arm's broken. Don't move it."

Kamil heard other sounds, other footsteps. But these were light, silken sounds, as of slippered feet walking with a delicate tread. The footsteps circled around her, paused.

"They're both dead," said a woman's voice, as cool as the steel fingers of the cyborg.

Kamil stared upward. Images were beginning to emerge from a fire-tinged blue haze.

"Of course they're dead," said the man. "You're not paying me to miss, Your Majesty."

Your Majesty . . .

Kamil leaned weakly back against the metal arm. Pain and shock left her without the ability to think. She couldn't understand what was happening, couldn't react to it.

"Who are you?" she whispered.

The woman knelt down. She was heavily veiled, wearing a chador—the long, flowing, body-enveloping garment of the deserts. The woman removed the veil from her face, let it fall.

Queen Astarte. Queen of the galaxy. Dion's wife.

"I am sorry that they hurt you," said Astarte gravely. "They moved much faster than I had anticipated they would."

Her gaze shifted from Kamil to the letter, still clasped in the useless hand. Blood oozed from the scratches made by the rosebush. Kamil saw the eyes shift, but there was nothing she could do about it.

Astarte reached out with slender fingers, plucked the letter from Kamil's limp grip. Traces of blood stained the crumpled paper. It was smudged with dirt from the attempt to bury it beneath the bush.

"We shouldn't hang around here long, Your Majesty," advised the cyborg. "We're lucky no one's spotted us before now. I'll put a field dressing on her arm. And I've got a drug here that'll perk up her a bit. At least so she can make it to the spaceplane."

"The drug won't harm her . . ."

"No, it's one of Raoul's concoctions."

"Very well." Astarte unfolded the letter.

"Don't . . . please . . ." Kamil made a feeble protest.

Astarte glanced at her, turned her attention to the letter. Kamil watched the purple eyes—beautiful eyes, she thought dreamily, through a haze of pain—track the writing, read every word, including the postscript.

It wasn't signed, but then, a wife would know her husband's handwriting.

A needle jabbed into the skin of Kamil's upper arm; a sensation of warmth flooded through the muscle, into her body. Pain began to ease away: the pain of her broken arm. The pain in her heart intensified. She was watching, with a dreadful kind of fascination, Astarte's face.

The queen was obviously skilled in keeping her emotions hidden beneath that suave and lovely mask. But for an instant, just an instant, the mask slid away, dropping like the veil. Hurt and betrayal, stark and terrible and cruel. It is one thing to suspect, another to hold the evidence in your hand.

Kamil's eyes filled with tears, not from the pain of her injury, which she could no longer feel, but from shame, guilt. The break in her arm would heal. This wound that she herself had inflicted on another mortal would never heal. No matter what happened, the pain would always be there.

"Sorry, sister," said the cyborg, mistaking her tears. "I don't have time to be gentle."

He was dressing her arm, wrapping it in a plastic sling that inflated at a touch. The sling was filled with cooling liquid that both stabilized the break and acted to reduce the swelling.

Kamil looked up at Astarte, wanted to say something, to offer some sort of explanation, but the words wouldn't come for the tears.

Astarte folded the letter carefully, tucked it inside the capacious folds of the chador. Her features were once again masklike.

"It was imprudent of him to write this. Imprudent of you to keep it. If my mother had gotten hold of it . . ." Astarte shook her head. "I could not have saved you, either of you. You would have both been lost."

She gathered the silken sweep of the chador around her, rose gracefully, stared down at her from what seemed to Kamil's drugged senses to be a great height.

"Is she almost ready to travel?"

"Yeah." The cyborg grunted.

"Travel?" Kamil repeated dazedly. "Where . . ."

"The one place you will be safe," said Astarte. "The one place where my mother dares not touch you."

The cyborg helped Kamil to her feet. She would have said she was too weak to stand, but once she was up and moving, she was amazed at how much better she felt.

"What about the bodies?" Astarte asked coolly.

Kamil looked down at her two attackers. Both lay dead. The flesh of their faces had been melted away, leaving charred bone, covered with blood and brains, exposed. A wave of dizziness swept over Kamil. She swayed on her feet.

"No, you don't, sister," said the cyborg, catching hold of her, shaking her. "I'll dispose of the corpses, Your Majesty. You take her away from here. Put those clothes we brought on her."

The cyborg was also dressed in the concealing robes of the desert dwellers, a *kafia* covering his head.

Astarte put an arm around Kamil, led her away from the gruesome remains lying in the rose garden. The queen was shorter than Kamil, barely reached her shoulder. But Astarte's grip on her was firm, her footsteps unfaltering. Kamil staggered like a drunken spacer, would have fallen if the queen had not supported her.

The two reached the garden wall. Kamil leaned weakly against the stonework. The queen pulled out a pack that had been stashed behind the wall. Rummaging inside it, she produced another chador and draped it over Kamil's unresisting body.

It was much like dressing a child. Kamil thrust her arm into the sleeve when Astarte told her to, obeyed the woman's commands without thought. Kamil couldn't think. The sight of the bodies had badly unnerved her; not even the stimulant could alleviate the effect.

It might have been her lying dead.

The chador's tight-fitting wristband wouldn't go over the battlefield sling. Astarte took hold of the fabric, ripped it at the seam, slid it up and over the arm.

Another bright flare of light came from the garden; a sizzling and popping sound, and a strong smell of burning flesh.

Both women stared at each other. Astarte's skin was pale; she caught her breath. Kamil dug her hand into the sharp stones of the wall to keep from fainting.

The cyborg returned, thrusting a lasgun inside the sleeve of his flowing robes.

Astarte lifted a veil and wrapped it around Kamil's nose and mouth. "Keep your face covered. If you have any thoughts of trying to escape, put them out of your mind. Remember, I have the letter. You hold Dion's fate in your hands. You can save him—"

"—by coming with you?" Kamil shook her head. She had regained her wits somewhat. She thought she understood. "You're planning to use me . . . some sort of plot to . . . to blackmail him. Force him to do what you want. I won't let you. Kill me . . . the way you did them."

Astarte regarded her without emotion. "Your death will accomplish nothing. He would be yours for all eternity then. Believe me, Daughter of Olfesky, I do not want to hurt my husband." The purple eyes shimmered above the veil. "I only want him back."

"Time to go, Your Majesty," said the cyborg grimly.

The three left the rose garden. Behind them, two thin spirals of smoke and a few ashes drifted up from the path, were caught by the wind and blown away.

When the headmaster woke, refreshed, from his nap and came out to walk in his garden, he would find nothing amiss except two charred patches on the ground where it appeared someone had been burning leaves.

Her face hidden by the veil, Kamil was hustled swiftly through the Academy grounds. She said nothing, made no attempt to escape—a futile move anyway, considering the cyborg held her in a grip of steel. No one paid any attention to the three. Many of the students and faculty came from arid planets, wore the traditional garments of their people.

Arriving at the spaceport, she was taken aboard a private spaceplane. The plane lifted off, was soon in the endless night of space.

Once they had made the Jump, the cyborg gave her another injection. This one, he warned, would knock her out.

"I'm going to set that broken bone, sister. I assume you don't want to be awake for the operation."

"No," said Kamil confusedly, "I don't want to be awake."

Darkness slid over her. The last thing she saw, before she lost consciousness, was Astarte's beautiful, expressionless face.

Chapter ·◆━◯━◆· Nine

Chaos and Ancient night, . . . as my way,
Lies through your spacious empire up to light,
Alone and without guide, half lost, I seek
What readiest paths lead where your gloomy bounds
Confine with Heaven . . .

John Milton, *Paradise Lost*

Derek Sagan opened the volksrocket's hatch, stood a few moments in the hatchway, before descending the few steps to the damp grass. What he could see of Vallombrosa was not much different in daylight than it had been in darkness, this due to the fact that a bank of gray fog hung over the hillside. Sagan could see the grass beneath his rocket, flattened and blackened from the touchdown. He could see the stand of trees that he had walked past last night and not much more beyond that. The pavilion, the other tents were all shrouded in the heavy mists.

Convenient, he thought, and walked back into his plane.

He gathered the objects he would need for the rite, wrapped them each carefully and reverently in black velvet. He could not handle them without thinking back to the last time he'd given the test: Dion's rite.

He remembered it clearly, far too clearly. One doesn't usually forget being kicked in the face by an Immortal foot. It proved, beyond question, that Dion was meant to be king.

"Or did it?" Sagan asked himself (or was he speaking to her unseen, but clearly felt presence?). He straightened from his task. "Or did it mean nothing more than that he was being set up to take the fall?"

He pondered the question. "If my theories are correct, this strange force Flaim Starfire controls is unstoppable. A force that is unseen, unheard, cannot be easily detected. It glides through solid matter with ease, leaves little trace of its passing behind. It plucked this volksrocket out of space and transported me here in less time than it takes to tell it. In addition,

Flaim is recruiting men and machines. With a strong army and navy behind him, and this terrible power at his command, he is invincible. One thing could stop him—the space-rotation bomb. But Dion will never use it. He'd die first. And he may well have the opportunity."

Sagan placed the objects in the black cloth scrip he had brought with him for the purpose. He tugged on the drawstring of the scrip, pulled it tightly, shut the bag.

He wondered again if he had truly seen Maigrey, if her spirit was with him, or if that brief flash of silver was something his mind—sickened by loneliness, grief, anger—had conjured up. The vision had been very real to him, but then most delusions are real to those who suffer from them.

Footsteps could be heard, outside the hatch. They were firm and strong, but lacked the quick, decisive stride of youth.

"Pantha," Sagan said to himself, not turning around.

The voice confirmed it.

"Good morning, my lord. I trust I do not disturb you?"

"I will be with you presently," called Sagan, taking his time.

"The fog is thick this morning. My prince feared you might have difficulty finding your way."

"I found my way to him across a galaxy, sir. I'm not likely to lose him in a mist."

Pantha laughed politely at the jest that had not been a jest. Sagan descended from the plane, shut the hatch behind him. The two men began to walk at a slow and leisurely pace up the hill.

"You want to find out how much I know," Sagan said.

"Naturally," Pantha replied, easily keeping pace with the Warlord, despite the almost forty years difference in ages.

"Know about what? The other world? The world of strange, dark matter."

Pantha glanced over at the Warlord. He did not appear surprised. "I told Flaim you would discover it."

"Let us say 'deduce' its existence. Just as you did, years ago."

Pantha sighed softly. "You cannot imagine the feeling of elation when I first discovered my theory was correct, when I first contacted *them*. All the tests, the readouts pointed to a second world, coexisting with this one. This planet—far more heavy than it should be, the wildly fluctuating gravitational fields. You know. You saw your own results. Like you, I deduced its existence, but how to prove it?"

They came to several boulders, which formed a crude circle. Pantha stopped.

"Could we talk a few moments, just the two of us? My prince is not ready yet. He is taking this rite quite seriously. He requested an hour or so to be alone with his thoughts."

"Quite proper," Sagan remarked. He seated himself on one of the rocks, laid the scrip at his feet on the wet grass.

"He is eager to impress you. Whereas I—" Pantha smiled, ruefully, wistfully, "I have been merely eager to talk to you."

Sagan said nothing, gazed steadily at the old man.

"He doesn't understand the wonder of this, you see." Pantha indicated, with a vague wave of a gnarled black hand, the world around them. "He was raised with it. This world holds no marvels for him. And the new ones, the recruits—once they're over their initial feelings of terror, once it's explained to them, they accept it.

"Do you know, my lord," Pantha continued, settling himself on a boulder, "that I wasn't the first to discover this planet? An early Earth exploration team found it, landed on it, set up a small scientific station to study it. They were the ones who named it Vallombrosa. They deduced what we deduced, you see. They theorized another world, a world of dark matter. They just didn't carry their theory far enough."

"To the extent that this dark-matter world was populated, you mean."

"Precisely, my lord. I have often wondered what reports—if any—they sent back to Earth. Certainly no record of this place was passed down to us. Perhaps they never made it safely back home. Or perhaps, if they did, they made a pact never to reveal what they had found. They left all their data of what happened to them here behind on a vidlog. I found it in the wreckage of the shelters.

"The log is quite frustrating to watch, actually. The innate, boneheaded logic of the twenty-first century. Since we can't see it or touch it or smell it or taste it, it cannot exist. Since it doesn't look like us, it can't possibly think or feel."

"Still," said Sagan, "if they *had* figured it out—"

"—I would be nowhere. I know that," Pantha interrupted testily. "I suppose I should be grateful they were so stupid. But their blind prejudice, their lack of imagination, irritates me. Here's an example of their report. I quote:

" 'When the universe began, two types of matter came into

being. Ordinary matter—what you and I are made up of—an(
strange dark matter. Dark matter interacts weakly with ordinary
matter, mostly through gravity. Dark matter is believed to be
more uniformly distributed through the universe than ordinary
matter. Planetary bodies made up of strange dark matter were
believed impossible. We have now, of course, disproved that
But life based on dark matter, as some have suggested, is pure
fantasy.'" Pantha snorted. "So much for uninvestigated logic
There is life on Vallombrosa, life made of strange dark matter."

"Vallombrosa. Valley of Ghosts." Sagan mused. "They
thought this world was haunted."

"Yes, indeed," Pantha said with a grim smile. "As I mentioned last night, the creatures—I call them strange dark-
matter creatures—are intensely curious. They'd never seen
beings like us before. They were simply studying the
scientists—as the scientists *should* have been studying them.

"You must view the vidlog. It's almost funny, like watching a
cheap ghost movie. Books suddenly leap up into the air, crash
to the floor. A microwave oven sails slowly and effortlessly out
a window. Toilets flush repeatedly and inexplicably. Lights flash
on and off. Computer disks are erased, ruined. And just when
these bizarre pranks started to wreak havoc with the minds of
those wretched scientists, one of them mysteriously dropped
dead."

"The creatures?"

"Yes. Oh, they didn't mean to kill the man, mind you. You reported noticing an odd feeling come over you at one point during your flight here. You felt 'compressed' was how you put it."

Pantha paused, glanced at Sagan as if expecting him to protest or question having his personal files invaded. When Sagan
did not, Pantha smiled and nodded.

"You understand, of course. I should have expected you to.
At any rate, I am glad you do. It makes things easier. Where
was I? Ah, yes. Feelings of being compressed. These creatures
are amazing. Their bodies are held together by what I can only
describe as coherent gravity fields. They appear to perceive the
world around them by sensing gravitational distortions
throughout their entire bodies. As a consequence, they have no
defined shape, but rearrange themselves in whatever way best
allows them to either sense or transmit gravity waves. In other
words they are all hands, all eyes, all brains. To move an object,

they create a gravitational field around it by wrapping them-selves around it."

"That was how they brought me here," Sagan interjected.

"Yes. The creatures wove a gravitational field around your plane. They move faster than the speed of light, using the Einstein-Rosen bridge to open up tunnels in space, through which they travel. And, as you might suppose, they can pass through matter virtually undetected.

"I say 'virtually' because, as the cyborg's men discovered during the raid on Snaga Ohme's, there *are* ways that their passing can be discovered. Whenever they go through solid matter, for example, the possibility exists that they will cause a change in the atomic structure. Ordinarily, such a change is slight, hardly noticed. But in the case of a living being—a human—the change could be fatal.

"The odds are extreme," Pantha said reassuringly. "I've cal-culated them, of course. The creatures have passed through me a thousand times, with no ill effects. Unfortunately, one of the scientists was not so lucky. He died instantly. And none of his colleagues could figure out how or why."

"That was when they decided to leave."

"Yes. And their decision to flee only made matters worse. Realizing their human specimens were departing, the creatures became quite frantic in their attempts to communicate with them. This, of course, resulted in some spectacular physical manifestations. These only increased the humans' panic. They were fortunate the creatures permitted them to leave at all. The creatures could have captured their ship, brought them back.

"They did follow them to Earth," Pantha went on, shifting to a more comfortable position on the rock. "They investigated the planet, found out all they needed to know. Psychic re-searchers of the time must have had a field day. When the studies were concluded, the creatures left. Human civilization posed no threat to them, you see, and once their curiosity was satisfied, they had no more interest in it. Or in us."

"Humans posed no threat," Sagan repeated.

"Yes," Pantha reiterated. "That was true *then*." He laid em-phasis on the last word.

"I see. So as long as we 'posed no threat' to them, they were content to leave us alone."

Pantha shrugged. "They are far more advanced beings than ourselves. It is difficult to judge them by our standards, but I would say that they are vastly more intelligent than we are or can ever hope to be. Their civilization is much older. We are to them what ants are to us. Unless the ant happens to develop a sting."

Now, at last, Sagan was beginning to understand. "The space-rotation bomb—the first weapon we have ever developed which they consider a threat. It could destroy them utterly."

"So they have postulated."

"That's why they raided Snaga Ohme's. They were searching for it."

"We were fairly certain the bomb transported to that vault was not the real bomb. Far too easy to locate. But the creatures wanted to make sure. They would like to have the bomb destroyed, but they have agreed to allow it to remain in existence, so long as Flaim has complete control of it. Once he locates the true bomb, the creatures will obtain it for him. Nothing can stop them. Nothing."

Dion, Dion, Sagan chided silently, bitterly. *If only you had taken my advice!*

"You speak of communicating with them," the Warlord said aloud, casually. "How did you manage that?"

"It took much time. Much patience. The story is a fascinating one." Pantha grinned slyly. "Perhaps someday I will have a chance to share it with you." He pushed himself up off the boulder. "Not now, however. We have been gone longer than I anticipated. My prince will be growing impatient."

Sagan accompanied Pantha up the hill. The mist lay thick and heavy still, curling about the trunks of the trees that lined their path. But the mists were beginning to lift from Sagan's mind. The path he must follow was becoming clearer to him every moment.

As I feared, nothing can stop them. Dion can surround that bomb with a fleet of a thousand warships, post a million men to guard it, lock it in a vault in the core of a world made of solid steel, and these creatures would slide right through it like butter.

Only one obstacle blocks Flaim's path to the throne. The young man currently sitting on it. Dion knows where the bomb is. And Flaim doesn't.

They arrived in the clearing outside the large pavilion. The ground where the bonfire had burned was a large circle of charred blackened wood, soft gray ash. Heat continued to radiate from it. Some of the large logs—not yet completely consumed—gave off thin trails of pale smoke.

Flaim was, as Pantha had predicted, waiting for them impatiently.

Sagan paused to regard the younger man intently. "Pantha has told me about the dark-matter creatures. You possess enormous power. Why do you want this initiation? Why do you care?"

"I do this for you, my lord," replied Flaim at once. The blue eyes narrowed, hardened, cooled. "And for him."

"Dion."

"Yes. He sees me now, but I am nothing but a shadow on his mind. I want him to see me clearly. I want him to understand me and my intentions. I want him to take me seriously."

"And me. What do you want of me?"

Flaim came to stand before him, laid both hands on Sagan's shoulders.

"You will give me the throne, my lord. You will place the crown on my head."

Sagan made no response.

Flaim, thinking perhaps that none was needed, lowered his hands, gestured. "The rite would be held inside the tent, if that suits you, my lord? Pantha has everything prepared."

As well that place as any other. Sagan entered the tent by himself, looked over preparations.

All was as it should be. Pantha had a good memory, for a rite he himself had taken over seventy years ago. The pavilion had been emptied of all furnishings: pillows, bolsters, blankets. In the center stood a small table. Sagan placed his scrip on the floor. Removing a black velvet cloth, he spread it over the table, then opened the scrip and began laying out and arranging the other objects he'd brought with him. He should have been offering up ritual prayers, but the words drifted out of his mind, like the smoke and the soft gray ash upon the wind.

Outside, he could hear Flaim pacing restlessly, impatiently.

"The rite will not necessarily grant you power, Prince Flaim," Sagan remarked, raising his voice to be heard. "It was never intended to do so. Developed by those of my Order, the Order of Adamant, the test was given to those of the Blood Royal on or near their entry into puberty. The test not only marked the passage from childhood to adulthood, but was a means of finding out if the person tested was truly Blood Royal."

"I know." Flaim came to stand beside the closed tent flap. "Pantha told me all about it. I am old to be taking it. But then so were you, so was my cousin. Perhaps it runs in our family," he added mockingly.

Sagan made no reply.

"The rite does not enhance one's power," Flaim continued, "but since it involves one's reactions under stress, it indicates how strong or weak one is in the power."

"I have the feeling you know your own strength, Your Highness," Sagan commented dryly.

"Yes, but I want to prove it to others," Flaim returned.

"The early priests believed the rite provided an indication of God's will," Sagan added after a pause.

"Yes, my lord. I am aware of that."

Sagan had completed arranging the objects on the black cloth. He stepped back, regarded them.

Is all correct, my lady? Is it as you remember? Words he'd spoken to Maigrey aboard *Phoenix*, before they'd given Dion his test.

No response. He walked out from the tent.

"Do you believe in God?" he asked Flaim.

The prince stared at him, startled by the question. A smile tugged at his lips; he seemed about to laugh. Then he saw that the Warlord was serious.

Flaim appeared uncomfortable. "How can I answer that, my lord?" He gestured at Sagan's black cassock. "Seeing you dressed as you are? A priest of the Order?"

"You can answer it truthfully," Sagan replied. "I dress as I do for my own reasons. My habit may reflect my beliefs . . . or it may disguise them."

"I see," said Flaim, regarding the Warlord with new understanding and respect. "Yes, what a perfect hiding place! And all the while you—"

"I asked you a question, Prince Starfire," Sagan interrupted.

"Forgive me, my lord. Here is my answer. I believe in myself. No omnipotent, omniscient being controls my destiny. Life is chance, coincidence. Thus we must always be ready to seize the moment"—he grabbed the air, tainted with smoke, twisted it in his clenched fist—"and turn it to our own advantage." He opened his hand, which was empty. "I make my own luck. If there is a cosmic power, my lord, it is within me."

Sagan inclined his head to acknowledge the answer. "We are ready for the rite of initiation."

Flaim smiled, excited, exhilarated.

"May Pantha come with me?"

Sagan glanced at the old man, who stood—silent, keen-eyed—near the dying fire.

"No. I am sorry. It is not permitted. Your will is too strong, sir," he said to Pantha. "You might inadvertently influence your prince."

Garth Pantha bowed, nodded.

"And I trust the strange dark-matter creatures will not inter-fere," Sagan added, casting his gaze around the pavilion, the hillside, the trees, the mists.

"Pantha has spoken to them," Flaim replied. "They do not, of course, understand, but they have agreed to leave the vicinity in order that their energies do not unduly influence the pro-ceedings."

"How very gracious of them," Sagan remarked wryly.

He realized, suddenly, what was wrong, why he was irritable and out of temper. Others were in control here. He was not—a new circumstance for the Warlord. Flaim might treat him as an honored guest, the prince might even look up to Sagan, admire him, accord him respect. But a turn of a key in the cell door makes the honored guest a prisoner. And even less effort makes the prisoner a corpse.

Sagan held open the tent flap. Flaim walked confidently in-side; the Warlord followed. Pulling the flap down, he secured it carefully, shutting out all traces of gray light that seeped in-side. The interior of the pavilion was suddenly extremely dark. Flaim couldn't see and came to a standstill, not wanting to bump into anything.

The Warlord took hold of the prince's arm, guided his steps to the table that stood in the center of the tent.

"At your feet," said Sagan, "you will find a robe. Take off your clothes and put it on. Take off your weapon, as well," he added, aware that Flaim wore the bloodsword at his side.

Flaim knelt down, felt for the robe. "Ah, the customary hair shirt," he said, grimacing at the feel of the rough cloth.

"It is not permissible for you to speak unless I ask you a di-rect question," Sagan reprimanded.

"Sorry," said Flaim in a low tone, a hint of a laugh in his voice. By the rustling sounds, he was changing his clothes.

Sagan made his way around the table, feeling the edges with his hand. Finding what he needed by touch, he lifted a white beeswax candle, lit it, placed it in a silver candleholder that stood at the end of the table. The other objects on the table remained hidden beneath a black cloth.

Flaim's head emerged from the crude, slit neckline of the garment. His face was flushed; the candle flame burned in the Starfire-blue eyes. His shining raven hair was tousled. He shook it back out of his face, squared his shoulders, smiled.

Looking into those eyes, Sagan saw another young man, saw Dion standing in precisely the same place. His face livid, his body shaking in uncontrollable fear, the boy had very nearly been sick.

I'm going to die, Dion had said.

Sagan lifted the cowl of his habit up over his head. He lit another candle, placed it at the opposite end of the table.

A white circle on the floor glistened in the light.

"Stand in the center of the circle," Sagan instructed. "Do not break the line."

Flaim did as he was instructed, moving forward into the circle of salt confidently, still smiling. He was enjoying this.

Dion had walked into the circle with trepidation, certain he was going to his death.

Sagan began to speak the ritual words. "Creator, one comes before you *who is on the verge of manhood* [No, that is ridiculous! leave it out]—who seeks to understand the mystery of his life [and that is not true, my lady. Look at his face. He understands all too well].... We of the Blood Royal have been granted talents beyond those of other men ... use our mental and physical prowess to protect and defend ... [I didn't, as you, my lady, reminded me. I used it to conquer. And so will this one]."

The rite continued. The four elements: earth, air, fire, water. "Man seeks control over each," Sagan intoned.

Flaim stood in the center of the circle, eager and expectant as a child about to receive a longed-for gift.

"This night, Flaim Starfire, you come to me ..." Sagan paused. "To *us*," he amended softly, grimly, acutely aware that he wasn't alone. "You come to us to be initiated into the mystery. You seek control of that which is beyond the control of most. If the Creator deems you worthy, you will be granted that control. [*And if He doesn't, I'll take it,* that's what you're thinking, Flaim, isn't it? Yes, I know. I remember thinking the same.]"

Reaching out his hand, Sagan removed the black cloth that covered the objects on the table. Candlelight gleamed off a silver wand, a silver pitcher filled with water, a silver dish filled with oil, a silver ball.

Flaim's hands flexed beneath the sleeves of the robe, his fingers twitched. He licked his lips, his breath came quick and hard.

Sagan reached for the silver wand. Maigrey had performed this part of the rite. Her hand had been the last to touch it. He picked it up.

"Air. The breath of life. The wind of destruction."

He moved the wand in a slow circle. The air around them began to stir, a wafting breeze that caused the candle flames to flicker. The wind strengthened, the candles began to smoke, the flames whipped around the wick. And then they were blown out.

Dion was suffocating. The boy, clutching his throat, was gasping for air and not finding any. There was terror in his eyes, which were bulging from his head. His lips were turning blue, his chest jerked, the muscles fighting frantically to sustain life. . . . The boy dropped to his knees. . . .

The prince laughed exultantly in the darkness and gulped in a deep breath.

The wind died. The candles flared back to life. Sagan placed the silver wand down upon the table.

"Earth," said Sagan. "Matter. You can control matter."

Lifting the silver globe from the table, he tossed it into the air. He exerted his will upon it. The metal globe hung suspended in the air above his head. Its appearance began to change. Razor-sharp spikes protruded from its surface.

"Place your hands beneath it," Sagan instructed.

Flaim did as he was commanded, extending both hands beneath the ball, which was studded with flesh-piercing spikes.

The globe began to drop.

"Hold," ordered Flaim, and the globe halted, hung above his hands.

"Fall," commanded Sagan, and the ball dropped.

A look of anger marred Flaim's face; the blue eyes flared as the candle flames had flared. He cast a glance at Sagan, a glance of enmity from one who does not like his will thwarted, bested. But Flaim did not move his hands. He held them steady, ready to catch the spiked ball.

The globe fell; the knife-sharp spikes made an eerie whistling sound in the air and a dull, soggy, plopping sound as they drove through flesh and muscle, tendon and bone. Blood spurted. Dion screamed. His hands were impaled on the silver globe.

The spikes withdrew an instant before they touched the prince's flesh. Flaim caught the ball with ease. He smiled at Sagan—a grim smile, a smile of triumph.

Sagan reached out to take hold of the silver ball.

Flaim clasped both hands around it, crushed it. He tossed the pieces, like bits of broken eggshell, on the black cloth.

"Water." Sagan lifted the pitcher. "From which comes life. Cup your palms." He poured water into Flaim's hands. "Drink."

The prince lifted his hands to his mouth, drank deeply.

"What did you taste?" Sagan asked.

"Blood," Flaim answered.

Upending the pitcher, Maigrey poured the water on Dion's injured hands. The cool liquid flowed over the palms, bringing relief from the pain, seemingly, for he closed his eyes, tears sprang from beneath the lids. The water mingled with the blood, washed it away.

"Fire. Sustainer. Destroyer."

The oil lamp burst into flame. Before Sagan could say a word, Flaim placed his hand over the fire, brought his hand down on top of the flames. The fire licked his flesh. He covered the lamp with his palm, smothering the flame, then lifted his palm, his right palm. It was red, already starting to blister from the self-inflicted burn. The five scars made by the needles of the bloodsword oozed a darkish liquid.

The expression on Flaim's face had not altered, not changed.

Dion never made a sound, but stared with a calm, terrible fascination at the flame covering his hands. The fire blazed, finally died. When it was out, the flesh of his hands was left whole, untouched, unblemished, healed.

"My lord," said Flaim, holding out his burned hand, "have I proven myself to you? Will you grant me your support?"

Sagan smoothed the black velvet cloth with his fingertips. He stared into the candle flame, which glowed steadfast, unwavering in the still air. His fingers brushed over a cool spot of water, splashed on the cloth. He cut himself on a jagged piece of metal—all that was left of the silver ball. He remained standing, unmoving, silent.

Flaim did not move, did not make a sound, though the pain of his injured hand must have been severe.

Sagan stirred, spoke aloud, but softly. "I helped put Dion Starfire on the throne. I pledged my allegiance, my loyalty to him. He knew—everyone knew—that I had misgivings about him, about his ability to rule. But Fate conspired against me." He looked at Flaim. "Chance, coincidence—call it what you will. I fell from grace. Dion rose. I left the world . . . to avoid temptation."

Sagan raised his hands, removed the cowl that covered his head, settled it back on his shoulders. Reaching out, he took hold of Flaim's hand, his right hand, his burned hand. Sagan grasped it, pressed it hard, tight.

Flaim tried to maintain his stoic demeanor, but the pressure of the Warlord's grip was too much. A gasp of agony escaped his lips. He flinched; a trickle of sweat trailed down his temple, glistened on his cheek.

But then he smiled, fierce, exultant. He straightened his shoulders, shook the black hair from his face. And he strengthened his grip on the Warlord's hand, pressing burned flesh to callused flesh, fresh scars left by the bloodsword matching long-unused scars.

"I came here searching for a king," said Derek Sagan. "I have found him."

Chapter ❖ Ten

In love alone we hate to find
Companions of our woe.
William Walsh, "Song, Of All the Torments"

Kamil awoke in a peaceful, quiet room of green-tinged shadows weaving back and forth against a far wall; of muted sunlight, bird song, and the gentle melody of a flute playing softly near her. She lay in a comfortable bed, with clean, sweet-smelling sheets, and stared around her in a serene, calm, and uncaring state—the aftereffects of the drug. She was drifting on the surface of a placid lake after a terrifying struggle with horrible things beneath its surface.

The green-tinged shadows were leaves and branches, stirred by a fragrant breeze. The flute music stopped. Kamil glanced in its direction.

A young woman, seated at a table near the window, had been playing. Seeing that Kamil was awake, the woman smiled at her and, taking the flute with her, left the room, shutting the door behind her.

Shortly after her departure, the flute music began again, repeating the same melody, as if the player were practicing it. The tune was simple and sweet, with the faint undercurrent of melancholy peculiar to the song of the flute, whose every breath seems a sigh. Kamil hummed it, lying in her bed, looking drowsily about her, and then she remembered everything.

Her broken arm lay across the coverlet, wrapped in a more sophisticated type of inflatable sling than the cyborg had used. The arm was numb, felt heavy and foreign; it didn't belong to her. Fearfully she moved it, was relieved to see her fingers wiggle. There was no pain; Kamil assumed this was due to whatever drugs they had been giving her.

She sat up and looked more closely around her room. Her clothes were neatly folded on a nearby chair. They'd been washed, apparently, for all traces of blood and dirt were gone. She was wearing some sort of sleeveless gown made of cotton.

It was comfortable, if not fancy. The room was a small bedroom, not much bigger than her dorm room back at the Academy.

Sliding out of bed, pausing a moment to recover from a wave of dizziness, Kamil padded softly to the door. Slowly, quietly, she tested the handle. Not locked. She crept over to the chair, grabbed her clothes, and dressed herself with considerable difficulty, encumbered by the sling and lacking the use of her right arm. It was especially frustrating attempting to button her shirt, but she managed and, sliding on her shoes, was just about to glide out the door when it opened and someone glided in.

Kamil sat down on the bed and tried to look as if she hadn't been going anywhere.

Astarte smiled coolly, but said nothing. The queen was wearing some type of loose-fitting white garment that fell in soft folds from her shoulders. A golden belt, made to look like sheaves of wheat, circled her slender waist. Her dress came to her ankles; golden sandals, matching the belt, covered her small feet. Her shining black hair was done up in an elaborate twist. Her eyes—with their vivid, glittering wine hue—seemed the only bright color in the softly colored room.

Another young woman, standing behind the queen, carried a tray draped with a white cloth. Astarte gestured. The young woman placed the tray down on the table. A delicious smell— fresh-baked bread—scented the air. Kamil gazed at it longingly, all thoughts of escape put on hold.

"Are you hungry, Daughter of Olefsky?" Astarte asked. "Yes, I thought you would be when you awoke. Xris advised us not to give you anything to eat until the drug wore off. He said you'd get along without food fine for a few days. You were given water, of course. You probably don't remember much about the trip, do you?"

Kamil shook her head. What she did remember, she'd just as soon forget.

Astarte sent the young woman out of the room, bid her shut the door. Advancing to the table, the queen removed the cover from the tray. Fresh fruit, cheese, a loaf of warm bread.

"I don't suppose it's the type of fare you're accustomed to eating," said Astarte, folding the covering cloth meticulously and placing it at the side of the tray. "Your people are carnivorous, I believe. We do not eat meat, particularly in the temple environs. I should not do so myself, but I am often forced to—a concession I made when I became queen. It would not do to offend a host—such as your father—by refusing what is served. The Goddess understands. Come, eat."

Kamil stared at the food, her mouth salivating, but she made no move to leave the bed.

Astarte shook her head. "You will accomplish nothing by starving yourself."

That made sense. Kamil stood up, went over to the small table, started to sit down. Then she realized she was in the presence of the queen, who was still standing. Kamil caught herself, stood deferentially.

Astarte smiled again, but this time her smile was strained. "You think it perfectly all right to make love to my husband, yet you wait for my permission to be seated in my presence."

Kamil flushed, embarrassed and guilty; angry that she was being made to feel embarrassed and guilty.

Folding her hands, Astarte sat down gracefully, her back straight, head high. "Go ahead, Olefsky's Daughter," she said, her tone no longer bitter, but sounding only resigned. "Sit down. Eat your meal."

Feeling foolish, but not knowing what else to do, impelled by her hunger, Kamil sat down in a chair opposite Astarte's. Lifting the bread, Kamil began to eat, then remembered her manners.

"Will . . . will you have some, Your . . . Your Majesty?" she offered awkwardly.

"No, thank you. I have dined. And don't call me that. It sounds . . . ludicrous." Astarte waved her hand. "I don't suppose you call my husband 'Your Majesty.' "

Kamil was chewing bread. She swallowed the piece, then laid her hand down on the table, the remainder of the bread uneaten. Her gaze fixed on her plate; her body grew cold, stiffening.

"I'm sorry," said Astarte suddenly.

She reached out her hand, rested it on Kamil's hand, which was still clutching the piece of bread. Astarte's long fingernails brushed Kamil's skin, their touch cold, a contrast to the warmth of her fingers.

"I'm being a bitter, vindictive wife." Astarte sighed. "That won't accomplish anything either. I don't want to alienate you, Olefsky's Daughter. Of course, we can't be friends. That *would* be ludicrous." She smiled briefly, wanly. "But we do have one thing in common. Dion. We both want what is best for him."

Kamil said nothing. Removing her hand slowly but gently from Astarte's touch, she resumed eating.

The queen drew in a deep breath, placed her hands once again in her lap. Whoever was playing the flute outside her door had started over. Kamil knew the melody well enough by now to flinch whenever she heard a wrong note.

"Your name is Maigrey Kamil," said Astarte. "But they don't call you Maigrey, do they?"

Kamil, her mouth filled with bread, shook her head.

"I never knew her," Astarte continued, sitting bolt upright, hands clasped in her lap. "My mother did. They were old enemies, fought during the Vapor-breather Wars. My mother despised her. She said Lady Maigrey was a coward who betrayed her commander, then ran away to hide from the consequences of her action. Of course, what my mother couldn't understand was how Lady Maigrey could have betrayed Derek Sagan. I think my mother was jealous. She wanted Sagan for herself. But that was not possible.

"Sagan admired and respected my mother, I think, but there was only one woman he could ever truly love—Lady Maigrey. Their love for each other was born when they were born. The Goddess meant them for each other. But the Evil One worked to thwart Her plans. Pride, jealousy, fear, mistrust—the weaknesses of our mortal flesh tore them apart. But love conquered, in the end. They are together now. In death, they have told each other what they could not say in life.

"I will call you Kamil," said the queen abruptly. "And you must call me Astarte."

"You don't love him," said Kamil softly, nervously tearing her bread into bits, her hunger assuaged. "You don't love him like . . . what you said, 'a love that was born when they were born.'"

"No, Kamil," said Astarte, the wine-colored eyes meeting hers steadfastly. "No, you are right. I don't love him like that. I never can. I never will."

"But I do!" Kamil threw the bread to her plate. "From the first moment I saw him—no, even before I saw him. When my father first told me about meeting him, I felt something for Dion then, though I didn't understand it. I'm afraid my father didn't think much of Dion at first. They met that night at Snaga

Ohme's, the night Ohme was murdered, the night Dion declared himself king. My father was talking to Lady Maigrey. Dion came up and accused her of betraying him because of her love for Sagan. Maigrey hit him."

Momentarily forgetting where she was, who was her audience, Kamil smiled, recalling the Bear's lively, boisterous account of the incident. "Lady Maigrey didn't just slap Dion. She socked him, according to my father. Knocked him back about five paces, cut his lip open. My father thought better of Dion after that, though. He defied that horrid old man, Abdiel, at the risk of his own life, and claimed the throne. When my father told the story, I could see Dion, though I'd never met him. I could see him so clearly. . . ."

"Yes," said Astarte quietly, "I can imagine."

Kamil recalled where she was. She sat hunched over her plate, toying with the uneaten fruit. She didn't look up. "You understand, then, that this isn't our fault. We didn't mean to hurt you. We don't want to hurt anyone. We have to be together. We were *meant* to be together."

"Yes, you were," said Astarte. "But you cannot."

Frustrated by the woman's calmness, thinking she'd prefer rage—at least she could understand rage—Kamil demanded, "Haven't you ever loved someone like this?"

"I have not met my soul's partner. I doubt if I ever will now. The Goddess obviously does not intend it. I was meant to do my duty, to be queen, to bear the heir to the throne."

Kamil stared at her. "Your Goddess intends you to be trapped in a loveless marriage? How can—"

"Not loveless," corrected Astarte. "I love Dion, in my own way. Oh, not the same way you love him, Kamil. I wish I could," she added wistfully.

The queen shook her head. "But I am giving way to self-pity, a weakness the Goddess abhors. I respect my husband. I respect him for the goodness inside him. I respect him for his high ideals and noble principles, for doing what he truly believes is right, for his self-sacrifice and dedication to the people. I admire him for his honor."

Kamil flushed again, bit her lip.

Astarte understood. "You think it's strange of me to talk of admiring him for his honor, when he's behaved most dishonorably to me. But I do. For I have seen how he suffers because of his betrayal of me. If he was not honorable, he would not care. And Dion does care, doesn't he, Kamil?"

Kamil pressed her lips together tightly, not to be lured into this trap.

"He cares. And so do you. I find myself liking you, Kamil."

Kamil found herself unable to return the compliment. She couldn't imagine "liking" Astarte. The woman was too remote, too distant. One might as well say one "liked" the moon.

"Where am I?" Kamil asked, when the silence between the two had grown uncomfortable. "Where have you brought me?"

"The Temple of the Goddess on the planet Ceres. Don't worry," Astarte added as Kamil stared in alarm and astonishment. "This is the one place where you will be safe. My mother dares not harm you here, on sacred grounds. You arrived in a coffin. I trust that is not an ill omen, but it was the only way I could smuggle you inside without mother's knowledge. Now, of course, she knows you are here. Her spies are everywhere. But I have spoken to her. No one dares shed blood in the Goddess's temple. She would curse the person for all eternity."

"So I'm only safe as long as I stay here?" Kamil looked around her.

"Oh, you need not keep to your room. The temple grounds are large and extensive. You may walk them freely. In fact, I will show you around now. Xris says you should take exercise, after your long confinement. Our Sacred Grove is quite beautiful. Would you like to see it?"

Kamil supposed she would. She felt the need to stretch her legs, the need to tire herself out, wear away the unhappy confusion roiling inside her.

They left her room, walked through corridors that were lined with latticed windows, permitting air and sunlight to enter freely. Wind chimes filled the air with their musical vibrations. They walked outdoors, into a garden whose beauty brought tears to Kamil's eyes. Snowcapped mountains soared above them. Far below, in a valley, the spires and towers of the main city of Ceres, also named Ceres, spread over the land.

The city was removed from the temple, kept at a distance. It was not a distance of disdain, but one of love and respect—the mother who permits her child to stand on his own, yet watches over him. A broad highway led from the city to the temple, a lifeline that was never cut.

The walled garden was vast and open to the skies. No tall

trees grew, for the Goddess was said to look down upon the garden and bless those who walked it and it would never do to impede Her sight. A feeling of peace and serenity always touched those who walked in it. Kamil felt it, in spite of herself, and she wrestled against it.

The two walked side by side, alone. The few people they met bowed in respect to Astarte, then left her presence with respectful consideration for her privacy. Astarte did not mention the last garden the two had walked together, for which Kamil was grateful, but she couldn't help thinking about it.

Astarte was explaining the benefit of some particular herb that grew along the pathways, when Kamil came to a sudden halt.

"This is all very pretty, Your Majesty"—she refused to call her by her given name—"but let's face it, I'm a prisoner. Is this how you plan to win Dion back? To use me as hostage?"

Astarte regarded her intently, then said softly, "What I have to say will not be easy for me to say or for you to hear. I want the Goddess to witness our conversation. Will you agree to that?"

"I . . . I suppose." Kamil faltered. "You know I don't believe in your Goddess," she added defensively.

"That is all right," Astarte returned, smiling. "She believes in you. Will you come?"

Kamil had no choice, apparently, not if she was going to find out what this woman had in mind.

They came to an arbor, covered with grape leaves. And here, it seemed, they had reached the end of the garden. The ground sloped upward steeply from this point, was covered with thick brush and trees.

Astarte led the way through the arbor. Parting a curtain of morning glory vines, she revealed a small path, hidden from sight from anyone loitering in the garden.

"This is the Walk of the High Priestess," she said. "It leads up there." She pointed. "To the Cavern of the Holy Goddess. Only I may go there, or those I bring with me. The climb is steep, but not treacherous, and you will be able to rest once we reach our destination. I will help you over the rough parts, Give my your hand."

Kamil protested that she could walk on her own and she did, up the first several meters. Then she found she needed help, needed two good arms to pull herself up over the rocks. Reluctantly, she gave Astarte her hand, allowed the queen to assist her.

Kamil was out of breath, hot and sweaty when they reached the top. The queen looked as cool as if she had been strolling the shaded corridors of the temple. But then, Kamil told herself irritably, Astarte probably makes this climb every day.

The cavern was dark, shadowed, smelled of moist rock and soil and water and smoke. It was large; a stone statue of the Goddess stood in the very back. Kamil could not see much, for very little light entered the cavern. A small flame flickered on an altar before the statue.

"Stay here, please," Astarte commanded.

Leaving Kamil at the front of the cavern, the queen moved to the back. She knelt before the Goddess, prayed quietly for several moments, placed an offering of flowers that she had gathered from the garden on the altar.

Returning, she brought a pitcher, which she filled at a running stream that bubbled near the cavern. She handed Kamil a cup, poured the water. It was sweet and cool. Kamil drank thirstily. The view from the cavern was breathtaking—encompassing the temple grounds and, far, far below, the city itself, all spread under the cloudless blue sky.

Kamil ignored it. "Very well," she said. "We're here. I'm your prisoner. You can hold me hostage. But I tell you right now it won't work."

"I know," said Astarte. "I am aware, as you are, that such a plan would not work. Dion would do anything, of course, to save your life. He would even, I think, give up the throne. And that must not happen. He is all that is holding the galaxy together. The chaos into which it would fall would be destructive, unimaginable. The Corasians wait for just such a moment. Ask the cyborg, Xris. He has recently returned from there. He knows."

Kamil was taken aback. "That's not true. Dion would never give up the throne."

"You don't believe so? What would *you* give up to save him?"

"I'm different," Kamil protested. "I'm nobody—"

She stopped, remembering.

When I was nobody, I didn't want to be. Now that I am king, I wish I was nobody again. Dion's words.

Though Kamil hadn't spoken them aloud, she knew she might as well have. Astarte heard her thoughts plainly, or perhaps saw them on her face.

"You see?" the queen said.

"He didn't mean it." Kamil defended him. "Everyone gets frustrated with his life sometimes. Wishes for a change."

"Would you love him if he were nobody?" Astarte asked softly.

"Yes," Kamil replied. She smiled, thinking back to the time she'd first met Dion. He'd been nobody then. A little boy again, playing in a lake. "I'd love him no matter what he was. But you wouldn't," she added accusingly, turning on Astarte. "You wouldn't have anything to do with him if he weren't king."

"What you say is true," Astarte agreed. "Though not precisely the way you mean it. Because he is king, I am queen—a role I do not seek for self-aggrandizement. I took it only after many hours of prayer. It was the Goddess's wish, that I could better serve her and also serve the people, work for their welfare, strive for peace. No matter what you think of me, you must admit I have at least done that much."

"Yes," answered Kamil readily, "and I've said as much to Dion. He agrees. You've been a perfect consort. But not the perfect wife. He doesn't love you! You don't love him! And using me to blackmail him isn't going to change that."

"You still do not understand, Kamil. I'm not going to use you to blackmail Dion. He doesn't know you are here. And he won't know. I'm not going to tell him."

"You won't have to," Kamil retorted. "The baroness, your mother, will tell him."

"As long as you are here, within the Goddess's hand, my mother has taken an oath to keep your whereabouts a secret. I chastised my mother severely for her attempt to murder you. It was an attempt I had not sanctioned, I had not approved. She undertook to act anyway, behind my back. She still thought of me as her daughter, you see. Now she knows better. Now she knows I am her queen."

"But what do you want of me, then?" Kamil wondered, confused. "Why am I here? People will miss me," she hedged. "When I don't come back to my dorm. When I don't show up for classes. The authorities will contact my parents. My father and mother will be frantic—"

"The Academy has been told you returned home for personal reasons, family business. As for your parents, I have spoken to your father and mother. I have explained to them exactly what I have done. I told them why and what I now intend to do."

Kamil gaped. "My father? . . ."

"They approve," Astarte continued gravely. "They have given me their blessing."

"I don't believe it." Kamil leaned against the cavern wall. She felt suddenly weak. "You're lying. This is a trick. My father would never permit—"

"Your father is a good man, an honorable man," Astarte interrupted. "Have you ever asked him how he felt about your illicit love affair with Dion? What would his answer be? Would he do such a thing himself? Would he break the vows he took to honor your mother?"

"No, he wouldn't. He loves my mother. And that's why he would understand," Kamil argued passionately. "I love Dion! He loves me! That's what's important."

"More important than stability, than order, than peace? More important than the lives of countless billions of people?"

"What do you want from me?" Kamil cried, turning away.

She found herself staring into the stone eyes of the goddess, stern and unwavering.

"I want you—of your own free will—to release Dion. I want you to tell him that this liaison is ended. You must be firm. You must mean it. Then, and only then, will he give you up and come back to me."

"I won't," Kamil said thickly. She didn't look at either Astarte or the statue. "I can't. That's like asking me to stop breathing. It would be like . . . like . . . dying. Except dying would be easier!" She flung herself back against the wall, winced at the pain that shot through her arm.

"Nevertheless, Kamil, it must be done. For his sake, you must make this sacrifice. I don't expect you to reach this conclusion immediately. It will require thought, prayer—to whatever deity you favor. Take your time. The peace and serenity of these surroundings will encourage you to look inward, come to know yourself. When you do, you will agree."

"Never," said Kamil firmly. "Our love is sacred—more sacred than some vows that you spoke with your lips, not your heart. Besides, you read the letter. Dion intends to start divorce proceedings—"

"He won't. His advisors will urge him against it. They will counsel time, patience, an attempt at reconciliation. I think he will listen to them. Especially now that I've muzzled Mother," Astarte added dryly.

She gazed long at Kamil, then said, "I may not love him as

you do, but I know him. I have faith in him to do what is best for his people. And I have faith in you. I think you are a good person, an honorable one. Eventually you, too, will determine what is right and you will have the courage to act upon your determination."

Kamil turned her back on the queen, started to walk back down the path. She slipped. Unable to catch herself with her broken arm, she fell heavily. Pain, frustration, anger at both Astarte and herself, fear, and unhappiness blinded her with bitter tears. Lying sprawled on the path, she wept.

Cool hands touched her; gentle arms cradled her.

"You can't keep me here forever!" Kamil gulped, pulling away.

"I don't intend to, Kamil. After a fortnight, you may leave in peace, no matter what your decision."

"You already know my decision. You may as well let me go now."

"We shall see. A lot may happen in a fortnight."

Don't count on it, Kamil said, but she said it to herself. She was tired, her arm throbbed painfully, her head ached. Her legs were scratched and bruised from the fall.

"Just leave me alone!" she mumbled. "I can get down by myself."

"There is an easier path," Astarte said. "A path we use during festival. It is on the opposite side of the cavern. The way is much longer, but the road is smoother. You may take either one you wish."

The queen left, wending her way down the steep and rocky path.

Kamil sat on the hillside. From somewhere below, the flute music resumed, pensive, unhappy. Kamil dried her tears, sighed. Her very own father, against her. He'd always seemed so understanding, so supportive and sympathetic. But then, she'd never told him that she and Dion had become lovers. Not because she was ashamed of it, but . . . well, it just wasn't the sort of thing girls discussed with their fathers. It wasn't his business. . . . It wasn't anybody's business!

If we were nobodies, nobody would care.

Kamil lay back on the ground, gazed through the leaves of the trees up into the empty sky.

There was her answer.

"If we were nobodies . . ."

Chapter ❖❖❖ *Eleven*

... and out of his mouth went a sharp two-edged sword.
The Bible, Revelation 1:14

Flaim gave a celebratory banquet to honor Sagan and his pledge of fealty to the prince. The meal was gracefully served by the prince himself, in homage to the two older men—his mentors and advisers. Food was placed on a large wooden tray on the tent floor. The tray revolved at the touch of a hand, bringing all the food upon it within reach of the guest.

The fare was simple, plain: cold meats, cheeses, breads, fruits, and candied nuts. It was intended to be eaten with the fingers, no plates or implements necessary. The men lounged on the floor, leaning against the silken embroidered bolsters. Outside the tent, another fire—this one much smaller than the bonfire of the previous night—blazed brightly. Drink was served in silver goblets.

"Wine for me, my prince," said Pantha, holding out his goblet. "Since you insist upon waiting on me."

"It is an honor, I assure you, dear friend. An honor to serve both of you—mentor, father; new friend, adviser. Which will you have, my lord? Wine or water?"

"Water, please, Your Highness."

"My choice, as well. I detest alcohol." Flaim poured cold water from an iced carafe for himself and Lord Sagan. "It clouds the senses, robs a man of control."

"At my age," Pantha remarked, sniffing critically at the wine, "a little clouding of the senses is a thing to be honored. I can afford the luxury of relaxation. Let other, younger, stronger hands do the work." He raised the glass of wine solemnly to the prince.

"I took a vow, when I joined holy orders, never to drink strong spirits," Sagan commented, giving the tray a gentle push to bring the apples within easy reach.

He appeared to be absorbed in his selection of the fruit. But, watching closely from beneath lowered eyelids, he saw Flaim and Pantha exchange glances. The old man drank his wine. Flaim, who had a hunk of cheese in his hand, laid it back down untasted.

Lifting an apple, Sagan rubbed the red skin on the sleeve of his cassock.

"About these vows of yours, my lord," said Flaim, leaning back, regarding the Warlord with a darkened countenance. "Pantha and I have been studying the Order of Adamant. We found information on it in some of his old reference files. I find that the priests and priestesses who belong to that Order must take a vow never to use weapons of destruction."

"That is so," said Sagan calmly. "Unless they happen to be a warrior priest, such as myself."

"Ah." Flaim's expression brightened. "Of course. That explains everything. I had not known you were a warrior priest, my lord."

"They were banned by His Majesty, I believe," Pantha stated, eyeing Sagan curiously, somewhat suspiciously.

"My ordination was kept secret. My father, who was a High Priest, foresaw the need of warrior priests in the dark days to come."

But did he? Sagan wondered to himself. Did my father foresee all this? If so, how he must have pitied his son!

"However," the Warlord continued, holding up the apple to the reflected light of the fire, studying its skin for flaws, "I have since renounced the status of warrior priest. My vows are now the same as all the others in the Order."

He bit into the apple, watched the two. Again, the exchange of glances. Sagan chewed the fruit, waited.

"But, my lord," said Flaim, shifting restlessly on the floor, "surely your pledge to me frees you from those vows. If it comes to war—I know we all hope it does not, but if it does—the Church would naturally side with the anointed king. I say 'the Church,' but, of course, I mean the archbishop. He and my cousin are devoted friends, I believe."

"Yes, Your Highness. The archbishop would most assuredly back Dion's claim, particularly since he knows the truth about yours."

Flaim waved that aside as unimportant. "As we have discussed, you will deal with that. In any case, my lord, your pledge to me frees you from these vows. You owe this Church no allegiance now. Your allegiance is to me."

"You misunderstand, Your Highness," said Sagan quietly. "I did not take these vows before the Church. I took them before God."

Flaim looked at Pantha, who merely raised his gray eyebrows and nodded toward the Warlord, silently counseling his young friend that the conversation was not finished.

The prince, frowning, turned back to Sagan.

"My lord—"

Sagan raised a hand. He tossed the half-eaten fruit down on the wooden tray. "Perhaps we could save time if Your Highness will tell me exactly what it is he wants of me."

Flaim stared down at the cheese, at the bread beside it, at the tray, at his water goblet. His handsome face was brooding, thoughtful. He glanced up once at Pantha, but it seemed that this time the old man withheld his counsel. The decision was left to the prince.

At length Flaim lifted his blue eyes. The firelight reflected in them seemed to spring up from the cheekbones, consume the eyes in flame.

"I need you as military adviser."

"I may advise. This does not break my vows."

"As general, field commander—"

"No, Your Highness. There are others as well qualified. You do not need me for that."

Flaim was silent again. His hand absently sent the tray revolving slowly around and around.

"I need you to bring my cousin here, to Vallombrosa. To me."

Sagan nodded. "I thought as much. And what do you want with him, my prince?"

"I mean him no harm," Flaim said earnestly. "I only want to talk to him. I want to meet him; I want him to meet me. I want him to see for himself that—of the two of us—I am the stronger, the better qualified to rule. I want a chance to avoid war, to persuade him to abdicate in my favor."

"As I told you before, my prince, Dion will never do that."

"I think he will." Flaim smiled. "I think he will have no choice."

"Ah, you have a plan."

"I would be a poor prince if I did not. Forgive me if I do not discuss it with you, my lord. As you yourself said, one cannot afford the luxury of trust. . . ."

Sagan inclined his head to indicate he understood perfectly. "You could arrange a formal meeting with His Majesty—"

Flaim shook his head, laughed. "He wouldn't let me within a hundred light-years of his sacred person. He'd be a fool if he did. And then there would be the attendant publicity. I would be cast as the long-lost relative, crawling from the darkness, seeking the light. When I stand in the sun, I want to be seen standing upright. I don't want the people to see me groveling at my cousin's feet. No. This meeting between us must be kept secret."

"Your Highness has what must be the galaxy's most effective secret police," Sagan said coolly. "The dark-matter creatures. As you said, nothing can stop them."

Flaim did not, apparently, comprehend for a moment. He stared at Sagan in some confusion. Then he smiled. "Ah, you are suggesting that we have the creatures deliver His Majesty. . . ."

"Much as they delivered me to you, Your Highness."

Flaim exchanged glances with Pantha, who gave a slight nod. "We considered that idea, my lord. We have, in fact, conducted experiments along those lines. We have had, from time to time, certain undesirable elements appear in our population— criminals, the mentally unstable, that sort. The dark-matter creatures proved most effective in removing them. Unfortunately, the creatures are not used to dealing with such fragile life-forms as ourselves. Many of the prisoners were irreparably damaged."

"Plucking a solid, massive object like a spaceplane from the heavens is one thing," Pantha offered. "Plucking a human being from his dinner table is quite another. The shock alone killed several."

"If His Majesty ever traveled by spaceplane alone . . ." Flaim shrugged. "But that, of course, is one thing he never does."

The prince leaned forward. "You, my lord, are the only person who can penetrate the circle of steel that surrounds the king. You alone can slip inside. You trained those men who guard His Majesty. Admit it, my lord, their real allegiance is still to you."

"As you said, I trained them," Sagan remarked, "and I would kill with my bare hands the first one who failed in his duty to the king whose life he has sworn to defend and protect. Those men would kill me without hesitation, at the king's command.

And he *would* command it. Dion doesn't trust me. I was his teacher, you see. I taught him that he cannot afford the luxury of trust. And if there was one lesson he learned of me," Sagan added dryly, "it was that."

Flaim was not pleased. He contained his anger well; he had self-control. But it was obvious he was not accustomed to having his plans thwarted. He gave the tray a sudden, sharp spin that sent it whirling, flung food in all directions. Bounding to his feet, he walked away, walked to the open tent flap, stared outside.

Sagan watched, interested in the reaction. "There is one person, however, who might be able to accomplish your objective, Prince Starfire. One person the king trusts implicitly—however misplaced that trust might be."

Flaim turned around. "Yes. Who is that?"

"A man named Mendaharin Tusca."

"Tusca." Flaim frowned. "That name sounds familiar—"

Pantha coughed, drawing attention to himself. "You recall the man, my prince. You saw the reports. He is known as Tusk—"

"Oh, yes." Flaim shook his head. "I think you are mistaken, my lord. We approached Tusca already. He wasn't interested in joining us. His wife's pregnant or some such thing. And he told our agent straight out that he and the king were no longer friends."

"Tusca lied," said Sagan.

Flaim regarded him with renewed interest. "Yes, my lord? Go on."

"The two are no longer close, certainly. That would hardly be proper—a mercenary soldier and the king. Dion knows the value of appearances. But if there is one person alive in this universe whom Dion considers a friend, one person he would trust with his life, it is Mendaharin Tusca."

"But," Pantha struck in, shrewd eyes glinting, "if this Tusca is close to His Majesty, the mercenary would not serve our purpose."

"I said Dion regarded Tusk as his friend. I did not say the feeling was mutual."

"But this man Tusk owes the king his life!"

"Precisely. How many friendships have been destroyed because one friend owed another money? The borrower comes to hate the lender, because of the power the lender holds over him."

"If you are right, my lord, this Tusk could prove exceedingly valuable to us," said Flaim after another exchange of glances with Pantha. "Is there a way to convince him to join us?"

"Yes, Your Highness," said Sagan.

Flaim waited expectantly.

The Warlord remained silent.

A rueful smile twisted the prince's lips. "Ah, I see, my lord. I'm being taught a little lesson here myself. The knife cuts both ways."

"It does, indeed, Your Highness. I promise you, however, that in a fortnight's time I will have Mendaharin Tusca standing before you, eager to carry out your commands."

"And you with him, my lord?" Flaim asked.

"Certainly, my prince," Sagan said. "It is my honor to serve you."

"Then nothing can stop me! Rise, Pantha. Rise, my lord. We will toast this occasion." Flaim grabbed the wine carafe, poured wine in the old man's goblet. He sloshed water into his own cup and that of the Warlord's.

Raising his goblet high, Flaim said with a laugh, "I give you the king! To His Majesty. God save the king!"

"God save the king," said Pantha reverently, tipping his glass toward Flaim.

"God save the king," Sagan echoed, and drank deeply. "And now, my prince, I bid you good night. I must prepare for my journey. If I have your leave to go—"

They exchanged farewells. The Warlord left the tent, walked down the hill. The mists had gone, blown away by a sharp, cold wind.

"And what do you think of him, my prince?" Pantha asked when the two were alone.

Flaim looked after the Warlord thoughtfully. He was a patch of darkness slashed into the fire's light. And then he was completely one with the darkness, disappeared into it.

"I must confess that I am disappointed," said Flaim coolly. "I had expected a warrior—an aging one, of course, but a warrior still. Instead, I see a broken old man, old before his time, older by far than you, my friend—in spirit, if not in years."

The prince shook his head, sighed. "A pity. One can still see the greatness in him. It flashes forth, from time to time, only to grow dim and flicker out."

"Your Highness must take into account the type of life Derek Sagan has been forced to lead these past few years. He speaks of taking this withdrawal from the world upon himself, but I have no doubt that your cousin Dion was responsible for Sagan's banishment."

Flaim was doubtful. "I cannot imagine such a man as Derek Sagan going meekly into exile."

"As you said, my prince, Sagan is not the man he was. He was Abdiel's captive for many months. Who knows what the mind-seizer did to the Warlord's brain? I see you looking dubious still, but you did not know the mind-seizers." Pantha was grim. "They were terrible, evil men. You owe your cousin a debt in that he removed this most formidable enemy from your path."

"And I shall repay my debt, you may be certain," Flaim said with a laugh. He bent down, picked up an apple, juggled it absently as he talked. "When our 'gentle cousin'—to use a term Shakespeare was so fond of—gives us the throne, he will be free to do what he likes with the remainder of his life. A prisoner, of course, but a prisoner in a gilded cage. He might even come to thank me. According to our spies, that wife of his will desert him once he is no longer king. Cousin Dion can have that mistress of his. Olefsky's daughter. What's her name—"

"Maigrey, my prince. Maigrey Kamil. Not to be confused with the Lady Maigrey."

"Now, there is a woman I would like to have met—the woman who could charm Derek Sagan."

"She would have liked to have met you," came a voice from the shadows, "when she could still use a sword."

Flaim glanced around swiftly. "Did you hear something?"

"Only the wind whipping through the tent, my prince," said Pantha.

"If so, the wind has found a tongue. I heard words . . ." Flaim was silent, listening intently.

"My prince, really . . ." Pantha began.

"Well, it's gone now. Never mind. Speaking of Sagan, can I trust him, do you think, my friend? As far as I trust anyone," he amended, grinning.

"I think so, my prince. If the king cast him into exile, Sagan will be happy to ally with the one who frees him. He was pleased with your offer of a command, that much was obvious. And who knows, Flaim? You might well restore him to true greatness. He might prove to be of real value. The acquisition of Tusca will be the test."

"Yes, that would simplify matters. But we will, of course, carry through with our other plan—just in case. The queen is on Ceres, I believe you said?"

"Yes, Your Highness. She left the planet for a brief trip in company with the cyborg, Xris. Our people attempted to follow them, but the cyborg is quite adept at evading pursuit."

"Pursuit? The queen doesn't know about our spies, does she?" Flaim demanded.

"No, certainly not, Your Highness. Unfortunately, our people seem to have stumbled onto some sort of private intrigue. Her Majesty is back on Ceres now, however, safely ensconced in the temple. There appears to be no immediate likelihood of her returning to the palace."

"Excellent. We must not move too soon. We don't want to make our cousin suspicious. We will see what Lord Sagan brings us."

"Yes, Your Highness."

"You know, it's a pity—" Flaim took a bite out of the apple. "Pah!" He spit it out. "Rotten."

"You were saying, my prince?"

"What? Oh, yes. As Sagan said, it is a pity that we cannot use the strange dark-matter creatures as our secret police. What excellent spies they would be! Unseen, unheard. We could send them to keep watch over Lord Sagan."

"Flesh-and-blood spies must serve the purpose there, my prince. Though I doubt that they'll bring us back much useful information, if they manage to keep track of him at all. Derek Sagan may be a shadow of the man he once was, but that shadow is still quite formidable."

"The creatures could be told to follow him."

"True, but what would that accomplish, my prince? It would be like sending a human to spy on the doings of a beehive. The dark-matter creatures cannot understand our languages. In fact, they have only a very limited concept of us as sentient beings. Always remember, Flaim, the creatures have no care for us. They use us, we use them—an alliance of mutual convenience, nothing more."

Flaim shrugged. "I bow to your judgment, my friend. And

now I must return to the alcazar. I have been gone far too long as it is. Will you remain here until the Warlord has departed, then supervise the dismantling of this?' Flaim gestured to the tent, the surroundings.

"Certainly, my prince. When that is done, I will join you."

Flaim pressed the hand of the older man. "Thank you, my friend. Your help has been of inestimable value."

Pantha, obviously pleased and touched, clasped the younger man's hand. Flaim departed, walking out of the tent with long, confident strides. He tossed the apple into the bonfire as he passed.

Book Three

Give me the crown.
Here, cousin, seize the crown. Here, cousin,
On this side my hand, and on that side yours.
Now is this golden crown like a deep well
That owes two buckets, filling one another,
The emptier ever dancing in the air,
The other, down, unseen, and full of water.
That bucket down and full of tears am I,
Drinking my griefs, while you mount up on high.
William Shakespeare, Richard II, Act IV, Scene i

Chapter ❖ One

I knew, and know my hour is come, but not
To render up my soul to such as thee . . .
                    George Gordon, Lord Byron, *Manfred*

The screen door slammed.

"Tusk! Where are you? Tusk!" Nola shouted.

"I'm giving the kid a bath," came Tusk's voice and a splash.

Nola threw the grocery sack she carried in the general vicinity of the kitchen table and headed for the small bathroom, located at the far end of the house. Reaching the door, she paused to catch her breath.

"Yeah, what?" Tusk squatted on the floor next to the bathtub. Water glistened on his face, trickled down his arms. Young John, seated in the tub, lifted up a small bucket filled with water. Grinning gleefully at his mother, he proceeded to upend it, deluging himself and his father.

"Jeez, this kid must be part dolphin—"

"Tusk . . ." Nola tried again.

Tusk looked up. "What the—" He jumped to his feet. "You've been *running?* In this heat? You thinkin' of tryin' out for a marathon? What sorta weird hormone's attacked you now? Here"—he put the lid down on the toilet seat—"Sit down. John, don't do that—"

"Tusk!" Nola grabbed hold of his arm, pinched him to emphasize the serious nature of what she had to say. "I stopped by the store . . . to get the milk for lunch . . ." She gasped for breath.

"Yeah, so?" Tusk glanced back at his son. "John, damn it, I've told you— Look at the mess you've made!"

"It's Link, Tusk!" Nola persisted. "He's in the Seldom Inn, in a high-stakes ante-up game. (John, your father told you not to do that.) I heard it from Rozzle. He stopped me as I went past his office. He tried to call, but since the phone's been disconnected . . ." Nola brushed back her sweat-damp curls. "Link's losing, Roz said. Big time."

307

"So what else is new?" Tusk grunted. He grabbed a towel, wiped off his face, then began mopping up the floor.

Nola leaned against the door frame. "Link's bet the spaceplane, Tusk. His half of it."

Tusk froze, towel in hand, water dripping on the floor. He stared at her.

"It's true, dear," she said bleakly. "Roz said he'd try to hold things off as long as possible, but it may already be too late. You better hurry."

Standing up, Tusk tossed the towel on the floor. "That son of a bitch!"

···❖❖❖○❖❖···

The Seldom Inn was a combination bar and motel located near the spaceport. Its customers were generally traveling salesmen, bored convention goers, commercial pilots on layovers, and private pilots who wanted some pleasant diversion. The Seldom Inn offered this in the form of cheap liquor; cheap food; moderately priced, moderately clean rooms; and a gambling casino—which is where the owner made his profits.

The owner, Rozzle Dozzle, was a tall, stringy man who looked as if he'd hung himself out to dry in the sun twenty years ago and forgotten to take himself back in. One of the wealthiest men in town, Rozzle dressed in pretty much whatever came to hand when he got up in the morning and was constantly being mistaken for one of his own janitorial staff—which mix-up appeared to afford him considerable amusement.

He had the reputation of being a fair employer and a good neighbor, so that if he ran a few rigged tables, employed a few slick dealers, fleeced a few strangers out of their credits, no one in town much minded. The locals knew which games to avoid. Rozzle was lenient as far as bar tabs were concerned and he always made certain regular customers left when they'd had enough. He was well liked and he could tell you within two numbers of the right of the decimal point how much money he'd made during his lifetime.

Tusk dashed in the inn's front door, vaulted the reception desk, nearly knocking down the startled clerk, and plunged into Rozzle's office.

"Where the hell is he?" Tusk shouted.

Rozzle jerked a thumb. "Upstairs. Sorry, Tusk. I tried my damnedest. You know how Link gets when he's been drinkin'.

And Banquo's been buyin' jump-juice for him like they was goin' to take it off the market."

"Link up there?"

"Yeah. Tusk, wait."

Rozzle was on his feet. He could move fast and, from dealing with juicers over the years, he was stronger, tougher, and more tenacious than he looked. Catching hold of Tusk's arm, he gave it a few good twists and a jerk to bring the mercenary to his senses.

"I got some good customers up there. Friends of mine. I can't let you go barging in, makin' a scene."

Tusk struggled ineffectively in Rozzle's grip, but finally gave up, was forced to cool from rapid boil to simmer.

"You okay?" Rozzle eyed him dubiously.

"Yeah!" Tusk rubbed his arm. "Yeah, I'm all right. Can I go up?"

"Long as you don't start bustin' up tables."

"Not tables. Heads. One head." Tusk clenched his fist.

"Link's a big boy, Tusk." Rozzle touched a button, spoke a few low words into a commlink. "He don't need his mommy."

"He needs a keeper!" Tusk glowered.

"I've fixed it. Just tap twice, softly, on the door. The Redhead'll let you in. And, Tusk. Look out for this Banquo. He's the big winner so far."

"Banquo?" Tusk screwed up his face. "I know him?"

"Naw. He's new around here. Came in last night. He don't look like much, but I got a feeling he's trouble."

Tusk nodded gloomily and headed for the upper floors.

Rozzle gazed after him, shook his head. "Tusk, my friend, meet your new partner."

◄─❍─►

Tusk tapped twice, softly, on the door. Rozzle's wife, known as the Redhead, a woman as round and short as he was tall and thin, and one of the best dealers in the business, opened the door.

The room was filled with tobacco smoke and the stale, sour smell of sweat. Sunlight filtered in through the cracks of a drawn window shade. A harsh nuke light shone down from the ceiling on a green baize-covered table.

"Game's over, I'm afraid, Tusk," the Redhead said quietly.

Tusk had no need to ask who'd lost. Link sat slumped in dejection, his elbows on the deal table, his head in his hands.

Stalking across the smoke-filled room, Tusk grabbed hold of his erstwhile partner, shook him.

"What the hell have you done?"

"I was hot, Tusk. Hot. I couldn't lose." Link didn't look up. "Then . . . you know how it goes. The cards went against me. I figured, though . . . only a matter of time." He stretched out his unsteady hand for a half-empty glass of jump-juice.

Tusk knocked the glass out of his reach, sent it smashing to the floor.

"Hey, no trouble." The Redhead waddled over.

"Then get him the hell outta here!" Tusk swore bitterly.

"Come on, pumpkin," the Redhead crooned. With an expert hand, she levered Link up out of the chair, steered his stumbling footsteps toward the door.

"A straight," Link said to no one in particular. "I had a goddam straight. How the hell'd he beat a goddam straight?"

Two other players, who didn't look any too happy themselves, gave Tusk a glance, then filed out of the room. The big winner remained behind, gathering up plastic credits, golden eagles, and paper cash.

He was a grossly overweight man with a coarse, jowly face, stubbly with a few days' growth of dark beard. He had tiny pig eyes, almost buried beneath layers of fat. But these eyes—when they turned on Tusk—were remarkable for their calculating shrewdness. And the man either had been involved in a terrible accident or was born with severe handicaps. He couldn't walk; he rode in what was commonly know as an airchair—a sophisticated wheelchair that traveled on cushions of air.

He had use of one hand and arm, apparently, for it was this hand that was scooping up the cash, depositing it in a bag attached to the arm of the chair. The other hand was immobile, locked in a fixed position over a computer keypad attached to the chair. His head and neck were held upright by a brace. He could not move his head, but was forced to swivel about in the chair to look directly at anyone, a movement which he made with startling speed. The fingers—surprisingly thin and long, considering the grossness of the body—flicked rapidly over the keypad. A synthesized voice spoke.

"You're Tusk, I take it?"

"Yeah," said Tusk morosely, shoving his hands in the pockets of his jeans. "That's me."

"I'm your new partner, sir," the mechanical voice told him. "Lazarus Banquo."

Tusk glanced again at the leering man, found he didn't much like looking at him, and glanced away. "Can't say that I'm pleased to meet you."

"No, sir, I don't suppose you are." Banquo made a sound in his chest, a sort of gurgling belch that was, perhaps, a chuckle.

His clothes were expensive, but they hadn't been washed in some time, to judge by the remains of various meals that adorned his tie and shirtfront. Judging by the smell, Banquo hadn't bothered to wash himself either.

Tusk took a step or two closer to the window. "Look, Mr. Banquo, I'll level with you. You didn't get yourself much of a prize. Our shuttle business is really just gettin' off the ground—"

"A veritable pun, sir! I appreciate it." Again the belching chuckle.

"Yeah, well." Tusk yanked the window open, drew in a deep breath. "Glad you got a sense of humor. Anyway, business hasn't been that great. We've got a few debts and now, without a co-pilot . . . I mean I take it you don't—"

"No, sir. Wouldn't dream of it. Capital. That's all I'm interested in, sir. Liquidate. Turn into cash. Nothing beats cash, sir. Nothing!" Banquo's good hand squeezed the money bag he held.

Tusk looked around grimly. "That's kinda what I had figured. I can't buy you out right away. But I could pay you some each month. . . ."

"A fair offer, sir, but not one I'm prepared to take. There's a consortium on planet . . . well, I won't say where . . . but they would offer me a hundred thousand eagles for my share of that Scimitar this minute, sir. This minute.

"Of course, sir," Banquo added with a jowly grin, "where my half goes, your half goes, sir. But they would be willing to pay you the same amount."

"A hundred thousand . . . Are you crazy?" Tusk stalked over to stand in front of the obese monstrosity, glared down at him. "It's worth fifty times that amount! One hundred times!"

"Then pay me, sir," Banquo said, the grin swallowed in layers of fat. The pig eyes were suddenly cold and dangerous.

"Pay me what my half is worth now, sir, and we will part company."

"You goddam bastard. You got Link drunk, then cheated him. I'll lay money those cards were—"

"Come, come, my dear sir," Banquo intervened. "Say nothing that you may regret later. We are, as it seems, at an impasse. Notwithstanding the wise advice of Solomon, we cannot very well cut the spaceplane in two. However, I begin to see the glimmerings of a solution. Escort me to my suite, where we may talk in peace."

The grotesque man clutched the bag close to him. "I feel rather nervous carrying this much cash. I have seen several unsavory characters running loose in this establishment."

"Look in a mirror," Tusk advised him, but he did so under his breath.

Banquo activated the air jets and the chair rose up off the floor and carried the hefty, immobile body out of the room. Tusk tagged along; he hadn't much choice.

"Not that I am defenseless, mind you, sir," Banquo's machine voice told him. The eyes regarded Tusk with cunning. Banquo patted the arm of his chair, and Tusk saw that it was really a beam rifle. "Computer-controlled. I have only to press this button. Fires forward or backward, sir. My own design."

Tusk grunted. They proceeded down the hallway to an elevator. Being cooped up in a small, stuffy elevator with Banquo was not a pleasant experience. Tusk held his breath as long as possible, was glad they only had to go up one flight.

The doors opened. The chair whirred along quietly down the corridor. Neither man spoke until they had reached Banquo's room. He fumbled in a pocket for the pass card, handed it to Tusk.

"If you would be so good, sir. My manservant quit, the ungrateful wretch. Abandoned me in this dreadful place. Come in, sir, come in."

Banquo glided in through the open door, entering what Rozzle termed a "sitting room," due to the presence of a couch and an understuffed armchair. The Seldom Inn had only two suites: the President's Suite—so named because some third-, fourth-, or fifth-world president had actually been forced to spend the night in it when his shuttlecraft developed anti-grav problems. The other suite was what Rozzle termed— unofficially—his High-Roller Special, and was set aside for those gamblers who took the game seriously. This one was a cut above the President's Suite, having three rooms: a bedroom, a small sitting room, and a bathroom, complete with a jet-tub and a private safe in the bedroom. In Banquo's case, the jet-tub was, apparently, a wasted feature.

"Shut the door, will you, sir? Take a look up and down the hall first. Excellent. All this money. One can't be too careful. If you would lock up securely . . ."

Tusk peered into the hall, reported it empty. He shut the door, activated the lock.

Banquo wheeled the chair to the bedroom door, came to a halt. Clutching the bag, he stared into the room nervously.

"Would you be so good as to check the bedroom, sir? Someone might have entered during my absence and be lurking in wait. One of the duties of my manservant, sir, is to investigate each room before I enter. I never go anywhere without prior investigation."

Tusk hesitated. He had the distinct and unpleasant feeling that the "solution" to their "problem" was going to involve Tusk's transformation from spacepilot to manservant. And Tusk was fully prepared to tell Banquo to take his half of the Scimitar and sell it to a scrap heap. What the hell? It was only a spaceplane. There were dozens more like it out there. Work a regular job for a couple of years, earn the cash . . . As for XJ, it'd serve the damn loudmouthed computer right.

Tusk walked into the bedroom, took a halfhearted glance around.

"Yeah, it's safe," he reported sullenly. "You can go in."

"Excellent, sir. Excellent. I take your word for it, you see." Banquo powered his chair into the bedroom. "If you will excuse me for a moment, sir, I have some personal business to dispose of." He patted the bag. "Don't be offended, sir, if I close the door and lock it. I trust you, sir. I truly do. But money is money and, in your dire position, the temptation might be too strong for you to overcome."

Tusk glowered, considered telling Banquo just where he could stash his filthy money. He swallowed his words, however, and couldn't help noticing how rotten they tasted on the way down.

"Help yourself to a drink, sir," Banquo called, peering around the door as he was shutting it. "You'll find a wide and varied selection there on the desk. Oh, and take a look out the window, please. I fancied I saw some derelict stragglers hanging about out there yesterday, staring up at my room. Oh, and make certain the window is shut and bolted."

Banquo closed the door. The lock clicked. Tusk heard the sound of the chair whirring across the floor, then silence.

He stood in the center of the sitting room, which smelled of freshly stirred-up dust and cheap furniture polish, and told himself to walk out the front door and never look back. He couldn't ever remember feeling this low. Not even the time when he and Nola were surrounded by mind-dead and Corasians and the Scimitar wouldn't make the liftoff.

"I'd've sold the damn plane for a handful of peanuts then. It damn near got me killed. What do I care? Let the bastard have it."

Tusk actually took a step toward the door. He and Nola had been married in that spaceplane. He'd rescued Dion from Sagan in that spaceplane. Dion had saved his friend's life in that spaceplane. . . .

Tusk brushed his hand across his eyes, realized he was actually crying, and cast a swift, embarrassed glance toward the bedroom door. It remained shut. Sighing, Tusk headed for the window. Might as well get used to obeying orders. He peered out between the cracks in the metal blinds, was rewarded with a magnificent view of the Seldom Inn's parking lot and the open-all-hours grocery store across the way.

Both were practically deserted. Vangelis' afternoon heat had driven everyone with any sense indoors. A gigantic lizard was meandering across the parking lot. A woman sat on a bench in front of the grocery store drinking a can of pop and fanning herself.

The window was shut and locked, had probably been shut and locked for the last twenty years. Behind him, he heard the door open.

"It's okay, Mr. Banquo. Hell, there's no one dumb enough to be out in this heat this time of—" Tusk turned around.

Derek Sagan stood in the bedroom door.

It was fortunate the window was shut, or Tusk would have fallen out of it.

As it was, he staggered back against it, crashing into the blinds, nearly bringing them down on his head. He gulped for air, couldn't find any. His chest felt like it was being squeezed in a vice.

"You're dead!" Tusk wheezed.

"Not quite," Sagan said. He walked over to Tusk, reached out his hand.

Tusk made a good attempt at climbing backward up the wall. "Don't! No—"

The Warlord took hold of the pilot's black arm.

Tusk gasped, flinched, expecting to feel corpselike fingers dragging him down into a marble crypt. But the hand that touched him was warm, its grip strong. Shivering, Tusk stared at it, his mouth opening and shutting.

"Flesh and blood," said Sagan grimly. Steering Tusk to a chair, he thrust him down into it. "Here, drink this." The Warlord grabbed a bottle, poured something in a glass, put it in Tusk's hand.

Tusk nearly dropped it. After fumbling with the glass for a moment, he tossed the contents down thankfully. He had no idea what it was, but the fiery burn in his throat stabilized him, though he was still confused as hell. He began to catch his breath, decided maybe he wasn't having a heart attack, after all. Just a stroke.

He picked up the bottle. His hand was shaking too much to hit the glass; he sloshed the liquor all over his pant legs. Tossing the glass, Tusk lifted the bottle to his lips, took another drink, and found he could actually look at Sagan without shuddering.

"Where's B-Banquo?" Tusk mumbled, his lips almost too numb to form the words.

Sagan cast a significant glance through the open door to the bedroom.

Tusk, peering that direction, saw the empty air-chair, a pile of clothes and padding, and a plasticskin mask, lying on the bed. He looked back at Sagan . . . and understood.

"Holy shit," he whispered in awe, and gulped another drink.

Sagan took the bottle, set it back on the desk. "We have important business to discuss, Mendaharin Tusca. I want my partner' sober."

"Your . . . partner . . ." Tusk stood up unsteadily, supported himself on the edge of the desk.

Sagan walked over to the window, began checking the vicinity. The Warlord was dressed in military fatigues—pants only— his chest and arms were bare. Tusk gazed in semi-drunken fascination at the scars on the man's arms and back and chest.

Battle scars, some of them; others appeared to have been self-inflicted.

"Yes, partner," said Sagan. Making certain the blind was securely shut once again, he turned to face Tusk. "Rather appropriate, don't you agree? Seeing that it was *my* Scimitar to begin with. I'm buying back my own stolen property."

"This ... this was a setup!" Tusk burbled. "You swindled Link ... on purpose!"

"Indeed." Sagan seated himself on the edge of the desk. "Sit down. We have a great deal to discuss. Perhaps you should breathe into a paper bag. ..."

Tusk muttered something pertaining to paper bags and their ultimate fate in the universe and collapsed back into the chair. He stared at Sagan, unable to believe, yet forced to believe; completely unable to comprehend.

"You're not dead," he said at last in wonder.

"I thought we settled that," Sagan remarked with some asperity.

"Yeah, yeah. Just ... just give me a minute, will you? You're not dead and you're half-owner in my plane. Not some clown named Lazarus Banquo who never existed, but you—Lord Sagan. Christ!"

Tusk put his head in his hands, shut his eyes. This procedure didn't help. When he opened them again, Derek Sagan was still sitting on the edge of the desk. "What the hell's going on here? Why the disguise? Why the setup? Does Dion know? This has something to do with him, right?"

Sagan almost smiled. The muscles at one corner of his mouth twitched; the dark eyes warmed briefly.

"Yes, this has something to do with Dion. You might say it has everything to do with Dion. You are going to enter the palace, Mendaharin Tusca, and abduct the king."

Tusk gawked, stared, then laughed,. "What's the punch line?"

"No joke," said Derek Sagan. "I am serious. Deadly serious. You don't think I'd spend day after day wearing that disguise"—he glanced in disgust at the remains of Lazarus Banquo—"if I were not serious?"

Now Sagan did smile, but the smile was dark and mocking. "Come, come, Tusca. You were about to agree to indenture yourself to the odious Mr. Banquo in return for the privilege of keeping your beloved plane. You will simply indenture yourself to me. Either that or pay me the cash you owe me."

Tusk was on his feet. "You know I can't. You knew that when you cooked up this scheme. Trying your old tricks again. Still trying to get hold of the crown for yourself. Well, you can count me out. I'll blow up the damn plane first. I'll blow myself up with it. Go to hell. Go *back* to hell."

Tusk made an unsteady lurch for the door. He had nearly reached it, was astonished that he had come this far and was still alive, when Sagan spoke.

"That was what I was hoping you would say."

Tusk stopped, half-turned, looked around. "What do you mean by that?"

"His Majesty is in deadly peril, Tusca. Together, you and I are going to try to save him. But we will be playing a dangerous game."

Sagan sounded sincere, Tusk had to give him that. Yet Derek Sagan was Blood Royal. He had the gift. He could be charming when he wanted, sound sincere when he wanted. When it suited his purpose.

The Warlord rose to his feet, reached into the pocket of his fatigues.

"Take it slow," Tusk said, hand on the lasgun he wore at his belt.

Sagan drew forth a small plastic computer disk. He held it up for Tusk to see.

Tusk kept his hand on his gun, made no move to take the disk.

The Warlord walked over to Tusk, slapped the computer disk into his palm.

"This is the deed to my half of the Scimitar. It's yours, Mendaharin Tusca. Free and clear. Take it and walk out that door. I won't stop you. I doubt if I could stop you," added Sagan wryly. "I'm not the man I once was."

Turning, he walked back over to the window, lifted one of the blinds, looked out. Tusk could see the scars on the man's back, as if he'd been struck repeatedly with a whip.

"Like hell you're not," Tusk muttered beneath his breath.

He juggled the disk, flipped it up and down. He knew it, recognized it. It was the deed, all right. The Scimitar was his again. All his. He could walk out that door this minute, except he knew now he wouldn't, and he knew Sagan knew.

"All right. If we're doing this for Dion, he must have given you some message for me, some little something that would make me know this is all legit. . . . We have a code, you see . . ."

The earring. He would have sent the small earring made in the shape of an eight-pointed star. Tusk's father had given it to him, to remind Tusk of a vow—a call to serve a monarchy in exile. He'd answered that call, reluctantly, but he'd answered. The call had changed his life. He'd given the star to Dion, the last time he and Tusk had met.

If you ever need me . . . Tusk had told him.

"Dion didn't send me," Sagan replied. "He doesn't know anything about this, and he mustn't. That's part of the game. They sent me to recruit you. It was my—"

"They who?"

Sagan was irritated. "You're not stupid, Tusca. I don't hire stupid people and once, for some misguided reason, I hired you. Who do you think 'they' are?"

"That outfit that calls itself the Ghost Legion? I'll give 'em credit. They're well-named. They dug *you* up from somewhere."

"What did you say?"

"Nothing, nothing." The more Tusk thought about this, the less sense it made. He shook his head, baffled. "So it *is* the Ghost Legion? They sent *you* to get *me?*"

"It was my idea, I must admit, but I allowed them to think it was their own. You are going to join Dion's enemies, Tusca. You must convince Dion that you are a traitor."

"Yeah, and maybe you're the traitor!" Tusk's head was throbbing. "I don't like this. I don't like any of it. How do you expect me to trust you? You had my father murdered. Damn near killed me—" He stopped. It had suddenly occurred to him that maybe he should be finding out a few things, pass them on to Dixter . . .

"Look, sir, my lord, if you'd give me more details, then I could decide for myself."

Sagan did not turn around. He shook his head.

"This is just dandy." Tusk swore. "You don't trust me. I sure as hell don't trust you—"

"It's not that, Mendaharin Tusca," Sagan interrupted, still keeping watch out the window. "You have a pregnant wife, a child. I presume you don't want them involved. Though," he added in a lower voice, "some people already think you know too much. Come here." He motioned toward the window.

Tusk hesitated a moment, then stepped forward.

"Look outside," Sagan said.

Suspecting a trick, Tusk peered out through the chink in the blind. "What the hell am I looking at beside a whole lotta concrete?"

"The woman sitting on the bench out in front of the grocery store fanning herself. Do you know her?"

Tusk looked at her intently—again. She'd thrown away the pop can. "No." He shrugged. "That doesn't mean a lot. We do a roaring tourist trade around here—"

"She knows you," Sagan said coolly. "She followed you here."

"From my home?"

"From your home. They know where you live. They've had you under surveillance for a week now."

Tusk eyed Sagan. "You did this to me."

"You did this to yourself, Tusca. When you befriended a seventeen-year-old boy and helped make him a king."

Tusk peered back out at the woman. It *was* odd, her sitting there like that in the middle of the day. "Meaning to say that I'm already involved, no matter what I decide."

"Perhaps." Sagan shrugged. "Perhaps not. They *might* forget about you . . . about your wife and child. . . ."

Tusk took another look at the woman on the bench. Irritably, he snapped the blind shut.

"This has all happened too fast. You gotta give me some time."

"We don't have time," said the Warlord. "They are watching you. I don't believe they have penetrated Banquo's disguise, but they'll soon figure out who I am and then they'll start watching me. This room is the one safe place where we can talk without being overheard."

"There's the Scimitar. . . ."

Sagan shook his head.

Tusk stared at him. "You're saying they've got it bugged? Naw, that's crazy!"

Sagan lifted an eyebrow. "Is it? Think back. Have you had any customers in the last two weeks?"

Tusk tried to think. He was beginning to feel as if he were sinking deeper and deeper into dark water.

"No. Business hasn't been all that great," he said glumly. "Hell! Wait a minute, though. They decided we weren't what

they had in mind, but they went on board, took a look around . . .
Shit!

"If you're right, I'm already in this." Tusk glowered. "I'm in
this up to my goddam neck. And I still think *you're* responsible!"

The Warlord had no comment. A slight smile tugged at his
lips; it did not warm the eyes.

Tusk turned on his heel, walked toward the door. He had his
hand on the handle, was opening the door when Sagan spoke.

"If you go home, they'll grab you, your wife and your child.
They can't afford to leave witnesses. On the other hand, if you
and Lazarus Banquo leave now, we can board the Scimitar and
be off-planet before they know what's happened. Once we're
away, you can send a message to your wife, warn her to flee to
a place of safety."

Tusk stood a moment, then he yanked open the door, stalked
out of the room, slammed the door shut behind him. Clutching
the computer disk in his hand, he tromped angrily down the
hall, took the fire stairs instead of the elevator, came storming
out into the front lobby.

Rozzle was standing at the reception desk. "I'm sorry, Tusk.
If there's anything . . ."

Tusk walked over to the front entrance. "Did Link get home
all right?" he asked over his shoulder.

"Yeah, I had one of the girls drive him. Tusk, I—"

Tusk's eyes flicked in the direction of the woman seated in
front of the grocery store. She sat fanning herself in the heat,
looking up and down the road as if she were waiting for someone.

Turning, he walked back to the desk. "Rozzle, do me a favor.
Send a message to Banquo. Tell him I've gone to get *our* Scimitar ready for liftoff. He can meet me there whenever he's
ready."

Rozzle grimaced, shook his head. "That fat bastard. Sure, I'll
tell him. Look, Tusk, again, I'm really sorry . . ."

"Forget it," Tusk said grimly. "It's not your fault."

He left the motel, walked across the parking lot. Climbing
into the jeep, he kicked it into gear, drove off. He took a quick
glance in the rearview mirror.

The woman was gone.

Chapter ❖ Two

By a knight of ghosts and shadows
I summoned am to tourney
Ten leagues beyond the wide world's end.
                    Anonymous, "Tom o'Bedlam"

"Open up, XJ!" Tusk bawled, banging on top of the Scimitar's hatch. "Hurry up! I'm about to fry out here in the sun!"

The hatch whirred open slowly. Tusk tumbled down the ladder. The Scimitar's interior was dark and sweltering hot.

"Tusk, is that you?" came an irritable voice, which sounded as if it had been awakened from a nap.

"Jeez, turn the air on, will you?" Tusk said mopping his brow with his shirttail. "It's like a goddam oven in here!"

"If you think I am going to waste fuel—"

"Shut up and do it," Tusk growled, in no mood to argue. "We've got a—" he swallowed, "new owner and he—"

"What?" XJ screeched.

"You heard me," said Tusk, glancing around the plane nervously. He knew he wouldn't be able to spot the listening devices, but he couldn't help looking. "Link lost his share of the spaceplane in an ante-up game. The new owner's coming to . . . uh . . . take it out for a spin. So get ready for liftoff. Oh, and while you're at it"—he tried to sound casual—"run the routine system check for bugs."

"New owner—! Link lost—! Bugs—" XJ's circuits were overloading. The computer sizzled and crackled incoherently. "There are no bugs on *my* plane. He won't find so much as a cockroach—"

Tusk swung himself down into the cockpit. Crouching over the computer, he hissed, "Listening devices, you RAMless idiot! Run the *routine program!*"

"Routine program? What routine—"

Tusk gave the computer a swift thump.

"Oh!" XJ's lights blinked viciously. "*That* routine program. Why didn't you say so? Not that I'll find any—I'll be damned."

321

Tusk grunted. Collapsing into the chair, he lowered his aching head into his hands.

"You want me to get rid of them?" XJ asked in subdued tones.

"No," Tusk snarled, "I want to keep them for pets!"

"Gee, aren't *we* in a mood today?" XJ said loftily.

There was silence, then the report. "All clear. Who planted them— What in the name of ROM are you doing?"

Tusk was staring at himself in one of the steel panels, poking and pulling at his skin.

"I think I am," he said.

"Am what? Crazy? Yeah, I could have told you—"

"No. My skin. I think I've turned white." Tusk put his nose to the steel plate, ran his hands over his face.

"Would you at least *try* to make sense?" XJ demanded irritably. "What happened to the plane? Who's the new owner? Someone with a brain, I trust."

"I've heard about things like this," Tusk said, examining his hands. "People have a sudden shock. Their hair turns white overnight—"

"*Hair* turns white! Hair! Hair! It happens to hair, not to skin, you moron. What happened to the plane?" XJ howled.

"Link got in an ante-up game—" Tusk began.

"Is that *him*?" XJ interrupted, shocked.

"Who?"

"The new owner. Outside. I can't believe this—"

"Switch on the cam," Tusk said, sounding nervous.

An image appeared on the vidscreen. It was Lazarus Banquo, in his air-chair, jetting across the tarmac.

Tusk jumped to his feet. "Open up the cargo bay. We'll get him on board through that."

"Shall I rig up a winch?" asked XJ sarcastically.

Tusk whipped around, glared at the computer. "You might be interested to know that he owns the half of the plane that has you in it."

"I'm not surprised," XJ retorted. "An intelligent, sensible-looking gentleman like that would immediately recognize my talents—"

Tusk left to open the cargo bay.

--◄■❍■►--

"A fine-looking plane, sir. Fine-looking," said Lazarus Banquo, rubbing his hands together. Safely ensconced inside the Scimitar, he drove his chair around the passenger compartment. "I see you've made a few improvements—"

"We took care of the bugs," Tusk interrupted. "You can . . . uh . . . make yourself comfortable now."

Without waiting for a response, he headed again for the cockpit and began running through his systems check. He could hear, up above, what sounded like a balloon deflating.

"We'll be ready for liftoff in about thirty minutes. Sorry it's taking so long, but I had all the systems shut down to save on fuel—"

"*My* idea, sir," the computer chimed in, talking in dulcet tones. "You'll find we run an extremely efficient ship, Mr. uh . . . I don't believe we have been introduced. Who is this gentleman, Tusca?"

XJ sent a mild electrical jolt through Tusk's fingers.

"Ouch! Jeez!" Tusk snatched his hand back. "You—!" He paused, then said sweetly, "I'm pretty busy right now, XJ. Why don't you go up and introduce yourself to our new owner?"

"I'll just do that." XJ popped into its remote unit.

Small arms wiggling, it soared up from the cockpit and into the Scimitar's main cabin. Tusk stood up to watch.

"How do you do, sir? I am XJ-27 and I'm the one who really runs—"

XJ's optics flared. It gave a wild *eep*, then, with a strange sound—a sort of an electronic gargle—the remote went dark and crashed to the deck with a thud.

The lights went out; air-conditioning and life-support systems shut down. Tusk fumbled for a nuke lamp. Switching the beam on, he climbed up the ladder, flashed the light around.

Lord Sagan stood on the deck. XJ's remote unit lay at his feet, wobbling back and forth. Then it slowly rolled to a stop.

"My God," said Tusk, awed, "I think you've killed it."

The Warlord actually smiled.

"If that's the case, I have an FNCB 67 in my volksrocket. We can make the transfer—"

Lights on the remote flickered, flashed on, went out, came back on, dimmed a moment, but the computer hung in there. Cool air began to blow into the cabin once again.

"Where . . . where am I?" asked XJ feebly.

"If we're finished with the theatrics," Sagan said grimly, "and *if* there's any water, I'm going to take a shower." He was still pulling plastiskin off his face.

"There's ... there's water, m-my lord," stammered XJ, a glitch fluttering its audio. "Lots of water. More water than you could possibly want ... ever."

The Warlord stripped off the remains of Lazarus Banquo, then squeezed himself into the small shower unit.

Tusk, trying hard to keep a straight face, went back down to the cockpit. XJ followed, the remote unit breathing down Tusk's neck.

"Why didn't you tell me?" the computer demanded, seething. "I could have shorted out! I think I did melt down two whole boards. Was that ... is that ... Derek Sagan?"

"Yes," said Tusk, flipping switches.

"Alive?" XJ's lights blinked nervously. "I mean ... you saw him, too, didn't you?"

"Alive as I am," said Tusk. "Maybe more. The sight of him just about sent *me* six feet under."

"*He* won the plane from Link? Sagan ... owns us?"

"Shhh! Keep your voice down. You might say we were his all along," Tusk muttered. Hearing the water begin to run, he breathed a little easier.

"This is your fault," said XJ in gloomy tones. "I know it is. What does he want with you?"

"Us," Tusk corrected. "You remember that Ghost Legion business?"

"Ghost Legion ..." XJ's light brightened. "They offered us a job. They were willing to pay good money—"

"We'll be lucky if we live to cash the check. I don't know much about the deal. He"—Tusk glanced back nervously at the shower door—"wouldn't tell me the details. But it has to do with Dion. The kid's in some kind of danger and—"

"From Sagan?"

"Jeez! Keep quiet, will you?" Tusk broke out in a cold sweat. "No, not from Sagan. At least Sagan says it's not from him. Damn, I wish I knew what was going on!"

"So who had the plane bugged? Did Sagan do that?"

Tusk shook his head. "Naw. He warned me about it. I don't know who, for sure, but I could make a guess—"

"The Ghost Legion."

"It's got to be. They asked me questions about Dion. I

thought I'd convinced them that he and I had called it quits, but either they didn't believe me or . . ."

"Or what?"

"Or Sagan convinced them otherwise. He got me into this on purpose."

"Because you could help Dion?"

Tusk was quiet a moment, then—after another glance at the shower door—he said softly, "Maybe because I can *get* to Dion. I know if I was Dion, I wouldn't let the Warlord within a light-year of me."

"You think Sagan's setting you up for the galaxy's biggest sucker? If so, he's come to the right place."

Tusk mulled this over. "I thought so, at first. Part of me still does. But part of me doesn't. You saw that elaborate scheme he cooked up to keep from being spotted himself. He fooled me—"

"I knew who he was. All along," XJ protested. "Recognized him the moment he appeared on the screen. I was just putting you on—"

Tusk ignored the computer. "And he's been living in the disguise for who knows how long? All that padding must weigh a metric ton. To say nothing of sitting cramped in that chair for hours on end, unable to move, his face all covered with plastiskin. . . ."

"Yeah, yeah," XJ snapped. "I'm in tears. So what's his story?"

"According to what I can piece together, Dion's in danger from this Ghost Legion. We're going to join, go along with their scheme, get Dion out in the end. At least that's what I *think* the Warlord's got in mind. He wouldn't tell me much."

"A double agent. Now, *there's* a good career move. If one side misses, the other's bound to get you. And you agreed to go in on this with him, didn't you?"

"What the hell choice did I have?" Tusk demanded bitterly. "They bugged the plane. Some woman followed me here—from home, XJ. From home."

"You're sure we're not getting paid?"

Tusk glared, didn't answer.

"I don't like this," said XJ.

"You don't see me dancin' around the fuckin' plane, do you?" Tusk demanded. He glanced back at the shower door again. "But I came up with a plan on the way here. I pretend to go along with Sagan, pretend like I'm working with him, keep an eye on him, find out what's going on. If anything looks funny, well ... I'm in a position to warn Dion. The way I got it figured is that I'll be pretending to be workin' for Sagan, pretending to be against Dion, when all the time I'll really be workin' for Dion, pretending to be working for Sagan, pretending to be against Dion."

"You call that a plan?"

"Yes."

"Well, I don't. I call it Let's Pretend There's Intelligent Life on this Spaceplane."

The water in the shower gurgled, spit, and dribbled to a stop.

"I could transmit a message to Dixter." XJ spoke so softly Tusk almost couldn't hear. "Sagan would never know."

"Yeah," Tusk whispered, "that's what I was thinking. But we got to figure out what to say ... Tell him—Wait! Shush."

The shower door opened. The Warlord stepped out, toweling himself off. He walked toward the cock-pit.

"Just about ready. Uh"—Tusk looked around—"what do you go by these days? I mean, what should I ... we ... call you?"

" 'My lord' will be satisfactory," replied Sagan, again almost smiling. "And when you meet the king's first cousin, you will refer to Prince Flaim as His Highness or His Royal Highness."

Tusk's jaw sagged.

"First cousin?" XJ's lights flickered in suspicion. "What first cousin? I know the genealogy of the Starfire family better than I know my own. Which, in case you're interested, I'm a direct descendant of a Unix-5000—"

"Shut up!" Tusk snarled. "Or you'll be an ex-direct descendant. What were you saying, my lord? The kid's got a first cousin? How? Where?"

"I'll spare you the lurid details. Suffice it to say that Amodius had a son—illegitimate, no rightful claim to the throne."

"But he wants it anyway." Tusk brightened. "And we're going to stop him!"

"No," Sagan replied coolly. "We're going to assist him. Keep telling yourself that. Over and over and over. I want you to be able to repeat it in your sleep."

"I don't think I'll be getting much sleep," Tusk muttered.

Sagan turned away, went to get dressed. "Lay in a course for Vallombrosa. Let me know when we're ready to make the Jump."

"Yes, my lord."

Glancing up, to make certain Sagan wasn't watching, Tusk began to type:

MESSAGE TO JOHN DIXTER. I'M BEING

"John Dixter is your son's godfather, I believe," said Derek Sagan. His voice floated down from the aft section of the spaceplane.

Tusk's fingers froze on the keyboard.

"Yeah." His throat constricted. He swallowed, tried again. "Yes, my lord," he managed. Sweat trickled down his collarbone.

"It would be a pity if something were to happen to him. Or his godson. Once we're out of orbit, you will send a message to your wife. I'll tell you what to say."

"Yes, my lord."

How the hell did he know? Tusk wondered bleakly. He couldn't have overheard XJ asking about Dixter. It's not possible. Not even for the Blood Royal. He knows what I'm thinking. That's what it is. He just plain bloody well knows what I'm thinking!

Words flashed across the computer screen.

I DON'T LIKE THIS. I WANT TO GO ON RECORD AS SAYING—I DON'T LIKE THIS!

"Put me down for one of the same," Tusk said softly.

Very, very softly.

Chapter ⚬⚭⚬ Three

Be near me when the sensuous frame
Is rack'd with pains that conquer trust;
And Time, a maniac scattering dust,
And life, a Fury slinging flame.
Alfred, Lord Tennyson, "In Memorium A.H.H."

Maigrey restlessly walked the vast halls of heaven, paced them back and forth, back and forth until the shining beings—whose patience is purportedly unending—heaved martyred sighs as they went about their duties.

Knowing the mind of God meant less than nothing to her now. She wanted desperately to know what was going on in the mind of Derek Sagan. And so, she left the beautiful, starlit halls (to the vast relief of those who dwelt there) and entered the physical plane, the land of the living, to take up her nightly vigil.

One with the darkness, she glided inside the Scimitar. The spaceplane was traveling the Lanes, which meant the occupants could sleep, leave the watch to the computer. Tusk slept restlessly, as he always did without Nola's comforting form beside him.

Maigrey glanced at him fondly, if somewhat worriedly, then took her place beside Sagan's bed.

He slept soundly, no longer disturbed by intrusive dreams, doubts, or indecision. He lay on his back, one arm flung over his head, the other lying across his chest. His breathing was deep, steady, even. He had made his choice, for good or for evil.

But this one night's rest could not make up for a score of wakeful nights. Their mark was on him. His face, strong and hard when awake, was haggard in repose, his eyes sunken. Only the lips, drawn to a thin, straight, dark line, remained tight, firm. Whatever purpose he had, whatever resolve he'd made, he would carry it through to the end.

" 'Broken old man,' " said Maigrey softly, recalling Flaim's derisive description, and she sighed in frustration. "I should be used to this. You never did explain anything to us. We were your squadron, your Golden Squadron. You expected us to obey orders, to react instantly to your command, without necessarily knowing why or what you had in mind. Because of the mind-link, I knew more than the others did about your plans. But there were times when you caught me by surprise. And though it was sometimes irritating, sometimes terrifying for us, we understood."

"Yeah, John, I'll getcha a drink of water," Tusk mumbled suddenly, starting to climb out of his bed.

"Go back to sleep!" XJ snapped.

"Sure thing, sweetheart." Tusk nodded obediently, crawled back onto the fold-out couch, wrapped his arms around a cushion, shut his eyes.

"I'm not your— Oh, forget it." XJ went back to work.

Maigrey was silent, until she was certain Tusk had fallen back to sleep. She moved nearer to Sagan, lowered her voice, until it was no more than a sigh from a shadow.

"It was second nature to you to keep as much of yourself locked away as possible. You told us what you thought we needed to know, nothing more. You couldn't trust. Not even us, who'd grown up with you. Not even me, who loved you."

She reached up to touch the scar on the flesh she wove from her memory of life. "In a way, I suppose, it was a compliment. You had faith in us to come through when you needed us. And we had faith in you. And it worked. All but once, when you took our loyalty too much for granted.

"I chose Amodius, my king, then—poor, unworthy king that he was. I was his Guardian, I had pledged my allegiance to him. And so had you. And when you saw that Abdiel meant to kill the king, you offered to guard him—a man you hated and despised—with your life.

"Surely you would do the same for Dion. You helped raise him, my lord. Not from boyhood to manhood, but from ordinary to divine. You found the spark within him and kindled it, and now it burns clear and bright; not a consuming holocaust, but a shining beacon, for all to follow.

"You can't be taken in my Flaim, despite the test. . . . I know you're not. I *know* you're not," she repeated angrily, to silence some inner, arguing voice.

But the voice refused to be silenced. She faltered, wavered.

"But then what is your plan, my lord? Tell it to me this once. Don't let me go into battle half-blind! I see only the faint outline. . . . Why, *why* is it necessary for you to bring the two of them together?

"The risk you run is enormous, and what do you hope to accomplish? There are alternatives. You could go to Dion, warn him *again* of his peril, tell him what you've discovered, *urge* him to use the space-rotation bomb. . . . "

Maigrey paused. "Use it against thousands of innocent people, whose only fault is that they are captive to one man's corrupt ambition." She sighed. "All right, so that's out."

She pondered. "You could warn him to take precautions against his cousin. To increase his bodyguard threefold, never stir from the palace, shut himself up like a hothouse plant. Yes, there's a solution. He'd lose the throne as surely as if he'd died on it. He might as well die on it.

"But is it wise for the two to confront each other? I don't understand, my lord. I don't understand. And I'm frightened."

She bowed her head. If the dead could cry, the touch of her tears, falling on his still hand, would have wakened him.

"You have a right to be angry. I feel your anger as I feel the temptation burn within you. How easy it would be to give up, let go, fall. How much more difficult to struggle on through the darkness alone, without the hope of light.

"I tried to give you hope, my lord. I tried to let you know you aren't alone, but I failed."

Maigrey reached out her hand to touch his. One thought, one wish, one command and she could wrench herself free of her ethereal bonds, plunge across the gulf, feel, clasp, hold. She could talk, listen, answer, reassure.

One spoken word . . .

The dark door swung open. The dark path appeared before her. The dark landscape of terror and travail and sorrow stood etched against a hideous sunrise.

Maigrey shrank back. Her hand fell to her side.

"How bitter is this separation. How vast and cold and empty the gulf that keeps us apart. I could cross it, but at what terrible risk . . . to us both.

"We are ghosts to each other now, my lord. Echoes of a voice, memories of a touch. . . .

"I can't stay with you. The temptation to touch you, to talk to you, is too great. I'll return to the alcazar. As Prince Flaim said, ghosts make wonderful spies. Wonderful, though ineffective."

She sighed. Her shadowy hand lay over his real one. "If you call on me, my lord, I will answer. If you need me, I will come to you."

His fingers moved slightly, as if in response, as if he would reach out to hold her.

But she was gone.

--◁■⟩◯C■▷--

The alcazar of Prince Flaim Starfire would have been classified as one of the wonders of the galaxy—had anyone else in the galaxy ever seen it (and been able to return to report of it). It was an enormous fortress, built entirely of the stone of Vallombrosa, stone that was the color of bleached bones. And not one wall stood perpendicular to another. On first seeing the alcazar most people mistook it for a naturally occurring rock formation put to practical use.

Closer observation would force them to reconsider. The fortress was far too well made to have been built by Nature, who tends to overlook details like doors, windows, and leaky roofs.

Though crudely and oddly constructed, the alcazar was solid. It might look as if half a mountain had been ripped out to form it, the rock smashed together and molded like clay. But the walls were solid, the joints tight, the rooms, with their crazily slanting floors, snug and dry. It was, in fact, the ideal fortress—strong as half a mountain, indistinguishable from the whole of the mountain.

The alcazar was constructed, but not by human hands. It had been "built," if one could use such a term, by the dark-matter creatures. It had been built by ghosts.

As to those who lived in the alcazar, or who orbited above it in the space stations, Valley of Ghosts was a most appropriate name, for the population of Vallombrosa was made up, for the most part, of those whom others in the galaxy had come to think of as ghosts.

When Garth Pantha returned to Vallombrosa, he was protector to a future monarch who had no subjects. But Pantha had foresight enough to know that one day, when Flaim was old enough to make a bid for power, he would need a loyal and willing population to back him up. And so Pantha began recruiting people to come to Vallombrosa.

He couldn't recruit them openly, of course, without tipping his hand, making himself and his strange dark-matter creatures known to the rest of the galaxy. His problem: How to bring people here who had no idea where they were going and who would be happy to stay here for years, living on space stations, isolated and cut off from the rest of civilization. Who would be desperate enough?

His answer: People on the verge of destruction. People facing imminent annihilation, hopeless people at the point of certain death, who would be grateful to the man who came to their rescue. Innumerable mysterious disappearances over the years were not mysteries on Vallombrosa.

Take, for example, the vanished population of Otos 4, which led to the intergalactic war with Rylkith and his vapor-breathers. The gigantic city of Otos 4 was under siege from its alien neighbors. The humans, on the verge of starvation, had been transmitting frantic appeals for the rest of the galaxy to come to their aid. King Amodius dithered, not wanting to start what he knew would be an intergalactic war.

Meanwhile, Garth Pantha arrived in Otos 4 in secrecy, under the protective cloak of the dark-matter creatures. He arranged for the entire population to be taken out of the city, again by the machinations of the creatures.

When the vapor-breathers landed, they found Otos 4 completely deserted. Not a living soul left. A billion people gone without a trace. Of course, no one believed the vapor-breathers. The galaxy assumed that Rylkith had destroyed all the humans in the city, which led to war.

Now, after all these years, Maigrey realized that Rylkith had been telling the truth.

"How many thousands died in that war for nothing?" she asked herself.

The deaths did not trouble Garth Pantha. The war was a perfect cover for his recruiting, as were all disasters, man-made or otherwise. The battleships that disappeared without a trace, the cruise ships in distress who were never heard from again, the planets whose suns were about to go nova. The people were all snatched from the jaws of certain death, whisked here, to this peaceful and beautiful—if strange—world.

Of course, they paid a price. They were not permitted to leave Vallombrosa, nor to have any contact whatsoever with the galaxy outside their world. And they could not live on the planet's surface, but were forced to reside in space stations which they either built or "acquired" from other planets.

Pantha had once tried to place people on Vallombrosa itself. But it proved far too difficult for any species made of solid matter to accustom itself to living long with those made of strange dark matter. The only people who lived on the planet's surface were those who worked in the alcazar, and they had to be rotated on a frequent basis for the sake of their own sanity.

But such minor inconveniences as living in a closed and artificial environment were infinitely preferable to the certain death these people had faced, and most were content to obey Pantha's laws. Any who were not content were removed by the dark-matter creatures.

To give Pantha credit—and later Flaim, when he grew old enough to take over the rule of Vallombrosa himself—he used this sort of drastic punishment sparingly, and then made generous reparations to the affected families. Those the prince removed were generally troublemakers, not particularly well liked anyway. And, as time passed, such removals grew fewer, were no longer needed.

Prince Starfire had the charisma of the Blood Royal, the charm of the Starfires. His people came to revere and respect him. They were wholly committed to his cause. Maigrey, who had hoped to find cracks of discontent, rebellion, was disappointed.

Dion Starfire was spoken of as the usurper. Flaim Starfire was known to be the true king.

Again and again, despite herself, she questioned Sagan's motives. "Why bring Dion here? The risks he runs are very great. If he should fail . . ."

Is that it, my lord? Do you want him to fail?

She refused to let herself consider that possibility. She had faith in him, if no one else did. But her faith brought her no peace. Instead, she spent the days and nights wandering the alcazar, a restless spirit, the perfect spy, gaining valuable information she could never put to use.

The dark-matter creatures were the true danger, the true threat—but then Sagan already knew that. Flaim's military might was impressive. It was certainly not sufficient to conquer a galaxy, however. If it weren't for the dark-matter creatures, he'd be just another planet-popping dictator, gobbling up territory, making life miserable for his neighbors.

The creatures were a powerful ally, but a capricious one. This was something Maigrey discovered, wondered if Sagan knew. The creatures acted out of no loyalty to Flaim. Maigrey doubted if the creatures even understood the prince's ambition, or cared about it one way or the other. She guessed that anyone who possessed the ability to communicate with the creatures could elicit their services, though what the creatures' motives might be in serving was unclear to her . . . and apparently to Garth Pantha as well.

It was, Maigrey thought with a certain grim amusement, like trying to fathom the mind of God.

Pantha and Flaim were discussing this very subject one day. The two generally spent their evenings alone together in one of the upper-level rooms of the alcazar known as the Hall. The room, with its weirdly canting stone walls, its oddly sloping stone ceiling, was large and spacious and chill. A huge wood-burning fireplace located at one end provided the only heat.

Those who lived and worked in the alcazar were subject to primitive living conditions. No central heating, no electricity, no modern conveniences of any type—apparently. Maigrey soon discovered that, like so much else about the bastard prince, the medieval life-style was a facade. Not a light bulb in the place, but the alcazar was fitted up with a sophisticated electronic surveillance system that would have brought tears of pride to the eyes of the late Snaga Ohme.

A secret inner room, located far below the alcazar—adjacent to the dungeons—was equipped with nuclear generators. Their power ran the surveillance system, which spied on all Flaim's employees and visitors, as well as a communications network, keeping Flaim in contact with the outside galaxy. Much of the equipment in the communications room was old and outdated, having been salvaged from Pantha's spaceplane. Here, Flaim had grown to manhood, watching the rest of humanity on a video screen.

Small wonder, thought Maigrey, that he knew them only as two-dimensional forms who could be shut off or turned on with a wave of the remote.

This night, Pantha and Flaim were discussing Flaim's future rule of the galaxy, discussing it in cool, matter-of-fact terms as a done deed, brushing off Dion as they might brush a drop of blood off the royal throne.

"You realize, my prince," Pantha was saying, "that the dark-matter creatures cannot be trusted. I would not be so quick to include them in your plans, nor make any plans dependent on them."

"I am perfectly aware of that," Flaim returned impatiently. "How could I be otherwise? You remind me of it daily! But I see no harm in figuring the creatures into my plans. They have served me in the past. Why should they not continue to serve me in the future? Besides, by then I will have the space-rotation bomb—"

"Which the creatures could easily destroy."

"They've agreed not to. Besides"—Flaim shrugged—"if they do, you will build another. You have already discovered the theory behind it. You need only examine the bomb itself to figure out how it works. At least so you've told me.

"At any rate, by that time I will be fully established on the throne, my other allies in place. You see, my friend, I am not totally dependent on the creatures. I merely plan to take advantage of their incredible powers, if they are still around."

Allies? Maigrey asked, suddenly intensely interested. What other allies?

Her question was not immediately answered. The fire was dying, the room growing darker and colder. Flaim rose from his chair. Grabbing a log, he tossed it on the glowing embers, stirred them up. The prince was accustomed to performing such menial tasks himself. There were no servants in the alcazar, only a person to do the cooking, and even then Flaim often decided to fix his meals himself. Garth Pantha had not pampered the boy. The man had raised Flaim to be self-sufficient, and it was well he did. People were a precious commodity on this world. The living on Vallombrosa had far more important tasks to perform than waiting hand and foot on His Royal Highness.

Pantha drew his heavy chair closer to the fire, warmed his gnarled hands at the brightening blaze.

"What allies?" Maigrey repeated, frustrated.

Flaim turned suddenly, advanced toward the back of the room. "I heard you," he shouted. "Where are you? *Who* are you?"

"My dear boy!" Pantha was staring at Flaim in astonishment.

"What are you? Where are you?" Flaim demanded.

He walked into the back part of the large room, into the

shadows. His blue eyes glittered; his gaze darted into every corner. He was not frightened so much as irritated, annoyed.

Maigrey held perfectly still. She had no idea what was happening or why. She had no notion how he knew she was here. He had earlier evinced awareness of her presence—in his tent in the forest—but she had discounted that incident, attributed it to an overactive imagination. Now she was forced to reconsider.

"I have heard you speak before now. I have seen you. I know you are here!" Flaim was starting to grow angry.

Pantha had risen to his feet, was regarding his young friend in concern. "Flaim, I assure you, we are quite alone—"

"No, my friend." Flaim stood in the center of the room, his hands on his hips, waiting. "We are *not* alone. I can't believe you haven't heard it! A woman's voice, low-pitched . . . and familiar. I swear I've heard it before . . . the vids, I think . . . the old ones. Damn! Why can't I place it?"

"I've heard nothing," said Pantha. "Perhaps the creatures—"

"Not them! I've known them and their ways since childhood. This is different. It's like a bug, buzzing in my ears. There now." Flaim paused, listening. "The voice is silent. Yes, you hear *me*, don't you, Lady?" he said to Maigrey, staring right at her. "Why won't you let me see you?"

"Or perhaps you're not permitted to do so," Flaim considered, his anger cooling. "Perhaps you are under some constraint. Forgive my hasty speech." He made a low bow. "I thank you for your attention, Lady, and bid you consider yourself a welcome guest in my house."

Laughing, he turned away.

Maigrey, considerably alarmed and perplexed, retreated to the darkest corner of the room, far from the fire's light, and even there she did not feel safe. Though Flaim resumed his chair and his conversation, his gaze occasionally swept the area, searching for her, aware that she had not left.

Blood Royal, she said to herself. But who could have supposed? . . . Yes, he knows me. Though he doesn't realize it yet. Pantha's old vids—those made of Sagan and me, when we were young. Flaim has watched them over and over again, studied them. And then later, vids taken when we were with Dion. . . . That's how you know me, Your Highness.

Now even Garth Pantha was glancing about nervously. "I must confess, you've unnerved me, my prince."

Flaim appeared amused. "In the Valley of Ghosts, we must expect ghosts, my dear friend."

"As a scientist, I can't accept that. And as a self-proclaimed atheist, neither should you."

"A belief in spirits does not necessarily imply a belief in any all-powerful being. Take the example of the fire. These ashes—they are dead to all appearances, the wood consumed, destroyed. Yet, hold your hand over them. You can feel warmth, energy still. I find it impossible to think that the boundless energy burning inside me will not outlast this frail shell of a body."

"A rather farfetched theory, my prince," said Pantha, relaxing, smiling. "I consider this my fault. I should have never indulged your penchant for horror stories as a child. This comes of too many hours spent reading H.P. Lovecraft. You say you recognize the voice. Not your mother, perhaps?"

"Have your joke, my friend. It is *not* my mother. I never heard my mother's voice and, I tell you, this voice is almost as familiar to me as your own. I can't place it yet. But it will come to me. She is silent now. I trust I haven't frightened her away."

"That would be a switch!" Pantha grinned broadly. "For the living to frighten the dead! I do not think—"

What he did not think was to remain unknown. An attractive woman had appeared in one of the large, open doorways. She stood silently, waiting to be noticed, waiting for permission to enter.

Pantha, seeing her, bit off his remark. Flaim motioned her to come forward with a graceful wave of his hand and the invariably charming smile.

"Enter, please, Captain Zorn."

She entered, handed him a sheet of paper. She wore the same uniform that was standard on Vallombrosa, a one-piece jumpsuit which emphasized her slim and elegant figure.

Maigrey, thankful for the interruption, was paying little attention. She was thinking that it might be best to leave the alcazar. If Flaim figured out who she was, the knowledge might make him distrustful of Sagan. Or might it have the opposite effect? Egotistic as he was, Flaim might convince himself she'd come from the nether regions to serve him. She was pondering the matter when she noticed an interesting tableaux being played out in front of her.

Garth Pantha was regarding Flaim with marked curiosity, a

curiosity that was almost eager, anxious, apparently occasioned by the entrance of Captain Zorn. Maigrey began to pay closer attention.

The woman was standing close, very close, to the prince. She had handed him a message, which he was perusing. A brief message, apparently, for he glanced up at her almost immediately, smiled again.

"Thank you, Captain. That will be all."

The woman bowed, turned on her heel with military precision, and left the room. But both Maigrey and Pantha had seen the ardor with which Captain Zorn regarded Flaim. And both had noticed the disappointment on her lovely features when she left. That disappointment was reflected on the face of Garth Pantha.

Flaim had been rereading his message. He looked up. "You will be interested in this. It is from Derek Sagan. It says—" He stopped, perplexed. "*Now* what's the matter? Oh, I see. *That* again."

"She is a lovely woman."

"I thought you had given this up," Flaim complained, irritated. "I grow quite tired of this."

"I had hoped these latest injections . . ."

"I haven't taken them," Flaim interrupted. He looked exasperated. "I should think you would be grateful I am not prey to this weakness. After all, look where such uncontrolled appetites led my father."

"To your birth!" Pantha countered. "Was that such a bad result?"

"No, but only because of *your* quick thinking and smooth talking, my friend. Otherwise, God knows what Amodius would have done with me. I am what I am, Pantha—asexual. I accepted the fact long ago. You should, too. What am I missing?"

"Pleasure—"

Flaim smiled derisively. "Two naked bodies, rubbing together for an hour or so? An animalistic urge that we've never quite overcome, designed purely to induce us to procreate."

He put his fingertips together, held them to his lips. "True pleasure, Pantha. True pleasure comes with imposing my will on another. Forcing even the most powerful to submit themselves to my dominant authority. That excites me. That stirs the fire in my brain, if not necessarily my loins."

"Such fire will not provide you with an heir," Pantha observed, displeased.

Flaim waved an uncaring hand. "Artificial insemination."

"You have no seed. You are sterile."

"Then I will come up with a suitable donor," Flaim said impatiently. "The father who raises the child is more important that the father who creates it, as you have long told me. As you yourself are living proof. What has brought all this up again?"

"The child would not be Blood Royal."

"That is not necessarily a drawback." Flaim stretched his legs to the fire. "I would not want a child as strong as myself, as ambitious. One could never trust such a child. When it grew up, I would be constantly looking over my shoulder. What was it Henry IV termed his son, Prince Hal—his 'nearest and dearest enemy.' I want a cowardly, timid child, who will be afraid to take the crown—even from my stiff, cold corpse."

"Such a child would hardly make a good ruler, my prince."

"It won't need to be. I will leave a galaxy ringed around with steel and fire, ruled by darkness. The Corasians will control the outer planets. The dark-matter creatures will maintain control over the Corasians and any other potentially dangerous elements in my own population. The people, who have no inkling that the Corasians have been brought here solely for my benefit, will be so fearful that they will literally beg me to declare martial law.

"I shall do so, of course, by establishing a vast, all-powerful military. By the time my supposed heir takes over at my death—which we all hope will be in the far, far-distant future—he will have little to do but smile and look gracious and keep his fist clenched."

Flaim's allies—Corasians! An ingenious plan. Maigrey was forced to compliment the prince. You permit these monsters to enter the galaxy, give them a few insignificant planets in payment, let them conquer a couple more every so often, just to make the Corasians happy and the people frightened. Fear keeps everyone cowering under the bed, keeps their eyes shut to what you are really doing.

"But all that is in the future," Flaim was saying. "Back to the present. The message." He held up the paper. "Guess what it says."

"I cannot, my prince."

"Lord Sagan. He has found Mendaharin Tusca, convinced him to join us. They are on their way here now, as we speak."

"And you believe him?" Pantha inquired testily.

"Why shouldn't I?"

"Because as you well know, my prince, our spies lost all contact with Derek Sagan. They reported Tusca had lost his ship in a poker game and was forced to take up company with a quadriplegic named Lazarus Banquo—"

"Lazarus Banquo!" Flaim began to laugh.

Pantha frowned, looked displeased.

"Lazarus Banquo," Flaim explained. "Now I understand. It was Sagan all along, of course. Don't you get the joke? I find it really quite funny—"

"I don't," Pantha retorted. "Sagan had some reason for assuming this bizarre disguise—"

"Of course he did. Millions know the Warlord by sight. But who would think to see him in a wheelchair? I begin to reconsider, my friend. Derek Sagan is not the broken-down old man I took him to be."

"No. This proves that he is considerably more dangerous."

"To my enemies, Pantha. To my enemies. And my 'nearest and dearest' enemy—my cousin Dion—is almost within my grasp."

"That remains to be seen," said Pantha, unconvinced. "And it brings up another point. You are so cautious of your unborn heir, my prince, what will you do with your cousin—the one person who could be a serious threat to you?"

"Once he's abdicated the throne? Once he's meekly handed over the crown?" Flaim laughed. "Who would want the weakling back? Who would follow his tattered, yellowed standard? Besides, as we've discussed, it will be necessary to keep our cousin around to make it all look legitimate. Blood is thicker than water, that sort of thing. We will set our cousin up in the alcazar here—trot him out every year as our adored relation. And speaking of relations, now that phase one's objective has been achieved, I believe we should implement phase two."

"The queen's—"

"Hush, my friend." Flaim glanced back into the shadows. "Who knows who is listening?"

Pantha looked startled, then rather anxious. "My prince, surely you don't truly believe—"

Flaim began to laugh again.

"Ah," said the old man, "you're teasing me."

"I can't help it, Pantha! You take everything so seriously. Besides, if there really are ghosties and ghoulies out there, what can they do to stop me? What can any of them do?"

The two men rose. Flaim carefully banked the fire, to keep the embers glowing preparatory to building the blaze up again in the morning.

"A long day," he said, clapping the older man on the shoulder. "Good night, my friend. Sleep well."

The prince turned toward the part of the room that was now, with the fading firelight, left in deepest shadow. "Good night to you, as well, Lady."

Grinning, he walked with Garth Pantha out the door.

Maigrey huddled alone in the darkness, a disembodied spirit afraid to make herself visible even to herself.

"The living scaring the dead," she whispered. "Not as far-fetched as you think, old man. This prince of yours terrifies me."

Chapter ❊❊❊ Four

We're not going to a church social.
The Magnificent Seven

Half-asleep, Xris lounged on his bed in the high-class hotel room on Ceres, watching a vid through a hazy cloud of tobacco smoke. The vid was a B-grade police thriller, with a premise as phony as the hero's hair. Xris had been a Fed himself, before the "accident" left him more machine than man, and he'd gotten a few laughs watching the hero break more laws in catching the criminal than the criminal had broken in the first place. They had reached the hovercopter chase sequence when the phone buzzed.

Xris activated the vidscreen to see who was calling.

A message came up on the screen: *Sorry, the caller isn't dialing from a vidphone.*

The phone continued to buzz. Xris picked up the handset, held it to his ear, said nothing.

Total silence at the end of a completed connection would be extremely disconcerting to most callers, especially those who had no business calling. But not this particular caller.

"Xris Cyborg," came the lilting, drugged voice.

Xris exhaled softly. "Raoul."

"And the Little One."

"Of course. One sixteen." He hung up.

After several minutes—longer than it would have taken ordinarily but, depending on what drug Raoul had ingested that morning, the Loti might be having difficulty reading the room numbers—there came a knock at the door.

Xris walked over, answered it. He didn't even bother to glance through the small peephole to make certain of his visitors' identity. He didn't need to. Raoul's perfume wafted through the closed door, began a contest to see which could smell worse—the perfume or the foul odor of the twist's smoke. Xris gave it even odds, opened the door.

342

"Xris Cyborg." Raoul blinked, as if amazed to see him. Perhaps he had forgotten where he was, why he had knocked.

The Loti flipped his long, silky black hair over his shoulders with a deft move of his delicate hands. He was dressed in crushed pink velvet knee breeches, tied with pink ribbons over a pair of white hose, ending in black dancing pumps. An orange velvet doublet, slashed open here and there to reveal puffs of pink silk, completed his ensemble. A pink lace bow was tied around his neck.

"Charming," said Xris. The Loti liked to be complimented on a new outfit.

"Thank you," Raoul replied, smoothing his hair.

He drifted into the room. (Now that the two were in close proximity, the perfume easily felled Xris's tobacco smoke.) The Little One shuffled along behind his friend. The long raincoat—which seemed to grow shabbier every time Xris saw it—dragged on the floor. Two bright eyes stared out at the cyborg from beneath the rim of the battered fedora.

Xris shut the door. "Yeah? What's up?"

"Very nice," said Raoul approvingly, glancing around the room. He sat down in a chair, made himself comfortable, crossing his legs at his shapely ankles, and began to blissfully contemplate a minuscule speck staining his white hose. "Look, a spot. That oaf who bumped up against me at the reception desk. Beast."

Raoul sniffed and, catching a glimpse of himself in the mirror opposite, pulled out a tube and touched up his lip gloss.

Wondering idly if Raoul was wearing the poisoned variety, Xris resumed his seat on the bed. The cyborg knew it was useless to try to hurry the Loti. Raoul would tell his own story in his own way and in his own time. The Little One, meanwhile, curled like a dog at Raoul's feet. The bright eyes vanished behind the raincoat's turned-up collar. He, she, or it (Xris still had no idea) was apparently going to sleep.

"I am certain you are wondering why we have transported ourselves this vast distance across a galaxy to speak to you in person, Xris Cyborg," began Raoul, licking one slender finger (making certain not to mar the lip gloss) and rubbing it on the invisible spot on his white hose. "Not that the Little One and I do not deem it a pleasure to once again see you, friend Xris."

Xris lit a twist, inhaled, breathed out, nodded, and waited.

Having gotten rather distracted, the Adonian paused a moment to collect his thoughts—tantamount to trying to catch butterflies without a net. Raoul glanced down gratefully at his companion, who had not spoken a word—aloud.

"Thank you for reminding me. Yes, that was it. We were residing with our comrades in the home of our late employer, Snaga Ohme—our comrades send their regards as well, Xris Cyborg. As I was saying, we were residing in the dwelling of our late employer, Snaga Ohme, when we received a most important message, highest priority, code number . . ." Raoul paused, looked vague, fluttered a hand, "I can never remember those silly numbers. At any rate, you may take my word for it that the message was considerably urgent."

He regarded Xris with limpid eyes.

"What was the message?" Xris asked, puffing on the twist.

Raoul's eyelids fluttered. He was wearing pink eye shadow. "Ah, yes. The message. Her Majesty, the queen, is in extreme danger. Possible kidnapping attempt."

"Son of a bitch," said Xris. He took the twist out of his mouth. "Who'd the message come from? And why didn't you just transmit it? You wasted maybe a day, day and a half getting here—"

"Ah, there is a reason for that, Xris Cyborg," interrupted Raoul, and the Loti's eyes were suddenly, disconcertingly sharp and shrewd. "The sender was most emphatic in insisting that this message be presented to you in person. We were therefore forced to assume that the sender did not want to take even the smallest chance that this message might be intercepted."

"Okay, I can see that. Who sent it? Dixter?"

Raoul shook his head. The silky hair slid down his shoulders. He brushed it carefully back. "We do not know who sent the message."

Xris stared, then frowned. "That's impossible. You said it was coded. Surely either Lee or Harry remembers the code numbers," he added with a sarcasm that he knew would be completely lost on the Adonian. "And if you didn't know who sent it, then why the devil—"

"Devil!" Raoul smiled in delight. "One might consider that appropriate." He nodded thoughtfully. "Yes, one might. As a matter of fact, Bernard recognized the code number, Xris Cyborg, though it had been many years since he had seen it. The code number belongs to the late Lord Derek Sagan."

Xris would have raised an eyebrow, both eyebrows, except

that he didn't have any eyebrows, only acid burns on his bald head. "Son of a bitch," he said again, speculatively. He put the twist back in his mouth.

"Bernard's precise words," said Raoul gravely.

"Must be a hoax."

"How is that possible, Xris Cyborg? Would anyone else have known Lord Sagan's code number?"

"Lady Maigrey knew it."

"Ah, yes, well . . ." Raoul replied, momentarily downcast. "I grew to be quite fond of the Lady Maigrey. So did the Little One. I trust she forgives us the unfortunate incident during which we once attempted to poison her. It was in the champagne. My late employer, Snaga Ohme, did not trust her. A disagreement over the precise ownership of the space-rotation bomb—"

What this had to do with anything was beyond Xris. He interrupted the Adonian's ramblings. "Does the Little One have any feelings about this message?"

"He was considerably upset. He is opposed to kidnapping, under most circumstances, and he has a high opinion of Her Majesty—"

"I don't mean that," Xris snapped. "I mean did he get any . . . you know—*feelings* . . . about who sent the goddam message!"

Raoul's eyes opened wide, evincing astonishment. "My, my, we are irritable." He paused a moment, glanced down at the Little One. "Is that so?" He looked back at Xris. "Well, well, well. Now I understand. I am sorry, friend Xris. I did not mean to unduly try your patience. Yes, the Little One did receive a sort of a feeling from the message. The Little One is of the opinion that the message could have quite possibly come from Lord Sagan."

"Quite possibly?" Xris repeated. "Just what the hell—"

The Little One lifted his head; the two bright eyes were once again visible. Xris wondered what all that sympathetic "well, well-ing" had been over and just exactly what Raoul was sorry about.

"Skip it," he said, mulling things over.

Sagan's body had never been recovered, nor any remnants of his spaceplane. Not that one usually found remnants of a plane after the Corasians had finished with it. Or body parts either. But Xris had always wondered. He'd always assumed that it would take a lot more than a bunch of lava-brained aliens to do in Derek Sagan.

"So let's suppose that Sagan is alive." He put the proposition to Raoul, who tried hard to look interested. "And he sent this message, using his old code number because that's the only one he knows, yet making it clear that he doesn't expect me to get curious about who sent it or why.

"Which I'm not," he added reassuringly, glancing around the room, just in case. Derek Sagan was one person the cyborg didn't intend to cross—dead or alive. "It's none of my business.

"But this about the queen," he continued. "This is my business."

Her Majesty was paying him to hang around on Ceres, in case she needed help with the king's mistress or to return the young woman to her home or whatever other plan Astarte had dreamed up. Women. Xris decided that never in his entire life would he understand them.

He recalled a conversation he'd had with her on their way back to Ceres after leaving the Academy.

"I know what I'd do if this were my wife's lover," he'd said, looking down at the comatose Kamil.

"Oh?" Astarte had regarded him with maddening calm. "Did your wife have lovers?"

"Huh?" Xris had stared at her. "We're not talking about me—"

Astarte had merely shrugged. "You brought it up. Shall I tell you what I think about your wife? That she has loved no one in her life but you. She still loves you. And you risked your life to save her from a horrible death. How wonderful you must have looked to her, alone and frightened in that terrible place. Like an angel. . . ."

At that point, Xris had walked out.

"What shall we do, friend Xris?" Raoul prodded the cyborg out of his reverie. "Are we to take this seriously? Should we alert the king? Warn Her Majesty—"

"It's not that simple," Xris muttered. He stood up, took a twist from his pocket, stared at it, shoved it back. Walking over to the window, he parted the curtain a centimeter, looked outside. "We can send a message to His Majesty through Dixter. Though I'm not sure what good that will do. His Majesty's there, the queen's here."

Raoul glanced in some astonishment around the room.

"In the Temple of the Goddess on Ceres," Xris explained.

"Oh . . ." Raoul smiled. "I see."

"Yeah. And that's the problem. The only people who can get inside that temple are holy types. Priests and priestesses, that sort."

"Not us?" Raoul was disappointed.

"No, not us."

"A pity. I did so want to meet Her Majesty. She has a trick of putting on liquid eyeliner. . . . I've attempted to emulate it, but I cannot seem to get it to look the way she does. I was going to ask her—"

"Some other time," said Xris dryly.

"I suppose. . . . Could we get a message to her? You must be in communication—"

"Her Majesty communicates with me. Not me with her. Especially now. These are Holy Days or something like that. The High Priestess is incommunicado."

"What about her mother, the baroness? A woman of great physical prowess. I've always imagined she'd be good with whips. . . ." Raoul sighed.

Xris was thinking, and it wasn't about Adonian "imaginings." People made vids out of those.

"No," said the cyborg at length. "Obviously Sagan—or whoever sent that damn message—doesn't want this spread all over the galaxy. And what could we say anyway? What have we got? A voice from the grave. DiLuna would laugh us off the planet."

He gave the matter more thought, made a decision. "I'll send a report to Dixter. See what he says. He may know something about this from his end. Then we'll *try* to get an audience with the queen."

Now that his mind was made up, Xris began to move with his customary speed. "We'll head back to the spaceport; my plane's parked there. I'll contact Dixter, pick up weapons. Speaking of which, you boys armed?"

"The usual," said Raoul, smiling.

"I don't think poison lip gloss is going to come in handy." Xris grunted. "What about him? He got that blowgun of his?"

"The Little One always carries it about his person. He finds it gives him a secure feeling. So much anger in the universe . . ."

"Yeah, it's a problem, all right. Bernard said you've made some improvement in shooting a lasgun."

"So long as the target is fairly large and makes no sudden movements, I have been known to come extremely close." Raoul rose to his feet, paused to study his shapely calves anxiously in the mirror. "Does that spot show?"

"You look lovely," the cyborg assured him, herding him and the Little One out the door.

"Thank you, friend Xris. As to the shooting," continued Raoul, considerably charmed with the subject, "I must admit I do believe I am improving. Lately, on the target range, I have only hit myself twice, the Little One once, and Bernard three times. I believe that is a personal best."

"Stick to lip gloss," Xris advised.

Large crowds lined the roads leading up to the mountain to the temple. This day of the week long festival celebrating the coming of spring was the day for the Procession of the Children. Everyone in the temple city was present to witness the parade of the Goddess's chosen, winding its slow and solemn way to the temple proper.

The parade was not, as one might suppose, a parade dedicated to the celebration of youth. All mortal beings are considered children of the Goddess. Those taking part in the procession (the only ones permitted inside the sacred precinct on this day) were the priests and priestesses who served the Goddess. They came from all over the galaxy, wherever the Goddess was honored. Each wore his or her own native dress and, as there were also many alien species in the parade, the procession was always a colorful and educational event.

Everyone attended. Businesses were closed. Transportation in and around and over the city of Ceres came to a virtual standstill. All major routes were blocked off. People lined the streets. Hover traffic was prohibited, ostensibly in keeping with the sacred nature of the day, in reality to prevent midair collisions over the parade route.

Xris reached the spaceport before air-space was shut down. In his ship, he made a quick call to Dixter, who was vague when it came to Derek Sagan, but emphatic in urging the cyborg to get to the temple—fast. And that, unfortunately, proved impossible. Airspace was now off-limits and ground traffic was backed up for kilometers. Xris commandeered a motorcycle, drove it as near the temple as possible. (Raoul, clinging to Xris tightly; the Little One, adhering to Raoul's back like a leech, was ecstatic.) When even the motorcycle got bogged down, Xris abandoned it. The three took to their feet.

The cyborg's strength cleaved a path through the throng, though he made few friends along the route. He pushed, shoved, and occasionally lifted people bodily out of his way. Those who thought at first they were going to be angry over being manhandled quickly changed their minds when they saw the sunlight shining off the cyborg's steel hand. Raoul and the Little One followed in the wake left by Xris's passing, stumbling over feet and legs and offering a babbling, everflowing stream of apologies.

"And these people call themselves religious!" Raoul stated, his cheeks and ears flushed red with exertion and indignation. "I've never *heard* such language! The Little One is quite shaken."

Xris glanced down at the small figure, saw that the fedora was trembling, the raincoat shivering. Raoul had hold of one of his friend's arms, was half-supporting, half-dragging him along.

"Tell the Little One I'm sorry, but I don't have time to be polite." Xris paused a moment to scan the situation.

They had reached the main road leading from the city to the temple. The head of the procession was still several meters behind them, moving along at a slow pace. The temple was in front of him.

Leading the procession were prominent people from all over the galaxy. Last year, the king himself had attended, walking the path with the rest of the faithful, endearing himself to the crowd. This year, pressures of state had forced His Majesty to forgo his appearance, but the prime minister was in attendance, as well as numerous members of the Galactic parliament, other religious leaders, and dignitaries and potentates from all over the galaxy.

The doors to the temple were open to receive them. Temple guards stood on the stairs; priests were on hand to welcome the faithful inside. Astarte, queen and High Priestess, was not visible. According to Dixter, she would be somewhere inside the temple proper, spending the day in devout prayer. She would not be seen at all, would not greet her guests until after sundown, when all would assemble in a large arena on the temple grounds.

"Now that we are here, friend Xris," said Raoul as he endeavored to soothe the wounded feelings of the Little One, "what do we do?"

"Beats the hell out of me," Xris stated, eyeing the situation with mounting frustration.

There was no way, absolutely no way—that Xris could see—to get inside. A reporter tried it, waving something in the air and jabbering about a press pass. One of the temple guards strong-armed the man, turned him over to the baroness's army. The reporter was hustled away without ceremony. The last Xris saw of the man, he was being made to eat his press pass. The cyborg swore beneath his breath, took out a twist, stuck it in his mouth, and began to chew on the end.

"Surely the queen is safe for the moment," Raoul commented. "No one would attempt anything in this mob, under the eyes of the galaxy." He cast a significant glance at the staring lenses of innumerable remote vidcams that hovered over the heads of the crowds.

"Who knows? If it was some sort of terrorist group, they'd like nothing better than to be splashed all over the vidscreen. Dixter took it seriously enough."

"He promised he would endeavor to warn Her Majesty of her danger," Raoul shouted, raising his voice to be heard above the roar of the crowd.

"I doubt if he'll meet with much success. No intrusion from the physical realm is allowed to interfere with the holy ceremonies, or something like that."

"What?" Raoul yelled.

Xris shook his head. *Forget it,* he mouthed.

The procession was nearing the temple. The crowd surged forward. The baroness's troops—guarding the parade route—shoved the people back. The Little One was bowled over and nearly trampled. Raoul hauled his friend to his feet. Xris caught hold of both of them, dragged them close to him. No one came too near the cyborg. Those who did gave the metal arm and leg—with their flashing lights and ominous beeping sounds—a startled glance and backed off as far as they could.

The head of the procession moved slowly toward them. In the vanguard was a double line of robed and hooded men and women, singing a hymn of praise to the Goddess, carrying fruits of Her bounty in their arms as offerings. Behind them marched the dignitaries. Among them, expressing his respect and reverence for a religion that had, in the old days, rivaled his own, walked the archbishop of the Order of Adamant. The days of animosity and intolerance between the two religions were over and, though certain radical members of each group continued to cause strife, the majority of clerics in both orders worked hard to maintain peace.

"Too bad we did not think to disguise ourselves," yelled Raoul in the cyborg's good ear.

Xris looked down at his own steel weapons hand, glanced at the lip-glossed and rouged Adonian, and snorted. "What as? Dancing girls?"

Raoul appeared about to comment on this, but the Little One suddenly tugged urgently on his sleeve. The raincoated arm lifted and a small hand emerged pointing at the passing group of singing men and women now filing inside the temple door. Raoul cocked his head toward his friend, then sidled close to the cyborg.

"Friend Xris," he said in a low, urgent tone, "the Little One tells me that those clerics are not thinking holy thoughts. They are hostile and full of evil intent."

"What?" Xris looked down at the empath. "Is he sure? You said he was shaken up—"

"He is certain," said Raoul. The drugged slur had disappeared from the voice; the shimmering eyes were actually in focus. "He says they carry weapons of destruction beneath their robes."

"And they're marching right into the temple!" Xris swore in frustration. "And here we stand."

"Alert the guards. . . ."

That was a possibility. Xris took one look at the heads of government, the arts, religion, moving up the hill. Once the shooting started . . . He shook his head. "They probably wouldn't believe us anyway. By the time we convinced them, it'd be too late. Damn it, we've got to get inside! I—By God!" he said suddenly, his gaze on the procession of dignitaries. "There's the answer. Brother Daniel!"

"Who? Where?" Raoul blinked his pink-lidded eyes.

"The archbishop! Brother Daniel. Don't you remember? With Lady Maigrey—"

"Ah, yes! Do you think he will remember us?"

"I don't see how he could ever forget," Xris said grimly. He was busy surreptitiously arming his weapons hand.

Raoul stood on tiptoe, waving the pink silken scarf he'd removed from around his neck. "Yoo-hoo! Brother Dani—"

"You idiot!" Xris grabbed hold of the Loti, dragged him down. "Don't draw attention to us! Not yet, at any rate. The Little One got any of those sleep-drugged darts on him?"

The fedora was bobbing up and down enthusiastically.

"He says yes."

"Tell him to load up. At my signal, go into one of your fits. Head for the archbishop. The Little One and I'll see you get a clear path. Got it?"

"Ah, yes!" Raoul glittered. "A fit. And what do I do when I get there? Do I get to kiss anyone?"

"No, damn it! Drop like rock. I'll handle it from there. The Little One know what to do?"

"Yes, he is most—"

"I don't care what he is. Those bastards are already inside. Wait till the archbishop gets opposite us . . . Ready . . . Now!"

Raoul sucked in a breath, let out a piercing shriek. Xris, knowing it was coming, was still unprepared for it. The Loti's scream was tortured, truly terrifying, and had the effect of causing those standing around him to make a concerted effort to get somewhere else. Even those in the procession came to a confused halt, heads craning to see what was going on.

Raoul was now twitching and foaming at the mouth and doing a spastic dance—the very image of a Loti on a bad trip.

Three of the baroness's guards started toward him. The Little One clapped his hand to his mouth. One of the guards winced, slapped at her neck as if she'd been stung by a bug. The next moment, she was prostrate on the ground. Her two companions had their hands out, ready to catch hold of the gyrating Raoul.

Xris grabbed one with his steel hand, sent a mild jolt of electricity through her body. She stiffened and collapsed, writhing on the ground. A kick of his steel leg sent the other guard crashing back into the milling crowd.

People fighting to get away from the Loti opened up a path that led right to the highway. Seemingly oblivious to what was going on, Raoul jerked and twisted rapidly out of the crowd, dove headfirst to the ground right in front of the archbishop, and, with another horrible scream, curled up in a fist-clenching pink velvet ball at the priest's feet.

Xris was right behind him. The cyborg threw his own body

protectively over Raoul, looked up into the archbishop's shocked face.

"Brother Daniel!" said Xris swiftly, speaking in the military argot used by the Warlord's men. "Remember us?"

Archbishop Fideles looked at him closely, gasped. "Xris!"

"Play along with me!" the cyborg told him. He raised his voice, switched to the language of Ceres. "The Adonian is dying! Give him your blessing, Holiness!"

The guards crowded around. Two of them seized hold of the archbishop, intent on guarding him from possible danger.

"An outrage! Remove this man! How dare you—"shouted another member of the Order of Adamant, who was also trying to drag the archbishop away.

The guards had lasguns aimed at Xris's head.

"Halt this madness!" Fideles demanded loudly and forcefully, his voice carrying over the tumult, as it had once carried in the confusion of battle. "You, Prior John. Stand away. Give this poor man air. And you call yourself God's minister." He cast a withering glance at the prior, who fell back in offended dignity.

"You, guards. Leave the poor man alone! Put away your weapons! You are on holy ground!

The guards, moving slowly and reluctantly, did as the archbishop commanded. They stood back, leaving a clear space around the prostrate man and his friends, though they kept their guns leveled at Xris. The crowd in front had fallen silent, trying their best to hear, shushing those in back who couldn't see and were demanding to know what was going on.

The archbishop knelt down, laid his hand on Raoul's forehead. Fideles was trying hard not to notice that Raoul had winked at him.

"What in the name of heaven, Xris—" Fideles began in an undertone.

"The queen's in danger." Xris leaned close to the archbishop, pretending to be ministering to the stricken Adonian. "Those clerics who went into the temple aren't clerics. The Little One spotted them."

"God save us!" Fideles exclaimed in horror. "Who sent you?"

"Lord Sagan," said Xris.

Dixter hadn't told the cyborg much, just enough.

Fideles stared, then closed his eyes in relief. "Thank God! I had not heard from him. I was beginning to think—"

"No time for that now, Brother!" Xris interrupted grimly. "Get us inside!"

"Yes, of course. You're right." Fideles gathered up his heavy ceremonial robes and rose to his feet. "This man is in desperate need of medical attention. Let him be carried into the temple."

"But Holiness! That is not possible!" One of the temple priests came dashing forward. "He is a Loti! It would be a sacrilege—"

"He is one of the Goddess's children, however unworthy!" Fideles returned sternly. "Far greater sacrilege if he dies out here on the temple steps."

Xris had lifted Raoul, was holding him tenderly. The Adonian looked quite pale and pitiful, his eyes closed, his body lifeless, his long black hair hanging almost to the ground. The Little One clung to Raoul's limp hand like a frightened child to its sick mother.

Either the priest was moved by true concern for a fellow mortal or by the thought (cleverly introduced by Fideles) of a Loti—surrounded by reporters—breathing his last on the temple steps. The priest gave orders for the wretched man to be carried inside. Guards surrounded them, hustled them swiftly into the temple, away from the curious eyes of the crowd and the vidcams.

Fideles looked after them worriedly. Forced to return to the ceremonial procession, the archbishop said and did what he was supposed to say and do. But those around him noted that he appeared worried and preoccupied. Prior John whispered that the incident had badly upset the Holy Father, and everyone was extremely kind and solicitous to the archbishop.

Little did Prior John know that the archbishop was trying his level best to figure out some way of shaking loose those obtuse fools and hurrying off to join his former comrades-in-arms.

Chapter ··❦·· Five

CHRIS: Go ahead, Lee. You don't owe anything to anybody.
LEE: Except to myself.

The Magnificent Seven

Kamil had been granted leave to attend the religious ceremonies if she chose, but she perversely declined, declaring that she would spend the day in her room. In truth, she would have liked to have seen the ceremonies and witnessed the rites, but refusing to do so gave her a feeling of control over her situation and she took a certain grim delight in exercising it.

Not that she lacked control. She was not a prisoner—at least not a prisoner of the queen's. Kamil could have walked out the enormous front doors of the temple at any time she chose. The cyborg, Xris, who had brought her here, was waiting—by the queen's command—to take her back, take her wherever she wanted to go. The bindings were off her arm. The limb was stiff, but healing well. Each day Kamil told herself that tomorrow would be the day she left.

Each day tomorrow came, and another tomorrow would be invoked.

Kamil offered various excuses to herself—Astarte would see reason, Astarte would agree to step aside, Astarte would this or Astarte would that.

But, of course, Astarte never would and Kamil knew it. The real reason she was staying here was that it was easy to stay here. If she left—when she left—Kamil would have to make a decision. She would have to face Dion, face herself, face the fact of them together. Their lovemaking, which had seemed so wonderful and beautiful and a little bit daring and thrilling, was now something tawdry and shabby, secretive and furtive. In the dark night, when she lay sleepless, tears drying on her cheeks, Kamil knew that she could never again think of only the two of them. From now on, there would always be a third person, watching silently, sadly from the shadows.

Kamil felt ashamed and guilty, and she hated feeling

ashamed, hated feeling guilty. It was Astarte who made her feel this way, and therefore Kamil found it convenient to hate Astarte.

"Why did you have to ruin everything?" Kamil had demanded of her rival one day, when they were walking together in the quiet solitude of the temple gardens. "Everything was fine. No one was getting hurt. Not you! You don't care about *him*. Not *Dion*. All you care about is the king. You can have the king. Let me have Dion."

Astarte had looked at her with those lovely clear eyes and there was sorrow in them. "I wish I could. For his sake, I wish I could. A part of him will be lonely when you are gone. A loneliness I can never fill. But it cannot be." She shook her head. "It must not be."

Then I'll take him! He'll divorce you! He's already considering it! Kamil had wanted to shout at her, but she hadn't. She had only walked away. Astarte's calmness, her understanding, her acceptance, her sorrow, baffled Kamil. It was like battling an enemy who throws down all her weapons and stands and stares at you. Refusing to surrender, yet refusing to fight.

Kamil was going over all this for the thousandth time in her mind, and had just decided that she would most definitely leave tomorrow, when the sounds of the approaching procession came in through her open window. Tired of her own company, glad for some distraction, she walked out to one of the high temple walls, from which she had an excellent view. Leaning over it, she watched with gloomy interest the thousands of people shifting and swaying far below.

The head of the procession was just entering the temple steps—a group of robed men and women, singing and bearing fruit and grains in tribute to the Goddess's bounty. Restless, Kamil was about to leave and return to her room when she noticed some sort of disturbance taking place down below.

The procession straggled to a halt. She couldn't make out what was happening; the crowd was swirling around in disorder. Then the mob parted. Guards shoved people back. The archbishop was involved, to judge by his ornate and colorful robes. And then a man was carrying what looked to be a garishly glad woman inside the temple.

Sunlight flashed off a metal arm. Kamil leaned perilously far out over the wall to get a better look. It *was* Xris! The cyborg was carrying a woman into the temple.

"How odd," Kamil said aloud, talking to herself. "How extremely odd. But then I'm not surprised someone was hurt. Considering the mass of people down there. Still, it's strange Xris should be involved. I wouldn't think he'd have been interested in this sort of thing."

The healers would be prepared to take care of whoever it was. The infirmary had been restocked with supplies for the event, more beds added. Religious ecstasy generally felled several of the more zealous. Apparently someone had been affected early.

But Xris involved . . . The more Kamil thought about it, the less sense it made.

"I'll just go see what's going on. I need to talk to Xris anyway," she added, somewhat ashamed of her own morbid curiosity. "I need to discuss plans for leaving. This will be the perfect opportunity."

The gardens and grounds were empty; most of the inhabitants were either on duty in the arena or busy in other parts of the temple. Kamil returned to the main building, entered through a side door, and passed quickly down the maze of hallways. She had learned her way around in the past days. The infirmary was located in a back wing off the main building. It had its own private garden and tropical solarium, complete with a pool of bubbling hot, healing waters.

Gliding soft-footed into the sickroom, Kamil cast a quick glance around. None of the healers took any particular notice of her; she had taken to dressing in the comfortable, loose-fitting gowns all the women wore. But she didn't see the cyborg. No one was in a state of quiet alarm; no one was fussing over a new patient.

"Now, this *is* odd," she stated to herself, "I would have thought they'd be here by now. I wonder what's going on." She left the infirmary, went back into the hall, turned, headed for the front entryway.

The halls she walked were empty. All was quiet within the temple walls, a quiet made eerie and unnatural by contrast with the cheering and singing that could be heard outside.

Kamil rounded a corner and was proceeding down the main hallway when a strange-looking personage clad in a too-long raincoat and a battered hat suddenly appeared out of nowhere, popping up directly in front of her like the evil demon pops up in a fairy tale. The person made no sound. Two astonishingly bright eyes stared at her.

Gasping in shock, Kamil nearly tumbled over the small figure. She tried to dodge around it . . . a hand clapped over her mouth. Strong arms dragged her into an empty room.

"Don't scream," said a faintly mechanical voice in grim tones. "I'm not going to hurt you. I need information and I need it fast. The life of your High Priestess is in danger."

The hand on her mouth loosened slightly. Kamil squirmed in the cyborg's hold, which was like a metal vice.

"Xris! It's me!" she mumbled, tugging at his hand.

And either he understood her or he had just taken a good look at her.

"Kamil?" he said in astonishment, letting her go.

Trying to recover from her shock and fright, she leaned dizzily against a wall.

Xris stared at her a moment, then grunted. "Sorry. I didn't recognize you in that getup."

"What's going on?" she demanded. "What are—" She stopped.

Another odd-looking figure had appeared at the cyborg's shoulder—the person Xris had carried into the temple. Male or female, Kamil couldn't tell at first glance, but it had to be one of the most extraordinary people she'd ever seen. And certainly one of the most colorful.

"The priestess who brought us here rests comfortably, friend Xris," said the flamboyant beauty. "I do not believe she has been permanently damaged. She has simply fainted—out of fear, I think. You were rather severe on her."

"I don't have time to play nice," Xris said. Half of a soggy twist drooped from his mouth. He regarded Kamil grimly. "Do *you* know where something called the Cavern of the Holy Goddess is?"

"Yes, I've been there, but—"

"Good." Xris gripped her by the arm, began propelling her across the room toward a window. "Where is it? Can you see it from here?"

"You can't go there!" Kamil protested. "Astarte's there, praying. She'll go there all day. We're forbidden to disturb her—"

She paused. "What do you mean, she's in danger?"

"Nothing. Forget it. Just show me where this damn cave is." He thrust her bodily at the window.

Kamil, frightened by his intensity, pointed. "Do you see that giant oak tree, the one way, way up the side of the cliff? That tree stands in front of the cavern. You can't see the cave. It's hidden."

"How do you get there?"

"A road leads to it. You can see part of it from here—that white trail leading up the mountainside. It's made of crushed marble. . . ."

"According to the Little One, the invaders know the way," said the pink velvet beauty. "They move with swiftness, purpose, and resolve."

Xris adjusted his mechanical eye, brought the road in focus, stared intently into the groves of trees and bushes at the foot of the sacred mountain. "Yeah, I can see 'em. That's the way they're headed, too." He glanced at Kamil. "I don't suppose there's another way to get up there?"

Kamil hadn't heard him. She was staring at the raincoated personage. "The Little One. I know you. And you must be Raoul. Dion told me about you—"

"Not now!" Xris said through clenched teeth, biting the end off the twist. "Well, sister? Is there another way?"

"Yes, there's another path," said Kamil slowly, making up her mind. "I've taken it. Astarte showed me. She and I used it."

"Give us directions."

"I couldn't. I can find it again, but only if I see where I'm going."

Xris eyed her speculatively. "All right. You lead."

Kamil turned, almost fell over the prostrate figure of the priestess.

"She'll be all right," said Xris. "Get going."

Kamil did so. They left the room, entered the hall, moving swiftly.

"I'll go on ahead," Xris said to Raoul when it became apparent that the Little One could not keep up. "You two follow as quick as you can. And stay in touch. Let me know what he knows. Use the commlink." The cyborg tapped his ear, glanced at the Little One.

"Yes, friend Xris," Raoul replied, waving his hand nonchalantly. "We will act as guardians of your rear end."

Xris grunted, shook his head, and spit out the remainder of the twist. He increased his pace, keeping his hand closed firmly over Kamil's arm, urging her along.

"You can let go of me," she told him. "I won't run off or cause trouble. You said Astarte was in danger. What do you mean? What invaders?"

"Just show me how to get up the mountain, sister."

"I will when you let go!" Kamil planted her feet, pulled back.

Xris eyed her, released his hold. Kamil kilted her long skirts up into the belt at her waist, started forward again at a run. The cyborg joined her, moving swiftly and easily, but with a strange, awkward gait, as if his mechanical leg were involved in a contest with the physical limb. It soon became obvious to Kamil that the cyborg could have run far faster had he wanted, but he was matching his pace to hers. Knowing the distance she would have to travel, she set her own pace at one she knew she could maintain.

They emerged from the main building. People saw them, shouted at them; a few attempted to follow, but none could catch up with them. Kamil led the way through the massive garden, heading for the grapevine-covered shrine that marked the entrance to the hidden path.

"What invaders?" she asked again.

Xris didn't answer, but his gaze flicked over to the north side of the mountain. Kamil glanced that way herself, thought she saw movement, but couldn't be certain.

"You don't trust me, do you?" she said.

"Should I?" The cyborg returned. "It would make life easier for you if she dropped out of the picture."

Kamil felt blood burning in her face, and it wasn't from the exertion of running. "I suppose I earned that." She couldn't look at him, kept her eyes on where she was going. "But I'm not that bad. I'm really not. If she is in danger and if there's anything I can do to help, I will. Put it this way: She saved my life. I owe her."

"Fair enough," said Xris. He wasn't even breathing hard. "How far is it?" He had glanced again in the direction of the north path. Now Kamil could see small figures, dwarfed by the mountainside, moving among the fir trees at the mountain's base.

"There . . . that little shrine." She was having to pause, to catch her breath. "Behind it. The path goes . . . almost straight up. That road they're on . . . takes longer, but it's easier."

"Got it," said Xris.

He scanned the cliff face, and though Kamil could see nothing herself, she guessed that the enhanced vision of the cyborg could pick out the small footpath, winding among the rocks and trees. Reaching the shrine, the two stopped. Kamil bent over—hands on her knees—to catch her breath. Xris was conversing with Raoul.

"They are beginning their ascent." The Adonian's voice could be heard faintly, coming from Xris's commlink. "There are twenty of them. Commandos. They have already killed one person—a priest—who tried to stop them."

"Killed!" Kamil looked involuntarily in the direction of the invaders.

She could see them winding up the path. They had abandoned their white robes, but they must have been wearing some sort of camouflage body armor, for they blended in well with the wilderness background. She saw a brief flash of bright light, heard the whip-shot echo of a laser blast ricochet off the rocks.

"What are they firing at now?" Xris asked Raoul.

"A small group of temple guards is chasing after them. I don't think they will be for long," Raoul reported.

"Those . . . the temple guards aren't armed!" Kamil protested. She saw them, in her mind's eye—mild and devout young men and women. The office of temple guard was given as a reward for scholarly pursuit. "They weren't really meant to guard anything." She felt sick.

"They're not. Not even keeping 'em busy," Xris muttered, frowning. "I'm going on up," he said to Raoul.

"I'm going with you," Kamil said, but she said it faintly and he didn't hear her.

"Be ready for my signal," he continued, talking to Raoul, then ended the transmission.

Circling around the shrine, he found the small path and began loping up it. Kamil wanted to follow, but she couldn't move. She stared at the snakelike line of men—murderers—moving with swift and practiced skill up the mountainside. They were heading for the cavern, heading for Astarte. And down below, the dead. People dead and dying. Kamil didn't know what she had expected from the intruders exactly, but it hadn't been death, violent death. Violence seemed ludicrous, out of place in these beautiful surroundings. This peaceful tranquillity should have prohibited such acts of terror.

"And she is alone, up there," Kamil whispered, the realization twisting cold inside her. "They've killed to get to her. Twenty of them. . . ."

Kamil began to run, started scrambling up the cliff face behind the cyborg. She couldn't have said why she followed, except that she was suddenly angry—angry at the fact that a place and a people dedicated to peace had been so savagely violated. And there was instinct—the instinct of the shieldmaiden, of Olefsky's daughter, to protect and defend. And then there was shame. She'd been stung by Xris's accusation. And though she told herself she didn't give a damn what some mercenary cyborg thought of her, she did care what she thought of herself.

Kamil had been raised in the mountains of her homeland. She caught up with Xris and kept up with him.

"Go back," he ordered, not stopping to look at her. "You'll only get in my way."

She ignored him, kept moving. Glancing at her, Xris said nothing more, shook his head.

The path was steep, but not difficult to climb. The two were making good time, but so were the commandos, forging up the opposite side of the mountain. Nothing, no one was stopping them now.

Reaching a flat, level piece of ground, Xris halted, grimly surveyed the enemy.

"We'll never make it!" Kamil gasped, pulling herself up over a sawtooth ledge to stand beside him. "What . . . what are you doing?"

"Going to slow them down. Give 'em something to think about." Xris had removed his cybernetic hand. Opening his weapons leg, he took out a hideous-looking device resembling a hand with three gigantic hollow fingers, those fingers cut off at the knuckles. He attached the hand swiftly, then inserted three small torpedolike objects into each finger.

"You got a good carrying voice?" he asked Kamil.

"Yes," she said, gulping. Her heart beat fast and light; the air she breathed was clear and pure and seemed to sparkle before her eyes; rocks and trees were flat, two-dimensional, cut out and pasted down against a blue sky.

"Pitch your voice toward those rocks over there and yell like the devil himself had hold of you."

"What . . . what do I yell?"

"Anything that comes into your head. It's not the words, it's the sound I want." He handed her a lasgun. "You shoot?"

"Yes. My brothers taught me. But I can't hit anything at this range. . . ."

"Doesn't matter. Just blast away. Raoul, we're going to turn ourselves into an army. You understand?"

"I understand, Xris Cyborg."

Raising his voice, Xris bellowed, "Commence firing!" His voice came tumbling down the cliff like a rockslide. He shouted again, kept shouting, "Take them from above! Outflank them!" Pointing his weapons hand in the air, he fired off the three rockets. They arced high into the air, exploded among the commandos, sent them scattering.

"Aye, aye, sir!" Kamil yelled, sudden excitement making her giddy. The echoes of her voice came shrilling back from a different direction, so loud that they startled her. She didn't recognize herself. "We're moving up behind them, sir!" Aiming the lasgun, she fired at a fir tree, set it ablaze.

"Good girl," said Xris. "Look, that's done it."

"What? I can't see." Kamil squinted. Then she did see.

The commandos, uncertain of where the attack was coming from or how large the force against them was, had halted. They were taking cover, deploying themselves along the path.

"It won't hold them for long," he said, and even as he spoke, Kamil saw the commandos steadily crawling their way upward. "But it'll slow 'em down. Come on, sister . . . if you're coming."

He began climbing again. Kamil stashed the lasgun in the belt of her robes and hurried after him, her feet slipping and stumbling, her hands sweaty. Her injured arm had begun to throb painfully. She ignored it.

Down below, she could see Raoul starting up the path, shrieking something unintelligible about "air strikes" at the top of his lungs, and suddenly another, deeper voice began thundering from ground level.

"Circle around behind them, men!"

Kamil, peering down below, was astonished to see the archbishop, hampered by the folds of his elaborate ceremonial robes, standing in the garden, waving his arms and shouting for all he was worth.

Xris smiled. "Good for you, Brother Daniel."

The cyborg stopped again farther up the mountainside, fired

off three more rockets. Kamil blasted away with the lasgun. More trees were burning; smoke was drifting up over the area.

In answer came an eerie, hair-raising whistling sound. Xris grabbed hold of Kamil, pulled her down flat on the ground. The mountain rocked beneath her, heaving up, falling back down. Splintered stone and bits of tree flew through the air. Dust and a bitter, acrid smoke filled her lungs and set her coughing. Dazed, it took her long moments to realize that they were under attack.

The ground had not stopped shaking before Xris—with a brief glance at her, to see if she was all right—was up and on his way again. Hardly knowing what she was doing, moving by instinct alone, she staggered after him. She could see the cavern now and thought she caught a flash of white near the entrance. Astarte must be wondering what was happening, or perhaps she'd already guessed. As queen, she must have lived every day with the knowledge that she was a potential target.

The whistling sound came again and this time Kamil knew what it was, reacted. She dove beneath an overhanging rock ledge, crowding her tall body under it as far as she could manage. The mountain shook and shuddered, rocks and boulders bounded down around her, a shattered tree trunk slid past.

And she heard, beneath her, a heartrending scream.

The scream was terrible, worse than the explosion. It stopped her breath. Horrified, Kamil crawled out from beneath her ledge, stared down below. Raoul was standing over the crumpled figure of his diminutive companion. A large bloodstain covered the back of the raincoat.

Raoul screamed again, a wail of sorrow and anguish; then he collapsed beside his friend. Black hair falling around his shoulders, Raoul gathered the Little One close, cradled the head—still wearing the battered fedora—close to his body.

The archbishop was hastening up the path, oblivious to the laser blasts bursting around him. One whizzed past Kamil, but she didn't even flinch. She was suddenly shaking so much she couldn't move.

"Go on, Xris!" the archbishop was yelling. "I'll take care of them! Go on!"

A strong hand grabbed Kamil's arm, pulled her along.

"Stay here! Keep under cover!" Xris ordered her, shoving her toward a grove of trees.

"No," she said through numb lips. "I'm coming."

And she came, though nothing made sense to her anymore. It was all fear and confusion and noise. She fixed her eyes on Xris and did what he did, went where he went, ducked when he ducked, ran when he ran.

They reached a ledge jutting out just beneath the cavern. Xris caught hold of Kamil, jerked her back when she would have crawled up and over without looking. He pointed and she understood. They would have to cover a large open patch of ground, with no cover anywhere, to reach the cave.

Astarte stood just inside the cavern's entrance, her soft white robes falling in folds around her. Her hands were on her hips; she was staring down the mountainside. And she didn't look frightened, as Kamil had expected. By her fixed expression and rigid stance, she was angry. So angry that it might have been her anger alone causing the mountain to shake.

"At least she has sense enough to keep out of the line of fire," Xris muttered.

He was pressed back against the ledge, absorbed in removing the rocket launcher from his arm, reattaching the weapons hand. Kamil held the lasgun, covering them both. She couldn't see the commandos, couldn't hear them.

"Are . . . are they gone?" she asked, daring to hope. "Did we frighten them off?"

Xris snorted. "Frighten? Hell, no. They're out there. Waiting to see what we do. They've probably guessed it was all phony, but they're not sure. They can't afford to take chances. Once we break cover, though, they'll know."

He twisted his head to look at the cave. "But if we can make it inside there, we can hold 'em off until DiLuna's forces get here."

He turned back to her. "I'm gonna run for it. You cover me. You can handle that, can't you, sister? You okay?"

"Yes," said Kamil, drawing a deep breath. "I'm okay. I can do it."

He smiled at her. Taking a twist from his pocket, he stuck it in his mouth. "We come out of this, I might have a job for you on my team." His tone grew bitter; he glanced back down the mountain. "Looks like there may be an opening. Ready?"

"I'm ready."

Xris gave her a final, reassuring nod, then pulled himself up over the rock ledge. Firing as he went—small torpedoes shooting out of his weapons hand—he dashed headlong for the cav-

ern. Kamil kept up a steady stream of laser blasts. The
commandos opened fire on Xris, but the cyborg crouched low
and ran for it, ducking into the cavern just as a tree behind him
burst into a ball of flame.

"Now, sister!" he shouted.

Smoke stung her eyes and filled her lungs. She heard more
rockets going off. Unable to see, impelled by sheer panic,
Kamil clambered over the ledge and hurtled toward the
blessed safety of the cavern. Xris ran out, stood in front of the
cave, blasting away.

A woman's hands caught Kamil, halted her mad forward
rush. For a moment all she could do was cling blindly to Astarte, gasp for breath, and try to understand that she was safe,
she'd made it.

"We're okay for the moment, Your Majesty," Xris said, dodging back inside. "You and Kamil go into the back of the cave.
Both of you keep down. I'll stop 'em at the entrance." He was
reloading his weapons hand, began shouting into the commlink.
"Raoul! Damn it, Raoul, come in!"

"Xris!" came a voice over the commlink. "This is the ar—
Brother Daniel. The queen? Is she safe?"

"For the time being. My guess is they want her alive, or else
they'd have killed her by now. Alert the baroness—"

"I already did. But she refuses to bring her forces inside the
temple grounds. It's against their law—"

"Law? The hell with that shit!" The cyborg swore.

The woods began to move. Shadows beneath the trees came
alive, began closing in. Kamil grabbed hold of Xris's good arm,
tugged and pointed. "Look . . ."

"I see. Get in the back, damn it!" Xris shouted at the queen.

"No," said Astarte calmly. "I will not. And put away your
weapons." Reaching out, she plucked Kamil's lasgun from her
hand, tossed it far back in the cave. "There will be no killing."

"Too late, Your Majesty," Xris said, keeping his eyes on the
commandos, who were moving nearer with each moment.
"There's already been killing. Some of your people are dead.
Maybe some of mine." He was back on the commlink. "Brother
Daniel, go to the baroness. Make her listen to reason. Tell her
we're surrounded, but we can hold out—"

"Archbishop, this is Astarte." The queen raised her voice to
be heard. "Tell my mother I am safe and well. I intend—"

"Xris!" Kamil cried.

Three figures, two men and a woman, had emerged from the swirling smoke. The men held beam rifles, the woman carried a lasgun, all leveled in the direction of the cavern.

Xris shoved the queen behind him, raised his weapons hand.

"No, Xris! I forbid it!" Astarte cried, grabbing hold of his arm. Her voice was stern and commanding. "There will be no more killing. Those who bring violence to these holy grounds will bring violence upon themselves."

She stepped out in front of the cyborg, moving swiftly, before he could stop her. "You have defiled sacred ground," she said to the invaders, her voice stern. "What do you want?"

One of the men came forward, actually raised his hand to touch his helmed forehead. "Captain Richard Dhure, Your Majesty. We'd like you to take a little trip with us, ma'am."

"If I agree to come with you, will you leave in peace? Will you stop the killing?"

"We never wanted to harm anyone, Your Majesty. But we have a job to do and that is to deliver you safe and sound to the chosen destination." Dhure was polite, respectful, and he never lowered his rifle. "If you'll come with us, ma'am, we'll be out of here in five minutes."

"Very well," Astarte agreed.

Deliberately keeping her body between that of the commandos and the cyborg, the queen walked toward the front of the cavern. Such was her calm, imperious air that Kamil stared at her, dazed, let her go.

"Stop her!" Xris ordered, out of the side of his mouth. "I'll take care of them."

Jolted to action, Kamil jumped forward, reached the queen's side. The cyborg dodged to his left, to get a clear shot at the leader.

A sniper, hidden in the woods, had apparently been waiting for just such a move. A single deadly beam sizzled into the cavern, struck Xris in the chest. The cyborg flew backward, landed heavily on the cavern floor.

The two women froze, immobilized, clinging involuntarily to each other. Xris lay motionless, his eyes closed, smoke rising from his burning shirt. The twist dangled from his flaccid lips. LED lights on the cybernetic arm flashed, the fingers twitched spasmodically.

"Oh, Xris . . ." Astarte pushed Kamil aside, tried to go back to him.

"This way, Your Majesty," called Captain Dhure. "Out front.
Like I said, we don't want to hurt anybody, but we have a job
to do. The next shot takes out your girlfriend here."

"Don't hurt her," Astarte commanded. She had stopped,
turned around. "I will come with you."

"Don't go," Kamil whispered.

Astarte smiled reassuringly. "I am in the hands of the Goddess," she said softly.

Kamil was numb with shock, shivering. She couldn't say a
word.

Astarte walked steadily out of the cave. But she had taken
only a few steps when she staggered, swayed on her feet.

"Careful," called the captain, halting his men, who had been
about to leap forward, "it may be a trick. You, girl"—he gestured with his rifle at Kamil—"help your mistress."

But Kamil was already there. She caught Astarte in her arms,
lowered her to the ground.

"Are you hurt?" Kamil asked anxiously.

Astarte shook her head, made a weak attempt to sit up.
"No ... I just felt faint. ... I'll be—"

Kamil's breath caught in her throat. She didn't know how she
knew, except that she had helped her mother bring six baby
brothers into this world. "You're pregnant!" she gasped.

"Hush!" Astarte gripped Kamil tightly. "Don't say anything.
No one must know. The Goddess has told me. 'The baby may
not be born ...' Promise me! Swear by your God!"

"Just rest. Don't talk anymore." Kamil looked up at the captain of the commandos. She didn't know what these people
wanted. Perhaps it would be best if they *didn't* know they had
an additional prize, that the queen was carrying the royal heir.
Was it Dion's child? Kamil swallowed hard, squeezed Astarte's
hand.

"I promise," she said softly, swiftly. "Her Majesty is ill," she
said to the captain. "She shouldn't be moved."

"We'll take good care of her. We have a medic on board."
Captain Dhure was saying something into a commlink. Looking
skyward, he made a lowering motion with his hand.

A dark shadow fell over them. A hovercopter was overhead.
At the captain's signal, the craft tilted, began descending sideways down the side of the mountain, using blasts of air to push
itself away from the rocks.

"Help me to stand," Astarte ordered.

Kamil regarded her anxiously. "Should you?"

"Yes. The dizziness is past."

Kamil did as the queen commanded, assisting Astarte to her feet. The captain kept one eye on them, another on the cave, but even he must have been able to determine that the cyborg wasn't faking.

The hovercopter reached ground level. Air jets blasted around them, whipped up dust and smoke, spreading the fires among the trees. It was difficult to stand in the fierce wind. Astarte's long hair came undone, blew into her face.

Kamil brushed stinging bits of rock and sand from her eyes, tried to see. When the hovercopter touched down, Captain Dhure firmly but respectfully led Astarte toward it.

Feeling helpless and wretched, Kamil watched the queen depart. Astarte walked with dignity, one hand holding her hair back from her face in order to see. The commandos treated her with deference. The queen might have been making a royal junket.

Suddenly, on impulse, with no clear idea what she was doing or why, Kamil ran forward.

"Let me go with her!" she shouted above the roar of the air jets.

Captain Dhure eyed her dubiously.

"I'm her ... her handmaiden," Kamil told him, saying the first thing that came into her mind.

Shieldmaiden ... handmaiden.

The captain didn't have much time for consideration. Perhaps it occurred to him that the queen might be more tractable if she had a companion along. He agreed with a wave of his hand, and Kamil ran to the copter. The queen was already inside. One of the commandos assisted Kamil.

"What are you doing?" Astarte stared at her.

"I'm coming with you."

"You don't need to do this."

"Yes, I do," said Kamil fiercely, and turned her head away, ending the conversation.

She knew, without asking, whose child the queen carried.

A soldier strapped Kamil securely into her seat. Another wrapped a blanket around the queen.

Captain Dhure climbed in. "Take 'er up," he told the pilot. "You patched through to the baroness? Yeah, put her on. Baroness, this is Captain Richard Dhure, Ghost Legion. We've taken your daughter hostage. . . . No, *you* listen to me, Baroness. Her Majesty is fine and she'll stay fine so long as you follow our instructions. We had hoped to keep this low-profile, but your people ruined that.

"This is what you tell the press: An assassination attempt was made today against Her Majesty, the queen. The attempt was foiled. The queen is safe and she has gone into hiding on this planet until you are assured that all the people involved have been captured . . ."

The copter lifted up, its motion erratic and jerky as it fended off the rocks. The noise of the jets drowned out whatever Dhure was saying. Kamil had heard enough anyway.

Clinging tightly to the sides of the seat, she stared down at the ground, which was falling away rapidly beneath her. Fires burned. Smoke was spreading through the temple gardens. Other hovercopters were whirring overhead, dropping down to pick up the remainder of the commando force left on the ground. They wouldn't be picking up all of them. She saw a few bodies, probably from Xris's rockets. Their retreat was swift and easy; no one made any attempt to stop them. The commandos left their dead behind.

Crowds had gathered in the temple gardens, were staring up at them. Kamil could see a small procession descending down the mountainside. It was led by the bright robes of the archbishop. Following after came the flamboyant pink of the Adonian, and beside him two healers bearing a litter holding a small raincoated body.

Other priests and healers were scaling the mountainside. They'd find Xris. Find him dead . . . alive . . .

And Astarte was carrying Dion's child.

Kamil suddenly began to cry.

A gentle hand, cool fingers, brushed against hers. Kamil wanted to shake the hand off, but its touch was comforting, eased the bleak unhappiness, the pain, the anger.

Kamil clasped her hand over Astarte's, held on fast.

Neither woman spoke. Below, in the temple gardens, smoke drifted among the trees like ghosts.

Chapter ❖ Six

The King has killed his heart.
William Shakespeare, *Henry V,* Act II, Scene i

Tusk climbed out of the Scimitar's hatch, descended slowly down the ladder, taking in everything around him as he went. He'd landed the spaceplane on a hangar deck in a warship, a ship of the same type and variety as the old *Phoenix.* The hangar bay was now shut and sealed. Breathable air was filling the chamber, and an honor guard was marching out across the deck to welcome them.

"At least that's what I hope they're doing," Tusk said to himself. He loosened his lasgun in its holster, marked places in the hangar bay he could use for cover.

The honor guard drew themselves up in formation, raised their weapons in salute, did not appear prepared to gun anyone down. Two officers stepped forward, bowed with utmost respect to Lord Sagan, who had left the plane first. They were all now waiting for Tusk.

Reaching the deck himself, Tusk was less than pleased to recognize his two former passengers—Commander Perrin and Captain Zorn.

"Welcome aboard, Tusca," said Cynthia with a cool smile and a firm handshake.

"Got any more scotch?" asked Don, broadly winking.

Tusk watched his hand clench into a fist—apparently of its own volition; knew that in about three seconds that fist would be giving good ol' Don something to wink about. Seeing Lord Sagan watching him without seeming to be watching him, Tusk forced a grin, uncurled his fingers, and permitted Don to wring his hand practically off at the wrist.

"How's the vacuum cleaner business?" Tusk asked.

"The vacuum—?" Don blinked, then his booming laugh echoed through the hangar bay. "Oh, you mean Mrs. Mopup? Ha, ha. That's a good one." He clapped Tusk on the shoulder. "She's fine. Just fine. She'll appreciate you asking."

371

"I'm so glad that you've decided to join us," said Cynthia. She turned back to Sagan and, unless Tusk was mistaken, the woman was regarding the Warlord with far more than professional interest. "My lord," she said in softer tones, "His Highness has asked that you would attend him immediately in the royal quarters. Commander Perrin will escort you there. I will take Commander Tusca to his quarters."

"I am at His Highness's command," said Sagan with a slight inclination of his head.

The Warlord was wearing the long black cassock of a priest of the Order of Adamant. Tusk had wondered at first at the change of costume—Sagan had dressed in fatigues during the trip across the galaxy. The cassock's long skirts were cumbersome and—to Tusk's mind—implied weakness. But now, standing on the hangar deck, Tusk revised his opinion. The black-robed man stood out in sharp contrast to the uniformed soldiers surrounding him. And the robes didn't imply weakness so much as latent power, a mysterious power that awed, frightened, and—apparently—attracted.

"Will you be dining with His Highness tonight, my lord?" Cynthia asked.

"I am entirely at His Highness' disposal," Sagan answered.

"Then perhaps I shall see you there, my lord," Cynthia replied, smiling.

Sagan bowed and walked off with Commander Perrin. The Warlord didn't give Tusk a backward glance.

"Just delivering the goods, aren't you?" Tusk said to Sagan's back, somewhat bitterly. It was all part of the act, of course, and Tusk had to admit that their entrance had played well. But somehow he hadn't expected his costar to walk off stage and leave him to face the audience alone.

The honor guard tromped after Lord Sagan. Tusk was left with Cynthia. He smiled at her and hoped his smile didn't look as sick as he felt.

"This way, Commander," Cynthia said formally. Though she was automatically returning Tusk's smile, her eyes had strayed once more to Derek Sagan.

And though Tusk was a happily married man, he couldn't help but feel somewhat slighted. My God! Sagan had to be sixty, at least!

"What'd you call me—Commander?" Tusk forced a laugh

that he was afraid sounded forced. "I thought we were close friends. After all, you did shoot me—"

"*I* didn't shoot you," said Cynthia, looking at Tusk with more interest.

"Well, your vacuum cleaner shot me," Tusk amended.

"Not the same." Cynthia moved close, twined her arm around his, drew him along. "If *I'd* shot you, you would have remembered it."

Jeez, this woman moved fast. Not five seconds earlier, she would have been lifting Sagan's skirts. Now her hips were rubbing against Tusk's as they walked along, side by side (practically cheek to cheek). Maybe she's been ordered to move fast, Tusk thought, which thought effectively shriveled any desire he might have felt. He grinned, gulped, and tried to look as if he were enjoying himself.

Only when they reached his quarters did it occur to him that he had no idea where he was. He hadn't bothered to keep track of where he was going and it was a hell of a big battleship. That was stupid. Damn stupid. And he prided himself on being levelheaded, skilled!

"Uh, this may sound dumb," he said, "but . . . where are we?"

Cynthia laughed pleasantly. The compliment had not been lost on her. "Officer's quarters. B deck." She led him to a door. "If you want, I'll draw you a map."

She drew him inside the small berth, shut the door behind them. At this point, Tusk expected to have to put up a fight for his honor. He fully intended to, of course; he was a happily married man. But, somewhat to his disappointment, Cynthia merely took a turn about the room, making certain everything was in order.

Smoothing out a wrinkle in a perfectly flat, smooth, and wrinkleless blanket, she said casually, "You've known Lord Sagan a long time. What do you think of him?"

Tusk dumped his gear on the deck, shrugged. His insides were tying themselves up in square knots. What the hell was she after?

"Nobody knows Derek Sagan," he said, which was, after all, the truth. "Least of all me."

"You served under him." Cynthia sat down on the bed.

Tusk sat down in a chair on the opposite side of the bed. "Way under him."

"You went AWOL—"

"Look, you know my life history. I don't see—"

"But because of the Usurper—"

"Who?" Tusk stared.

"The Usurper. Dion Starfire. Because of him, you and Sagan became friends."

"Not friends," said Tusk. "Never *friends*." He laid emphasis on the word and knew he meant it.

Cynthia looked surprised. "But you came with him—"

"Because I needed the cash. Plain and simple."

"We offered you cash."

"Yeah, and shot me in the bargain. Are you here to interrogate me, Captain?"

"Call me Cynthia, please," she said. "And you can't blame us for being curious about why you changed your mind."

"And maybe making sure I *did* change my mind." Tusk was growing angry, found himself resenting the fact that she didn't trust him. Not that she should trust him, but, damn it, she didn't know that! "If you're wondering how much money His Highness is paying me, I guess you better take that up with him."

Cynthia rose languidly to her feet. Coming over to stand in front of Tusk—which put him at about eye level with her extremely slender waist and softly rounded stomach—she rested her hands lightly on his shoulders.

"Don't be mad, Tusk. I know what His Highness is paying you. It's less than you deserve." She ran one long fingernail slowly up his neck, under his chin, tilted his head back, forcing him to look at her. Her lips pursed, she leaned over him. "The reception takes place at 1800. That's about an hour from now. It'll give you time to shower and shave. Dress uniform. You'll find yours in the closet there. I hope it fits." She ran her hands over his shoulders. "I think I remembered your size pretty well. I'll be back to escort you."

Placing her finger playfully on his lips, she turned and walked out of the room. The door shut behind her.

Tusk remained seated in the chair, unable to move. For a minute he was afraid he was going to get the shakes. His shirt was soaked with sweat; he was shivering. He went over every word, tried to see if he had slipped up anywhere. No, it all rang true. Or did it? Maybe he shouldn't have gotten angry. Maybe that had been too much. Or maybe not enough. Maybe he should have stormed around, punched the wall.

"Every minute! Every hour I'm around her, around any of them, I'll have to watch myself, watch every goddam word I say!" He flung himself back in the chair, accidentally banged his head on the wall. "How the hell did I get myself into this?"

It was when he found himself tugging on his earlobe, tugging at an earring that wasn't there, an earring in the shape of an eight-pointed star, that Tusk said several bad words and went to take a shower.

He'd have to look up that word—*Usurper.*

◦◦◦◦◦

Tusk had forgotten how much he detested dress uniforms. Ordinarily they either choked him or pinched him or an interesting combination of both. This one didn't do either. It was worse. It was a one-piece nightmare that slid over him like a second skin, and he knew the moment he squirmed into it that this second skin and his original skin weren't going to get on well at all. He was still wriggling uncomfortably when a buzz came at the door.

"Me," said Cynthia, and walked in.

"You got something against privacy around here?" Tusk demanded, scratching at his left arm. He'd made an attempt to lock his door, discovered it wouldn't.

"You got something to hide?" Cynthia returned. She ran her gaze appreciatively over Tusk's lithe, firm body. "No, I'd say you didn't. We're very informal around here, Tusk. I don't suppose Derek Sagan would approve. He was a strict disciplinarian, wasn't he? Which might be nice under some circumstances." She paused a moment, smiled slightly, then shrugged. "But that isn't Prince Flaim's style."

Back to Sagan again. What was going on? Was she hoping to play each of them off the other? Fishing for information? Or was she simply a woman in love?

Tusk studied himself gloomily in the mirror. He looked like his young son, decked out for the night in his stretchy pajamas. The thought made Tusk desperately homesick. He hoped Nola and John were okay. He'd only talked to them once—via Rozzle—right after they'd left Vangelis, prior to making the Jump. At Sagan's "advice," Tusk had told Nola about Link losing the plane to Lazarus Banquo.

"I'm going to go with Banquo," he'd said, "and try to work out a deal to get my Scimitar back."

It was the first time in his life he'd lied to her, and he knew she knew he was lying. He'd been thankful Rozzle didn't believe in vidphones; at least he hadn't had to try to feed her that line face-to-face. He had heard in her voice that she was scared—not for herself, but for him. Remembering that he'd been followed from their house, Tusk tried to impress on Nola that she needed to be a little bit scared for herself.

It hadn't been easy, with Sagan breathing down his neck, but Tusk had managed to tip her off. At least he hoped she'd gotten the message.

"I'm sorry I'm not going to be able to go to Marek's party tonight, sweetheart," he'd told her. "But you go and take John with you. He can wear that bunny rabbit costume you made him. You know, the one with the tail. The jeep's at the spaceport. Drive careful, sweetheart. Love you."

He'd signed off quickly, before she could say anything. Marek wasn't having a party. But he did have a vacation villa up in the mountains, one he'd been trying to get Nola and Tusk to use for a holiday. And she was bound to pick up on the word "tail" and his warning to "drive careful," since John didn't own a bunny rabbit costume.

Either that or she'd think he was on the juice again. God! He wished she were here with him now. They were a team, a damn good team. She had a way of steadying him, of giving him confidence in himself, of . . .

"And they say women are vain!" Cynthia commented, coming up behind Tusk.

He realized he'd been standing there this whole time staring at himself in the mirror.

"I just want to make a good impression, that's all," he said. "What's he like, this prince of yours?"

"Yours, too, I hope," Cynthia countered.

Tusk turned around, faced her. "Yeah, well, right now it's strictly business with me." He'd decided in the shower that he shouldn't appear to be a pushover.

"That's because you haven't met him yet," said Cynthia. Her flirty, playful attitude was gone. She was subdued, awed. "He's an incredible person. He is handsome, charming, strong, intelligent. He has no vices, no weaknesses. He is completely focused on one thing—being king." She looked up at Tusk earnestly, almost fanatically. "Flaim Starfire will be an incredible king."

Dangerous, Sagan had said of the prince. Yes, Tusk thought, any man who could inspire loyalty like this in followers like Cynthia would well be classified as dangerous. Come to think of it, any man Derek Sagan termed dangerous must be . . . well . . .

dangerous. And there had been respect in Sagan's voice, the same respect Tusk heard echoed in Cynthia's. . . .

Derek Sagan had never termed Dion dangerous.

Tusk's insides began to twist again. *What if I'm alone in this? What if Sagan's laughing at me? What if they're all laughing at me? I net Dion for them and look around for help and they all laugh at me.*

"My, you *are* nervous," said Cynthia, resting her hand on his arm.

"Yeah, I . . . I guess I am," said Tusk. "I'm not much used to being around royalty."

"But you're half Blood Royal yourself," Cynthia observed. "We know all about you, Mendaharin Tusca." She put her arm through his. "Calm down. You'll soon be as devoted to the prince as the rest of us. I promise you, once you meet him, this won't be 'strictly business' for you any longer."

"You don't think so, huh?" Tusk said, trying out a light laugh.

"I don't think so. I *know* so," said Cynthia earnestly.

·-·◁▷◯◁▷·-·

An hour later, standing talking to the prince, Tusk was beginning to wonder himself. Flaim Starfire was exactly what everyone had said he was. He slid down the throat as easily and hotly as jump-juice, left you feeling slightly intoxicated by the whole experience.

"Mendaharin Tusca, what an honor to meet you at last." Flaim stopped Tusk from his awkward bow, extended a hand, shook Tusk's warmly. The Starfire-blue eyes were brilliant, mesmerizing. The prince's smile was sincere, his handshake firm, dignified. "I cannot tell you how delighted I am you decided to join with us. I know—" his smile warmed, dazzled, "I know you're 'strictly business,' but I hope to win you to my cause. Come, I want to speak to you a moment in private."

Many people were hovering around the prince, waiting, begging for a share of that smile. But they all seemed to evaporate the moment the prince gave the signal. Flaim placed one hand on Tusk's shoulder, drew him off to a corner by himself. Tusk felt Sagan's eyes on him, although the Warlord was standing in the far corner of the vast room, engaged in polite conversation. Sagan started moving in Tusk's direction, but was deflected by Cynthia. Taking hold of Sagan's arm, she began introducing him to other guests.

And that was the last Tusk saw of the Warlord for the time being. Flaim led him to a steelglass viewscreen, presenting a marvelous view of the prince's large fleet of ships and the space stations in orbit around Vallombrosa.

"I am pleased you have decided to undertake this delicate task for me, Tusca," said Flaim with a gravity that was every bit as becoming as his smile, "because I think you alone can convince my cousin of how much I look forward to meeting him. I know that the two of you have not been close in these past years. . . ." He paused, looked at Tusk expectantly.

"Yeah, I mean, yes, Your Highness. I guess you could say that. It's just that he's so high and a king and all and I'm . . . well . . . you can't say it was really like we were mad at each other or anything . . ." Tusk was floundering, hoped someone would cast him a line.

Flaim came to his rescue. "Exactly. Change in circumstance, the passing of time, friends drift apart. It's no one's fault. A misunderstanding. And this will give you a chance to renew your friendship with Dion, Tusca. And you'll be doing both of us a great favor by bringing us together at last."

"At gunpoint," Tusk said, his mouth moving before his brain was in gear.

Flaim appeared more amused than offended. "I heard that you were candid, Tusca. Up front. You say what you think. I like that quality very much, far better than mindless flattery. And I trust that the use of force will not be necessary. For one thing, I don't believe His Majesty would harm you, do you, Tusca?"

Tusk shook his head, guilty and uncomfortable.

"No, of course he wouldn't. And there is another reason. Come. There's someone I want you to meet."

Confused and dazed, feeling as if he'd drunk too much wine and shouldn't be driving himself home, Tusk glanced about for assistance. He was relieved to note that Sagan—with the smoothness and skill of a longtime naval commander—had steered Cynthia onto the shoals of conversation with several high-ranking officers, and then had promptly and politely left her to her fate. Tusk had a last glimpse of Sagan bearing down on them, when he was forced to turn his attention back to the prince.

The reception room aboard His Highness's ship *Flare* was vast, intended for the diplomatic functions that often took place on naval vessels. Such ships were highly suited—when not at war—to the shunting of diplomats back and forth between planets. The room was furnished with the obligatory round tables and uncomfortable chairs, designed for the sole purpose of bringing together total strangers to stare blankly at each other while they sipped lukewarm drinks and ate food off toothpicks.

Prince Flaim was moving toward one of these tables, located apart from all the others, in a far corner of the room. Tusk had already observed this table and its occupants and had been curious about them for several reasons. The two people sitting at the table were women. They were both dressed in white gowns (when everyone else was in uniform) and there was something familiar about one of them, though Tusk couldn't figure out what, because she sat with her back to him. No one came near these two women, but that may have been because several men stood near the table. The men did not carry weapons, but they had the stance and quiet watchfulness of guards—whether bodyguards or prison guards was hard to tell.

The women didn't seem to be enjoying themselves, from what Tusk could see. Each had a drink before her, and food, but neither was eating. Both appeared tense, ill at ease, and both appeared determined to ignore what was happening around them. They did not seem to be finding much comfort in each other's company, however. They weren't talking to anyone, not even each other. An elderly black gentleman sat with them, smiling on them both, apparently trying to do what he could to entertain them.

At the sight of Flaim approaching, the three guards backed off. Tusk recognized one of them as Captain Dhure. The captain acknowledged Tusk with a friendly smile and a nod, but said nothing, seeing that Tusk was being escorted by the prince. The elderly black gentleman rose to his feet. He, too, seemed vaguely familiar to Tusk, but he didn't have time to think where he knew him. Flaim was making introductions.

"Her Majesty, the queen."

The shock went through Tusk like a laser blast. He'd never met Astarte, but he'd seen her on the vids, before his machine had been repossessed. At first he thought confusedly that this must be some type of trick, for his benefit, maybe an impostor . . . but he had to abandon the idea.

There was no mistaking, no imitating Astarte's startling beauty, or the cool, imperious attitude with which she snubbed him. Flaim bowed before her, accorded her respect, paid her homage as if she were on her own royal barge, of her own free will. Astarte accepted his homage as no more than her due, but with the set jaw and rigidly held emotional control of one who knows that it's all mockery.

The prince's game plan was obvious to Tusk now. Had Sagan known about this move? Had he been behind it? Or was he as taken by surprise as Tusk? The Warlord had come up to stand behind them. Tusk sensed the man's presence, though he couldn't see him. Flaim was introducing the elderly black gentleman, whose name Tusk recognized, though he was too distraught to try to place how he knew him.

Flaim didn't introduce the other woman; probably the queen's servant, Tusk concluded, glancing at her without much interest. Then he noticed that the woman had her head turned away, her hand before it. She was shielding her face, deliberately trying to prevent him from noticing her. Which, of course, made him notice her. There *was* something about her that had seemed familiar. . . .

And then he knew.

Tusk gasped, sucked in his breath. "Kamil! What the hell—"

"No, sir, you must be mistaken," murmured Kamil. She flashed him a pleading glance, gave her head a quick shake. Her eyes darted swiftly to Flaim, then back to Tusk again. "My name is Diana—"

"What is this?" Flaim asked with sudden interest, looking from one to the other. "Do you know this woman, Tusca?"

Tusk glanced around. Sagan was watching him through half-closed eyelids. The Warlord's expression was impassive, but Tusk could see the sudden rigidity in the body, the slight twitch of the thin lips. Tusk had blundered, apparently, but what had he done? What the devil was going on anyway? And what in heaven's name was he supposed to do about it?

He thought fast. There was only one thing he could do now. "Her name's not Diana. It's Kamil," he said harshly. "Maigrey Kamil Olefsky. She's a friend of the royal family—"

"Indeed she is!" said Flaim, turning and regarding Kamil with marked interest. "What strange chance has thrown this prize into our hands? I would dearly love to know *this* story," he added, exchanging amused glances with the elderly black man.

Tusk still didn't understand, though everyone else seemed to, judging by the knowing smiles. He tried to look knowing himself, but he felt like the only person at the party who doesn't get the host's dirty joke and has to laugh politely anyway.

Flaim turned back to him. "Tusca, my friend. Thank you for

enlightening us. Now you will be able to tell His Majesty, when you see him, that we are entertaining not only his wife as our guest, but his mistress as well."

Mistress! Tusk, shocked and disbelieving, looked from one woman to the other, to Astarte—pale but unmoved—to Kamil—flushed and angry and wretched—and he had his answer.

"Close. Very close," Sagan murmured grimly, but Tusk heard approval in the voice, and he relaxed somewhat.

Kamil couldn't have gone on with this deception long. The prince was undoubtedly having some sort of ID check run on her. It was just a matter of time. And this revelation had, without doubt, raised Tusk a notch with the prince. Flaim was regarding the mercenary with new respect.

"If you will excuse me, Your Majesty," Flaim said, bowing to the queen with grace, "I must steal Pantha away from you for a moment."

The elderly man, Garth Pantha (*that's* who he was, Tusk realized) bowed and left the queen, came to join Flaim and Tusk. The prince laid a hand on Tusk's shoulder.

"You have already proved yourself invaluable, Tusca. You have my thanks and"—Flaim smiled—"my apologies for any uncomfortable moments you might have experienced since coming aboard. Captain Zorn was only obeying orders. I trust that from now on you two will be very good friends."

Calling off the dogs, are you? Tusk said, but he said it in his head.

"My Lord Sagan," continued the prince, "Pantha and I must greet the rest of our guests. Perhaps you and Tusca would be so kind as to entertain Her Majesty?"

Sagan bowed his acquiescence and there was nothing Tusk could do but bow his as well. The Warlord turned toward the queen, but not before he had cast a sharp, swift glance at Tusk.

Tusk didn't need the warning. Undoubtedly, either the two women or the table or all three were wired for sound. Feeling as if his skin-tight uniform were crawling over his body, Tusk set his face in what he hoped was a go-to-hell expression and accompanied the Warlord to the table.

Astarte had no intention of being entertained by either of them, however. Rising to her feet, she turned her back on them, faced Captain Dhure. "I find these people odious. I will retire now."

"There is no need for that, Your Majesty," Sagan interrupted, bowing. "We would not want to deprive the rest of the assemblage of the pleasure of your company. We will withdraw."

"His Highness would like you to remain, Your Majesty," added Captain Dhure respectfully.

"On display?" Astarte said, her beautiful lip curling.

"When one has the jewel of the universe in one's possession, one naturally wishes to show it off," replied Captain Dhure gallantly. "Isn't that true, my lord?"

"An interesting analogy. I once heard the late Snaga Ohme say almost the same thing about a jewel he owned. A starjewel, given to him by the Lady Maigrey. Your godmother, I believe," he added, with a bow for Kamil.

"Don't speak her name!" Kamil flared angrily. Trembling and earnest, she faced the Warlord. "You're not only betraying Dion, you're betraying her! She sacrificed her life to save Dion. She loved him. For some reason, she loved you!"

Sagan stood unmoved. He regarded Kamil in silence. The dark eyes were rarely lit by any inner light, but now the darkness in them was cold and intense. It cloaked him, and it seemed that he cast the darkness over them, like a pall.

Kamil shrank beneath the chill and steadfast gaze.

"You are a child," Sagan said to her finally. "You know nothing about love and sacrifice. But you will." He looked back to the queen. "Your Majesty," he said, bowing deeply.

"My lord," she said stiffly, barely deigning to recognize him.

He flicked a glance at Kamil, but said nothing more to her. Turning, he walked off.

No one spoke. Astarte watched him go, her brow furrowed, her expression thoughtful. Kamil stood staring after him. She looked dazed and shattered and frightened. Tusk had gone hot all over; now he was cold. He had no idea what any of that had been about, wondered if Sagan himself knew.

"I need a drink," Tusk said, planning to make his escape back to his quarters. "If you ladies will excuse me." He gave an awkward bow, turned on his heel, and bumped right into Cynthia.

"Hello," she said, smiling at him. Resting her hands on his arm, she turned him around. "Introduce me."

"Uh, I don't think I'm real welcome here right now," Tusk said to her in a low tone, hoping she'd take the hint and leave.

"You're not," said Kamil, recovering herself. She looked at him now with more sadness than anger. "How could you betray him, Tusk? You're Dion's friend—"

"Yeah? He's been a real good friend these last three years, hasn't he?" Tusk sneered, conscious of Cynthia's hands on his arm, of her eyes watching, her ears listening. "I helped put that damn crown on his head and what thanks do I get? He leaves me and my wife and kid to practically starve."

"But if you'd only asked him, Tusk! If you'd told him—"

"Come crawling to him like a goddam beggar? He would have liked that! I already owe him my life. I can imagine what'd it'd be like owing him money! Naw, I make my own way in this galaxy. Let's go," he said to Cynthia. "This company's too rich for my blood. I'll buy you a drink."

Startled at himself, Tusk was thankful to escape. He'd sounded and noted very convincing. Too damn convincing. The words had come from somewhere deep and ugly inside him, spewed out as if he'd stuck a needle in a festering sore. Had he meant what he'd said? Did he resent Dion? Was he jealous of him?

Am I here because Sagan forced me into it? Tusk wondered uneasily. Or am I secretly looking forward to seeing Dion take a fall?

"That's stupid. I'm turning paranoid," Tusk muttered, running a hand over his tightly curled hair. "I don't trust Sagan. Now I'm even beginning not to trust myself!"

"What did you say?" Cynthia leaned near.

"Nothin', nothin'," Tusk mumbled.

"Don't let her upset you." Cynthia cast an amused glance back at the two women, who sat together disconsolately, for show, on display. "As Lord Sagan said, one is a child. And the Usurper's wife is a spoiled bitch. You're doing the right thing, Tusca. And you know it."

"Yeah, I know it," said Tusk.

He snagged his drink, would have liked about fourteen more, but knew better. A half-hour spent showing Cynthia John's baby pictures got rid of her. Prince Flaim was no longer interested in him. Sagan had long since made his excuses and left. Kamil and Astarte were eventually permitted to return to wherever it was they were being held prisoner. Tusk took the opportunity of slipping out himself, made his lonely way back to what he was beginning to see was his own prison cell.

Lying on his bed, he poked at his inner sores with a mental needle. Finally convinced that he was a thoroughly rotten human being, Tusk drifted into an uneasy and troubled sleep.

Chapter ·◄►❍ Seven

O villains, vipers, damned without redemption!
Dogs easily won to fawn on any man!
Snakes in my heart-blood warmed that sting my heart!
   William Shakespeare, *Richard II*, Act III, Scene ii

Dion sat in his office, affixing his signature to the daily stack of official documents, moving his old-fashioned ink pen to this line and that as D'argent indicated with a gentle murmur, a gesture of his hand. When the process was finished, D'argent gathered the papers—many of them handsomely decorated with the royal seal—handed them to a servbot, and began to straighten up His Majesty's desk.

This complete, D'argent dispatched the servbot about its business. When it had whirred itself out of the room, the secretary said in a low voice, "Sir John Dixter is waiting to see you, Your Majesty."

"Very good. Cancel the rest of my morning appointments."

"Yes, sir. However ..."

Dion, absorbed in reading a report, looked up. "What is it, D'argent?"

"You do have the appointment with Mendaharin Tusca this morning, sir. Shall I cancel it, as well?"

Dion relaxed, sat back in his chair, smiled tiredly. "I'd forgotten that was today. The first time he's come to visit in three years. No, don't cancel Tusk. Plan on serving luncheon."

"Yes, sir."

"And you've summoned the prime minister?"

"He will be here this afternoon, Your Majesty."

"You better schedule a news conference for early this evening." Dion rubbed the palm of his right hand, scratched at the inflamed scars. "We should have an announcement for the press by then."

"Yes, sir. Would Your Majesty like more hot tea?"

"Thank you," Dion said absently.

The teacup beside him was still full, its liquid cold and untasted. D'argent whisked it away, returned with a steaming pot of tea, another one of coffee for the Lord of the Admiralty, and the Lord Admiral himself.

Dion rose to meet him. The two shook hands.

"Any news, sir?" the king asked.

"No, Your Majesty," Dixter answered heavily. "I'm sorry."

Sighing in frustration, Dion sat back down. D'argent poured the tea and the coffee, waited a moment to see if there would be anything else, then departed, gliding silently from the room.

"The baroness has effectively cut Ceres off from the rest of the galaxy," Dixter continued. "All transgalactic shipping has been halted, all spaceplanes grounded. No one is allowed to land on the planet or leave it. Communications with the outside, including her own systems, have been severed. Of course, this makes a certain amount of sense if there truly was a conspiracy to murder the queen—"

"But not me!" Dion said angrily, slamming his hand on the desk, causing his tea to slosh over the rim of the cup into the saucer. "She has no right to refuse to communicate with me!"

"Rightly or wrongly, Dion," said Dixter, "DiLuna blames you for what has happened—"

"What *has* happened?" the king demanded, frustrated. "Do we even know? How is Astarte? Is she safe, well? Does DiLuna have any idea who made the attack? If there even *was* an attack—"

"There was," Dixter said grimly. "That's been confirmed by all our sources."

"Then why does DiLuna blame me?"

Dixter's expression was grave. "The baroness has just issued a communiqué. It came as I was leaving. I brought it along." He handed a printed transcript to the king.

Dion read it. His face registered shock, disbelief. He reread it more slowly, then looked up at Dixter.

"Xris? The Xris we know? The cyborg who helped the Lady Maigrey, who risked his life to save Tusk? No, I can't believe it!"

"Nor can I. But he's been arrested, charged with the crime, tried, and convicted. DiLuna doesn't waste time. I'm surprised he hasn't been executed by now."

Dion studied the communiqué in perplexity. " 'The queen is in retreat, praying for the souls of the dead.' " He looked up, glowering. "We must find out the truth. What the hell are those undercover people of yours doing?"

"They're our best, Dion," Dixter said gently. "But there are problems. The incident took place inside the Holy Temple. It was immediately sealed off. Our people aren't priests or priestesses. They have no way to get inside, would probably be killed if they tried. This is a serious offense. Blood was spilled on sacred ground. The people of Ceres are angry and afraid. Afraid of the Goddess's wrath."

"To say nothing of DiLuna's," Dion muttered.

"That, too." Dixter smiled wanly.

"If only I knew Astarte was safe! If only I could talk to her!" Dion started to rub his right palm again, forced himself to stop. He clasped his hands tightly together on top of the desk. "I should have been there. I should have been with her. It was my place."

"There was nothing you could have done—" Dixter began lamely.

"But you agree, I should have been there," Dion said quietly. "At least I'd know the truth about what happened, instead of being kept in the dark. The baroness wouldn't be able to make me look like a fool. Though that's precisely what I've been."

Standing up, he walked over to the window, stared out of it. Tourists swarmed over the sidewalk below. A small cluster of them had their heads craned, looking upward, gawking at the top floors. Their guide was undoubtedly informing them that His Majesty was at work behind those steelglass windows this very moment.

"I thought I had it all under control. Everything was going along fine, I thought—because that's what I wanted to think. Talk about passion blinding you. It blinded me to duty, responsibility, honor. I've hurt Astarte. And I never meant to. She didn't deserve it. If she was cold and distant, whose fault was that? I shut her out of my life deliberately, then blamed her for slamming the door when she left."

And Kamil, he added to himself, brooding. I love her. I'd lay down my life for her. Yet I hurt her, too. I hurt her as surely as if I'd run the bloodsword through her. All for my own selfish desires. I should have been strong enough, loved her enough to let her go.

"Now everything is falling apart," he continued aloud. "I'm as bad as my uncle. How can I expect to bring order and stability to the kingdom if I can't bring it to my own life?" he finished bitterly.

"Don't be too hard on yourself, son," Dixter admonished. "You're young. You're human—"

"No," Dion countered, glancing around. "I am Blood Royal. I am a king. Kings don't have the luxury of being young, human, in love. Nor can they afford the luxury of self-pity." He stared gloomily out the window.

"No, they can't," Dixter said bluntly. "Let's face it, Your Majesty, DiLuna could be making things a lot worse for you. Where's the war she threatened? She said she was going to declare her systems independent, yank her representatives out of parliament. Has she done any of that? No. And I almost wish she had."

"Why?" Dion turned to him.

"I think it's a bad sign. DiLuna's not acting out of anger. She's *re*acting—out of fear. And as long as I've known her, I've never known her to be afraid of anything."

"All the more reason to find out the truth!" Dion clenched his fist. "If we sent in warships—"

Dixter shook his head. "There'd be a fight; at the very least a confrontation. Any attempt to force her hand will only make matters worse. We have to be patient. And you have to set the example, Your Majesty. Six major systems had dignitaries on Ceres for the festival. Clergy, ambassadors, government officials—all being detained on the planet 'for their own protection,' according to DiLuna. That includes the archbishop, by the way. The systems are edgy about this. If they see that you're starting to panic—"

"—we could end up with a galactic conflict." Dion sighed, frustrated. "I'll be patient. I'll continue to work through diplomatic channels. It's all I can do, I suppose." He stared unseeing out the window, thinking, trying to find some other way.

Dixter was silent, letting the king consider the matter.

"Xris! Of all people!" Dion repeated. "What was he doing there? Did he tell you?"

Dixter shook his head. "No, Your Majesty. Except that he had advance knowledge of the attack. He contacted me that very day, said someone had sent an anonymous warning, in code, to his men at Snaga Ohme's. Warned that an attack might be made on the queen. Strange thing about that warning, though. The code used was Derek Sagan's old code."

"Sagan!" Dion turned to face Dixter. "But how— Why—"

"I have no idea, son." Dixter looked exhausted. He hadn't slept in three nights. "Except that I do recall telling Sagan that Xris and his team were working for us—independently. I told him if he needed help—unofficial help—he could contact them."

Dion was chilled. "That means that my cousin may be behind this." He considered, then shook his head in frustration. "No, it doesn't make sense. None of it makes sense. Why would my cousin want to murder Astarte? What could he hope to gain by such a heinous action? The people love her. . . ."

"There's something else, too, Your Majesty," Dixter said. "The attacks on the outposts. They may be connected."

Dion left the window, came back to his desk, sat down. "Connected? How? Your coffee's cold, sir. Let me warm it for you."

He reached for the coffeepot with his right hand. Seeing the hand for the first time in the light, Dixter stared.

"My God, son! What happened?"

Dion glanced at his palm. The five puncture wounds were swollen; ugly red streaks extended from them like the rays of a small, fiery sun. "I have no idea. But it's been getting worse. The pain and the burning is almost unbearable."

"The bloodsword—"

"I haven't used the bloodsword, not since Sagan advised me against it. The dreams have been getting worse, too. I see my cousin. See him so clearly. . . ."

Dion's hand was shaking. He set the coffeepot back down with a sharp clatter, almost dropping it. "What about the outposts?"

"Three have been attacked. All in one area, as I told you."

"Around Vallombrosa."

"Yes, Your Majesty."

Dion looked back at his hand. "And you said there was something strange about these attacks—"

"Yes, Your Majesty. Reports are beginning to come in. We've interviewed the survivors. They said it was like . . . like . . ." Dixter hesitated.

"Like what?"

"Like being attacked by ghosts."

"Ghosts again!" Dion swore softly in frustration.

"Yes, ghosts again. There was no warning. No one saw anything coming. Suddenly metal buildings were crushed like beer cans. Spaceplanes crumpled into twisted rubble. The ground split wide open. And then . . . nothing."

"No strike force, no assault, no landing."

"Nothing," Dixter reiterated. "But there could have been. The outpost is finished, useless. All land-based weapons systems were either destroyed outright or their electrical systems so badly scrambled that they're unable to function. All shields were knocked out." He shook his head. "A group of kindergartners could have marched into that base and taken it over."

"And no enemy was ever sighted?"

"No, Your Majesty. There were several interesting and instructive points in the attack: wild gravity fluctuations, people reporting feeling 'heavy' or 'compressed,' slight changes in radiation levels . . ."

"And all the outposts attacked are located near Vallombrosa. My cousin's come out of hiding, it seems." Dion rubbed at his hand. "Sagan was right. I should have used the space-rotation bomb."

"That was never a consideration and you know it."

"My inherent weakness," Dion said bitterly.

Dixter shifted uneasily in his chair. "Speaking of Sagan, have *you* heard from him?"

"No. Not a word."

"You don't think he's . . ." Dixter hesitated.

"What? Shifted allegiance? You said he sent a warning about the queen—"

"*Maybe* he sent it. And it didn't arrive in time for us to do anything. That may have been a cover."

"I wonder—did I ever really *have* his allegiance to begin with? Where was he when I first became king? When I needed his advice and counsel? He simply . . . walked off. Left me to struggle with all this alone."

"I think he had his own struggle, son," Dixter said.

"A struggle he may have lost," Dion said grimly.

A faint buzz sounded. A red light flashed on a panel at Dion's right hand, below eye level.

"Security alert." Dion flicked on the commlink. "Captain Cato. What's going on?"

"Security reports a disturbance in the tourist area, Your Majesty. Some drugged-up Loti left the group and wandered into a secured area. He's been apprehended."

"Loti!" John Dixter was immediately attentive. "That's odd. Captain, this is the Lord Admiral. Do you recall a Loti by the name of Raoul? He worked for Snaga Ohme."

"Good God!" Dion murmured.

"The Adonian? Yes, my lord."

"Would you recognize him?"

"Of course, my lord. There aren't many like him, thank goodness."

"Find out if he's the one they caught down there. Report back immediately."

"Yes, my lord."

"Was Raoul with Xris on Ceres?" Dion asked.

"He could well have been," Dixter answered.

The two men said nothing further, waited in uneasy silence until the call came through.

The king answered swiftly.

"It's Raoul, Your Majesty," returned Cato. "He insists on talking to you."

"Bring him straight up. The back route."

"Yes, sir."

Long minutes passed, longer than the ticking clock counted them. A portion of the wall at the rear of Dion's office slid open. Cato entered, half-leading, half-carrying a stumbling, weakly moving Adonian.

Dion thought that at first the centurion had made a mistake. This wasn't Raoul! The Loti's usually sleek black hair was ragged and unkempt, trailed over his face. The pink velvet costume was rumpled and torn and covered with ominous splotchy stains. His painted-nailed hands shook; his whole body shook. Cato lowered him gently into a chair.

"Raoul?" Dion asked in disbelief.

"It's him, sire," said Cato, speaking in a soft voice, as if the Adonian mustn't hear. "Though it took me a while to make sure. He's been through hell, from the looks of him. I wanted to take him to the infirmary, but he keeps saying he has to see you."

"Yes," said Raoul, lifting his head. The movement, it seemed, took a great effort. "Yes, I had to see you, Your Majesty." He closed his eyes. A shudder ran through his body. His hands twitched.

"Summon the doctor," Dion ordered Cato.

"No, Your . . . Your Majesty," interposed Raoul weakly. "Thank you, but . . . no. It . . . wouldn't help. It's the drugs, you see. Or rather, the lack thereof." The Loti's eyes were shadowed, red-rimmed. But they were focused, clear, and in pain. "I have come from Ceres—" His words were broken off by a spell of coughing.

Dion poured a glass of water. Cato passed it to the Loti, assisted him while he drank it.

"How did you manage to escape, Raoul?" John Dixter asked, after a glance at Dion. "All flights are grounded."

Raoul gave a wan smile. "There is always a way for one of my talents." He drew a deep breath. "Brother Daniel . . . helped me. He has been arguing with . . . the baroness. Trying to convince her to . . . tell you the truth. But she's afraid. So afraid. Brother Daniel said . . . you had to know. And so I came."

He could no longer continue talking. He grimaced, gasped in pain. His hands clenched and unclenched spasmodically.

"The doctor could give you something—"

"No!" Raoul grasped hold of Dion's arm, held on tightly. "No, I . . . must make certain . . . I tell this right."

"What is the truth, then, Raoul?" Dion asked sternly. "What did Brother Daniel send you to tell us?"

Raoul shook the black hair out of his face. "The queen has been taken hostage."

"Hostage?" Dixter repeated, seeing Dion too stunned to speak. "Who did it?"

Raoul's gaze held fast to the king, never leaving Dion's face. "I don't know. DiLuna knows, but she won't say. They told her . . . they told her they would kill the queen if word got out. And so the baroness . . . made up this story. Xris . . . Xris was there. He tried to stop—" Raoul choked, coughed again.

"Xris tried to stop them," Dion filled in the pause.

"They shot him and, unfortunately, they hit one of the few remaining human parts left to him." Raoul blinked his eyes rapidly. "He clings to life. He is stubborn that way. But he has not yet regained consciousness. Brother Daniel says that the baroness is using the cyborg as some sort of goat—"

"Scapegoat?" Dion suggested.

"Perhaps. I don't know. Very little of this has any meaning for me. You . . . note the absence of my partner?" Raoul glanced at the empty space beside him. He even reached out an unsteady hand to touch something that wasn't there.

Dion remembered the small, raincoated figure, the battered

hat. "The Little One," he said softly, at last beginning to understand. "Is he . . . He isn't . . ."

"Not dead!" Raoul said swiftly. "Not yet. But perhaps . . . while I am gone." He closed his eyes again, shivered. "Brother Daniel promised he would stay with him and . . . wouldn't let him be afraid. You had to know. And I was the only one to come."

"Thank you, Raoul," Dion said, putting his hand over the Loti's trembling wrist. "You have performed an invaluable service. I'm sorry about Xris. Sorry about the Little One. If there is anything I can do—"

"You could come to them!" Raoul clung to Dion. "Your hands are the hands of the healer."

Dion looked grim. "I doubt if the baroness would permit it."

"She will. She must. Brother Daniel will talk to her!"

"Perhaps," said Dion thoughtfully. He exchanged glances with Dixter. "Perhaps that *would* be the best way, sir. She could hardly refuse an errand of mercy. I will see what can be done, Raoul. Now, if you'll go with Cato to the doctor—"

"I thank you, Your Majesty, but no." Raoul stood up. He nearly fell, put out a hand to steady himself on the back of the chair. He warded off Cato's assistance. "Forgive me. I don't mean to be rude. But I'm going back."

"Back? Back where? To Ceres?" Dion shook his head. "I'm sorry, Raoul, but that's not possible. The planet's under a self-imposed blockade. There's no way."

"For a person like me," said Raoul simply, "there is always a way. It may not be legal, but there is a way. I promised him, you see. I promised him I would come back quickly."

He appeared stronger, as if he were gathering up the various fragments of himself, putting himself back together. He even touched his hair, made a feeble and ineffectual attempt to smooth it. "It was . . . nice seeing you again, Your Majesty. I will tell Brother Daniel you are coming."

Turning, he launched himself across the floor, heading for the front entrance.

Cato looked at Dion questioningly.

Dion motioned with his hand. "Take him out the back. Have some of your men keep an eye on him. Don't interfere with him—unless he tries to kill someone," the king added, remembering Raoul's dubious talents.

"Yes, Your Majesty."

Cato caught hold of Raoul, steered him gently around a couch, headed him in the direction of the disguised door. Raoul suffered himself to be led, gave Dion a sad, sweet smile as he departed.

"So my cousin is holding the queen hostage," Dion said grimly when the two were alone.

Dixter's expression was grave. "You don't know that for certain, Your Majesty. I'll try again to establish some sort of communication with DiLuna. Maybe I can use this new information as a lever—"

"Tell her I know the truth now and I will come to Ceres to investigate. And I'll bring every warship I have in the galaxy with me. I don't give a damn about confrontation. Tell her I care about one thing—Her Majesty's safe recovery."

Dixter nodded, and left.

Dion returned to his desk, sat down, and tried to work. At length, though, he gave up. He couldn't concentrate. His thoughts kept going to Astarte. He thought of her captive, frightened, alone. And from there his thoughts sank deeper, into darker waters.

Surely they wouldn't harm her. Her usefulness to her kidnappers—whoever they were—would preclude that. They must plan to try to exchange her for . . . what?

Dion scratched his palm.

The crown. Astarte knows what I must say. We've discussed what I must do if she is ever taken hostage. She'll know I must abandon her to her fate. But she'll think I don't care. She'll think that losing her won't matter to me, because I don't love her. Perhaps she'll think I'll be glad. . . .

"Oh, God!" he cried in silent agony. "Am *I* guilty of this crime? Did I wish this? Did I secretly want this to happen?"

"Your Majesty . . ."

Dion gave a violent start, looked up. D'argent stood before the desk.

"I'm sorry, sir," said D'argent, concerned. "I thought you heard me come in."

"No . . . I . . . I must have dozed off," said Dion confusedly, wiping sweat from his face. "What is it?"

"Mendaharin Tusca is here to see you, sir. Shall I send him in?"

"Yes, please."

D'argent left. Dion sat in silence a moment; then he reached inside the top right-hand desk drawer, drew out a small, elegant box made of rich azure blue leather stamped with gold. The box had originally held Dion's wedding ring. Now it contained a single earring, fashioned in the shape of an eight-pointed star. Opening the box was like opening the door to memory. Dion stared at the small star, sighed.

"Strange, how Tusk always comes when I'm in trouble," he said to himself. "I can't tell him anything about this, of course, but just seeing him—"

"Mendaharin Tusca," D'argent announced.

Looking abashed and out of place, his hands jammed into his pockets, Tusk stood inside the door.

"Thank you, D'argent," Dion said, standing up. He placed the box with the earring down on the desk. "That will be all."

The secretary left the room, crossing behind Tusk, who took a step or two farther inside the office, then came to a halt, looked at Dion uncertainly. The mercenary was dressed much as Dion remembered, wearing battle fatigues over a green T-shirt and regulation boots, acquired from army-navy surplus. Two objects were new: a large, shining belt buckle in the shape of a snake, which was rather grotesque, and a pendant—a smiling lion-faced sun. Dion recognized the pendant as one of the cheap souvenirs popular on Minas Tares.

The king was somewhat puzzled by the sight; he'd never known Tusk to wear any jewelry except the one tiny earring in the shape of an eight-pointed star—which was currently resting on the king's desk. But he decided that maybe this was Tusk's idea of a joke.

"My friend." Dion crossed over to meet him. Extending his hand, he clasped Tusk's, shook it warmly. "How are you? How's Nola and the baby? And XJ?"

"Uh, fine," said Tusk, returning the handshake briefly, breaking loose as soon as he could manage. He thrust his hands back into the pockets of his fatigues, hunched his shoulders, glanced nervously about the spacious, richly appointed, elegant office. "They're all fine," he repeated mechanically. "Jeez, this is huge. Bigger'n my house."

Dion led Tusk to a comfortable chair in front of an ornate fireplace. "I forgot. You haven't seen this part of the castle yet, have you?"

"No, they were . . . uh . . . still remodeling when Nola and I came last time." He stood awkwardly, staring at the chair.

"Please, sit down," Dion said. "No formalities between us."

Tusk sat down, sat perched on the edge. Dion pulled up a chair near that of his friend. "Would you like something to drink? I can ring for D'argent—"

"No, no, thanks." Tusk licked his lips.

"We'll have luncheon served in about half an hour. I can't visit with you long, I'm afraid. Not as long as I'd like. You don't know, my friend," said Dion after a moment's pause, "how good it is to see you."

"Yeah. Well, it's ... uh ... good to see you, too, kid. I mean, Your ... uh ... Majesty." Tusk shifted uneasily in the chair. He eyed Dion. "Maybe I shouldn't be saying this, but you don't look real good."

" 'Uneasy lies the head that wears the crown,' you know," said Dion with the practiced smile. "Pressures of the job. You can't imagine," he added, voice softer, the smile fading, "how many times I've thought about you. About the old days. When it was just you and me and XJ. When I was ordinary."

Tusk ceased his restless fidgeting, regarded Dion with an odd intensity. "You were never ordinary, kid. You were then what you are now. Like that comet Dixter used to talk about. The rest of us just sorta got caught up as you flew by. And I wish to God we never had!" he exclaimed suddenly, fiercely, bounding out of the chair.

Hands in his pockets, he headed aimlessly for the windows. "These things open?" he asked abruptly. "It's stuffy in here."

"No," said Dion, rising, looking after his friend in concern. "Security reasons, of course. They're laserproof steelglass, like on the old *Phoenix*."

"Able to withstand a bomb blast, I suppose," Tusk muttered. He was standing with his back to Dion, working at something with his hands, working swiftly and deftly, to judge by the motion.

"Yes, something like that." Dion took a step forward across the sculptured carpeting, decorated with the royal seal. "Tusk— are you in some kind of trouble?"

"No," said Tusk, turning around. His voice was steady now, his demeanor calm. Sunlight glinted off a metal object he held in his hand—an object he pointed at Dion. "You are."

Dion stared in disbelief. "What are you talking about? Tusk, if this is some kind of joke—"

"No joke, kid," said Tusk grimly. "And just hold it right there,

will you? You see this?" He exhibited the object in his palm. It
had been the snake belt buckle, was a belt buckle no longer.
"You remember that gun you used to try to kill Sagan that night
at Snaga Ohme's? The one Abdiel designed to get past the
Adonian's security?"

"Yes." Dion stared at his friend.

"This is something like it. Almost. Runs off a little tiny nuke
cell in my watch." Tusk held up his wrist. "Not as fancy or as
powerful as the gun you carried, but this one works the same
way. Except that it only fires in one direction—where I point
it."

"Are you going to use it on me?" Dion asked steadily.

He couldn't believe he was this calm. None of this was
real—that was the reason. None of this made sense. He was
waiting for Tusk to laugh and tell him that the gun was really
a chocolate bar. . . .

"Are you going to kill me?" Dion persisted.

"No, kid. We need you alive. But I'll use it on anyone who
thinks they'd like to try being a hero. Like that secretary of
yours, for instance. Or maybe Cato or Crassus or any of the rest
of the boys.

"You see, kid," Tusk continued, keeping the gun aimed at
Dion, "we're going to be taking a little trip. Now, you can make
this real easy and safe for everyone concerned, or you can
cause trouble. In which case, a lot of people will die. Including
your wife," he added.

And now everything began to come together.

"I could kill you right now, Tusk," said Dion quietly.

"Yeah, I know," Tusk said, glancing around the room. "You
got all these fancy security devices, hidden lasguns and so
forth. What is it—one word and I'm a dead man?" He shook
his head. "But you won't."

"No, you're right, I won't," said Dion softly. "I couldn't.
That's why they chose you, isn't it?"

"Yeah," said Tusk with a brief, bitter laugh, "that's why they
chose me."

"Whose idea was it?"

"Sagan's."

Dion sighed. His shoulders slumped. He began to massage
his burning, aching right hand. "And Astarte? She's safe?"

"So far," Tusk said. "Kamil, too."

"Kamil!" Dion looked up swiftly. "How—? No! That's not possible. . . ."

"It is, kid," said Tusk, almost gently. "I know. I saw her. I . . . uh . . . talked to her."

"Dear God!" Dion murmured in agony. "What have I done? What have I done?"

He leaned against his desk for support, stared down unseeing at the objects on it. Then he focused on one of them. Smiling wanly, he reached out. . . .

"Steady," warned Tusk, moving a step closer.

"It's . . . nothing," said Dion. He picked up a small blue leather box. Flicking it open, he held it out for inspection. "You see? Nothing."

Tusk looked inside. A spasm of pain crossed his face. Keeping the gun aimed at Dion, he took the small eight-pointed star out of the box. He stared at the star; then, slowly, deliberately, he closed his hand over it.

"What a sucker I used to be."

He shoved the earring in his pocket.

"Come on, Your Majesty," he said harshly, waving the gun. "Quit stalling. And don't think I'm gonna get sentimental, either. What went down between us was a long time ago. Times have changed. So have you. So have I."

Dion shook his head. "It won't work, Tusk. I'm not going with you. I don't know what my cousin wants from me, but he won't get it. These men, my guards"—the king glanced toward the door—"are pledged to die—not for me, but for what I represent. I'm not just a person, Tusk. I'm the king."

Tusk grunted. "*They're* pledged to die for you; it comes with the job. But what about all these other people you got livin' in this mother castle? How many are there—a few hundred? And what about this city? Another coupla thousand? Men, women, little kids? They pledged to die for you?

"You heard about what happened to those military outposts? I give the signal and the same thing happens here, Your Majesty. Buildings squashed like some giant something stepped on 'em. Quakes that go clear off the damn scale. I've seen the 'ghosts' work, kid. I saw one of the outposts get hit. It's weird. Kind of spooky. The only sounds you hear are the screams of the dying."

"Ghosts?" said Dion.

"His Highness calls 'em strange dark-matter creatures. They

do his bidding. The blood that was spilled in the palace the night of the Revolution will be nothing compared to what the creatures will do if he unleashes them. And two of the bodies they'd find in the rubble will be your wife's and Kamil's."

"I don't have much choice, then, do I?" Dion said in quiet defeat. "What does my cousin want with me?"

"Family reunion, maybe," said Tusk. "I don't know. And I don't care. My job is to bring you. That's it."

"I can't just leave, disappear. . . ."

"You won't. You're going to Ceres, to be with your wife. A religious retreat. Give thanks for her 'escape from death.' We'll arrange a live broadcast to the galaxy once we're on board ship. And don't worry. You won't be gone long. A coupla days ought to wrap this business up.

"Now"—he motioned with the gun at the commlink—"tell your secretary you're leaving, coming with me for old time's sake. We'll use the back route, take the unmarked limo to the spaceport. You'll be doing the driving. Tell your chauffeur we won't be needing him today."

"You've done your homework, I see," said Dion, reaching for the commlink.

"Not me. Derek Sagan. I think he knows you better'n you know yourself, kid." Tusk grunted, gestured again. "Talk. And don't try anything fancy."

"D'argent, I'm . . . going to be out of the office for a while. I need some time to myself. Tusk and I are going to the spaceport to see the old Scimitar. Inform the Prime Minister that I'll meet with him tomorrow. And call off this evening's press conference."

"Very good, sir," came D'argent's cool voice. "And shall I reschedule your five o'clock appointment with Mr. Gold?"

Dion hesitated, glanced at Tusk.

The mercenary regarded him grimly.

"No," the king said, after a moment. "No. I will be back in time to meet with . . . Mr. Gold."

He ended the communication, straightened, stood up.

"What was that Gold business?" Tusk asked suspiciously. "Some type of code?"

"Yes. D'argent suspects something's wrong. He's highly intuitive. If I'd said to him 'Yes, reschedule'—"

"—the room'd be crawling with guards. Only they'd be dead

guards before long. This secretary won't do anything on his own, will he? Won't decide to be a hero?"

"No, D'argent obeys my commands. Besides, I've told him everything was all right."

Tusk continued to regard Dion with doubt. "I hope you're telling the truth. For all our sakes."

"Tusk—" Dion began.

Tusk glowered, frowned, motioned toward the hidden door. "Get movin', kid."

"You will address me as 'Your Majesty,'" Dion said.

"Yeah? Well, maybe not for long." Tusk's grin was stiff, like rigor mortis had set in. "I just found out what the word *usurper* means. Oh, and bring the bloodsword. His Highness's orders."

The secret panel slid open. The king, carrying the bloodsword, walked through it.

Tusk followed along closely behind.

Chapter ⊸⊶∘⊷⊶ Eight

God save the king! Will no man say, amen?
William Shakespeare, *Richard II*, Act IV, Scene i

Once on board the Scimitar, Tusk barely spoke to Dion. The mercenary spent most of his time flirting with his attractive co-pilot, introduced to the king as Captain Cynthia Zorn. XJ was also quiet and appeared to be in low spirits, an unusual condition for the loquacious and irascible computer. Tusk attributed this to the sustaining of a recent shock that had disrupted its systems.

The Scimitar had changed, too. The hard-fighting spaceplane now resembled a spacegoing motel. Dion recognized hardly anything about it, except the cockpit. And he wasn't allowed there.

He had little time to feel nostalgic for the old days, however. Safely out in deep space, certain that they were not being followed, the Scimitar joined up with a warship. Dion was received on board without either honor or ceremony. He was immediately escorted to a communications room. There he was handed a prepared script, which he was told to read as written. Any deviation and he would face reprisals of an unspecified nature.

He had no intention of rebelling. Giving the matter serious thought during his trip on the Scimitar, Dion decided that the best way was to go along with his cousin, make the required broadcast. To do anything else would start rumors flying, set the media wondering and speculating, and cause panic among major systems already unnerved by the supposed attempt on the queen's life. Dion could count on Admiral Dixter and the prime minister to deal with situations which might arise in the king's absence. Meanwhile, he would deal with this family matter.

A family matter. That was how he came to view it. An ugly, dark, insidious inheritance, bequeathed to him by his unfortunate uncle. The sins of the fathers, visited upon the heads of

400

the unsuspecting sons. This hadn't been Dion's fault, but it was now his responsibility. A family matter. He was the only one capable of dealing with his cousin.

"Capable . . ." Dion repeated with a twisted smile. He looked at his right hand, the inflamed scars. "He rages inside me, taunting, teasing, provoking, constantly probing my mind for its secrets. And what do I do in return? How do I affect him? A shadow on his mind, perhaps, nothing more than that. I can't do more!" Dion argued. "I can't focus on him."

The king stared at his reflection—a ghostlike image wavering in the steelglass, insubstantial and ephemeral against the cold blackness of space. "He slid into my mind through the cracks, through the self-doubts, the constant questioning, the inner turmoil. And he has none of these. His mind is honed and sharp and unflawed. It is a weapon he can use with skill and agility. Like a weapon, it lacks compassion. But what has compassion ever brought me," he questioned bitterly, "except sleepless nights?

"He is the epitome of the Blood Royal, the perfect ruler: soulless, uncaring, practical, fearless. He is what Sagan wanted me to be," Dion added with a grim, disparaging look at his pale, flat twin in the glass. "And my lord has apparently now found a king he can honor.

"But surely *you* don't honor my cousin, do you, Lady? He isn't what you meant for me to be." His voice softened. He thought of Maigrey, appearing to him in her silver armor, her hand upraised in warning. "Yet where are you? Why don't you come to me now, as you came to me once before? Surely this isn't what You want a king to be?" he asked of the impenetrable, eternal darkness. "Surely this isn't what You intend? Will You help me? Support my cause?"

He waited, listening for the still small voice within to bring comfort, reassurance.

Nothing. Silence.

"Very well," said Dion after a moment. He clenched his fist over the scarred and wounded palm. "This is a family matter, left for me . . . alone."

◦•◦⊂⊃◦•◦

Dion made his broadcast, told the people their king was going on a private religious retreat, assured them he would be gone for only a few days, asked for their prayers and their un-

derstanding. It was a good speech, touching, well written, and
sounded very much as though Dion had constructed it himself.
The cadence, the rhythm, the music of the words, the declama-
tion of a thought, all these might have been Dion's. But they
weren't. They were Flaim's.

Having never known any close blood relations, Dion had
never been forced to question what part of him was truly himself and what part he owed to genetics. He had always imagined, fondly, that he was a unique and singular creation. Now
suddenly he was confronted with the disquieting fact that perhaps he was merely one in a long, long line. . . .

When the broadcast was complete, the warship entered the
Lanes, made the Jump to Vallombrosa.

·-◄■)ɔ◯⊂■>·-

An armed guard escorted Dion from the warship to the fortress palace of the prince located on Vallombrosa. The king was
shown to his quarters—a suite of rooms located deep in the interior of the strange, labyrinthine building, which had no reason or logic to its design but appeared to have been scooped up
and thrown together by the children of giants.

His rooms were large and chill and sparsely furnished. His
door locked on the outside. Guards stood in front of it.

Dion was gazing bleakly at his uncomfortable surroundings
when the guard thrust open the door.

An elderly black man entered. He bowed politely, introduced
himself as Garth Pantha, the prince's aide and mentor. Pantha
was respectful, deferential, and asked Dion if he would be so
kind as to favor them with his presence before dinner.

"Your wife," Pantha added gravely, "is most anxious to see for
herself that you have arrived safely."

Dion replied coldly, "I will most assuredly come."

Pantha led him into a large, high-ceiling hall, with flagstone
floors, tapestry-covered stone walls. A huge fireplace stood at
one end; a roaring blaze gave light and warmth. The room
seemed filled with people.

Confused and slightly disoriented by his bizarre surroundings, Dion could not, for a moment, place any of them. He saw
disembodied heads and faces; eyes, familiar eyes, stranger's
eyes. No one spoke.

And then suddenly he was aware of Astarte's eyes, of Kamil's shining hair, of Sagan's face emerging from darkness, of Tusk turned sideways, not looking at him.

Walking toward Dion, moving with the same gait, the same grace, was his own shadow.

"Dion Starfire," said Flaim, gazing at him intently. "I am your cousin. We meet, at long last."

Ties of blood. A reminder of a father and a mother, of grandparents; an extension into the past, bringing forth the future. Not alone, not free-floating, but bound to past generations by an umbilical cord that might be cut, could never be severed.

A hunger that had been born with Dion, that he lived with all his life, was suddenly, strangely satisfied.

"My cousin," Flaim said in soft, tremulous tone.

He reached out his hands, grasped hold of Dion. It was obvious that Flaim was moved by similar emotions, obvious as well that such emotions were unexpected.

Leaning near, Flaim kissed Dion's cheek.

Dion accepted his cousin's kiss, not moving, not returning it, only staring.

"You are as I pictured you," continued Flaim, studying Dion with eager eyes. "Except taller. Yes, I had always thought of myself as being the taller of the two of us. Perhaps because I am the elder." He smiled, charming, ingratiating. The smile was his alone, had no part in the family bloodline. "But let me hear you speak, cousin. We even talk alike. I know, I've heard you on the vids. Don't you think so?"

"Yes," said Dion, dazzled and deeply troubled. "Yes, we talk . . . alike."

"Why, we might be brothers instead of cousins. I suppose that comes from the fact that my mother is also my aunt. But I am being selfish. I have other guests to consider, and I must share you with them. We will have more time, cousin, much more time, I hope, to get to know each other better. Her Gracious Majesty, the queen, has been much concerned about your safety."

Pale and composed, Astarte rose to meet Dion, made him a formal curtsy. Standing behind the queen, keeping to the background, was Kamil. She didn't look at him. By her flushed face and deprecating demeanor, she was wishing she could vanish and be forgotten, like the sparks of the fire going up the chimney.

Any meeting of these three was bound to be embarrassing,

awkward. Dion was aware of everyone's eyes watching him. He guessed that they must be laughing, mocking.

I deserve this, he thought, and it was this knowledge that impelled him to walk steadily forward. This is my punishment.

He went up to his wife, held out his hand to her, clasped her hand—small, white hand—in his.

"I trust you are well, madam. They haven't harmed you?"

"No, sire," she answered him coolly, and it hurt him to know that they met in this crisis as strangers.

The room was suddenly unbearably hot, the walls trembled and leaned in over him, the floor shivered beneath him. He turned to Kamil, barely aware of what he was doing or saying.

"Princess Olefsky"—it was the mirror image that spoke—"I hope you are well? You have not been harmed?"

Her close-cropped hair shone silver in the firelight, the golden eyes shimmered with tears. Dion was reminded of the first time he'd met her, of the first evening they'd spent together in her father's castle, the first night they'd known they loved each other. How long ago it seemed, and innocent—an innocence forever lost.

"Thank you, Your Majesty," Kamil murmured. "I am quite well."

Her face was flushed crimson. Dion could think of nothing else to say that wasn't saying too much. He turned back to his wife.

Astarte had not been watching. She had distanced herself, was staring off into another part of the room, as might a stranger suddenly thrust upon two close friends at a boring party. He took her hand again to regain her attention, but the touch was cold.

"Madam," he said, acutely aware he sounded artificial, reading again from a prepared script, "I am sorry about this, about all of this."

"You have nothing with which to reproach yourself, sire," said Astarte quietly. "This was not your doing."

But it was, and he did, and he knew he was looking less and less a king at the very moment he needed to be a king.

"I am your prisoner." Dion turned to Flaim. "Release Her Majesty and the princess. You don't need them any longer. Return them safely to their homes."

Flaim, smiling, stepped gracefully between the husband and wife. The prince took Astarte's hand in one of his, Dion's hand in the other. "I wouldn't think of it. Our family is all together now. We will not soon be separated, I hope. Please, everyone be seated. Cousin Dion."

Releasing their hands, Flaim drew up a chair for the king, close to the fire. "No one can sit down until you do, you know, cousin. Surely you won't keep us all standing?"

"What is it you want of me?" Dion demanded. He continued to stand, and though he was keeping his anger sheathed, he permitted a part of the sharp-honed blade to show. "End this ridiculous farce. You have brought me here by force. You have kidnapped my wife. You are a killer, a murderer. People died in the Temple of the Goddess; people died on those outposts you attacked. What is it you want?"

"Oh, excellent speech! Quite powerful." Flaim was enthused. "I must learn to emulate your style. No, no, dear cousin, I truly mean that. I have had so little contact with the public at large. I am too informal. I must learn to act the part of a king every waking minute. Well," he added, with a sly glance at Kamil, "perhaps not *every* minute."

Kamil flushed, turned her face away. Dion opened his mouth, realized that to speak would only make matters worse, kept silent.

"Come, come!" Flaim laughed disarmingly. "Don't be angry, cousin. We are all adults. Kings before you have had their mistresses. No one thought the worse of them for it. And if you insist on standing, cousin, why, then, we will all stand, though it is rather hard on the elder among us." He glanced at Pantha and at Derek Sagan. "And uncomfortable for your wife. She has been somewhat unwell."

"No, truly, I am fine," Astarte protested swiftly. She pushed herself upright. She had been leaning on the arm of the chair.

Dion, his jaw set, assisted his wife to be seated, then sat down himself, stiffly and rigidly. The rest of the company did likewise, with the exception of Sagan, who drifted farther back among the shadows, keeping watch over them, in Dion's mind, like his dark angel.

The same thought, or something similar, might have entered Flaim's head, for he suddenly rose to his feet again, looked directly into the back of the room. "Excuse me, cousin, but there is someone else I forgot to acknowledge. I am pleased you have joined us, my Lady Maigrey."

Dion started, stared. She wasn't there, of course. No one was there. That part of the room was empty. Dion was beginning to think his cousin was mad, when he saw Sagan's face, dark and thoughtful and brooding, saw the man's gaze stare with piercing intensity into the shadows, as if they were a veil and he might part them.

"You must forgive my prince," said Garth Pantha with an embarrassed laugh. "He fancies he is visited by a ghost."

"But I am. No fancy. Nor am I mad. Am I, cousin?" Flaim turned to Dion. "You've seen her, haven't you? Lord Sagan told me you had. You see, Pantha? I am not alone.

"I've heard her speak," Flaim continued. "Oh, not to me. She talks to herself, I think. Pantha is skeptical, but then, he is a scientist, which means he is skeptical by definition. I consider her visit a great honor. I didn't recognize her at first, for which I hope her ladyship forgives me," he added, bowing to the shadows. "But then I recalled where I had heard that voice. So distinctive, deep and low for a woman's.

"I am not certain why she has come, however. In whom does she take an interest? I like to think it is me, but perhaps I flatter myself unduly. You will, I trust, be so good as to include the Lady in your conversation."

Laughing, Flaim resumed his seat and whether he was laughing at them or at himself, Dion couldn't tell.

"What were we discussing?" Flaim glanced at Dion. "Yes, I recall. You were asking, I believe, cousin, what it was I wanted of you. Why, I want to be king. It is as simple as that. As the only heir of Amodius Starfire, who was anointed king when he died, the crown belongs rightfully to me, not the son of a younger brother."

"You are wrong. You have no claim," Dion answered calmly. "And you know it. You are illegitimate, born of an incestuous relationship. No one in this galaxy would recognize such a claim."

"When you put it like that, no," Flaim conceded, smiling ingenuously. "But, as I said, we are all adults. Adults are well aware their children are not prepared to understand and deal with certain harsh realties of life. Therefore we hide unpleasant truths from them. We tell small lies to keep their innocent trust in us intact. My mother was *not* the king's sister. My birth *was* legitimized. And you, dear cousin, are *not* having an illicit love affair with the daughter of an old friend."

Half-blinded by tears, Kamil rose, started to leave. Astarte caught hold of her.

"Stay, Kamil," said the queen. "Don't let him frighten you. He does not frighten me."

She kept fast hold of Kamil, who sank down in her chair. Wiping her tears away, she tried to look calm and self-possessed.

Dion's heart ached for her pain, though he did not dare show it. He was grateful to Astarte for maintaining not only her own dignity, but her husband's as well. Little as he deserved it.

"So you intend to blackmail me, is that it?" Dion asked.

"Such a harsh word." Flaim grimaced, shook his head. "An arrangement of mutual convenience to us both. Here is what will happen. You will acknowledge my claims publicly, peacefully abdicate the throne in my favor. And you will leave with your own reputation and honor unsullied, to live in peace with this wife . . . or another, if you so choose."

Dion shook his head. "I will not make such an arrangement. You will have no hold over me. I'll go public. I'll admit my disgrace—"

"And I will stand by him," said Astarte, clasping Kamil's hand even tighter. "The people will understand, as I do. My husband is guilty only of loving a woman most deserving of being loved. They will understand. Dion Starfire is king; he was meant to be king. He has heaven's mandate—"

"Does he?" Flaim interrupted, with a smile that was no longer charming. "Does Dion Starfire have heaven's mandate? Will you answer this for us, my Lord Sagan?"

Sagan stepped out of the shadows. He moved slowly, deliberately, his dark-eyed gaze fixed steadfastly on the king.

Dion watched, guarded, wary.

Sagan came to stand before him, looked down at him. "Your cousin, Flaim, took the same test you did. He did not blench, he did not tremble. He didn't bleed or nearly die. He caught the silver ball and crushed it. Who is the stronger? Which of you, do you suppose, does God intend to be king?"

"Which does He, my lord?" Dion asked quietly.

"Look into your heart," Sagan advised. "And know the truth."

"So much for heaven's mandate," said Flaim lightly. "God—it seems—has turned His back on you, cousin."

"As have my friends, apparently," said Dion, his gaze shifting from Sagan to Tusk.

Tusk was still not looking at him. Hunched forward, he stared moodily into the fire.

"Then I am alone," said Dion simply. "But the lion is alone, so you once told me, my lord. I will die alone, if need be, but I will die a king. I will not give you what you ask, cousin. I cannot believe God demands this sacrifice of me," he added, with a defiant glance at Sagan.

"He has demanded others as dear, Your Majesty," Sagan replied quietly.

Dion stared at him, suddenly thoughtful.

Flaim smiled expansively. "I must say I am quite impressed with you, cousin. I applaud your courage, your resolve. It speaks well of our family. However, since I don't believe in this God of yours, what He demands or does not demand means little to me. The rite proved to Lord Sagan that I have the strength and the ability to rule. I see I must spend the next few days proving myself to you, cousin Dion.

"You shake your head. You look doubtful. You don't think I can. I accept the challenge.

"But now"—Flaim slapped the arms of the chair, sprang jauntily to his feet—"you are tired. Your journey has been long and stressful, worried as you must have been about your wife. Now that you find her safe and sound, I am sure you are looking forward to getting some well-deserved sleep. We will continue our discussion tomorrow, and perhaps engage in a little light exercise, to keep us both in shape.

"You brought your bloodsword, I hope, cousin?"

Dion cast a swift glance at Sagan, saw the Warlord watching him intently, a flicker of fire in the depths of the otherwise dark, chill eyes.

"Yes," said Dion, his left hand going automatically to his right palm. He caught himself, clenched his fist. "Yes, I brought it. But—"

"Good." Flaim rubbed his hands together in expectation. "Excellent. I am like a child with a new playmate. Now, at last, I can quit sparring with my shadow.

"Your Majesty." Flaim bowed to Astarte, who had risen with cold dignity. "I trust you will spend a pleasant night. I am sorry that you and your husband must be quartered in separate bedrooms, but I find that the hours spent in solitary thought are the most productive. And I want you all to think a great deal. Pantha, would you escort our cousin back to his room?"

Dion had been hoping for some chance to talk privately with Astarte, but that was not to be allowed, apparently. There was nothing to do but make the best of it, go along. To do anything else would impair his dignity, do him more harm than good. He walked over to Astarte. Taking her hand in his, he brought her hand to his lips, kissed it gently.

"Don't worry, madam," he said to her softly. "Everything's going to be all right."

"Yes, sire," she said to him, smiling, if only to keep her lips from trembling, "I know it will be."

He smiled back, reassuring, released her hand. He would have said something to Kamil, but she was already hurrying out the door.

A part of him died then. A part that was young and hopeful and filled with golden dreams. A part that had once played, naked and free, in a blue lake on a distant world. No matter what happened now, he had lost her.

He was truly alone.

Chapter ❖❖❖ Nine

Night, the shadow of light,
And Life, the shadow of death.
Algernon Charles Swinburne, *Atlanta in Calydon*

"*Dead* of night," Tusk said to himself nervously, peering intently into the darkness. "What a stupid expression. I wonder who the bright person was who thought that one up."

He was standing irresolutely out in the hallway, his hand on the door handle, urging himself to shut it and get moving. But the hall was so intensely dark and so intensely silent, so intensely dead, that he lingered by the door, hanging on to the handle as something solid and real.

"It's all this talk about ghosts. I don't believe in ghosts. Any type of ghosts. Not even some weird dark-matter type of ghost," he said, but he said it quietly, and continued to peer nervously down the hall, continued to hang on to the door handle.

Staring down the empty hall, Tusk imagined the creatures roaming it. Maybe one was passing through him right now. Or maybe he might walk into one. He'd been told, by Garth Pantha, that the creatures could kill. *Not that they would mean to,* he'd assured Tusk. *Your death would be accidental.*

"But it'd be a little late to accept their apologies." He wiped away a trickle of cold sweat that was running down his neck, soaking his T-shirt. "Still, if they are spooking up the place, they could be in my bedroom, for all I know. My chances are as good out here as anywhere, I suppose."

Tusk made his decision, shut the door, and set out. He staggered as he walked. He had his story ready, in case the guards stopped him. Two swigs of jump-juice taken before the expedition had not only bolstered his courage but provided an authentic smell to his breath.

He was thankful he didn't have far to go and that he'd made this trip once before by daylight; otherwise he would have been hopelessly lost. Tusk didn't think much of the ghosts' no-

410

tion of architectural design. The alcazar could more aptly be described as a warren than a fortress. The hallways were like runs in burrows—winding, bending, slanting up, sloping down.

Tusk located his destination by counting doors and even then he wasn't certain he'd found the right one—all the doors in this place looked alike. He hesitated a moment before knocking, wishing he'd swallowed two bottles of jump-juice instead of two swigs. But he couldn't stand here long; his hesitation would look strange to anyone who was watching. Tusk banged on the door.

"Cynthia!" he bawled in a loud and drunken voice. "Lemme in! Itsh Tusk."

He heard footsteps, slow and heavy, cross the stone floor inside the room. Tusk's heart beat faster; his T-shirt was wringing wet. He gulped in a huge breath, was just about to bang on the door again, when it opened.

Lord Sagan stood framed in the doorway.

"Cynthia!" Tusk bawled again, then focused in on the tall, stern, glowering figure of the Warlord. "Cynthia?" He peered around Sagan. "You there?"

"You have the wrong room, Tusca," said the Warlord. "And what are you doing roaming the halls in this inebriated condition? I've told you before—"

Grabbing hold of Tusk's shirt, Sagan dragged the mercenary inside, slammed the door shut behind him.

"Yes, what is it?" Sagan demanded coldly.

"Can we talk?" Tusk glanced nervously around. "Is it safe?"

"The electronic surveillance devices in this room have, unfortunately, developed a malfunction, some type of distortion whose source cannot be located. Yes, it is safe to talk here. But make it fast and keep your voice down. The night watch saw you in the cameras located in the halls. They will be here any minute."

Tusk jammed his hands in his pockets. Shoulders hunched, he faced the Warlord. "I don't like this. We've got to do something."

"Unless I am mistaken, we *are* doing something," Sagan responded dryly. "And 'liking it' was never part of the deal."

Turning away, he walked to a desk, where he had set up a portable computer. He sat down, turned his attention to information that appeared on the screen. "If that's all, you may leave."

Tusk, growing a little angry, followed.

"It's not all. Not by a long shot. I got an idea," he said to Sagan's back. "Let's bust everyone outta here. Now. Tonight. You know where Dion's being held, and the queen—"

"They are in separate wings, as far apart as is physically possible," commented the Warlord. "Guards are posted at each door. The halls are under surveillance. The rooms are bugged. And then there are always the strange dark-matter creatures. Now, how do you propose we 'bust' everyone out?"

"There's a way," Tusk turned sullenly, pacing about the small, misshapen room. "There's always a way. Hell, you and the Lady got the kid off a Corasian mothership!"

Sagan was obviously not interested in reminiscing about the past. "You know the plan," he said coldly. "We stay with it."

"No, I don't know the goddam plan!" Tusk stated, coming around to face the Warlord's back again. "You won't tell me!"

"You know your part of it. That's all that is essential. I can always"—Sagan's voice hardened—"arrange for *you* to leave."

"You know I won't. Not while the kid's here. Not after *I* was the one who brought him here."

"Then we have nothing further to discuss. It is time you returned to your room. Your coming here was foolish to begin with."

"My getting involved in this whole fuckin' scheme was foolish to begin with! Look, my lord," he continued, more subdued, "let me at least tell Dion we're on his side—"

"No!" Sagan stood up, rounded on Tusk. The Warlord's expression was fey, chilling. "You will say nothing to him. Nothing."

Tusk fell back a pace, then halted, determined to hold his ground. "You saw Dion tonight! He thinks he's in this alone—"

"Precisely what I want him to think."

"What are you after? This isn't another goddam test, is it?" Tusk demanded. Anger was bolstering the jump-juice, which was bolstering his courage.

Sagan smiled, thin-lipped, dark and bitter. "You might say it is. Though not necessarily Dion's."

Tusk didn't understand. Shaking his head in disgust, he started for the door, "I'm gonna tell him—"

"How like your father you are," Lord Sagan said, sneering. The remark was obviously not meant as a compliment.

Hot blood rushed to Tusk's head. He whipped back around, hands clenched. "You bastard! How dare—"

He made a jab with his fist.

A hand like steel-toothed jaws snapped over his, crushing, sobering.

"Keep your voice down. And listen to me. By telling Dion we are here to help him, you tell Flaim. It is that simple. Tomorrow, Flaim will convince Dion to use the bloodsword—"

"He won't," Tusk mumbled, wincing, "The kid knows better—"

"He may have no choice," Sagan interrupted grimly. "And when Dion inserts the needles of the bloodsword into his hand, Flaim will insert his mind into Dion's. The two will be irrevocably linked. Dion would reveal us. He couldn't help himself. Our lives—yours and mine—would be forfeit. And then the king would be very truly alone. Now, do you still want to tell him?"

Tusk stood speechless. The hot blood of fury was draining rapidly from his head, leaving him sick and chill.

Seeing he had calmed down, Sagan released his hold on him. "Are you gonna try to help Dion tomorrow, then?" Tusk demanded. "Keep him from using the sword?"

"I will do what I have to do," Sagan answered. "And I will expect you to do the same."

Tusk eyed him bitterly, nursed his bruised and aching hand. "You calculating son of a bitch. I don't have any choice, do I? You got me good. At least you think you do. But I'll be watching you. Remember that. I'll be watching!"

Yanking open the door, Tusk came face-to-face with a guard.

"Is everything all right, my lord Sagan?" asked the guard. "We received a report that a man was wandering the halls, creating a disturbance—"

"He's drunk, that's all." Sagan gave Tusk a shove that sent him staggering into the guard's arms. "He came here in a jealous rage. See to it that he gets back to his room safely."

"Yes, my lord," said the guard.

Sagan slammed shut the door.

The guard assisted Tusk to his feet, accompanied him back to his room.

Yeah, thought Tusk, lying on his bed, staring bleakly into the darkness, I'm sure keeping my eyes on you. . . .

Kamil lay in her bed in the dark in the dead of the night. She was wrapped in her blanket. Her knees were drawn up to her chest, her arms wrapped around the hard and lumpy pillow. Her thoughts were fixed on one idea.

If only I could talk to Dion alone for just a few moments. It would all be so easy. . . .

"I've been looking at this all wrong. Tusk did Dion a favor, bringing him here. Why couldn't I see that before? I'll find a way to talk with him tomorrow. There has to be a way—"

"Are you awake?" asked Astarte softly.

Kamil flinched, frowned. She'd been keeping as still as possible, pretending she was asleep. But she must have spoken her thoughts aloud, or at least whispered them. Should she keep silent? Or answer?

Her muscles were stiff and cramped from lying in one position. She turned over on her back.

"I'm sorry. I didn't mean to wake you."

"You didn't," Astarte replied. "I've been lying here awake a long time."

"You should try to sleep," Kamil said tersely. "You'll end up making yourself sick."

"I've been praying for Dion."

"Well, you should be sleeping," Kamil snapped. "Both for your sake and the baby's."

"Don't coddle me, Kamil. Pregnancy doesn't make a woman weak and fragile. My people believe pregnancy makes a woman strong. After all, you lock a precious jewel in a strongbox, not a delicate glass case. My mother had armor specially designed for her to wear to battle when she was pregnant.

"Back in the early days, the women of Ceres had to go on with their lives, you see," Astarte explained. "We had no choice. Grain had to be harvested, shelters built, towns defended. The men were too valuable to risk losing. New life is a great gift, but the universe does not come to a halt because one woman is going to have a child."

"Not even a royal child," Kamil muttered. She knew she sounded bitter, vindictive, but she couldn't help herself.

"Not even then," said Astarte softly.

Kamil sat up in bed. Fumbling for the matches, she lit the candle by her bedside. The room the women shared was like every other room in the alcazar, stone walls and floor and ceiling, no windows, a heavy oaken door. Woven mats spread over

the floors and walls did little to either cheer the room or alleviate the chill. Climbing out of bed, shivering, Kamil padded
over to poke at the glowering coals in the fireplace.

"You're being awfully casual about this pregnancy." She
spoke almost accusingly. "You want this baby. More than anything in your life, you want this child. And you're lying there
praying!"

"What would you have me do?" Astarte asked, sitting up.
"When there is a need and a time for action, one takes action.
When there is not a need or when one is incapable of taking
action, one has patience . . . and faith."

Her words were confident, but she sighed as she said them.
Taking up the candle, Kamil walked over to stand at the foot of
Astarte's bed.

"You're not as cool about this as you'd like me to believe. Or
you'd like yourself to believe."

"The failing is mine, then," said Astarte. "I'm afraid, Kamil.
Afraid for Dion . . . afraid for my child. The Goddess sent me
a vision the night the baby was conceived. In my vision, Dion
and I were making love. I saw Dion's face . . . at the moment
of conception. And then he disappeared. All was dark, and then
I saw another face. It hung over me and leered at me."

Kamil perched gingerly on the edge of the bed, placed the
candle on the floor.

"What does that mean?" she asked harshly. The thought of
the two of them . . . together . . . twisted her up inside. "That
Dion isn't the father?"

"Oh, he's the father," Astarte replied in a calm, passionless
voice.

"Then I don't understand," Kamil said irritably.

"I don't either." Astarte lifted her lovely eyes. "The face of
the other man was the face of Dion's cousin—Flaim."

Kamil stared at her in perplexity. "How could it? You'd never
seen him—"

"I didn't know who the man was. Now I do. This vision was
the reason I left Dion," Astarte continued. "I had to get away.
I had to open myself to the Goddess, rid myself of any distract-
ing thoughts or feelings. I hoped she would make the vision
clear. At least now I can put a name to the stranger's face." She
shivered.

Kamil almost said something, stammered, fell silent.

She couldn't believe she was thinking what she was thinking.

If I'd been listening to this tale of visions and faces in dreams in broad daylight, I would have laughed at myself for taking what Astarte says seriously. It was a dream she had—nothing more.

But here, in this eerie, cold, dark room of stone, lit only by the light of a dying fire and a candle, trapped, afraid for myself and for Dion—for him more than myself, it is suddenly very easy to believe.

And Kamil wanted most desperately to believe.

"What?" Astarte pressed her. "Do you have an idea?"

"Maybe the Goddess is trying to tell you that there is a way out of this. All Dion has to do is give up the crown. Abdicate. You have what you want from him. He's given you a baby. Flaim can have what he wants—to be king."

"And would he be a good one, do you think?" Astarte asked, frowning. "After what he did to us? To my people? A man who resorts to murder, abduction—"

"He did that out of necessity," Kamil argued. "Rulers have to do things that they don't like sometimes. Read Machiavelli. Dion has. Rulers have to be ruthless sometimes."

"Do they? Is Dion ruthless?" Astarte asked softly.

"No, he isn't," said Kamil, triumphant, "and that's why he suffers so. What Lord Sagan said tonight, about the test, makes sense. Which of the cousins proved strongest? Flaim did. Dion isn't really suited to being a king. He takes everyone's burdens on himself. He worries about people. He tries to reason with them when he should be firm, tell them right out what to do and what not to do. And then make them do it."

"It seems to me you have described a very good ruler, albeit"—Astarte sighed—"an unhappy man."

"There, you see." Kamil tried to convince herself.

"Dion has been a good king," Astarte pursued. "He has tried to bring peace, order, stability to the galaxy and, for the most part, he has succeeded."

"He has succeeded," Kamil repeated bitterly. "And look what it's done for him!"

She picked up the candle and stalked angrily back to her bed. Blowing out the flame, she set the candle down on the bedstand with a sharp clatter, then crawled into the covers and crouched beneath them like a cornered animal, wanting to leap and rend and tear.

"Why don't you hate me, Astarte?" Kamil demanded suddenly. "It would be easier. . . ."

"So you could hate me back? I don't hate you, but I do envy you, if that's any comfort." Astarte slid down among her sheets.

"*You* envy me," Kamil repeated, scoffing.

"Yes, envy. Tell me"—Astarte's voice was altered, tight, sad—"tell me how you love Dion."

Kamil was at first startled, then offended, then suspicious. But then she thought angrily, Why not?

"All right. I'll tell you. When I hold him in my arms, I'm jealous of the very flesh and bones of him that get in my way. I want to gather him, all of him, inside me and keep him there forever. And when he's inside me, I want to flow over him, seep inside him, become the blood that nourishes him, the air that sustains him. This is how I love him. I care about him. Only him. He's all that matters to me. I don't care about any of the rest."

"Do you see now why I envy you?" Astarte asked.

Neither said anything more. Neither realized she had said too much.

⋯⊰⋅⊱◯⊰⋅⊱⋯

Two men sat in a brightly lit room in the dead of night, listening.

"There you have it, my friend!" cried Flaim triumphantly. Leaning back in his chair, he smiled at Garth Pantha. "Problem solved. A royal heir. With my face. Prefabricated, so to speak. No fuss, no bother. Her Majesty is pregnant. What truly remarkable luck. I would be a fool not to take advantage of it."

"By doing what, my prince?"

"By altering my plans slightly. I must marry her, of course."

"Of course." Pantha shrugged. "Which presumes she does not already have a husband."

"Of course."

"Which presumes that blood is *not* thicker than water."

"When my cousin's blood is spilled," Flaim, said, smiling, "I will provide you with a sample for analysis."

Pantha grunted. "Tusca went to visit Sagan tonight."

"I am aware of that. He was drunk."

"Tusca's clever."

"Not clever enough to keep himself out of Sagan's clutches. Perhaps Tusca has reconsidered, wants to toss in his hand. If he ever wants to see *his* wife and child again, he knows he'd better keep his money in the game."

"Has that electronic malfunction in the Warlord's room been cleared up?"

"No, my friend, nor will it be." Flaim laid a soothing hand on Pantha's thin shoulder. "It is Sagan's doing, of course."

"If he had nothing to hide, he would not bother!" Pantha said testily.

"What do *you* have to hide, then, my friend?" Flaim asked, teasing. "Is the equipment in *your* room functional?"

"You are being flippant," Pantha rebuked, stern and displeased. "The matter is serious—"

"I am aware of that," Flaim returned. A flash of cold steel in the voice silenced the older man. "Tomorrow will be the test. Sagan will prove his loyalty to me tomorrow. Once my cousin Dion lays his hand upon the bloodsword, he is finished. Sagan knows this, and if he tries in any way to dissuade him . . ." Flaim shrugged.

Pantha shook his head, unconvinced.

"You will see, my friend. You will see. Sagan is mine. And now let us leave this darkness to our Lady-friend, if she is here, and make our way to our beds."

Flaim made a graceful bow to the shadows and left the surveillance room and the night to the dead.

Chapter ·••◦◦◦•· Ten

Two stars keep not their motion in one sphere ...
William Shakespeare, *King Henry VI*, Part One, Act V,
Scene iv

At midday, Vallombrosa's double sun hung directly over the alcazar. The sky was cloudless, as if sucked dry by the heat. The suns—one yellow and large, the other small and red— glared on Vallombrosa with a perpetual, leering squint. Arms of flames, red and yellow, swirled from one sun to the other, disembodied hands, holding floating eyeballs.

The suns had reached their zenith, stared down upon a large courtyard located in the center of the alcazar. Built roughly along the lines of a quadrangle surrounded by tall, bleached-bone-colored stone walls, the courtyard was open to the air and was the alcazar's recreation area.

Black streaks on the walls marked where hard rubber balls had bounced. Lines in the gravel drew the crude boundaries for some sort of game. Rows of wooden benches, for the convenience of spectators, sheltered beneath an overhang, huddled in the shadows.

But there were few shadows today. The suns, directly overhead, bathed the arena in hot, harsh light that reflected with blinding brilliance off the hard-packed playing field, the bleached white walls. The heat was not oppressive, for the air was cold, the suns warmed the grounds pleasantly. But Sagan blinked in the bright light when he emerged with the prince from the building's dark interior, pulled his cowl over his head.

Flaim was charming. He might have been leading his guests onto the lawn of a manor house to play at croquet until tea time. He was particularly attentive to Astarte. The prince led the queen by the hand (with the utmost deference and respect) to a bench in a far corner, one of the few shaded areas in the quad. He fussed over her comfort, ordered cushions brought to ease the hardness of the bench's wooden surface, and offered

419

refreshments. All of his attentions were politely and chillingly declined.

Baroness DiLunda had always openly despised this priestess daughter of hers, considering her soft and weak. Sagan, watching Astarte maintain her dignity and composure in this seemingly hopeless and dangerous situation, would have advised the baroness to reconsider her assessment.

Kamil sat down beside the queen. Sagan had not, until now, met Olefsky's daughter, Maigrey's godchild. He eyed the slender, boyish woman with a feeling of relief. He had steeled himself to see in her a resemblance to Maigrey, if not in form (which would have been unlikely) then in spirit. He looked for Maigrey's brash, reckless courage, her fierce pride and love of honor, all tempered by the glimmer of laughter in the sea-gray eyes.

This girl (Sagan thought of her as a girl, though Kamil must be near twenty-one) might yet come by such qualities. But she didn't possess them now. Or if she did, they had been consumed by love, whose fire, out of control, often consumed what gave it life. Kamil appeared to have little interest in what was going on. Her eyes and attention were only for Dion, fixed on him alone. Sagan knew Maigrey was present; he could hear the faint music of the sad, sweet chord vibrating in the still air. He wondered what she thought of this goddaughter.

Sagan turned his glance away from Kamil. He was glad to feel nothing. It would make things easier, later on.

Pantha came into the courtyard, carrying with him a large wooden box. He spoke a few quiet words to Flaim—who was continuing to make various attempts to try to talk to the haughty queen. The old man took his seat in the sunlight, basking in it like an elderly cat. He placed the box on the bench beside him.

Dion entered last, accompanied by Tusk. The mercenary was sullen and silent and had one hand wrapped up in a bandage.

"I bumped into a wall," he muttered in response to Flaim's question.

The prince turned back to the queen, and so missed Tusk's glowering gaze shift to Sagan.

The Warlord's jaw set. Tusk was going to be a problem. But he was a problem that could be dealt with, when the time came.

Sagan, clad in the stiff folds of a black cassock, walked across the courtyard and stood with his back to the wall, feet planted wide apart, his hands clasped behind his back, his face hidden in the shadows of his cowl. He closed his eyes against the sun's glare, retreated deep into himself, dragged into the depths of his soul all inconvenient and dangerous thoughts and feelings, locked them away and shut heavy doors of discipline and resolve upon them. Though he himself would not handle a bloodsword, the two using them would be acutely sensitive to each other and, Sagan guessed, one of them, at least, would try to probe his mind as well.

What he found there would be exactly what Sagan wanted him to find.

"Quite a merry party, eh, cousin?" Flaim was commenting to Dion when the Warlord returned to the level of upper consciousness.

The prince had left the queen and was strolling forward to stand near Dion. Flaim was wearing tight leather pants, tall black boots, and a white shirt with long flowing sleeves and an open V-neck, of a style popular with duelists in vids. "That will be all for now, Tusca, thank you. Would you like to stay and watch? Perhaps you'd care to join Pantha. . . ."

Sagan caught Tusk's eye, made a brief movement with his head. The mercenary gave some mumbled excuse, lounged over to post himself beside Sagan. Crossing his arms, Tusk leaned back against the wall. The mercenary's eyes were red and puffy and he blinked them constantly against the light.

One good thing about Tusca, Sagan remarked to himself with satisfaction, he doesn't look in the least dangerous.

"And now, cousin," Flaim resumed, smiling at Dion, who hadn't spoken a word, "we will take a little light exercise, for the amusement of ourselves and our guests. You have no idea how long I have been looking forward to this. Being forced to practice day in and day out with one's shadow is incredibly dull. How I have longed for a partner to test my skills! Pantha, my friend, if you would be so kind . . ."

Pantha rose to his feet. Opening the box, he drew out the two bloodswords and brought them forward. Flaim, meanwhile, was scraping out a circle on the hard pavement with the heel of his boot.

"Not precisely accurate, but good enough for our purposes. This is not a formal duel, after all, but only a friendly practice session. I believe that is close to the correct diameter, my lord?" He turned deferentially to Sagan.

"Near enough, Your Highness," said Sagan, who had barely glanced at it.

Flaim lifted his bloodsword—the sword that had once been Pantha's—from the box. The two bloodswords were almost identical in appearance, except that one—Dion's—was decorated with the engraving of an eight-pointed star, signifying that it had once belonged to a Guardian.

Dion reached out his hand and took hold of his sword, being careful to keep the needles clear of his flesh. He held it a moment, studied it carefully, as if making certain it was truly his. Then, moving slowly and deliberately, he replaced the sword in the box.

Pantha looked questioningly at Flaim. The prince shrugged, gestured. Pantha set the box down on the ground between the two men, went back to his seat.

Flaim buckled his sword around his waist, cast the circle a critical glance once again, walked about it experimentally, peered up at the suns, as if to determine how the light would affect him, then looked back at his cousin.

Dion stood calmly, relaxed, made no motion to retrieve his sword.

Flaim studied his cousin with interest. The prince had not expected such a response, apparently, seemed not quite certain what to make of it. Shrugging again, he smiled again, squinting in the sunlight, and inserted the needles of the sword into his hand. He winced a bit, caught his breath; the pain is intense, but quickly over—for those who are meant by genetic design to use the swords.

For those who are not, it can kill.

"Surely you will try a few passes with me, cousin," Flaim urged. His face reflected the warm and tingling sensation that comes after the pain, when the micromachines are surging into the bloodstream, connecting the weapon with the brain, making it another limb, respondent to the brain's command.

"No," replied Dion.

"Oh, come, come," Flaim pleaded, still charming. "We need not even bother with the rules, if you don't want. A couple of passes . . . to get the blood flowing."

He activated the sword as he spoke the words. The hot blade

flared, hummed, loud and discordant in the still air. Swift as thought, Flaim slashed the fiery blade past Dion.

Dion fell back, stumbling, averting his face or the sword would have blinded him.

As it was, the blade scorched his skin. Everyone in the silent courtyard heard the sizzle, smelled the burning flesh.

Kamil gasped and started to jump to her feet. Astarte caught hold of the girl's wrist, pulled her down.

Tusk shifted his weight, uncrossed his arms, jammed his hands into his pockets. He glanced over at Sagan, who was very careful to take no notice.

Flaim shook his head in concern. "I am deeply sorry, cousin. Forgive me. I didn't mean to hurt you. Just provoke you a bit. Come, this is poor sport! Pick up your sword."

Dion brought the back of his hand to his injured cheek, glanced at the blood on his fingers.

"I will not fight you, cousin. If you are going to kill me, then you must do it in cold blood." Dion looked at Sagan as he spoke, perhaps thinking back to a time when the Warlord had said almost those very same words to him.

Sagan permitted the memory to enter his mind; it might prove useful. But any emotions attached to it were stripped away, leaving it skeletal, bare.

"Kill you? Yes, cousin, I could kill you. I could slay you where you stand." Flaim spoke impatiently. He lowered the bloodsword; then, abruptly, he switched the sword off. "But I don't want to. Your death would serve no purpose. It would be a waste."

Reaching out with the warm, strong, persuasive clasp of an elder, wiser, more knowledgeable brother, he embraced Dion, drew him near.

"Abdicate the throne, cousin. Give me the crown. We both know I am the worthier of the two. Give me the trouble, the crushing responsibility. Give me the sleepless nights, the lonely days. I am the stronger. I will bear the burden. You have only to live the rest of your life in peace"—he glanced obliquely at Kamil—"with one who loves you."

Dion's brows drew low over the blue eyes; his lips parted, as though he would answer. Flaim gripped him tighter, moved nearer, forestalled him.

"You have much to live for. More than you might think. Did you know, cousin, that your wife is pregnant? Yes, she bears your child. No trick, cousin. Look at her. You will see the truth."

Dion was astounded. Involuntarily, he turned his head to look at his wife.

Astarte knew, though she could not possibly have heard, what Flaim had just said to her husband. And at that moment, the queen's composure failed her. The blood mounted to her face, staining it crimson, then fled, making her deathly pale by contrast. She opened her mouth, but no words came out.

Beside her, Kamil sat rigid, flushed, her head bowed, unable to look at Dion, unable to see anything else.

Dion sighed, a sigh that seemed to come from the echoing empty well of the past three years.

"I will make you a deal, cousin," said Flaim softly. He spoke in Dion's ear, but the flow of the Blood Royal through both their veins and through the bloodsword brought his words to Derek Sagan. "Give me the throne and I will make your child heir. I swear it. I will swear to it in public, sign papers, whatever you would have me do. I can't father children of my own, you see."

Dion shook his head.

"Listen, cousin." Flaim's voice altered subtly, became softly lethal. "I would seriously consider this offer if I were you. Because either way I will have what I want. If I must kill you and marry the grieving widow, I will. She won't marry me, you say? Oh, yes. She'll have no choice. Not if she wants her child to be king! Come, cousin! Give me the crown! Don't make me kill you!"

Dion lifted the blue eyes, looked into the blue eyes that must have been like looking into his own reflection. "No."

Flaim glared at him, the prince's blue eyes flaring with thwarted desire. He dropped his hand from Dion's arm and, turning, paced once about the courtyard, his expression dark and frowning.

"Then I have no choice," he said, but he spoke reluctantly and he did not look at Dion as he said the words.

Suddenly, struck by an idea, he turned on his heel, faced the king.

"I tell you what, cousin. We will settle this as princes of the blood settled such disputes a thousand years ago. We will fight for the right to wear the crown. The victor takes the throne. What do you say to this? Who knows?" Flaim laughed lightly.

"*You* might kill *me*. And then all your problems would be solved."

Dion was tempted. Sagan could see the temptation in his face, feel it in the young man's heart. The king hesitated, considering.

No one in the courtyard spoke. The only sound was the distant echo of music, now troubled and played in a minor key, and the faint rustle of the stiff folds of Sagan's cassock.

Dion glanced again in the Warlord's direction. Sagan said nothing, either aloud or silently through the blood. But Dion must have heard anyway. Or perhaps he had finally learned to listen to his heart, as Sagan had advised him.

"I will not hazard what is not mine to wager. I am the rightful king. I believe I was destined to be king." He glanced again at Sagan; this time his gaze was troubled. "Though some might dispute it. I will not fight."

Flaim was frustrated, more than angry. Scratching his head, he took another turn about the courtyard, then came to stand in front of Sagan.

"My lord, how is this to be resolved, short of murder? Have you any suggestion?"

"I do, Your Highness," said Sagan smoothly. His shadowed eyes did not leave Dion, even to look at the prince, to whom he spoke. "In the ancient days, to which you referred, a king might name a champion to fight in his stead."

"A champion," said Flaim, appearing to consider, but his voice took on a cool note. "I trust your lordship is not offering himself . . ."

"No, Highness," said Sagan, bowing. "My vows prohibit me from bearing arms. But there is one who would be honored, I believe, to fight for the king's cause." His gaze shifted from Dion and went across the courtyard to Kamil.

Flaim had not expected this. He was suspicious, dubious. Then, suddenly, he grinned broadly.

"Well done, my lord," he said softly beneath his breath, with a chuckle.

Turning on his heel, he walked over to the box, which lay at the king's feet. Flaim grasped hold of Dion's bloodsword, lifted it out of the box—taking care not to touch the five sharp needles.

"Tusca, bring forth the king's champion," he ordered.

Tusk jerked bolt upright, gawked. "What?"

"Bring forth the king's champion!" Flaim instructed him, somewhat impatiently.

"You've all gone nuts," Tusk said in disgust, and leaned back against the wall.

"Do it!" Sagan shot out of the corner of his mouth.

"Do what?" Tusk scowled at him. "Rush out and polish up my plate mail? Come back with my two-handed broadsword? This is the stupidest—"

Sagan left the wall against which he'd been standing. Ignoring Tusk, the Warlord stalked over to Kamil, who was staring in confusion, not understanding. Well, she soon would. It would be interesting to see how she reacted. He hoped, for Maigrey's sake, she would accord herself bravely.

Sagan grabbed hold of Kamil's right wrist.

Astarte clasped hold of the girl's other arm protectively, glared at the Warlord with a bold defiance that would have done her warrior mother credit.

"Let her go!" she demanded.

"Do not interfere, Your Majesty," Sagan told her coldly.

He stared at the queen, exerting the influence of the Blood Royal over her. Astarte paled; her hand slid limply away.

Sagan yanked Kamil to her feet. The girl stumbled, and held back; he was forced to drag her over to Flaim. Grasping Kamil firmly around her shoulders with his left arm, Sagan took hold of her right arm, thrust forward her right hand, palm up.

"Give her the weapon, Your Highness."

Flaim held the needles of the bloodsword poised above Kamil's flesh and looked questioningly at Dion.

Behind him, Sagan heard Tusk surging forward. "Are you mad? Do you know what that'll do to her? It'll kill her! You bastard! I didn't agree to—"

Sagan shifted his hold on Kamil, struck Tusk a backhanded blow against the side of his head.

Tusk hit the ground, as if he'd been felled by lightning. Shaking his head, he made a feeble effort to get up. Blood dripped from his mouth. He groaned, collapsed, lay still. Sagan paid no further attention to him.

Flaim was holding Kamil's hand firmly, forcing the palm open by pressing down on the thumb joint, bending the wrist. The girl gasped from the pain, but did not cry out. She didn't struggle, knowing it would be ineffectual against the strength of the Warlord. She stared in terrible fascination at the needles, glittering in the light of the double suns, at the strange double shadows they cast over her flesh.

Does she know what terrible death she faces? Sagan wondered curiously.

Yes, she knows. She lifted her eyes and looked at Dion.

He had gone white, so pale it seemed he might have died where he stood. No color at all was left in him, except the flaming hair. Wet with sweat, his hair trailed down over his face like rivulets of blood. He stared at the needles and at Kamil's hand, and he breathed suddenly, very hard and heavily.

"I saw Marcus die," he whispered.

"Not by the bloodsword," Sagan returned. "You saw him die swiftly, mercifully, by your own hand. And he was in the early stages of the disease, before the cancer had spread like poison through the body. Three days he would have lingered; no drugs to ease his terribly agony. Of all the deaths a man can die, this death is said to be the worst. A man . . . or a woman."

Flaim forced Kamil's hand nearer the sharp needles. She flinched, and Sagan felt her shudder in his grasp, but she still did not cry out. She averted her face from the sight of the deadly needles, or perhaps to keep from influencing Dion, keep him from seeing the fear she couldn't help but feel.

Sagan was pleased with the girl's courage . . . for Maigrey's sake.

"What will it be, cousin?" Flaim demanded. "Will *you* fight for your crown? Or will she?"

Dion stared at Sagan, a searching look. The Warlord felt the mental probe, was careful to keep all inner doors sealed, shuttered, barred. He assumed he had done so, was somewhat surprised and considerably displeased to see a faint flicker of light in the despairing blue eyes. It was gone swiftly. The eyes dimmed, looked away. Then, as if he'd found the answer to his unspoken question, the king reached out and snatched the bloodsword from Flaim's grasp.

Dion thrust the needles into his own hand. The spasm of pain that crossed his face was only partly caused by the needles entering his flesh. The more bitter pain came—as was obvious from the last, dark glance he cast at Sagan—from betrayal.

The Warlord released his hold on Kamil abruptly, with little care. Weak and trembling, now that the danger was past, the girl staggered and nearly fell. It was Flaim who gallantly caught hold of her, led her back to her bench with a few soothing words of apology. She only shook her head, availing herself of his support because it was either that or fall down on her hands and knees.

Astarte received her gently, drew her down on the bench, said something to her that no one else could hear. Kamil shook her head and pulled away. Slumped against the wall, huddled on the bench, she stared bleakly at the ground.

Because of me. Her lips formed the words. *Because of me.*

Girlish innocence had apparently come to a swift and painful end.

Tusk, groaning, was regaining consciousness. The Warlord bent down, grasped the mercenary by the combat vest he wore, and dragged him out of the sun into the meager shade of a wall.

"You bastard . . ." Tusk mumbled through split and swollen lips.

"I had no choice. You nearly got us all killed," Sagan said softly, coldly, talking under cover of the sound made by Tusk's body scraping across the courtyard. "One more stupid stunt like that and I will have no choice but to destroy you."

Tusk started to say something.

"Shut up," Sagan told him.

Yanking the mercenary to a seated position, the Warlord shoved him back against the wall. Tusk caught himself, barely saved himself from falling. Propping himself up, he rubbed his jaw, spit out a tooth, and groaned again.

Flaim walked jauntily back to the circle. He appeared inordinately pleased, was sweeping the bloodsword this way and that, loosening up his arm.

"Perhaps, my lord, you would go over the rules of combat. For my sake," he added, with an apologetic smile for Dion. "Since I have never been privileged enough to witness a duel, as has my cousin."

Again the memories. The duel: Sagan and Maigrey. And he knew he wasn't the only one who was remembering, for he heard the music, faintly sweet and sorrowful.

"Combat must take place within the circle," intoned the Warlord, speaking coolly, impassively, sinking memory deep. "A combatant may step outside the circle to rest. The other may not pursue him. Two rest periods are permitted. Then it is a fight to the finish. If a combatant steps outside the circle after the two rest periods, he is deemed to have surrendered and therefore lost the match."

The Warlord said this last offhand, with a slight curl of the lip. Surrender might exist in the rule book, but it was an option never seriously considered.

Flaim stepped into the circle. His face was flushed with excitement and exhilaration. Dion did not enter the circle yet. He was still pale, still shaken from the confrontation over Kamil. He glanced at her once or twice, worried, to see if she was all right.

"The kid better concentrate on what he's doing," came a muttered voice at Sagan's shoulder.

Tusk had pulled himself to a standing position, was slouched against the wall at the Warlord's side.

"Never did understand how those damn swords worked," Tusk continued casually, too casually. "Dad tried to explain it once, but, hell, what did I care? You mind going over it now?"

"Why?" Sagan asked dryly, his gaze fixed on Dion. "You thinking of using one?"

Tusk shrugged. "A guy never knows when information like that might come in handy."

Sagan was glad the folds of the cowl hid his smile. "When the swordsman grasps the hilt, those five prongs inject a virus into the bloodstream. In the Blood Royal—someone with the correct blood type and DNA structure—the virus opens channels that parallel the normal nerve channels and eventually reach the brain. Micromachines are injected, making connection with the body's lymphatic systems to draw energy from the body's cells to power the weapon. The energy comes from adenosine tri—"

"Skip the science lecture," Tusk interrupted, scowling. "My head aches enough as it is. I thought the damn thing had its own external energy source."

"It does, but once that is depleted, the sword draws on the body's energy."

"Uh-huh." Tusk faced him, dark eyes red-rimmed, one of them starting to swell shut. "I know what happens if someone who isn't Blood Royal uses it. What about me? Half-and-half."

Sagan shook his head. "I can't say. No studies were ever done that I know of. Half-breeds weren't considered of much importance. I wouldn't advise it, however," he added quietly. "You would probably be able to use it, though not very well.

And you would risk contracting the disease. Only in a mild form. . . ."

"I might live for months, eh?" Tusk asked with interest.

"If you were lucky," Sagan replied. "If not, you might last for years."

Tusk regarded the Warlord thoughtfully, probably trying to decide if he was bluffing or telling the truth. The mercenary jammed his hands back in his pockets, gloomily hunched his shoulders, and turned his attention to the duel.

Dion had at last pulled himself together. Now that he was forced to take this action, he must know that he would have to kill his cousin. Kill . . . to keep from being killed.

Both bloodswords activated. The thoughts of each cousin rushed into Sagan, ran through him, mingled with his own thoughts in a boiling confusion as difficult to separate as it would be to separate the mingled strains of blood.

He had to be careful, very, very careful. Fortunately, the two were concentrating heavily on each other, would pay little attention to him—a broken old man. He settled back to watch the duel.

The two saluted each other; Flaim bowed, as ritual demanded. Dion, however, merely inclined his head. A king still. Each assumed the correct stance, blades burning. Blue flame held blue flame, blue eyes held blue eyes. The thoughts were already probing, though the swords were still. Then Dion lunged; Flaim parried, and the battle began.

The two are evenly matched, Sagan decided after the first few moments. Advantages, disadvantages canceled each other out. Dion had the advantage of having sparred against a living, breathing, thinking opponent (Sagan himself had been the young man's tutor), whereas Flaim had only fought against his own imagination. But Dion, busy and preoccupied with the cares of kingship, was out of practice. He had not used the bloodsword in action in years. Flaim, by contrast, had practiced daily, following the routine pattern Pantha had taught him, a routine that kept both body and mind in prime condition.

Dion remembered his tutelage, opened aggressively, attacking with spirit and skill, and soon forced his opponent to go on the defensive. Flaim's blade disappeared, the weapon shifting—with the swiftness of thought—from bright blade to invisible shield.

The use of the shield required far more energy than the

blade, drained the sword's reserves, would soon start to drain the body's. Dion's swift and furious onslaught actually forced Flaim backward, caused him to step outside the circle.

"Hold!" Sagan called, palm raised outward.

Dion fell back, resting, breathing hard.

Flaim, looking grim and defiant, leapt back into the circle immediately and, having learned his lesson, went on the offensive. A flurry of blows made the eyes ache trying to follow them. Dion's foot slipped once, but he shielded himself, held Flaim's battering attack off until he could regain his balance. With a tricky maneuver (one Sagan recognized as his own), Dion dove under Flaim's guard with a slashing stab that might well have ended both the duel and the prince's life.

A skillful diving roll carried Flaim out of danger . . . and out of the circle.

"Hold," Sagan called out for the second time. "If you step out again, Your Highness," he cautioned the prince grimly, "you forfeit and must surrender."

"I understand. Thank you, my lord," Flaim said.

Dion's blow had cut open the prince's white shirt; it hung around his body in bloody tatters. His left knee was slashed open.

Both combatants were sweating; Dion's shirt clung to him. He wiped his hair out of his face. Of the two, Flaim appeared the more fatigued, however, and he had certainly taken the most serious injuries. He limped when he walked back into the circle.

Dion did not look triumphant, however. He was watching Flaim warily, cautiously, knowing that these duels were—as Sagan had once told him—one-tenth physical and nine-tenths mental. Flaim seemed in just a little too much pain, he was limping just a little too weakly, breathing just a bit too heavily.

Dion was on his guard, therefore, when Flaim suddenly regained his strength with a bound and, grinning, swept into the circle with slashing fury. Dion shielded, came back to the offensive. Flaim shielded, came back.

The duel went on. Tusk rubbed his eyes, wincing at the bright light. Astarte and Kamil watched silently, both very properly fearful of breaking Dion's concentration. Each woman was instinctively, perhaps unknowingly, clasping tight hold of the other's hand.

Pantha watched with no more than a placid interest, as if he were already certain of the end.

Dion stepped outside the circle, but was back in before Sagan could call a halt. Though the king knew the misstep counted against him, he chose not to take advantage of the rest period—to rest himself was to give his opponent the opportunity to do the same. Dion's blade flamed and vanished, attacking far more than defending. He was in control of the fight. It was as if some angel with a flaming sword had descended from heaven to do battle for the king.

He burned with a pure, holy fire. Imbued with the rightness of his cause, the knowledge that he was light battling darkness, he fought with valor and skill.

Watching Dion, Sagan remembered. He knew that look—it had once been his own. He could feel again the exhilaration of battle that brought with it a strange calm, an air of detachment. Let go of fear and advance to meet death. Step partway into the silent realm, stand straddling the border. And when you do so, you become vibrantly aware of life, from the cloudless sky above to the tiny, glistening drop of blood on the ground at your feet. Let go of fear and the soul floats free, the mind is clear and fixed and the flaring blade is the fatal embodiment of thought.

"Well done, boy," Derek Sagan said, deep, deep within.

But Dion heard. The blue eyes, brighter than the fire of suns, turned upon Sagan and the king's smile was that of one exalted.

And then Flaim stepped out of the circle and fell upon one knee, raising his hand over his head, the classic position of surrender. He shut off his bloodsword.

It took Sagan a moment for his soul to rejoin his body. He felt the flesh's heavy dead weight acutely, dragging him down; came back with a bitter sigh.

"Hold!" he called, harsh and strident.

He stepped into the circle, between the combatants—one standing tall, the other bent-kneed on the ground. Dion, breathing heavily, could not speak. He had lowered his sword, but the blade hummed. His face was expressionless; his own soul still floated far above. He seemed not to understand that he had won.

No one in the courtyard spoke; Kamil and Astarte were confused. Never having seen a duel, they were uncertain what this meant. Tusk, having—or so Sagan hoped—learned his lesson, was watching the Warlord for a cue. Garth Pantha knew. He'd seen bloodsword duels before, likely fought in a few. He sat unmoved, watching with detached interest.

"By the rules of the contest, by stepping outside the circle, by shutting off your sword, you, Flaim Starfire, admit defeat," Sagan informed him.

"Oh, yes," said Flaim, with a laugh. Rising gracefully to his feet, he bowed to the king. "Thank you, cousin. I thoroughly enjoyed myself. Pantha."

The elderly man came forward, bearing the box. He opened the lid. Flaim laid his bloodsword inside. Shaking the raven hair out of his face, he smiled at the queen, who still neither moved nor spoke.

"I am certain the ladies enjoyed it," he added, with a bow and a flourish for Her Majesty.

"Then I have won," said Dion, appearing to suddenly realize it himself. "You renounce your claim to the throne. You will let us go free."

"I'll let you go . . . to the devil."

Flaim had taken a soft leather glove from Pantha, was pulling the glove on over his hand, over the puncture wounds left by the bloodsword.

"I won," Dion repeated grimly.

"You lost," Flaim told him. "You lost the true battle, cousin. The one we were fighting in our minds. I penetrated your secrets. I now know the location of the space-rotation bomb. I know where you've hidden it. Pantha, you must contact the dark-matter creatures, send them to fetch the prize."

Dion stared, white with shock and disbelief and terrible understanding. "A ruse," he whispered. "All a ruse."

"Yes, cousin." Flaim laughed. "A ruse. To goad you into using the bloodsword, to trick you into revealing the location of the bomb."

The bloodsword flared blue. Dion made a sudden lunge at the prince, sweeping the sword in a slashing arc.

Derek Sagan stood in his way, blocked his path. Sliding expertly inside Dion's guard, the Warlord caught hold of the king's sword arm, hurled him off balance.

Dion stumbled, fell, landing heavily on his hip on the ground.

"Don't be a fool!" Sagan told him. He cast a significant glance around the courtyard.

Dion looked up. Armed men were running into the courtyard, their lasguns drawn and aimed—some at the king, others at the queen and Kamil.

Dion's shoulders sagged in defeat. "Your advice comes rather late, my lord," he said bitterly.

Chapter ❖ *Eleven*

You may my glories and my state depose,
But not my griefs; still am I King of those.
                        William Shakespeare,
                Richard II, Act IV, Scene i

"I must ask you to hand over the sword, Your Majesty," said Sagan.

Dion rose slowly and stiffly to his feet. Shutting off the bloodsword, he thrust the hilt back into its sheath, unbuckled the belt and removed it from around his waist. He carefully wrapped the belt around the hilt, silently handed the bloodsword to the Warlord.

Sagan replaced the sword in the box, alongside Flaim's. Pantha shut the lid, tucked the box under his arm.

"My lord Sagan, I thank you especially for your assistance in this matter." Flaim cast a triumphant glance at Pantha as he said this. "We will meet in two hours. By that time, the bomb should be in our possession. We have plans to finalize. Would you be interested in hearing them, cousin?"

Dion made no response.

"It seems the Corasians are about to invade the galaxy," Flaim continued. "Yes, cousin, within a few days, your Lord Admiral will start receiving reports that the enemy has crossed the Void and is preparing to attack. You, Your Majesty, will heroically and valiantly defend the galaxy by detonating the space-rotation bomb in the middle of the Corasian invasion force.

"Alas, cousin." Flaim spread wide his hands. "A terrible accident. You yourself are killed in the explosion. You die, a martyr to the cause, having saved your people. Your funeral will be most impressive. And I will be there, the next Starfire in line, to take the throne. The people will welcome me with tears in their eyes. Especially, as it will turn out, when they learn that the Corasian threat has not ended."

"You've allied yourself with the enemy," said Dion, quiet, the quiet of despair.

"By necessity. Kings must do things out of necessity," Flaim said, with a sly glance toward Kamil. "The Corasians will be granted certain planets—secretly, of course—to do with as they please. In return, they will 'retreat' on command, return when needed, keeping the galaxy in a suitable state of turmoil and fear that only I can quell.

"But your soul may rest easily, cousin. I do intend to keep my promise to you. I will marry the queen and raise your child to be heir. And if Her Majesty proves so indelicate as to refuse me, then her planet will be one of the first to fall victim to the enemy."

"I don't suppose she will refuse," said Dion, his eyes on his wife.

"An ingenious plan, don't you think, cousin?"

"Most ingenious," Dion agreed.

"I wish I could take credit for it." Flaim shrugged. "But I have Lord Sagan to thank."

"Indeed?" Dion—his expression troubled, thoughtful—turned to the Warlord.

Sagan bowed in acknowledgment.

Dion gazed at him for long moments. Then, the shadow falling dark over him, he lowered his head and stared down at the ground. "I see."

"Guards, attend Her Majesty. Escort her back to her quarters," Flaim commanded. "But perhaps Princess Olefsky would like to remain a moment, recover from the shock of her ordeal. For which I do apologize. I think she should be allowed to have a few words alone with the king. Tusca, remain with my cousin, take him back to his room whenever he is ready."

Tusk, standing against the wall, nodded sullenly.

Orders issued, Flaim left the courtyard, accompanied by Pantha and the box. Two female guards came to take charge of Astarte. The queen crossed the courtyard with her accustomed dignity and cool aplomb. But she hesitated when she neared Dion.

He remained standing in the center of the courtyard, inside the circle, his head bowed, rubbing the palm of his right hand.

Astarte stopped beside him, seemed to want to speak, to offer comfort. She reached out her hand.

He didn't see it, didn't look up.

But, after all, what comfort can *I* give him? I'm a stranger. . . . Her words were unspoken, but they were written on her face. Her hand fell to her side. She sighed and started past.

Dion, hearing her sigh, became aware of her. He caught hold of her hand, looked at her steadily, intently.

"Astarte, are you all right? The child—" He faltered a moment, then said gently, "Our child—" He couldn't go on.

Astarte's pale face flooded with color. She was radiant, beautiful, life beating within the confines of death and despair. "Our child is fine. I am fine," she said to him, clasping his hand tightly. "Don't worry about us."

He couldn't speak, but brought her hand to his lips, then pressed it against his cheek. Astarte's eyes filled with tears. He smiled at her reassuringly. She returned the smile, blinked back the tears, and, with regal bearing, walked out of the courtyard.

Kamil remained sitting on the bench, staring at Dion, her heart and soul in her eyes. Dion glanced at her, shook his head, stared back down at the bare ground beneath his feet, at the drops of blood in the circle.

The courtyard emptied of people. Sagan, heading for one of the buildings, walked past Tusca. The mercenary looked sick, sat hunch-shouldered on the bench.

"I hope to hell you know what you're doing," Tusk said in a low voice, through split and blood-caked lips.

Ignoring him, the Warlord continued on. Tusk didn't bother to repeat himself. He sat unmoving on the bench.

Sagan entered one of the buildings adjacent to the courtyard. He walked through the corridor, whose windows looked out upon the courtyard, taking care that his footsteps were loud and heavy. Pausing at the end of the hall, he turned and silently doubled back. Keeping in the shadows, he took his place near a window, as near as he could get to the circle in which the king remained. Kamil had joined Dion now, was standing beside him.

The air was calm, sound carried well, and the Warlord had excellent hearing. Still, he might have had difficulty eavesdropping on their conversation had not Kamil inadvertently assisted him. Glancing mistrustfully at Tusk, she took hold of Dion's limp hand and, tugging him into responsiveness, drew him away from the mercenary. Her movement took them nearer Sagan, so near he was forced to retreat a step or two back deeper into the shadows to avoid being seen.

Her words took the Warlord by surprise, apparently startled Dion, too.

"Dion," she said to him firmly, her voice pitched low, "you've got to find a way to escape."

He raised his head, roused from his despairing lethargy.

"Listen to me first, before you say no," she continued swiftly. "I have an idea. A good one. When Tusk comes to take you back, grab his weapon. Force him to fly us out of here in the Scimitar. We'll rescue Astarte, take her with us. Tusk knows all the passwords, all the codes. His spaceplane is parked near the alcazar.

"He'll do it. I know he will!" Kamil gulped for air, nervous excitement stealing away her breath. "He doesn't like this, any of this. You saw him. He tried to help me. It was only Sagan, knocking him senseless, who made him back off. We'll escape and . . . and . . ." She paused, uncertain.

"And what?" Dion asked, smiling sadly.

"Well," she said, faltering, "you'll have to go into hiding. Flaim would be searching for you. But meanwhile we could raise armies against him. My father would help, and the baroness—"

"Until the bomb exploded. Or the strange dark-matter creatures attacked them. Or the Corasians invaded. No," said Dion quietly, "your father might want to help. But he couldn't. He'd be too busy fighting for his own survival."

Kamil was silent, faced with irrefutable logic. Her hands twisted together. Then her expression hardened. "We just stay in hiding, then. Don't bother about fighting Flaim. Or else wait a few years. Wait until you are stronger and he is weaker. Wait until he makes a mistake. Wait until Sagan turns on him and they're at each other's throats. It's bound to happen," she pointed out with grim and bitter certainty. "Sagan betrayed you. It's only a matter of time before he betrays Flaim."

Dion shook his head, his face again thoughtful, dark, and troubled. He glanced—oddly enough—at Tusk. The mercenary hadn't moved. But he was watching them from beneath half-closed eyelids.

"What will I do during that time I'm 'hiding'?" Dion asked.

"Why, you'll . . . Well, I guess you could . . . We . . . we'd . . ." Kamil looked foolish, then irritated. "What does it matter what you'd do? We'd just go on living, waiting . . ."

"Try to see the road ahead," Dion told her. "Go on. Look into the future. What will I do? Wait on tables? Sell computer chips door-to-door? Where will I go that I won't be recognized? You are asking me to exile myself, live in constant fear, live again without a name."

He shook his head. "You forget, Kamil, I was raised like that. I lived seventeen years of my life in hiding. I won't go back. And I won't raise a child of mine like that."

She was frustrated, unwilling to give up. "It would only be for a little while—"

"Kamil." He spoke to her gently, reaching out and taking hold of her arms. "You can't see down that road because that road doesn't exist for me. I am king. When the archbishop placed the crown on my head, the scepter in my hand, I accepted a responsibility. I took it upon myself to be the people's protector. I can't flee and leave them to their fate. What would I say to them? That I ran away when there was danger, came back when it was safe?"

Kamil tried to say something, but he held her tightly, silenced her with his earnestness.

"There would be no return for me, Kamil. If I throw away the crown in fear, how could I ever reclaim it?"

"At least you'd be alive," she told him, not looking up at him.

"Would I?" he asked tiredly. He dropped his hands from her shoulders. The weariness was evident on his pallid face. "Would it matter?"

"Yes, it would matter!" Kamil returned. "What nonsense—to say you might as well die as not be king. You lived seventeen years without knowing you were a king and you were happy. You told me you were. You had your books and your music and . . . and someone who loved you."

She faltered a moment at that, then, taking a breath, returned to the fray, stronger for her momentary weakness. "Platus never wanted you to be king. You told me that, too. He wanted you to be an ordinary man, doing what you could for people in ordinary ways. *That's* what truly counts in this life. If every ordinary person lived his life respecting others, their rights and their feelings, then we wouldn't need kings.

"You were happy being ordinary until Derek Sagan came along. He murdered Platus, but he did something worse to you that night. He murdered the good, the quiet, the ordinary part of you!"

She choked back a sob. Dion put his arms around her again,

drew her close. She rested her head on his breast. But he stared out over her head, his thoughts far away. His lips moved. Sagan, attuned to the thought, heard the silent words he himself had said to Dion years ago.

I came to rescue you. . . .

But Kamil was also attuned to the thought, though it was love's ear that was quick to hear it, not the telepathic ear produced by genetic design.

She pushed herself away from him, looked up into his face. "That's it, isn't it?" she said softly. "That's why you're ready to throw your life away. What Sagan said."

"What do you mean?" Dion said, startled and troubled.

"About you failing the test. You believe him. You don't think you're good enough. You've let Sagan convince you that you don't deserve to be king. You think, like him, that your cousin's better than you are and so you're just going to crawl away and die!" Kamil was angry now, her anger driven by her fear.

Dion had grown pale and silent during her attack, but her words seemed to give him pause, made him think. "Perhaps you're right. Believe what Sagan says," he repeated, musing. "He never lied to me, no matter what else he did. . . ."

His gaze went to Tusk, who had either fallen asleep or passed out again. Dion withdrew into himself, took himself far away from spying ears, loving or otherwise. Sagan couldn't read the young man's thoughts, but he could guess them, and the Warlord frowned in the darkness.

"Oh, Dion, you can't think that!" Kamil cried, alarmed. "Flaim will be a dreadful ruler, cruel and vicious. Like he was today. Astarte told me so. I didn't want to believe her, but I see now what she meant."

Dion, looking back to her, smiled in spite of himself. "A fine counselor you are," he said, gently teasing. "One minute I shouldn't be king and the next minute I should. Which is it to be? You can't have it both ways, my dear."

"I know. I'm sorry. I don't understand any of this horrible mess. I shouldn't have tried to lecture you. I've probably done more harm than good."

Kamil sighed forlornly. Then, putting her arms around him, holding him, she said quietly, "I understand only that I love you and I'm afraid for you. We have a chance to escape. Take it. Once we're away from here, then everything will work itself out. I know it will."

Dion hesitated, tempted.

Sagan watched in silence. Knowing that he could intervene anytime he chose to prevent such a rash and hasty act, he was curious to hear the king's response.

"No, Kamil," said Dion. His hesitation had lasted only a moment. He wasn't uncertain of his decision; he was reluctant to destroy the hope shining in her loving eyes. "I have to stay and see this through. I have to catch that damn silver ball," he added with a bitter smile. "If I am meant to die, then it will be with dignity, as a king. I won't die shot in the back, caught running away."

Sagan's eye caught movement in a distant doorway, saw two shadows cross a window. Tusk, who had not been sleeping, saw them, too. Rising to his feet, rubbing his aching jaw, he slouched over to Dion.

"C'mon, kid," he said in a low voice. "Someone's lookin' for you." His gaze flicked to his left, over his shoulder.

Dion turned to Kamil. "Will you—"

"No, go on," she said, and her tone was cool. She didn't understand, was afraid and feeling helpless, and because she was afraid and helpless, she was angry. "I'll stay here awhile. I like it outdoors . . . in the sunshine."

She turned her back on him. Dion looked at her, obviously wanting to say something to do or make everything right. Realizing this was impossible, he walked away with Tusk. The two crossed the courtyard, stepped over the circle, and disappeared into the alcazar.

Kamil held herself stiff and rigid until she could no longer hear the echoes of their footsteps. Then, thinking herself alone, she sagged down on the bench, lay on it like a heartsick child, and began to cry—hurting, despairing sobs that wrenched her body.

Sagan waited, still, silent in the darkness. He was not disappointed. A flash of silver appeared very near the weeping girl, a silver armored guardian, standing vigil over her grief.

He watched a moment longer, then left his post, taking care that his footsteps were quiet and muffled, not to disturb either of them.

Chapter ❖ Twelve

The game's afoot ...
William Shakespeare, *King Henry V,* Act III, Scene i

Sagan arrived early for his meeting with the prince. Flaim, in excellent humor, welcomed the Warlord cordially and even Garth Pantha seemed to unbend and greet Sagan with cordiality.

They met in the communications room of the alcazar, the one place in the fortress where they could be sure of talking without interruption, for no one—not even the guards—were permitted to enter this room, on pain of death. It was the first time Sagan himself had been accorded such an honor. He knew, of course, that he had been tested and gathered that he had passed.

He looked around with curiosity; that would be only natural. But he had to keep from appearing too curious, which would have aroused suspicion. It was from this room Garth Pantha communicated with the dark-matter creatures. The Warlord's gaze darted swiftly from one complex machine to another, from vidscreen to commlink, from old outdated equipment to new. He recognized everything, saw nothing strange, no familiar equipment being put to unfamiliar use.

Pantha was watching him, and Sagan had the distinct impression the sharp old man knew what the Warlord was searching for. Pantha placed the tips of his fingers together, gazed at Sagan over them with an amused smile, like a parent watching a child search the house for a hidden birthday gift.

Go ahead, he seemed to challenge silently. *Look all you want. You'll never find it.*

Sagan, in answer, fixed his gaze on Flaim and kept it there.

". . . truly remarkable," the prince was saying. "Did you see my cousin's face when you dragged Kamil up to me? I was almost afraid for a moment you had gone too far, my lord. It occurred to me that, caught up in the chivalrous mood of the moment, our cousin might take it into his head to thwart my

441

wicked design on the woman he loves by killing himself. Which would have put an undoubted crimp in my plans."

"There was little fear of that, Your Highness," said Sagan. "Dion is not a fool."

"No, I don't suppose you would have lavished what time and care on him as you did if he were. And I must admit, it all worked marvelously. Taken up in the heat and excitement of the contest, he reacted as you predicted. He lowered the guard on his mental processes to concentrate on the physical. I was able to slip through quickly and easily, penetrate his mind and discover the location of the bomb. The dark-matter creatures have been dispatched and should be back . . ." He glanced at Pantha.

"Any moment now, Your Highness."

"They will bring it here," said Flaim, gesturing to a marble stand that stood in the center of the room. "I am eager, most eager, to see it. So is Pantha. He has made quite a study of it, did he tell you, my lord?"

Sagan was not surprised. "Indeed, sir? You obtained information on it from the Corasians, I presume."

Pantha nodded acknowledgment. "The information Abdiel was able to glean from you, my lord."

Sagan did not like the reminder. Pantha was quick to notice. The elderly man grew grave. "An evil man, Abdiel. I sleep sounder nights knowing he is destroyed."

"Yet you're not above using the information he gained, no matter how he gained it."

"As a scientist yourself, my lord, surely you would agree that valuable information should not be wasted simply because it was obtained in a manner we might not approve. After all, we owe our very existence as Blood Royal, as genetically superior beings, to experiments done by the Nazis in their concentration camps."

"Which might suggest something to somebody," Sagan remarked.

Pantha frowned, wondering if he was being insulted. Then—eyeing Sagan closely—the old man apparently decided that the Warlord was making a joke and let it pass.

"Considering the way in which the information was obtained," Sagan went on coolly, "didn't you fear that some of it might not be accurate? That I might have deliberately lied to him?"

"That was to be expected. But with my technical expertise—almost as great as your own, my lord, or so I flatter myself—I was able to determine what was workable and what was not. Something the Corasians were never able to figure out, which was why they have not been able to produce a space-rotation bomb of their own. I discovered, for example, the cyborg's 'arming' device. I must say I had a good laugh out of that. And you should see the monstrosity the techno-moronic Corasians created because of it. I lacked only one thing—"

"A working model."

"Yes. And now that is being supplied. I believe, mind you"—Pantha raised a bony index finger—"that I could have developed a working bomb myself. I am very close. But this will make it all so much easier."

Sagan regarded the man intently, wondered if he was telling the truth; if so, how much? Pantha was adept at keeping his thoughts hidden; he had not used the bloodsword in years. Might have been afraid to do so, after his disappearance. There was no way even Derek Sagan could penetrate that old and cagey mind. But he guessed that Pantha did have some knowledge of the bomb, though probably not as much as he boasted, else why the desperate need to get his hands on the real thing?

Which might make matters awkward. Still . . .

Sagan trampled his thoughts down swiftly, shoved them back inside his mental strongbox. He could still feel Flaim's quick, jabbing probes, like uncomfortable surges of electric current passing almost continually through him.

An interruption came in the conversation. Sagan experienced the unpleasant compressed sensation he had learned by now to associate with the dark-matter creatures. At the very same instant, the space-rotation bomb appeared out of nowhere, resting securely on the top of the marble stand.

He had not seen it since that fateful night Lady Maigrey had convinced him—and others—she was planning to detonate it. A trick, as it turned out. But a trick that had won Dion the prize.

Sagan, coming forward to look at the bomb, lifted his hand involuntarily to the starjewel he wore around his neck. And, as he did so, he saw Garth Pantha do the same; the old man's hand going to his neck.

There gleamed the Star of the Guardian. A rare jewel, the secret of whose creation died with the priests of the old Order of Adamant . . . and the triggering device on the space-rotation bomb.

Garth Pantha was in possession of a starjewel. Probably, aside from Sagan's own, the last one in existence. How? Pantha had not been a Guardian, and only the Guardians received the coveted, mystical starjewel. Amodius, of course. He must have given his favorite this valuable token of esteem and friendship. Or perhaps as payment for removing the unwanted fruit of the king's sins.

Awkward indeed.

Flaim was gloating over the bomb like a doting mother over a new baby—hovering near it, afraid to touch it. Pantha regarded the prince with amusement.

"You may pick it up, Your Highness. It is quite harmless, when not armed."

Flaim lifted the bomb gingerly. It did not look like what it was—the ultimate destructive force in the universe. A solid crystal cube, about ten centimeters in height and width, it might have been mistaken for a lady's jewel box—of a rather bizarre design. Embedded in the crystal was a pyramid made of pure gold. A small flat computer keyboard containing twenty-six small keys was affixed to the top of the crystal. The point of the pyramid connected to the underside of the keyboard.

"Even when armed," said Sagan, "the correct code would have to be entered in order to detonate it."

" 'The center cannot hold,' " quoted Garth Pantha.

Sagan cast him a swift glance.

"One of Abdiel's earliest acquisitions," Pantha explained, almost apologetically. "Obtained first from the Lady Maigrey, confirmed through yourself. I was not familiar with the quotation, not being a student of ancient literature. However, I discovered it in my files. One of Yeats's poems, I believe. A most apt quote, considering the way in which the bomb works.

"The quarks of the atom pulled apart, the color bond which holds them together stretched to its limit, the space between them rotated in such a way that, upon release, the quarks rushing back together collide, totally annihilating matter. In theory, it could tear a hole in the fabric of the universe. Quite ingenious."

Sagan acknowledged the compliment with an oblique nod, all the while wondering how the fact that Pantha knew the key to exploding the bomb would affect his plans, not daring to give the matter thought. The Warlord turned to the prince.

"You have the bomb now and the knowledge and the capability of detonating it. In what capacity can I serve Your Highness?"

"Let us be seated," suggested Flaim, "and discuss this comfortably." He replaced the bomb back on its marble stand, gave it one more covetous glance, then sat down at a table. He indicated chairs. Sagan took one located directly opposite the electronically controlled and guarded door that was the room's only entrance, only egress.

"You, my lord, will take command of the fleet," Flaim told him. "I want to move ships into position in key areas of the galaxy—Minas Tares, the Houses of Parliament, DiLuna's system. I have taken your advice and disguised my ships to resemble those of the Royal Navy. But I want to take no chances. I want to keep out of detection range of any naval vessels. Can this be done?"

"Certainly, Your Highness."

"When the king's death is announced, my ships will then be ready to move into position. I don't anticipate any trouble, except perhaps from DiLuna . . .?" Flaim looked at Sagan questioningly.

"Astarte can handle her mother," Sagan responded. "The queen is shrewd and ambitious. She wants her child to be king. I do not foresee DiLuna or her allies giving you any difficulty."

"Excellent." Flaim leaned back comfortably in his chair.

"However, such a plan will require your entire fleet, Your Highness," said Sagan. "We will not be able to spare even one single ship to guard Vallombrosa."

"The dark-matter creatures will guard it, such as it is." Flaim glanced around the room with disfavor. "I, for one, do not intend to ever come back here. All my people will come with me. The one thing I regret is the loss of the ship that will be carrying the king."

"We discussed other options," Sagan said. "Are you, perhaps, reconsidering?"

"No, no, my lord. You're absolutely right. Any other way of disposing with His Majesty would look far too suspicious. The ship has been fitted out to match the king's royal flagship. The crew has even been issued copies of official naval uniforms—

not that there will be enough left of them to identify. If what you say is true, the blast will vaporize them."

"It is never wise to take chances, Your Highness. You must remember that this bomb has, for obvious reasons, never been tested. We are not certain precisely what it will do. It would be a shame to have your hopes dashed by the discovery of a fragment of a body clad in the wrong uniform."

"You have made your point. All has been attended to. Any debris found floating in space will confirm the tragedy: The royal flagship blew up, lost, with all hands on board."

"A pity about the crew," Sagan commented.

"Yes, I will lose some good people. But they have all pledged to give their lives to me. I shall miss the ship more." Flaim sighed, frowned. "I can get men far more cheaply and easily than a naval vessel."

"If all goes well, Your Highness, you will soon have the Royal Fleet under your command," Sagan reminded him.

"True." The prince glanced again at the bomb and smiled. "I do not foresee anything going wrong, do you, my lord?"

"Certainly not, Your Highness."

"Pantha, have we forgotten anything? Any final details we need to discuss?"

"No, my prince. Your orders have been issued. By tomorrow morning, all will be in readiness. This is the last night you will spend on Vallombrosa, Flaim," Pantha added in a softened tone.

Flaim stood up. Reaching out his hands, he grasped hold of the old man's. The moment was special between them. Sagan politely moved away to give them privacy, walked over to stand near the door.

"The goal we have worked for all these years is within sight, my friend," Flaim said. "The crown is almost within my grasp. I am reaching out for it, even now. Do not think me ungrateful when I say I never want to return to Vallombrosa. It is you who have always taught me that we never look back, only ahead."

"I know, Flaim. I know," Pantha said softly. He looked around the room and shook his head. "Many were the hours I sat here and stared in hatred at these walls. I—who had roamed a galaxy, who had riches and wealth beyond belief— had imprisoned myself inside a chill and dismal cavern.

"I thought I would go mad in those early days," he continued. "Oftentimes I sat here bitterly regretting the fact that I hadn't died in that fake explosion. And then you would toddle into the room." Pantha looked at Flaim with a sad and wistful smile. "Excited about some discovery—a bug, a rock, a half-dead flower. You were a beautiful child, strong, healthy, intelligent. I would tell you everything I knew—the scientific names, the chemical composition—and you understood, young as you were.

" 'What a king you will be,' I would say as I lifted you into my arms. 'What a magnificent king.' No, Flaim, my son"— Pantha had tears in his eyes—"I do not ever want to return to Vallombrosa either. There were too many times I thought I would die here. Still, its memory will be blessed."

Sagan, embarrassed, cleared his throat.

"Your Highness—"

Flaim turned a tear-streaked face, looked somewhat ashamed. "Forgive me, my lord. Of course, you have duties to attend to. You don't want to stand around watching Pantha and I make fools of ourselves. You have leave to go."

Sagan bowed, turned toward the door.

Flaim activated the control. The door slid open. The Warlord walked out. The door shut and sealed behind him.

Sagan took a moment to study it from the outside, then, nodding to himself, left with what he had come planning to obtain—a complete knowledge of how the door operated, including its security devices and alarms.

He had already checked on the other two doors he would need to open this night. Both were simple—plain and ordinary bolt locks. Returning to his room, the Warlord lay down upon his bed, prepared to slip into the quiet meditative state that was, for him, more restful than sleep.

And much safer.

Fortunately, Flaim would have a lot on his mind tonight. Composing himself for rest, Sagan reflected on the fact that sentiment was a ruinous emotion.

Chapter ❈ Thirteen

Look into my face; my name is Might-have-been;
I am also called No-more, Too-late, Farewell.
                    Dante Gabriel Rossetti, "A Superscription"

It was a quiet night in the alcazar. Quiet as far as those guarding the halls and corridors were concerned. There were, of course, the usual disturbances, usual for a planet the dark-matter creatures roamed: an entire shelf of books was thrown down in Pantha's library; several dishes were broken in the kitchen; motion was detected in a corridor, but no visual confirmation could be made by the guard who went to inspect; a minor disruption occurred in the electrical system of the communications room. The electricity shut off, but then flashed on practically before the system had time to register the interruption. Again, on inspection, nothing untoward was found.

The guards shrugged, shook their heads, and muttered that they would be glad to leave Vallombrosa.

The night was not particularly quiet for any of the rest of the inhabitants of the alcazar, with the exception of Flaim, who slept soundly and dreamed of glory. Pantha spent the night in his room, studying computer analysis of the space-rotation bomb. By morning, he was confident he could make another. Astarte, her regal facade shattered, cried herself to sleep. Kamil sat up with the queen until Astarte, worn out and exhausted, finally slept. Unhappy and restless, Kamil lay down on her bed, staring into the darkness, drifting in and out of a feverish doze, dreaming strange dreams of a woman with pale hair and silver armor.

Pantha had provided Tusk with medication to ease the pain of his injured head. Tusk swallowed the tablets, wished they could ease the ache in his heart, and flung himself down dispiritedly on his bed. His thoughts writhed in his brain like snakes in a pit. He didn't trust Sagan, then he did. He would free Dion, then he wouldn't. He was going to fly to Dixter for help, then he wasn't. He flipped and flopped and was sorry he'd taken the medication. Pantha had warned him—rather tersely—not to mix it with jump-juice.

Having at last decided gloomily that he was going to be up all night and he better make the best of it, Tusk immediately fell sound asleep. He was dreaming that a tall, dark figure loomed over him when a strong hand, clapped tightly over his mouth, brought him to heart-stopping wakefulness.

Tusk thrashed out. A weight like someone had landed a spaceplane on his chest pressed him into the bed.

"Don't move!" cautioned a voice in his ear. "Don't make a sound. Listen."

Tusk, recognizing the voice, did as it commanded. He had little choice in the matter. His bruised lips, covered by the hand, hurt like the devil. He could barely hear over the pounding in his ears. Try as he might, he couldn't see a thing in the darkness.

"Make certain you board the king's ship tomorrow," the voice breathed directly into Tusk's ear. "I understand that you have become friendly with several members of the crew?"

Tusk nodded.

"Tell them that they are being sent on a suicide mission. Tell them that the space-rotation bomb is aboard the ship and that Flaim intends to detonate it, destroying the king and the crew. You will convince them of the danger and persuade them to take over the ship.

"You will need proof. When Flaim and Pantha leave the ship, I will discover where they've hidden the bomb. It will be armed and set to explode when the ship reaches its destination. You will show the bomb to your comrades. That should be proof enough."

And then the hand was gone, the voice was silenced, the dark form no longer present.

Tusk lay still a moment, wondering if he'd been dreaming. But the slowly subsiding racing of his heart was real; so was the fear, which was rapidly being replaced by excitement and grim satisfaction. Now, at last, he had something to do, something positive to do. It wouldn't be easy, but if all else failed, he'd fly Dion off in the Scimitar, shoot their way out.

They'd done it before.

Relaxing, sighing deeply, Tusk whispered a good-night to Nola, as he always did, even when she wasn't lying beside him, then rolled over and slept.

Dion lay awake all night, staring into the darkness. He, too, saw—or thought he saw—the woman in silver armor.

"I made the right decision, didn't I, my lady?" he asked.

She didn't answer, but he didn't expect her to. After all, it had not really been a question.

He was still awake when the twin suns lifted up over the walls of the alcazar and the guards came to his door.

The rattle of a key sounded in the door lock. Astarte and Kamil looked at each other. Astarte held out her hand. Kamil took hold of it. They stood waiting. The door opened. Dion, accompanied by armed guards and Flaim, entered the room.

He looked at Astarte. "I am being permitted to say good-bye to you, madam," he told her quietly.

Astarte's lauded beauty was gone. She was small and crumpled, her eyelids heavy and red and swollen from weeping, her lips gray and colorless. They trembled when she spoke. Her hair was disheveled, uncombed.

But despite the fact that they were in a prison cell surrounded by armed guards, and he was about to be killed and she was about to become the wife of his murderer, she was still queen and he was king and they had an audience.

Astarte drew herself up with dignity, cast an imperious glance at Flaim. "Please, leave us alone."

"Certainly," said Flaim. "The guards will be right outside the door, should either of you require anything." The prince turned to Kamil. "You acquitted yourself with remarkable courage yesterday. I therefore give you a choice—life or death. You may either stay with the queen and enter her service permanently or you may travel with the king."

"Stay with Astarte, Kamil," said Dion swiftly. "I want you to."

"Please, Kamil." Astarte turned to her. "Please, stay with me."

"No," said Kamil, not looking at either of them. "I'm going with the king."

"Kamil—" Dion began, his face troubled.

"If you don't mind," Kamil interrupted, speaking to Flaim, "I think I would like to leave now."

Flaim was all sympathy and understanding. "We are boarding the Royal Flagship. The guards will be happy to escort you."

Her back rigid, Kamil walked out of the room without saying a word to either person she left behind.

"Her Majesty will be traveling in my flagship," Flaim told Dion. "I will do everything in my power to make her journey comfortable. We will be returning to Minas Tares. It would be best for the queen to be in the palace when word comes of the tragedy. And, of course, I want to be near at hand."

Dion made no response. Flaim turned to leave. Pausing, he turned again, came back.

"Damn it, cousin! Don't make me do this! Abdicate the throne. Go live with that girl. Most men would give their lives for love like hers. What's being king compared to that?"

"My duty," said Dion. "My responsibility." He glanced at Flaim. "You understand. It's what we were born to, bred to. What would our lives be without it?"

"Nothing, of course." Flaim regarded him with admiration. "You are right, cousin. I do understand. Forgive me. I won't trouble you about it again.

"Five minutes," he said, and shut the door behind him.

Dion and Astarte looked at each other, shy and awkward as they had been on that first unhappy night together. Then Dion reached out his hands to his wife.

"Can you forgive me for being a blind fool?" he asked.

She clasped hold of his hands, held on to him tightly. "Only if you can forgive me for being a selfish monster."

He gathered her close. He had never noticed before how fragile she felt in his arms, yet how strong.

"It was my mother's fault, for coercing you into this marriage," Astarte whispered.

"I used to think so," Dion replied. "But now I'm not certain. Maybe some god . . . or goddess had a hand in this."

He stroked her hair. This was the first time he'd ever seen it mussed. "Astarte," he said softly, "as hard as my death will be, it will be easy compared to your life."

"Don't . . ." Her eyes filled with tears.

"Hush, listen to me. You could escape this marriage. Flaim won't pursue it. He'll have too many other concerns. I could urge you to do this, but I'm not going to.

"You possess power—the power of your faith, the power of being yourself. The people admire you. You can use this power to glove my cousin's iron fist. He won't like it. He'll fight you. But he won't be able to stop you. Work long and hard, slowly and subtly, and you will build up a resistance to my cousin's tyranny that will be invincible. Perhaps, in years to come, you can overthrow him."

"With the help of our child."

"Our child. My only regret . . . is that I will never . . ." Dion faltered, his strength failing him for a moment, "never see . . ."

He couldn't speak. He could only hold on to his wife and she to him. Sadly, their silence said more than three years of spoken words.

"Time to go, Usurper." The guard thrust open the door.

Astarte drew back from her husband's grasp. Smoothing her hair, she stood tall and upright, her eyes dry, a smile on her lips. They might have been parting for the day's duties. She extended her hand. The fingers were chill, but the hand was steady.

"God go with you, sire," she said softly.

He took her hand, pressed it to his lips. "May the Goddess be with you, madame. And with our child."

He turned and left her. The door shut behind him. She heard the key grate in the lock.

"I won't cry," she said, pressing her hands over her womb. "I won't cry. I won't make myself sick. For the child's sake. Everything I do from now on will be for the child's sake."

She sank to her knees, clasped her hands in prayer. "Blessed Goddess, you fought at the side of the heroes at Troy, you brought us safely through the heavens to our world, you sustained us through the dark times when all seemed hopeless. Blessed Goddess, send angels to fight at my husband's side—"

The key rattled in the lock. Thinking it might be Flaim coming to escort her to the ship, Astarte sprang to her feet. She drew herself up haughtily.

"You have leave to enter," she said, for form's sake only. The door was already opening.

"Tusca!" She gasped, startled.

Entering the room, Tusk crossed over to her. "Dion thought you might like this to remember him by."

He pressed something into her hand and winked—at least she thought he winked. It was hard to tell; one eye was swollen almost shut. Before she had time to ask a question or say a word, he was gone.

Astarte opened her palm. In it lay a silver earring, formed in the shape of an eight-pointed star.

Book Four

Turning and turning in the widening gyre
The falcon cannot hear the falconer;
Things fall apart; the center cannot hold;
Mere anarchy is loosed upon the world,
The blood-dimmed tide is loosed, and everywhere
The ceremony of innocence is drowned;
The best lack all conviction, while the worst
Are full of passionate intensity. . . .
                    William Butler Yeats, "The Second Coming"

Chapter ·◆◆◆· One

Things fall apart . . .
William Butler Yeats, "The Second Coming"

Vallombrosa was now truly a ghost planet. The alcazar was deserted, stood empty beneath the double suns. All personal effects, all data files (primarily Pantha's) had been transferred secretly to the *Flare*.

Her Majesty the queen was also transported to *Flare*, to be taken back to Minas Tares. Those who observed her noted that she was pale, but calm and composed. It was well known that the royal marriage had not been a particularly happy one.

The space-rotation bomb was taken aboard the ship carrying His Majesty. Pantha himself carried the bomb aboard, concealed in the same box that held the two bloodswords.

The brief interruption of the electricity to the door of the communication room during the night had been reported to him. He was at first concerned, but finding on investigation that nothing had been disturbed, that the space-rotation bomb was still there, he decided that it must have been the dark-matter creatures.

"They have an extreme interest in the bomb," Pantha told Flaim as they traveled to what Flaim was terming, between themselves, the "ghost" ship. "They were probably checking on its safety."

Flaim was displeased. "I don't like to think of them getting close to it. They won't harm it, will they?"

"They didn't harm it transporting it to you, my prince. I told them that we intend to destroy the bomb in a distant part of the galaxy, far from their own world. They intimated their satisfaction."

"They won't be happy when we build another."

"Precisely why we *won't* build it on Vallombrosa. I doubt if they'll ever discover it. They wouldn't have known of this bomb if I hadn't warned them of it.

"They are really rather provincial beings, I believe. Attached to their own homeland, with no ambitions or design on any others. As long as they can be assured Vallombrosa—and by extension their own world—is safe, they will be content."

Arriving on board the "ghost" ship, Pantha took the bomb to Flaim's quarters. Here they would leave the bomb, armed, the code punched in, to tick away the seconds of the lives of everyone on board.

"What will you tell the crew?" Pantha asked.

Flaim smiled. "My speech is all prepared. I will tell them that we are embarking on a great enterprise, one that will carry them to eternal glory. I have obtained secret intelligence, gleaned from the dark-matter creatures, warning of an impending Corasian invasion. Not even the Royal Navy knows of this threatened attack—which will be the truth; the Corasians are still in their own galaxy.

"I will take it upon myself to thwart the enemy's plans and drive them back to their own galaxy. When the people of the galaxy learn that I have saved them, they will be only too eager to grant me any demands that I might make upon them. And I will demand to be made king. That's what I will say to them."

"Won't they wonder why the Usurper is on board?"

Flaim shrugged. "I don't trust him out of my sight."

"And when we flee the ship?"

"We're inspecting the fleet."

Preparations were made to leave orbit. Everything was in readiness. Lord Sagan had arrived on board, as had Dion. Flaim ordered his cousin and Lord Sagan to join the prince in his cabin to hear the speech.

The prince made his speech over the vidcom, to the cheers and applause of the assembled crew. None of them had any doubt at all but that Flaim Starfire would soon be king and that their fortunes would be made.

"How was that, Pantha?" Flaim asked when he was finished. He glanced around. "Where's Pantha?"

"He was called to the bridge, an urgent summons," said Sagan. "The speech was quite good, Your Highness. You played down the death of the Usurper, I noticed." An oblique glance at Dion, who sat unmoving, expressionless.

"I took your advice, my lord. As you said, some may still have a soft spot in their hearts for my cousin." Flaim nodded politely in Dion's direction. "They wouldn't stand for seeing him executed, but if he dies in battle . . ." The prince shrugged.

Sagan nodded in understanding. The three were seated in Flaim's private quarters aboard the "ghost" ship. Only two people, Flaim and Pantha, had access to these quarters—an arrangement similar to one Derek Sagan had once used aboard the *Phoenix*. Now the former Warlord was relegated to a small berth in the officer's part of the ship. He stood looking out the steelglass window at Vallombrosa, still in sight, and permitted himself the luxury of memory.

He was—as he had always been before a battle—calm, relaxed. His senses were heightened. All objects in his sight seemed sharp-edged, bathed in bright light. He could hear words unspoken, attune himself to the thoughts of those near him, keep his own thoughts shrouded in darkness. All was going well, according to plan. Tusk and his Scimitar were safely aboard; the Warlord had ascertained as much. He could trust Tusk to handle his end—the mercenary had a powerful incentive and he was a good man. Dependable, like his father.

Sagan had now only to wait and be patient, something he'd never been very good at when younger. He glanced down at his arm. Hidden beneath the knife-edged crease of the sleeve of his uniform (disguised as that of an admiral of the Royal Navy) were countless scars. Self-inflicted wounds, intended to remind him of his own mortality, his own frailty, intended to remind him of his duty to God. Patience. Yes, he had learned patience.

Or at least he had learned to conceal his impatience.

Garth Pantha entered through the large double doors.

"My friend!" Flaim began exuberantly, stopped at the expression on the elderly man's face. "Something's gone wrong, hasn't it? What?" He rose to his feet, leveraging himself out of his chair with a shove of his hands. "What is it? Wait. Call the guards to escort my cousin back—"

Pantha halted the prince's command with a swift gesture. "Your cousin should stay, my prince. He . . . may be needed."

Flaim answered with a frown. "What is it, then? Speak. What's wrong?"

"The dark-matter creatures, Your Highness."

Flaim glanced involuntarily in the direction of a large vault. "Not the space-rota—"

"No, not that," Pantha interrupted hastily. "I . . . I really don't know how to tell you this, my prince. It is all . . . most inexplicable. I don't understand . . ."

"Just tell me!" Flaim snapped.

"We have received a report—it has gone galaxy-wide, Your Highness—that the system of Bidaldi, in the center of the galaxy, has been attacked by a mysterious force. From all indications it appears that every major city in the Bidaldi system was destroyed by horrific nuclear war. Yet there were no explosions, no radiation. Buildings have been leveled, people killed. The death toll, Your Highness, is said to be in the millions."

"Dear God!" murmured Dion softly.

No one else spoke, all silent, pondering.

"Bidaldi is a populous system." Dion was the first to break the silence. "And a wealthy one. They are located in the center of a Lane convergence. And they are peaceful. They have no enemies—"

"Everyone has enemies," Flaim returned. "What does this have to do with us?"

Pantha wiped sweat from his face; his wrinkled black skin glistened. He swallowed, tried to speak, paused to lick his lips. "Your Highness . . . I'm afraid it has everything to do with us."

Flaim stared at him. "No!" he protested, aghast. "You can't be serious! The dark-matter creatures?"

"All evidence points to it, Flaim," said Pantha. The man looked suddenly ancient. He sat down heavily in a chair. His hands shook. "I have studied the data as it came in. Due to the fact that we're tapped into the Royal Naval channels, I was able to intercept the navy's official communications. Instruments on Bidaldi recorded wild and inexplicable fluctuations in the gravitational readings. These are all now back to normal. Survivors report people dropping dead of no apparent cause. And there is more evidence. I would not tell you this, my prince, if I was not absolutely certain." Pantha shook his head. "There can be no doubt, I'm afraid. The dark-matter creatures attacked and destroyed Bidaldi."

"But why? What do they possibly hope to gain? You said they weren't ambitious!"

"I didn't think they were! And it doesn't look as if they've gained anything. They have abandoned the planet, apparently." Pantha lowered his head into his hands. "After they wreaked havoc on it, maimed and slaughtered, they just left. . . ."

"Perhaps they're *not* ambitious," said Dion slowly, considering. "Or if they are, ambitious only for their own survival. You taught them, cousin, how easy we flesh-and-blood mortals are to destroy. The bomb taught them to fear us. Perhaps their only goal is to see to it that we will not be a threat to them again."

Flaim cast him a swift, baleful glance. Going to the commlink, he contacted the guards standing duty outside the door. "Return the Usurper to his quarters."

Pantha lifted a haggard face. "The people will be expecting their king to make a public pronouncement on the tragedy. If he doesn't, they will suspect something is wrong—"

"I'll deal with that when the time comes!" Flaim said angrily. "Guards, take him."

Dion stood up to leave. "The creatures have slipped from your leash, cousin—if they were ever really on one. How much longer before they turn on you?"

The king left, the guards marching him back to his quarters that were, in essence, his prison. Once he was gone, Flaim began pacing the room.

"This is intolerable! If I am linked to this disaster, it could ruin me."

Wheeling, he came to stand in front of Pantha. Gripping the old man by his shoulders, Flaim jerked him to an upright position. "You have to talk to them. Now! Find out what the devil is going on! Tell them to stop immediately. Tell them . . ." Flaim fell silent.

"My prince?" Pantha looked at him.

"Hush, wait. . . . My lord." Flaim turned to Derek Sagan.

The Warlord stood before the viewscreen, staring out at Vallombrosa. He had said nothing at the news, which appeared to have made very little impression on him. Now he looked deferentially around at the prince.

"Your Highness?"

"My lord, if the space-rotation bomb was exploded here on Vallombrosa, would it destroy the creatures and their world utterly?"

"Without a doubt, Your Highness. The creatures know that, which is why they fear it. It would be a shame, however, to lose such valuable allies. . . ."

"Yes, that is true," Flaim replied, frowning. "They are an integral part of my plans. Well, we will consider that only as a last alternative. Pantha, you must go and speak to them."

"I would be careful what I said to them, sir," Sagan remarked. "I would do nothing to make them nervous or afraid."

"I quite agree, my lord," Pantha said grimly.

Pantha left the prince's quarters. Flaim continued pacing.

Damn it all! Sagan swore silently, bitterly. All was going too well. I should have expected this to happen, seen it coming. Of course the creatures would be fearful, suspicious, wonder what is going on. It is natural that they make their fear known, but I didn't suppose they would show this much cunning. Obviously they know more about our psychology than Pantha credits them. And what will Flaim do about it?

He glanced over at the prince, who was deep in thought—and not being very careful of his thoughts. Sagan could follow every twist and turn.

So that is your the solution, Prince. The Warlord had to admit it was a sensible solution, though it certainly made things damn complicated for himself.

The doors opened. Pantha entered.

Flaim looked up, startled. "That was quick. What did they say?"

"I was unable to contact them, my prince." Pantha appeared troubled. "Which is strange, considering—"

"Damn the considering!" Flaim shouted impatiently. "What do you mean you can't contact them? Won't they answer?"

"No, Flaim," said Pantha quietly, a hint of rebuke in his deep voice. "They will not. They are not in the ship's vicinity. Perhaps if I returned to the planet's surface . . ."

Flaim struggled inwardly, finally regained a modicum of self-control. "Do so, then. Leave now. You can take my shuttle. I will expect you back this night."

Pantha shook his head. "Your Highness . . . this may take some time. Consider that communication with the creatures is, under the best of circumstances, difficult . . ."

"At 0600, then," Flaim said. "That will give you all night. We dare not wait longer. Damn it, Pantha, if *you* were able to deduce the dark-matter creatures were responsible for the slaughter on Bidaldi, others may do so."

True enough, Sagan thought to himself. Dixter already has reason to suspect Vallombrosa. It will be only a matter of time before he reaches a similar conclusion—if he hasn't done so already. The admiral must have discovered by now that the king isn't taking a holiday on Ceres.

Sagan frowned. I hope to God the entire Royal Navy isn't about to descend on us.

"What do you think, my lord?" Flaim asked abruptly.

"I agree with Pantha's earlier statement. The king's silence on this tragedy on Bidaldi will look extremely odd," Sagan said, hoping to buy time. "People will begin to ask questions."

"You had better hurry, Pantha," Flaim said. "Report back to me in the morning. As for the king's silence, he may soon be forever silent. My lord, contact the commanders of the fleet. Tell them that plans have been altered. We will remain in orbit around Vallombrosa until tomorrow morning, at which time they will receive further orders."

"Yes, Your Highness."

Sagan was glad to leave. He needed to be alone, to think this out. He moved through the ship, part of him oblivious to its familiar sights and sounds, part of him paying close attention to them, noting all that went on around him. But he did not go immediately to the communications room to contact the other commanders, as he had been ordered.

Sagan took a detour to the flight deck. He was, he told the officer on duty, making a surprise inspection. All pilots were to report to their craft. The word went out, the pilots came running. The Warlord made his tour. On one occasion, he stopped to upbraid the hapless pilot of an old Scimitar on the condition of his plane.

"All hell's broken loose. The timetable's moved up," Sagan said in a low undertone as he ducked beneath the Scimitar's belly.

"To when?" Tusk whispered.

"Tomorrow morning."

Tusk gawked. "Tomorrow! You can't be—"

"Have that attended to immediately, Commander," Sagan said loudly.

"Yes, my lord." Tusk saluted, managing to look as if he'd just been chewed up and spit out. Not difficult, considering what he'd just learned.

"Tomorrow morning!" he repeated, groaning, when the Warlord had continued on. "Shit!"

Chapter ⋅❖⊰◗◖⊱❖⋅ Two

Death be not proud . . .
For those whom thou think'st thou dost overthrow,
Die not, poor death, nor yet canst thou kill me.

           Donne, *Holy Sonnets*

Kamil sat on the hard bed in the tiny cubicle that was her prison cell, going over her plan time and again in her head. She was going to escape, rescue Dion, find Tusk and make him fly them out of here. The middle part of her plan was good, so was the end—flawless as far as she could judge. Free Dion. Fly away. It was getting *to* the middle and the end that was proving difficult. Before she could free Dion, she had to free herself. And she couldn't get out of her room.

An armed guard stood posted outside her door. Kamil had observed him closely when he brought in and later took away her untasted evening meal. She'd had some vague idea of jumping him at that point, but she'd been daunted by both his physical size, which was impressive and, more important, his cold disinterest in her. He would obviously just as soon kill her as look at her.

He was an older man, in his forties, one of the prince's trusted inner circle. He was a battle-scarred veteran, looked as if he'd fought his way to the galaxy's center and back.

Frustrated, Kamil flung herself down on the bed, which was already rumpled from her fevered thrashings. She had to save Dion, whether he wanted saving or not.

"He's thinking all wrong," she said to the wall. "He isn't thinking at all. He's acting out of emotion. When he's free from danger, away from Flaim—away from Derek Sagan," she added grimly, "Dion will see everything clearly. He may be mad at me at first," she admitted, "but he'll eventually come to see that I've done the right thing."

She would save Dion from himself . . . if only she could get out her door.

Lying on her bed, she made plan after plan, only to discard

them all. At last, tired from running frantically around and around the wheel that never seemed to take her away, Kamil closed her eyes. She couldn't remember when she'd slept last . . . or eaten anything. The wheel began to turn slower and slower. Now it was rocking back and forth, back and forth. She had the impression someone was in the room with her, though the door hadn't opened.

Kamil wasn't frightened. She'd seen this person before.

"Where have you been?" Kamil demanded accusingly.

"Here, all the time," was the mild response.

"Then why haven't you helped us? A godmother has a sacred duty to her godchild. Why don't you help me?"

Kamil was fretting, whining like a sick child. But she felt like a sick child, frightened and alone. Two tears crept out from beneath her eyelids. "Don't just stand there and look at me, Lady. I need you! I have to save Dion . . ."

"You won't save him by crying," she said.

Kamil started, was suddenly wide awake, thinking she'd heard a voice.

"If you're determined to do this, get up," the voice commanded, and it was clear and cool as the lake near Kamil's home. "You haven't much time."

Slowly, Kamil sat up. Slowly, she opened her eyes. A woman clad in shining silver stood beside the bed. Long, pale hair fell over silver armor. Gray eyes were cool and clear as the voice; a scar marred the right side of her face.

Kamil blinked, rubbed her hands into her eyes. When she opened them again, the woman was still there.

"Lady Maigrey," Kamil whispered.

The woman inclined her head in acknowledgment.

"You . . . you've come to help me?"

"Advise you," Maigrey corrected. "I am prohibited from direct interference or involvement. However"—she smiled slightly; the smile twisted the scar on her face—"since you *are* my godchild and since, as you say, the duty is a sacred one, I am allowed a certain amount of mice and pumpkins."

"Mice and pumpkins . . ." Kamil echoed, confused, not understanding. If this was a dream, she should insist on it making more sense.

"Never mind." Maigrey went on briskly, "What is it exactly you are trying to do?"

Kamil found herself explaining her plan. "Am I doing the right thing?" she asked, in conclusion. "Will this work?"

Lady Maigrey shook her head. "I cannot say. I do not see the future, nor would I be allowed to tell you if I did. Free will and all that," she added, with a rueful smile. "You must decide for yourself whether or not to take this risk. For, child, the risk is very great, the danger very real."

"I know," said Kamil somberly, staring down at her clenched hands. She looked back up at the lady. "But it will be worth it. I have to save him. If I can do that, whatever happens to me doesn't matter. *You* know, Lady," she urged persuasively. "You understand. You were in love like this when you were alive. Or so my father told me."

"*When* I was alive? . . ." Maigrey repeated softly. "Love is the one part of us death cannot kill."

"I'm sorry, Lady." Kamil was touched by the woman's sorrow. "Derek Sagan's betrayed you, as well as Dion. If he—"

"Are you going to try to escape?" Maigrey interrupted coldly. "Or perhaps you'd prefer to sit and chat?"

"No, I'm ready." Kamil left her bed. But now she was feeling nervous. Her stomach fluttered; her hands began to sweat. She glanced uneasily at the door. "What . . . what do I do?" She wiped her hands on the white gown she still wore.

"Scream," Maigrey instructed. "Scream loudly and like you mean it. The guard will enter, his gun drawn. I don't suppose you happened to notice if he was right- or left-handed?"

"N-no," Kamil stammered, trying to think back. "I believe . . . right-handed."

"If you had never seen him, knew he was human, you would assume he was right-handed and trust in the odds. As it turns out, this man is left-handed, so you would have lost. Get into the habit of looking, observing," Maigrey admonished her pupil. "You never know when such information could mean the difference between life and death. Stand over there. By the door."

Kamil did as she was told. Her heart was racing; her stomach had gone from flutters to upheavals. She was afraid she might be sick. She couldn't disgrace herself in front of this gray-eyed woman, however. She clenched her fists, dug her nails into her flesh, and looked at Maigrey attentively.

"When you scream, he will enter with his weapon drawn.

You will have a split second to react. You are on his left-hand side. Grab his gun, yank it from his hand, and shoot him."

"Shoot him," Kamil repeated through numb lips.

"Shoot him," Maigrey said firmly. "He will probably have the weapon set on stun, but you can't count on it, so make up your mind right now that you are going to kill him. That way, if you do, it won't come as a shock."

"Kill him," said Kamil. She thought of him, of that hard face, and she banished the memory quickly. "Kill. Yes, I'm going to shoot, kill."

"Good. You've fired a lasgun before?"

Kamil nodded, thinking back to Xris. She grew calmer, glad to be reminded of that time. She'd come through that action all right. He'd praised her, in fact. "Yes, I've fired a lasgun before. Xris said—"

"Good," Maigrey cut in crisply. "Ready?"

Kamil nodded, unable to speak. Her throat was so dry, she wondered how she would manage to force any sound out. She was faint, shaking, but it was now or never. Drawing a deep breath, she screamed.

Her voice cracked; she choked. Desperate, aware of the gray eyes regarding her with detached speculation, Kamil drew another breath, screamed again. Her pent-up fear and frustration found an outlet. The sound was astonishing, almost frightened her.

The door burst open. The guard entered, his weapon drawn, as Maigrey had predicted. He was bigger than Kamil had first thought. She was tall, but he towered over her by a head. The hand that held the gun was massive and strong. He wasn't looking at her, didn't see her, but was searching swiftly and expertly around the small room. It wouldn't be long before he found her, crouched, frightened, unable to move, hiding behind the door. . . .

Suddenly the man's mouth gaped open. His eyes bulged; he fell back a pace.

Lady Maigrey stood in front of him, silver armor gleaming, pale hair stirring, as if in an ethereal wind. She gazed at the man without a word.

Kamil flung herself on the guard with a strength born of desperation. She grabbed his hand, wrenched the gun from it with an ease she hadn't expected, turned the weapon on him . . . and froze.

It was one thing to shoot in the heat of battle, fire at targets you couldn't see. It was quite another to shoot an unarmed man who was only an arm's length away, staring straight at you.

If the man had remained standing still, Kamil probably couldn't have gone through with it. But the guard—angry and embarrassed—reacted instinctively to his danger. He lunged at Kamil.

Terrified, Kamil fired.

The blast knocked the man backward. He fell against the partially opened door, slid to the floor, and lay there.

Kamil began to shake.

"Stop that!" Maigrey snapped. "Shut the door!"

Kamil did as she was told, stepping gingerly over the body to do so. She knew he was dead.

"Take off his uniform," Maigrey ordered. "And put it on. Quickly, child! Quickly! Don't think about it," she added. "Just do it."

Kamil did as she was told. "Dion," she repeated over and over. "I have to get to Dion. He's all that matters."

Kneeling down beside the man, she rolled the body over, face up, and started to divest him of his uniform. She noticed then that he was alive. Sighing in relief, she worked swiftly.

Soon his uniform was off him and on her. The uniform was a jumpsuit, stretchy, made to fit a variety of sizes, and so Kamil didn't look as odd in it as she had expected.

"The helmet," Maigrey reminded her.

Kamil grabbed it, jammed it on her head. It smelled of sweat and some sort of disinfectant shampoo. She started for the door.

"Wait a minute. You're not finished here. Bind his wrists behind his back. Rip up that gown of yours. Wrap his head in the pillowcase to muffle his voice when he comes to. Don't worry. He won't smother."

Kamil had to wrestle the inert and almost naked heavy body. Fortunately, she was accustomed to roughhousing with her brothers, and so that part, while distasteful, wasn't anything she couldn't handle. She made a neat job of the knots; stood up, sweating.

"Now?"

"Now," said Maigrey.

Kamil started to open the door, hesitated. "Will you be with me?"

"You won't see me," Maigrey said. "But I will be with you."

Nodding, Kamil yanked open the door. She started to look up and down the corridor, then remembered that—in her uniform—she had a perfect right to be here. She sauntered casually out of the room, locked and sealed the door behind her. She set off down the corridor.

"When do they change guards?" a voice in her ear asked.

"At 2400," Kamil answered. "If they keep to their usual schedule. I *did* find that out," she added, rather defensively.

"Good for you. Hopefully, no one will miss him until then. Which gives you time. Do you know where Tusk's quarters are?"

"No, but I figured I could ask. That wouldn't look strange, would it? I mean, with all the confusion of coming on board . . ."

"Perfectly normal. You have a talent for this."

Kamil flushed, pleased. Then she shook her head. "But I froze back there. When he came in with the gun. If he hadn't seen you . . ." She paused. "You did that on purpose, to save me. . . ."

"Mice and pumpkins," Maigrey told her. "But the ball ends at midnight, child, so you had better hurry."

⊷⊷⊱◈⊰⊶⊶

"Cynthia, it's like this," Tusk was saying. "This prince that you admire so much is nothing more than a double-crossing, cold-blooded murderer. He's sending every one of us to his or her respective graves. No, I take that back. There won't be enough left of us to put in a grave. Not enough to put in an eyedropper. You've heard of the space-rotation bomb? Well, the prince has it and it's on board ship right now and he's planning to blow it up tomorrow morning after breakfast . . . Fuck it."

Tusk tromped around his tiny room, kicked a chair in passing for good measure.

"She'll never buy it," he told his reflection in the small steelglass porthole, out of which he could see Vallombrosa, looking like one of young John's rubber balls. "And I've got 'til morning to convince her? Shit!" He kicked the chair again. "I wonder what the hell went wrong? Why didn't Sagan tell me?

" 'Course that woulda been a first," Tusk went on bitterly. "He hasn't told me one goddam thing from start to finish. And this just might be the finish. Go out with a great big bang. 'Do it by morning,' " he mimicked.

Tusk glanced at the time. "Well, I'm not getting anywhere here. Wonder where good ol' Cynthia'll be this time of night? Her quarters, probably. Maybe something brilliant'll come to me on the way there—"

He was just about to open the door when the door opened on its own.

One of the prince's guards stood there, his gun leveled at Tusk's breast.

Tusk raised his hands in the air. "What the—"

The door slid shut. The guard removed his helmet.

"It's me, Tusk. I want you to take me to Dion."

"Kamil!" Tusk collapsed back against the bulkhead, clutching his chest. "Jeez! I wish people'd quit doing this to me! My heart can't take much more of this. And just what the hell are you doing?" he demanded irritably. "Why don't you go back—"

Tusk lunged, made a swift and expert grab for the lasgun, intending to snatch it away before she knew what hit her. Unfortunately, he was the one who got hit. She brought the gun down hard on his hand, cracked his knuckles.

Tusk yelped. "Where'd you learn that?"

"Never mind. Now take me to Dion."

"Oh, for the love of—" Tusk sighed, exasperated. "Look, Kamil, I got things to do. Important things. You don't understand what's going on. And I can't explain now. Just take my word for it, everything's under control."

He couldn't believe he'd just said that with a straight face. "Okay? Okay. I'll take you back to your room and—"

"You'll take me to Dion," she repeated for the third time, pointing the gun at him. "I've shot one man already."

"What the hell do you think you're going to do once you get there?" Tusk demanded. "He won't go with you. He's already told you that once. Yeah, I heard that conversation you two had. You plan to knock him out cold and haul him off while he's unconscious?"

"If I have to," Kamil said, her jaw setting. She gestured with the gun toward his leather flight jacket, lying over a chair. "Put that on. And get your gear. We're leaving."

Tusk, shrugging, did as he was told. Kamil put her helmet back on, gestured with the gun at the door. "Go on. Open it. Keep your hands in the air. You're my prisoner. A traitor. You're to be locked up with the king."

"You say so, sweetheart." Tusk shook his head. Slinging his

pack over his shoulder, he walked out of the room and into the corridor. Kamil followed, the gun jammed into his back.

--◁═⊃◯◖═▷--

Kamil had no idea where they were going. They marched down the corridor, down several corridors, took a lift, marched down another corridor. People stared at them, but no one interfered, most probably figuring the less they knew about this the better.

She kept close watch, afraid Tusk would try some sort of trick, maybe lead her back to her own room. She dared not ask Lady Maigrey, for fear Tusk would overhear, and the lady was keeping silent, perhaps for the same reason.

But they obviously weren't going to the detention center.

"This isn't the way to the prison cells," she said in a low voice to Tusk, after they'd just passed the Officer's Club.

"Dion's not being held in the brig," Tusk said out of the corner of his mouth. "Flaim wants to keep him close by, keep an eye on him."

That made sense, Kamil supposed. And it gave her something else to worry about. Running into the prince would be unfortunate.

"Faster," she said to Tusk.

He obeyed, shaking his head. They rounded a corner. The number of people roaming the corridors had steadily decreased. The corridor they turned into was empty, except for two guards standing duty in front of a door located at the very end.

Kamil's heart quickened with excitement.

Tusk strode forward. The guards came to attention, looked at Tusk and his escort quizzically.

"I'm to lock this man up with the ki—Usurper," Kamil told them. "Open up."

Rather to her surprise and considerably to her relief, the guard obeyed her without question. One said something into a commlink. The door slid open.

Lord Derek Sagan stood inside.

Chapter ❀❀❀ Three

And I would hear yet once before I perish
The voice which was my music—Speak to me!
George Gordon, Lord Byron, *Manfred*

"What's this?" Sagan demanded. "What have you done now?
Gotten yourself arrested?"

Tusk jerked a thumb back at Kamil. "Claims I owe her
money."

"Do you?"

"Maybe. I thought it was just a friendly game." Tusk
shrugged. "Anyway, I haven't got it. I told her that, being my
employer, you held the plastic."

"We will discuss this in private," Sagan said grimly.

Kamil was caught. She could do nothing, and her mentor appeared to have forsaken her. She walked into the Warlord's
quarters. The door slid shut behind her.

Tusk disarmed her easily. "Guess who?" He took off her helmet.

Kamil emerged, flushed, defiant. "You bastard," she said to
Tusk.

"Sorry, sister." He sounded bone tired. "I'm only doing my
job. She drew this on me." He handed the lasgun over to
Sagan. "Ordered me to take her to Dion. I think she's got some
idea of bustin' the kid out. Don't ask me how she got loose." He
glanced at her, shook her head. "Maybe she's been takin' a cor-
respondence course in commando training. Learn to Kill for
Fun and Profit. Anyhow, she made a pretty neat job of it."

"Indeed." Sagan eyed her with interest.

"I figured I better bring her here. You'd know how to keep
her outta mischief. Either that or I could lock her up on board
the Scimitar. XJ'd watch her."

"I don't think that would be a good idea," the Warlord responded wryly. "Her instructor might be prepared to give her
flight lessons." His tone grew stern. "Does anyone know you're
gone?"

She stood mute, refusing to talk.

"There was probably a guard," Tusk offered. "She said something about shooting one guy already. They won't find him until they change guard at 2400—"

"Unless he's supposed to report in on the hour," Sagan said. He was silent, thoughtful, then looked up at Tusk. "Go to the girl's quarters. I'll deactivate the security lock. Enter and dispose of that guard—"

"What am I supposed to do with him? Flush him down the toilet?"

"I don't care what you do with him," Sagan snapped, irritated at the interruption. "Just arrange it so that no one finds him for at least twelve hours. Then fix the girl's room to make it appear that she's left. Permanently. Do you understand?"

"No, but that never seems to bother anyone," Tusk muttered.

Sagan chose to ignore him.

"When that is finished, you must proceed with the plan."

"Why tonight, if you don't mind my askin'—"

"There is a possibility—a very good possibility—that Flaim will detonate the bomb tomorrow."

Tusk swore. "Great! That's just fuckin' great!" He swore again, then said, "Let's suppose that by some miracle I get everyone convinced that they want to seize control of the ship. Just when are we supposed to do it?"

"You will know."

"How?"

Tusk waited for an answer, but the Warlord remained silent.

"You're not even going to give me a damn signal?" Tusk shouted.

"Keep your voice down. The less you know, Tusca, the better for you and everyone. Don't worry," Sagan added dryly, "you won't have any trouble recognizing it."

"A bomb blast does sorta tend to get your attention," Tusk said bitterly. He sighed. "This is goddam impossible. Look, my Lord, Kamil here's got a good idea. Why don't we just spring the kid, take him—and us—out of danger?"

"First, Dion would not go. Second, I doubt if even you, Mendaharin Tusca, could shoot your way through a fleet of warships. Third, you will need a ship of this size and a loyal crew in order to rescue the queen. Fourth, there are the dark-matter creatures. What do you intend to do about them? Fifth, you would not achieve the major objective."

"Which is?" Tusk asked. He looked subdued.

"My problem. And we are running out of time. I suggest you get on with it."

Sagan turned to the computer, called up data on the security system.

Kamil, bewildered and amazed and apparently forgotten, had shrunk back into a corner.

Tusk started to leave, paused by the door. "You're aware, my lord, that Cynthia may just decide I'm a traitor and shoot me on the spot?"

Sagan did not glance around. "That is a risk. But one I'm willing to take."

"Yeah, well, just so you don't eat your heart out worryin' about me." Tusk glowered, glanced over at Kamil. "Say hello to your dad and brothers for me. And don't *you* worry, everything's going to be okay."

"Contact me on the bloodlink I gave you when you have the ship secure," the Warlord ordered, as Tusk put his hand on the door control.

Tusk snorted. "You've got a helluva lot of confidence in me."

"As I told your earlier," Sagan replied, "there is much of your father in you."

Tusk stared at him, open-mouthed. Then he shook his head and left.

The Warlord continued to work on the computer. Worn out by fear and excitement, Kamil began to shake.

"I've been a fool," she said in a small voice.

Sagan made no response. He might not have heard her.

Kamil rubbed her burning eyes, leaned her head back. She was too hot. There seemed far too little air to breathe. She tugged at the tight-fitting body armor.

"Sit down. Lower your head between your knees," Sagan instructed, still not bothering to look at her.

Kamil did as she was told, sinking down to sit on the deck. She rested her arms on her knees, her back bent, her head almost touching the deck. Surprisingly, she felt better.

Sagan switched on the commlink. "Put me through to Prince Starfire. Yes, it's urgent. Tell him the Olefsky girl has tried to escape."

Kamil was on her feet. "No! They'll take me back—"

Sagan flashed her a warning glance, raised a warding hand.

"Yes, Your Highness. I have her. The girl had help. The man

who was supposed to be guarding her has disappeared. No, she hasn't told me who her accomplice was—so far. I will continue to interrogate her." A pause, listening. Then, "I think it best if she remains in my custody, Your Highness. At least until I discover who assisted her. I have moved her to a different cell block and doubled the guard. Very good, Your Highness. Has Pantha reported back?"

Sagan listened again. His expression grew dark, the eyes shadowed. His lips tightened until they were nothing more than a thin slash across his face. The shadow spread from him throughout the room.

"I see." Sagan spoke quietly. "The creatures told him that. What does he think?"

Again silence. His gaze abstracted, he stared into the shadows.

"I am afraid I must agree with him," the Warlord replied. "The creatures are no longer to be trusted. They have become a distinct menace. We are all in danger. Is Pantha still in the alcazar?"

The Warlord's expression darkened still further, eyes narrowed. A flame flickered deep within. His voice betrayed no hint of his obvious disquiet. "Yes, I find that odd myself. But at least if the creatures are not around this ship, we are safe for the moment. When will Pantha return?"

He asked the question casually enough, but his hand clenched tightly as he waited for the answer. When it came, he relaxed, the fingers uncurled. He smiled, dark and mirthless. "Probably the wisest course, although I doubt if he will accomplish much by remaining on Vallombrosa longer. I am going to go make the rounds of the other ships in the fleet, place them on full-alert status. . . .

"I will endeavor to do so, Your Highness," he added after another pause, "and I appreciate the compliment, but if I am late, I suggest you proceed. Pantha's starjewel will arm the bomb as well as mine."

The transmission ended. Sagan stood in silence, staring at nothing, absorbed in his thoughts, which must have been terrible ones, to judge by his expression. Kamil was careful to keep quiet, not to disturb him, though she was frantic to know what was happening.

At last he seemed to reach some inner decision. His face hardened, became again unreadable. The fire in the eyes shut off, the source feeding it removed.

"Tell me, please?" Kamil ventured.

Sagan eyed her, shrugged. "Flaim's going to detonate the bomb tomorrow morning. Instead of dying while defending the galaxy from the Corasians, Dion will die defending it from the dark-matter creatures."

"But you're going to stop him!" Kamil said, excitement surging through her. "You and Tusk. You're going to take over the ship! You *didn't* betray Dion. You've done all this, risked all this for his sake. The Lady Maigrey knew. That's why she said what she said about love. I didn't understand—"

"What did she say?" Sagan asked abruptly.

Kamil hadn't meant to mention that. She flushed and stammered, embarrassed. "You—you're going to think I'm crazy. She wasn't real. How could she be real? I haven't slept in nights. And sleep deprivation causes hallucinations. They're very. . . ."

He took a step toward her. "You saw her?"

"I . . . I thought I did."

Kamil was too frightened to try to argue further. He was so intense, rigid; his eyes seized her, wrung her soul.

"What did she say?" He laid distinct emphasis on each word, as if he forged each out of steel, linked them together in an iron chain.

Her throat and mouth were dry. She swallowed again. The expression on his face, the look in his eyes were terrifying.

"She said, 'Love is the one part of us death cannot kill.' "

He closed his eyes and sighed. The sigh was deep and anguished, drawn up from some dark part of his being.

Kamil caught a glimpse of it on his face—savage and hopeless. Shuddering, appalled, she lowered her head, unable to look at him, his pain too intense for her to bear.

Only when she heard him moving purposefully about the cabin did she dare look again. He had gone into an adjoining room. The door slid shut behind him. Kamil waited, nervous, apprehensive. That look of his, that terrible look, like one past hope. Suppose she'd been wrong; Maigrey had been wrong. Suppose he'd sent Tusk off to certain death. . . .

The Warlord returned. He was clad in a flight suit.

"Put your helmet back on," he ordered, lifting it and handing it to her.

She tried to, but her hands were shaking. She fumbled with the strap. He watched her impassively, made no move to assist.

"What are we going to do?" she asked.

"Leave," he said.

"Leave the ship?" She stared, aghast "Leave Dion here to die! No! I won't come! I won't let you—"

"You have a choice, young woman," he interrupted, the chill in his voice effectively silencing her. "Either come with me now or I will kill you now. I dare not let you remain behind. Left on your own, you have the power to do too much mischief." He laid heavy, ironic emphasis on the words "on your own."

Kamil was in no doubt that he meant what he said. And although she was prepared to give her life for Dion, she wasn't quite ready to do so now.

"I'll go," she answered meekly.

"Keep silent. Follow my lead. Don't question anything I say or do." He handed her back the lasgun. "You know how to shoot that, I presume?"

Kamil stared at it, stared up at him. "Yes, my lord." Her lips moved, but no sound came out.

He nodded. "Switch it off stun. From now on, if you have to shoot, you will have to kill."

She did so. She could kill him now. He was unarmed. He had turned away from her; his hand was on the door control. Kamil raised the gun.

But she couldn't fire.

She had heard stories about the charismatic power of the Blood Royal. How they could subvert, charm, persuade. Did he hold her in thrall by some form of genetically engineered enchantment? Or perhaps it was just common sense, telling her that she was lost if she killed him now. Perhaps it was an unseen hand, laid on her own.

Perhaps it was the voice, soft, like music.

Kamil thrust the gun in the holster.

Sagan opened the door, propelled her out, one strong hand firm on her shoulder. The guards snapped to attention.

"The money will be transferred to your account," Sagan was saying. "If you take my advice, Lieutenant, you will not lend him any more. Tusca is an irresponsible drunkard, but he does have his uses. You are due to go on duty shortly, you said. There is a small service you can render me. I have a prisoner to transfer.

"The name is Olefsky, Maigrey Kamil. . . ."

Chapter ❦❦❦ Four

Disorder, horror, fear and mutiny
Shall here inhabit . . .
William Shakespeare, *Richard II*, Act IV, Scene i

"How do I get myself into these messes?" Tusk asked of no one in particular. "I was born under an unlucky star, as mother used to say. She was right. A goddam eight-pointed star."

He found and disposed of the inconvenient guard, who was still unconscious in Kamil's quarters. Tusk hoisted the man to his feet, dragged him out of the room and through the ship, expressing loudly what he thought about guys who couldn't hold their jump-juice.

The guard—restunned—was now taking a long nap in Tusk's shower stall.

Tusk continued commiserating with himself. "This whole damn end of the galaxy's about to blow sky high and I'm doing *Mutiny on the Bounty*. If I was smart, I'd say the hell with this, the hell with all of 'em, and fly my black ass off this floating time bomb."

The thought appealed to him and he toyed with it.

"Sagan says Dion won't go along with it," Tusk remarked to the door of the lift taking him to the officer's quarters. "Well, Kamil's got a point. One good clunk over the head would stop the arguing real quick. As for warships? What's a few dozen warships? Hell, the kid and I took on the whole Corasian galaxy."

Tusk luxuriated in this scheme for the few seconds it took the lift to whisk him upward.

What the hell? It passed the time.

He located Cynthia's room. She was out, but an electronic message flashing across the memo screen above the hand scanner advised all interested parties that Captain Zorn could be found in the officer's club.

Tusk had pumped himself up to make his presentation. Now he sighed like a deflated balloon. He'd have to delay their talk until he pried Cynthia out of the bar, steered her somewhere private. Fortunately, he knew how to manage that. He just hoped Nola would understand.

Arriving at the club, which looked like every other officer's club on board a naval vessel, Tusk peered around until he finally spotted Cynthia's blond head. She was sitting at a booth in the back of the club, practically hidden in a shadowy corner. Perrin and Dhure were with her.

"Figures!" Tusk muttered gloomily. "I suppose the prince himself'll come waltzin' in here next."

The three were deep in conversation, leaning over the table, their heads together. The music was loud, thumping through the metal deck.

Tusk was strongly tempted to take a detour to the bar for a quick one to help his nerves. He'd been trying to ignore the fact that his hands had started shaking the moment he'd walked off the lift. He glanced at the time.

No time. He continued heading for the table. Whatever it was these three were discussing, it must be serious. None of them heard him approach, or even noticed him until he was standing right in front of them.

"Hullo," he said.

He might have tossed a grenade into their midst. Cynthia jerked up, her startled face white against the dark leather of the high-backed booth. Perrin upset his glass, spilled his scotch. Only Dhure retained his accustomed calm. He nodded at Tusk.

"What can I do for you, Tusca?"

"Could I buy you all a drink?" He sat down, though no one had asked him to or particularly appeared to want him.

Cynthia and Perrin exchanged glances, and Tusk was suddenly struck by one of those flashes of insight that flares like lightning from the murky clouds of the subconscious. He had no idea what they'd been discussing, but he knew instinctively there was trouble and trouble might play into his hands if he was careful . . . very careful.

He took a seat next to Cynthia, gave his order to Dhure, who slid his card into the drink dispenser, punched in a rum and cola (a drink Tusk couldn't stand; he wouldn't be tempted to overindulge). Dhure handed the drink over. Tusk drank a gulp, kept control of his facial muscles to avoid grimacing.

"So, what's up?" he asked, playing nervously with his glass. "You guys look kinda off center."

All three exchanged glances this time. Then Cynthia said cautiously, "You haven't heard?"

"Heard what?" Tusk countered, taking another gulp that went down the wrong pipe.

They waited until he had finished half-strangling himself, then Cynthia—after still another round of glances with her cohorts—shrugged. "You might as well know, I suppose. It'll be all over the ship by morning."

"Maybe and maybe not," Tusk said, beneath his breath, taking care that they all heard him.

Cynthia raised an eyebrow.

Tusk shook his head. "I'll tell you later. You first."

"You've heard already, then. About Bidaldi?"

Tusk stared "Bidaldi? No, what's Bidaldi got to do with anything?"

"It's been attacked," said Perrin, and for the first time since Tusk had met him, good old Don wasn't smiling. Tusk considered it a distinct improvement. "Pretty near wiped out, from the reports we've heard."

"Attacked?" Tusk was truly astounded. "Who attacked it? Not Corasians. The Bidaldi system's in the center of the galaxy—"

"The Ghost Legion," said Dhure.

Tusk blinked. "I get it. We went to war and nobody bothered to tell me."

"Not us," Cynthia said, lowering her voice, casting a cautious look over her shoulder. "The real Ghost Legion. The dark-matter creatures."

"Is the prince out of his goddam mind?"

"Keep your voice down," Dhure advised.

"His Highness didn't have anything to do with it!" Cynthia flared. "The creatures acted on their own. He's as upset about it as anyone."

"Yeah, I'll bet he is," Tusk said. He lifted the drink, but his hand began to shake, so he was forced to set it back down. He was really putting himself into the part.

"Don't you dare—" Cynthia began angrily, but Dhure flashed her a look, and she subsided.

"What's wrong, Tusca?" Dhure asked with that maddening calm. "You look like you've heard some bad news yourself. Obviously not about Bidaldi."

"Naw, though it all fits now. All makes sense." Tusk twirled the glass around and around in the puddle of condensation that had collected beneath it. "I got to tell someone." He lifted his eyes, met theirs. "Though it could get me in a hell of a lot of trouble."

He laughed, a cracked laugh that he cut off quickly. "Yeah, as if I could be in *more* trouble. Or any of us could." He was silent a moment, considering, decided just to plunge ahead. "You got any idea what mission this ship's on?"

"We're going to stop a Corasian attack," began Dhure, apparently having elected himself spokesman.

"I mean the real mission," Tusk said.

Everyone looked at everyone else again. Then they all looked at Tusk.

Tusk mopped his forehead with his sleeve. "You've heard of the space-rotation bomb?"

They all nodded.

"Did you know it's aboard?"

Nobody said anything.

"Yeah," he went on, with another nervous laugh, "it's on board all right. And tomorrow morning, sometime around breakfast, it's going to go off."

The silence was so intense Tusk could have sworn he heard the ice in his drink melt. "Makes sense, when you stop to think about it. Takes care of the dark-matter creatures. And the king. And those of us who know the truth about Bidaldi."

"Usurper," Cynthia corrected automatically. "I don't believe it," she said flatly.

"How did you hear this, Tusca?" Dhure asked coolly. "Lord Sagan tell you?"

Tusk snorted. "Sagan wouldn't tell me the password to get into hell. Not that I'm likely to need it. I figure I'm a shoo-in. I'm his flunky. About to be his ex-flunky. Let's just say"—the mercenary slid the glass back and forth over the table—"that I overheard something I shouldn't have."

"What do you plan to do?"

"Me?" Tusk raised his head. "I'm gettin' the hell out of here. I was on my way to my plane, in fact, when I thought . . . Well, you guys have treated me okay. So I figured I'd give you the tip-off. And now"—Tusk breathed a sigh—"I'm outta here. Adios. It's been fun."

He stood up.

"You're not going anywhere, Tusca," Perrin said quietly.

Tusk put his hand on the lasgun. "Don't try stopping me—"

"Not me. The order just went out. All planes are grounded. No one leaves without His Highness's permission."

Tusk sat back down. "That does it, then. The tomb's sealed. What's the reason?"

"Security. With the Usurper on board. Lord Sagan's orders."

That bastard! Tusk thought. So this is how much he trusts me. Or maybe this is all part of the scheme. This is how he gets to be king. Double-crosses all of us.

Tusk's hand went nervously to the tiny device he wore embedded in his left wrist. A "bloodlink," Sagan had termed it, a communications device that drew its energy from Tusk's own body. He was, after all, half Blood Royal. The device was crude, but then—as Sagan had put it—so was Tusk.

I could ask. . . . Tusk was tempted. I could find out . . . not that he'd tell me. And what would I gain? I'm still trapped on this mother death ship!

"You can't be right," Cynthia said suddenly, startling Tusk. He wondered for a minute how she'd known what he was thinking about. But she was puzzling out her own loyalties, it seemed. "Flaim Starfire gave those orders. He's on board this ship himself. He wouldn't blow himself up!"

"You bet he won't," Tusk growled. "He'll be on the first plane off this crate. That's the plan. You watch. This is how'll it'll play. First, the fleet'll get orders to hit hyperspace. Then His Highness'll leave, catch the last ship out. And we're left behind on our lonesome, with that damn bomb ticking our lives away."

Tusk saw them exchange glances again. His gaze fixed morosely on his glass of watery rum and cola. He had them on the hook. All he had to do was reel them in. But sometimes that was the toughest part.

"I got an idea," he said.

Again, silence. Again, the eyes.

"The king—I mean the . . . uh . . . Usurper—knows how to disarm the bomb. When His Highness and the fleet are gone, we free Dion, let him disarm it. And we take over the ship."

"But that would be mutiny," Cynthia protested. "We'd be traitors."

"If the bomb is set to go off, like Tusk says," Dhure pointed out, "then *we're* the ones who've been betrayed."

Cynthia's face hardened.

Tusk had the feeling it was time to leave, let them flop and wriggle on the hook for a while. If he stayed longer—in his "unnerved" state—it might start to look phony. Besides, suddenly he wanted very much to be out of that room. The bar was starting to seem extremely small.

"Where are you going?" Perrin asked as Tusk stood up.

"Beats me," Tusk said, rubbing the back of his neck. "Maybe back to my plane. Maybe wait till morning, try to make a break for it. If you guys aren't in this with me . . ."

He looked around. Cynthia was defiant. Perrin wouldn't meet his eyes. Dhure only shook his head, but whether he meant no, he wasn't in this, or yes, he was, but he had to convince the other two, Tusk couldn't decide.

Figuring he'd done all he could—and far more than he'd expected—he said "Be seein' ya" and left.

He kept walking until he was far enough away from the lounge that none of the three were likely to find him. He had no clear idea where he was going, though he knew well enough where he wasn't—his quarters or his spaceplane. If the three decided against him, turned him in as a traitor, those would be the first places the guards would search.

Rounding a corner, Tusk looked up and stiffened. Two guards stood at the end of the corridor in front of a sealed door.

"So that's what you had in mind," he said, meaning himself. Dion's prison cell.

The guards hadn't noticed him yet. Tusk ducked down an adjacent corridor, flattened himself against the bulkheads. Did Dion know what was going on? Had he any idea? Had Sagan told him?

"No," Tusk answered that question quickly enough. "Of course not." He looked at his watch—0300 hours. He didn't have much time.

Dion should know. He had a right to know. He needed to be prepared. Surely it couldn't make any difference now. Flaim probably wasn't going to be wanting to try out his bloodsword technique any time soon.

"And besides," Tusk said somberly, admitting the real reason, "if anything *does* go wrong, I don't want him to die thinkin' he's alone."

Emerging from the corridor, he strode rapidly down the hall toward the king's cell.

The guards knew Tusk by sight from the alcazar. One, in fact, had assisted the mercenary back to his room the night he'd been "drunk."

Tusk grinned, to show they were all friends.

"You sober tonight?" the guard asked.

"Yeah. I'm on duty." Tusk grimaced; then he looked at them expectantly. "Well?"

"Well what?"

"You're supposed to let me inside there."

"Sorry, friend. Orders are: No visitors."

Tusk shook his head, swore. "Now, goddam it. Talk about inefficient. . . . They were supposed to let you guys know. Lord Sagan sent me. Word is that the Usurper's escaped."

One of the guards laughed. The other shook his head. "Hell, I think you are drunk. Unless he's turned himself invisible and can walk through a nullgrav steel door, he's still in that room where I left him an hour ago. Safely tucked in bed."

"He's Blood Royal," Tusk returned grimly. "In case you've forgotten. Those goddamn genetic wonders can do tricky things." He relaxed, once more on their side. "Look, I believe you, but Lord Sagan's got this idea in his head and I won't have any peace myself tonight unless I can go back and tell his lordship that, yeah, I saw the king—I mean the Usurper—and he's sleepin' like a babe.

"What'll it hurt? You open the door, let me walk in, have a few words with him to make sure it *is* him. You'll have me locked in there."

He pointed to the commlink. "Lord Sagan's order'll be comin' over in a minute." Tusk paused, frowned. "Or maybe you're questioning his lordship's—"

"No, no," said the guard, looking tense. "Like you said, you'll be locked in there. I guess it couldn't do any harm. Give me your lasgun, though."

Tusk unbuckled it, handed it over. To do otherwise would seem suspicious. He even submitted to being scanned and hand searched. Not finding any other weapons, the guards passed him through, unlocking the door by a series of complicated code commands they took care Tusk couldn't see.

The room was dark. Dion was lying in bed, eyes closed. Light from the corridor illuminated his face and Tusk had a sudden memory of the first night Dion had spent aboard the Scimitar. Tusk remembered seeing him lying in the hammock in exactly the same position. One arm over his forehead, the flaming red-gold hair spilling out from beneath it. His breathing was deep and even. He was sleeping soundly, without worry, without fear. It seemed a shame to wake him.

The room went all blurry. Tusk blinked his eyes.

"Shut the door," he said, voice harsh.

"Not too long," the guard responded. Then he added, "It sure as hell looks like him."

"Yeah, well, it would, wouldn't it?" Tusk snapped.

He hit the controls himself, left the guard to figure that one out.

Dim light from stars and one of Vallombrosa's moons lit his way. Dion's hair, in the starlight, was the dark crimson of fresh blood. Tusk stood beside the bed. His mouth was dry. He wondered suddenly what the hell he was going to say.

Reaching out his hand, he started to shake Dion's shoulder.

"Yes, Tusk. What is it?"

"You're awake," Tusk said inanely.

Dion sighed, sat up, shook his hair out of his face. "I heard you come in. I was dozing, I guess. I wasn't sure if it was you or part of a dream I was having. What is it? What do you want?"

When he'd first spoken, Dion had sounded like his old self. Like nothing had happened between them. But now, with the questions, his voice was cold, suspicious. The blue eyes glinted, white starlight reflecting off diamond-hard edges.

"I don't have much time." Tusk was having trouble breathing. "Look, kid, I got to tell you—"

The door whipped open. Light flared. Half-blinded, Tusk slid around, his hand going instinctively for his lasgun seconds before he recalled that he wasn't wearing it and that reaching for it would look all wrong. He shifted the move to bring his hand to his eyes, squinting and peering.

"What the—"

"Is that the Usurper?" the guard asked. He didn't sound sarcastic. Coming up behind him were six more guards. All had beam rifles. Three were pointed at Dion. Three were pointed at Tusk.

"Yeah, it's him," Tusk answered. He started to edge his way out the door. "Guess I'll be heading back to make my report—"

"Don't move," said the guard. To Dion. "Get dressed."

"Why?" Dion asked calmly.

"Prince Starfire wants to see you. Be quick about it."

"Do you mind if I have some privacy?" Dion asked coldly.

The guard considered it, then shook his head. "You"—he ordered Tusk—"out."

"Not until I hear from Lord Sagan," Tusk said. Leaning against a bulkhead, he crossed his arms over his chest, made it clear he wasn't moving.

The guard wasn't likely to shoot one of Sagan's henchmen, at least not without orders from someone higher up. The guard shut the door, left Tusk and Dion alone.

Dion dressed with exemplary care. Tusk, attempting to look put upon and disgruntled, wondered morosely how Dion had managed to keep the black uniform clean and pressed. He even added the purple sash, the lion's-head pin, and other royal accoutrements that had been, previous to this, stored away in a borrowed box.

He knows, Tusk realized suddenly. He knows.

Dion moved over to Tusk. Hand on his arm, he put his mouth to Tusk's ear. "The room is bugged. What were you going to tell me?"

"Good-bye," Tusk said quietly.

Chapter ·◄━⊃◯⊂━►· Five

Surely some revelation is at hand . . .
William Butler Yeats, "The Second Coming"

"Why have you brought him?" Flaim demanded of the guards, staring at Tusk. "I didn't send for this man."

The captain looked to Garth Pantha.

"I did, Your Highness," Pantha said quietly. "He obtained entry to your cousin's room, saying something to the effect that Lord Sagan was fearful your cousin had escaped. The guard on duty let him in, but reported the matter to his superior, who reported it to me, shortly after I arrived back on board. I didn't like the sound of it. I believe we should hear his story."

"Very good, Captain. That will be all." Flaim waited until the guards had gone, then looked at Tusk intently. "Lord Sagan thought my cousin had escaped?"

"Yeah. I mean, yes, Your Highness," Tusk stammered.

The mercenary would have given his Scimitar, with his right arm thrown in for good measure, to know if Cynthia had talked, maybe told Pantha. Tusk had to keep shoveling, however, even if what he was pitching turned out to be dirt from his own grave.

"You know how Lord Sagan gets," Tusk continued. "Well, maybe you don't. *Paranoid's* a good word for it. Comes up with these wild ideas. Dreams 'em, he says. He had a dream that he saw the kid, that is the king, here—or rather the Usurper— walk smack through a locked door. Now, he figures that, being Blood Royal, the kid, that is the king, I mean the Usurper, just might be able to—"

"That will do," Flaim interrupted coolly. "I will ask Lord Sagan when he arrives what he 'figured.' "

"You've sent for him?" Pantha asked. "I thought you said he'd left the ship to place the fleet on alert status."

"He should be back by now. Captain Zorn has gone to locate him."

Cynthia, huh? Tusk thought. So she was here, talking to His Highness. Well, that's torn it.

Tusk waited for the prince to have him arrested, hauled off, put in irons, but Flaim turned away, no longer interested. He had his own worries, apparently. The prince's face was grim. Whatever was going on, he wasn't happy about it. Neither was Garth Pantha. The elderly man sat hunched in a chair. He looked worn out, almost ill.

And Sagan's not gonna be any too thrilled to hear that I was caught talking to Dion, Tusk said to himself gloomily. And just what the hell has Sagan been doing all this time anyway? When is this signal of his going to come—not that I can do much about it when it does. And what is the goddamn signal?

Then Tusk remembered the bloodlink attached to his wrist. Lifting his left hand, he wiped his sweating face slowly.

"If you're counting on me seizing control of this goddam ship, you're in for a major surprise," he said softly into the small round metal disk implanted in his flesh. "A major, major surprise. I must have failed. Cynthia must have talked. Yeah, we're all in for a surprise. A bizillion-megaton surprise—"

Flaim was looking over at him.

Tusk coughed loudly, ceased talking. He'd said all he needed to say anyway. And speaking of a bizillion megatons, there it was. Sitting on a glass-topped table, like a goddam crystal knickknack.

The space-rotation bomb.

The last time Tusk had seen it, he and Dion had been transporting it for safekeeping to Bear Olefsky's planet. Tusk stared at the bomb. His mouth, his entire body seemed to go dry. Had Dion seen it? Tusk shifted his gaze to the king.

Dion was standing at the steelglass viewscreen, staring out at Vallombrosa. How often had Tusk watched Dion stand like that—hands clasped behind his back, eyes on distant stars, communing with who? Himself, his reflection—a pale ghost in the steelglass—or a God he had only just come to know? How could he be so calm? He must have seen the damn bomb. He had walked right past it.

Tusk was suddenly tempted to pick up the crystal cube and hurl it with all his strength into the wall. A stupid move. He wouldn't accomplish anything—the impact wouldn't hurt the bomb in the least—and before he could get his hands on it he'd likely be dead.

Flaim was armed with his bloodsword. Garth Pantha sat in the chair opposite and though the old man didn't look too good—sort of gray and shriveled—he could probably still handle that lasgun he was wearing. Not to mention guards posted outside who could be within shooting range in three seconds flat.

"But at least I'd be doing something," Tusk muttered, "Other than standing here, waiting to be blown back to my original components."

The skin around the bloodlink itched. He jammed his hands into his pockets to keep them from doing something stupid, like scratching at the metal disk, drawing attention to it.

And then it popped into his head to ask brightly, "Say, Prince, old chap, how much time have we got left?" Tusk was alarmed to feel the words in his throat, knew he was going to blurt them out. He gave another hacking cough, which startled everyone in the room.

"Got anything to drink?" he croaked.

Flaim cast him a disgusted look, motioned to a well-stocked bar in a corner.

Tusk walked over, grabbed a glass, shoved it under a spigot, and hit the first dispenser button he came to. Colorless liquid poured into the glass, probably vodka. Tusk wasn't choosy at this point. He picked it up, brought it to his lips.

After all, what the hell did it matter? Might as well go out with a bang. Tusk stared at himself in the metal reflection of the drink dispenser. His hand started to shake. He slammed the glass down, sloshing vodka over his fingers. Dumping out the liquor, he filled the glass with water, then discovered he couldn't drink it.

The double doors opened, Cynthia entered. She glanced at Tusk, glanced swiftly away again.

"Where the devil is Lord Sagan?" Flaim demanded impatiently.

"He has not returned yet, Your Highness. He's been to the other ships. He left *Flare* about an hour ago. The fleet is on full alert. I can only assume Lord Sagan is en route back here. He has not responded to any of my attempts to contact him."

"Odd," Flaim said, frowning.

"Possibly not, Your Highness," Cynthia replied. "The spaceplane Lord Sagan took has had trouble in the past with its two-way communication."

"We do not need him, my prince," Pantha said. He motioned the prince to come near him. He and Flaim spoke together, keeping their voices down.

Cynthia remained standing at attention, but her eyes shifted to Tusk. She didn't flush with guilt or look smug. Maybe he was wrong. Maybe she hadn't given him away.

Tusk looked pointedly—very pointedly—at the space-rotation bomb sitting on the glass-topped table. Cynthia followed his gaze. Would she know what it was? The damn thing looked so innocuous. . . .

Acting bored, Tusk sauntered over to the table. "Say, this is pretty fancy. What is it?" He reached out his hand.

"Don't touch that!" Pantha's hoarse shout startled even Tusk, who had been expecting it.

He snatched his hand back. "Sure. No problem. I'll just go fix myself another drink. Anyone else want one?"

Pantha didn't bother to answer. He turned back to Flaim, but Tusk noticed that the old man moved his position to keep an eye on the bomb.

Tusk strolled over to the bar. He had shown Cynthia—or rather Pantha had shown her—that the crystal cube was something special, something extremely valuable. Hopefully, Cynthia would add the cube and Pantha's reaction together and come up with the right answer.

He couldn't tell, by her expression, if he'd accomplished anything other than draw attention to himself. Tusk poured himself a bourbon, and this time he drank it.

"We will give Lord Sagan fifteen more minutes," Flaim told Pantha at last. "Then we will proceed. Captain Zorn, return to the flight deck, await my lord there. On his arrival, bring him here immediately."

"Yes, Your Highness." Bowing, Cynthia left the prince's presence. She did not so much as glance in Tusk's direction again.

Dion spoke, though he didn't turn around. "I take it that the dark-matter creatures have refused to cooperate?"

"Pantha was finally able to communicate with them," Flaim replied. "They have determined that we 'aliens' are a threat to their existence. It seems that they discovered—we have no idea how—Pantha's plans to build more space-rotation bombs. The creatures will destroy all humanity first before they permit such a thing."

"And so you will destroy them."

"No, cousin," said Flaim, with a smile, "*you* will destroy them."

"Unfortunately destroying myself at the same time."

"A terrible tragedy. One which the galaxy will mourn, even as they proclaim you a hero. I have sent for Lord Sagan to arm the bomb, set the detonation code. I thought you would like to witness that small ceremony before I lock the bomb up in that vault and leave. At least the knowledge that you are ridding the universe of these murderous creatures should provide you with some comfort in your final moments. What is it now, Pantha?" Flaim sounded irritated.

The old man was staring, frowning, at the bomb.

"I still find it strange that the creatures are not around here, keeping an eye on it, so to speak."

"How do you know they're not around?" Flaim asked. "They refused to answer your first communications, even when you tried them from Vallombrosa."

"The ship's sensor readings would indicate their presence. Nothing." Pantha shook his head. "Absolutely nothing."

"Perhaps they don't know what the bomb is. You didn't tell them when you sent them for it—"

"They know," Pantha said grimly. "They knew the first bomb they took was a fake, though they brought it back anyway. They sense the power."

"Even though it's not armed?"

"The power is still there. Arming the bomb accelerates it, moves it higher on the scale. I don't like this. I wonder what they're up to. . . ."

Flaim suddenly sucked in a breath. His face went white, the blood draining from it all at once, as if a vein in his throat had been cut.

The prince hurled himself at Dion. Grabbing hold of him, Flaim spun him around, flung him back against the steelglass.

The two stared at each other, a duel waging between them not the less deadly because it was fought in silence, without weapons.

"Pantha," Flaim commanded, hands clenched to fists, "arm the bomb."

"Now, Your Highness?" Pantha was staring at the prince in shock. "But Lord Sagan—"

"Damn Lord Sagan!" Flaim cried. Foam flecked his lips. "You fool, don't you understand? Arm the bomb!"

An expression of horror contorted the old man's face.

"My God!" he whispered.

He grabbed hold of the crystal cube with its glittering gold pyramid. Yanking the starjewel from around his neck, breaking the chain that held it, Pantha attempted to fit the jewel into the bomb.

His palsied hands trembled; he could not make the jewel fit. Flaim swore savagely. Pantha managed, by dint of sheer force of will, to control his shaking long enough to thrust the starjewel into the bomb. He punched in the code, stared at it— grim, intent. And then he hurled the bomb to the floor.

Tusk's heart stopped. Blue-yellow flame burst before his eyes and he thought for a horrifying instant that the bomb had gone off. When he could see again, he realized that it was his over-heated brain that had gone nova, not the bomb. It was lying on the floor at the old man's feet.

Now that he could think semirationally, Tusk remembered that the bomb couldn't explode just on impact. He stared at the crystal cube. Suddenly, at last, he was beginning to understand.

"You are right, my prince," Pantha said, disbelief and anger cracking his voice, "this bomb is harmless. *This* bomb is the fake."

Chapter ·◄◄►◄► Six

Oh, God of battles, steel my soldiers' hearts . . .
William Shakespeare, *King Henry V*, Act IV, Scene i

The bomb's a fake. The damn thing's a fake! We're not in any danger of being blown up. We never were. *This* is the signal. Tusk latched onto the first large chunk of coherent thought that bobbed past.

This is the signal!

Now is when I'm supposed to take over the ship!

He almost laughed out loud.

"I think we know why Lord Sagan has not yet returned," Flaim remarked.

"He switched bombs," said Pantha blankly.

"It had to be him, of course."

"He switched bombs!" Pantha repeated, as if he still couldn't believe it.

"I should have destroyed the fake! I thought it might prove useful . . . when we developed bombs of our own. I never supposed, never imagined . . ."

"The disruption in the electrical system . . ." Pantha continued the bitter litany. "And the fact that the dark-matter creatures were not here, on board ship. I wondered . . ." His fist clenched. "But I should have known!" He looked up, dazed. "And how did you know, Flaim?"

"My gentle cousin!" Flaim was staring at Dion. "I saw this in his mind, the day we fought that stupid duel. He had faith, you see. I couldn't believe it. I *laughed* at it. You simpleton, I told him. After everything Sagan's done to you . . . and still you trust him.

"Have you considered that your trust may be misplaced, cousin? It is just possible that Derek Sagan has betrayed us both. Used *us* to recover what he lost."

Dion made no response.

Flaim turned from him with a curse. Dion took advantage of

the moment to cast a swift, questioning glance at Tusk: What is Sagan's plan?

Tusk poured himself another drink. I wish the hell I knew—

A strong hand grabbed his shoulder, twisted him around. Flaim stood in front of him, practically toe-to-toe.

"What do you know about this?" Flaim demanded coldly. "What is Sagan's plan?"

"Damn it, you two are just plain weird!" Tusk looked from one cousin to the other. "How the hell should I know what his plan is?"

He grinned, shrugged. Now that the worst was over, he felt unbelievably calm. "Let's face it, Your Highness, if you were Derek Sagan, would you tell me *your* plans?"

"He does have a point," Pantha observed dryly.

"He does." Flaim regarded Tusk grimly. "But I don't believe him. However, we will soon discover the truth." He activated the commlink, but before he could say a word, a voice came over.

"Your Highness! I must speak to you. I have news about Lord Sagan."

"Cynthia!" Tusk whispered. Maybe there was hope, after all.

"Enter!" Flaim commanded.

She came in, a beam rifle in her hand. Her expression was grim, tense. She didn't even look at Tusk. He swallowed his hope, poured himself another.

"Your Highness! The fleet has made the Jump! They've all gone into hyperspace! Lord Sagan's orders. Was this by your ..." Cynthia had been about to say *command* but the prince's look of astonishment, kindling to white-hot fury, answered her question.

"The queen's ship?" Flaim could barely speak coherently.

"Yes, Your Highness." Cynthia swallowed, licked her lips. "And it was apparently given instructions to change course—"

"Damn!" Flaim exploded. It seemed for a minute as though the blast of his rage might tear him apart, but he managed to contain the damage, pick up the pieces. He rounded on Dion. "You have very little reason to smile, cousin. A minor setback that will soon be put right."

He turned to Cynthia. "This man"—Flaim gestured at Tusk—"is to be placed under arrest. He is a traitor."

Cynthia responded instantly, moved to stand beside Tusk. He

lowered his head, rubbed the back of his neck, tugged casually at his left earlobe.

Dion stood near the viewscreen. He had not moved. His thoughts were far away, perhaps with his queen and his unborn child. But he was paying more attention than he appeared. He had been watching Tusk obliquely and now, catching sight of the seemingly insignificant gesture, the king began rubbing his right palm.

"Take him to interrogation," Flaim was continuing. "I want to know . . ." The prince paused, as if uncertain how to proceed.

"Yeah, what is it you want to know, Your Highness?" Tusk interjected loudly. "The location of the *real* space rotation bomb? Not the phony—"

"The prisoner is not to talk, Captain Zorn," Flaim interrupted. "Unless he has something to say."

"Not the phony bomb, like the one you found—"

Cynthia slammed the butt of the beam rifle into Tusk's stomach. The blow doubled him over. She struck him again in the back of the neck, sent him crashing to the deck. And suddenly Pantha was on top of him.

"He's wired. He has to be! Yes!" Pantha caught hold of Tusk's wrist. He ripped out the metal disk, leaving five tiny spots of blood glistening on Tusk's black skin.

Pantha held the disk for the prince to see. "A bloodlink! He's been in contact with Sagan this entire time! And . . . Your Highness!" the old man cried, straightening. "I *know* where the bomb is. Where it has to be! In the alcazar."

"Bah!" Flaim snarled impatiently. "Sagan could have hidden it anywhere—"

"From us, yes, but *not* from the dark-matter creatures! They would keep close watch on the bomb. And *they* are still on Vallombrosa. Therefore the bomb is still on Vallombrosa."

Flaim paused to consider this, apparently decided it made sense. "What will the creatures do if he removes it?"

"I have no idea, Your Highness. They might try to stop him. They might simply accompany him to his next destination."

"Would they seize it from him if you ordered them?"

"Perhaps," said Pantha hesitantly, "but you must remember, Flaim, that the creatures are no longer taking orders from you. In fact, I begin to think that they have been *using* you. They used you to locate the bomb for them—"

"They brought it back to me, to Vallombrosa."

"The logical place. Here they would be able to keep it safe. They paid no attention to you when it seemed you were about to leave. They knew the real bomb was staying behind. I do not think—"

"Enough! I understand," Flaim snarled, irritated, his ego bruised and hurting. "So they were using me. Answer my question! Will the creatures recover the bomb?"

"They might take the bomb from Sagan, my prince," Pantha said gravely, "but I doubt very much if they would give it to you. You must go after it yourself."

"I can never reach the alcazar in time. It will not take Sagan long to retrieve the bomb and then leave."

"You can, Your Highness, if the creatures transported you. There would be a risk, but you could be there in seconds."

"An excellent idea. Talk to them, Pantha!" the prince urged, with mounting excitement, increasing anger. "The creatures may not be here, but they are certainly listening. Convince them to take me back to Vallombrosa. Wait! Perhaps we could simply tell them to stop him—"

"I would not advise it, Your Highness." Pantha was halfway out the door. "Their idea of stopping him might be to drop the alcazar on top of him . . . and the bomb."

"Promise them anything. Tell them I'll *give* them the space-rotation bomb, if that is what they want. It is the man *I* want." Flaim ground the words with his teeth, as if he were grinding flesh.

Lying on the deck at Cynthia's feet, Tusk looked at Dion. The king had not moved, stood rubbing his palm. Tusk rolled over on his back.

"Yeah, Your Highness, I guess you *are* kinda eager to get your hands on Lord Sagan. No one's ever played you for a sucker before, have they? So now you and the dark-matter boys are heading down to Vallombrosa—"

"Shut him up!" Flaim ordered irritably.

Cynthia walked over to carry out instructions, raised her foot to kick him in the mouth.

Tusk rolled, lunged, made a grab for Cynthia. The instant Dion saw Tusk move, the king sprang at Flaim, grappling for the bloodsword. His hands closed over the hilt. Flaim's hands closed over Dion's wrists. The two struggled.

Tusk got his hands around Cynthia's ankle, tried to drag her foot out from under her. He might as well have tried to pull a steel beam out of the deck. Cynthia knew this move, apparently. She smashed the heel of her free boot down hard on Tusk's hands, breaking his grip and maybe his fingers, kicked him in the face for good measure.

Turning from an agonized Tusk, Cynthia took a moment to determine the status of the battle between the cousins. She latched onto Dion from behind, dragged him off Flaim, flung the king backward.

Dion staggered, regained his balance, surged forward once again.

Cynthia lifted the beam rifle, fired.

The blast caught the king in the chest, sent him reeling into the couch. He collapsed onto the cushions, hung there a moment. His limp body slid from the couch to the deck.

"Kid!" Tusk made a feeble attempt to reach him.

Cynthia planted her foot on his chest, pinned him to the deck.

"You haven't killed him?" Flaim demanded harshly. "I may need him."

"No, Your Highness. My rifle was set on stun."

Flaim smiled grimly, drew several deep, heavy breaths. "Excellent."

Tusk's skull throbbed with pain. His mouth was split open; his jaw ached, his hand hurt. Cynthia's back was to the prince. She was looking down at Tusk. He searched her face, hoping for some sign, some softening of the tight-clenched jaw, a flicker of the eyelid.

Nothing. She wasn't looking *at* him, apparently, but through him.

Tusk blinked rapidly, tried to focus his blurred eyes. It was a struggle to remain conscious, and then he wondered why he bothered. He'd done all he could, and that hadn't been much. He'd failed.

So what else was new? Just one more failure in a long series of failures. At least this one was likely going to be his last. . . .

"Your Highness!" Garth Pantha came bursting back into the room, his robes whipping around his ankles. "The creatures are considering. They insist on speaking to—"

He stopped, stared in blank astonishment.

The prince was hauling Dion to his feet. The king was groggy, but he was conscious, appeared unhurt.

Flaim motioned to Pantha to come assist him. "We'll take my

cousin with us. Sagan won't do anything rash if he sees that the life of his precious king is in danger."

The prince had firm hold of Dion by one arm, Pantha took the other. Looking dazed and faint, Dion sagged limply between the two.

"What about Tusca, Your Highness?" Cynthia asked.

"Take him to interrogation. Find out what you can. Then, if he's not dead yet, kill him."

"Yes, Your Highness."

Tusk shut his eyes. Death sentence, huh? He really ought to do something about that. And he would, when he woke up . . . He heard Pantha and Flaim leave, dragging Dion with them. He heard the soft whoosh of the doors opening, sliding shut. . . .

She jabbed him with her toe. "On your feet."

Tusk rolled over, groaning loudly. He looked over at Dion . . . who wasn't there. No one was there.

Tusk blinked. "Where the—?"

"They've gone to stop Lord Sagan. On your feet," Cynthia repeated flatly.

He stood up, wiped blood from his mouth. "Now's our chance. We—"

"Shut up. Turn around." Cynthia pressed the rifle into the small of his back. "Keep your hands in the air. And don't try anything."

Four guards had entered the room, posted themselves at the double doors.

He lifted his hands.

"March," Cynthia said.

Tusk marched.

Four guards. I'll wait till I'm near the doors, then I'll jump her, get the gun away. The guards won't dare shoot me, for fear of hitting her. And good ol' Cynthia'll be my ticket outta here.

Tusk tensed, ready to spring. Then, "Shit!" he breathed.

A short, squat mechanical device trundled in through the open door.

It was his old friend—Mrs. Mopup.

The killer vacuum cleaner had at least one of her nozzles aimed right at Tusk. The four guards had turned their attention away from him, were looking at Mrs. Mopup, and grinning.

"Keep moving," Cynthia ordered. Her rifle jabbed him painfully. "You don't want to upset Mrs. Mopup."

Tusk made up his mind. Killer vacuum cleaner or no, he was damned if he was going to die screaming in some cell disrupter. He muttered a response, which was colorful, graphic, and would certainly *not* be included in a book of a famous hero's last words.

He took a step, planted his feet, and hurled himself sideways. Cynthia's forward momentum carried her on ahead. She started to turn. Tusk, twisting like a cat, jumped for her. His hands closed over the gun barrel; he tried to wrench it from her grip.

"You bloody fool!" Cynthia gasped.

Holding on to the gun, she jerked it from his grasp. The guards had stopped laughing and were dashing to her rescue. Cynthia lashed out with her foot, caught Tusk in the solar plexus, sent him crashing to the floor. The next moment, she landed squarely on top of him.

"Mrs. Mopup!" Cynthia shouted. "Shoot!"

Mrs. Mopup fired, four times, in four different directions simultaneously.

Chapter ❖ Seven

> . . . Many things answered me—
> Spirits and men—but thou wert silent all.
> Yet speak to me! . . .
>
> George Gordon, Lord Byron, *Manfred*

Emerging from the hatch of the commandeered spaceplane, Kamil gazed in wary, distrustful astonishment at the alcazar looming black against the brightening dawn. "What are we doing back here?"

"I left something behind," Sagan said, standing on the tarmac.

She stared at him in astonishment. "I thought we were going to save Dion. How can we—"

"If you're coming with me, hurry up," he told her coldly.

Kamil hesitated, frustrated. The journey to Vallombrosa had been accomplished in silence. His dark demeanor awed her, daunted her. Should she go? Or stay? What could she do if she went?

What can I do if I stay? she thought bitterly.

Kamil hurried, but she was awkward and slow-moving descending the ladder. Sagan's long strides had carried him to the entrance of the alcazar before Kamil was halfway to the ground. Afraid of being left behind, knowing she would certainly lose her way through the erratic jumble of corridors, Kamil slipped and slid the rest of the way down the ladder. Then she had to run to catch him.

"What was it you left here, my lord?" she asked, not really expecting an answer, but not liking the eerie silence of the halls of the abandoned alcazar.

"The space-rotation bomb," he replied.

"No," she said, not daring to hope. "It's on the ship. Flaim took the bomb on board."

"That one is fake. This one is real."

Kamil came to a halt, weak-kneed with relief. Dion was safe!

Her eyes flooded with tears. She dashed them away hurriedly, before he could see them, and hastened to catch up again.

It was black as night in the alcazar. Sagan switched on a nuke light, handed another to her. She flashed the light around, trying to figure out where she was, but she had no idea. She had never been able to find her way around. The oddly angled, distorted hallways had always reminded her unpleasantly of a fever-dream she'd once had. Sagan, however, moved ahead confidently.

"Will you tell me what's going on? Please, my lord?" Kamil asked him timidly. "I think I have the right to know."

"I switched bombs," he answered her—again to her astonishment.

But she had the feeling he was not talking to her. He was talking through her to someone else. So vivid was the impression, Kamil glanced to her left, half-expecting to catch sight of the lady. No one walked beside her, but the impression did not go away.

"Flaim didn't give a damn about convincing Dion to abdicate the throne. He wanted the space-rotation bomb and, in order to obtain it, he had to probe deeply into his cousin's mind, far deeper than he was able to do from a distance. That was his real reason for wanting to get hold of Dion.

"And it was my reason for bringing them together. My reason for forcing Dion to participate in the contest. I planned to switch the real bomb for the fake one. But in order to do that, I had to have the real bomb. Dion would never hand it over to me; nor should he. But Flaim would—unintentionally.

"I made the switch the night before we left Vallombrosa. Prince Flaim retrieved the bomb the next morning. He didn't know then that he was carrying the fake. He couldn't know. No one could who did not examine the bomb carefully. And then he would have had to know what to look for. Garth Pantha would have recognized the difference, but he had no reason to examine it. Why would he?

"If all had gone as I first planned," Sagan continued, talking to the lady, one longtime friend and companion to another, "Flaim would not have discovered the switch until he was on the other side of the galaxy, prepared to blow up the Corasians. I would arm the bomb and Pantha and Flaim would flee to safety. The bomb would not, of course, go off. Tusca and his mutineers would seize control of the ship, battle the Corasians if necessary, and return with the king to fight the pretender.

"That was my plan, my Lady," he said quietly, apparently completely forgetting Kamil's presence. "But the dark-matter creatures forced the issue and so I had to alter it. It is a pity they must be destroyed. They were undoubtedly harmless until they came in contact with humans. We contaminate everything we touch, it seems."

"What will we do now?" Kamil asked, speaking for herself. She had the feeling the Lady—if she was truly here—already knew the answer.

Kamil's voice reminded him of her presence. He glanced at her, made no mention of the fact that he had been talking to someone else. Probably he had not even realized it. But now he spoke to Kamil.

"I am going to arm the bomb and set it to explode—after we've left the planet."

"Won't the dark-matter creatures try to stop the bomb from going off?"

"They can't. Once the cycle is started, only the person who knows the code can stop the bomb from detonating. My guess is that *if* the creatures figure out it is armed and set to explode, they will be afraid to touch it, afraid they might set it off.

"Actually," he continued, "exploding the bomb at this location will prove far safer for the galaxy. According to my calculations, the anomaly of the strange dark matter should contain the power of the blast. Reduce its destructive force."

"But Vallombrosa will be gone?" Kamil looked around.

"Oh, yes," Sagan said dryly. "I simply meant the blast would no longer possess the force needed to tear a hole in the fabric of the universe."

"I see." Kamil swallowed. "And . . . after that . . . we'll return to the ship?" Back to Dion, she thought, but did not say. "What will we do then?"

"If Tusca has seized control, we simply walk on board. If not, then I will take over myself. In that eventuality, Flaim will probably escape us. And His Majesty will have a continuing fight on his hands. But in the end, Flaim will fall. He does not have the makings of a true king."

"Yet you said he passed the test. . . ."

Sagan glanced at her; a dark smile touched the thin lips. "Perhaps I lied."

"You should tell that to Dion, then," Kamil pointed out. "When this is over."

"He knows," Sagan said quietly. "He told you."

Kamil remembered her conversation with Dion in the courtyard. *You can't see down that road because that road doesn't exist for me,* he'd said to her then. *I am king.*

She flushed uncomfortably, fell silent.

They continued moving farther into the alcazar. The fortress was truly ghostly now. Unseen eyes watched them, unheard voices cursed them, silent footfalls accompanied them. A door opened as they passed by. Some distance ahead, another slammed shut.

Nerves taut, Kamil's hand fidgeted around the lasgun. She walked behind the Warlord and to his left, instinctively leaving his weapon hand free—though he was not armed—instinctively covering his back. She didn't even know she was doing it until she saw him give her an approving look.

"Your father has taught you well."

"Oh, this . . ." Kamil smiled shyly, pleased with his praise, glad to talk again. Their talk drowned out the whispers. "Actually, it was my mother. She is a shieldwife. Something I guess I'll never be," she added softly with a sigh, "no matter what happens."

"You have loved and been loved," Sagan said. "That is what's important."

Kamil, surprised, couldn't answer immediately. Perhaps Sagan had surprised himself with his comment because he pressed his lips tightly together, as if to keep a check on them.

A table tipped over as they walked past. A chair skittered across a floor.

She turned, nervously flashing the light behind her.

"The dark-matter creatures," Sagan told her. "They are watching us."

Kamil found herself walking at his side, almost touching him. He glanced over at her, frowned. Blushing, she fell back to her former position.

The silence, which wasn't silent, was unnerving.

"You were loved," Kamil said. "And you loved."

"Not enough," he answered.

A porcelain vase lurched to the floor, shattered. Kamil gritted her teeth, shut her eyes to what was going on in the darkness around her. She edged closer to him. "I don't understand."

Perhaps he needed the sound of living voices as much as she did. Or perhaps he was again talking through her to someone else. . . .

"We both loved other things more, and that came near destroying us."

"What things?"

"Power, for one. Glory, for another. Pride, ambition, the need to control everything around us." He looked down at the five scars on his hand. "Not surprising. We were bred to it. 'The taint in our blood,' my lady used to say. But that's no excuse. Dion was bred to it, as well. And he has turned out differently. *Glorie à Dieu.*"

"That's the reason you're doing this for him?" Kamil spoke hesitantly.

Sagan flicked her a brief glance, then looked away. "My lady sacrificed her life for him. Left him as a sacred charge in my care. If I had no other reason, I would guard him because of that alone. But Maigrey was right. Dion will be our redemption. Because of him, the Blood Royal will no longer be remembered with a curse. I have pride enough left in me to appreciate that.

"Not that I wasn't tempted," he added after a moment's thoughtful silence, talking again to his unseen companion.

"Flaim would have given me everything he promised. I would have been Warlord of a vast and powerful armada. But I saw how it would end. I would not be satisfied unless I had it all. Unless my power was absolute. I would challenge him . . . and he, being younger, stronger, would have defeated me. I would have fallen in ignominy and shame. I would rather die."

His expression was suddenly chill and cruel. Kamil caught a glimpse of the man he might become, of the man he had once been. She wasn't certain now that she trusted him. Which man was the truth? Did he know?

Kamil kept still after that, deciding she preferred the unquiet silence to any more disturbing revelations.

Sagan was also apparently no longer inclined to talk. He had come to a halt. Kamil, looking around, now recognized where she was—the great hall, where Flaim had brought them on that first terrible night.

The Warlord appeared displeased now, and impatient, and

once Kamil thought she heard him mutter. "I should have heard by now. Something's gone wrong."

She was frightened then; afraid for Tusk and for Dion. She ventured a question, but he ignored her. He shoved open the doors, entered the room.

The strong beams of the nuke lamps reflected brightly off the huge fireplace, the furniture, the near walls. She sent the light stabbing into the vastness of the hall, was sorry she'd done so. The darkness seemed to suck the light into its maw and swallow it. Kamil lowered the light swiftly, kept the beam on the floor directly ahead of her.

Sagan entered the room, his light flashing here and there along the wall. He walked across the stone floor, came to a tapestry. He pulled the embroidered and moth-eaten cloth aside, revealing a small door.

He looked back behind, flashed the lamp around the room briefly, then returned it to the door. He focused his light on the door handle. Reaching out, he plucked a small piece of black cloth from between the door and the frame. He nodded, satisfied. "Undisturbed. Flaim never thought to check. I'm going in here. Keep watch," he ordered.

Kamil stared inside when he opened the door, caught only a swift glimpse of the room's interior. It appeared to be a storage room. He shut the door.

Shivering, trying to tell herself that she didn't mind being alone in this terrible place, Kamil drew her lasgun and took up a position near the door. She even remembered to check the gun's setting, make certain it was on kill, not stun.

She stood in the empty hall, listening to the perturbed stirrings of the dark-matter creatures, stirrings that seemed suddenly to become angry, dangerous.

Kamil licked dry lips, held tightly to the gun, tried to keep her hand from shaking. With every breath she drew, a sharp pang of fear jabbed beneath her rib cage.

She recalled an old saying of her father's—something to the effect that the enemy climbing over the wall was always less frightening than the enemy hiding in the hills, and she suddenly realized its truth. She would have given a great deal for a real, live, solid, substantial person right now—be it friend or foe.

And then she heard Sagan's voice coming from within the

room, heard him swear a brief, bitter oath. Footsteps crossed the room. He yanked the door open.

"What—" Kamil began, but the question died on her lips. Despair and fear squeezed her heart.

"Flaim has discovered the fake. He and Pantha are on their way here . . . may be here already."

"Dion?" She asked it without a voice, only her lips moving. "Tusk?"

"They are bringing Dion here. Tusca has failed. I've lost contact with him. He may already be dead."

Sagan walked back into the storage room.

Kamil, not knowing what to do, stood staring into the whispering darkness until she felt it start to close in around her. It was trying to steal her breath, to suffocate her. She crept into the storage room, nearer the light, nearer Sagan.

His nuke lamp rested on top of a table, its harsh beam shining on a crystal cube with a golden pyramid in its center. A row of tiny buttons, each with a strange character on it, were positioned on the top of the cube.

He held in his hand a dark and ugly jewel, carved into the shape of an eight-pointed star. The jewel was revulsive to look upon, conjured horrible images in her mind. She saw a hideous, distorted twin of herself, evil, perverted, dancing on her own grave. Now she understood the expression on his face; fey, dire, doomed. He was seeing himself.

Kamil shuddered. She didn't want to look at the jewel, didn't want to look at him. Yet, she discovered, she couldn't look anywhere else. Her gaze was held by the jewel, by his face, both terrible and awful. She shut her eyes, but that didn't work, for she could still see the jewel's dark light and, worse, she felt as if she were slowly falling into its dark heart.

Opening her eyes, she asked him softly, "What . . . what are you doing?"

His large, strong fingers moving with incongruous delicacy, Sagan carefully embedded the jewel in the bomb, fitting it into a star-shaped depression obviously intended to receive it.

"Arming the bomb." He did not look at her. "You should return to the spaceplane."

"I couldn't. I don't know the way. I'd get lost."

"Your godmother will assist you," he said dryly. "She will see to it that you escape Vallombrosa safely."

Kamil only shook her head. "No, my lord. I'll stay."

He said nothing more. He began to punch in the code, repeating the words as he depressed each button. "'The center cannot—'"

Kamil heard movement behind her—real movement, solid movement.

Sagan lifted his head. Kamil turned, her lasgun drawn and aimed.

Dion and Flaim stood in the doorway. Kamil had a clear shot. But which was which? The white light of the nuke lamp reduced all complexities to simple shapes formed of brilliance and shadow, reduced the two cousins to one. The Starfire flared white-hot—all-consuming in one, blazing with a clear, pure light in the other. But it burned in the blood of both. And, for an instant, both looked uncannily alike.

Startled, uncertain, Kamil hesitated. In that instant, Flaim drew the bloodsword, held it in front of him, its shield activated.

"Take your hands away from the bomb, my lord. Keep them still. Make no move. Not so much as the flicker of an eyelid. Or His Majesty dies. You"—Flaim's eyes flicked to her, returned immediately to the Warlord—"throw down the gun."

Bitterly reproaching herself for her failure, Kamil held on to the gun more out of frustration than because she hoped to be able to do anything with it.

"Throw it down!" Flaim commanded.

"Do as he says," Sagan told her.

Half-blinded by tears, Kamil hurled the gun away from her. It slid across the floor, banged up against Flaim's foot.

A third person emerged from the darkness. Garth Pantha bent down, picked up the gun, thrust it into the belt of his robes.

"Move away from the bomb. Come out in the open, my lord," Flaim ordered. "Keep your hands where I can see them. Both of you—move!"

The prince began backing up, motioning with the bloodsword for the two inside the storage room to follow. He kept fast hold of Dion, pulled him along with him.

Dion was pale, dazed and groggy. He stumbled when he walked. He didn't even seem startled to see Kamil. He only looked bewildered, almost stupefied. And then his eyes rolled back, his head lolled on his shoulders. He fell to the floor, on his hands and knees. Flaim loosened his grip.

"Watch him, Pantha!"

Drawing Kamil's lasgun, Pantha held it to the king's head. "Keep walking, my lord!" Flaim ordered.

The Warlord emerged from the storage room. Kamil followed at his left, a pace or two behind and to one side. The part of the hall in which they stood was lit by the eerie blue glow of the bloodsword, the bright white glow of the nuke lamp. But most of the rest of the vast hall was in darkness, as though a gigantic hand was cupped over them, sheltering the light from a whispering wind.

Flaim made a gesture. "Pantha, go inside the room. Get the bomb. It's sitting on the table. And while he is doing that, you, my lord, will die."

Pantha left to obey the prince's commands. Flaim advanced on Sagan.

Dion lifted his head slowly. His eyes were alert, flaring blue. His fainting spell had all been an act, Kamil realized confusedly, but what could he do?

Attack Flaim with his bare hands, if nothing else. Dion gathered his energy and strength within himself. Coiled like a wild beast, he prepared for a desperate lunge.

Sagan looked at Dion, smiled slightly, shook his head. The dark, shadowed eyes shifted to Pantha, who was hurrying toward the storage room.

There lies your duty, Dion, his look said plainly. Kamil could almost hear the unspoken words. *You cannot save me.*

Dion understood. So did Kamil. Fear, anguish, and helpless frustration choked her throat. She longed to do something, but she had no idea what. She was afraid to interfere, afraid of destroying whatever slim hope they all had.

Face pale, jaw set, Dion altered his stance slightly, shifted his attention to Garth Pantha.

Flaim raised the bloodsword. The blade flared a brilliant blue. Sagan stood motionless, bathed in the blinding light, unarmed, unable, unwilling to defend himself.

"Now, child," spoke a cool, low voice in Kamil's ear, "be ready."

Chapter ❖ *Eight*

And so our scene must to the battle fly . . .
William Shakespeare, *King Henry V*, Act IV, Chorus

Bright white light blossomed around Tusk. He stared into it, awed, blind.

"I always heard," he said to himself, "that when you die, you move toward a white light. This is it. They're right. It *is* kinda pretty."

A heavy weight pressed down on his chest, but there was no pain. He waited to be absorbed into the light, to move off down the tunnel, to be welcomed by . . . oh, say, his father, maybe.

The heavy weight lifted from his chest. A shadow loomed before his dazzled eyes. A voice spoke. It wasn't his father, it was a woman.

Well, thought Tusk, this is almost as good. So long as she leaves before Nola gets here.

The woman leaned close to him and spoke again.

"Just what the hell were you trying to do?"

Tusk was confused. From all he'd heard, people weren't supposed to talk that way up here. The woman slapped him across the face.

Yep, he was definitely in the wrong place.

"Wake up. Snap out of it."

And now he noticed that the bright light had gone out. He had a brief and extremely unpleasant sensation of being rolled down a narrow black tube. He hit bottom and the impact jolted him awake. Alarms were buzzing raucously; the sound stabbed into his head. He looked up. Three people stood over him.

"I'm alive," he said, hoping for confirmation.

"No thanks to you," Cynthia snapped. "Of all the idiots— I had everything under control and then you—" Seething, unable to complete a sentence, she glared at him, then turned away. "We better shut off those damn alarms. We'll have every guard in the place down on us. Don, explain what's going on to the bridge.... I don't know. Make up something. You're good at that. Rick and I'll drag the bodies inside."

Tusk—still lying on the deck, still trying to figure out what had happened—watched dazedly. Perrin, on his way to the commlink, stepped over Tusk, grinned.

"Want a drink? You look like you could use one."

Dhure gave him a nod and half-salute as he walked past. He and Cynthia began dragging the smoking bodies of the guards into the prince's quarters.

"At least these weren't any of our guys," Cynthia said.

"We would have had to take them out anyway," Dhure commented. The last of the bodies was inside. He glanced down at the blood and bits of charred flesh left lying on the deck, shook his head. "There's a few more fanatics like them left on board, too. We don't have much time."

"Shut the doors," Cynthia ordered.

Perrin was on the commlink, talking to the ship's commander in soothing tones. Dhure walked over to Tusk, squatted down beside him.

"You okay?"

"Yeah, I think so." Tusk felt gingerly all over his body, couldn't find any holes. With Dhure's assistance, the mercenary staggered to his feet.

Cynthia glared at him again. "What the devil did you go and jump me for anyway? I'm on your side!"

"And how the devil was I supposed to know that?" Tusk demanded irritably, remembering. His hands started to shake. No, he said to himself angrily. Not now! "You could have given me the high sign—"

"Not with ..." Cynthia stopped. "Not with Flaim watching," she said quietly. She didn't look a whole lot better than he felt. "I intended to get you out of here, past the guards. Then we were going to meet up with Don and Rick and—"

Tusk patted her shoulder. "I'm sorry. I didn't know. I had visions of myself locked in some damn cell disrupter—"

"What's done is done." Cynthia cut him off.

"... must have got her wires crossed, sir," Don's voice drifted over to them. "The damn thing went berserk...."

Tusk grinned. "Good ol' Mrs. Mopup."

Cynthia smiled, but her smile didn't last long. She shook her head and sighed. Her gaze went involuntarily to the crystal cube with its golden pyramid, lying on the floor.

"It's not . . . not the real one?"

"So they say." Tusk wasn't about to go take a better look. "Anyone got an extra lasgun I can borrow?"

Cynthia popped open Mrs. Mopup's chest cavity, produced a lasgun and holster. "There's another beam rifle in here, as well. Disassembled. But it wouldn't take long—" -

"No, thanks." Tusk shook his head. "I got a couple in the Scimitar."

"Damn, this is an ugly thing." Dhure, squatting down beside the crystal cube, was careful not to touch it. "You sure it's fake?"

"I'm not sure of anything anymore," Tusk said grimly. "Pantha seemed to think it was a phony and my guess is he wouldn't have gone off and left it if it wasn't, but I wouldn't touch it. Especially the jewel."

The starjewel was lying on the floor, tangled in its chain. The glittering gem, carved of a rare gemstone by a process long kept secret by the High Priests of the Order of Adamant, was now dead and forgotten, as the priests themselves were dead and forgotten.

" 'A starjewel could never be accidentally lost or misplaced,' " Tusk said, hearing the echo of his father's voice, " 'but if it is willfully given up by its owner, it will start to die.' There's supposed to be a curse on anyone who takes a jewel that isn't rightfully his or her own."

"Who would want it?" Cynthia asked with a shudder.

The jewel's fiery heart was already beginning to flicker and diminish. Soon it would turn black and hideous to look upon. Tusk thought of his father's starjewel. It had shone clear and bright, its white light shining cold and pure amid the consuming flames of his funeral pyre. Even when the body had been reduced to ash, the jewel was unharmed, untouched. They had placed it in his tomb with the burial urn.

"Yeah," Tusk said, "who would want one?" Reaching down, he picked up the small metal disk, the bloodlink. He stuffed it in a pocket, buckled on the holster. "Can you get me flight clearance? Or do I have to shoot my way out?"

"You can get clearance." Don Perrin sauntered over, a glass of scotch in his hand. "The commander thinks Prince Flaim is still on board. His Highness is too busy to talk right now. So I'm relaying His Highness's commands. I'll tell the flight deck you're leaving the ship on His Highness's orders. Where did they all go anyway?"

"Vallombrosa," Tusk said, heading for the doors.

"And that's where you're going, isn't it?" Cynthia said.

"It's my job to rescue the king," he said.

"You mean the Usur . . ." Her voice died. She swallowed. "You've been on his side all along. You and Lord Sagan."

"It was Sagan's plan," Tusk said, shrugging. "I just did what I was told."

"I'm glad," Cynthia said suddenly. "I know it sounds silly, but even when you were supposedly on our side, I didn't much like you—betraying your friend like that."

"I didn't much like myself. You three are taking over this ship, right? What's your next move?"

"Mrs. Mopup will pay a visit to the bridge." Perrin stared into his glass, sloshed ice around. "Things could get real ugly."

"I doubt if it'll come to that," Captain Dhure said. "Once we explain what we know, the rest of the crew will listen to reason."

"And when they do, if you'll take my advice, you'll get this ship outta here. The real space-rotation bomb's down there"— Tusk gestured out the viewscreen toward Vallombrosa—"and the devil himself only knows what could happen. And, would you do me a favor? See if you can locate the queen. Take care of her, will you? If anything goes wrong . . . say Flaim manages to come out of this. . . ."

Dhure nodded. "Don't worry. I think we understand our prince a little better now than we used to. And ourselves even more. We'll see to it that Her Majesty's safe. It's the least we can do, to make up for what we did on Ceres."

"Thanks." Tusk nodded, turned to go. Then he paused, looked back at Cynthia. "Why did you do this for me? What made you change your mind?"

"I'm not sure. The creatures attacking Bidaldi. The other ships leaving and this one staying behind. The bomb on board, like you said. All of it happening just like you said. That. And him."

"Dion." Tusk guessed.

"The more I was around him . . . I can't explain it. But he *is* king. Do you understand?"

"No," said Tusk, shaking his head. "I never did."

"And you," she said. "I'm sorry I had to rough you up."

"I'm not," he told her, smiling. "I'm a happily married man."
He touched his split lip. "This makes it easier to say good-bye.
Take care of yourselves."

Careful to keep clear of Mrs. Mopup, Tusk edged his way
around the vacuum cleaner and left the prince's quarters, heading for his Scimitar.

"Yeah, he is king," Tusk commented on his way out. "And I
can't do a damn thing about it. Except maybe stop hating him
for it." Wincing, he inserted the tiny needles of the bloodlink
into his arm. "It's okay, my lord," he reported. "We've taken the
ship. I'm on my way."

Chapter ·❖❖◦ Nine

Things fall apart . . .
William Butler Yeats, "The Second Coming"

Flaim advanced, swinging the bloodsword in a flaming arc.
"Knock him off his feet, Kamil!" Maigrey's voice jolted
through the young woman like an electric shock. "Dive! Roll
into him!"

Kamil had no time to think, no time to prepare. She saw immediately the wisdom of the lady's plan and acted. Springing at
him in a diving, twisting roll, Kamil drove her right shoulder
into Flaim's knees.

Her move caught the prince off guard, took him completely
by surprise. Flaim pitched forward. His swing went wild.

The Warlord started to turn, to fall back, as Kamil dashed
forward. The arcing flame of the bloodsword struck him, but
the blow was not lethal, as it would have been if Flaim had
connected. The blade sliced into Sagan's left side.

He gasped in pain, put his hand over the wound. Blood
spilled over his fingers. Smiling grimly, he banished the pain,
forgot about it.

"Well done, my lady," he said, and started for the storage
room.

Dion ran past him, hoping to stop the old man before he
could reach the bomb.

"Pantha! Look out!" the prince shouted, struggling to regain
his feet.

Pantha turned around, lifted the lasgun . . .

Dion slammed into the old man, grabbed Pantha's hand. The
two rolled on the floor, wrestling for the gun.

Flaim started to go to his friend's aid, but Kamil lunged for
him, grabbed hold of his leg, tried to drag him back down. The
prince kicked at her savagely, endeavoring to free himself.
Cursing, he lifted the bloodsword over her head.

"Drop it!" roared Tusk.

The mercenary stood in the doorway, peering into the flaring light, the baffling darkness. He saw the blue flash of the sword, caught a glimpse of Kamil, her face bruised and bloodied, yet still clinging to Flaim.

"Drop it!" Tusk yelled again, and then he fired.

The sword's light disappeared. Flaim shifted from attack to defense. Tusk's shot burst harmlessly on the prince's shield, but it gave Kamil time to get out of the way. She crawled on her hands and knees, then fell flat, limp, unconscious. Tusk dashed to help her, firing again, forcing Flaim to use his weapon to protect himself.

Pantha fought Dion with the strength of despair. But Tusk's shout and firing distracted him.

"Flaim?" Pantha tried to find his prince. His deathlike grip on the gun relaxed.

Dion wrestled it from him, jumped to his feet, and made a dash for the storage room.

Derek Sagan was there ahead of him. He held the bomb in a blood-stained hand.

"I'll cover you, my—" Dion began.

Sagan shouted in warning.

A blow smote Dion from behind, sent him staggering to his knees. Flaim hurtled past the king, bloodsword again flaring blue. He was no longer interested in Dion. The prince wanted the bomb—and his revenge on the man who had betrayed him.

Tusk stood protectively over Kamil, peering into the flaring light, trying desperately to see. His lasgun was raised, but he didn't dare shoot, for fear of hitting either Sagan or the king.

Dion was on his feet again. He surged forward, caught a confused glimpse of Flaim and Sagan, of blue fire reflected in the bomb's crystal . . .

And then darkness.

Dion halted so suddenly, he nearly fell over.

Nothing in the room but darkness. The prince and Sagan were gone.

"I'll be a son of a bitch," Tusk breathed in awe.

Splatters of blood marked the place where the two had—only seconds before—been standing. They had both disappeared, as if they had been swept up by the whispering shadows.

"What the—" Tusk began.

"The dark-matter creatures!" Pantha howled, his voice rising to a triumphant shriek. "They have him!" Whirling, robes flapping, the old man raced for the doors.

Dion started to run after him.

Tusk grabbed on to his sleeve. "Kid! Wait! Let him go! Who knows where the hell the creatures took Sagan?"

"Pantha knows, obviously," Dion said grimly. "I'll follow— Dear God! No!"

They'd come out of the storage room. Tusk was carrying the nuke lamp, flashing it around. The light beamed on Kamil's body lying on the floor.

Her face was battered almost beyond recognition, swollen, bruised. A dark streak of blood trickled down from her skull. One arm was twisted at a strange angle, the fingers of her left hand were broken and bleeding; jagged bone shone white in the harsh light.

Dion took a step toward her, then stopped. Anguished, he looked in the direction of Garth Pantha.

"Kid! She's hurt bad!" Tusk said urgently. He knelt beside her, was examining her with gentle hands. "I think her skull's fractured."

"Take her back to your plane, Tusk. I'll be there as soon as I can." Dion turned away.

"That won't be soon enough!" Tusk told his back. "She's dying!"

Dion stopped. He put his hands over his eyes, shuddered. Then, not looking back, he started forward again.

"Your duty lies here, my king," came a clear voice.

A woman, clad in silver armor, appeared before him.

"Nope," Tusk muttered in a tight voice, "I don't believe it. I do not believe it."

"My lady!" Dion stared at her in awe.

"Let the others continue the battle, Dion. Your task is to heal the wounds. Your duty is to your subjects, to Kamil and Tusk, to your wife and child. Take Tusk and Kamil out of here. Lead them to safety."

"But . . . Sagan, Flaim . . ."

"The bomb is armed. The code has been entered. My lord has only to add one more letter—the last letter of the last word—and the bomb will detonate."

Dion was silent a moment. Then he said, "He won't be able to escape, will he?"

"No," Maigrey answered quietly. "But all is as it should be.

Once, long ago, he pledged his life to his king. This day, he will keep his vow."

Dion hesitated. He looked again at Kamil. Tears filled his eyes. He looked back at Maigrey. "I can't leave him to die alone."

"He won't be alone," she said softly. She rested her hand on the hilt of the bloodsword at her side. "And now you must hurry. My lord will buy you what time he can, but you don't have long. Farewell, my king."

"I won't see you again, will I?"

"No, Dion. It is time for your Guardians to leave you. You need us no longer. May God bless and keep Your Majesty."

And then she was gone, as if she had never been.

Except that Dion could see, in his dazzled vision, the bright, argent glow of her armor, gleaming cold and pure, like the moon.

Chapter ❖❖◯❖◐❖ Ten

Though much is taken, much abides; and though
We are not now that strength which in old days
Moved earth and heaven, that which we are, we are:
One equal temper of heroic hearts,
Made weak by time and fate, but strong in will
To strive, to seek, to find, and not to yield.

Alfred, Lord Tennyson, *Ulysses*

It seemed to Sagan that he had shut his eyes in the great hall, blinked to find himself somewhere else. The movement was so swift that he had no sensation of it at all, beyond the strange feelings elicited by the proximity of the dark-matter creatures. That, and their fear and their anger.

They seethed around him, invisible, but he could sense their threat, like smelling thunder on a still summer night. He wondered how they knew their danger had increased. Undoubtedly they could sense the heightened energy of the armed bomb. But why didn't they take it, why take him with it?

Afraid. Perhaps afraid that they might accidentally set it off. For they have no concept of how it works—only the knowledge that, unless it can be stopped, they are doomed.

And so they had brought him here, away from help. And they had brought his enemy with him.

It took Flaim a moment to assimilate where he was. He, too, glanced around in astonishment. Then recognition dawned.

Moonlight streamed in through a barred window, illuminated five cells, which were actually nothing more than five small caverns scooped out of the solid rock of the planet's interior. Iron bars stood before each cell. The bars had been driven into the ground like javelins thrown by some immensely powerful hand. The five cells formed a crude star shape around a center open area: two facing each other, one at the head. A five-pointed star, locked in a dungeon.

"How suitable," said Sagan to himself.

He put his hand to his injured side. The wound was serious,

deep, but not mortal. He had lost a lot of blood, but he felt no pain. He had learned when he was a boy how to thrust pain down into the depths of his being, how to ignore it, banish it from his mind. His wound was an irritant only, a stiffness in his left side that hampered swift movement, a catch in his breathing every now and then, when his discipline slipped.

He could fight with such a wound, could hold his own against an enemy—even an enemy young and strong and uninjured, like the one standing before him. But Sagan was not armed. He held the bomb, and it was armed, the code was entered. He had only to add one more letter and it would explode, destroying Flaim, destroying the dark-matter creatures, destroying itself.

Unless he could gain time, the bomb would also destroy his king.

Flaim knew where he was now, what had happened. He smiled at Sagan grimly. "You're finished, my lord. You have no weapon. Put the bomb down, surrender."

"I surrendered only once in my life," Sagan replied. "Long ago, when I was young. To a man called Abdiel. A mistake. I swore I would never do it again. If you want the bomb, you must kill me."

Sagan held the bomb in front of him, in his left hand. He put his right hand on top of it, on top of the row of buttons. "And you must act swiftly. Your aim must be certain. You must kill me before I press this one button. Once I touch it, the bomb will detonate in five minutes."

"Hardly time enough for your precious king to escape," Flaim said, unconcerned. He advanced, bloodsword blazing. "And I don't need to kill you. All I have to do is sever your hand from your body. And I think—"

Still talking, hoping to distract him, Flaim lunged.

But Sagan had been watching the prince's eyes, not listening to his voice. He saw the blow coming. Springing aside, Sagan hurled the bomb at Flaim.

The bomb's crystal case flared in the sword's light. Nothing could harm it, not even the bloodsword. Without the code punched in, the bomb would land harmlessly on the floor.

But Flaim reacted involuntarily, as Sagan had hoped he would.

Seeing the bomb flying at him, the prince arrested his stroke to avoid hitting the bomb. He cringed involuntarily as it tumbled to the floor.

"My lord!" a voice cried. "You have a weapon now!"

She stood before him, pale hair, sea-gray eyes, shining silver armor. A bloodsword spun in the air, flung from her hand to his hand—a move the two had spent endless hours practicing together.

He caught it without thinking, just as he had responded without thinking to Kamil's diving roll. In his mind, she had been Maigrey and they had been in Abdiel's prison, or on the Corasian mothership, or in any other of the countless battles they had fought together.

It was not surprising that she was with him and that she had thrown him her weapon.

He caught it, inserted the needles into his hand, felt the painful, stimulating warmth of the micromachines surging into his body, felt the sword become one with his mind.

The weapon flared blue. Flaim fell back before the Warlord. The prince's baleful gaze darted around the cell block. He could not see her, but he knew she was there.

"So, Lady," the prince said, "I wondered how long you could stay out of this fight without interfering. And you, my lord." Flaim took a defensive stance. "What about your vow to forgo the use of weapons?"

"I've broken so many vows in my life," Sagan responded, watching the eyes, "one more isn't likely to make much difference."

"You're an old man." Flaim sneered. "Old and weak and hurting. How long do you think you can last against me?"

"Dion is returning to the warship with Tusk," Maigrey said to Sagan, her voice singing its sweet, familiar music in his mind. "They need time to reach the plane, leave orbit, and enter the Lanes."

"Long enough, Your Highness," Sagan responded.

They circled around each other, around the bomb, lying on the floor between them.

A feint. No takers.

Another feint. A quick strike.

A flurry of blows, blue sparks flaring.

Shield, attack.

Attack, shield.

Around and around.

Watch the eyes. Watch the eyes.

And on and on and on.

Buying time.

Sagan's wound reopened, started bleeding. He was conscious of pain now, pain he could no longer ignore. He was growing weak from blood loss. The weakness and the pain affected his use of the bloodsword. Keeping the shield up took more energy, greater concentration.

Soon, he knew, it would take more energy than he possessed. A broken old man.

Flaim saw his opponent's weakness, saw it in small mistakes—in missed footing, in strokes that pulled up short. The prince redoubled his attack. The Warlord's skill and experience kept him alive, were all that kept him alive against Flaim's strength and agility and youth.

On and on and on.

Watch the eyes . . .

Watch . . . the . . . eyes . . .

The Warlord was nearing the end, and Flaim knew it. The prince was setting a trap, pretending to be weakening himself, hoping to draw Sagan into making a rash move that would leave him open, unguarded.

It was old gambit, well executed . . . except that at the last moment, the trap closed over the trapper.

Sagan lunged, struck.

Flaim flung himself down, threw himself flat on the floor. The bloodsword flared in a flaming arc over his head.

And then the bastard prince should have died at the Warlord's hand, as had so many before him. But Sagan lacked the strength to press home his advantage. He staggered back against the wall, drew a ragged breath, tried to clear the mists that were fast dimming his vision.

Maigrey was with him, watching him. He could see her now, see her so very clearly. She had remained silent, not moving, knowing better than to do or say anything that might distract him. The moonlight shone on her pale hair, shone on the silver armor. She was starlight, pure, cold, ethereal.

His eyes went to her and beyond her, out the barred window, into the night skies. Another star—or what seemed a star—lifted off from the planet's surface, rose into the heavens.

Sagan followed it with his gaze. It was, like her, the only light he could now see.

"Dion," she said to him softly.

The light of the spaceplane flared, blazed a fiery trail, like a comet across the night sky. The light soared—a brilliant and radiant light that glinted off blue eyes like moonlight on a frozen sea. It shone warm and red-golden in the center of the galaxy like a lion-faced sun. It would burn long and bright, and when its glow faded into peaceful darkness, other lights would have been kindled from it, their bright fires illuminating hearts, keeping back the fear of night.

The light vanished. The spaceplane had entered hyperspace.

"My lord!" Maigrey shouted a warning.

Flaim was on his feet, lunging. The bloodsword's lethal light flared, blinding. Sagan raised his sword, activated his shield. His own light burst, then died.

Flaim's sword entered the Warlord's body, drove Sagan back against the wall, pinned him.

The prince stared at him a moment in grim triumph, then yanked the flaring blade free.

A gush of dark blood spewed out. Horrible, searing agony ripped at Sagan with fiery claws. He doubled over, his hands clutching his wound, trying vainly to hold on to his life, which flowed out, red, over his fingers.

Maigrey stood watching, silent, unmoving, the tears the dead could not shed shining like starjewels in her gray eyes.

The prince stepped back to gloat over his victory, stepped back to watch his enemy die.

Sagan reached out his hand . . .

"Flaim! Stop him! Stop him!" Pantha screamed from the prison entryway.

Flaim—seeing at last the Warlord's intention—flung himself at the dying man.

Too late.

Sagan's bloodstained hand grasped hold of the bomb, fumbled for the button, the fourth one from the beginning of row twenty-six.

The one marked with the symbol *d*.

Convulsively, gasping, eyes closed against the burning pain of death, he pressed the button down.

Thin beams of light, like tiny threads of starfire, radiated outward. They extended from the starjewel, planted in the bomb's heart, to the golden pyramid. When the light touched the pyramid, the bomb began to make a faint sound, as if humming to itself.

Flaim stared at it, his eyes wide in horror. "Stop it!" he breathed.

Sagan lay on the floor. "Five minutes," he said, and the words came out a whisper, stained with his life's blood.

"We must get out of here!" Pantha screeched. He caught hold of Flaim, fingers like talons. "The creatures! The creatures can save us. Quickly, my prince. We must reach the room! We must communicate with them."

Flaim flung the old man away from him.

"Why?" he demanded savagely, standing over Sagan. "Why? *I* was everything *you* wanted to be!"

"That is why," Sagan answered.

"Flaim!" Pantha begged.

The prince glared at Sagan in impotent outrage; then, turning, he ran from the star-shaped prison. Pantha dashed after him.

Maigrey watched them leave, then shut the door.

Kneeling on the floor beside the Warlord, she drew off her blue cloak, folded it, gently placed the bundle beneath his head. He groaned in agony when she lifted him. She took hold of his right hand, brought it to her lips, clasped her own right hand tightly around it.

He looked up at her.

"You're not crying, are you?" he asked, with a faint touch of irritation.

"No, my lord," she said softly. "I'm not crying. I can't."

The beams of light in the bomb grew stronger, brighter. The humming grew louder, was harsh and discordant.

Sagan looked at it and his face blenched. He couldn't help but think of the end, the blast, the one unspeakable, horrifying moment of unendurable agony before the blessed solace of death.

Maigrey saw his glance. She leaned forward; her pale hair fell around him like a curtain, hiding death from sight.

The floor and walls began to shake, shuddering as if in terror. A crash and a rumble came from somewhere in the alcazar. Rock dust drifted down over them. And out of the night—a hideous shriek of rage, a despairing wail of terror.

"The creatures have answered Flaim's plea," Maigrey said.

He tried to speak, but blood flowed from his mouth. He choked, fell back, shuddering.

"Hold fast to me, my lord," she said. "I'm here."

He gripped her hand hard. The spasm passed. Everything else seemed to be fading from his sight, was drowning in darkness. Everything except her. She shone more clearly, became more real to him each passing moment.

"What did you give up to come to me, my lady?" he asked her. Their minds spoke. His voice was silenced forever.

"Nothing that matters, my lord," she answered.

Lifting his left hand with a great effort, he smoothed back the pale cloud of hair, touched her cheek, ran his fingers along the scar. He left a crimson mark, his own blood.

"Your soul. You are damned, my lady, as I am damned."

"My soul was never mine to lose, my lord. It was yours. Always yours."

He smiled, a true smile. And then he stiffened. A stifled cry of wrenching agony escaped his lips. The pain was unendurable.

"Not long now," Maigrey said softly.

The starfire light inside the crystal case shone brightly, pulsed stronger than his own torn and wounded heart.

"Don't leave me," he breathed.

"I won't," she promised.

She bent over him, put her arms around him. She lay her head on his breast.

"Ever."

The center cannot hold.

Chapter ❖⊰◦⊱❖ Eleven

KING: I tell thee truly, herald,
    I know not if the day be ours ...
HERALD: The day is yours.
    William Shakespeare, *King Henry V,* Act IV, Scene vii

The Scimitar shot through the Lanes. The silence on board the spaceplane was one with the silence of the eternal night around it. The only words spoken were terse conversations between Tusk and the computer, figuring the fastest way possible to get the plane off Vallombrosa and into hyperspace.

Dion had carried Kamil from the alcazar. He made her comfortable on the bed, as comfortable as possible; she was wandering, now, in her mind. He sat beside her in a chair. So many miracles were needed now; what gave him the right to ask for this, in particular? His thoughts went back to the golden-tinged day he'd met her. He'd been so lonely then. Searching desperately for someone to love, for someone to love him. He had found her. She had found him.

His shieldmaid. As in the dream, she had fallen, protecting him. As in the dream, he would pick up his weapon and go forward, leaving her behind.

He held her hand and her wild ravings ceased. But she sank into a frightening sleep, which seemed far too deep. Try as he might, he could not rouse her.

He was aware of Tusk, standing at his shoulder.

"We're ready to make the Jump. Is she ... is she any better?"

Dion shook his head.

Tusk, who could see things for himself, laid his hand in silent sympathy on his friend's shoulder, then returned hastily back to the cockpit.

Dion listlessly strapped himself in, made Kamil secure. He had long ago learned to cope with the effects of leaping into hyperspace. Leaning back in his chair, he forced himself to relax, closed his eyes.

They were fighting together, side by side. The battle raged around them. Friends and comrades fell, struck down, dead, dying. And then there came a lull. The horrific noise of slaugh-

ter ceased. The enemy was gone. The two of them stood alone
on the field, resting, waiting for the next onslaught. They could
hear the din of terrible trumpets. It was coming. He drew his
bloodied sword, advanced to meet it. He turned to smile one
last time at his shieldmaid.

But she had laid down the shield, laid it at his feet. Reaching
out her hand, she took the sword from him, to wield it for herself.

"The shield is yours, sire, to defend and protect. It is my
place to continue the fight. Good-bye, Dion. . . ."

"Dion . . ."

He jolted awake. Kamil lay propped up on one elbow, her
hand on his arm, shaking him. Her face was bruised and covered with blood, but her eyes were clear and focused and alert
and puzzled.

"You're all right!" he breathed.

"I'm fine," she said, "except for a splitting headache. And,
oh, Dion, I had the strangest dream . . ."

⋯⟨⊃⟩⟨⊂⟩⋯

The Scimitar was in the Lanes, putting light-years between
them and the Vale of Ghosts. They were safe. Unless the universe ripped apart—always a possibility, however remote, with
the space-rotation bomb.

The three of them could do nothing now but wait. Kamil ignored pleadings to stay in bed. A shot from Tusk's medkit eased
the pain in her head. She came forward, to be with Dion and
Tusk. They huddled together in the small cramped cockpit,
waited in silence. To try to put into words what they had seen,
what they had been through, what they faced would have de-
meaned it, diminished it. And so they spoke of it in silence,
heart to heart, and found far greater comfort.

It was Tusk, sitting in the pilot's chair, who first broke the silence, broke it softly, reluctantly. "We're coming up on the
point you wanted to leave the Lanes, kid. Do you— Shall I . . .
take us out?"

"Yes," said Dion.

"Get hold of Dixter, fast," Tusk told XJ.

XJ obeyed without adding its normal sarcastic comment. Either the computer was impressed with the awful solemnity and
tension of the situation or else the threat Tusk had muttered
under his breath when they first came aboard had been dreadful enough to at last muzzle XJ-27.

"Sir John Dixter, Your Majesty," announced the computer in a tone that could almost have been called respectful.

"Dion! Son!" Dixter appeared to be struggling against a need to reach out and embrace the vidscreen, a need to reassure himself that Dion was real. "I heard what happened! Are you all right? And Tusk and—"

"We're fine, for the moment. All fine. How did you know—"

"Her Majesty." Dixter's expression was grim. "She's been in contact with us. Yes, she's safe. Sagan spoke to her on board the ship, told her what he planned. He also gave her the names of some people she might be able to count on—friends of ours, Tusk, from the old days. Gorbag the Jarun, some of the other mercenary pilots.

"They'd all grown disenchanted with the prince, especially when they heard that the dark-matter creatures were running amuck. The queen was able to persuade them to help her seize control of the ship. They did so, without bloodshed. She's a remarkable woman, Dion," Dixter said with enthusiasm, speaking before he thought.

He looked uncomfortable immediately after.

"Yes, sir," said Dion, smiling, "she is."

Kamil stood up suddenly from the co-pilot's chair where Dion had ordered her to sit. "You belong there," she told him. "Tusk . . . might need your help."

"Kamil . . ."

"No, it's all right. Really." She smiled at him.

"Kid?" Tusk twisted around.

"Yes, I'm here," said Dion briskly.

He took the co-pilot's seat, continued talking to Dixter. "You know, then, sir, what Sagan planned to do. How he switched bombs. He was going to detonate the space-rotation bomb harmlessly, far, far out in some remote part of the galaxy. But . . . it didn't quite work out."

Dion cleared his throat, his voice choked by the ache of fear and dread inside him. "Flaim discovered the plan at the last minute, went to Vallombrosa to try to stop Sagan. We escaped. My lord . . . did not."

"Yes, son," said John Dixter. "I know. You see . . ." He hesitated, rubbed his jaw.

"Tell me," Dion commanded. "What happened?"

"Vallombrosa's not there anymore, son. The planet's gone—as though it had never been. Nothing left of it, that we can detect. Of course, we can only scan it from a distance. We don't dare send in recon planes. Not yet. Sagan was correct in his postulation that the dark matter would contain the blast. He theorized that the dark matter would act like a shield, prevent the chain reaction from continuing throughout the galaxy. Destruction was confined to a relatively limited area."

"To Vallombrosa."

"I'm sorry, son," Dixter said. "There's a possibility, of course, that Sagan could have escaped. . . ."

Dion stood up.

Tusk glanced at him, shook his head, looked away.

Kamil reached out a hand to him. Dion didn't see it. He walked blindly to the ladder, climbed it—apparently by feel alone—disappeared up into what had once been the gunner's bubble, was now the observation dome.

⋯◁═╳◯═╳▷⋯

Dion sat in the bubble, staring out into space, its dark deadly blackness sparkling with myriad roaring furnaces of suns. Immense fires that give birth to life, sustained life, destroyed life. Viewed from this distance, the suns were nothing but tiny white sparks in the vastness of the universe.

In the vastness of the mind of God.

Vallombrosa. Valley of Ghosts. Gone as if it had never been. His cousin. Gone, too.

Dion looked at his right palm. The five wounds were no longer swollen, had ceased to pain him. Soon they would fade to nothing but five white scars on his hand, for he would never use the bloodsword again.

Derek Sagan.

Dion stared into the darkness and its coldly burning stars and thought of the man whose darkness had cast a shadow over the king's own life, a shadow that had forced Dion to close his eyes, look inward, see his own darkness. Only then had he been able to open his eyes, see beyond the darkness, to the light.

Well done, boy.

He heard the words echo in his mind, heard them again, as he had heard them clearly that day of the duel. It was then that he had known for certain that Sagan had not betrayed his oath, that he was his king's Guardian, as he had sworn so long ago. It was this faith Flaim had seen inside Dion, though his cousin had not been able to recognize it. It was this faith that had, Dion supposed, cost Sagan his life.

I can weep for him, Dion thought, but I can't grieve. As Maigrey said, all is as it should be. There is a rightness about it, a suitability. A fittingness, in the mind of God.

He knew it, though he couldn't explain how. It was as if a door had opened and he had been permitted a swift glance inside before it slammed shut again.

Cold fingers touched his hand; Kamil's hand closed over his. He drew her up, into the bubble, to sit beside him. There was a rightness about this, too. He couldn't grieve.

"She and Sagan are together again, aren't they?" Kamil said softly.

"Yes," answered Dion.

"As we will be together . . . someday," Kamil said.

"Someday," Dion held her hand fast.

" 'You have loved and been loved,' " Kamil said, almost to herself. "I understand now what he meant."

"We should be thankful," Dion said, his eyes on the stars. "What happened to them would have happened to us. We would have been torn apart by anger, fear, misunderstanding. We would have ended up hating each other. Hating ourselves. That won't happen to us now. When we say good-bye . . ."

He faltered. Her hand pressed his, giving him courage.

He continued on steadily. "When we say good-bye, it will be with love and trust."

"Kid?" Tusk peered up at them from down below. "Sorry to interrupt, kid—I mean, Your Majesty. I guess I better get used to saying that. I've made contact with Her Majesty's ship. The queen's anxious to see you. The captain wants to know when you're planning to come aboard and should he lay in a course for Ceres or back to Minas Tares? And Dixter needs to talk to you about the Corasian attack."

Dion rose. "Her Majesty and I will be going to Ceres. We're going to give thanks. To both God and the Goddess."

"Sure thing, kid," Tusk said. "I mean, Your Maj— Oh, the hell with it. You know what I mean." He disappeared back down into the cockpit.

"Yes," said Dion softly. "I know what you mean."

He turned to Kamil. "Good-bye," he said, kissed her gently, and left.

"Good-bye," she told him, after he had gone.

Chapter ❊◦❊ *Twelve*

Heaven's last, best gift . . .
John Milton, *Paradise Lost*

"You'll come to visit us—Astarte and I. You and Nola and your family."

"Royal command?" Tusk grinned.

"Yes." Dion replied gravely. "Royal command."

"Sure, we'll come," Tusk said, and meant it.

"Often."

"Well, as often as we can. What with the business . . ." He sighed, ran his hand through his tightly curled hair, cast a harried glance around the Scimitar. "Back to vacuum cleaner salesmen, I guess."

Dion smiled as if he knew a secret, started to say something, then shook his head. "Good-bye, Tusk."

The mercenary started to shake hands, but Dion clasped his friend in his arms.

Tusk patted Dion on the back. "Good-bye, kid. Good luck." He paused, then said awkwardly, "I wish . . . I wish it all could have turned out different. . . ."

"All is as it was meant to be, Tusk," said Dion quietly.

"Yeah, I guess so." Tusk sounded dubious. Backing off, he wiped his nose, turned his head away.

Dion looked over at Kamil, who had been standing near him, silent, waiting. He reached out his hand. She took it. They held fast to each other for the length of a heartbeat.

She smiled at him, reassuring. "You better go," she said. "They're waiting for you."

Their hands parted.

Dion climbed swiftly up the ladder leading out of the Scimitar. At the top, he paused, took one last look around.

"Good-bye, XJ," he called.

There came a sort of a croak and a wheeze. The lights flickered and went out. The hatch whirred slowly open.

Standing in the darkness, Tusk heard the roar of the crowd on the flight deck of *Flare*, cheering the appearance of their king. When the lights came back on, Dion was gone.

"Well," said Tusk to himself with a sigh, a smile. "That's that."

◦◦⊰⊱◦◦

The ceremonies were over. The crowds had dispersed. XJ was in a high state of indignation.

"I've never seen such a mob! It's ... unmilitary. And some fool reporter actually had the nerve to sit his fat fanny down on my wing! He won't do that again soon. I sent about sixty volts through him."

Tusk grinned, shook his head. "We've got clearance. Lay in a course for the Academy. And then—home."

Kamil sat beside him in the co-pilot's chair. She was brisk and purposefully cheerful. "I've already got the course plotted, Tusk. I needed ... something to do." Her smile slipped a moment, but then it was back. "You're sure you don't mind taking me back to school? I know how eager you are to see your family—"

"No trouble at all, kid. It's on the way."

"Admiral Dixter on line," the computer reported.

The admiral's face appeared on the vidscreen.

"We got His Majesty safely delivered, sir," Tusk reported. "Any word on the Corasians?"

"We've arranged a welcome-to-the-galaxy party. A surprise party. I don't think they'll be bothering us for a long, long time."

"Good, good," Tusk said, nodding. "I ... I don't suppose, you've heard from Nola?" he asked wistfully.

Dixter's grim face relaxed in a smile. "As a matter of fact, I have. After you told me where you thought she might be hiding, I made contact with Marek. Nola's fine, other than being worried about you. Your son's fine. And speaking of Nola, ... Tusk, this may not be the time to bring this up, but there's something I'd like you to think about.

"Three years ago, His Majesty offered you a commission in the Royal Navy. I know you turned it down, but I wish you'd reconsider. I could use an adjutant, Tusk. Someone I could trust. Someone His Majesty can trust. I'm not that many years away from retirement—"

"Whoah!" Tusk sat back, stared at the vidscreen in alarm, even terror.

"I don't mean you'd take over right away," Dixter said, smiling. "I expect to be around a while. Quite a while. Say at least another twenty years. But when I do leave, I'd feel better knowing you were the one who'd be sitting in my chair."

Tusk was in a state of shock. So was XJ apparently. For once, neither of them had anything to say.

"You don't have to give me your answer now, son," Dixter advised, seeing that Tusk was in no shape to talk anyway. "Discuss it with Nola. You'd have to move to Minas Tares, of course. But it's a beautiful city. Nola would like it here. And the children would have the very best educational opportunities. Like I said, think it over."

Tusk tugged on his left earlobe. The eight-pointed star earring was back, a gift from a grateful Astarte.

"I know this is gonna sound weird, sir. But, if I took it—and I'm not saying I am—but if I did, would there uh ... be a place somewhere for Link? He's a jerk and an ass and a blowhard, but he's a pretty good pilot and if he had somethin' to occupy his mind other than cards and the juice, I think he might turn out okay."

"I believe we could find a place for Link," Dixter said gravely.

"Now, just a minute." XJ had also recovered. "Excuse me, sir, but you haven't mentioned the most important factor. How much does this job pay us? Are uniforms included? What about cleaning and pressing? And am I going to have to be reprogrammed for military protocol, because I—"

"You!" Tusk exploded. "Us? If I do take this, you're going into dry dock with the Scimitar and maybe, if you're lucky, I'll take you out in sixteen years when it's time to teach young John how to fly—"

"Dry dock!"

The lights on the ship went dark. Life support shut down.

"Dry dock," the computer repeated in ominous tones. "If you ever want to see any kind of a dock again, Men-da-ha-rin Toosca, you'll forget you ever said those two words in my hearing.

"As for commissioning *you*," the computer continued, seething, "it's obvious that the admiral's doing that simply in order to get me."

The lights came back on. The soft whir of life-support began again.

"I'm getting tired of this spaceplane anyway," XJ went on peevishly. "It's never been the same since you 'remodeled' it. I think I'd like a desk job. Yes, that would be a good place for me. Right on top of your desk, at your fingertips. Feel free anytime, Admiral, to step in and ask my advice. Tell His Majesty, too. I imagine you both will be coming to consult me frequently.

"As for you, Tusk, I'll answer your phone calls and screen your visitors. . . ."

Tusk groaned, laid his head on his arms on the console.

"Excuse me, Admiral Dixter." Kamil was deferential, abashed at being in the presence of such a great man.

"You're Olefsky's daughter, aren't you?"

"Maigrey Kamil, sir," she said, relaxing, attracted by the warmth in his eyes, reassured by the sad, faint smile that touched his lips when he spoke her name. "I was wondering if you knew . . . if you had any information. The cyborg, Xris, and the little empath . . . they were hurt on Ceres. . . ."

Dixter nodded. "I just passed this message on to His Majesty. Archbishop Fideles informs me that Xris is recovering. And the Little One has pulled through. Raoul bought lime-green toreador pants to celebrate."

"That's good," she said, smiling. "I'm glad. Give them both my best. And tell Xris that someday, I may take him up on his offer."

"I'll do that. Your father and mother send their love, by the way. They said to tell you they were both very proud of you. And Kamil," he added, "there's an opening in flight school for you—anytime you're ready."

Kamil flushed with astonishment, pleasure. "Truly, sir?"

"You come with the highest recommendation," the admiral said. "From His Majesty."

Kamil's eyes filled with tears. Mumbling something about leaving Tusk and Dixter to talk in private, she hastily left the cockpit, climbed the ladder leading up to the main cabin.

Once alone, she thought she was going to cry.

"No," she said, resolutely. "I won't. This is what I wanted."

All is as it was meant to be.

"I wish I could believe that," she said suddenly, with a sigh, a frown. "If I could . . ."

That was odd. There was something on the bed, a bundle. She was positive it hadn't been there a moment before.

Her first impulse was to call Tusk.

She didn't, however. She drew near, cautious, wondering.

It was hard, angular, and had been wrapped neatly in the folds of an azure blue velvet cape.

Reverent, awed, Kamil gently lifted the soft blue fabric, drew it aside.

Shining, silver armor.

Epilogue

One short sleep past, we wake eternally,
And death shall be no more; death, thou shalt die.
> John Donne, *Holy Sonnets*

The radiant being entered the halls of heaven with slow and solemn tread. The shining light of the Presence cast long shadows behind the two who stood in judgment. The awful majesty of heaven shone full upon them, but they did not flinch or lower their eyes before it.

They stood together, gold and silver. They stood tall, proud, defiant.

The radiant being sighed.

Ascending the throne of judgment, the being commanded, "My lord, come forward."

Sagan left Maigrey's side, came to stand before heaven, alone.

The radiant being looked down on him from a great height.

"My lord, you have done wrong. Not uncommon in mortals, but in you I see no repentance. I hear no plea for forgiveness."

Lord Sagan made no response, did not lift his eyes to look into the bright light.

"You knew the will of God, my lord."

"I did," Sagan replied.

"You deliberately thwarted it."

Sagan pressed his lips together, was silent. Fire flickered in the dark eyes. Then he said, "I did."

"No, he didn't!" Maigrey protested. She started to take a step forward, to come to his side. "My lord *didn't* thwart God's will! He sacrificed his life—"

"But I did." Lord Sagan halted her with a warding, upraised hand. And now he lifted his gaze, regarded the being grimly. "You see, my lady, Dion was meant to die."

"That can't be true," Maigrey faltered, staring upward.

"It is," Sagan said. "That was the portent of the test. Flaim, a king. Dion, a martyr. That was the plan."

"But why?" Maigrey demanded.

"And do you ask God to explain His ways to you?" The personage was severe, implacable. "My lord, we might take a merciful view of this matter, if we were convinced that you acted out of compassion, selfless love, loyalty—as did Lady Maigrey. Since you have kept your heart deliberately concealed from our view, you are the only one who knows the truth. Was it this which led you to defy God?

"Or did you act out of pride, out of arrogance, out of a need to demonstrate your own power? Did you thwart God's will, my lord, simply to show Him that you could?"

Sagan smiled, dark, twisted. He made no other answer.

"Which is it, my lord?" The personage was stern.

"Whatever you want to believe of me," Sagan answered.

The radiant being gazed down at him in sadness. "I offer you, my lord, one more chance. Confess, repent, be redeemed."

Sagan stared straight ahead. He did not lift his eyes. Or lower them.

The personage sighed a second time.

"Very well, then. I have no choice but to deem you guilty.

"Lady Maigrey, come forward. You deliberately broke your covenant with God. You crossed from this blessed realm to the physical. You interfered with the living and thus you, too, thwarted God's will. Do you repent, my lady? Do you ask for forgiveness? Think well before you reply. Recall the terrible punishment you face."

A portal opened before her.

"Look into it, my lady. I repeat here what I said to you once before. Into that dread world you will be cast. You will not be permitted to return to this blessed realm, except by a path that is long and difficult and filled with pain. Many are those who have perished on it, to live in dreadful torment and agony, bereft of all hope of comfort, peace, redemption. That is the fate you face. And you face it alone."

Maigrey stared down the path that led from light into darkness. At the terrible sight, defiance seeped out of her, like her heart's blood flowing. Her eyes lowered; she could not face it. Her head bowed. Her hands clasped together, holding tightly to her fast-diminishing courage.

Sagan, too, stared down that path and, strong as he was, he

blenched, paled. But he stepped forward, came to stand by her side.

"She will not go alone," he said.

"Is that your choice, my lord?" the radiant being asked.

"It is."

"And is this your choice, my lady? Or will you repent?"

"How can you ask that of me?" She raised her eyes. "I would go to him again, if he needed me, though all hell barred my way."

"You may well face that test," said the personage sadly.

"Then go with him now, my lady. And you go with her, my lord. This much mercy We will show. The way back is open to you. The path is dark and dangerous, but it is clearly marked. If you look for it, you will find it. But the road will not be easy. May God go with you."

"He needn't bother," said Sagan.

He turned to Maigrey. Bowing, he extended his hand to her. "My lady?"

She placed her hand in his. "My lord."

Neither looking back, the two entered the darkness, together.

"At least," said the radiant being to the Immortal Watching Eye, "we've accomplished that much."

The portal closed behind them. The personage descended from the throne. He was stopped, at the bottom, by a thin man with a careworn face.

"Yes, Platus? What is it?"

"They saved Dion's life. They kept a cruel and heartless man from becoming king. How is this wrong?"

"Thousands of years ago, a man was crucified by cruel and heartless men. What would have happened if someone had intervened to save him?"

"I don't know," said Platus softly. "Perhaps he would have lived an ordinary, happy life."

"But that was not the plan."

Platus shook his head. "I don't understand."

"Of course, you don't, child," the radiant being said kindly. "God is the beginning and the end. You are only the middle."

Acknowledgments

I am pleased to acknowledge the use of invaluable notes written by Gary Pack, noted physicist, who was the first to discover and explain the anomaly of the strange dark-matter creatures.

Many thanks also to Nicole Harsch; Mike Sekuta; Janet Pack; Gary Pack; Captain Richard Dhur, Royal Canadian Artillery; and Captain Don Perrin, retired, Royal Canadian Artillery, for staging the last battle scene.

I would like to credit an editorial written by Richard Brookhiser, senior editor, *National Review*, that appeared in *Time* magazine, November 11, 1991, titled "Why Not Bring Back the Czars?" for inspiration.

Many, many thanks to Steve Youll for wonderful cover art and for his support and encouragement. I'm thankful he gave up his career as a starship pilot.

To David Cole—there should be an award for great copy-editors. You'd get my vote!

And finally, to Amy Stout—my editor at Bantam/Spectra for many years. We miss you, Amy. Maigrey and Sagan and Dion and Tusk and XJ and I all miss you. God bless.

About the Author

Born in Independence, Missouri, MARGARET WEIS graduated from the University of Missouri and worked as a book editor before teaming up with Tracy Hickman to develop the *Dragonlance* novels and the *Deathgate* books. Margaret lives in a renovated barn in Wisconsin with her teenage daughter, Elizabeth Baldwin, and two dogs and one cat, where she is working on a new novel. She enjoys reading (especially Charles Dickens), opera, and snow-shoeing.